WINDWARD PASSAGE

WINDWARD PASSAGE

A NOVEL BY **Mark Brewer**

Crown Publishers, Inc., New York

Printed in the United States of America
Published simultaneously in Canada by
General Publishing Company Limited

Designed by Rhea Braunstein

Library of Congress Cataloging in Publication Data

Brewer, Mark.
   Windward passage.

   I.   Title.
PZ4.B84715Wi [PS3552.R4213]   813'.5'4   77-26675
ISBN 0-517-53304-9

for LINDA

Part One

chapter 1

i

JOE Eiler remembered the day when Sidell and Insinger first conspired. They were all in Aspen then. But when Joe started telling
me the entire story a few years later, he was so far from that place
and his chances of ever seeing it again were so remote he described
it rather sadly. He loved to tell it though. After a few drinks were
down and his feeling was right, he would even relate in curious
detail scenes that he never actually saw. In some cases, of course,
Joe knew what occurred from having discussed it with one or two
of the others, but there was a lot he just seemed to know. Eiler was
an unusual fellow. I doubt any of it happened much differently
than he said. As much as possible, I'll try to put it down the way he
gave it to me, except for the names. I am aided a little by the fact
that I knew these characters too, the ones that matter, and knew
them fairly well. And I have been where they were and done a little of
what they attempted. Under the circumstances it is best not to say
more than that.

As Joe recalled, it was a singular Aspen day. It was bright, dry,
January—skiers on the slopes of Ajax were carving, tumbling,
streaking. It was the sort of day that makes Aspen's reputation as
the finest ski area in America indisputable, when that sun-
drenched thinness of air gives even simple pleasures a certain high
excitement. Joe loved the place. Set among its crown of alps far
above the world, it is a crossroad for great extremes of wealth,
desire, aspiration and fulfillment. Few who pass there are not

inspired, if only in recreation, to pursuits greater and faster than the normal train of life below. And on a quick, sunlit winter day, the power of the place—the promise of its height—seem almost too much.

But, despite the fine conditions, Jack Sidell had not left his rooms at Aspen Block that day. Nor had he skied the day before. That afternoon, as the street below his window filled with boisterous traffic, he sat quietly on the couch, back erect, fingers tapping softly on his thighs. He had sat there almost an hour, retracing the nearly final plans he had developed over past months, and he was satisfied that they were as well laid as they could be at this stage. Sidell tended to worry, but for the next several minutes he smiled faintly, feeling that combination of eagerness and fear that always accompanied the acceptance of challenge.

His watch still showed thirty minutes until he was to meet Insinger, and he stood abruptly, needing some activitiy. He was tired of waiting, felt like he'd been waiting years. He killed a little time in his meticulous way, watering his plants, poking the fire, straightening a few drafts he'd made that morning.

Women adored Jack's apartment. Everyone admired it. It was handsome and artistically arranged. And it fit Jack well. He was tall and graceful, and he possessed what Eiler once called "heroic good looks." He had broad, smooth features and dark brown hair that was always rather long and well styled. He was a careful, casual dresser, and he wore very good clothes. There were plenty of women who adored Jack and didn't give a damn about his apartment.

Jack sat again, glanced once more at his watch, and decided he might as well have a few lines. He crossed the room, took the short stairway two steps at a time to the bedroom, which overlooked the lower rooms like a loft, and retrieved the glass vial of cocaine from among the articles on his dresser. As he turned back to the stairs though, he stopped and looked at the vial a moment, shook the few grams of shiny powder and put it back.

Four months earlier, Jack Sidell had completed an architectural degree at the University of Colorado, where he had been an all-league football player and a talented student. His prospects had been promising but, to him, uninviting. The Broncos had drafted him, and they needed another wide receiver. But there were too many uncontrollable factors in that choice, chiefly the likelihood of being maimed by some huge fast psychotic. And he was tired of the game. A few of his professors had offered entrees to reputable firms, where he could perform the internship required

2

for licensing by the A.I.A. He had agonized over those opportunities because architecture was his love, but the notion of designing banks and car parks for two years had seemed like an upholstered purgatory. Another plan, in slow gestation through his final semester, was far preferable.

In the past year, he had completed a number of designs that had been professionally admired, and, if he had the capital to construct them independently, he was confident he could launch a reputation and career and escape the rigors of menial apprenticeship. He had no doubt of his ability to pull it off, but he had nowhere near enough money. During the past summer, however, while he was finishing his last courses at the university in Boulder, he had been asked by an old acquaintance to participate in a dope deal. Like almost anyone in Boulder, Jack often used marijuana and ventured an occasional hit of acid, but he had never been a dealer. He had always intended that, if he ever got into dealing, it would have to be worth the risk. But the right deal had never materialized.

That summer, though, he had been asked to arrange the transportation of a fairly large shipment of marijuana from a point in the Mexican desert to a point in the Arizona desert. It was simple, exacting, and lucrative. And that was just the way Jack liked things. He had located and contracted a pilot, constructed a plausible alibi for a Mexican sojourn, picked up the stuff just north of Hermasillo, set it down in the dark of night just south of Tucson, doubled back to clear customs at Nogales, and over the next two months collected payments totaling a little under forty thousand dollars.

It was nice work, and naturally as he wrestled with the problem of trying to break in at the top as an architect, it had occurred to him that it could be done again—on a much larger scale. And in addition to his ability and inclination to perform such tasks, he possessed two other attributes that he knew could get him the money he needed. He was an expert sailor. And he knew Tom Caval.

ii

"Yeah, I don't know what your chances might be on a deal like that, but I think we can get 'em to give it their best consideration. Talk to 'em about it, you know." Burt Melton hesitated, chewed at the side of his mouth, and listened. "We'll do it then," he answered, full of encouragement and mutual purpose. "Right. Right. Okay. Look though, I guess I need to get a check from you. You know. Yeah. Sure." He smiled. "Just have her drop it by tomorrow morning then. Great. Great. Give you a call. Bye."

Melton put the receiver away and exhaled a satisfied whistle as he leaned back. On the verge of laughter he said aloud, "What a shithead." He rolled his eyes upward, then sat forward to scribble a quick half-page of notes on legal pad, which he tore away and deposited with several others at a corner of his large desk. Still smiling, he got up and approached the broad window that fronted his office with a view of Ajax Mountain, still dotted with skiers making final runs. He wore square-toed boots with Vibram soles, flared continental denims, a maroon sweater over a white turtleneck, and with his long blonde hair he looked very much like the successful young Aspen lawyer that he was, mining the reserves of real estate development, the present treasure of that area.

A moment later, concluding that his last phone call had been business enough for the day, he stepped to the door and called, "Hey Marcus, buy you a drink."

He leaned in the doorway until Mark Insinger appeared from the small, windowless office at the back of the hall.

"I'll have to pass that up. Uh, thanks anyway." Insinger stood rather uncertainly and spoke without Melton's throaty, fraternal tone. "I've got a little meeting this afternoon."

"Guess you do." Melton lifted his eyebrows noticing Mark was turned out with more than usual care in tailored corduroy slacks and a bright laundered collar outside his sweater. "Want to use this office?"

Mark said, "Sure," having known it would be offered. "I guess so. Thanks."

"What's goin' on?" Melton called as he left the door to get his parka. "Big deal?"

"Could be. Could be." Insinger knew Melton would be smiling, though he couldn't see him. Mark's infrequent appearances at the small rear office were always a source of humor, depending, as they did, much more on the quality of skiing on a given day or the nature of recent female acquaintances than on the promise of occasional divorces or contracts. Melton and his partner, who occupied another plush office midway on the hall, sometimes wondered how Mark Insinger had managed to insinuate himself into their association, but Mark had been around Aspen long enough for them to accept him, and they had mutual friends.

4

"I may do a corporation for some people," Mark added when Melton returned to sight, pulling on his parka.

"Yeah? Anybody I know?"

"I don't believe you do." Insinger savored his curiosity. "I don't think you do."

Melton smiled at him, wondering what he was up to, noting again that Mark Insinger had always seemed to be waiting for something. He playfully warned Mark not to make too much money, then told Annie at the front desk which calls should be passed on to him at home.

A few minutes later, telling Annie "No calls" as he went past, Insinger moved into the larger office. Annie was amused. Mark dropped his pad and case on the big desk and looked about with an appreciative smile. A twelve-by-eight blue and red Bokhara rug mellowed the high gloss random-width maple floorboards. There were highly finished teak shelves on either wall, one filled with legal references, the other with bestsellers and leather-bound classics. Between the desk and window, two ultra-suede and polished steel couches faced each other across a low marble table, and the commanding view of the slopes spoke of privilege expensively displayed.

Mark depressed a pedal beneath the legal works, and an array of Heineken appeared in a small refrigerator. Back when he was hustling through law school many people had thought this was the sort of office Mark would someday occupy. For a while now, those people had ceased in that thinking.

Mark Insinger had also attended the University of Colorado, but he had finished a law degree with a master's in tax a full three years before Jack Sidell had arrived in Boulder. He had worked hard in school, and his family had looked forward to his prosperity and the aid he could give their businesses. But once he had returned to Chicago and been accepted into an old and conservative firm, his life had ached to a halt. Work at the firm was painfully remote and boring; the partners who directed him seemed like mere shadows of their enterprising clients; and through a long Chicago winter Mark Insinger had felt like the shadow of shadows.

He had stuck it out for a year though, until his first vacation, which he spent in Hawaii. Lahaina seemed very much like paradise, and a friend from Boulder introduced him to a Honolulu attorney who suggested Mark might be interested in joining a project he was directing. It was a study of the social impact of laws relating to marijuana sponsored by the state bar association. Even though the position was little more than that of assistant and glorified law clerk, it was exciting against his recent background. He accepted immediately.

Insinger's tenure at Boulder had largely preceded the marijuana binge of the late sixties, and he had tried the stuff, but never actually used it. But, during his ten months in the islands, he quickly began to smoke, first socially and then regularly. The work for the study was tolerably interesting, and the out islands and exotic nights of Hawaii restored a spirit to his life that he had longed for while growing old in Chicago at an early age. Through colleagues, he met several dealers who relaxed in Hawaii between operations or used it as their base. He was fascinated with their fast wealth, the daring of their business, and the apparent ease of their lives. After several months, he became a discreet friend in a circle that revolved around two or three of these young entrepreneurs. He partied with them frequently and spent occasional weekends on some yacht or at a Molokai retreat. By the time his work with the study was finished, it had begun to seem as bourgeois as the firm back in Chicago, and he was thoroughly enamoured of the risky adventures of the smuggling life. Legal work in any fashion he considered dull and safe by comparison. Yet he lacked the money or expertise to think he could find outside the law a chance to earn enough money to live in the style he had come to admire.

He had been about to accept a position with a San Francisco firm, returning to tax and securities, when he had run into one of his fast island acquaintances who was departing on a skiing vacation after a lucrative transaction. It was all Mark needed. As quickly as he had forgotten Chicago he declined San Francisco and left with his friend for Aspen.

For more than a year, up until the afternoon when he awaited Jack Sidell, he had skied constantly, caroused almost every night, and went through a parade of loose company and rare Aspen women. Yet too frequently he had had pause to consider what a piddling waste he was making of his law career, how unproductive he had become. He was living the life, but there was no substance. There was all the promise and flair, but no real action to give it meaning. Somehow, though—and perhaps just to excuse his expensive sloth and self-indulgence—he had believed that if he remained long enough among the people and circumstances he desired, he would someday find a way to make it all work.

And surely enough, he had met Tom Caval, had become his

6

friend, and this day would become his partner. With that would come money, the tropics, hotels, adventure, and fluffy haired, round assed women with just that little space of daylight high between their thighs.

When the front office door opened that day, Mark Insinger gazed dreamily out the wide window, but much further than the mere darkening slopes of Ajax.

iii

Jack Sidell had met Mark Insinger only once before, at one of Tom Caval's select debauches. Caval had grinned fiendishly as he assured them they'd be getting to know each other quite well. Jack had thought there was a little of the weasel in Mark Insinger, perhaps because of his narrow features, which tended to twitch when he grew nervous or intent. But Insinger was thoughtful and calculating and a lawyer, so Jack was willing to wait and see.

Jack stopped just inside the door when Annie showed him in. "Hello, Mister Insinger. Nice office you have here."

"How are you, Jack?" Mark smiled self-consciously from the center of the room. The twitch in his eyebrows caused him to flinch slightly every few seconds. He spoke at a careful rate. "This is Melton's office, actually, but it's kind of a nice place to discuss business."

"Yeah." Sidell glanced around and walked toward the window. "Nice view of the mountain." Jack hated to make false compliments. He found the place ostentatious, so he mentioned the view.

"Would you like a beer?" Mark asked. "There's some liquor if you want a drink."

Jack said beer was fine, and Mark poured two into mugs and set them on the marble table, as Jack sat on one couch. Mark got his note pad from the desk and sat on the other couch. There was a little more small talk, and then Mark, seeing that Jack seemed ready, simply smiled at him and waited. Both of them were nervous though. There was a precipitous anxiety in the silence.

Jack Sidell drilled himself again on what and what not to say, on what and what not to allow, and once again forced his thoughts into order. As always the effort tightened his body and face, as if from physical exertion. He had suffered dyslexia as a child, had had misunderstood inabilities in reading and coordination, and had overcome them mainly through will and determination. Reading and especially business deals still required great concentration though. In addition, a defensiveness he had borne since childhood made him almost painfully anxious as he sat across from a fast thinking lawyer. His eyes were fixed on the books behind Mark Insinger, and he said nothing for nearly a full minute.

"How much has Caval told you?" Jack finally asked. "About — the project."

Mark exhaled with the slightest impatience. "Well, I understand it involves a boat and a considerable amount of—uh— cargo. Now, what Tommy wants me to do is to learn the details from you, and then set up some way to take care of things."

Mark looked steadily at Sidell, who scowled a little because he did not care to hear Caval called Tommy.

"Like for instance the boat," Mark continued. "A boat of any large size is a red flag to the I.R.S. It attracts attention because it represents a lot of money. So we'll have to form a corporation with some sort of plausible purpose for buying a boat."

Sidell leaned forward, preparing to comment but still appeared apprehensive, so Mark kept going.

"It's a fairly simple matter to set up a legitimate corporation without the government knowing who the actual principals are or where the money came from. It's the best way to do it. And it's not hard. No real problems."

"Okay. Fine." Jack turned the mug slowly between both hands and studied Insinger's narrow face and the flinch in his brow with uncertain misgivings. Yet he liked the quiet pace of Mark's voice. He answered in the sharp staccato in which he normally spoke. "I was thinking we could set things up as a charter service. For taking people on trips, day sails, turns around the harbor, or whatever we want to say. That explains a boat, office, communications equipment, all the stuff we'd need."

Mark nodded. "That sounds like it might be the number." He lit a cigarette. "But it might take something a little different too, depending on how much equipment we need to purchase. So, why don't we start with how much we're going to pick up, where we'll pick it up, where we'll bring it in, how we'll —"

"Alright," Jack cut in. He took a cigarette from the pocket of his wool shirt and looked as if he might just leave without another word. After a thoughtful drag he stood up and walked a slow circle by the bookshelves, toward the window, and back to the couch. Mark could not imagine what was bothering him.

Jack moved with the studied physical dignity of an accomplished, slightly egotistical athlete, and Mark admired him as he paced smoothly around the room. All through his youth Mark had wished he were larger, more athletic. In Jack Sidell he also saw a thoughtfulness and a scientific attitude toward danger that intrigued him. He enjoyed the knowledge that Sidell needed him.

When Jack sat again, he spoke with a sudden defensiveness that often startled people. "I want to get this straight before we go on. I'm not a dealer. I don't have anything to do with this stuff after it's off-loaded. That's your business, or Caval's, or whoever. I'm just the captain of a boat that's going to take on a cargo in international waters and off-load it in international waters. Now if we make a corporation or whatever, I don't want it to show anything different than that."

"Sure. I understand." Mark Insinger smiled and nodded like a good lawyer. "I don't think that's any problem." A smuggler, not a dealer, he thought. A nice distinction, but one the law did not observe.

"Okay," Jack's voice softened. "I just wanted you to know. I don't have anything to do with the distribution."

That was not precisely true, but accurate enough for the present, so Sidell pulled a deep breath and began again.

"So, as it stands, we plan to take on a load in southern Mexico. Guerrero. Probably near Acapulco. Around Zihuatanejo maybe. There's a nice little harbor there and some coves that might do, but anyway the load will be taken to the West Coast. Probably northern California, but I haven't really checked that out yet. Might be as far up as Seattle. We don't need to know that yet." Jack paused a moment. "We'll be moving five tons."

Insinger's lips pursed slightly, but that was a mannerism that occurred every ten or twenty seconds no matter what was said. He looked back into Sidell's eyes as unaffected as if Jack had mentioned five pounds of laundry. Inwardly, however, Mark worked the figures as quickly as the computer he was not often without. Two million easy, he registered. He was glad suddenly that Caval had not yet wanted to discuss amounts or cuts, that he'd said they would work things out. Two million was a nice figure to work with. He countered Sidell's eyes with a question.

"What kind of boat does that require?"

"Motor sailor." Jack took the last of his beer and sat back. "At least forty feet, with a good diesel and some room."

"Room for cargo." Mark leaned forward.

"Sure."

"What does that go for? A boat like that."

"Thirty thousand anyway."

"Is that a lot?"

"Not really." Sidell leaned forward too. "Even for that much, she'll probably need some work."

She, thought Insinger. He liked that. It reminded him of his friends in Hawaii. Their boats had always been female.

"We need a good boat," Jack went on. "No way around that. It's a tough one coming up."

"Coming up from Mexico," Mark assumed.

"Yeah. Sure. The wind and seas are against that trip. You take them head-on. That's work for a boat. You can start leaking, use up your fuel, ruin the cargo—anything. Loaded, we could pop a board and go down."

"Pop a board, uh?" Mark Insinger's brow flinched, and his lips pursed for an instant. "Why couldn't we get a fiber-glass boat? Do they cost more?"

"No. Maybe less." Jack hunkered forward a little, extending his hands, a tolerant gesture. "But we need a wood boat. An older boat. Nice looking. Charm. I mean, this is supposed to be a charter deal. Who the hell wants to go out on some new plastic job?"

Insinger shrugged his agreement. His ignorance of such matters did not bother him.

"What about getting it out to the boat?"

"That's the Mexicans' problem. And Tom's, I guess. Yours too maybe."

"We do have to get it off, though. I guess that's not your problem either."

"Well—" Jack Sidell turned his head uncomfortably, but Insinger kept him in his gaze. Jack and Caval had agreed that Caval would take care of everything except pickup and delivery. And Jack didn't like the idea that Tom Caval might get more out of him than they'd agreed. But he was concerned about the shuttling. "I would use a Bertram," he answered suddenly. "That's a big sport cruiser—the best one. Two of them maybe. Maybe just one if we find a good spot. So you can run twice or three times."

"Are they like fishing boats?"

"Yeah, sport fisherman. Lots of space below decks. Nice cabins. Nice main salon. Twin engine jobs. They can haul ass. But you need someone who knows the things."

"Sure," Mark nodded with more enthusiasm, as he noted the Bertrams on his pad. Sidell kept glancing nervously at the yellow sheets whenever Mark wrote. Mark stood up slowly and set his shoulders with a deep breath. For the past two weeks, whenever he had thought—dreamed—of the project, it had been of a big speedboat rushing ashore through the darkness with a load. And he had been driving it.

Mark got two more beers, set one politely before Sidell and sat again. "What you have described," he said, carefully pouring into the mug held in his other hand, "what would you say it might cost?"

"No way of telling," Jack answered quickly. He had not wanted to worry about expense, and Caval had assured him there was no need to.

"We have to establish some kind of cost pattern."

"You can't do it with any accuracy," Jack objected.

"Even so—"

"Well look, I was told there was plenty of money to do this thing. And to do it well. If you don't have enough money, then there's going to be fuck-ups. I don't care to have any part of that."

The thing Jack cared least for in Tom Caval was that he had no sense of perfection. He just rammed things through. Jack believed in doing things first class, with the best equipment, or not at all. He had approached Caval with his plan primarily because he knew Caval had the money to do it well.

"Right, right," Mark was nodding. "I know." He was beginning to regard Sidell as a thoroughbred who started easily. "But let's just see how many of the basic costs we can list. So we'll know when money is needed and how much. So we can be sure there won't be any fuck-ups."

Jack sat back again and thought perhaps he'd been a little hasty. Yet he still felt he had to watch out. He had set certain requirements for the operation and meant to respect them. In those areas in which he had managed to excel, it had been only through tight planning and execution: by studying charts and sticking to courses, by running pass patterns as carefully as he drew plans for a building. He was relaxing a little with Mark though, as most people did. Jack liked him in a way, was a little curious about him. For the next hour and a half, the two men laboriously pieced together the general logistics of the operation they had each separately looked forward to for so long.

There was the corporation—attorney's fees, office rental, furniture leases, communication equipment, business cards, telephone, answering service, stationary, at least minimal advertising, and the expense of those things. Then there was the boat—the finding, surveying, and purchase; the registry, refurbishing, and maintenance; and finally, the outfitting, provisions, and fuel. There were trucks, houses for operations and distributions, and much more. And to these Insinger added rough estimates for trips to Mexico and purchase of "the dope."

Jack Sidell enjoyed the attention to detail. He set forth the major tasks in order of necessity, and Insinger, through his own knowledge, questions, and inference, supplemented the main costs with long lists of expenses such as hotels, meals, and transportation, each carefully noted. Finally Jack relaxed and finished another beer while Mark's fingers traveled quietly over the keys of his calculator. He spent several minutes totaling it all. Then, to Sidell's satisfaction, he did it all again.

"I guess that's close enough for now," Mark said at last.

"What'd you get?"

"Around a hundred eighty thousand."

"That sounds about right."

"It's there," Insinger smiled. He was certain Tom Caval had the money. Mark had never seen a more extravagant dealer—and only few men of any sort with more apparent wealth. And Mark marveled always that Caval was so young, that this gaudy enigma who had drawn himself and Jack Sidell outside the law was only twenty-two years old. Even Jack was twenty-three then. Mark was almost thirty, so despite his admiration for both Caval and Sidell he enjoyed feeling a paternal relationship to the deal, looked forward to integrating their raw talents into a sophisticated operation. The money was there to do it. And, at the moment, Mark felt it was his money too, which was very pleasant. He blinked a few times and focused again on Jack Sidell. "How soon do you plan to head for San Diego?"

"I'll leave—," Jack thought a moment, "day after tomorrow. I'll look around for an office too. I'll be down in a good area for it, and I can check to see it's unobstructed for the radios."

"That'd be good." Insinger's lips pursed judiciously a few times. "Then—uh—Tom and I will be out in about ten days, maybe a little more, to start the corporation. And we can check out the office and take a look at some boats."

They smiled at each other across the table, each in his own way satisfied that the enterprise was soundly begun.

"How much money will you need?"

Sidell thought ahead. "Expenses, rental car, the office, good faith on a boat—three thousand."

12

"I'll get it to you tomorrow." Insinger paused, nodding silently. His brow twitched. "Shall we get out of here and have a drink on it?"

At Andre's the crowd was thick and loud, and a band was playing in the corner, but Sidell and Insinger moved through it unaffected, preoccupied, almost oblivious, their plans already having propelled them into a higher, faster orbit.

Insinger bought a couple of Cuervos, and they made their way toward a table that was just clearing, but lost it to more eager customers. They found a place to stand along the wall.

"Well," Mark raised his glass, "to easy money?"

Jack smiled indulgently. "I don't think anybody ever made this kind of dough without trouble."

"Okay," Mark grinned. "To trouble."

Jack would have preferred to drink simply to fortune, but he felt brash and like Insinger he was sure nothing could stop them. He laughed and lifted his Cuervo.

"Trouble."

chapter 2

i

JACK Sidell was waiting at the gate in San Diego when Joe Eiler came off the plane. Sidell stood with his feet set apart, hands easy on his hips, and on his face a narrow smile that registered surprise whenever Joe Eiler appeared when and where he had said he would. To Joe Eiler, seeing Jack was always good, somehow refreshing. Sidell had been in the sun a lot, the first few buttons of his shirt were open, his jeans were laundered, and his hair was cut smooth and full, just covering his ears. The Prince Charming cut, Joe used to kid him. Joe generally felt a bit scruffy by comparison—and was.

"Mister Eiler."

"Hello Jack. You're looking good."

They didn't bother to shake hands. They simply smiled and looked each other over before heading for the terminal. They were built the same way except that Joe was a couple of inches shorter and weighed a little less. He had high cheekbones and a square chin, but his smile was a little crooked, and there was something unsettling about the premature crow's feet around his gray eyes. They were very pale eyes, and Joe's gaze could be ice. His hair was light reddish brown, healthy thick hair, but rarely cut well. He was wearing charcoal wool slacks, black cowboy boots, a turtleneck, and a brown ski parka. He almost always dressed that way, regardless of weather, and generally looked like he'd been in the clothes a few days.

"You look tired," Jack said as they started to walk.

"I could use some sleep."

"The grip a little heavy?" Jack wondered with a smile. Joe's small, worn leather bag pulled at his left shoulder.

"My life savings," Joe cracked. Eiler had just moved fifty kilos and was carrying among his change of clothes about seven thousand dollars in odd sized bills.

Jack shook his head. "Why don't you get a safe-deposit box?"

"Why don't you get a job?" Eiler waited for Jack to smile. "See if any of those things you draw will stand up."

"They will. In fact, I was messing around with a little house the other night. Sort of a mountain retreat. It looked like you. I want you to see it."

"Lot of exits, uh?"

Jack laughed. "And a secret tunnel that goes to the airport." He laughed harder.

"Hilarious." Joe kept glancing out of the corners of his eyes as they moved through the sparse crowd.

"Maybe you can afford to have me build it for you when we finish this project."

"Sounds like a great deal. Payment in kind, uh? You'll build me a hideout."

Jack was still chuckling when they reached the exit and made for the parking lot. There was not a cloud in the sky, and Joe felt like he'd arrived from another planet.

"Found a boat yet, captain?"

"I've looked at a few, but no real prospects yet. I found a place that will be good for an office though. We'll go by later."

"Okay. Caval in town?"

"Yes. Got in yesterday."

"So, what's the deal?"

"We'll go see Caval and Insinger, talk over a few things, then go do the corporation."

14

There was an optimism in Sidell's long gait, as if great things awaited doing that day, all within his capability. Eiler felt good keeping up with him. Near the front of the lot, Sidell walked up to a spanking new, burgundy Citroen, sleek as a panther, and stopped to put Eiler's bag in the trunk.

"Nice," Joe allowed after he was in.

"Just got it," Jack grinned at him. "They're great cars. Incredibly precise. Especially for being French."

Eiler shrugged, and the engine revved with a mean whine as they backed up. "This that Maserati engine?" Sidell nodded, and they sped away. Joe wondered how Sidell would account for the purchase, but was sure he had it covered. Sidell's family in Boston was wealthy, and although they were very strict about Jack's making his own way, Joe figured they came in handy for explaining income. He didn't bother to ask. They rarely spoke of such things. He fiddled with the seat until it let back nearly prone, and Jack touched a button so the sunroof hummed open. Eiler smiled into the ether.

"How was Denver?" Sidell asked.

"Jesus."

"Yeah?"

"I got the job done." Eiler sounded weary of his profession.

"I'm sure, but did you get paid?"

"There's a few loose ends I have to go back for, but I always collect."

"What a shitty business," Jack said, real distance in his voice.

"Well don't say it now, captain."

"You know what I mean. Staying at that end like you do, hustling the stuff, all those people."

"Soldier class, I guess."

"Bullshit."

"Plenty of that." Eiler closed his eyes and smelled the Pacific, as the Citroen stretched its legs on the freeway. "So how's Tom Caval?" Joe pronounced the name with cool distaste and posed the question rhetorically, the way one might ask, upon arrival in Paris, "How is the Eiffel Tower?"

"Haven't seen him much. He just got in yesterday. I had dinner with him last night, but he had people there, and he was busy impressing them. I left pretty quick. I can't take it when he's holding court."

"Yeah, I know. This is a big baby you're talking about, my friend. You think Caval can run it?"

The question annoyed Sidell. "I'm here," he said.

They kept south on the freeway, snaking through the traffic, Jack's arms straight to the wheel, and they didn't speak for a few minutes. Jack brought the middle finger of his left hand to his lips and squeezed the nail carefully between his teeth, methodically from one end to the other, and Joe knew he was still gauging Tom Caval.

Joe had known Jack Sidell for five years and knew how Jack thought. Joe had known Caval almost that long, but not as well, and had never been Caval's friend. Joe had known Mark Insinger only a few months, but he liked Mark. There were not many people Joe ever liked. And there was not much affection wasted on Joe either.

Joe Eiler had met Jack through football at the university. Eiler had started off on a scholarship as a pretty fair halfback from Wichita Falls, and they played together as freshmen. They both played well, but by spring the coaches had determined that football was not the most important thing in Eiler's life. They decided not to waste any more money. Marijuana was the great collegiate pastime of those days, so when the scholarship money ran out, Joe gradually began dealing, and then quit school. In the process, he met Tom Caval.

By the time Jack showed up in Aspen with this scheme in his head, Joe had, from time to time, started hanging around there too and Jack recruited him. Joe had said of course he'd go. It sounded like a hell of an adventure—and a lot of money, more money than either of them could imagine. But Eiler had stipulated that Jack must be the boss. Eiler would be his man. He would invest in the cargo and sail and be paid as crew. But he wanted Jack to set it up and deal with Caval.

It was Joe Eiler who had introduced Jack to the Tucson deal that had whetted Jack's appetite for this enterprise. Joe had liked the way Jack worked. Sidell had a good head for detail and strategy, and his appearance and comportment commanded respect, even from police. Jack was also a worrier. He knew when to stop worrying and act, but he fretted until the last minute, and Joe liked that.

Eiler had been involved in the Tucson deal, but as usual in a lesser, stateside capacity. Joe was sort of knocking around the dope business then, getting by. He had lost inspiration for anything more. He had always done pretty well in the business though and had never been busted in the States. Two years earlier, Joe had been doing very well. He had married a girl in Boulder, and everything seemed on the rise. Joe was different then—and she was, by any standard, a prize. They were happy, but she came from a family that had never made a dishonest nickel, so the business always bothered her, especially as things got bigger. Of course she had wanted him to quit, thought he had such talent for other things. And Joe always said he would stop someday.

Finally, he made out well in some cocaine, and that was to be the end. She had just gotten pregnant, and they decided to go to Mexico for a vacation. They stuck a little coke and a few hits of acid in her purse. Fun for the trip. It was so simple. Some young narc in Cuernavaca figured they might be a mark. He found the stuff in her purse, and he and his partner hauled them up to Lecumberri prison in Mexico City. They scared her into signing a confession about the cocaine. And when she did, they gave her a Coca-Cola. They had put all the acid in the Coca-Cola, and then they fucked her for two days. She must have gotten pretty sloppy on them, because they finally dumped her in a little hotel on the edge of the city. She killed herself there, hacked up her wrists with a broken glass.

When they found her, they just deported Joe. He took the body back to her family. For months he tried to do something about it. He managed to find a girl who had been there and told him what happened, but the government didn't care, and nothing ever came of it. Joe Eiler never gave a damn about anything after that— certainly not about being a honcho in any dope deal.

They were off the freeway, shooting through the run-down Mexican neighborhood near the waterfront. Joe turned away from the window.

"So where's he staying?"

"The Del," said Jack. "Where else."

"Oh yeah? Well, that'll be nice." Tom Caval always stayed at the best hotels—or at least what he thought were best—and frequently booked the best suite they offered. If you had to see him for some reason, it was one of his more appreciable qualities.

"How your plans going?" Joe asked a moment later. They were cutting along the wharfs and warehouses toward the bridge.

"It's a little early yet, but it looks pretty good. I've got a crew figured out. I know the kind of equipment we'll need. And I can move a good piece of cargo without having to mess around like you do."

"Oh, I hope so. God forbid you should have to—"

"You know what I mean."

Joe laughed a little, but Sidell was pretty serious. Eiler was characteristically sarcastic, especially in serious situations.

"Look," Jack shifted the topic, "on these corporation papers, we need you to sign as one of the officers."

"You signing?"

"Sure. I'm president of the thing. You'll be vice-president."

"At last. Success. I assume these won't be our names."

"Of course not. Insinger's got it all worked out. It's no problem." When Joe nodded, Jack said, "He's got a name for you, but I don't know it."

"So what's your name?" Joe grinned.

"Slade. Jack Slade."

Sidell said it perfectly straight, as if they'd just met, but Joe couldn't help sneering. "What the hell have you been reading?"

"Nothing wrong with that." He wasn't going to let Joe get him going.

"Sure. I guess not. I'll be James Bond, okay?"

"Be serious for Christ's sake, will you?"

"Alright. Make it Jimmy Bond."

"Don't be an ass."

Jack reached the sweeping arched bridge, and it lifted them above the harbor, away from the waterfront and the city and the freeway. It provided a fitting introduction to the view of verdant Coronado, dominated by the neo-Victorian mansion that is the Hotel Del Coronado—to cognoscenti, The Del. Across the bridge, they wound through broad streets of the meticulously kept houses that had grown up around the hotel since it was built at the turn of the century. They drove slowly past the front entrance of The Del, where white overalled attendants ogled at the car. Jack parked it himself. No spic teenager was driving Jack's chariot. And the keys might have provided access to Joe's bag. Coming from the lot, they had the front view of the place, the sprawling dignified array of white wood gables, dormers, spires, cupolas, gingerbread shingle work, and long pillared verandas, all topped with a weathered red roof and appointed with splendid gardening. Going up the steps, Sidell felt inspired and confident. It was a setting equal to his own designs that day.

Inside, Jack went to the desk to see what rooms Caval had and to give a call, so Eiler strayed for a look around. In such places, no matter how he dressed, Joe always felt everyone knew he was running some scam. But Jack was born to it and moved like he owned the place—and could have convinced most people of it. Joe wandered dreamily amid the richness of the lobby with its red leather couches and walls and ceilings of paneled mahogany. He had once been there for a few days with his wife, so the nostalgia was acute, ached even against his defenses.

The Del had been a favorite of the famous for years, had been frequented by foreign dignitaries, and had hosted a state dinner or two. But most of all it seemed to Joe Eiler a place to be in love. He'd heard it said King Edward VIII had met his lady there, for whom he had eschewed an empire. There was that romantic, early-century elegance about the place, and that morning it seemed wasted on the tourists in synthetic fabrics. But despite them, there was still a sense of Teddy Roosevelt and Scott Fitzgerald; of Astors, Armours, and Vanderbilts; long decadent nights; epic parties; Glen Miller; and a fig for care.

"Nice work, don't you think?"

Joe nodded. Jack had come up beside him at an entrance to the huge main dining room.

"Did you notice the ceiling?" Sidell strode into the empty center, beneath the great crown-shaped light fixtures, where his voice echoed. "I love it. No visible supports, no pillars." He gestured the length and breadth of the arched ceiling. "It was an amazing feat in its day. Still is, if you consider the equipment they had then. Bold. The guy who built this had some balls." He kept looking up, telling Joe something about the blonde wood—and that it was all pegged rather than nailed. Then he said, more to himself than to Eiler, "Vision and balls. That's what it takes."

And money, Joe thought—which is why we're here.

Mark Insinger answered the door and exchanged pleasant greetings. He looked content and much more confident than he had as a shiftless, hip lawyer back in Aspen, when he'd longed for some action equal to his ability, and especially to his dreams. Mark was dressing with more care since the project began, wearing more expensive clothes, and paying more attention to detail, rising to the occasion.

As Sidell and Eiler entered the sitting room of the suite, there was a letter desk on their left, a small fireplace on the far right between the bedroom entrances and, against the near wall on their right, a round oak table with four captain's chairs. Straight ahead of them lay Tom Caval, on a couch, in a brown velour bathrobe with a hood, propped up on two pillows. Tom was a startlingly handsome young man, the kind who turned heads on the street. He had a rich olive complexion with improbably sharp, predatory features

19

and full, jet-black hair that seemed incapable of being mussed and very rarely was. Tom was short, but tightly built and well proportioned. And he possessed an energy, and an opinion of himself, that made his presence dominating.

Tom Caval had started school in Boulder a year later than Jack Sidell and Joe Eiler, but it had not held his interest long. Tom got into the business about the same time Joe did. He and Joe even did a few deals together back then, but Joe soon quit that. Caval was too domineering, too manipulative. He always made more money than Joe—part of which Joe thought was his. Tom managed the same thing with everyone. In a couple of years, he seemed to be running everything that came into Boulder and to have a piece of everything in Denver. Tom was one of those people for whom the world seemed custom-tailored.

He came from a wealthy family of lawyers in Chicago, who held valuable real estate around the lake and had close connections with certain of Chicago's Italian businessmen who were greatly suspect among law enforcement circles. It was a matter Tom always enjoyed mentioning for purposes of intimidation, and he used it often, the way some businessmen invoke the prospect of litigation. Moreover, Tom loved thinking of himself as an independent young Mafioso. He always attracted a crowd of friends who admired his beauty, his wealth, his appetites. And he played the role for them, relishing his tempers and his expenditures, openly celebrating his illegal successes.

All his life, Tom Caval had gotten what he wanted. And he always wanted more. No matter what audacious schemes he had attempted, he had almost never failed. Hence, he had derived an unshakeable confidence that there was nothing he could not do. That, along with his other attributes, chiefly money and uncanny good luck, had produced one of the most aggressive, greedy, flamboyant, successful dope dealers in the country.

When Tom Caval had started making big money, he moved to Aspen where he opened a stylish shop specializing in French skis and the finest European equipment and, of course, acquired a sleek circle of retainers. Within a year, he had other shops in Steamboat, Glenwood, and Vail. By that time he had regular flights coming in from Mexico, netting him one or two hundred thousand dollars a crack. It was nice business, but the government had been bearing down on the Mexican air traffic, and Tommy was getting restless. He wanted to do something new, different, bigger, and a boat deal had seemed like just the thing.

20

Tom smiled and nodded a silent hello as Jack Sidell and Joe Eiler entered, but his eyes centered on Jack. Jack casually approached the couch as he looked around. There was a tangible current of resistance between them, but it did not immediately flash.

"How are you, Tom?" Jack took a seat at the round table and glanced at the room-service breakfast dishes on the coffee table. He was irritated by people who weren't up and dressed at least by nine.

"Great, Jack." Tom's smile grew carefully. "Yourself?"

"Okay. You just getting up?"

Caval burst at the tone of Jack's voice. "I already played two sets of tennis and swam in the ocean this morning." Tom had a very short fuse and always yelled, almost screamed. This punk, he thought; I made enough in the last two weeks alone to buy and sell his ass. "What the hell have you done?"

"Oh, nothing that important."

Caval just laughed his odd laugh, a series of brief nasal noises. It was as if he didn't have time, or might miss something, or somehow be taken advantage of if he let loose. So he concentrated it through his nose and got it over with. It made most people very nervous.

Mark Insinger and Joe Eiler had been about to ask each other about Aspen, how things were, but it was impossible. The exchange between Caval and Sidell gripped the room.

"You got a boat?"

"Not yet."

"No?"

"We need the *right* boat," Jack emphasized. "That takes some careful looking, but I'll find it."

Caval smiled and nodded twice slowly. But he was peeved and suddenly impatient and felt like yelling again. He hadn't made a fortune in smuggling by sweating every goddamn fine point. The guys who did that screwed around until the cops got there, or else nothing ever happened at all, or if it did it never came off until fucking Christmas. You just get out there and do it! He was on the verge of saying so, but stopped himself—and smiled secretively instead.

"I've got an office picked out," Jack added. "It's good."

"Good and clear for the radios?" Caval inquired softly.

"Sure," Jack strained. He did not like to be questioned. "It's up high, right at the beach. We've got access to the roof too."

"That's good. We'll go see it today."

"Right. I've found a guy who does electronics too. Good man. He sells radio sets, sets them up for fishing fleets."

"I already got a guy for that stuff."

"This is different, Tom. This guy is a marine specialist."

"Okay." Caval lifted his eyebrows. Marine specialist, he thought. Jesus. Let's hire the fuckin' navy.

They stared for a moment longer, but the room began to relax. Mark and Joe started to talk about the skiing and a few ladies they both knew.

"You guys want coffee?" Caval asked. Mark and Jack nodded. "I ordered some—wherever the hell it is."

Tom grabbed the phone on the coffee table and was starting to give Room Service hell when there was a knock at the door. Mark admitted the coffee, and Tom dropped the receiver in place without a word.

When the boy had left with the breakfast tray, Jack Sidell set himself before Caval, preparing defensively for business, and said, "How about going over these corporation papers? I have some questions I need answered." Being part of the corporation, even fictitiously, ran counter to Jack's plans. Insinger had convinced him to do it, but, characteristically, Jack meant to be very careful.

"That's Mark," Caval waved his hand. "That's all Mark. I don't know any of that stuff. You guys work it out."

Mark Insinger filled his cup and looked up anxiously, yet spoke with the slow soothing tone he'd learned to use with Sidell. "Alright," he blinked. "We'll be seeing this lawyer at one, so I suppose we'd better go over them."

Mark joined Jack at the table, opened his briefcase and took out a file of papers. He had a corporate statement and three or four copies. Joe Eiler stepped over long enough to glance through one copy, while Mark explained that signing the papers as an officer involved only a very limited risk. Joe laughed at that, but made no objection. They were to be Coastal Enterprises Inc., a leisure corporation, and Joe would be Joseph P. Ellsworth. Joe observed that the name wouldn't clash with the monogram on his pajamas, but it sure wasn't as cool as Jack Slade. There were brief indulgent smiles, and then Joe left the rest of it to Mark and Jack. He regarded the corporate front as a game Sidell and Insinger played to make each other feel better. He figured if they pulled the deal off right it wouldn't make any difference—and if they didn't, the corporation wouldn't do a damn bit of good. He walked to the french doors beside the couch and looked down at the courtyard while he smoked a cigarette.

22

Tom Caval lay on the couch and watched Insinger and Sidell at the table. Joe had never seen Tom either still or silent, but that morning Tom lay comfortably, with his arms folded, engrossed for almost half an hour with Sidell and Insinger's careful exploration of each detail of the corporate front.

Like any financer in the realm of narcotics, Tom Caval had begun his career directing a lot of hippies and half-bright outlaw entrepreneurs, most of whom he would not have condescended to dine with. He had used them well though, better each time, and now he gloated over the fact that he was embarking on a multimillion-dollar deal. And now his employees—as he thought of them—were skilled and well educated young men capable of leadership in almost any business.

When Jack and Mark began to retrace a few matters, Caval turned over onto his elbow to face Joe, who sat at the writing desk, making some notes for phone calls.

"Joe Eiler," he said, smiling curiously. It was the first indication that he realized Joe was present. "You been doing okay lately?"

"Fair." Joe turned to face him.

Caval made precisely two of his laughs. "I hear you're getting pretty big in Denver now."

"Not really."

"Yeah?"

"Yeah. I don't need to get big."

"No?"

"No."

They kept each other's eyes a moment, and then a confused disgust crept onto Tom's face. He was something of a Nietzschean, although he could not have known it, since any sort of philosophy would have bored and infuriated him. He came by it naturally, knew innately that he was superior, and strove always toward the superman who controlled, made things happen, existed above and directed other lesser humans. And anyone with remotely equal capabilities—who eschewed such power—was offensive to him, as if they were suggesting that he, Tom Caval, was less than he believed himself to be. Tom rose without another word and went to his bedroom to dress.

ii

Caval drove to the lawyer's office in the rented Chevrolet. As usual he kept the accelerator close to the floor. His excellent eyesight, reflexes, and luck kept his driving from being terrifying, but it was always scary. As they were hurtling through downtown traffic at forty and fifty, Sidell kept asking in annoyed tones if the damn thing wouldn't go any faster. And each time Sidell asked, Caval spitefully did manage to go a little faster.

Things went smoothly enough with the lawyer, though the man was not very impressed in the beginning. He was polite, but condescending, and had a round face and round, horn-rimmed glasses, through which he seemed to object to everything.

Mark Insinger did not care for the man, even though he had been dependably recommended. Even though Mark explained that he too was an attorney, but not a member of the California bar, the lawyer was bothered that Mark had drawn the corporate papers himself and was seeking only his imprimatur. He took every opportunity to pick at fine points as though they were crucial oversights. He affected boredom and a desire to hurry the interview to an end until, when matters were almost finished, Mark took a manila envelope from his case.

"I have some funds here for the corporation." He waited for the lawyer's eyes to rise from the thickened envelope. The man was suddenly keen. "To cover initial costs and expenses. And, of course, your fees. I'd like you to open an account for us today." Mark handed him the envelope. "The bank downstairs will be fine."

Mark went on about the nature of the account, and the lawyer was nodding eagerly as he looked into the envelope. He opened his mouth slightly, then took a new look at his clients. He poured the contents onto his desk, and the money arrived with little thuds, fifteen packets of hundreds, fifty in each, mostly used looking bills. Tiny beads of sweat appeared on his upper lip. He sat back a moment and fingered his tie and stared at what was likely more cash than he had ever seen in one place. Slade, Templin, and Ellsworth, he must have thought. Who the Christ are these young dogs with their open shirts and their hair and their bag of loot?

"How much is that?" He smiled and made a nervous gesture with his hand.

"Seventy-five," said Mark, omitting the obvious.

Joe Eiler thought: Concentrates the attention doesn't it, you stiff. The lawyer smiled and said, "Hmm-hmm." Like most attorneys, he was exhilarated by the feeling of being close to the limits of the law, and seventy-five thousand cash had to be very close.

Jack Sidell drew a long breath of embarrassment. He thought

24

it was a crude and flashy way to operate—typical of Caval. But given the source of the funds, there was no alternative.

"Well," the lawyer bestirred himself. "I'll call Bill Hanson downstairs—he's a vice-president—and have my secretary take this down." He lifted his eyebrows and looked carefully at each of them. "There will be cards to sign of course." They all nodded. "So then. We'll get a receipt and get this going. As soon as they—uh—get it counted."

On the sidewalk an hour later, Tom Caval studied his left wrist. When his three partners approached, Tom directed attention to a new gold digital watch, which he had bought when he'd grown impatient waiting for them. When it occurred to him to inquire about the lawyer, Mark reported that it had gone well. "Bet he liked that money," Caval smiled.

"He took notice," Mark nodded. "He took notice of that. He wasn't too interested in us at first, but I think he'll be taking our calls."

Caval quickly made his nervous laugh, and he and Mark Insinger leered at each other. Tom Caval loved money, especially cash. He habitually carried remarkable sums of it, literally thousands, and was never shy about letting people see it. And, at that point, particularly, Mark Insinger was fascinated by the money. He and Caval had still not discussed what portion of the project's return would be his, but it was the immediacy of the cash that kept Mark at Caval's call, under his power.

iii

They visited the office Jack Sidell had picked out, and Mark Insinger, relishing his new name of Templin, rented it for the corporation. Then they returned to the Del Coronado. Back in Caval's suite, they smoked a few joints and joked easily as they made further plans. Jack studiously paced the room. Joe poured a few drinks from his traveling bottle of scotch and seemed to bide the time suspiciously, as though awaiting some action he instinctively distrusted. Mark made notes at Caval's direction. Caval lounged on the couch and savored his power and the amusement of a new and larger challenge like a young general, certain of success, relaxing with his officers early in a campaign.

Their confidence was tempered only when Sidell, as Eiler had insisted, broached the prospect of a bust. Who would be responsible? Who paid attorneys to keep everyone quiet? Caval inflated with pride and demolished the problem, insisting that he would hire the best attorneys for everyone involved, that no one would be left in the open. Tom's assurances were always made with indignance. Nevertheless they discussed the matter several minutes and were just dropping it when the phone rang. Joe Eiler laughed loudly when it happened. Caval began an agitated, cryptic conversation. At the end of it, after some long, studied curses, he told them one of his drivers had been in a wreck driving up from Arizona and gotten busted with a load. Eiler laughed harder than before and poured another drink. Caval had great ability to infect others with the importance of his affairs, and the staggering coincidence was scarcely remarked as he grabbed the phone again. Eiler took a good belt and wondered if fate filled all Tommy's inside straights.

Caval was a dynamo for the next twenty minutes. He called associates, gave warnings, orders, called his attorney at home, then Western Union. Finally, he amazed even Eiler by producing the necessary two thousand dollars from his wallet, with several bills to spare, and said, "Let's go; Western Union closes in fifteen minutes." They chased him down the stairs and through the lobby, and were barely in the car as he pulled away. They squealed around corners and roared down the middle of streets. In a moment they were back on the bridge, reducing its long arc at a shuddering ninety-five miles per hour. Caval turned to yell at Eiler and Sidell in the back seat: "This is the way I operate, man. I know how to handle busts. You got to move before they do. I know how to run a deal."

Jack Sidell merely nodded. He did not mind the speed now. It was necessary speed. And he had to admire the skill with which Caval piloted the big sedan. In the front seat Mark Insinger quivered as he tried to recount the money while they shot through red lights and stop signs, pausing only an instant to check for traffic or cops, but he loved it. Like Jack, Mark was captured by the action, brought all the more under Caval's spell. Joe thought it was a great show.

chapter 3

i

THE airport at Panama City was the hottest, most humid place Insinger could ever remember being. Yet it was chaotic, swarming with dark people who hustled through the heat around him, their language overwhelming his spare knowledge of Spanish. Normally he could have adjusted to the heat, drunk a cold beer, but events over the last several days had put him off balance. He felt adrift, and, for the moment at least, did not know where he was going. Things had changed. Sitting on one of the bright plastic chairs, an eye on the bags, he strained to hear news of the delayed flight. But he was beginning to wonder if they would ever take it. Caval, in a voice much too loud for Mark's nerves, sounded as if he might change things further.

"You know, maybe we oughta do this thing from here. From Panama." He savored the assurance that he could do anything he wanted, needed only to give the order. "Panama Red," he mused. "They grow great stuff down here. I bet we could move it like hell. Anything with a name moves great. You know." He snapped his fingers. "Whatta ya call that?"

"I don't know," Mark shook his head. "Product identification."

"Right. That. But I think there isn't that much market for 'Red' anymore. I could tell you some stuff about movin' that shit a couple of years ago though. Hell, we called everything 'Red.' We were gonna paint some stuff red one time. With goddamn food coloring!" Caval broke into his snorting laughter. "The 'Red' thing cooled off though. I don't think it moves anymore. Whatta ya think?" He didn't bother to await Mark's answer. "No, I don't think it's hot anymore. I think Colombian's the deal."

Tom shifted attention suddenly. "Where the fuck are all these people goin'?" He surveyed the crowd with amused disgust, like a cattleman regarding an inferior herd. Overweight women sat spread-kneed, supporting gigantic bosoms. Thin, nervous husbands with thick mustaches listened for something and watched from the corners of their eyes. Swollen-stomached children noisily misbehaved. Slick-haired young men with white pants and big watches hurried everywhere. Large men in hot looking suits seemed to signal each other with glances.

27

Caval shrugged at it all and then savored aloud: "Colombian. Colombian." Uneasily Mark watched him consider the glory. For a few minutes Tom seemed to be dreaming of the expedition successfully completed, of the personal triumph, the grand entry in the tally of his fulfillment. Tom's eyes glazed a little. He must have heard himself saying one day, "Yeah, I brought in tons of Colombian. Five tons. I made millions." Hell, seven tons, he must have thought. Eight. Ten tons! Tom must have liked the sound of ten tons.

"Yeah, Colombian really moves," he said aloud to Insinger. "You just say the name and they pay the price. We could move more than we figured you know. We could run a lot bigger deal."

Mark barely nodded. At least it's still Colombia, he sighed— whatever the hell it will mean. Mark wondered how Caval, who was usually so fastidious that the slightest discomfort enraged him, could stand there sweating like a horse and not complain. Tom's tight Lacoste shirt was soaked, his dark sculpted features glistened. A drop of sweat occasionally fell from the sharp end of his nose. Yet he would not sit, be still. He had to stand, talk, stare among the crowd with variations of amazement, distaste, affection. "I'm gonna check out the duty-free store," he decided abruptly. "Stay with the stuff, uh?"

"Son of a bitch is wired," Mark mumbled. He watched Caval move through the crowd, noticeably faster than anyone else, the wallet in his back pocket fat with hundreds. Though Mark hardly shared Tom's enthusiasm, there was a sharp excitement about their mission. He toyed frequently with images of laden trucks grumbling through the jungle to a deserted beach, of negotiations in broken Spanish at small dark houses with dangerous men. But too many unknown factors had accumulated, and he sensed a danger in it all, to which Caval seemed oblivious. At regular, brief intervals, Mark's brow twitched distractedly.

Ten days earlier, shortly after their return from San Diego, Mark had received a brief summoning call from Caval, and they had met that night at Caval's house on Red Mountain across Aspen from the slopes. "We're goin' to Colombia," Caval said as soon as Mark entered the room. He hadn't even had time to say hello to tall, quiet Marshall Heard, who seemed never to be far from Tom and whose sinister rectangular face always reminded Mark of an Easter Island statue. Teresa was there, too, Caval's young woman, whose beauty seemed like a painting since she was even more quiet than Marshall Heard—as if Tom subdued the speech in anyone who was around him long enough. Mark had nodded self-consciously at them, then sat at an end of the couch where Caval lay. "Okay," he blinked at the fire, then at Caval, "why are we going to Colombia?"

Caval had put it out quickly and simply. The decision had been made. They were going to do the deal out of Colombia, so they were going down there to set it up. Tomorrow. He wanted Mark to make flight arrangements and find out about anything such as shots or passports that might be necessary. When Mark inquired whether Caval knew anyone in Colombia, Tom had answered irritably. He had a contact. In Cartagena. Where is that, Mark had wondered. "On the coast, man!" And there was a weight to Caval's words that ended the discussion. Caval had talked to Heard for a moment about some other matter, then he picked up the phone and soon Mark had left.

That night Mark had felt uneasy, surprised at the news, uncertain what his role would be there, but a taste for it grew. South America! Still, Caval had well-organized contacts in Mexico. But Mark had no idea he had any in Colombia. Moreover, he had never counted on going anywhere to meet primary sources, but that night as he packed and called airlines he thought of tiled verandas in the shade, dusky women, and it was alright. The more he thought about it, it was great. He barely slept.

Next morning he told Caval they would need passports, which neither possessed, so they must go first to Denver or Los Angeles. A small matter, said Caval. They would go to L.A., get the passports as quickly as possible, and talk to Sidell about the new plans. They took a flight to Denver, narrowly caught one for Los Angeles, and by midafternoon were settled in Newport Beach.

Jack had driven up through the hazy coastal balm, exercising the Citroen at ninety and a hundred most of the way. He enjoyed the outing and wondered what was up. But, as he sat across from Caval near the pool at the Newporter, he had not been impressed.

"Sure. Colombian moves great. But have you looked at a map?"

"Course I have," Caval had snapped. "What the hell—"

"Well—" Jack took a pen and drew a crude map on a napkin. "Cartagena's like here. You want me to go through the Panama Canal?"

Insinger laughed. Caval stiffened.

"Look goddamnit, on a deal this size, they'll get it the hell over to the other side. Wherever we want it. Or we'll deal with somebody else." Tom had spoken as if it required nothing more than a long ride across town.

"I don't think they would, Tommy." Mark had been diplomatic. "Too much country to cross. Too many security problems, payoffs."

"Bullshit. They'll do it if we say so."

"I can't see it," Jack shook his head. "If we score down there, it looks like an East Coast trip to me."

"Maybe it'll have to be." Tom could always find an offensive. "Can you handle that?"

"Look. We get a decent boat, and I can sail it anywhere."

"I'll remember that," Caval had smiled.

"Just let me know which end of which continent a little in advance."

Not until the passengers for Bogotá had been directed to the international gate did Caval return. He carried a new Nikon camera, perhaps the most expensive single item in the duty-free store. He said it would make them more believable as tourists. A fine precaution, Mark thought.

Once they had applied for passports back in L.A., it had taken a week to get them on a rush order. That left little to do but hang around the pool at the Newporter, drinking beer and making frequent trips to the room for a reefer or a snort of coke from Caval's ample vial. Mark had tried to start several conversations about the contact in Cartagena, but Caval would say only that he knew the man through his Mexican suppliers. At various times, Mark asked how the Mexicans had come to know a Colombian source, and if there weren't a lot of pretty gruesome rip-offs down there. Caval had reacted as if Mark were prying or doubting him, and he passed it off each time saying, "Don't worry. I know what I'm doing."

After two days, Caval had gone back to Colorado on pretense of looking after his shops, which Mark had never known him to do, and he did not return until the morning of their flight to Panama. Bored, anxious, and full of questions, Mark had asked pointedly on the plane whether the man in Cartagena was the actual grower or a middleman, if he or someone else would transport the dope to their boat, if the man was familiar with maritime patrols. Caval had replied evasively.

"We're gonna go down and work it out with him," Tom said finally. "I've got plenty to worry about without you grilling me. If you don't like the deal, you can get out. I need somebody who'll help me. Not question every goddamn thing."

A few moments later though, Caval had been jovial again, talking of frivolous matters, of wanting someday to have retreats on the finest coasts through Central America, the north of Colombia, and in the Caribbean islands. His desire for possession never knew bounds.

By the time they came in over steamy marshes and lagoons to land at Barranquilla, Mark realized completely that he was not to be a counselor or a coexecutive in this exploit, but an assistant under direction. He had to accept that, but going into strange, quite possibly dangerous territory without knowing what was going on did not sit well at all. Yet after awhile, as he stood in the open rear door of the plane, when most of the passengers had departed and the men among those who remained aboard for the trip to Bogotá shared bottles of scotch or *aguardiente*, he accepted that too.

The heat, the trade wind strong in the afternoon, the soldiers with carbines on the runway, even the carelessness and danger he kept sensing suddenly made him bold. He spoke Spanish to a few men, bummed a cupful of scotch. Later, approaching the plateau of Bogotá above the broad valley of the Magdalena, where towering cumulus stood like monuments to vast untameable beauty, both Tom and Mark felt the ancient lure that draws men to distant lands to steal away simple goods for illicit treasure.

ii

When he killed the light at his bedside and slipped off his pants, Mark could barely see her movements as she undressed. Then he could see the thin brass of the bedstead and for an instant her teeth, before her soft curves moved onto the bed as easily as a familiar cat. "Hi," he said again. They had said only that when she entered. She moved up a little, tucked her legs beneath her. She still spoke only with her dark eyes, her wet smile, as she bent slightly toward him. Her left hand touched his stomach. The right played inside his thigh, then slipped up to his buttocks. Her middle finger went right to his rectum, where it played every nerve and muscle of his body, so that he tensed at first and caught hold of the brass above his head. Then he liked it, breathed, "Jesus, sweetie, where you going?" As if in answer, she folded on him with the slow grace of a swan. Her mouth was hot and firm on the head of it for several moments, her teeth hinting, threatening before she took the rest of it, salivating, lubricating, her finger still playing, and her motion on him coming just a little faster each time. He gripped the brass and muttered, "God-o-mighty, mama, god-o-mighty," kept saying it louder until finally, with a long delectable groan, he delivered.

She did not pause, she used her teeth, lightly over all of it, and then just across the top, and had him laughing and swearing that he couldn't stand it until his head lay over with a silent smile.

"You Americano?" She moved even with him. Insinger moaned affirmatively. "I like," she smiled. "*Tu fumas*?" Mark said, "Sure," and turned slowly to the bed table and lit one of the reefers. They used only half of it before, to Mark's surprise, the soft crook of her third and little fingers brought him fully back. She moved across him, held his arms away, while she traced the inside of his lips with her tongue and put him in without a hand. Artistry, was all he could think.

Earlier, when they had arrived at the Tequendama, they had secured a suite, and Caval was quickly on the phone to the States. Mark had gone down to the lobby, and then for a short walk outside. He had not had any idea how large Bogotá was, how advanced. Nor had he been prepared to find the weather cool, the streets full of hurrying people, the majority dapper in continental styles. He had laughed at himself for having expected burros, serapes, and hot inactivity. Occasionally, on the long drive from the airport, there had been a donkey or small horse pulling some ancient cart through the evening shadows beside the road, but in the city he was impressed by a sophistication that reminded him of European capitals. And he admired the women, with their casual elegance and skin like soft *café con leche*. So, when he returned to the rooms and Caval wondered how they should pass the evening, there had been swift agreement. From the doorman, Caval had obtained an address said to be the best in the city, a plush old hotel limited in purpose to the sexual pleasures, where secretaries and students supplemented their incomes.

There was a knock at the door after the girl had left, and Mark went naked across the room and admitted Caval, clad in underwear. "Look at this little refreshment they've got." Tom moved to one of the chairs beside a small table. It seemed to Insinger the first time he had ever seen Caval relaxed. Tom actually chuckled unhurriedly as he unfolded a small package of thin blue paper and displayed shiny white cocaine. They each inhaled two or three small piles through a rolled bill. Mark's front teeth and upper lip went numb quickly, his foot tapped to an unheard beat. Sitting naked in the chair, he felt powerful.

"Nice stuff uh? Only cost about thirty bucks for all that. It'd be about two hundred in the States."

"Yes, quite nice," Insinger answered distantly. "I can't get over that woman. An artist."

"That's what the man said." Caval laughed, still easier than usual.

"I think I'll have another."

"You gotta be kidding. Mine did a number. I couldn't get it up."

"Hell, I may never feel like this again." Mark went eagerly for the phone. He thought it must be the climate; coke usually stayed him.

Caval waited until she appeared, then went back to the next room with the cocaine for company. The second woman was younger than the other, but a little heavier, with an excited, more amateur expression. Mark put her on the bed with her buttocks at the edge and placed her legs over his shoulders. They went at it hard and fast and lay gasping in a hold like wrestlers at the end.

Mark had two more women that night, many scotches on ice, more cocaine, and a couple of reefers. Caval stayed in the other room, listening to brassy Colombian rock music on the radio and considering his fortune. He ingested nearly the total of the blue package and was almost paralyzed when Mark helped him out the front door and into a cab at 4:00 A.M.

iii

They slept past noon and almost missed the plane to Cartagena—only made it because Caval pounded the back of the driver's seat and exhorted him as one would a horse. Insinger suffered contentedly in the back seat. It was late afternoon and still quite hot when they checked into the Del Caribe, the oldest hotel on the Boca Grande strip, a grand edifice built to resemble the Spanish battlements which surround the Old City. The rooms they took were spacious, with shuttered windows, red tile floors, and wooden ceiling fans. Caval looked around, shrugged, and went immediately down to the large palm-lined pool in the inner courtyard. When Mark joined him he still felt weak and thick, yet he was anxious to know when they would call the contact and where and when they would meet him. But Caval avoided his eyes, talked of other things. With a continuing effort Mark kept from pressing him. Maybe that's what the business requires, he thought. You just keep cool, don't ask questions, be ready for anything. There was a hard, mercenary romance to that, which Mark assumed as best he could, and he simply lay there letting the sun purge his excess.

Insinger habitually required at least an hour to shower and change clothes before supper, so people waiting for him inevitably went ahead before he finished and he caught up later. Thus he emerged that evening from the elevator and looked for Caval in the lobby, then at the poolside restaurant, before finding him outside in front of the hotel. He was talking to one of three middle-aged men in filthy muslin suits who hawked cigarettes, gum, assorted mementos from small shelves propped up by rocks on the ground near the hotel entrance. In particular, Tom spoke to the thin, unshaven man who had greeted them that afternoon with a convulsion of furtive winks and smiles, promising to get them anything they wanted. Mark couldn't imagine what they were discussing, so he moved near them and looked at the man's goods as he listened. The man seemed confused, and Caval sounded insistent.

"No, man, I mean *mucho. Mucho!*"

"Si. Yes. I bring to you."

"No. Come on. *Mira.* Like this *mucho.*" Caval bent down and drew figures in the dirt beside a walkway that led through hedges to the street. The old man was astounded.

"Kilos," Caval hissed. "That many kilos."

Mark's mouth fell open. The old man regarded Caval's gleaming eyes with a boundless consternation, then stared perplexedly at the figures and shook his head.

Jesus, thought Insinger, the guy just thinks he's crazy. Maybe he is. Goddamn.

Caval finally shrugged and left the old man shaking his head at the dirt. "Come on," he said to Mark as he passed, "let's eat."

At dinner Tom kept kidding him about his exploits of the previous night, but Mark finally could not keep his silence. He lowered his voice, but spoke firmly.

"Tom, why in the hell are you talking to some jerk like that when we've already got a man?"

"I thought he might know something."

"But if we already—"

"The guy we got is for sure. An ace in the hole. But we may be able to do a lot better. There's got to be plenty of sources. So we'll just look around the place a little and see what we can find out."

"That's dangerous as hell."

"All of this is dangerous." Tom laughed as quickly and stiffly as ever. "But I know what I'm doin'. I've done goddamn well in this business—and not by being safe."

The next morning they rented motorcycles from a small agency beside the hotel and began, in Caval's words, "to check things out." Insinger felt painfully conspicuous and frightened as they left, but kept telling himself to be bold. If they failed here, if he couldn't hack it, couldn't help get the deal underway, it might all fall through.

Before they had even left Boca Grande, the vacation district along the beach west of the Old City, Caval stopped to question a young man. The kid nodded carefully at first, but shook his head in amazement when Caval came to particulars. Caval smiled, took off again. Soon they reached the old section, three and four hundred years old, surrounded by gray fortress walls with broad parapets. The streets were narrow and crowded with traffic, most of it on foot, and the buildings were all constructed touching at the sides with pipe roofs, ornate masonry, balconies overlooking the street. There was a mysterious air to it, all the little doorways and alleys, the lack of signs, the similarity of building fronts hiding who knows what within. They worked through the streets for almost an hour, stopping at certain corners to watch the traffic and be watched in return. The sun grew quite hot, and they were both tense and spoke very little.

There was something palpable, something in the volume of activity, the sea of bright colors, dark features and dark glasses, sharp resentful glances. And it warned that this was no place for two gringos to be hustling a deal on the street.

Caval sensed it all, yet never doubted he could locate a source. He figured they wanted him as badly as he wanted them. You make yourself visible and see what comes. It was his brass and his luck that made Caval so sure of himself, but he thought of it as his ability, his talent for manipulating the factors of chance, his gift for attracting fortune. All he had to do was go out and claim it.

As they stopped at corners, sitting on the bikes, they were approached twice, but one man knew only cocaine. Caval spoke to the other one quite a while before deciding irritably that he was of no use. He started speeding back toward Boca Grande, riding angrily, and he nearly collided with a bus at the traffic circle. They were close to the hotel when he pulled over suddenly at a large open restaurant. It was about noon, but there were few people. As they sat and ordered beer, Tom kept watching two men, roughly in their thirties, sitting together nearby. Whether it was their hair, their shirts, their mannerisms or their speech that interested him, even Caval could not have said. He sensed what he wanted. Insinger watched him approach their table, nod hello, and sit as casually as an old friend. The men listened a moment, and their faces hardened. Then suddenly they stood up and walked away down the street without a single glance behind them, leaving Caval alone at the table.

"Don't look at me like that," Caval snapped a few moments later. "I can smell cops. I know 'em. I know more about this stuff than you ever will. I started like this, man. I went down to goddamn Culiacán to find my own sources when everybody said I'd either get busted or killed. But I did it. And now none of those assholes could touch my business in their dreams."

Mark took a deep breath and said something placating, but he did not like the sound of Caval's talk—although he had no doubt it was true.

When they had drunk a few beers the sun was blazing in full, but they went back to the Old City. It seemed to Insinger they wound continually among the same streets, passed the same faces, which grew more curious each time, then sinister. They spoke at length to two men—or rather Caval spoke while Mark waited at a short distance and thought about prison, death, sunstroke—then briefly with a third, but none of it came to anything. When they got back to the hotel and turned in the bikes, they were both tired and baked in sweat. Caval was angry and stalked away, leaving Mark to pay, but he had enough. The hell with being cool, he thought. This is crazy, goddamn suicidal.

When Insinger reached the rooms, Caval was on his way to the pool in his swim suit with a towel around his neck.

"Wait a minute," Mark told him.

Caval shut the door but leaned against it.

"I would say, on the strength of a day's investigation, that one does not easily locate sources around here. Not for the amount we want. Moreover I would say on the basis of observation and inference that we could very likely get our nuts cut off walking around asking for a few tons of dope."

Caval chuckled with a sawing sound. Mark continued with the same patient effort to be calm, but his brow and upper lip flinched in earnest.

"So why do we not simply call the man here and see what he has to offer? If it's not good enough, then—"

"Because there is no man here. I don't know anybody here except you." Caval leered. He enjoyed this. "So what we gotta do is find one. Just like we were looking today. And if not here, then in another town, until we find one." He turned to go but stopped, adding, "And don't think for a minute I won't find one."

iv

Insinger rose early the next morning and shaved and showered with what was, for him, remarkable dispatch. With the help of a young woman at the front desk, he located an attorney who spoke English, talked with him briefly on the phone, and then took a cab to his office in the Old City. He was an elderly, dark-haired man in a handsome beige suit. His English left almost as much to be desired as Insinger's Spanish, but Mark made him understand that he and an associate represented a California corporation which was interested in coastal real estate to be developed as a resort. It was the only thing he had been able to think of as a cover, but at least it could link them to a local attorney who might be helpful in case of trouble. The old gentleman agreed to be ready to examine contracts or deeds, and when Mark gave him $100 U.S. as a retainer, the man became positively excited with the idea, gave great encouragement, and offered to introduce Mark to several men of importance. He would have talked all day, but Mark said he had another appointment, obtained a receipt, and was on his way with several of the man's cards in his pocket.

It was almost eleven when he returned to the Del Caribe, and he expected to find Caval by the pool. Instead, he saw him in the open restaurant behind the pool, sitting with what looked to Mark at first like a disheveled woman. As he rounded the pool among sunbathers on wooden recliners, he saw instead that it was a flaming American hippie, of a sort rarely seen even in the States. As Mark stopped at a short distance to look at him, his face twitched with embarrassment and anger. The guy was dirty, unshaven for days, had a cloud of ragged brown hair, wore baggy muslin pants that were torn at the side and rolled up to his knees, beat-up canvas slippers with rope soles, and a blousy red shirt tied at the waist. A baboon could not have attracted more attention, and other guests nearby and even the waiters were clearly offended.

"What in the hell is this?" Mark sat down wearily.

"This," Caval growled in warning, "is our friend. His name's Jeb."

Jeb had a meal before him and ate with a vengeance. He looked up to nod at Mark, and there was a glint in his eyes that spoke of far too much acid.

"Jeb's gonna help us. He's been around Colombia now for quite a while. And he has a friend who knows a grower over in Saint Marta."

"Yeah," Jeb grunted, bolted a mouthful of food. "That's right, man. I been around Colombia a long time. My friend can help you guys out."

"Far out," Mark said carefully. "How long have you been here?"

"Well," Jeb chewed, "not more than about four months maybe—but a lot in real time, you know?"

"No."

"Soul time." He looked deadly serious, eyes fired. "I've spent soul time in the jungle. I had to find myself before I could find my way out."

Mark turned pleading eyes to Caval.

"He and another guy got lost in the jungle around Saint Marta," Caval smiled. "Didn't have anything on 'em except acid, so they ate that." Tom cackled. Jeb kept eating. "I guess they were pretty fried for a few days."

"Apparently. Do you know this grower, whoever he is?"

"No, but my friend knows him good. He's told me about him. I'll take you guys to see him."

"He lives here? Your friend?"

"Yeah. I don't know an address or anything, but I can find it."

Mark looked darkly at Caval, but Caval shrugged his shoulders and smiled. "Why not? You never know."

They rented a jeep from an agency in the hotel lobby and, guided by Jeb's ever-changing directions, felt their way through the old section and around the harbor to a sprawl of squalid shacks and crumbling adobes collected around dismal dirt roads at the foot of a small mountain.

"I don't remember exactly where his place is, but if we just drive around awhile I can find it."

"You speak Spanish?" Mark asked from the back seat.

"Not really, but I know a lot of words."

"That ought to be handy."

They moved slowly among the roads, most of which turned out

to be dead ends, for almost an hour. The small, crude homes were without doors or windows and looked empty except for an occasional chair, perhaps a table. Old women sat before almost every portal; small naked children were everywhere; young men hung around in groups, always sitting or leaning; there were no young women in evidence. Jeb craned out to examine every place they passed. Dark faces looked back at the strange gringo and his prosperous companions with acute distrust. The jeep left them in a miasma of brown dust.

"I don't think they like us much," said Mark.

"Shit on 'em," Caval snapped. "I don't care. I'm gonna find this guy if he's here. Jeb says all the real growing goes on up around Saint Marta."

"Santa Marta."

"Whatever. He says there's mountains there and the best stuff in the country comes from around there. You heard of *Mona*? That stuff called *Mona*? Blonde stuff?" Insinger shrugged. "That's where it comes from."

A few minutes later Jeb yelled to stop. "Back up, man. That's it back there."

They stopped before a small place constructed of wood and mud plaster and little different from others except that the edges of the door and window openings had been painted blue long ago. Jeb got out and went to the door and called hello before he entered. Caval took the Nikon—he had taken only two or three random pictures since he bought it—and followed Jeb. Insinger stayed at the jeep, and half a dozen naked children gathered noisily. Three young men in their late teens came silently across the road, then were joined by two more from another house. Mark nodded at them, ignored the begging of the children.

Inside Jeb struggled in Spanish with a haggard old woman, who sat in a straight wood chair and wore a pale ragged chemise. In a small rear room, there were objects on the floor, but there was virtually nothing else in the place, except the old woman and her chair. It seemed novel to Tom Caval. He showed the old woman his camera and took her picture.

"He's not here," Jeb said with a look of discovery. "But she says he's down that way. I'll go look for him."

Caval took another picture of the old woman, lost interest, and went back outside where more children and young men had gathered. He looked over the young men, and they looked back with predatory scorn. Mark's eyes were blinking at them. Caval's features tightened a little more than usual. Out of the corner of his mouth he said to Mark, "I guess we're on their turf." Nevertheless his eyes flashed; he grinned. The situation amused him.

Mark thought that was it. The four largest ones stood before the others. They had thin, steely muscles and hateful expressions. Their glances traveled from Caval to the camera to each other. Caval's presence, especially his appearance, seemed to challenge them. Mark's fear jerked in his throat. The heat, the dirt, the vulnerability, the primitive enmity were everything he had hazily foreseen. Against the menace of the young men, the camera glittered like a lure in the murderous sun.

"*Fotografía*," Caval said suddenly, lifting the camera. "You." He pointed at the meanest-looking one.

Mayhem crossed the kid's face, and the scene was very still. Then someone behind him said something that made everyone laugh, and the big guy looked embarrassed. Caval snapped him. Everyone laughed again. Then another of the tough ones stepped in front and flexed his muscles. Caval snapped and everyone laughed. Suddenly it all changed. The camera transformed the energy. It was theirs, too, for their pleasure, their enrichment. It acknowledged their importance. Tom took pictures of the young men, then of groups of the children—all, Insinger noticed, without ever touching the focus, f-stop, or lens speed—and managed to keep the group happily occupied until they saw Jeb returning with his friend.

Miguel, the friend, was thin, with oily black hair and a fatigued but attentive expression. A front tooth was missing, and he wore only sunglasses and dirty black trousers and carried a faded pink shirt. Jeb presented him proudly, and Caval instantly noticed the old needle tracks on Miguel's forearms, then smiled at him as they all moved into the room with the old woman.

"This *hombre* in Saint Marta," Caval began deliberately, "he has *mucho* marijuana?"

Miguel nodded easily. Jeb gave a broad smile.

"*Cinqo mille kilos?*" Insinger ventured.

"As much as you want," Miguel said in Spanish.

"It's good. *Es bueno?*"

"*El mejor.*"

"Good," Caval grinned. "You know where this *hombre* lives in Saint Marta? You know this *hombre?*"

Jeb translated the question, and Miguel nodded.

Caval turned to Mark. "Let's go."

40

"It's a long way. We don't know the road. You think this guy's for real?"

"I think he may be. And maybe Saint Marta's the place to be anyway."

When they asked Miguel to take them to the man though, he looked pained, said it was a journey of six or seven hours and very hot. Caval regarded him coldly.

"*Te gusta morphina?*" Tom asked him.

Miguel's lips parted reflexively in a wan smile. "*Sí. Como no? Morphina.*"

Caval grinned at him again, then turned to Jeb. "Tell him I'll set him to some shit when we see the *hombre.*"

After passing the hotel to leave a deposit and say they would not be back that night nor possibly the next, they started for Santa Marta. With Miguel in front to give Caval directions and Mark and Jeb in back, they jockied out the main streets among beat-up Fords and Chevies, black and yellow taxis, and hulking orange buses with garish decorations painted on the sides. They passed tiny stores, food stands, auto repair yards, KC Cola concessions with groups of people loitering in front, then on further outskirts, conflagrations of shanties even worse than Miguel's neighborhood. Insinger wasn't too excited to be trundling off across Colombia with an acid freak and a goddamn junkie, but it seemed better than roaming the streets. For the time being, though, it was worse to have to listen to Jeb. He told Mark about his astral trip in the jungle of the Sierra, how he'd seen his soul arrayed in the heavens and known his oneness with the earth, even how he had presaged being of service to brothers from America. "Soul truth, man, soul truth," he kept saying. Mark was relieved when they reached the highway and Caval accelerated so that the mechanical whine of the drive train and the flapping canvas roof made talking impossible.

Mark fished in his shirt pocket for cigarettes, and the rental agency's information card came out with the pack. He glanced through it after lighting up and smiled at the lame English. He had already noticed that, when a Colombian hotel or restaurant wanted to show class, they would use English on a sign or menu, and always screwed it up: "Vehicles are new, mechanically checked, and washed before rental for to assure you of a pleasant trip." He smirked and shook his head, but the next line made him cringe. "After paying U.S. $2,66 daily you obtain protection against damage by shock and total robbery." Jesus Christ! He dropped the card as if it were the Black Spot. Not flat tires or engine trouble, he thought, but shock and goddamn Total Robbery! What the hell's going on out here? He was pretty sure they meant to convey collision and theft, but who the hell knew? He took a deep breath, and his lips began to twitch. Shock, he figured, would be when *bandidos* opened up on that crate with automatic weapons. Total robbery's when they leave us standing in the road in our underwear. If we're lucky. He wondered if Caval thought the camera would help then.

The road from Cartagena to Barranquilla was well-traveled by cars and taxis and wide colorful buses, by pedestrians, and by men or boys riding burros or urging them forward under some load. Caval drove with uncharacteristic caution at first, but soon seeing that no one else did, he began to pass at will, using his horn as the others did, pressing the jeep to its maximum.

They had not traveled far when the roadside became thick with jungle foliage. Mountains appeared, small, sudden, scalloped, and rough-looking, with dark green cover. Occasionally, houses were grouped together, made of long branches and mud plaster. Some were painted brown, a few with red trim, others a sort of turquoise *azul*, and all of them were crowded near the road. Giant palms stood above everything in random bunches, and there were other towering trees with massive trunks supporting broad expanses of sparse, layered leaves. Burros wandered freely along the roadside, apparently available to anyone. Most of them stood motionless, heads down as if in prayer. The traffic took its toll among them, evidenced by an occasional pile of guts in the weeds along the shoulder, upon which gray-faced vultures arrogantly watched the traffic.

It was profoundly hot. They saw no one working, except men following burros loaded with bananas or firewood or else riding with a sad expression, ankles crossed over the beast's neck, a stick held over its head. Other people sat idly in doorways or beside wounded cars, walked slowly along the road, or sat in couples leaning against each other's backs for support.

At first Mark looked upon the passing spectacle with the resignation of a condemned man. Gradually though, the primitive energy that seemed to telescope the centuries made him feel daring, demanded strength, tantalized him with a rare sense of adventure. His fear subsided, but not much. Every few minutes, inspired by the raw feel of the land, Caval turned in his seat to yell at Mark with a ferocious grin. "Can you believe this country? We're gettin' into it now. We're gonna find that dope, by God!" Mark would only nod. He's crazy, Mark thought, really crazy.

42

They passed through a few villages with close rows of houses, small *almacéns*, and open produce stands. People walked in the middle of the road and moved at the sound of Caval's horn with slow, passive indignance. Beyond the halfway point to Barranquilla, the higher ground was rough grazing land for thin, white, high-shouldered cattle, and the lower fields were mostly planted in bananas. Twice they came upon boys displaying squares of red cloth, and Miguel told Caval to slow down. Then around the next curve, they would find twenty or thirty head of cattle being driven down the road by tough-looking *vaqueros* on small sorrels, and Caval would have to stop.

The third time they stopped for cattle, the jeep started up again sluggishly. Caval thought he'd left it in high gear, but when he saw he hadn't, he glanced darkly at Insinger. For the next twenty minutes, Mark listened to the engine, and he was sure they were losing power. Then they reached a good hill and could only labor up it in second.

"I got her floored," Caval screamed. He beat the dashboard. "This goddamn thing."

"I bet it's the head gasket," Insinger said. His brow and upper lip began to flinch. "Better slow down 'til we get somewhere or we'll be walking."

Miguel had started to scratch, and he shook his head, as if he'd known something would go wrong.

"This could be a karmic trip," Jeb observed earnestly.

"Fuck you," Mark sighed. Head gaskets, he recalled unpleasantly—four-cylinder jeeps always blow head gaskets when maniacs drive them at top speed. I wonder what he'll do now.

When they finally rolled into a small village with the jeep barely managing thirty kilometers, Insinger felt total robbery was in store. They reached a dusty lot with a long shack, bound on one side by an old truck being repaired and on the other by a great collection of discarded auto parts, bodies, engine cases. Mark and Caval left Jeb and Miguel with the jeep and found the *gerente* inside the shack. As they described the trouble to him, mostly in sign language, two men working on the truck joined them, then a third appeared. The manager agreed it was the head gasket, and said there was no problem. The other men drifted away, and Caval and Insinger waited while the manager searched among cluttered shelves of parts in the rear of the shack. Absorbed for the next several minutes in their limited options, Caval decided that if they couldn't get the jeep fixed immediately they would limp on to Barranquilla, rent another one and keep going.

Miguel could not have cared less, but Jeb had a feeling something was wrong when the two men approached purposefully from the old truck, one carrying a socket wrench and the other a pair of rusty crescents, and raised the hood. The third man joined them with other tools, and another emerged from the shade at the rear of the shack. Then distributor cables, spark plugs, carburetors, manifold, valve covers, nuts, bolts, washers, tappets, collars, and springs were removed so swiftly by all those hands and cast so carelessly to the ground that Jeb stood amazed as if by a display of magic.

Just as the head itself and the bogus gasket were examined briefly then dropped in the dirt, the *gerente* shrugged and regretted that there were no appropriate gaskets on hand. Caval was trying to ask a question when Insinger yelled, "Hey. What the hell?"

When they reached the jeep, one of the mechanics displayed the blackened gasket, shredded on one side.

Caval nodded bitterly. "*Gracias,* motherfucker. Looks like you get the job."

"Why didn't you do anything?" Insinger snapped at Jeb.

"Man, it happened so fast. Like they just came and—"

"Okay. Hell," said Caval, "it's already done." He surveyed the half-dismantled engine with a certain admiration for the way he'd been taken. "They made boobs outta us, didn't they?" The *gerente* arrived from the shack and made a show of scolding the mechanics as they skulked back to the shade. "Awright. Awright," Caval stopped him, "don't rub it in."

"The bastards," Mark grumbled. "What do you wanna do? Think we oughta stay here and see if they'll fix it?"

"No. I ain't hangin' around this dump. We got business. We'll call the agency. It's their goddamn jeep."

"We might get a taxi," Jeb suggested.

"Great idea," said Mark. "So far you've been invaluable."

"No, man, they're cheap here."

"Yeah?" Caval turned.

"Sure. You can take one from Barranquilla to Santa Marta for just four hundred pesos. You might get one to take you from here for about six hundred."

"Awright. Hell yes." Caval came alive again. "We're not that far from Barranquilla. You and Miguel go find a telephone and call one. We'll pay 'em a thousand goddamn pesos." Tom regarded pesos as little different than bottle caps. He turned to Miguel. "Taxi. *Comprende?* Taxi. *Tu vas* telephone. *Telefono* taxi in Barranquilla. *Para ir* Saint Marta. *Comprende?*"

44

Miguel's slow eyes grew with wonder. They realized he had probably never even ridden in a cab, and to call one out from Barranquilla seemed beyond his conception. He would as readily have summoned the *Queen Mary*.

"Jesus," Caval rolled his eyes. "Go with him, Jeb, and make damn sure he gets the place right and tell 'em to make it pronto. Can you handle that?"

Jeb agreed, and the *gerente* cheerfully told them of a telephone nearby. As the pair departed, Caval shook his head after them, then looked down the road toward Barranquilla. "You can't let shit like this stop ya. You gotta stay after it—stay on top of it."

Watching the intensity of Tom's sweating features, Mark felt suddenly that Caval was not out of his element at all. Even his tennis shirt soaked with perspiration and the flashy running shoes were not unlike the dress of the few younger Colombians Mark had seen who obviously had money or ambition or both. And Caval was as fervently oblivious to national boundaries or customs as a zealous missionary. Anywhere the rich moved brazenly through poverty and squalor in search of more riches was Tom Caval's turf. For the first time Mark was confident they would score. He could not imagine how, but he was sure it would happen.

A moment later, Caval turned to the jeep again, and he and Mark broke up laughing. They were after millions. A used-up jeep was not much more than an empty beer bottle. Caval said, "I bet they turn that pup to spare parts in a New York minute."

They waited two hours—roasting in the jeep, sending Miguel for *gaseosas,* and warding off a horde of beggar children—before the taxi cruised into view. Caval sprang from the jeep and ran screaming into the road, frightening the driver so that he nearly fled. "Christ," Mark sighed, "does he think the guy won't know it's us?"

It was dusk, the sun to their left an enormous orange globe, as they neared Barranquilla and passed small ranchos with arched wooden entrances at the roadside proclaiming names like Rancho Maria, Las Americas, Villa Hermosa. The cab was an old Chevelle so they could talk easily, but they were wary of the driver and tired from the sun and the trip. They were silent winding through the quiet residential back streets of the city and then waiting at the river in a long line of vehicles for the ferry. It was dark when the crude barge motored slowly, angularly across the mile-wide Magdalena. The driver sped on for the last two hours to Santa Marta, and darkness hid the marshes, where cattle stood shoulder-deep and men fished shoulder-deep beside them, hid also the sudden

45

majestic Sierra Nevada, the northern extreme of the Andes, which ringed Santa Marta at the edge of the Caribbean.

Miguel directed the driver to Rodadero, a resort town on the beach just west of Santa Marta. It was a quiet bay with four hotels, one real street, and a promenade along the beach with a few shops and restaurants.

Caval was possessed. He could smell a score. His features were so intense, his speech so quick, and his movements so sudden that Mark was a little afraid of him. Caval paid the cab as if he had a plane to catch, then Miguel made him understand that they had to go somewhere to get in touch with the man.

"I'll go with you," Jeb volunteered.

"Yeah, he'd love that." Caval turned to Insinger. In the warm darkness, the wide dirt lane was empty except for a parked jeep, a battered flatbed truck, and dust from the departing taxi. Wind rustled in the palms, and Mark had a sense of being watched. Caval spoke in a low hiss. "You guys stay over at that restaurant. We gotta go someplace—I think he said a goddamn bowling alley—to see if the guy's around. I'll be back an' we'll get a hotel."

For almost an hour, Insinger sat drinking beer on a folding chair in a dirty, open cafe on the promenade. He was too tired to worry about Caval or even himself, and Jeb gave him little chance. He braided the left front side of his hair and told Mark about the clarity of his LSD vision and of the soul of Colombia. "It's all happenin' out there in the jungle," he concluded.

"Yeah," Mark sighed, "that's what they tell me."

"Who?" Jeb asked.

"Shut up, will you?"

Caval returned more excitedly than he'd left, his jaw set, fists clenching regularly.

"Where's Miguel?" Mark asked him.

"I gave him some dough an' he split." Caval would not sit. "I met the *hombre*. Talked to him. Not for very long. But he says it won't be any problem. He's got a big damn farm or sumthin' where he grows it. I'm gonna meet him in about an hour at some restaurant across the highway. He's gonna have a sample, an' we'll work things out."

"Far out, man," Jeb beamed. "Good karma, uh? I knew it was good karma."

Caval said, "Shut up."

"You think he's for real," Mark asked carefully.

"Definitely. He's wearin' a nice suit. Young guy though. About

46

thirty-five. He owns the goddamn restaurant we're goin' to. I know he's for real. I told ya I'd do it, didn't I?" Tom tried to grin, but his face seemed paralyzed with tension. "I told ya."

<h1 style="text-align:center">V</h1>

There was a vacant lot full of discarded building materials behind the hotel, and they were only on the second floor. "I could jump if I have to," Mark promised himself. Every few minutes for the past hour, he had heard heavy footsteps and strange voices in the hallway. His heart froze each time. He kept thinking of police bursting in and carrying him off to some hell of a prison. And that was the best of it. He figured anyone who learned of gringos wanting tons of dope would think they'd have enough money on them—which they did—to justify mayhem. He had torturous images of the door being broken in off its hinges, big dark Colombians rushing in with a flurry of machetes, his arm hacked off as he raised it in defense, his skull cleaved.

"You're in it now, man," he shook it off again, slapped a mosquito. "Just quit worrying. Don't freak out. Be cool."

It was hot. There was an air conditioner in the other room, but Caval had wanted to bring the man there. In this room, there was only a square hole near the ceiling in the outside wall, where the air conditioner had once been and through which flies, moths, and endless mosquitos now entered at will. "What a dump," Mark thought. "Now he decides to be discreet. Crazy bastard. He sure as hell found a man though. But what a way to do business."

"Damnit," he said aloud, slapping another mosquito. He already had a dozen bites on his ankles, forearms, and face. Jeb sat cross-legged on the other bed and babbled until Mark wanted to strangle him.

"I think all Colombia is like an astral trip," he started again. "Without all the American stuff around you, you can really see who you are. I bet while you're here you see how uptight you are."

Mark jumped up from the bed. "I'll tell you how uptight I'm gettin' right now, you cocksucker. Now shut your damn mouth."

"Wow," Jeb sighed. He observed Mark as if from a great distance, then rolled onto his back. "Too much."

A few minutes later, Mark heard the door open in the next room. His breath caught at the sound. He pressed himself to the wall, but they turned on the air conditioner, so he could hear very little. Caval's voice was so strained Mark barely recognized it at first, even feared for an instant that it might not be him. For the next half hour, he caught only bits of the conversation.

"*Si, bonita . . . muy bonita . . . Mona . . . Mona . . . No hay problema . . . Todo seguro . . . Todo . . . Diez . . . Diez mille kilos . . .* Come back, *comprende? . . . Comprende? . . .* big boat . . . *grande . . . Si,* come back, *yo regresso . . .*"

Then suddenly the voices were saying goodbye. Insinger sprang to the door, eager for a glance at the man. Looking out he saw a slim man, not tall, walking quickly down the narrow hallway. He wore a light brown suit, dark black hair well cut in back, and for an instant Mark glimpsed high cheekbones and a thick mustache as the *hombre* turned the corner and was gone.

Caval stood at the center of the room, his face dark with dirt and the sun, features still rigid as he stared at the black window. In his left hand he held a large plastic bag containing about two pounds of marijuana, and Mark thought he was trembling slightly.

"Check it out," Tom snapped, then tossed Mark the bag. He continued staring away, proud of himself, more certain than ever that he would make millions.

Mark nodded slowly at the stuff but with authentic admiration. It was moist, golden tops. He had never seen stuff as good. He fondled it, smelled it.

"*Mona,*" Caval pronounced carefully, "*La Mona.*"

"So it's on?"

"*Seguro.* It's on. For July. We can pick it up in July. A little north of here. Right on the water."

Mark wanted to ask if he were sure a deal so casually arranged was safe. But Caval was still so taut, the room so dominated by his energy, Mark feared he'd succumb to a seizure.

"Well, it's awful fine stuff," he said instead.

"The best. The best there is!"

Jeb knocked, and Caval let him in.

"Hey man, everything go okay?"

"Yeah. Great. Thanks a lot. Here." Tom grabbed a handful of the grass and pressed it into Jeb's hands. "Go relax. Get stoned. Here's some papers."

"Thanks, man. I'm glad it worked. I'm glad I could help you brothers out." To Insinger he looked more preposterous than ever in his baggy, rolled-up pants and canvas slippers.

48

"Sure. Yeah. You were terrific," said Caval. "In fact," he grabbed the bag, put a small amount on the bed beside Mark and thrust the bag at Jeb. "Here. I want you to have this stuff."

"Wow! Far out, man." Caval moved him toward the door as he spoke. "I knew if we could just—"

"Really. Thanks. We got business. See ya later, uh?" Caval closed the door, and they never saw Jeb again.

"Let's smoke the shit." Caval tossed Mark the other pack of papers the man had given him, then sat beside him on the bed, but stiffly, perched as if ready to launch himself into the air.

"How's the price?" Mark inquired gently a few moments later as he licked the finished reefer.

"Good. Forty or fifty a kilo. I think they do things in pounds here though. I'm comin' back down in a couple weeks. We'll work it out for sure then. All the details."

"Good. That's good." It was all Mark could say. After everything else, it was so simple, so improbable, was ended so quickly.

Mark smoked the first third. Nothing happened. Then it fell from his fingers. To his immediate amazement Caval smoked the entire remainder. Mark's perception distorted, the room seemed to brighten, his mind could not hold a thought or image. For an instant the paranoia returned. Now they'll come, he realized. But he was too tired for fear, and too many other things raced through his mind.

"Why is that goddamn air conditioner so loud?" Tom demanded. Mark looked around as if awakened from sleep. It seemed only a mild hum to him. "What the hell's wrong with it?" Caval growled through his teeth. "Goddamnit." He jumped from the bed in a rage. The unit was high in the wall above a small vanity. "Shut up, you bastard!" he screamed at it. Then he leaped and smashed it with his fist, which actually did make it loud. "Shut up!" He hit it again and again and again, until the battered machine was truly noisy. He started to hit it yet again, then stopped still, sighed, turned, and fell facedown, unconscious, on the bed.

Numbed by the dope and conditioned by the behaviors he had witnessed for the past week, Mark endured the outburst with oceanic patience. When Caval lay still on the bed, his back lifting irregularly with his breath, Mark went to the suffering machine and pulled its plug. He said, "Good night, Tom."

chapter 4

i

"LOOK at that boat!" The man sat with others, American friends on vacation, at the outer bar on Morning Star beach. "My goodness," said his wife, who was half-crocked on sweet rum drinks, "how dramatic." Their friends also commented, squinting out at a large boat with crimson sails a mile off shore, just beyond the reef. Even regulars along both sides of the bar, who had seen it around the islands for the past two years, paused from drinks and conversation to watch. The bartender did not stop mixing, but also turned to watch. His glossy black features crinkled with a smile, and he spoke the soft, quick tones of the island.

"She some boat, dat one. She really is. Name *Leda*. Old one too, you know. Hundred years maybe, maybe more." The first man asked where it was from. "Oh, yah, she from here now, you know, at de Yacht Haven. It's a woman own her." The couples before him registered some surprise. "Yah, it's a woman own her. Young one too, you know. And she bring it here herself, across de oceans, from Europe. Somewhere," he shrugged, "I don't know."

The boat they watched coming in from St. John was an old Baltic trader that ran eighty feet from the dinghy on the stern to the bowsprit nodding imperceptibly at the small swell as it approached the harbor at Charlotte Amalie. She was a stout old boat, indeed just seventy-five years old, nearly twenty feet wide, strong-looking even from a considerable distance. The hull was black, and the broad red sails were gaff-rigged on two masts. Two headsails, also red, stretched from the bow back and upward to the mainmast, as the *Leda* moved steadily across the view from Morning Star. She was a rare sight among yachts in the Caribbean, and in anyone she stirred at least a few thoughts of times long gone.

"Can it be chartered?" one of the men asked.

"Oh, I don't know 'bout dat, you know. I don't think so, but you could as' de woman."

Sidell watched the boat intently. "Sure," he mumbled. "Coastal Enterprises. My card." Jack liked the way she looked, loved old boats, yet he knew they could be great trouble. All I know now is that she actually floats, he thought. But he was happy to have seen her. He had arrived in St. Thomas that morning—a day early—

and had gone to Morning Star hoping the boat would come in while there was still light. He looked forward to examining her the next afternoon.

ii

Leda was a big boat and not easily piloted, but Margaret Emery leaned casually against the wheelhouse, played the breeze coming over the starboard quarter with only her left hand, and smoked a cigarette. Ahead of her, Harry leaned against the mizzenmast on one meaty arm and looked toward the harbor. Since no one else was aboard, Harry wore only a bathing suit, and the straps that fastened an artificial leg to his right knee were visible. Two Irish setters, Ariel and Belina, lay on their sides near his feet.

Had it ever been Margaret Emery's intention to be conventionally beautiful, she could have done it well. Her features were narrow and pretty, and she had a soft mouth and striking blue eyes. Her blond hair was streaked almost white from the sun and forever windblown. She was tall, and her waistline was a little full, but such things never bothered her. She had large breasts that had never known a bra and therefore hung easily against her ribs. She had broad hips and slim, strong legs—good sea legs. She wore white-soled sailing moccasins, cut-off jeans, and a muslin blouse.

Margaret and Harry scarcely spoke as they neared the harbor, even though they were good, playful friends. They had had a nice time in St. John, but were not returning under very happy circumstances. Margaret did not care much for St. Thomas in the first place. Too commercial, she felt, and too many Americans. She preferred the "down islands," as she loved to say, the Grenadines, St. Lucia, St. Vincent, in particular Bequia. However, with painful reluctance, she was having to sell *Leda*—sell her very life, it seemed—so she had listed it with brokers in the States, then had to come up to St. Thomas to receive prospective buyers.

Selling her boat was the most difficult thing Margaret had had to do in her life. She was only twenty-two when she had bought it in Denmark. She and Jesse, who was far away now and another pain, had lived on *Leda* through a freezing Alborg winter, when the boat was little more than hull and decks. From the beginning the boat had been everything, had held all the rest together. They had built a new deck with skylights over the old cargo hatches, replaced the masts, turned the big cargo hold below into a main salon, remade

51

her above in her former image. In the spring, they had done the rigging, the red sails, and that summer, with three friends, they had sailed the Atlantic, gravitated to the Caribees.

Two years in the islands had been one long, warm springtime. There were always friends, new and old, living on *Leda* or on other boats nearby. Someone was always coming or going. There was always cause for celebration, always some new island, cove, beach, village to be visited and befriended, added to the kingdom. Margaret was written about in magazines. There seemed no end to friends and Mount Gay rum—and, of course, *Leda*.

Boats, however, especially large old wooden boats, are expensive. They must regularly be drydocked, painted, in other ways maintained. And for a while that had been no problem. Margaret's father was a wealthy man who had judiciously married a succession of wealthy women. Even when Margaret's mother, the second wife, had remarried and became estranged, there had been money from her father when it was needed. But for the past year she had not seen him often. And when she did, he had spoken of financial troubles, though they had not been apparent. But money did become a problem for her. She had carried some cargo between islands, but made little at it. She had chartered the boat a few times, but hated it. She was not a woman to work for money. As always with the Caribbean boat crowd, there had been talk of smuggling, long dreams prosperous and adventurous played at night like games. But the people Margaret knew—handsome, tanned young men and women, most from privileged backgrounds—were ultimately not the type to risk their time and money, nor especially their lives.

Margaret had always paid a crew of three or four friends, but had been unable to afford it for the past several months. There was only Harry now, and he worked on other boats during the days. *Leda* needed paint, drydock, work on the rigging and engine. Margaret had always sworn never to keep the boat longer than she could properly care for it, so finally she had listed it.

Simultaneously it seemed, familiar faces grew scarce. Some other boats were sold; old couples divided and departed. Some finally went to businesses and normal lives back home; some simply went elsewhere. Of course, there were always new faces, but without the old common friendships, the treasure of shared experience. The scene was breaking up, as such things do, but to Margaret it seemed like the end of a very special era—her own. And now *Leda* was going too. When she allowed herself to think of it, and she was romantic enough to do so often, it was as if the last of the jeweled sand was running out of the glass.

Margaret kept her course and passed outside of Hassle Island, which divides the broad mouth of the harbor. Harry went below and started the old diesel. When they were almost past the island, he went to the bow and brought down the headsails. He was a big strong, orange-bearded man, and the false leg did not hinder him. He was well known in racing circles as an excellent crewman, and otherwise a good man in a pinch. He slackened the sheets, releasing the main and mizzen sails, as Margaret brought them about to the wind and motored into the lee of the island. She idled the engine and hurried forward to help lower the main. Harry took the throat line, which pulled the heavy gaff up the mast. Margaret freed it for him and then took the peak line. With *Leda*'s simple rigging and old wood blocks, Harry's part required brute strength on the line to keep the huge gaff from crashing downward once it was released. The peak line, running to the outer end of the gaff, was much easier but still hard work. They strained against the weight, as the sail slid slowly into a red heap. They worked the same on the mizzen. Every muscle in Harry's body stood out rock hard, and not a lot of women could have done Margaret's part. The task was never meant for only two people.

"How's the squash?" Margaret panted with a smile when they finished. She wondered that he could work at all with the head he must have after last night.

"What squash?" He grinned over his shoulder at her as she hustled back to the wheel, a grin that showed the pain.

Two days earlier they had sailed—mostly motored—over to St. John and had anchored about noon at Trunk Bay, one of those rare St. John beaches where the water is pale opal and emerald and turquoise over the reefs and white sand. Unexpectedly, Libby and George had been on the beach. They were old friends of Margaret's from New York, and they were with another couple Margaret had met two or three times on Bequia. It was a wonderful surprise, just what Margaret had needed when they swam out to the boat. They had a great time drinking and swimming naked off the boat, then they motored over to Caneel Bay where Libby and George and their friends were staying, and George bought dinner for everyone. The next day, they had gone out for a short sail, and Libby and George had other friends at Caneel who came along. They had a party that night, with strangers coming out in small craft to join them, people all over the decks, cassette tapes blasting, the salon crowded with people lying on cushions, sitting at the long oak table Jesse had built in Denmark, fornicating in the forecastle and in the staterooms, an infinity of gin and scotch and Mount Gay rum and island marijuana.

This morning, however, she had had to call Yacht Haven back in Charlotte to see if there were any messages. And, indeed, there was a prospective buyer arriving the next day. She did not know at first if she could stand another one. The last one had come the day before they left for St. John. She had known on sight she would not sell to him. He was a sleek little man with Gucci shoes and a leather briefcase. She had picked him up in the dinghy at Yacht Haven and collected Harry from the big racing boat where he worked. They had raised the sails for him, started the engine. Then, of course, he took her to dinner at Bluebeard's. He drank too much. Like the others, he seemed less interested in the boat than in the captain's ass, and when Harry headed for bed in one of the staterooms off the salon where they sat, the man unburdened himself. Winking like an idiot, teeth and lips glazed with saliva, eyes dull from scotch, he said he wanted to buy the boat, but only if Margaret would stay aboard. Margaret had not really heard the last of his proposition. Shortly the man had blown his dinner, and Margaret aimed him toward a berth.

iii

"Did she come?" Sidell always enunciated carefully on the telephone.

"Came kickin'." Joe answered. He was sleepy, looking out the window at rain. It was much earlier where he was. This bastard's in St. Thomas, he remembered.

"What do you mean kicking?"

"Just that it was good. Everything's okay."

"Good. You will be in touch with him, right?"

"Definitely. Today. Whatta ya doin' there? I hope you're warm enough."

"Looking at a boat." Jack brightened. "It may be a good one for us."

"Okay."

"If I get her, can you be down here in two weeks or so? There will be a lot of work to do."

"Sure. This number, okay? And have a Rum Collins double for me, will ya?"

54

"Right. I'll be in touch. Take care."

Jack hung up smiling. He checked out of the hotel and with his cylindrical canvas bag headed for Yacht Haven in a cab. Everything was going well.

Not too happily, Jack had left San Diego two weeks earlier, after Caval and Insinger had returned from Colombia and it was certain the cargo would be taken to the East Coast. He had done a lot of groundwork for nothing, yet he knew the East Coast well, especially New England, and felt it was more suitable. He had gone to Florida to look at boats, stopping in Aspen to discuss matters with Caval. Then he and Eiler had met in Denver.

The load being doubled to ten tons meant of course a larger boat, and Jack was somewhat concerned about how long it would take to off-load, but mainly he wanted to own more of the cargo. Caval had agreed in the beginning that he could buy as much cargo as he wanted from the source, but Jack lacked cash to increase his share. At wholesale, ten tons of Colombian would generate some four million dollars, and if he was going to haul the stuff, Jack wanted a good chunk of the proceeds. Joe Eiler happened to have money in another deal going down in Tucson with the same people Jack had first worked with several months before. It was a similar deal—even with the same pilot Jack had recruited—bringing in thirty-five-dollar Mexican kilos, and Jack wanted in. He and Joe had sat into the early morning drawing figures on notepaper. In total, the Colombian deal represented an enormous amount of money, and there would be great movements of cash and dope. By glimpses, that night, they had each realized for the first time how large a mountain they were climbing. Millions. Hundreds of thousands. In cash. In accounts receivable. Big cash transactions. With trust and threat and no rules. No escrows, no contracts, no banks, no lawyers, no cops. Raw commerce. At several points they had simply stared in silence, as if muted by the sight of some phenomenal peak in the distance.

Jack had $30,000 set aside to buy cargo. At the expected price of $20 per pound, it would give him 1,500 pounds of dope—which, at $200 per pound wholesale, could bring in half a million dollars. In addition, he had a small group of investors for whom he was buying $100,000 worth of cargo—about 5,000 pounds—for which he was to be paid 20 percent of wholesale value upon delivery, bringing him another $200,000. Jack's potential take was $700,000. But, that night in Denver, he could see a great deal more.

Jack was nervous that night, chewed his fingers as he calcu-

55

lated. Joe thought the numbers were getting to him. With the load doubled, it was as if it were all a big poker game and Caval had doubled the stakes. So Jack wanted to run half his $30,000 in the Mexican deal. It could bring him roughly $90,000 to add to his personal investment in the Colombian cargo—and raise his gross to over $1,500,000.

Joe had leaned forward on the couch that night in Denver and poured himself more scotch. For the past hour he had not bothered with ice. Joe's apartment was a two-bedroom place in an old neighborhood, but there was not much furniture. He never stayed long in Denver. The nights were still sharp then, and the nearly empty living room was cold, so the whiskey helped. Sidell had been working on the cognac all night, and he wore one of Joe's parkas. On the single bare wood Parson's table that served as Eiler's dining table and desk were the bottles, the ashtray loaded with butts, Joe's fifteen-dollar calculator, and all the scraps of paper that presaged their fortune. Joe let a gulp of scotch burn its way down before he said, "All your problems will get bigger. Taxes, transportation, security, collection. Jesus," he shook his head, "collection. All of 'em gonna get a lot bigger."

"I know that." Jack nodded sternly. "But I'm not going to do this again, so I'm going to make it good. And I'm not hauling a giant load of goddamn dope up here just so Tom Caval can make millions."

Joe agreed, but almost sorrowfully. He had long ago learned to distrust the swift growth of profit on paper. "Things never seem to work out the way you're thinking," he said. "They just never do. Even stuff the size of this Mexican deal never comes off without a hitch. They just don't."

"Our other deal did." Jack's eyes were insistent.

"Yeah." Joe took another swig. "Well, you had a nice position there. Everybody else was hot, and you didn't have to sell dope."

"No," Jack stated inarguably. "If you set things up right, they work."

"Is that right?" Eiler grinned. Maybe he was right, Joe thought. Maybe Jack was one of those people who just know how to make it happen.

Jack moved on. "If I can get a piece of this Tucson deal, I know people in L.A. who'll buy it. I know they will. And they're good. No bullshit. They want to move a lot of the Colombian too. And they know how to operate. But I'd need somebody to deliver and collect for me. I'll be busy as hell."

"Well look—" Joe smiled patiently, but he was becoming a little more interested. "Even if you could get in this deal, and it's pretty late, who's going to do that for you? Not me. I'll have my own problems."

"But listen." Jack bent forward, forearms on his knees. Joe could hear him thinking, and it amused him as always. When Sidell thought hard, it was not like wheels spinning but like big chiseled chunks of hard thought sliding into place in the masonry of his plans. "If you'll go in on this with me like we're going in on the Colombian, these people will buy your stuff too. And they're good. They'll pay most of it right up front. You won't have to be hustling around all over the place. Then you could do the transportation and collection and then meet me down south."

"I've already made arrangements with people around here."

"Screw it. This would be a lot better. I promise you."

"No. These are old friends." Joe was adamant but already wishing he didn't have to be. It sounded too fast, but it still sounded good.

"Well what if these L.A. people picked up my stuff in Tucson?"

"No way," Joe shook his head. "Ramone doesn't know these people, and I can't hang around Tucson, you know that."

"Don't you know someone who could deliver to L.A. from the plane?"

There was an urgency in Jack's voice that infected Joe. As he thought for a moment, his gray eyes paled further, and the thick red-brown hair stood tousled above his tired features. He knocked off the last of his scotch and poured more. "Cavin O'Neal," he said. Jack nodded. "Cavin would do it," Joe went on. "He's in Aspen. He's driven stuff for me before. I don't like him much, but he's good. He doesn't fuck up."

"Well, let's get him and do it," Jack resounded. "He could make five grand."

Joe watched him thoughtfully with a cynical squint. Jack's determination, even his good looks, the stylish ease with which he dressed and wore his hair, bore a promise. It was a prospect of accomplishments on a grand scale, executed with class. Princely maneuvers. Joe had eschewed those ambitions long ago, after Mexico, but the lure sneaked back through his hardened outlook now. He was a little surprised at his own thoughts: Move most of the stuff through these L.A. people in one transaction; have O'Neal drive it out; just bring enough back here to take care of a few people; have time; get back to the apartment in San Francisco for a while; wait for the L.A. people to get through; and then head for the islands. It beat hell out of the way he had settled for doing business the last couple of years. He had five grand in the Mexican deal. Working through these L.A. people, if they were as good as Jack said, he could make it thirty thousand for the Colombian. He could make half a million in the end if all went well. Half a million, Joe thought. Maybe Jack's right. The big one. I could quit. I don't believe I'm saying that. Does that ever really happen? Joe took another long sip of the scotch.

"Who are the L.A. people?"

Jack smiled victoriously. "There's about four of them who work together, but the main person is Peggy Canon."

Joe looked sick. "Peggy Canon," he covered his eyes. Then whined again, "Peggy Canon. Jesus Christ, couldn't your mother do it?" Peggy had gone to C.U., and Joe remembered her mainly from his freshman year, a nice looking little thing, heiress of some manufacturing kingdom, chased by the frat boys, always dressed like a magazine ad. She had gotten around a little, but he could not think of her as anything more than a sophisticated sorority girl.

"Come on," Jack demanded. He poured himself more cognac. "You knew her a long time ago. You think I'd risk this with her if she wasn't—"

"I'm beginning to wonder."

"No. Come on. I ran into her in San Diego. She stayed a couple of days, and we got pretty friendly, and she told me what she's into these days."

Joe kept questioning him, but Sidell said he had gone up to L.A. with her, had seen a small warehouse she owned for storage. "She had a ton of shit in there when I saw it," he said. He also said she had about half a dozen guys working for her, ordered them around like a brigade commander, and had a sharp head for figures and for staying out of trouble. "She has a little of the old man in her. She'll do this to get a piece of the Colombian."

Joe Eiler shook his head. "Jesus. Is everybody in the dope business these days?"

The next three days moved swiftly. Jack had got Peggy by phone the next day, and she was ready, even offered to send some money for assurance, but Jack told her not to bother. They flew to Aspen in the afternoon, and Eiler found O'Neal the next morning. Joe had known Cavin would be having breakfast late at Andre's, being a cool local guy with the dolls who worked there. Joe had never liked O'Neal. Cavin was too predictable, too fashionable, too

58

willing to please his peers. But Joe didn't like anyone much, and O'Neal's character was what made him good for the job. He agreed to fly to Phoenix, rent a Winnebago, meet Joe outside Tucson to be taken to the load, drive on to L.A., fly home, and be paid a few weeks later. Five thousand.

The dope was the hang-up. Eiler had reached Ramone in New Mexico even before Jack called L.A. But they were talking about more than eight hundred pounds of additional cargo, which would make the plane overweight. And Ramone didn't know if he could get the extra stuff, or if the pilot would fly overweight. Before they had hung up Ramone, with a slight Mexican accent and a passive singsong affection in his voice, said, "What you start pushin' things for, Joe? What you doin'?"

"Nuthin', Ray," Joe told him. "I just fell in with the wrong crowd."

The third day they returned to Jack's place, devoid then of his plants, his stereo, and the wood and brass antiques he collected. He planned to be on the move quite a while. They had gone to Carbondale, where Jack took $15,000 from a deposit box. Eiler was going through the motions with him, but if it all came together he'd kiss his own ass. But they had not been inside the front door a full minute when the phone rang and Ramone's little sister told Joe all he had to do was bring the money. Joe sat on the couch overwhelmed and nearly speechless, excited and at once amazed that the business could still excite him. It hardly seemed that a full day had passed and everything had slammed into place with the massive precision of Jack's cogitation. Joe could feel it in the room, could see it in the glint of Jack's brown eyes, the thrill of setting something big and fast into motion.

"Whew. Jesus." Joe headed for the kitchen. "Got some whiskey in here?"

Jack nodded silently. He bit the nail of his left middle finger and thought ahead.

iv

St. Thomas in the afternoon, sitting in Yacht Haven with a *cuba libre*, waiting for Margaret Emery. Jack Sidell was a happy man. Nothing pleased him more than to be among boats, and he had spent the last hour walking along the docks nearby, talking with owners and crewmen. The bar was loud. The crowd in the islands starts early, and the bullshit was already high. Jack spoke occasionally to a few people but chiefly awaited his appointment and enjoyed the scene. A good, raucous sailing crowd was much of what the islands were to him. He'd been going to the Caribbean for years, to the Bahamas, the Virgins, the Grenadines, first as a boy on his father's boat, then moving boats north for summers and back down south for winters, as a crewman at first and the last few times as a captain. Jack cherished the islands from Puerto Rico to St. Vincent because it was sailing country; life revolved around boats and always had. There was the infinity of coves, beaches, islands; the trades; the squalls; the sunsets. And anyplace where people who lived and worked on boats got together to drink was alright with Jack.

Most pleasing to Jack, however, was the fact that he was buying a boat. He might not buy the one he'd come to see, the big raw-boned girl that stood out among the others at her mooring in the harbor, but everything was set. He'd be buying some boat soon, and it would be a good one. For years he had dreamed of buying his own boat, and he knew it would happen now. To Jack Sidell, a big, well-designed sailing boat with a strong diesel, a boat capable of going anywhere a man had the guts and the ability to take her embodied the principal aspirations of his life. Independence, adventure, and money.

Jack recognized Margaret Emery when she came in. He'd once seen an article about her with pictures in some sailing magazine, but also the bartender and others in the crowd called hello to her. She spoke briefly to one man, called to another that she'd seen Libby and George at St. John, and he said he'd heard about their party. She laughed, surveyed the bar, caught Jack's eyes a moment, then looked elsewhere. Not until the bartender nodded at Jack did she walk toward him, smiling but unsure.

"Jack Slade?" she inquired softly. Her voice lifted the question with a sort of British inflection, acquired more as style than habit.

"Right."

"Margaret Emery."

They shook hands, traded pleasantries. She had expected an older man of course, even another one with Guccis, so Jack was an interesting surprise. Several people watched them talk, wondered if the young guy would be buying *Leda*.

"Saw you coming in yesterday. How was St. John?"

"Oh great. Too bad you didn't come earlier. We had a wonderful party on *Leda*."

"So I hear. Where were you, Caneel?"

60

"Yes. Caneel and Trunk Bay. Do you know the islands?"

They had a few drinks and talked of sailing and the Caribbean. They knew the same boats it turned out, the same bars in Fort-de-France, Soufrière and St. George, liked the same smaller, out of the way islands like Isles des Saintes and Bequia. They enjoyed each other. Jack liked her eyes and the accent she'd picked up. Margaret avoided talking about *Leda,* though. It was difficult for her to think of Jack as a real buyer, because he was young—and because she had hoped to sell it to someone like Jack. But finally Jack brought it up. They drank up and took the dinghy with its little Seagull motor and puttered over to get Harry. He was working on *Belial,* a sleek seventy-foot racing ketch. Harry came on deck, dirty and sweaty from working, and watched Jack hungrily studying the boat from the dinghy.

"You know her?" Harry asked when they were introduced. His voice was high but rough.

"Yup. I raced against her once off Nantucket."

"That right? When was it?"

"Chased her actually. It was that regatta they had in, uh, sixty-eight."

"Sure. I was aboard."

"Congratulations." Jack kept admiring the boat.

"Yeah. Was a good race. We hauled ever'body that day." Harry looked Jack over a little closer, then winked at Margaret.

For the next ten minutes, they talked about the design of the boat, the rigging, layout, past owners, other things that would have bored almost anyone else except them.

When they reached *Leda,* Jack was amazed, intrigued with her size. Built for large cargos but comparatively empty then, she lay high in the water so the length of the broad black hull seemed enormous, almost swollen. When he'd climbed aboard, Jack stood for a few minutes with one hand on the ratlines of the mainmast and looked around the deck. He marveled at how old everything was, how large and simple. It had the feel and appearance of an antique, yet everything was strong and working.

Margaret went to the after cabin to straighten a few things. Harry moved around instinctively, seeing that extra lines were coiled and out of the way, equipment properly stowed. Margaret's setters had barked crazily at Jack when he first came aboard, but then followed Harry around the deck with great interest. "*Some* dogs," Jack had remarked as they arrived. He knew of no animal less equipped mentally than an Irish setter.

When Margaret emerged from the cabin, she began to show

61

Jack around, told him when things were built or last repaired or which pieces of equipment had been given her by friends in Denmark. At the very stern was the steering box with the wheel on its front and the chains inside that worked the massive outhung rudder. An arm's length before the wheel was a trunk cabin, which rose five feet above the deck housing the after cabin and an engine room. The cabin was entered from the left rear—port astern Jack might have said—by a three-step companionway. Inside, the forward wall held a clothes locker, a chart table, and shelves for the radio equipment. She had had it paneled in teak, and there was a dark old feel to the place that suggested rum and flintlock pistols. There were low bunks on either side, the starboard berth set against the wide timbers of the hull, on which was a shelf of paperbacks, some photographs and postcards, and a pencil sketch of Jesse. In the rear of the cabin, beneath the level of the desk beside the companionway, the stem of the boat was visible, a giant spine made from a single huge oak. Jack loved it. Everything was stout, and unlike pleasure craft, there was plenty of space everywhere. He could stand erect and walk around in the cabin, and elsewhere the boat had been built to accommodate men working.

When they came out of the cabin and went around to the engine room, Harry was walking toward them, and the dogs raced up, collided, and fell over each other at Margaret's feet. "Start the engine, captain?" With all prospective buyers Harry maintained appearances of order.

"I'm in no hurry," said Jack. Harry looked like he'd put in a full day. "You look like you could use a beer."

Harry agreed and went below, telling them to holler when they needed him. Jack went to the narrow hatch of the engine room, just ahead of the cabin. He peered in and saw the strange-looking, old Grenaa diesel set deep in the hull, its two big cylinders standing like a pair of fire hydrants, its flywheel like something off a locomotive. Again there was plenty of space for working, and Jack could see the tanks for oil and fuel on either side. The engine room was about eight feet wide and extended twelve feet to the galley and cargo hold, which had been converted to a salon. The forward half of the engine space was divided between a large storeroom on the starboard side, opposite which was the head, water tank, and workbench.

On deck, the mizzenmast stood just ahead of the trunk cabin, and there at midships the deck was twenty feet wide. Between the masts lay the new deck which had been built over the old cargo hatches. Twelve feet wide and eighteen feet long it rose a foot above the main deck, with skylights looking down on the salon. Ahead of the new deck were equipment lockers, a forward deck pump, then the tall mainmast, rigged with wooden hoops. Ahead of the mast were open deck, the forecastle hatch, and at the bow, a great iron windlass.

Jack was a little overwhelmed. A lot of boat, he kept thinking as they moved around. A great deal of boat here. It would be perfect for a charter boat, even better for his real purpose, but with all the old equipment and probably a thousand idiosyncracies, it would take a long time to know her well. And he would have to know his boat well. Colombia to New England is a long haul, much further than he had ever sailed.

They went below through the main hatch set on the starboard side aft in the new deck, then down the broad companionway to the salon, which stretched some thirty feet between the foot of each mast. On the port side aft, beside the passage to the engine room, was the galley, with stove, icebox, cupboards, and a counter that separated it from the rest of the area. The starboard side of the salon was largely taken up by a long oak table, capable of seating twelve. The dark wide boards of the hull and the deck beams gave the rough warmth of an old inn. There was plenty of light from the skylights, though, and more room than Jack had ever felt in a sailboat. There was a bright batik tapestry, photographs, and sketches on the bulkheads, a shelf of books, big cushions, simple wood stools, and some cane chairs.

On either side at the forward end of the salon were two fair-size staterooms and, between them, a narrow passage over the bilge, which slipped around the mainmast and into the forecastle. There were bunks on both sides there, angling forward with the contour of the hull as it neared the bow, and in the center was the forepeak with lockers for stowing sails, the anchor chain, and big docking lines.

"You have quite a boat here, lady," Jack concluded as they moved back to the salon. He sat down at the table. Harry lay against a cushion reading. "She is, isn't she," Margaret answered. She stood before Jack a moment, not really looking at him, with a sad expression. She loved showing the boat, especially to someone who could appreciate it, but of course it reminded her of having to sell it. The drinks at Yacht Haven were wearing off too, and that made it easy for her spirits to flag. "Can I fix you a drink?" she asked. She didn't want to start the engine. Jack said, "Yes," and she poured Mount Gay and Coca-Cola and sliced a lime.

"This would really be a fine boat for what we're going to do," Jack said when she sat at the table. As yet he had made no mention of his purpose. "I have a corporation with some other guys. We're starting a charter service."

"Really?" She smiled, yet thought of mongrel kids running all over the boat. "Where?"

"San Diego. That will be home base anyway."

Margaret thought it a little odd that he'd be so far from California, and Jack was aware of it, but she didn't say anything. Instead she told him of a few other traders, sister ships that were on the West Coast at Marina del Rey or Sausalito. They spoke a while about different sizes and types of traders, how they handled, how other people had arranged them. Harry fell asleep. The dogs lay above on the new deck, occasionally peering down through the skylights.

Margaret made two more strong drinks and told Jack how *Leda* had been scuttled during the German occupation of Denmark, how they had cut her masts and put in the larger engine after the war, and built a pilot house in place of the original after cabin to keep out the Baltic winter.

"I can't stand to sell her," Margaret said finally. Her light blue eyes looked steadily at Jack. "But I can't afford to keep her anymore. And I'd rather not have her than not take care of her. But I'm not just selling to anybody. I've actually turned down two good offers. I'm not selling to someone who doesn't know anything and who'll let her run amok. And I don't want to sell her to smugglers or something, who wouldn't care about her and get her sunk in South America or seized by Customs."

"Why don't you smuggle with her?" Jack put the question lightly, but he meant it. "You could make enough money to keep her."

"No," she said distantly. "I don't even smoke marijuana. I wouldn't even know where to begin. And I'm really just not the type. I don't like it." She was quiet a moment, then added, "But I wish there were some way to keep her."

"I'm sure," said Jack. He felt a measured compassion for her. He admired the way she lived, and he liked her. He was sure she'd had a wonderful time with the boat, but having to sell it was her tough luck, and he didn't care to hear all about it. A few minutes later, to break the silence, he said, "I'd like to take a look at that diesel."

64

"Oh sure. I'll start her up. It's quite a process."

They finished the drinks, and Jack stiffened his shoulders at the slug of rum that had accumulated in the bottom. They were both a little tight. Harry stirred as they got up, but Margaret told him to stay put.

The engine sat low in the bilge, but the cylinders stood up almost to Jack's shoulders. Each one had a piston more than twelve inches in diameter. The exposed flywheel was about three feet across, and the lower half turned deep in the bilge. Describing the process as she went, Margaret lit and inserted tapers in the top of each cylinder to heat things up, then adjusted valves, fed in compressed air from a separate cylinder, set the flywheel to its timing mark. Jack stood close by, trying to keep track. Margaret turned on the spark. With the rum, however, she had neglected to pump the bilge, which was always the first step, so as the engine started with slow, deep, powerful chugs, the flywheel showered both of them with bilgewater. Margaret gave a scream of surprise and turned it off, then folded in laughter as she looked at Jack, who stood beside the flywheel perfectly still with the front of his clothes soaked and water dripping from his perfectly expressionless face. Margaret could not stop laughing. Jack did not move.

"Pump the bilge, captain," came Harry's tired voice.

"No shit," Jack yelled.

"Oh my god," Margaret tried to recover, started laughing again when she looked at Jack, then suddenly hugged him for a moment. "I'm sorry, really. Oh lawdie, lawdie," she spoke like the Bequia women, "I haven't done that in so long."

"I'm honored."

"It's the drinks."

"I'm sure it was my fault."

"It was. Really. Usually the buyers get drunk. But you've gone and got the captain drunk."

She got a towel, then said she'd pump the bilge and restart the engine. Jack said he'd seen enough to wait until morning, so she suggested he change clothes while she made some dinner. Jack changed in the port cabin, and Margaret made some rice and a hot curry. Harry awoke long enough to clean up a full plate.

After dinner, Jack and Margaret took cushions up to the deck and sat against the starboard rail. A hundred lights winked from other boats in the harbor; thousands blazed in the busy lower streets of Charlotte; and thousands more glittered on the mountainside, many colored. There was no moon yet, and the heavens were crowded and bright with stars. It was warm, and there was a faint, soft breeze. To the west, in the distance, the sky glowed above San Juan.

They talked only of sailing and the islands. When it became cooler, Jack put his arm around her. Margaret liked the way he felt, liked his size, the direct manner of his speech. And though she did not realize it then, there was purpose about Jack that the men she had known had lacked, and she liked that too. "I'm tired," she said finally. "I'm going to bed."

"To bed, uh?"

"Yes. I am tired." She had a faintly plaintive tone. She leaned to kiss him.

"Okay," he said. "Sleep well."

The next morning they had coffee on deck. Then they toured the boat again, as Jack made notes about repairs needed, spatial arrangements and equipment. Margaret started the engine successfully and told him more about the beast than he could remember. Finally they discussed price, and Jack was sure she'd settle for $35,000. Margaret made sandwiches for lunch, then Jack went with her to run the dogs. She borrowed a car, as always, from the bartender at Yacht Haven, and they drove high into the hills west of town, where there was a windswept meadow with ruins dating back to the buccaneers. They had a good time and were quickly growing close. Margaret liked it, more than liked it as things went on. But Jack felt compelled to maintain a certain distance.

They picked up Harry on the way back to *Leda* and went out for a sail. The wind was up well so they raised all but the topsails and went far out in the direction of St. Croix. The boat could not really go into the wind, nor come about nearly as easily as the boats Jack had known—in fact, in a decent sea, she would not come about at all without the engine. But when he took the wheel Jack felt a rare excitement and the power of her great mass moving through the water, and he wanted that boat.

The thrill of it actually began when he was cranking the old windlass with Harry and built up with the undulation of the broad deck and the deep grumbling chook-chook-chook-chook of the diesel as they motored out to open water. It was more than the pleasure of sailing again, more than the Caribbean spread out before him, rugged and bright blue in the thick heat of tropical sun. It was that boat. He raised the sails with Harry, and they made a course south-southeast. Then Jack stood back at the wheel with

66

Margaret, as she set the size and strength of the old craft against the endless wind and sea. The trade poured dependably over the port side; whitecaps in the swell threw themselves at the surging hull. Margaret's yellow hair flagged in the breeze, blew across her face as they half-yelled back and forth about the way *Leda* handled. Harry moved about with his quick, heavy gimp-step and red-bearded grin. There was fun in the feel of it, but once Jack took the wheel, he knew a far more serious and challenging excitement. His hip set against the wheelhouse, he watched the great intricate bulk of sail, masts, rigging, and deck guided by ponderous response to his hands upon the wheel as they drove ahead. This was not sport. *Leda* worked at it with ancient determination that foretold the ageless labor of his adventure.

They took a taxi to town that night, climbed the steps up to the old hotel called 1829 and ate on the veranda. Red bougainvillea grew on the railing by the table, and there were darker scarlet hibiscus in a hedge of vines across the roadway. They talked quietly and dreamily, like lovers, as they ate. Afterward they walked among the darkened upper streets of the town, narrow and vaulted with old stucco buildings close on either side, looked upon by balconies of wrought iron or carved wood railings with tall, shuttered french doors.

Light warm breezes twisted like lace across the harbor as they sat on deck. Jack wanted to sleep outside and pulled the extra mattress out of the aft cabin. He lay down on it and, without a word, she joined him. They kissed and shared a long exploratory smile, and he took her clothes off. She wore almost nothing, just cut-off jeans and a blouse. She lay on her back and felt his arm and stomach as he slid off his pants. Margaret was a good size woman with wide hips and big bosoms, yet as he moved onto her, she seemed soft and weaker and somehow much smaller. She murmured, "Don't be rough." She lay her head back with a sigh and her legs found the backs of his. She made a high, faint sound as he went into her, kept her hands at his ribs, then opened her eyes to the stars, with her face beside his, and pulled her arms tight across his back, and they moved very slowly.

V

Jack put out his cigarette and placed the call. He had spent all morning and the previous day thinking about it, figuring it, worrying over it, but he had decided. There was a good schooner there in Fort Myers near his motel and a larger one in San Juan, but they were much more expensive and would be very crowded with ten tons. *Leda* was the one he wanted. There would be a lot of work to do on her though, and a lot of getting to know her, and he would need Margaret for that. The morning he had left Charlotte Amalie a week earlier he had felt as if he and Margaret had been together years. She was making coffee and everything was "we." It had made him uncomfortable, even a little frightened. He was a man who did one thing at a time, and he had not wanted a binding romance in this bargain. "But if she wants to play house for a while," he had finally concluded, "then that'll be alright."

The operator called back within a half hour and put Margaret on the line.

"Hello."

"Jack?"

"Yes. How are you?"

"I'm fine. Are you well?"

"Sure. Listen. Uh. My name is Jack Sidell."

"Just today, or all week long?" From her playful tone Jack could tell she was excited he had called.

"No. That *is* my name. There are a few other things I didn't relate accurately."

She was still playful. "Did you call to say that, Jack?"

"Yes." He had to laugh a little too. "That and another thing. You said there was a business you didn't like."

"I'd like it with you."

"Good."

They both laughed then, with an almost childish embarrassment.

"I want to buy the boat."

"Okay. I'll sell it to you."

"But I want to know if you will stay on the boat until I know her well."

"Of course I will."

"Good." Jack took a relieved breath. "Then I'll be down in a couple of days, and we need to get going and get her on slip."

"Great." Her voice softened. "See you soon."

"See you then."

"Bye Jack."

Just like that, she thought as she hung up. Just like that. Then she started laughing, really laughing, felt like she'd gotten a reprieve at the very gallows. Her mind gamboled with fantasies of what lay ahead, and she was happy again.

vi

When Joe Eiler's phone rang that day, he didn't want to answer it. He lay in bed propped up on one arm and just stared at it in the other room. It rang about twelve times before he finally went to the straight chair opposite the couch and picked it up. When he answered, a voice he knew only by telephone began without prelude.

"You may have a problem, amigo. Your friend still hasn't showed up yet."

"Yeah. I'd say that sounded like a problem."

"You never know though. He may have just had to lay low for a few days for some reason."

"Yeah. You never know. A little vacation."

"He still may show up this afternoon or tonight. I like to be positive, you know."

"So do I. You want me to call you tonight or you call me?"

"No, I'll call you, that's okay. Be optimistic, huh?"

"Be serious. G'bye."

Eiler negligently dropped the receiver and stood motionless a moment. Then his face tightened, and his voice grated in his throat like the utterance of some animal when he said the name Cavin O'Neal. In a sudden rage he stepped back and yelled, "Shit!" and kicked the chair. The phone struck the floor with a loud ding just as the chair hit the TV and knocked it off the smaller table. The breaking glass shocked him. "Oh great. Terrific!" There was a basketball game he had wanted to watch that night. Then even having thought of that made him sick. He went to the couch and dropped. He had to close his eyes almost a full minute before he could think. You stupid bastard. You knew. You knew.

With Peggy Canon willing to pay fifty more bucks per kilo than he was in for in Denver, Joe had decided to move it all out to L.A. He had told the people in Denver that he'd be putting them onto some Colombian in just a month or two. Then you really got cool, he thought. You were going to sit back and direct it. Broker it. No more hustling around.

He had simply loaded up O'Neal outside Tucson and then flown up to San Francisco for a while, to relax before going down to pick up the profits. "Like Tommy Caval or something," he muttered.

With a bitter, guilty lament he shouted into the empty room: "God-damnit. Goddamnit. Oh Jack, goddamnit, look at all this bullshit."

chapter 5

i

AS he walked along the Rue des Ecoles, life seemed to Robert Cole brand new. When he had left town two weeks earlier, Paris had been cold and gray with rain, but now in mid April the trees were budding, and there were flowers on doorsteps and window ledges. Everyone he passed looked happy, expectant, dressed as if it were a bit warmer than it actually was, and the air was sweet with the offer of spring. Cole felt like running the last blocks, then shouting up at the building when he reached it, "Helen, it's springtime. We are new!" He laughed aloud at himself. People on the street would think he was silly. She already knew he was.

When Cole started up the stairs, his sister Lynette could feel it on the third floor. She hurried to finish a seam as his footfalls grew stronger. She designed clothes and had been in Paris for the past year trying her wings. "Hey!" he bellowed when he entered, and she was already crossing the small room to greet him. Cole was a bear of a man—over six feet and 230 pounds, with a great chest, thick brown hair, and a big curly mustache. He hugged her until she begged him to stop.

"So how was Switzerland?"

"Great. Wonderful." His eyes sparkled. Everything about him bristled with energy. "Where's Helen?"

Lynette's voice fell. "She's gone, Bob."

"Gone?" In an instant the winter returned in his eyes.

"She went home, Bob. It was best. She was so unhappy."

"So was I." There was anger as sudden as the sadness in his voice. "But we could've—" He leaned backward against the wall by the door, finally tired from traveling by train since the previous afternoon. "I just knew she'd be here. I don't know. I just wanted her to be here so bad."

"She's not gone forever. You'll see her again."

Robert felt cheated though, and he only nodded and went to lie on the divan. This day, he believed, would have made a difference.

"Jack's called here for you twice," Lynette said a few minutes later, when she'd returned to sewing. "From Puerto Rico, and he left a number."

Robert mumbled an incoherent reply, so Lynette let it go. He and Helen had been living together for two years. They'd been having troubles lately, but he had believed such things always happen and that they would work it out. He loved her enough to work anything out, but now he sensed with a painful emptiness that it was over. Irretrievably. He clenched his huge fists against the agony of his heart. His lips trembled like a child's as he pressed them together, and tears squeezed forth from his tightly shut eyes.

Robert had worked as a carpenter in Marblehead, and Helen had cared for the apartment and cooked. They had gone camping in the autumns when the New England foliage was high in color, skied whenever they could in winter, and sailed with friends on small boats during the summers. Their happiness had been so simple he had never realized how fragile it was.

During the late summer Helen had become melancholy and uninterested, but could not say why. Often he had found her crying, and when they made love, nothing happened. So after Christmas when the weather ended most of his work, they had come to Paris to stay with Lynette. Travel sometimes heals such problems, but only temporarily, and when the novelty of Paris passed, there was only its iron gray winter and again the sadness in Helen's eyes. Finally Robert had suggested they go to the Alps, as though they could keep journeying out of the morass, but she had said, "You go."

He thought the separation might help. But then he had spent a week with a farmer and his family just above Gstaad, living in the beehive behind the house, and everything became as clear as the alpine mornings. He and Helen had no continuity, no future. That was the whole thing. His work only led to more work, the apartment was temporary, there was no thought of children, no plans. Clearly, he understood that they had just been passing time, not really living, and he had headed back to Paris certain that they could begin again, stronger than ever. New. The smell of springtime in the countryside coming in the train windows had assured him he was right. It seemed impossible he was wrong. He lay silently on his back for nearly an hour before Lynette's words came back to him.

"You said Jack called?"

"He's called twice. He's in Puerto Rico. I have the number."

"Puerto Rico?"

"San Juan. The number's under the phone."

Maybe, Robert thought, just maybe. He got up and took the slip of paper from beneath the receiver. The Nautical Club, he read. A smile came cautiously.

"He said to get in touch as soon as you can."

"Goddamn," Cole murmured. He was afraid of wanting again, and then suddenly unafraid, as if there were really nothing to lose then—and perhaps everything to gain. He sat down immediately and placed the call.

Jack Sidell was Helen's older brother. Although they had known each other for two years, Robert and Jack had probably spent no more than four full days together. Yet they liked and trusted each other, and whenever they met, they were good friends. They had also sailed together on two occasions, and Jack had seen that Robert knew what he was doing. Not long afterward, Jack had asked him if he might ever be interested in sailing a load of marijuana. Jack told him he could make ten thousand if he sailed as first mate and a lot more if he wanted to move some cargo. Robert told him he'd be ready to go any time, but that had been almost six months ago, and he'd stopped thinking about it. Still he had never doubted that sooner or later it would come to pass. Because Jack was that way, and if Jack were not that way, Robert would never have said he would do it.

He slept a little, and then paced the small apartment all afternoon, waiting for the call. Finally the operator rang back and said she could not get through to San Juan but would keep trying. Near nine that night when another operator called to say it was still impossible, Robert thought a few moments and then called Air France.

This could be the beginning, he kept thinking. This could be what he had felt so strongly. There would be this, and then the money from it, and then he would make the rest of it happen.

He flew to New York the next morning, caught the shuttle to Boston and went to the apartment of some friends. That afternoon his call was returned.

"Hey buster, what're you doing down there?"

"I'm working," said Jack. "I have a boat here. Can you come down?" The connection was terrible. Jack's voice faded in and out of static.

"Sure I can," Cole yelled through the interference. "I'm ready. Is this what we talked about?"

"Yes. There is a lot of work to do though. Where are you?"

"I'm back in Boston. I can be there tomorrow."

"Good. Come on. How have you been?"

"Okay. Helen went home."

"Well . . . maybe she can come down later."

"Sure. Right. Listen, I'll see you tomorrow. This is expensive bullshit. Where do I go?"

ii

Early the following afternoon, Cole's taxi turned through the cyclone fence gate entering Isla Grande. They passed long barrackslike buildings, then turned left and made their way down a wide gravel roadway between deep holes filled with water from the last downpours. It was bounded on one side by shacks and garages and aircraft hangars and on the other side by about a square mile of continuous rows of more idle truck trailers than Cole had ever seen in his life. They continued past the small airboat terminal, more shacks, abandoned equipment of every description and more idle truck trailers, until they reached the water's edge at the north end of the small peninsula. They turned right and splashed through deeper ruts and holes past half-sunk boat hulls rusting in the shallow water and still more idle trailers and finally encountered an archway proclaiming with inscrutable pride, San Juan Shipyard.

Cole paid the fare and stood beneath the archway with his bag. About forty yards directly ahead of him, the first thing he saw was an enormous pile of junk. Even from the entrance he could see big rats, not darting among the refuse but moving rather casually. Close to the gate on his left was a low wood building that looked like offices, and opposite that was a long open garage, apparently for welding and other maintenance, but so cluttered it was impossible to tell for sure. He could see only a few men working, but others — wiry Puerto Ricans wearing only pants or shorts — stood or squatted in patches of shade. Several desperate looking dogs skulked in and out of sight.

Seeing the slips just beyond it, Cole walked toward the central junkpile. There were other garages nearby, as cluttered as the other, and more junk piles. The two slips, with rail tracks and dollies with iron wheels for pulling boats out of the water, were both vacant. A fishing boat waited at the foot of one slip, and a small freighter at the other, and behind them half a dozen other boats of various types waited in the dark, still water. Cole surveyed it all and judged the place a disaster. A damned hot one. Sweat ran off his forehead and down his back. He could not imagine Jack Sidell, always so clean and meticulous, spending more than an hour there.

Jack had in fact spent the preceding three weeks there and hated every minute of it. He and Margaret and two friends of Margaret's from St. Thomas, who were hired to help work on the boat, had spent the first week waiting to get on slip, living on the boat in thick damp heat, while the rats moved in and the mosquitos ate well each night. Then they spent ten days on slip while the bottom was recaulked and painted, and Margaret's friends painted the topside while Margaret and Jack worked on the engine. Caval had been in town much of the time, staying at the Caribe Hilton, and he came to the boat occasionally in his tennis whites to ask Jack, covered with sweat and grease, how things were progressing.

For the past week, Jack had been waiting for either Cole or Eiler to arrive, so he could return to Boston and along with Insinger scout out a landing site. He was packing his bag in the aft cabin, hoping he could make the 3:30 flight to New York, when Margaret yelled that Cole was there.

Sidell greeted him with a serious, preoccupied enthusiasm and introduced Margaret's friends, Fred and Rita, then showed him around the boat. It was not at all the sort of boat Cole had expected—a big pleasure yacht—but he was as fascinated as Jack had been with the size and age and practicality of *Leda*. When they reached the main salon, Cole looked around at the dark timbers and light streaming in the skylights and said in a hushed voice, "This is a smuggling boat; a real goddamn smuggling boat."

Jack and Margaret agreed, and they made small talk a while before Jack went up to see where Fred and Rita were working and then told Robert how the deal would run.

"Ten tons." Cole looked steadily at Jack when he finished. "From Colombia."

"Right."

"That's a lot of dope. And a hell of a lot of money."

"A great deal," Jack nodded. "Maybe trouble too. Colombia. You never know."

"Sure."

"Well?"

"I'm ready," Cole stated. "I'm ready to go."

"Good. Now there's one other thing I have to show you because we have to get going. Fred knows all the work that needs to be done and there's a list in the after cabin."

"You're both leaving?" Cole looked at Margaret.

"I have to go to Denmark to get some parts for the engine," she explained.

Robert said, "Oh," and they laughed at the look on his face.

"We need a new piston rod and a few other things, and it's just easier and faster to go to the factory." Margaret shrugged.

"I suppose so." Cole had a stern set-jawed expression whenever he didn't completely understand something. "Whose footin' the bill on all this?"

"You'll meet him," said Jack. "Let me show you this other stuff."

Margaret went to call a cab, and Cole followed Jack out the hatch behind her and back to the cabin.

"You'll stay in here." Jack closed the door and latched it. "And here's the main thing you have to keep an eye on." He lifted the mattress on the starboard bunk, slid one of the slats aside, and pulled up a green plastic garbage bag filled like a good-size pillow and knotted at the top. Cole smiled thinking it was the marijuana supply for the expedition, but then Jack pushed it at him like a medicine ball, and it was heavy and bulky and obviously not dope. Robert undid the knot looking curiously at Jack. In a moment, he was looking in at cash in packets of fifties and hundreds tied with rubber bands. "Okay," he said in a low voice. "How much?"

"About a hundred an' forty thousand. Give or take a few hundred."

"What d'you want me to do with it?"

"Guard it," Jack answered carefully. "If you need anything for the boat or for yourself take it out of there. But Fred and Rita don't know about it. They don't know about anything. They think it's the charter deal I told you about. And I don't know if you noticed, but this wouldn't be a very pleasant place if anyone knew you had this kind of dough."

"I noticed. But that's alright. Nobody'll touch it."

Twenty minutes later, saying they'd each be back in about a week, Jack and Margaret were heading for the gate with their bags. Robert became engrossed in *Leda* and spent the rest of the afternoon looking her over. That night he became acquainted with Fred and Rita over dinner, and with the rats and mosquitos. They talked and drank a little Mount Gay, and Robert quickly grew weary. He excused himself, said he'd been traveling a lot in the past few days. He went to the cabin and dropped on the bunk with a painful longing for Helen to be there. He stopped thinking of her only when he noticed uncomfortably that there was no pillow. Then a smile formed beneath his bushy mustache, and he retrieved the green plastic sack. He lay his head against it, folded his arms across his chest and began to laugh.

iii

Sidell carried a cup of instant coffee and walked through the dining room to the stairs that descended into the long living room. He was still a little groggy from the late hours one always kept in the company of Mark Insinger. But he had awakened in the master bedroom and seen the early sun bright on the white mist rising from the sound and could sleep no more. He lay and watched it through the glass doors awhile, then rose and managed to coax a small blaze from the few coals remaining in the fireplace before going to shave. He had felt almost the same exhilaration he knew a month earlier, the first morning he awoke on *Leda*.

Jack paused on the stairs with his coffee to look at a painting of a ship under full sail and two murals, bright-colored and busy, on his right beside the grand piano. At the foot of the short stairs, he stopped to feast on the room before him. It was a huge room, at least twenty feet by forty, yet it had a feeling of leisured ease. There were full-length windows along either side, which looked out on the forested shoreline, a large granite fireplace midway on the right, and bamboo furniture with big floral pattern cushions. At the far end of the room, glass thermalpane doors opened onto the sound. Jack slid them open and stepped onto the weathered deck just above the edge of the water. He sipped his coffee and studied the rocky shore nearby. Green mountains with forests of pine and birch extended along either side of the sound, which was perhaps two miles wide at the broadest point, until they seemed to meet in the distance where the narrow mouth of the inlet admitted the North Atlantic.

Jack dreamed of sailing *Leda* in there, of anchoring her in front of the house. He could almost see her added to the view. For a few delicious moments, he dreamed of owning the boat and the house. He looked inside again at the relaxed elegance of the main room, then again at its spectacular position on the sound. He resolved firmly that he would have both someday. Not the same ones perhaps, but similar. Then he allowed himself to accept that for the time being, at least, he already had them. More than most men have in a lifetime, he thought.

The house was known as Far Prospect, and was formerly the estate of a prominent actress who had been the daughter of a wealthy Eastern clan. It sat on Mount Desert Island off the north coast of Maine at the head of Soames Sound, said to be the only natural fjord in the United States. Designed by the leading architect of an earlier time, it was strikingly modern in its day and was still quite unusual. It was regarded by some as the first cantilevered house, built so as to thrust the long glass-walled living room out over the water. Sidell, of course, would not have been happier with a king's castle.

He and Insinger had spent two days driving up the coast from Boston, then three more in Bar Harbor, mostly in a motel room. Jack knew the Maine coast, and it offered a multitude of deep water coves and inlets. Along the coast to the south however, they had found nothing like the sort of large secluded house near the water that they needed. Jack had finally reasoned that Mount Desert Island, long a haven of the very wealthy and the site of numerous mansions and fabulous estates, was the obvious place to look.

Passing himself off as a law professor needing a place to work on the writing of a textbook, Insinger had called on several realtors and outlined what he wanted. Then he and Jack had played casino for the next three days, while the realtors called back to say that what they wanted was impossible. It was already late spring, and the few such places available to rent were already taken. They were getting desperate, and Jack owed Mark a good deal of money, when one realtor finally called to say that an author who had been renting the Far Prospect place for several summers had backed out at the last moment. The name was enough for Sidell. He had sailed into Soames Sound once with his father and knew the house. Once they'd seen it, Jack and Mark made no effort to hide their joy. The realtor had been a little curious at the sight of two men who had previously conducted themselves with such sobriety suddenly embracing on the front deck, exclaiming together, "This is perfect . . . just goddamn perfect!" Insinger rented it on the spot, through August, and produced five hundred as deposit and said they'd spend the night. The realtor figured they were fags but had no objection to the money.

Two shy, thin classical musicians from Greenwich Village, a young man and woman each with long curly hair and thick, wire-rim spectacles, had been living in the house as caretakers through the winter. They behaved like servants as soon as Mark and Jack began rooting around the place as if they'd owned it for years. That night, after the woman made a dinner, they played for the new tenants. Mark and Jack in the big cane easy chairs, sat before a fire, drank the better part of a fifth of bourbon, and talked in low voices about shuttling and storing the cargo. The musicians filled the room with Beethoven sonatas and Chopin, then Schubert in duet.

The sun was well up and fog nearly gone from the mountains when Insinger found Jack beneath the house. "Figured it out?" he called. Jack told him to come take a look, and Mark, stepping carefully with his coffee, joined him at the big triangular concrete block that supported the outer half of the main room.

"It's like us," Mark observed, after Jack had explained it and they sat looking across the water. "No visible means of support."

"Yeah," Jack smiled. It made him think of Eiler again though, as he had been frequently. Where the Christ is he? It's been a month. "I guess so," he agreed with Mark, "unless you know where to look."

They talked a few minutes about the music last night and the possibilities of breakfast.

"So you're going to drive the shuttle boat, eh?" Jack asked abruptly.

"Sure." Mark blinked self-consciously. "Why not?" He was aware Jack knew he had almost no familiarity with boats.

"We're going to need about a fifty-footer now." Jack seemed to be warning him. "Big twin-engine job, like a Hatteras or a Pacemaker. There's not a whole lot to operating them, but you'll have to practice. And study. Study Loran. Study charts. You'll have to know all the coast around here."

"Don't worry. I'll do it. I don't think the sound here will be any problem, but I'll know that inlet out there damn well. Will we be without lights?"

"Don't know," Jack pursed his lips. "Sometimes that attracts more attention. Sometimes it just doesn't make any difference. But maybe so. You never can tell."

"I'll make sure I can do it either way." Mark's confidence required an effort.

"Okay. Sure. But you've got to know the coast both ways from here too. And the waters beyond. If it's rough we'll get blown around loading. You'll have to be able to find your way back. In the dark, at least. And it could easily be rough weather besides. We'll be a good ways off the coast, too. You've got to know that boat in rough water. How she handles. Believe me, two big boats side by side in bad water is no party. And she'll have a real load on when you come in. Sometimes fifteen miles can be a hell of a long way."

"I'm certain it can. I'll be ready though." Sitting beneath the house looking out toward the Atlantic, Mark was eager to get a boat, to be stationed there at the house, running out to sea each day, until he knew it all perfectly and feared nothing. He wanted Sidell to admire his work. "Think you'll be able to help me some?" he asked. "Just make a few runs out there to acquaint me with it?"

"No. I'll have too much to do. Whoever you get the boat from will show you all about it. But you should keep an eye out for somebody around here who can teach you the immediate area. I'll be up to my ass with *Leda.*" Jack grinned at him. "You ought to see that baby."

"Well, I am looking forward to it. You think we should inquire around here about a boat?"

"No. You'd have to answer too many questions. Better if you just show up with a boat some day. People around here gossip like hell, but they respect privacy too. I know a big boat broker in Boston who handles stuff all up and down the seaboard. He'd be best."

"Okay," Mark nodded. "That's perfect. I have to spend some time down there anyway, getting a couple of houses to rent. Let's head down there today and get started."

Sidell agreed. "But let's get some breakfast first. Then we ought to make some more definite plans for temporary storage here. Plot it out. And then check out the roads and see what we have for neighbors."

"Sounds *bueno* to me, Jack." Even when excited, Insinger spoke slowly and deliberately. He nodded again, blinking, slightly surprised. "You know, I think this is all going to fall into place. I really do."

"Yeah. It will if we do things right."

At this point, Sidell did not believe in luck.

iv

Enrico's was crowded, San Francisco beautiful in the clear May weather. It was a warm day with a cool breeze, and the Broadway strip was vibrant and busy in the early afternoon—which is roughly morning for most people there. Joe felt a little silly sitting at a table near the sidewalk as if he were trying to get picked up, and he was not fond of the place in daytime. He liked it in the early morning hours when the creatures came out. He went there sometimes with a lady he knew who worked late, and they would drink coffee and cognac. In daytime though, there were mostly tourists at that time of year and nothing weird happening on the street. He finally went inside to the bar to wait for Sleig.

Almost a month earlier, once he was sure that O'Neal had split with the load, Joe had called Ken Sleig. He was a private investigator and worked with the best firm in the city. Kenny was a short Jewish guy with a round boyish face, and he was quite a detective. Despite his rather angelic appearance, he was absolutely fearless, and Joe knew of things Kenny had done that he himself would not have considered as a remote possibility. Kenny also bought large quantities of cocaine from time to time. Joe figured his wife used the stuff more than Kenny did, but that was how they had met and become friends. In addition, like all investigators, Kenny was bored as hell by most of his work, so he was usually easy for an interesting job. He also had an occasional moral sense, and when Joe told him about O'Neal, he had said, "Sure, I'll help you find the son of a bitch. I'll go easy on the expenses too."

Kenny's idea of "easy" was merely Beaujolais with his supper, but he was good, had contacts everywhere, and Joe needed his help. The guilt was haunting Joe. He felt responsible for the rip-off, but he also blamed himself for Jack Sidell's getting into the business at all, and he was beginning to regret that. Sleig had agreed to look around on the coast, and Eiler went back to Tucson, even though the drug authorities there had promised to leave whatever was left of him out in the desert if they ever saw him again. But Joe thought O'Neal might have doubled back, so he had spent a nervous week trying to find out if there were any big amounts of Mexican, priced to move fast. But Tucson was always full of those. He went on to Denver for almost two weeks, doing the same things he'd done in Tucson, but with the same luck. Finally he went to Aspen on a longshot, got Jack's old girlfriend to let him into the place at Aspen Block, and sat drinking scotch in the window for four days, hoping O'Neal would walk by. He finally realized miserably that O'Neal would probably not return to Aspen in that decade and headed home.

When Kenny arrived, and they had said their hellos, Joe asked, "Why the hell do we meet here? Just so I can pay a buck twenty for beer?"

"Not at all." Sleig sipped his drink. "They make the best Campari and soda in town."

"Horseshit. Nobody makes that crap taste good. You drink it because it makes you feel like Interpol."

"Now Joe, you're in a nasty mood and—"

"You found nothing, right?"

"Right." Kenny nodded into his glass, then looked Joe in the eye. "I tried hard. Really. He's not around."

"I know you did." Joe struck the bar with his fist. "Fuck!"

Everyone inside looked at them.

"Joe, d'ya mind?" Kenny looked away as if he hadn't noticed the outburst. When he turned back, he said, "I was in San Diego a week. In L.A. a week—and in a dump of a hotel—and I had people here looking the whole time. Finally I went up to Seattle for a week. He's not around. I'm sorry. He's probably sitting on the shit until it cools. Or else he went all the way back East with it."

Eiler just nodded and ordered a scotch.

"Goddamn, I thought I had him in Seattle though. Big shipment of Mexican poop just hit town. I had to arrange to buy ten keys of the stuff to see the people, but it wasn't him. Just some weird hippies. Hell, I almost forgot and left that junk in the trunk of the rental car. Had to throw it out on the freeway, for Christ's sake."

"Should've brought it back and sold it. You could've covered my bill."

"Beneath my dignity at the very least, Joe. And what with your assurances—" Sleig gestured smoothly with one hand. "Not bad stuff though."

"What'd you pay?" Joe asked out of habit.

"Oh hell, when I saw it wasn't the guy, I said I was the cops. Everybody lie on the floor, you know. I was packing, so I figured what the hell. They looked easy. Well, shit for brains, they did it. Stuff was sitting there all bagged up, so I just took it and split."

"Jesus Christ." Joe looked at the ceiling. He didn't believe it, but with Sleig it was possible. "You might have at least brought it back and let me sell it."

Sleig shrugged. "Joe—"

They talked awhile about where O'Neal might be hiding, what sort of guy he was, how Joe might find him, but it was just talk. Joe finally said he was leaving.

"Uhh, Joe," Kenny purred. "There remains the small matter of—"

"Yeah, right. I'll bring it over tomorrow."

Sleig closed his eyes as though in pain. "Let's just call it two thousand, Joe."

"I'm moved." Eiler smiled for the first time in a month. "That's okay though. I'll pay what we said."

"Alright," said Kenny. "Sorry, Joe."

chapter 6

i

INSINGER glared at his watch. "We're going to miss the flight again."

Ralph Thorton sat across from him in the small living room, leaning forward on the couch to watch a baseball game on TV. He answered, but was more interested in the pitcher's windup.

"Quit worryin' now, Mark. He'll be here in a minute. Check the runner damnit!"

The pitcher delivered, and the Pirate batter laced the ball over third base and sent it bounding toward the left-field corner.

"Get it, you slow bastard!" Thorton railed at the Cubs' fielder. "Home it, now." Ralph jumped up. "Home that baby!"

The Pirate runner was just hitting third when the fielder threw, but the throw was low, took a slowing bounce before the shortstop cut it off and fired home. The run scored easily, and the batter went to second with a double.

"You rag-arm," Thorton howled at the fielder, no longer visible on the screen. "You rag-arm busher! Jesus." He turned to Insinger. "Why don't they get rid o' him? Hell, the guy can't hit nuthin'. Runs like my grandmother. And I coulda pegged that ball home just then when I was ten years old."

"It's a terrible thing, Ralph, but I don't give a damn."

Ralph's girlfriend Katie laughed almost silently beside Mark, but Thorton roared, a raw belly laugh. Ralph loved to laugh. Whenever he got mad he would always prefer to be laughing, but when he was mad it usually went badly for something or someone.

"You're right, Mark. I get too excited over these silly games." He switched the set off.

"That's the truth," Katie mumbled. Ralph grinned at her and shrugged, but her face and her timid tone showed at least a little danger in making such a remark in company.

"He's gonna be here in just a little bit," Ralph assured Mark. "Don't worry. He was real sorry about yesterday and us missin' the plane an' all. And he's a good man. He's never late usually, 'cept he had a little trouble gettin' that AR-fifteen, but I want that thing."

"I'm still afraid you're going to have too much hardware in those bags. It's going to weigh a ton."

"C'mon now, Mark," he gave Insinger's knee a brotherly grip. "I got it all figured out. I broke down the twelve-gauge, and it's in with Katie's stuff and so's the thirty-eight and all the pistol ammo. I'll have the Reuger and the AR and the machine and their ammos in my two bags. Hell, I can carry that like a pillow." Ralph liked details and plans. Whenever he did something, he wanted to feel that it was just right, and he had learned that the hard way. "They're not x-rayin' bags at O'Hare. They're gonna start, but they haven't yet. I checked all that out. And once they're on here, we're free into Saint Tom. If they say anythin' about the bag bein' heavy, I just say it's my scuba gear, right?" He laughed loudly.

"I guess it's okay," said Mark. It's not my ass if they get caught, he figured. I'm a separate traveler, and I don't know them. I have my own cargo to worry about.

Caval had instructed Mark to meet Marshall Heard in Chicago to pick up funds for Thorton's hardware and deliver the remainder to Caval in St. Thomas. Mark had expected a sizeable amount of cash but had not been prepared for Heard to hand him a briefcase packed with $56,000. "Fifty-six even," Heard had stated. "Watch yourself." Then he left. It was the sort of thing Mark had dreamed of, the sort of task he had believed would be one of his specialties in the deal, and at first he frequently took time to gaze at the fifty-six packets and adjust their arrangement. But hanging around Thorton's house for three days had given him a case of nerves, and Ralph's big, hard-eyed, mean-spirited friends, who came and went like wolves, flat scared him. Now even flying to St. Thomas, without the pressure of having to cross any borders, made him jumpy. He blinked several times and said, "But if we're going to miss that plane again today, I need to call down there and tell Caval."

"We won't miss it. We'll get there on time." Ralph was starting to pace though. "And when we do," he stopped to grin, "it'll be just like a little party headin' down to the ol' islands for a vacation. Right, honey?"

Katie smiled and nodded. She was slender and pretty, with a nice figure, brown eyes, and long, light-brown hair. She did not speak much, but listened well. Whenever Ralph asked her about something that had happened when she had been present, she could always say in her hard Chicago accent something like, "He said fifty rounds the first time, but today he just said forty." "Is that right?" Ralph might ask, and she would nod. She was sweet and shy, and she loved taking care of Ralph and being subordinate, but she was tough too. She didn't mind carrying guns in her suitcase.

"Honey," Ralph asked, "would ya get us a couple more beers?"

She nodded getting up. "I'll call O'Hare too an' see if the plane's gonna be on time and check our reservations." Mark admired her ass as she left the room.

"She's a good little girl," Ralph winked at Mark. He loved her, and he paid for their little house in one of the near suburbs of Chicago, bought the food, her clothes, took her on trips, so he saw no reason why she should not wait on him. He never spoke roughly to her before others.

Ralph Thorton was a compact bomb of a man. He was only about five-six but weighed one eighty-five. He had a slender waist and short legs, so the weight was in massive shoulders and arms. He had grown up in downtown Chicago, and from the time he was seventeen, he had worked as a steel rigger on the construction of bridges, overpasses, and tall buildings, and as a bouncer in rough bars at night. His knuckles showed white, jagged scars, and in one brawl a broken beer bottle had left a narrow pink line from the corner of his left eye down to the round point of his jaw. A small piece of glass had lodged in his eye, harming his vision even after two operations, and ended his days in the lucrative high-construction trade. That was when he had decided, in the funda-

mental religious terms in which he viewed life, that God was showing him that he should be happier and easier going. He quit drinking so much and did in fact become much more jovial and tolerant
and slow—at least slower—to anger. He began to get into
marijuana at about the same time and, for the past few years, had
moved a lot of weight in Chicago. And people didn't cross Ralph
Thorton. Chiefly for that reason, he had become a friend and ally of
Tom Caval.

Ralph had been vacationing in Aspen when Caval and Sidell
had begun the enterprise, and subsequently he had skied a lot with
Jack. They had become good friends and were wild company on the
slopes. Jack had skied most of his life and could knife down the
most difficult slope with speed and style. Ralph was new to the
sport, but kept up through his phenomenal agility and total absence of fear. Jack felt Ralph would make an excellent crewman for
the voyage, so he had raised the matter with him even before Caval
did. And Ralph, who liked Jack, said of course he'd go. Ralph liked
Jack in much the same way he liked Tom Caval. They were sort of
pretty boys, and educated, and born with bank books up their
asses. But they were still good guys, and he wouldn't have minded
coming up the easy way himself. He believed Jack was the perfect
kind of guy to be the boat captain, and Tommy was the right kind of
boss for a really big deal.

"Alright now, here he is," Ralph clapped his hands when he
saw the car enter the driveway. "Let's get ready to go, gang."

The man lifted a large wicker clothes basket full of laundry out
of his back seat, and Ralph kidded him about it when he came in.
In the laundry, there was a .45 calibre Thompson submachine gun
with three long clips of thirty rounds each and the Colt AR-15
semiautomatic carbine with three square twenty-round clips.

"If it takes more than these babies," Ralph laughed as Insinger
paid the man, "our asses'll be cheap anyhow."

ii

Joe Eiler could hear that rough belly laughter of Ralph's as he
walked the last dark block to Joe's bar a few days later in Charlotte
Amalie. He was not eager to see Jack. But he had to see him
sometime, had put it off too long already, but if possible he planned
to put off the story one more day.

Joe's bar sat on a corner just up the hill from all the shops and the more commercial taverns on the lower main streets. It was a dark, dirty, rough place, devoted solely to determined drinking. There were usually two or three scruffy young people dancing to loud music from the jukebox near the open corner entrance, and almost always some pompous limey carrying on inside, who fancied himself the world's most courageous sailer and a gift to the ladies. That night, however, the loud voices and constant laughter from one table in the corner of the front section dominated the place. Jack and Margaret and Robert Cole and Ralph and Katie sat around the table, all tanned and lusty and bold, and at least half-loaded. Joe stopped in the doorway to watch them a moment. They had a chosen, special, fearless air; they owned the bar, the town, the whole goddamn island. The sea awaited them.

"Why there's that polecat," Thorton bellowed when he saw Eiler. The others laughed, and Ralph jumped and grabbed Joe's hand as he came to the table. Sidell turned around with his face full of both relief and anger. Ralph squinted fiercely into Joe's eyes: "Good to see ya again, Joe."

"Long time, Ralph. How you been?"

"Great. I wanna tell ya something," Ralph said confidentially, then his voice grew loud again, "but first say hello to these pirates."

Joe had never met either Margaret or Robert Cole, and he waited until they were introduced before turning to Jack.

"Where you been, Jack?" They shook hands and held on as Jack spoke.

"You bastard," he smiled. "Don't you say that. What happened?"

"We've expected you every day for the past month," Margaret said. Everyone laughed. They were laughing at everything that night.

"Hell, I knew he'd get here," Thorton yelled.

"Well?" Jack's face straightened.

Joe didn't know how he managed to smile, but he did. He supposed it was the company and not wanting to spoil what looked like a good time, which he hadn't had in a while. "If it'll keep for a month, I guess it'll keep 'til tomorrow, uh?"

Jack nodded happily. He was a very private man, and he had only wanted a sign and eagerly took Joe's smile for it. Thorton suddenly hammered the table with his fist and forearm, and the dozen or so other people in the place nearly dove for cover.

"Bartender!" he roared and grabbed Joe's shoulders. "Can't

you see how thirsty this man is? Get some more o' that queer rum over here." Everyone laughed. "And don't let that goddamned jukebox go off!"

Joe did not really know Thorton, but their paths had crossed a few times in Denver and Aspen, and Joe knew of him. Ralph was still on his feet, and he gripped Joe's hand again and squeezed it tighter than before. "You and me have just seen each other around a few times really, Joe," Ralph spoke seriously. He was a passionate man and spoke loud enough to quiet the others for a moment as if making a testimonial. "But I always knew you was a good man, and I had a feelin' we might get together on somethin' someday, and I'm just glad it's gonna be here with these people on this thing and—" Ralph trailed off, having embarrassed himself along with everyone else. Cole held his heart and gasped sarcastically. Jack said, "Give him a big kiss, Ralph." Thorton laughed louder than any of them and didn't let go of Joe's hand until he finished.

"Here." The bartender arrived suddenly and banged a plastic bucket of ice and a full bottle of Mount Gay on the table. "Kill yourselves."

When they finished laughing at that, Joe felt compelled to tell Thorton he felt the same way, then he said hello to Katie. "You get prettier every time I see you. Why you hang around with this lout?"

Thorton put his head back and laughed, and Katie shook her head, "I wonder sometimes."

"Where'd you catch that gorilla you got on the boat?" Joe turned to Jack as he sat down. They seemed to laugh harder each time. Joe could tell they were going to laugh all night.

"You mean he still had the boat under him?" Cole asked. More laughter.

"Yeah," Joe said, "at least when I came up. He was torturing a guitar for some reason."

Jack spit rum all over himself, and the others fell back and forth against the table howling.

Joe had flown into San Juan that afternoon, learned at the Nautical Club that Mr. Slade had returned to Charlotte, obtained a fair description of *Leda* and caught the last airboat to St. Thomas. He made it to Yacht Haven, where the boat was temporarily at the docks and stood for several minutes marveling at her. He could hear the laborious twanging of a novice guitarist somewhere. When he yelled Jack's name, a huge figure emerged from the main hatch. He was bigger than Robert Cole, six-four and two hundred sixty or seventy pounds. His name, he reported, was Billy Delight. He had a rather opaque stare, as he told Eiler where Jack was and tried to give directions. After a few minutes of it, during which Joe nodded and looked around the deck, he said he'd find it. Joe learned later that Delight was not really stupid but inexpressive and therefore generally thought to be stupid. But he was definitely clumsy, and on a boat that is not an endearing quality for a man his size. Delight had worked for Caval, but in the process came to owe Caval money, and Caval had decided Billy could work off the debt by being a crew member and summoned him to San Juan. Delight was unbelievably strong, even for his size, and could usually follow orders, so Jack took him on. Billy quickly distinguished himself, however, by tripping, knocking people over, dropping things, pulling lines so taut they parted, and he even fell overboard once in San Juan, while looking at the stars through binoculars.

"What did you think of *Leda*?" Jack asked.

"Hell of a boat," Joe allowed. "It was dark though. I didn't look around much."

"That's good," Cole said. "Delight would've tripped and knocked you overboard."

"I kept my distance. But I'd say, from the look of things, we all ought to be wearing eye patches and peg legs. Maybe we will before we're through."

They all laughed, and Thorton said, "That's a helluva thing to say. Here. Take some o' this." He refilled Joe's glass and splashed in a piece of ice.

"Better than what you said." Margaret elbowed Ralph in the shoulder and turned to Eiler. "We took him all over the boat, showed him everything, and when we finally sat down below, he said, 'Jack, do ya really think this ol' tub'll make it?' I could have—"

"Now Maggie," Ralph put his arm around her. "That was before I knew her. I've gotten to know her now, an' I'd go anywhere on her."

"Oh hell, you should have heard Caval when he first saw her," said Jack. He drained his glass and poured more. "He wanted a half million dollar yacht, right? He says, 'You spend all this fuckin' time and money,' " Jack imitated Caval screaming, " 'and you buy this *wreck*!' " Jack was getting pretty loose.

"I wanted to wring his neck," said Margaret. Joe was enjoying her melodious inflections. "Jack and I are covered with grease from working on the engine, and we're living with rats in this hot dump of a shipyard—"

"That's the truth," Cole threw in.

"—and here's Caval," she spat his name, "in his white tennis costume, calling my pride and joy a wreck. I wanted to crack his skull with the wrench."

"Well now Maggie," Ralph started, "if a guy don't know nothing about boats—"

"I nearly did crack his head when he showed up with those goddamn scales that day," Cole took over. "Gimme the bottle, will ya?" He lowered his voice. "We're all being cool, right? Don't want to attract any attention. There's people working on the boat that don't know anything. And here comes Caval in a taxi one day, with a truck following him that's loaded with these great big, goddamn, industrial, fucking *scales!* I could've killed him. I said, 'You stupid, crazy son of a bitch, what the hell are you doing?' Well, he didn't like that much."

"No," Thorton shook his head, "Tommy Caval don't like to be talked to like that by nobody."

"Well, I told him I didn't give a damn who owned the boat, it was a stupid thing to do, but he hasn't said a word to me since."

"Yeah." Jack was already pouring another one, and he topped off Joe's. "He talks about security, and then he pulls something like that. And after he called her a wreck, he finds out that people around here are more interested in *Leda* than any other boat in the harbor. So he starts wanting everyone to know it's his boat, bringing them down to see it and everything. Real secure, uh? Like what's he doing up at Bluebeard's if he's got this boat?" Jack looked darkly at Thorton. "And now this bullshit about paying more for *security* down there. I don't want to hear any more about security."

Great, Joe thought, Caval raises the price. I wonder if that bastard knows we got ripped off.

"Yeah, I know. You're right," Ralph nodded but wanted to get the conversation back to happier matters. "Hell, we got all the security we need right there on ol' *Leda.*"

Joe laughed with the others, figuring from what he knew of Thorton that he'd brought a small arsenal.

"Christ," said Cole, turning to Joe. "This guy and whatsisname—Insinger—arrive like the marines. We got so much security, it makes me nervous." From the way they laughed, everyone seemed to know Cole didn't care much for the guns. Cole added, "I think we could take St. John."

Jack said, "No problem. Let's do it." He poured more rum for himself and Joe. He was getting smashed. Eiler had rarely seen him that way, and it amused him.

"Yes, we'll steam into Caneel," Margaret laughed, "with Caval sitting in the bow, in his tennis costume, on his deck chair, and demand surrender."

"That was the limit," Jack shouted at Joe above the laughter. "Caval decides there's not comfortable enough furniture on board, so he brings down these tacky canvas deck chairs with goddamn yachting insignias on the back, so he can sit on deck without getting his pants dirty."

"My chairs aren't good enough," Margaret cut in loudly. "And then he has a great, bloody Naugahyde couch brought out in a truck to the dock and insists we load it down below. Because he doesn't think the furniture is nice enough."

"He thinks that makes it more like a yacht," said Cole.

Ralph chuckled deeply. "Yeah, ol' Tommy likes his comfort."

"That's not all he likes," Jack grumbled.

"Now damnit," Thorton growled jovially, "let's quit talkin' like this. We're all here together now and we oughta be havin' fun, insteada gripin' about each other like this."

There was mild agreement, then Cole said, "Okay, but I think I need to pitch Caval in the bay once, just to freshen him up."

They laughed of course. "Well, that's awright," Ralph said, "I think I might like to see that." He put his head back and laughed again at the idea. Then he suddenly hammered the table. "Bartender," he bellowed. "Play that damn jukebox, or I'll throw it in the street."

The man did not doubt him. He played several quarters worth and turned the volume up all the way. They loved it. Ralph poured more rum all around, then stood and toasted: "To the crew!"

"The crew," they chorused.

They were rare that night. They carried on well into the morning. The last moment Eiler could accurately recall was when Jack was explaining something in great but barely coherent detail—*Leda*'s engine perhaps. Margaret's forehead was on the table, arms hanging at her sides, her hair blowing slightly in a breeze that came through the doorway. Katie sat perfectly upright with eyes closed and a faint smile on her lips, not really asleep, but afloat. Ralph inquired thickly whether Jack was talking to Joe, and Joe answered with some difficulty that he'd thought he was talking to Ralph. At precisely that moment, Cole fell backward in his chair, unconscious. Joe had no recollection of how they returned to the boat and never bothered to ask. But his clothes were wet the next morning. They told him that, as a gesture of welcome, Jack and Ralph had flung him into the bay.

iii

There was a communion of pain and nausea that morning. They leaned and lurched around the galley while Margaret made coffee. When she started to attempt a real breakfast though, Joe could not bear the thought. "Where's Jack?" he asked her.

"He's in pretty good shape somehow. In the aft cabin I think, putting up a shelf."

"I guess that's in the back, uh?"

"Right," she nodded.

Joe was desperate for a little humor before talking to Jack. "You mean starboard?"

"Go away," she mumbled. "Go away."

Joe was oblivious to the harbor and the bright warm day and the features of that old boat as he went to the cabin.

"Good morning," said Jack. He was turning a screw into the forward wall to fasten the base of a shelf. It looked impossible to Joe. But the drunk seemed to have purged Jack. And, for the moment at least, he looked busy and content. "Why don't you shut the door?"

"What passes?"

"Shelf for the Loran," Sidell nodded at some electronic device on the starboard bunk beside him. "It's going to be real handy when we get around here on our way back."

"Nice little cabin you got here, skipper."

"Yeah, I really like it. If you'd drug your ass down here when you were supposed to, you could have taken one of the other cabins. Those forward berths won't be too comfortable going to Curaçao."

"Story of my life. We're going to Curaçao?"

"Yeah," Jack kept turning the screw, "we'll wait there until everything's ready. Take on supplies. Prepare everything."

Tell him and get it over with, Joe thought, so you can go back to sleep before you puke. His head was throbbing. Before Joe could swallow and speak Jack asked, "So how did it go? And what the hell took you so long?" He kept working.

"Sit down and cut that out for a minute, will ya?"

Jack turned quickly. "What's wrong?"

"O'Neal split."

"No," Jack breathed, then shook his head. "No way."

Joe looked up at the wide deck planks overhead and just nodded.

"No fucking way, Joe. Come on! No way."

"Definitely. I been tryin' to catch him for more than a month, but I can't find him. He ripped us good."

Jack kept shaking his head, until he realized completely that it was true. "Shit!" he shouted. "Shit, shit, shit!" He threw the screwdriver as hard as he could. It ricocheted off the walls, and Joe thought for an instant Jack had thrown it at him. Never go in business with your friends, Joe remembered. They stared at each other. The disaster had a shocking presence, like a close death.

"He never showed in L.A., Jack. Soon as I knew he'd split, I hired a friend of mine who's an investigator. He's a good man, and he knows dope, has contacts all over. He looked all over the Coast. I went to Tucson, Denver, Aspen. We looked every way we could. He's just gone."

Jack had dropped onto the berth across from him and sat staring as Joe spoke.

"It was my fault. Completely. That's all there is to it. I should've driven with him to L.A. But I didn't. He'd worked with me before. You know. Hell, we were almost friends."

"Almost friends," Jack snarled bitterly. "Almost friends." Joe had never heard that cynicism in his voice before. "You think Peggy—"

"No, Jack. Kenny had 'em watched good."

"Who's Kenny?" he snapped. His fists were clinched so that the skin over his knuckles was white.

"He's my friend, the investigator."

Jack just sat for a moment, lips drawn tight. Then in a fury, he turned on the bunk and rammed his fist into the teak. Joe thought he probably broke his hand, but he showed no pain.

"That won't help, my friend. I already tried it."

"Well, what *are* you going to do?"

"I've already done it. It didn't work. But when I catch him, I'll cut his balls off."

"Oh great. That'll be great. Let me have one of 'em, will you?" Jack was quiet a moment, then said, "That's almost everything. Almost everything."

Jack's fifteen thousand cash was gone, of course. But it was much more than that. The fifteen would have been one hundred thousand through the Mexican deal. And the one hundred thousand invested in the Colombian venture could have brought a million dollars. Jack sat there trying to realize that he had lost a million dollars.

Joe had had plenty of time for realization. He figured Jack still had the other fifteen thousand, which could bring about two hundred grand, and his cut from his investors stood to bring in that much again. Jack could still make nearly half a million, and Joe tried to think of some way to say that, without having Jack knock the shit out of him. Hell, it's a lot better than I'm going to do, Joe thought. With what was left after his own losses and Sleig, Joe would be lucky to make twenty grand hustling.

"You still got the other fifteen, don't ya?"

"Yeah." Jack did not look at him. "Want to invest it for me?"

"Don't talk to me like that, you bastard. I'm almost broke." Nasty son of a bitch when he's mad, Joe thought. Joe had never really seen him mad. "What about your people who wanted to put that money in?"

Jack took a deep breath and stood up before he spoke. "Yeah, they're still in. I've got their money. I can't believe it," he muttered. "I just can't believe it. That punk. That goddamn punk motherfucker . . ." Jack trailed off in vicious obscenities.

"Let's just save it, man. We'll find him sooner or later."

"Sure," he glanced at Eiler skeptically, "then what are you going to do?"

"Let's just save it. What's this about Caval paying security in Colombia?"

"Oh Christ!" Jack had forgotten. "What bullshit!" He sat on the bunk again. "He's talking about the price going up to cover the cops down there. To pay 'em off, so there won't be any problems. Says it's going to raise the price per pound to thirty bucks. Maybe even more."

"That's crazy." There was not much traffic from Colombia at that time, but Eiler knew people who had moved weight from there. "Nobody pays that much. Especially on a load this size. That's just goddamn crazy."

"No kidding."

"Besides," Joe argued, feeling what remained of his investment shrinking with the price increase, "you said your deal with him was for twenty dollars a pound. No matter what."

"Right." Jack looked weak, looked worse than Eiler felt. "He says the deal's changed now. Because he didn't know before about paying the cops and customs. He says we'll get popped for sure on a deal this big if he doesn't pay the cops."

"The deal's changed. What horseshit. Isn't that just like Caval? Isn't that just like that son of a bitch?"

"Yeah, I guess."

"He always screws you."

That was exactly why Joe had stipulated in the beginning that Jack do the dealing with Caval. Joe had never had any success at it, but he had been sure Jack could handle him. Jack was straightforward and unbending. Joe generally knew precisely what he should demand and what he could settle for, but it rarely came out right, and it never had with Tom Caval. Joe was simply a lousy businessman, but Jack was not. Or so Joe believed. He waited for Jack to say what he would do.

"You know," Jack squinted at him, "I think he's going to skim from the price you and me and Ralph pay so he can buy more. I think he hasn't got as much money as he thought. He's really been bitchy about money lately. The sky was the limit at first, but now he really wants to cut it."

"It's quite possible. What're you gonna tell him?"

"I don't know." Jack looked at his hands, shook his head, then chewed his left middle finger. "I don't know."

Eiler didn't like the way he sounded, but figured he was just stunned from the bad news. If Jack paid thirty dollars a pound, Joe computed, his profit would drop to somewhere near three hundred thousand. And that was a long way from what he'd planned. Sidell had seen a great deal of money go out the window.

"Jack." Joe had grown edgy in the silence. "You're not going to take this shit about the price are you?"

"What do you suggest I do?" he snapped.

"Jack, come on. The deal was twenty bucks a pound regardless."

"And what if he just won't do it?"

"Oh Jack, for Christ's sake, I can't believe you're talking like this."

"Well, what if he won't, goddamnit?"

"If he can change the deal all of a sudden, we can change it too. No twenty dollars a pound, no boat. No boat, no deal."

Jack looked away and tested the possibility. It would be complicated and nasty. It was possible, but there was Thorton and Delight. And Caval had paid for the boat, corporation or not.

"No," he scowled. "I'm not going to start that crap. That would be endless. Everything would go to hell."

"Looks to me like it already has." They were getting loud.

"Just you, so far."

"Shove it, Jack. You wanted more. You wanted to press the deal. You knew it could happen. You're a big boy."

"Anything can always happen."

There was abrupt silence. They had never spoken to each other the way they had in the last few minutes. It made both of them a little sicker, but there seemed no way around it. For a moment though, the old friendship returned to Jack's voice.

"So how do you stand now?"

"Oh hell," Joe rolled his eyes. "Total loss. Plus having to pay the investigator a bundle. I'm hard at it to scrape up five thousand for this thing."

"Well, the investigator guy is your goddamn problem. O'Neal was your man."

"Are you kidding," Joe snarled. "You sound like Tom Caval."

"Fuck you!" Jack yelled.

"Fuck yourself, Jack." Eiler opened the door to leave.

"Thanks anyway," Jack said. "You already have."

iv

She really doesn't give a damn about him, Insinger observed. He sat on the deck, his back against the mizzenmast, watching Helen Sidell. She had just arrived that afternoon. Everyone sat around the deck visiting happily. Jack leaned back across the skylights, and Margaret and Ralph and Katie were there. Billy Delight was running wires up from below, to connect the small speakers of his beloved cassette player. Caval and Teresa sat in the deck chairs. Margaret was going to make a big dinner that night, and several of her friends were coming.

Robert Cole had been a nerve case for the last ten days, since he'd called Helen and she'd said she would come. He was an affectionate man, and he liked to take care of a woman. As the group lounged about, joking and carrying on over one thing and another, he stayed close to her, got her drinks. He hugged her often and kissed her and told her without embarrassment before the others how happy he was she had come.

Mark Insinger knew something of their history from a conversation with Jack and knew that Cole had wanted her to come down and try it again, at least until it was time to head for Curaçao. Mark could not have cared less about them, until he saw Helen. He was on the boat that afternoon when she arrived with Cole from the airport.

Helen Sidell was beautiful. She had dark chestnut hair that fell just below her shoulders and smooth, round features. She was small, but her figure was delightful. Her legs seemed long in proportion to the rest of her tiny frame, and they were smooth and already tanned. She wore jeans cut off just at the abrupt curve of her butt. Her white gauze blouse was only halfway buttoned, with the tails tied at her navel, and the nipples of her circular breasts were outlined. Mark had watched her with a hunger.

"Oh, how wonderful," she had gasped from the dock beside *Leda,* when she first arrived. "Oh Jack," she hugged her brother as he greeted her, "she's marvelous!" She moved around the deck quickly and gracefully, drinking up everything she touched and saw, her eyes lit with a quick, rich, infectious enthusiasm. When she came up from seeing the salon and cabins, there was passion and desire in her outstretched arms, as if she would embrace, consume in her enthusiasm, the entire boat. "Oh gawd, Jack, she's absolutely too much."

"No kidding," Insinger had mumbled. He had marked well, as he watched her moving around, that slight open space high between the thighs where her legs did not touch, which he always considered the feature of a woman well-built for bed. But there was more to it than that, and Mark was surprised by the suddenness with which he felt it. The more he saw her that afternoon, the more interested he became. He saw something in Helen he had never realized he wanted until he saw it in her. It was a passion, a desire, she possessed—a romantic enthusiasm. Mark suddenly felt he had always wanted that in a woman, had always wanted to excite that desire and be inspired by it in return. He could not keep his eyes off her that afternoon. She did not speak much, but was not shy. And when she did speak, it was with an eager, sensual appreciation of what was happening—and a longing for more.

"Wouldn't it be great, though," she said at one point, "to have the boat all the time, and live on her and sail everywhere, and just do this sort of thing whenever you needed the money?"

Margaret agreed, of course, and she and Helen got on well from the start, but more reality was recognized in the mild laughter of the others. Jack knew he might even have to sink *Leda* somewhere once the deal was down, though he would never say it before Margaret.

She wants so much, Mark observed. And he could see that Robert Cole was not going to be the man who gave it. Even though Robert stayed close to her, often stroked her back or squeezed her thigh, she was almost oblivious to his affection. She was interested in more: the boat, the group, Caval, Delight, the grand promise of it all. Mark felt for Cole, and he could see how much, but how hopelessly, the man loved her. But he could also see that Helen had come down to have fun, not to have Cole again. And that, Mark foresaw, ought to be a fine mess.

Mark partook of the visiting that day from a distance. He sat with the group as they talked and drank and made laughing projections about hurricanes and attacks by the Colombian navy, but he entered the conversation little. He felt aloof from them. He was not of the crew, would not be making the voyage. He was with Caval, was management, stayed at Bluebeard's, whence problems came. Caval sat with them too and burst frequently into the conversation, always it seemed, with some relevant knowledge or experience that was better than whatever had been previously mentioned. Often, he began by saying, "Hell, that's nuthin, once I was. . . ." Mark knew that with the exception of Ralph and Delight, who liked Caval's cocky flamboyance, the others would rather he were not there. Helen, however, was as interested in Caval as in everything else, but to Mark she was with the others and—for the moment at least—unreachable.

Near sunset other people began arriving: Fred and Rita, who had worked on the boat in San Juan; Harry; friends of Margaret's from other boats, or from Yacht Haven or Charlie Brown's; and crazy island people she and Jack and Robert had met. The crowd on deck grew steadily, and talk turned almost exclusively to the islands, mutual friends, the life. They all seemed to know that Caval was the owner, and that, according to Jack and Margaret, he was a pain in the ass. The conversation left him behind, and when he entered it a few times to mention Colombia or somewhere he was sure they'd never been, he was treated with that combination of indulgence and contempt that young sailing people invariably feel for the rich owner who knows nothing about the boat, does not live on it, and to them does not deserve it.

While everyone else stood or sat or leaned against whatever was handy, Caval sat on his deck chair, self-possessed and too handsome. In the chair beside him was Teresa, silent as ever except for an occasional whisper in Tom's ear, elegant in white pants rolled up a little to keep the cuffs from getting soiled, a silk scarf covering all her black hair, her face as always stunning, but with makeup. She too was as alien to the crowd as the ring of small diamonds she wore on one hand or the rare crescent emerald set in gold on the other.

Caval sensed perfectly his separateness from the gathering. These punks and their loose chicks, he thought, with their hair bleached and blown all over, lying around like dogs. So they've been all around these islands. So they know all about boats. So big fucking deal. They couldn't get off their ass and earn enough money to own a boat like this themselves, or do a tenth of the other stuff I do.

Mark saw it all clearly too. He acutely felt his association with Caval. Margaret was below, cooking; Delight was playing music; things were warming up; and Mark knew there was going to be a good time. But he knew Caval would want to leave. And, of course, if life were simple, Mark would just stay there. But it wasn't. When Caval called to him, "Hey, let's get going," he nodded wistfully and got to his feet. Some people nearby looked around momentarily. Delight said, "Aren't you guys going to stay?" And Mark saw Cole roll his eyes at Jack. Mark silently gestured to the few people he knew or had spoken to. And then he caught Helen's eyes. He smiled as if to say, "Things are seldom as they seem." She smiled back, curiously, deliciously.

V

There was a good party on *Leda* that night. About twenty people were carrying on noisily around the big table when Eiler arrived. The salon felt like a crowded old tavern, full of laughter and smoke and music. Joe purposefully arrived late, because of the tension between him and Jack. He hadn't cared to spoil the re-union with Helen. The whole crew seemed to know Joe had fouled things up. Jack would never have told them, but even a big boat is a small place, and more is felt than said.

For the next two weeks, though, there was little time for any bad feelings. Jack was having a lot of the rigging replaced or strengthened, and there were a hundred things to prepare. He hired a wiry old blue-black islander to do the rigging, and Cole and Thorton helped him every day. Robert knew rigging pretty well, and so did Ralph, from his steelworking days. Lines were ropes to Thorton, and blocks were pulleys, but he knew what he was doing. Jack and Margaret took care of logistics. They plotted courses and figured times, determined what sort of auxiliary pumps and first aid equipment were needed, and procured them. They were rarely apart. Despite Jack's earlier reticence, they were in love—but perhaps more in love with what they were doing. Helen and Katie sunbathed mostly and went to the beaches, but they also figured a menu for the voyage. They did a lot of the cooking and the shopping for meals. Jack and Robert studied celestial navigation and practiced with a sextant. Aside from the immediate business, Joe and Jack did not speak. They could never think of anything worth saying.

Eiler and Billy Delight were the roustabouts. They were extra hands and backs when needed. They kept the boat clean and ran errands. It all interfered with Billy's principal desires, however, which were to listen to tapes or play his guitar or to be swimming or lying in the sun or fooling around with Helen. Delight was a happy, careless young man, huge and powerful, but with rosy cheeks highlighting his big, ruddy face. He was never angry, and he liked to laugh along with the others at his own comical errors. He had grown up in Florida and had never found anything in life more important than sunshine and water and girls. No one was ever too sure how he'd fallen in with Caval, and Billy's only businesslike attribute was that he never talked about himself nor certainly what he did for money. He was never known to speak of anything more serious than a beer or a song or a nice pair. In fact, Delight had known an associate of Caval's who sold a lot of dope around Fort Lauderdale, and since Billy never objected to flying anywhere with a couple of suitcases full of grass, Caval had gradually taken him over. Any sort of work was merely an unpleasant necessity to Billy, however. He never did it for adventure or desire for money, and he never showed the slightest interest in the underlying reason for his presence on *Leda.* Joe Eiler saw Billy every morning, and yet each time Billy would say, "Hey Joe, how ya doin'?" as if they hadn't seen each other in weeks. Then he'd usually add something like: "Say, if Jack doesn't have a lot of bullshit for us to do today, let's go over to Morningstar." He always made Joe feel like he was living in the jock dorm again.

During those last two weeks in Charlotte, *Leda* was a busy place, with people constantly coming and going, a hundred things to do, and a rich expectation in the air. And most of the time, although Insinger and Caval had taken away most of it, there was still a lot of money. They ate and drank as much as and whatever they wanted, and Jack spared no expense where the boat was concerned. Caval screamed over every expenditure—especially safely items like extra pumps, flares, life rafts, and survival rations—but Jack intended to have the best equipment. His purchases did on occasion seem extravagant.

One day he and Cole went to buy an Avon inflatable boat they could use as a runabout and if necessary as a lifeboat. At the equipment store, however, they encountered a sixteen-foot Boston Whaler, and Cole easily persuaded Jack it was more like what they needed. Naturally it required a motor, so they bought a fifty-horse outboard, in case they needed heavy service. Then Jack figured as long as they had this nice boat, they might as well get some recreation out of it. Caval nearly broke a blood vessel in his head when he happened to look out over the bay from his rooms at Bluebeard's while Sidell was water-skiing.

They were good times in Charlotte—as inspiring and alluring, yet as tenuous, as a rainbow—with the deal awaiting them at the end. They were happy as they worked, always drinking beer and listening to music. At night there was Joe's or Charlie Brown's or any other bar they wanted. And with comrades the size of Thorton and Cole and Delight, one could say or do nearly anything one liked. And they always did.

Insinger had been right about Helen though. And everyone except those who mattered most sensed that sooner or later there would be trouble over her. Robert thought she was still his woman, and from the beginning, it was clear she thought otherwise. They slept together in the starboard cabin the first two nights, then Helen started sleeping on deck where Delight bedded or on Caval's couch or on one of the bunks in the forward space where Eiler slept. She had been there only a few days when Joe walked into the salon as she was arguing with Bob: "Why can't I have the cabin to myself? I am a woman. You might at least let me have some privacy." Since Joe was there, Cole said nothing, but his eyes pleaded with her. The pain he feared—and Cole was a man who feared few things—was inevitable though, whether or not Helen had her own bedroom. The boat, the Caribbean, the business at hand all offered Helen as much adventure as anyone else, and she wanted it all. There was an abandon about it that she breathed deeply. She refused to allow Robert to regulate her life. For two years she had been virtually married to him. She had filled her life with one man,

100

and one day found it empty. She was ready to play. She was a sensuous and affectionate young woman. If she liked someone she wanted to grab hold, feel them, wrestle a little, even with her brother. But with a woman like her, it could never be innocent.

Eiler was leaning over the engine room hatch one day, handing Jack something, and she came up and pinched him hard enough that Joe howled and took after her. He caught her up in the bow and put her down on the deck. She struggled, yelping and laughing, as Joe pinched her several times with great relish. She always wore almost nothing, just a very small blue and red bikini, and she had a marvelous feel to her. When Joe stopped, his hands stayed a moment on those delectable thighs. Ralph and the old islander and Katie laughed at them. It was just fun. But Cole was a suffering man, and when Joe saw the vulnerable suspicion in his face, he felt like hell.

That sort of thing seemed to happen frequently, with either Eiler or Billy, and whenever Robert was nearby it warped for a while the entire atmosphere of the boat. With great effort Eiler restrained himself on those nights Helen slept in the close forecastle. She was never one for modest disrobing. It was hard work looking Cole in the eye the next day. But Joe would, because he liked Cole, and they had a long way to go together, and Joe didn't want Helen between them. It was even harder to ignore her when she wanted to frolic, but Joe tried.

Billy Delight did not try. Or at least what efforts he made were quite different. Helen liked him. He was so big, so muscular, and in a way handsome. All that he-man flesh was as attractive to her as she was to him. And since Billy hated working, he took every opportunity to hang around with her. Often he went up to her right in front of Robert and took hold of her, mauled her, bit her on the neck or shoulder. Helen liked it. Cole seethed. Billy went to the beach with her too sometimes when the others were working. Several nights Billy talked her into going to town with him, and they always stayed late. There were a few nights when everyone sat on deck puffing a reefer or sipping Mount Gay as they talked, and somehow Helen would end up below in the starboard cabin, listening to Billy play his guitar. Even something in the rough, ill-practiced manner he played fitted her fancy. Every coarsely romantic note was audible on deck, even if a tape or the radio were playing, because each one tortured Cole and everyone knew it. But the worst was when the music ceased altogether. Eiler tried to explain the situation to Billy once, but he was as eager and unknowing as Helen. "She's not his ol' lady anymore," Billy answered with a confused resentment. "I can't help it if she likes me more than him." In similar confusion perhaps, Robert thought somehow it would work out, that he and Helen would resume their former love, and it was a sad thing to witness.

Whatever Helen did with Eiler or Billy was simply playing, but during the last week in St. Thomas, she became genuinely attracted to Mark Insinger. Caval had left for Santa Marta and further negotiations, so Mark came almost every day to *Leda,* where he would rather have stayed the entire time. To Helen, he was much different than the others, staying at Bluebeard's high on the hill, where the old stone watchtower of the pirates was visible from the harbor. Mark was always well dressed in laundered pants and shirt, even though he stripped them off in favor of whatever shorts he could find around the boat. He was not boisterous and physical like the rest of them. He often seemed distant. Helen also saw him as the right hand of Tom Caval, whom Bob and Jack disliked for reasons that were obvious to her, and it made Mark something like forbidden fruit. Mark was physically different too, smaller and wirier. She never felt as if she could play with him as she did with Eiler or Billy.

Insinger was indeed different from the others in several respects. He was older, in his thirties. He had made some large decisions before, had built some things and torn them down, had tossed a profession and burned some bridges. Mark had more chips on the table, and perhaps a little more of himself at stake. So he was more serious and frequently worried. Even at times when they were all getting loaded and laughing it up, bold as young dogs, there was always a certain gravity about Mark that set him off. All this intrigued Helen. She had never seen it before, and it fascinated her. He was mysterious to her. His thin, nervous features were darkly tanned, as if he were of some Latin blood, and he seemed to Helen much more of a smuggler, a man outside the law, than any of the others.

Mark was aware of the problems with Robert Cole. He also knew Jack did not want his little sister involved in the deal. She would be going back to Boston soon, though, and Mark intended to make contact with her. He never doubted he could attract her, so he was patient. When he came to the boat he remained aloof, only quietly interested in their preparations or whatever fun they might be having at night, and he made no overtures. He waited for her to come to him—just as he had awaited this venture.

102

One night shortly before they were to leave for Curaçao, Mark and Joe leaned against the boom of the mainmast looking out across the harbor. They discussed the process of transferring the purchase money, then Eiler saw Jack and Robert in the stern taking a reading with the sextant and went to join them.

Mark had noticed Helen down below, looking up at them through the skylights as they talked. He sat on the new deck as Joe left and thought, I'll bet she comes up here. A few minutes later she did.

"What are you plotting?" she joked softly. She sat so that their arms and legs touched. They had rarely spoken before.

"To sell you into white slavery."

"Is that right?" she grinned with surprise. "Where?"

"Oh . . . ," Mark looked into her eyes, and they had many colors—blue, light brown, green, flecks of yellow—"my apartment in Aspen."

"Well that doesn't sound too bad. Maybe I'll sell myself." Her voice was low but very feminine. "If the price is good."

They laughed together. The caress of her thigh and the night air and the lights of Charlotte reflecting on the water made Mark wish Robert Cole were in Antarctica. He felt impossibly drawn to her; his body ached for her.

"I do wonder what you're thinking whenever I see you," she said. "You're always so quiet. Like you're always planning something."

Mark shrugged, but he loved her attention. "Just your slavery," he quipped.

"No," she protested. "Really."

Insinger thought, oh Jesus, honey, but said, "I don't know. Why?"

"I just wonder what you're thinking. I guess I wonder what you do. You're different from these guys. From Jack and Joe and Ralph."

"And Billy Delight?" Mark smiled and pronounced the name with irony. He thought Delight was a musclebound idiot, and it had made him sick the few times he had seen him with Helen.

"Quite different from Billy," she smiled back. "You're kind of mysterious."

Mark snorted at the idea and looked out across the water again—mysteriously.

"You are," she said. "But maybe you try."

"Well, I'm glad you finally noticed."

"I thought you would be."

"You ought to see me in my trench coat."

"I'll bet."

Mark painfully wanted to touch her, put his arms around her, and he knew she'd welcome it, wanted it. But not yet, he thought.

"Really," she leaned even closer to him, lowered her voice. "What do you do?"

"Mostly make phone calls, it seems. And try to figure things out."

"What things?"

"Just things. Mostly money."

"So you're in charge of the money, uh?"

"Sort of," Mark blinked. It was not wholly inaccurate. "Mainly transferring money lately."

"And I'll bet you won't tell me about it."

"There's not much to tell, really," Mark smiled. "But it's not the sort of thing to be discussed."

Helen closed her eyes and nodded knowingly. Mark could tell she'd give anything to be in on the deal. He knew she thought he probably entered Colombia by parachute clutching a briefcase full of cash and an Uzi submachine gun. But that was alright.

"Are you going to Curaçao with us?" she asked.

"I'm going to Curaçao, but not with you all."

"Other business, uh?" she grinned.

"Yeah. I didn't think you were going."

"Just for the sail. Jack doesn't want me to, but I love to sail, so I talked him into it. I'll be going back to Boston pretty soon after that though."

"So will I," said Mark. "We should get together. I have a lot of things to do around there."

"Where?" Helen knew nothing of Far Prospect.

"Just around Boston. I'll call you."

Helen smiled at him curiously and nodded. They were quiet a few moments. Helen leaned back on her elbows and gazed at the night sky. Her leg stayed casually against Mark's. Mark looked astern and saw Robert Cole looking back at him.

"I love the stars down here," Helen sat up and lifted her arms to the sky. The moon was new and the night glittered magically. "Don't you want to just reach out and take them? Hold them somehow?"

Mark said nothing, only smiled and nodded. He thought he'd heard that line in some musical.

"Sometimes I think the most beautiful things are the saddest

104

things," she went on. "You want them so badly. I do anyway. But you can never really have them."

Mark took an indulgent breath. He looked upward a moment and was not particularly impressed. He felt much older than Helen. He said, "No. I don't agree. You're being romantic. No, not romantic. Fatalistic. Beauty is the easiest thing to possess. The more beautiful, the easier. You can make it a part of you. Have it always with you." Helen kept looking up as he spoke. "With other things, like material things, it's the reaching out that it's all about. Reaching out and taking the most beautiful thing you can see or imagine is what life is all about. It's the wanting and the striving," he concluded. Mark blinked and smiled at himself. He was rarely given to philosophy. Moreover he was struck that it was the first thing he'd said to a woman in years that he had not said before to another woman.

"Is that what you're doing?" She studied his face.

"Sure." He blinked and nodded. "Yeah. Sure."

"What are you reaching for? Tell me."

"Good question," Mark smiled. He thought it was one of those questions you never stop to ask, and it took someone as impetuous or naive as Helen to bring it up. He wanted to tell her though, at least try, but not with Cole and everything else. He would save it. "A great deal," he answered. "But let's discuss it in Boston, if you really want to, okay? I have to talk to Jack about something and then make a call. We'll talk another time."

"Promise?"

"Sure." He stood suddenly, could not stand to be so near her any longer. "Promise."

iv

Joe Eiler awakened two days later at the sound of Sidell's voice and sat up squint-eyed on the bunk.

"What're you gonna do, keelhaul me?"

Jack smiled at him for the first time since Eiler had told him of O'Neal. "Not yet. Caval's back. I'm going to see him this afternoon. You too, if you want to come. I think you should. There's a lot to do. We'll be leaving day after tomorrow so let's clean up the spilled milk and figure out what we're going to do."

"Okay. Let me go to the head and get a cup of coffee."

When Joe returned to the forecastle, Jack was perched on his bunk. As Joe sipped coffee, they figured how much money they still had and how to keep it until the deal went down. The money was on hand. In addition to about $480 Joe had brought for expenses he had $5,000 for cargo, which was almost everything he had, and it was locked in his suitcase. Before returning to Puerto Rico from Far Prospect, Jack had picked up the hundred thousand from his investor in New York, then flown to Colorado to get the fifteen thousand he still had in the Carbondale safe-deposit box outside Aspen. He had brought it all with him and kept it beneath his bunk, as he had kept Caval's loot. Caval's cash was gone. Mark Insinger had made arrangements with a bank in Curaçao through which Caval planned to run the exchange, and Tom had flown the money to the Antilles in three separate trips, being met at the airport each time by a representative of the bank. Eiler and Sidell agreed to keep the money with them and decide in Curaçao whether to pool it with Caval's right away or see what developed. It didn't seem difficult, so Joe went on to the real matter. "Are we eatin' this price rise? I think you're right about him skimming on us. I bet he's paying twenty a pound."

"I don't know. Maybe. I've thought about it a lot though," Jack rubbed his forehead, "and I don't think we have much choice. Definitely, I'm going to press him about our original deal." He stiffened and sounded a lot better than he had the first time they discussed it. "I'm making him stick to it if I can, but if he just won't, I'm afraid we're screwed."

"Maybe not. Maybe we wait until Billy and Ralph and Katie are ashore some way and we take the boat." Jack was already shaking his head, but Eiler went on. "I've been thinking too. We split to Venezuela, La Guaira or Maracaibo. There's a million boats around there. I speak Spanish ten times better than Caval and Insinger put together, and I'll go to Colombia and get a new goddamn contact and we'll run our own deal. If Tommy wants to start breaking deals, let's screw him first."

Jack studied him nervously before he spoke, as though he saw something he was afraid of. "That's shitty, Joe," he spoke softly. "It really is. To hell with Billy, alright, but we'd be screwing Ralph, too. And the fact is that Caval has the money to run the deal. He has half the communication equipment, he pays the rent on Far Prospect, he's paying for the houses to distribute the stuff, for the fuel we need, provisions, everything. It would take all our money just to do that stuff."

"We could get back to the States and get more."

"Joe. Come on. You're not like that. Just because we got ripped off . . ." He didn't finish the sentence. "Even if we do all the things

106

you're saying, it would be a lousy rip-off deal. Even with the price rise, we've still got Far Prospect and a good crew. Things are organized, and there's money to do it. We can still make damn good money. I'm not throwing away my plans."

Right then Joe was so tired of dope dealing he could have vomited. For days he had really hoped Jack would agree to take everything and split. Now he remembered he was talking to Jack Sidell—Jack, who it had once been a pleasure to be with because he wasn't up to his ass in hustling and scheming. Joe felt ashamed of his suggestions. "Okay, man. I told you in the beginning it was your ballgame. I'm on for the duration. We'll play it your way."

When they got out of the cab in front of Bluebeard's late that afternoon Joe felt like he was going to see the spider in its web. In favor of a room from which he could see *Leda*, Caval had given up a suite. The room was luxurious and large however. Jack and Eiler sat in chairs by a small table, and Caval lay across the broad bed, wearing only a pair of white pants. The lights of the harbor far below were visible through the glass doors of the balcony. Caval plainly enjoyed having summoned them to his aerie. The small talk passed quickly.

"The price is thirty bucks a pound," Caval stated.

"How come nobody else pays that much?" Jack leaned forward and looked steadily at Caval. "Even for much smaller loads."

"I don't know what the hell other people pay," Caval snarled.

"They pay twenty."

"You've been to Colombia an' you know all about it, huh?"

"I know what other guys pay. How come it costs you thirty?"

"Because I'm payin' everybody off," Tom shouted. "I'm payin' the *Aduana* so we don't get busted, an' I'm paying' so they'll cover the loading. Protect the loading. Everybody knows when a deal this big goes down. If you don't take care of things you either get busted or highjacked."

"Maybe so," Jack said skeptically, "but fifty percent is a hell of a lot of money for that."

"Yeah? Well, I don't know how the hell you'd know. Those guys down there ain't dumb, man. They know how much the load is worth in the States. They ain't just hangin' around crackin' coffee beans. They want their piece too. So the price is thirty bucks."

"You're paying thirty bucks a pound?" Jack threw the question at him like a knife.

"Right, Jack." Caval regarded him with a smirk. "That's exactly right."

Jack stared at him silently and Caval stared back. Eiler

couldn't tell if Caval was lying or not. Under the circumstances it made no difference. Caval knew better than Jack that he controlled the deal. If he said he was paying for security and the price was going up, that's all there was to it. It was a *fait accompli,* a fact to deal with as surely as if the ocean had frozen. To Caval truth was not a factor. This was business. He knew Jack well enough to know he wouldn't run out on the deal, but Joe kept thinking how nice it would be to see Caval's face some morning when he looked out and saw the boat leaving.

Jack spoke again sharply. "What about the fact that your deal with me is for twenty dollars?"

"I can't get it for twenty, goddamnit. It's thirty."

"No," Jack stayed with him. "Paying security is your problem. The deal we made in Aspen is for as much as I want to buy for twenty dollars."

Jack was pressing as far as he could without actually threatening to take the boat or walk out. The room was filled with the energy of their dislike. There were shock waves when either of them spoke.

"I can't do it anymore," Caval snapped. "The price is thirty. I'm not making separate payments. The cost of security is in the price. The price is thirty."

"Well you're breaking our deal. I don't like it."

"What's this bullshit about breaking the deal?" Caval jumped up and stood on the bed looking down at Jack, his voice shrill and loud. "I didn't break anything. The deal just changed."

"We made a deal, Tom. You're obligated to stick to it."

"Bull-fucking-shit!" Caval screamed. "At first we said you get to buy at the same price I buy. Then I thought it was twenty, so we said twenty. But now it's thirty. I'm not obligated to do anything. What, have I broken some rules? So I have to sell my load to you for twenty bucks an' lose my ass? You're crazy!"

They stared silently. Jack thought again of what Joe had suggested, but kept coming up with the same conclusions.

Caval was thoroughly contemptuous: this crap about the breaking of the deal, like they'd taken some hippie oath. There were no obligations in this business.

"You guys got ripped off, didn't you?"

Jack sat back at the knowing question, as if slapped in the face. Eiler's eyes devoured Caval. "Where'd you hear that?" Joe demanded.

"I heard it." He looked Eiler over carefully.

"Where? Who told you?"

"Someplace. I heard it, that's all."

"I'd like to know where and from whom."

"Whatta ya wanna call 'em up?" Caval asked sarcastically.

"Yeah, as a matter of fact."

"Tough shit." He smiled for an instant. "Man, if you can't find O'Neal that's your problem. And just because you got ripped off and the price rise hurts you, I'm not *obligated*," he puked the word, "to break my ass sellin' to you at twenty stinkin' bucks."

Caval stepped down off the bed and walked in front of them toward the glass doors. He studied his hands and visibly flexed the narrow, well defined muscles in his arms. Sadly he admitted, "The price rise hurts me too."

Joe ransacked his mind trying to figure out how Caval could have known about O'Neal. He wanted to hang him off the balcony and make him talk. Jack sat perfectly still though, his face expressionless. He was mortified. His private business had been revealed. He felt like a novice who'd gotten burned trying to pull a fast shuffle. The humiliation of having Caval lord it over him was almost unbearable.

"You guys are a pain in the ass." Caval kept looking out the glass doors. "Ya know I could get a plane and do this deal a lot easier than all this bullshit scene I'm runnin' here." Neither Jack nor Eiler said anything. Caval turned and said, "What the hell though. Come on. Let's get this together and get it on."

"What are you doing on money with these guys?" Jack asked. His tone acknowledged that the battle was over and he'd lost.

"Whatta ya mean? I'm givin' it to 'em. Whatta ya—"

"No, damnit. How?"

"Oh. We got it in the bank in Curaçao. We'll transfer it to their account in the same bank when everything's set. Now can you get it together for a June pickup?"

"I've got it together now," Jack answered angrily. "I could leave for Colombia tonight. You just get it together on the place and the date and the goddamn price."

"Awright. Okay." Caval retreated artfully, his voice suddenly conciliatory. "The price is thirty. That's absolutely definite. I'm taking the last of my money to Curaçao tomorrow, and we'll meet there an' you guys can put your money in the bank too. Then I'll go to Colombia to take care of the final touches. We'll station Ralph at the Hilton in Curaçao so I can contact him at any time. And as soon as everything's ready to go down there, I'll give you the day, the exact location, and the hour."

Caval added every detail he could bring to mind, his voice smooth and pleasant, rather charming. Caval was always at his best when he was dictating what would happen, and he enjoyed making it all sound as if it were the cleanest, high-class, big-money dope deal that ever went down.

chapter 7

i

"SHE likes it," Jack thought of *Leda* as her old mass undulated with the sea. "She wants it." Leaving Charlotte the previous day, they had picked up a strong trade right out of the harbor. It had remained as constant as the dominating sun all that day, had picked up in the late afternoon, and blown steadily through the night. There hadn't been a hint of bad weather. The breeze had slackened this morning, but was growing again, as surely as the sun's passage. It was almost noon, and Jack could see a line of weather in the extreme distance, but it was far to the east and south. "It won't change," he had observed earlier to Joe. He sensed it somehow. He had been in those waters many times. "We may have this same tack all the way," he had reckoned. *Leda* seemed to feel it too. Sidell and that old boat were attuned to the sea like fellow travelers on a highway they knew well.

The headsails were up, the four diagonally in a line, scarlet and full of the wind, reaching ahead toward the bow, pulling. The main and the mizzensail seemed vast in the air ahead of Jack, even against the blues of the sea and sky, and they received the wind with a low hum. *Leda*'s timbers creaked happily, and the rigging whistled at it all. There was just enough swell so that it seemed to excite her, her great rough beauty bounding southward in a sensual hurry, the sun and wind and sea primordially intent on her passage to South America.

Sidell could have existed eternally in that setting. He kept the big wheel with the crook of his left elbow, his hip set against the wheelhouse, barefoot, his jeans rolled up below his knees, no shirt, and he felt as perfectly made for the situation as *Leda* was for the elements that had made her.

Margaret came up from the salon, then to the stern, and eased against Jack's side. He put his arm around her waist and brought her close. She spoke sweetly to him, saying how good it was to be at sea again. Jack just nodded. He seldom attempted to describe his thoughts. He simply held her there, until he could tell she felt it all too.

Margaret had looked forward to being at sea with Jack, just as she had looked forward to being in love with him when he had called from Florida. The two things grew together—another voyage. Jack was not quite the same. Margaret seemed perfect against his side just then or when they were working or drinking or making love. She was as perfect for him as *Leda* was. And in a way he loved her, had come to have far greater affection for her than when he had presaged it all in a Fort Myers motel. But theirs was a love of wanderers, of people whose lives are always changing, for whom the loving of places and people must be only for the present. Margaret knew it, as well as *Leda* knew the feel of a strong wind. And even though she knew the pain and loneliness that came equally with the rapturous freedom of it when it was right, she accepted with a wistful certainty that she could never happily retreat to conventional life. She took love eagerly when it came and did not look too far ahead.

Jack by nature liked to see ahead, thought in terms of strong things building and lasting. For the past three years he had had one woman without interruption. With difficulty, he had made her separate when he began the venture, the way a man leaves a wife to go to sea or war, recognizing—perhaps not unhappily—that it might well be forever. In matters of the heart, Jack instinctively preferred to bet all his chips or none at all. So his love for Margaret remained a little off balance. The transience of it restrained him slightly, but the perfect present was sweet.

"I don't know where it will go," he had demurred to Eiler the night before. With his typical edge, Joe had referred to Margaret as Jack's wife. It was late, their first night at sea, and they had stood together just forward of the mainmast, savoring the strong wind, the awesome vastness of the sea at night, and *Leda*'s heaving mass. There was a fine thrill of the timelessness of their adventure, and it seemed to inspire Jack to more candor than he normally allowed himself. "I'm starting not to care so much where it goes or how it ends. But just how it happens, you know? Maybe the sea lends you that acceptance. Or maybe she demands it."

Joe smiled at Jack's self-consciousness. "And you're becoming poetic to boot."

"Go to hell. It's true, though. I never thought like this before. Catch as catch can. But now there doesn't seem to be any other way. The making of plans is not so holy anymore. There's a lot of things in this deal that you just can't plan on."

Eiler mumbled some sort of agreement. In the momentary consternation of Jack's features, Joe saw his old friend challenge the assumptions that had led him into this business with such confidence: that there were dependable forces and relationships in the world, which a capable man could plot and measure, and thereby control his life. Joe wondered if that were true in any sort of life—but he knew damn well it wasn't in the dope business. Being outside the law was like being at sea. You could plot and measure all you wanted, but survival and success depended more on the ability to act decisively when factors suddenly changed. Joe was glad Jack was beginning to see it. He was afraid though that Jack's vision of himself and the world were going to take a beating in this business. He thought of discussing it, but as most people do on important matters, he had let it go.

It was around noon the next day when Margaret joined Sidell at the helm. Jack had been at it since early morning, so she took over and told him that Thorton was boiling eggs for lunch. Perpetually hungry, Jack hurried forward, but he was equally interested in seeing how Eiler and Thorton were getting along, what they thought of it all after the first twenty-four hours.

"All squared away up here, skipper." Eiler greeted him with a smirk and a careless salute. He sat against the new deck beneath the mainsail with his face in the wind and the sun baking him.

"Looks like it," Jack replied. There was always a sardonic tone when Eiler and Sidell spoke, but with an open friendliness Jack asked, "What do you think?"

"She's a jewel, man. Just a big, rough, beautiful jewel."

Jack nodded as he sat in one of the cane chairs Thorton had brought up from below. He didn't know if Joe was talking about the sea or *Leda* or all of it, but it made no difference. "We're getting down to business now," he smiled.

Margaret let them off the wind a little just then, and they noticeably picked up speed. "Awright!" Joe yelled and clapped his hands once. "Let's move this baby." *Leda* stalked the swells, almost leap-frogging them with a huge playfulness but crushed some into explosive splashes that shot high above her sides and became fine cool spray on deck.

112

"That woman can drive this thing." Jack hooked his thumb astern.

Joe said, "I hope like hell you can too."

Jack sneered at him. "That's the least of our worries." Joe smiled at his confidence. He agreed of course but would never have said so.

Ralph Thorton came out of the main hatch beside them with the necks of four beers wedged between the thick short fingers of one hand and a big bowl full of boiled eggs in the other. "Now goddamnit," he half shouted as he put the eggs and beers in front of them, "this is how men was meant to live. Ain't it, Jack? I salted 'em good, Joe."

"Definitely." Jack took most of an egg in one bite and followed it with beer.

"Joe and I was just sayin' earlier," Ralph sat beside Eiler and leaned forward to see Jack, "that we ought to be doing this kind of stuff all the time. I said, 'Shit, yes. Guys like us are made for it.' "

"I was thinking the same thing a few minutes ago, Ralph. The exact same thing." Jack grinned at him, nearly laughing at Ralph's enthusiasm.

"Were you?" Ralph smiled ferociously. "Hell, yes, you were." He took a long swig. "It's great, man. It's just great." Ralph looked over his shoulder. "Come get your beer an' eggs, Cole."

Cole looked back at them lazily over his shoulder and started to get up. He lay on the deck ahead of them, sunbathing with Helen, who was close beside him. Katie was nearby too, taking the sun on her back. Helen had been different for the past few days, since the night she had talked with Mark Insinger. She'd been much quieter than usual and rather reserved. It was something Mark had said, or perhaps just the way she felt with him. Somehow it had suggested that she act a little older and more serious, than running around the boat playing grabass with everyone. It had made her a little uncertain of herself too, and reflexively she had gravitated back to Robert. She had slept in the starboard cabin with him the last two nights, not with passion but with a familiar comfort. Robert felt in it a sort of Indian Summer: they were underway; Caval was far away; the sailing was perfect; he was first mate; and he could feel his woman coming back. He was positive again and in control of his life.

"What about Katie and me?" Helen called. "Don't we get any?"

"Why you sea hags," Thorton growled, "you're lucky we let you up on deck." Helen made a face at him and lay down again.

"You're really gettin' into it, aren't you, little guy?" Cole pushed Ralph's head as he came over.

"Look out, big boy," Thorton tried to grab his arm, but Cole pulled away. "Look out."

"Watch yourself," Eiler warned Cole. "Ralph an' I are just a couple of pirates now."

"Hell yes," Ralph laughed.

"Pirates," Cole snorted. "Soon as we see a little weather, you'll be sick babies." They cursed him playfully, and he added, "Just don't mess with the first mate."

Thorton put his head back and laughed, his mouth full of egg, then said, "It does make ya feel like that, don't it, Jack? This ol' boat and everything? Like we're pirates, don't it?"

Jack smiled. "I guess we are."

"Freebooters," Cole raised his bottle. An entire egg disappeared behind his shaggy mustache.

"Damn right," Thorton bellowed. He would have made a great pirate.

Billy Delight came up on deck about then. He had gotten badly sunburned the previous day and did not feel too well in general. He did not care much for sailing. He stood by as they talked, looking swollen and a little vulnerable. Eiler saw he was gazing at Helen's body warming in the sun, then noticed Cole watching Billy with a much different expression. Joe ignored it. "It does give you the feeling," he said, "once you get out far from land that anything goes. That you can do anything you're big enough to handle."

Jack agreed less anxiously than the others. He knew it was a two-way street. "Sure," he nodded, "this was real pirate country around here, alright. The whole Caribbean. Europe and the Mediterranean were pretty much civilized and under control then, but here it was wide open. And perfect for ships too. You've got all the Antilles, to the north and east, and the Americas in every other direction. The trades are always blowing, and there was always cargo to rip off and thousands of places to split once you did."

"I bet it was great," Ralph said.

Cole was still watching Delight.

"Yeah," Jack shrugged, "but it worked both ways. You couldn't just go wandering around. If someone came up on you with a bigger, faster boat or several boats or just more guns, you got to eat it. I'm not sure that would be so great."

"Hell, I'd take it," said Ralph.

114

"I guess we are," Joe remarked. "If someone messed with us on the way back, we couldn't exactly call the Coast Guard." They were quiet a moment. It was not a matter they cared to consider just then, except for Thorton.

"Speakin' of which," he blurted excitedly, "let's get them irons out an' make sure they're all in good order, whatta ya say, Jack?"

Jack shrugged, and Ralph jumped up and went below. "Bring that magnum," Jack yelled after him.

"The guns, eh?" said Delight. He sat down beside Eiler on the new deck, facing Cole.

"No. He meant the tire irons," said Cole. "Case we have to fix a flat."

Billy stared at Robert a moment, then looked away, toward Helen as it happened. He knew Cole did not like him. Jack looked at Robert a moment, then glanced warily at Joe. There had been tension between Cole and Delight all along over Helen, but it had never come close to real violence. Right then, though, Jack and Eiler could both feel it coming.

"Yeah," Billy mumbled, "I guess we oughta know the guns pretty well."

"There's something else you better know," Cole told him. "And that's that I don't want you messing with that woman anymore."

The sun seemed suddenly hotter, the air around them heavy, the rolling nod of the deck threatening.

Billy said, "Oh yeah?"

"Yeah. She's my woman."

"Well, I don't think she sees it that way."

The two men stared, and the air was static with inevitable violence. Ralph emerged from the main hatch, and Joe could see in his face that he sensed the trouble. He had the .41 magnum stuck in the waist of his cut-off jeans, held the AR-15 in one hand and the Thompson in the other. Jack took a deep nervous breath. If Cole and Delight were going to fight, it would be bad enough without having the guns around.

Cole said, "I don't care anymore what she thinks. I'm just telling you right now, one man to another, don't mess with her anymore. We've got a long way to go, and if we're going to get along, that's the way it'll have to be. I don't want any trouble, but I don't care."

Cole and Delight were especially awesome in size just then, rigid with anger and fear, and they all knew it would be a hell of a fight to break up, but they had to let them get it out. Ralph carefully

115

set the carbine and the pistol between himself and Jack.

"If you keep her between us, there will be trouble, man, and I don't care."

Perhaps deciding to cool it off, Billy said lightly, "What trouble?" Characteristically, he picked just the wrong thing to say.

"I'll show you what fuckin' trouble." Cole got to his feet in a hurry, and so did Billy and the others.

"You bastards!" Eiler's voice was panicky. "Now come on—"

At that very second, when nothing would have stopped them, Thorton turned cooly and fired an ear-splitting blast from the submachine gun off the side. The shock ripped it all open, tore all attention away from Cole and Delight, who jumped apart at the sound. Delight looked at Thorton with a cowlike expression. Both girls sat up, scared to death. One of them had screamed, and Margaret was yelling from the wheel. Jack seemed to have known what was happening. He wore an odd smile, but Joe saw his hands trembling. Joe nearly had a heart attack, until he realized that Ralph had it under control. The air rang.

"What the hell?" Robert demanded. He kept looking back and forth from Thorton to Delight.

"What the hell yourself," Ralph snapped. "You guys get your shit together. We got business a lot more important than your damn love lives." Then he smiled. "And right now we're tryin' to have a little fun."

Ralph picked up his beer from the deck, drained it, and threw it far out ahead of them so it came riding back on the swell. He fired one short blast, and again everything was rent by the noise. He missed, though, and the bright green bottle disappeared a moment. When it reappeared an instant later, Ralph crouched and gripped the weapon more securely. His second blast smashed the bottle to nothing. An astounding shot with a gun like that. Jack and Eiler cheered, and with great relief. Even Billy and Robert suddenly smiled.

"That's a lot more like it," Ralph grinned proudly. "Here, Cole." He thrust the Thompson at him. Jack and Eiler caught their breath, not so sure he wouldn't use it on Delight, but Joe finished his beer in a gulp and threw it out as Ralph had done. Cole chopped up the water around it, but the green bottle bobbed away unharmed.

"Jesus," said Eiler, "those bullets are precious. Let's use the shotgun. We got plenty of shells for it and about a hundred empty beers."

116

"Hell I forgot. You're right," said Ralph. Jack agreed, eager to keep things from returning to their former state.

When Eiler returned with the twelve-gauge and the garbage sack, Helen and Katie had come over to stand on the new deck. There was still tension in the air, and the girls looked uneasy, especially Helen, who must have heard a lot of what happened. It changed though. They all took turns standing at the rail, firing at bottles thrown out over their heads from behind. The bottles would ride up on the wind a moment before they faded quickly on the wake, and they hit a lot of them. The shotgun was an old Remington automatic, and they blasted away with it, laughing and kidding each other and emptying more beers. It transformed the tension into excitement, and the metallic jolt of the gun, the report and smell of powder, the small pop of bottles, and the cheers when one was hit felt like the height of sport. Billy and Robert managed to ignore each other. Katie hit three bottles in a row without wasting a shot, then merely smiled and said, "My daddy used to take me with him duck hunting." Bob went back and took the wheel so Margaret could shoot, and she was a good shot too, having known a few private skeet ranges. It was great fun, and they fired until there were no more empty bottles. Then Jack picked up the magnum, a Reuger .41, and said he'd like to try a bottle. Joe finished another beer and hurled it high over the side, and Jack, firing with both hands, hit it in the air. It was too much. They cheered wildly. Jack played it up, shrugged as if he'd expected nothing else. It was the luckiest goddamn shot Ralph had ever seen, but he laughed and shouted, "We're hot, by Jesus. Red hot!"

ii

The sailing continued perfectly. The weather was steady, and they barely touched the sails. They made good time, so by the third day out, they expected to reach Curaçao late that night. The boat was going well, only taking on a little water, the sources of which could be easily patched, the Jack had no complaints. There was really little to do. Eiler and Thorton were like tourists on a cruise, and Jack occasionally had to look for things that needed cleaning up or some adjustment in the sails just to keep them sober. In the afternoon of the third day, Joe and Ralph sat with their feet on the rail, talking and looking idly out to sea, with the wind in their faces, rocking with the great slow motion of the deck. Jack and Robert were back at the wheel, Margaret was asleep, and Katie was starting some dinner. Joe could hear Delight below in the forecastle, practicing his guitar, keeping to himself. Helen joined Ralph and Joe on the deck. Joe kidded her a little about the previous day's trouble, saying she was too damn sexy for her own good. The order of the boat seemed reliable enough just then that they laughed over it. After awhile, Helen went below to bring up a few more beers, and shortly Joe heard Billy's guitar fall silent. Perhaps Delight wanted to prove what he had said to Cole the day before, or perhaps he was simply unable to stay away from her. Much later, when he told Joe about it, he said he encountered her by accident and couldn't resist.

Billy came into the salon just as Helen was leaving the galley with two beers in one hand and another bottle in the other. Billy moved playfully in front of her and took her waist in his large hands. He bent to kiss her, but she moved saying, "Come on, Billy, let me go." Her interest in Delight had passed to almost nothing, but Billy's desire for her remained. And he had always been able to turn her on. He held the small of her back with one hand and pressed his face to her neck. The other hand slipped into her bikini, the big fingers into that silky hair, seeking the sweet wet warmth he had often known. Joe heard her say, "Billy, come on, stop it," but nothing more. Billy knew how she liked it, knew just how she liked it. Her eyes fell shut and her pelvis reached helplessly out to him, while by some rude fate Robert Cole came forward along the starboard side to the hatch above them. His face roiled violently at what he witnessed. "You bastard!" he shouted. "You son of a bitch!"

Robert was stricken for a moment by what he saw. It just gave Thorton time to get to the hatch and keep him from going down after Billy. "I'm gonna kill *both* of you," Cole yelled. Ralph struggled to restrain him. The day before, there would have been no holding him, and he might indeed have killed them. But now he was more upset than angry, more hurt. And just when he had thought it would work out.

"Damnit," Ralph shouted in his face. "You guys're gonna ruin the whole deal if you don't quit this."

"I don't give a damn about this deal anymore," Cole yelled back at him. He pulled out of Ralph's grasp and headed back to the stern.

Leda was an unpleasant place the rest of that afternoon and evening. Thankfully, Cole and Delight stayed away from each other, but the ambience of the boat was poisoned. Jack and Ralph and Eiler sat for awhile near the bow at sunset, and Sidell said Robert was badly shaken, not mad anymore but damaged, the first emotional casualty of the venture. They agreed then that Helen had to go, or else they would lose Cole, the only experienced crewman, or something worse would happen. They all felt a threat, a dread that seemed deeper than the problems they discussed. It felt as though things might come apart completely, and that night they did.

They sighted Curaçao about midnight, coming in toward the southeast point of the island. Soon afterward a light drizzle of rain began. Jack had mentioned earlier that there was some problem with the charts, that they were old and simple, but it seemed relatively unimportant. Jack decided they should simply feel their way around to the south and go in by the lights of Willemstad, the old port city. Cole was at the helm as they neared the eastern point. There were lights visible on the land, and he and Jack decided to use them as a bearing. They didn't realize that the lights were on high ground considerably inland.

Ralph and Katie and Margaret and Joe sat around the table in the salon. They had smoked a few joints, grown hungry, and were just finishing off some toasted peanut butter sandwiches. Delight was reading in the forecastle, and Helen lay asleep on Caval's couch. The first big ground swell came suddenly and felt as if something had plucked *Leda* into the air and then dropped her back in the water. Dishes scattered across the table, and Helen was lifted into the air above the couch. They heard Cole yelling, and Margaret scrambled up the companionway to the deck. Delight came stumbling out from the forecastle, but no one below said a word. It was as if some monster had grabbed them. The second ground swell came even stronger, lifting both the table and couch in the air. Then it felt as if they were plunging over a cliff.

Jack had clambered out of the aft cabin when he felt the first one. There was panic in Cole's voice: "We gotta come about. It's the shore. We're gonna run aground. We gotta come about."

Jack was already running forward to see how close they were. He shouted at Cole to hold the course. *Leda* could come about only slowly, even in the best conditions, and because of her bulk could be beaten back by waves or wind. So Sidell had to get the engine started first, if there was time. In the darkness and mist, he could not see well, but the surf sounded far enough away. He yelled at

Margaret to be ready to free the sheets. Ralph and Eiler were just coming up as Jack raced back to the engine room and told them to help Margaret.

"Damnit, we've gotta come about," Cole yelled at him. "We gotta come about."

"We can't," Jack yelled back as he jumped down the hatch. "Wait for the engine."

"We're gonna wreck it!" Cole kept yelling. "We're gonna wreck this goddamn thing!"

They were all in shock. Every few seconds the ground swells seemed to push them over a cliff. Ralph and Margaret and Eiler hung onto the ratlines on either side of the wet deck trying to see ahead. Billy, Katie, and Helen came on deck too. The boat felt crowded, disorganized, and doomed. They were all yelling questions at each other, but above the noise were Cole's desperate cries.

"Jack, we're gonna hit. We're gonna wreck!"

Jack had switched on the bilge pump, hooked up the compressed air, frantically lit the tapers, and put them in the cylinder heads. He was setting the timing mark on the big flywheel. The time it all took was maddening, and Cole's shouts were unnerving. He's shot, Jack told himself. All this crap with Helen has ruined him. He set the pressure valve and plucked out the tapers. "Come on now, you bitch." The old diesel sometimes started in reverse.

Margaret and Delight had gone back to the mizzen, and Ralph and Joe stayed ready at the mainsail, but confused and unsure what to do. Another ground swell heaved them slowly and violently. Right then Joe expected the crash of the hull against the rocks, but it didn't come.

Cole sounded hysterical. "Margaret, I'm bringin' her about. I'm bringin' her about."

"No!" Margaret screamed back. "Wait for the engine!"

They rose with another swell, and the surf sounded as close as the bowsprit, but suddenly they heard the deep metallic chugs of the diesel. Jack flew out of the engine room hatch yelling, "Now! Now come!"

Cole started to turn the wheel, and Jack was already around to the back of the cabin setting the pitch of the propeller with one hand and giving full throttle with the other. Then the engine died.

"Bring her back," Jack ordered Cole as he reset the throttle and screw. "I'll start it again."

Jack started for the engine room, but Cole simply froze and yelled, "No!"

120

Jack turned back, his own voice breaking with fear, and shouted, "You start it Margaret." He took the wheel from Cole and kept them headed for the rocks. He could see no choice.

As Margaret jumped down to the engine, Eiler could see the massive rocks of the shore only fifty yards ahead. It was like the death throe of some huge animal as they lurched on another swell. Joe looked around at Ralph and said, "We're fucked."

The pitching of *Leda*'s deck, the drizzle, the sound of surf ahead, of furniture and supplies crashing around below, the chaos and shouting on deck all had the numbing feel of inescapable disaster. But if the diesel had started once, even briefly, it could be restarted with far greater ease, and Margaret knew the thing perfectly. It began to chug again with miraculous speed, and Jack yelled, "Come about!"

He turned hard to starboard, and Eiler and Thorton freed the sheets and prepared to reset the sail once they were about. As they turned though, with the engine pushing and the rocks near enough to spit on, they lifted on another swell. It took them sideways; the boat rolled violently to port. Eiler figured that was it. He lost his footing, his legs struck something, he was thrown backward across the deck and landed hard against the port gunwhale. He glimpsed Katie and Helen in a heap on the deck nearby. Overhead the mainsail boom swung toward him as if they were rolling over. Then suddenly it swung back, caught the wind, and they were about. By the time Joe was up and helping Ralph set the sail, they were completely turned and with the diesel's help struggling slowly away from the shore.

Jack's arms trembled as he set a course. He felt weak and breathless. He kept mumbling, "I've got to get this boat under control."

Cole stood nearby, silent, one hand on top of the aft cabin, the other distractedly rubbing his forehead. He was undone to the marrow of his bones. He knew better than anyone how badly he had acted, but there was nothing to say. It had seemed a few moments earlier that everything had led up to the rocks. He wanted to say he was sorry for the panic. Then he wanted to say he was leaving as soon as they made port. But he felt as if he could not even speak and went below to his cabin instead.

When Cole had gone the others gathered in the stern. Joe tried to kid Jack about setting course for the harbor next time, instead of merely aiming for the island. But it was humor with great effort and still not funny. They just stood around gasping and staring at each other, having scared the wits out of themselves. And at bottom they all knew the worst of it—they could not really pull it off.

Even so, things loosened up a little once they came around to the lee of the island. Hell, they were alive. The boat was in one piece. They could see the harbor entrance. It was narrow, like a canal, dividing the city and lined with glittering lights of buildings close by the water. Arches of white lights sparkled along the top of the old pontoon bridge that opened and closed the harbor like a great gate. It all shined dreamlike in the darkness.

They were advised by radio to wait until morning to enter, so they moved out a safe distance and anchored. Before they slept Jack and Eiler tried to convince each other it was still possible. They agreed that the biggest task before them was to keep the crew together. The chance of it though seemed improbably remote. Cole would most likely want to leave, and Delight had never really wanted to be there in the first place. Now there was their open enmity as well. And Ralph, who was best of them at keeping things enthusiastic, would be leaving the boat to stay at the Hilton to await Caval's call. But Jack said he was sending Helen home immediately. That would allow them to try to get everyone working together again. "We can do it," he said. He said it with the same determination with which he had told Cole to keep the course when they were heading for the rocks.

When Eiler finally went to the forecastle to sleep, Helen's bags were packed beside her bunk. Joe could hear her sobbing in the sleeping bag but said nothing to her. The next morning Helen and Cole remained below, while the rest of them sat on deck drinking coffee as they watched great, ponderous freighters entering the harbor ahead of them.

When they finally entered, they passed the Intercontinental Hotel, which overlooked the harbor mouth from old fortress walls, then the old yellow colonial buildings and the tall narrow Dutch buildings very close to the water. The city was alluring and mysterious. As they made for the customs dock, the old pontoon bridge swung slowly shut behind them, like a trap with which the harbor swallowed them up. It seemed ominously permanent.

iii

The dark bare feet were silent on the red tiles as the old man approached the hammock suspended from hooks in the white

122

plaster ceiling of the veranda. The veranda extended about sixty feet along the front of the house, and broad archways in front looked across the sand to the deep cool blue of the Caribbean. "Señor Caval," the man said, pronouncing it Cabal.

"Hey *amigo,*" Caval looked up. He had been daydreaming, not really asleep. He wore only tennis shorts and was darkly tanned. *"Que pasa?"*

"Do you want dinner?" the old man inquired in Spanish.

"Is Umberto here? Is Umberto coming?" Caval's Spanish was simple and uninflected, and he asked the question with dulled interest, not expecting positive answers but having acquired the habit of asking.

"No." The old man shook his head with the indulgent, mildly amused expression with which he always answered that question. *"A la finca,"* he said. At the farm.

"Bueno," said Tom. He sat up in the hammock and looked down the beach through the archways. He could see Eduardo sitting in his yellow motorboat with his brother and two girls, so he told the old man, "No. No dinner, but a beer, eh?"

After Caval had met the others in Curaçao with Insinger and they had set up the bank accounts and communications procedures, he had returned to Santa Marta. He had given the grower, whom he'd come to know as Umberto, proof that the money was on hand and told him the boat would leave Curaçao when Umberto showed him the load, ready to go. The following day Umberto had taken Tom to see the stuff. They drove inland in Umberto's Nissan Patrol for four hours before reaching the *finca,* bumping over steep curving dirt roads through thick jungle, loud with the cries of strange birds. It was lush hill country at the foot of the Sierra, most of it planted in melons, and they drove between fields until they reached a slowly rising hillside covered with rows of marijuana.

The stuff was almost shoulder height then, the rows perhaps a yard apart, and on sight Caval figured there were about ten acres of it. Short wiry *braceros* with fierce eyes, carrying machetes or old rifles, seemed to appear from nowhere and followed them among the rows. Umberto showed Caval that the plants were still largely green, having not yet turned completely to the pale gold they would become by the time the flowers and seed pods appeared. *"Verdadora,"* Umberto called them, and then said in English, "They are children." He showed Caval that they would grow up to be *Mona.* Tom had not been terribly impressed. He had seen marijuana fields in Mexico, and although this was rather special, the primary thing

123

he noticed about the fields was that they were hotter than any-where he ever cared to be. "Yeah. *Bueno, bueno,* but *quando? Quando?*" When.

With an expression of pain and helplessness, Umberto had shrugged his shoulders in a way that Colombians of all classes do when a matter is subject only to the indomitable elements of their land, of which they are one of the most imponderable. Then with a smile he said, "We wait." Colombians love to wait. Waiting orga-nizes life, slows it down, provides time for activities other than labor. Tom Caval hated nothing more than to wait. For anything. And yet in that setting, even he had got used to it.

The day after Caval had seen the fields, the old man, who was now fetching a beer, had arrived at the Irotama Hotel with a jeep, and he took Tom and his bags to the beach at Rodadero. There they got into a motorboat and headed around the eastern point of the bay to a small stretch of beach called Playa Blanca. Four large houses and a tiny cantina stand were the only structures, backed against the steep pale cliffs that overlooked the beach and curved slightly to protect the houses from winds and rough seas and made the privileged area inaccessible except by boat or, with some diffi-culty, by foot. The houses there were owned by prosperous families from Bogotá or Barranquilla or Medillin who used them only dur-ing the holiday seasons of Christmas and January and in July. The grower, Umberto Parilla, was the eldest son of a family with consid-erable interests in Santa Marta and Barranquilla. He was a pleas-ant looking man of about thirty-five with dark brown hair and a straight mustache. He was well educated and spoke far more French than English. He was a casual, unhurried man, assured of his position and ability. Since the family was not coming for the July holidays that were just beginning, he had insisted that Tom occupy their Playa Blanca house and simply advise the old man, Ignacio, of anything he needed.

It was Umberto's young cousin Alvaro, a lesser member of the family, who Tom had met that first night in Rodadero while In-singer suffered with Jeb in the adjacent room. During two sub-sequent visits, Tom had met Umberto. Normally matters would have been left to Alvaro, but Umberto was no less taken than most people by the wealth and energy and good looks of this young American, so he had chosen to conduct the business himself. It was also a much larger deal than Alvaro had ever handled, and Umberto had not failed to notice the facility for crafty moves that gleamed in Caval's eyes. Nevertheless Umberto never gave the slightest indication that he and Tom were involved in anything unlawful. He behaved in a courtly, gracious manner, as though they were merely doing normal business that he had decided to conduct on a personal social level. That way it would be pleasant for the visiting Señor Caval, and Umberto would always know where he was.

By the end of a week, Caval had almost gone mad. Scenic beauty did not move him; he did not care for hot weather; he much preferred swimming pools to salt water populated by God knows what sort of marine beasts. He asked Ignacio so frequently where Señor Parilla was in those first days that Ignacio finally began to say that Don Umberto was either at the farm or in Barranquilla, although he actually had no idea. Gradually though, Caval grew accustomed to his setting, and by the time he had been there two weeks he loved it. Ignacio was a marvelous cook, and he grilled the finest steaks or prepared the freshest fish available anytime Caval desired. He also kept the house clean, hung up Caval's clothes or took them to the laundry, ferried him to Rodadero in the family motorboat on command, and from there would drive him in to Santa Marta or anywhere else he wanted to go. In addition, on the shortest notice Ignacio could disappear in the motorboat and return within an hour or two with the freshest marijuana or the finest *noventa percenta* cocaine. And Tom Caval did love service and good dope.

For the first time in his life, Tom found he could relax. He could lie in the hammock or sit in one of the big wicker chairs on the porch for hours, never grow nervous, and often be unable even to recall of what he had been thinking. In truth, he realized, he was tired of his businesses in Aspen, rather tired of Teresa, and very tired of bothering over the details of his venture with Sidell and Insinger. He cultivated an exquisite pleasure in doing nothing but watching the beach and the sea while his fortune grew golden in the faraway hills.

Life at Playa Blanca seemed only to get better. During the second week of his stay, the other families began arriving, bringing motorboats and small sailboats and children and cousins of all ages. Rodadero grew crowded, and each day young people with boats came to Playa Blanca to visit friends there or simply to enjoy the superior setting. Tom met Eduardo Torreros and his brother, whose name Tom could never remember. They were from Bogotá and owned the nicest house at Playa Blanca. Eduardo was a muscular kid in his early twenties, and everyone knew him. He had a

125

large yellow motorboat and numerous girlfriends. Tom and Eduardo became friends, and Tom often went skiing with Eduardo and others. Tom in turn would invite them to his house, where Ignacio would prepare dinners and make drinks as they sat about the large living room listening to cassettes. Tom also had four bedrooms, which made him a very popular host. Although he never mentioned what sort of business he was involved in with Umberto, everyone seemed to know, and they accepted him with both curiosity and admiration as an American adventurer. Tom enjoyed that immensely. One of those who accepted him was Marisa, a thin, dark-eyed, eighteen-year-old daughter of one of the Playa Blanca families. She was from Medellin, and her shiny black hair and young body were a delight. Her family would not let her go out alone with the gringo, of course, but she and Tom became close friends during the day, swimming and water-skiing. One day, while swimming alone away from the others, they took off each other's bathing suits, and late that night Tom was awakened by a tapping at his window. The late visits became a fairly regular pleasure, and Tom's life seemed perfect. At times he felt content enough to let the dope grow fifty feet tall.

Ignacio delivered the beer in a bottle wrapped carefully in two napkins. Tom took a sip and said in understandable Spanish, "I think I go to see if Eduardo and his friends want to go to Rodadero to eat." Ignacio nodded. Pretty damn good *Español*, Caval assured himself. "How long I am here, Ignacio?" Tom could not remember.

"Three weeks, more or less," the old man answered.

"Yeah, three weeks I guess." Tom shook his head thoughtfully. "*Bueno,* man. *Mas tarde,* eh?"

Ignacio smiled as Tom rolled out of the hammock and walked down the beach toward Eduardo's *lancha.*

Three weeks. Jesus. Tom thought of Ralph and Jack and Eiler. Bet they wonder what the hell's goin' on. Well, I have to wait, so they can wait too. I'd call, but I'd just have to listen to how much money Sidell wants for some goddamn safety equipment or something. I bet he was a lifeguard in high school. Yeah, that's Jack. A lifeguard. Safety first. Don't have anything to tell 'em anyway. Ralph's at the Hilton, so I'm sure he's happy. They got bars anywhere, so Eiler's good. The hell with Delight and that other big asshole. And Jack and that bitch have their boat, which is so cool, so they oughta be happy as hogs. Bet they wish like hell they were back in St. Thomas, though. Didn't know how good they had it back there. Bet they do now. Bet they remember who was payin' the bills, too.

126

Curaçao ain't quite the same. God, what a dump where they parked that thing.

chapter 8

MARK awoke without awareness of the passage. He looked around the room. At the clock. Seven. He smiled. Put his feet on the floor. He had made a point of rising every morning at seven since he'd come to Far Prospect, and now did not even require the alarm. It seemed like the first time in his life he had eagerly left bed.

He moved to the heavy wood and glass door and quietly slid it open. From the deck he could see the length of the sound, with its faint summer haze not yet dispersing. Each morning for the past several days he'd gone out on the deck with a special, almost childlike anticipation. Even though he knew it was impossible, he thought one morning he might see *Leda*'s red sails, like a kid dreams of snow in July. At any rate, they were due. He had had no word from Caval since leaving Curaçao, but there could have been reasons Tom did not want to call. Anyway Tom was supposed to be moving up the coast in a van, to make radio contact with *Leda*.

Mark lingered a few moments to smell the morning, the birch and the pine and the sea. It felt good to stand naked with the rounded green mountains stretching ahead of him along the sound. His body felt attuned to the setting. He had run two and a half miles each morning since he arrived, and he did sit-ups, push-ups and pull-ups on the front deck. He had quit smoking; his wind was good. He was more than ready. If he had to he could unload half the cargo by himself. He was down to about one hundred and forty-five pounds, and the muscles of his stomach made hard ridges. Veins stood out on his forearms and along his biceps.

He looked fondly out at his boat, another morning ritual. Sometimes he could hardly believe it was all true. The white Pacemaker, forty-six feet long, sat still and ready at its mooring pot in front of the house. Through the broker in Boston he had learned of the boat and the elderly Harvard professor who wanted to rent it out for the summer months. The boat had already been at Mount Desert, and all Mark had to do was pick it up in Northeast Harbor, take a few lessons from the old man, and bring her around to the house. Mark quickly fell in love with the big cruiser. The clean, modern style of it was more to his liking than the rough and physically demanding *Leda*. He much preferred the salon of the Pacemaker, with its divan and armchairs and stereo. She was uptown. And she was powerful. It quickened his pulse each time he turned on the system and pressed the starters and the big Cummins diesels burst alive with hoarse explosions and shots of water from the exhausts. He liked to put the throttles on full and feel the big boat squat and bore toward top speed, raked back defiantly with the engines roaring. Most of all though, he liked to move slowly about the island, growling in and out of harbors and coves at low speed, sleek and mysterious.

Mark walked to the bathroom with a conscious satisfaction. There was still a continual twist of smoke in the fireplace. Some notes he'd made were on the writing table beside the bookshelves, which held leather bound collections of Dickens, Poe, Cooper, Bulwer, and Mrs. Browning. He had been reading Spengler's *Decline of the West*. Each successive day seemed to exist on a progressively higher plane of capability.

Mark let the shower jets hit him full in the face for a few moments, so he could hear nothing but the frantic water, and he jumped, startled, when she touched him.

"Oh gawd," she shrunk away to a corner of the stall, "it's so cold."

"No it's not. Just get used to it. Come here." He tried to pull her toward him, but she wouldn't let him.

"Just a little hotter," she pleaded. She was still squinting sleepily, and the way she tried to cover herself from the water was almost pitiful. "Please. Just a little hotter. Please."

He turned on more hot. She drew toward him and the heat with soft sounds. "What are you doing up?"

"I heard you." She slipped her arms around him, and with their faces together they let the water drill against them. Wet and soft, uninhibited, as if she knew as well as he that no posture could diminish her beauty, the appeal of her body was magic to him. She was the first woman he'd ever known whose flesh he could not imagine ever tiring of. She reached down with one hand and held him for a moment. "My goodness," she purred. He was always incapable of speech at such moments. Sliding with the water, their mouths found each other. Their teeth touched; their tongues engaged with languid amusement. They coupled as inevitably as two magnets brought close. He set his legs apart, stiffened his back as her hands joined tightly behind his neck. She pulled herself up. He caught her legs beneath the knees, and she pressed her mouth to his ear as he put it in. He felt suddenly propelled by an inexhaustible resource of energy. No infinity of repetition could lessen the thrill of entering her. He could have howled in primordial ecstacy but murmured only, "Ohh, Helen . . . Helen . . ."

When Mark had returned to Mount Desert Island from Curaçao, he expected *Leda* to be leaving for Colombia in a week. Allowing for the passage, the shipment would arrive off the Maine coast in three to four weeks. Finding a boat had turned out to be simple, so Mark had quickly moved his attention to renting two houses in Boston, one for negotiations and one for transactions. The latter had to be well protected from view, yet be near an entrance to the Mass Pike. And the other simply needed to be not too far from the transaction house. The first two days Mark had the Pacemaker, he had taken the *Globe* and a city map with him as he ran out to the mouth of the sound and beyond. Coming back he stopped midway in the sound, drifted in the calm water and drank a few beers as he checked ads and made notes. With his house visible at the head of the sound and the long green mountains on either side, it was pleasant business.

He drove to Boston, laboriously checked fourteen houses he'd found in the papers, and that evening paid three months' rent on two of them. As further planned, he then drove to the nearest phone. But several minutes passed before he got out of the car. He had said he'd look her up, but he thought it might be best to let it go until another time. Jack didn't want her anywhere near the operation, especially now. And maybe that was best. Maybe you ought to let it wait, he thought. Just tell her something to keep her going. Since his arrival at Far Prospect though, Mark had wanted her there, envisioned her there, felt her there. He had known somehow she would go there with him. And, as he debated outside the phone booth, he finally did not know if he could return without her. He called the number she had given him, but there was no answer. On a chance he dialed the number of Jack's parents, and she picked it up. It was not a pleasant or expectant greeting, however, and Mark immediately felt defensive and foolish. Helen had returned to Boston with the guilty knowledge that she might have wrecked her brother's enterprise. In addition she had developed an aversion to it all, a resentment of it, as if since she could not have all of it, she didn't want any of it. Mark tried to be casual, but in the end he argued her into going out to dinner.

By the time they'd had a few drinks and were at a table at Locke-Ober, Helen was telling Mark about the trip to Curaçao. Unashamedly, she told him of the trouble and the way it had affected Robert, yet told it with a distance, as if she described a disaster striking some far city. The waiter interrupted and when he left, she concluded, "I know I caused a lot of trouble for you and Jack. For the deal. I wish I could make up for it. I will if there's anything I can do. If you need anything done here, just tell me, okay? Otherwise, all I can say is, nobody knows anything about it because of me. I don't talk about things."

Mark could see how badly she wanted to be some sort of operative, and he thought she would be good at it. "I'm relieved. We were afraid we'd have to vaporize you."

"I knew it when you called." They began to laugh. "They've sent Insinger. It's the big payoff."

They had savored the humor. Their eyes had played across the table. The solidly elegant trappings of the old restaurant were to Mark a perfect setting for her, and she began again to see in him the worldly detachment that had drawn her once before.

Mark did not begin to tell her about Far Prospect until they had finished the meal. She had listened quietly and awaited with a slightly puzzled amusement what she knew would follow.

"If you have the time and you really do want to help a little," Mark said after the coffee was served, "you might come up there. There's a lot to do, and . . ." He stopped himself. He was going to say that a woman would make things look more normal, but he couldn't. Chickenshit, he scorned himself. Say it straight. "Well," he started again, never having taken his eyes from hers, "to tell the truth, everything important has been done. There's really nothing to do now. I'm just passing time until they get here. It's a beautiful place. Why don't you come up and spend some time? You could drive up with me tonight."

The inclination of her head, the merest beginning of a smile—and just then Mark would have killed for her, burned cities.

"I do just happen to cook," she had said.

When they had finished, they held tightly, leaning in a corner of the shower with the water still beating on the tile.

"You're killing my back," she said finally.

130

He let her down and leaned into the corner, his eyes softly shut. She moved into the water and dreamily dropped her head back letting the jets comb her hair. "You going to run?"

"Uhh . . . definitely."

She was smiling as he opened his eyes.

ii

Ill-defined clouds proceeded monotonously from the northeast. Joe Eiler sat on deck, watching resentfully as they passed. In the distance they seemed to promise one great cloud, a weather system, as though it might rain, as if something might happen, but it was illusion. They simply came over one at a time, suggested coolness as they blocked the sun a moment, but then rode on leaving the relentless sun in their wakes. Joe had begun to feel that each day strove toward some dismal climax, whereupon it would be humid noon for eternity.

There is no haven for big pleasure craft in Willemstad, which is one of the world's busiest commercial harbors. Upon arrival *Leda* had been directed into the bowels of Otrabanda, the eastern sector, where they docked at an old wharf lined with warehouses. The area was surrounded and completely dominated by oil tankers, freighters, tugs and oil storage tanks—all of which combined to prevent any breeze from finding them as they baked in the stench of crude oil. Beside them at the wharf was an enormous old freighter, perhaps four hundred feet long, abandoned. It was a monument to rust, abuse, and inactivity that hulked above them always. On the other side was a wretched tug operated and lived on by what Ralph had described, before happily departing for the Hilton, as the shiftiest-looking bunch of Spanish niggers he'd ever seen.

They had been there roughly four weeks. They had moved only once, to test the radios between the Boston Whaler and *Leda* at a distance of four or five miles, and in the process discovered serious engine trouble. For the past two weeks that had added filthy, seemingly endless work to the boredom and general unpleasantness of waiting for Caval.

They had not eaten regularly or well. The few good restaurants were far away in town, expensive, and required at least clean dress, and they did a bad job of buying food. The first week had been busy with the final planning of supplies and learning where to buy them when they were ready to leave, with buying lumber to shore up the cargo and extra gasoline tanks and spare parts for the pumps. For the last three weeks though, there had only been the waiting and the engine trouble.

Morale was bad enough to match the setting. Each day Jack radiated a stronger sense of loathing for the situation. He liked good food, clean clothes, and recreation, and he accepted their absence only if he were camping or at sea. He had none of those things in Curaçao.

Cole's life was ruined. With Helen had gone all his interest in the venture and he kept on only because he would never walk out in the middle of a deal. He had soured on all of it, yet he still had to work with Billy Delight every day on the engine. To Cole the deal had become a wound that festered a little more each day. Nevertheless he usually managed a gruff humor, which sometimes seemed like the only thing that kept any of them going.

Ralph remained gung ho, even though he grew glassy-eyed and forgetful from four weeks of lying in the sun by a hotel pool waiting for a phone call. Whenever the others went out to see him for a swim and a shower, he did his best to raise their spirits, but a month with no word from Caval was hard on his optimism.

Margaret was devoted to both *Leda* and Jack, but she had never bargained for Otrabanda. Nor was it anywhere in her nature to confine herself to unpleasantness for more than a few hours just because someone was going to call. Messages could be left, calls forwarded. Four weeks in Otrabanda was as pointless to her as some Hindu exercise in suffering. She could take it as well as any of them, but she did so only because of Jack and *Leda*. She believed of course that, when the deal was over, she and Jack and *Leda* would sail away to Bequia with plenty of cash.

Billy Delight never had a clear understanding of what was happening. To do so would have required too much serious thought. He didn't seem to mind Curaçao, though. They were just a bunch of guys on a boat having a good time. But there just wasn't much to do there, and St. Thomas had been a lot more fun.

Eiler liked Willemstad, with its old buildings and loud little bars and lithe black girls in thin swaying skirts with their hair tied up in colorful scarves. But he rarely got to town. As for the deal itself, Joe had no other prospects.

Sitting on deck that morning, Joe grew depressed by the fact he had no other place to be, no one waiting. It made him prey to his memory of his wife. The heat reminded him of her family's place outside the city in summer—sitting by the pool with elm trees shading it, listening to the girls preparing a meal, saddling a quarter horse near sunset for a ride through the pastures, loving her on a warm night. It was sweet to remember, until inevitably it forced him to recognize that he would never have her again, that she was dead, that he had let her be killed, that she had suffered terribly.

Joe was weak that morning. He kept seeing her face. But the image kept changing to that obscene horror, that ugly death, and he felt himself coming apart. He was about to start crying, and he feared that more than anything. He had not cried in so long that if he started he felt he would never stop, that what tenuous little remained of his life would end up in a cross-sleeved jacket. The effort to suppress it choked him, and he trembled as if shivering from cold in the face of that cruel sun.

Sidell approached just then. "There any coffee?" Jack was sleepy. It was about eleven, but he had worked late on the engine. He was still greasy from it, unshaven for several days, and already sweaty from the mere effort of getting up.

"I don't know." Joe's voice quaked.

"Well, is . . . What's the matter with you?"

Joe just closed his eyes and shook his head. "If there's coffee bring me some, will ya?"

"Yeah. Sure." Jack looked at him carefully before going below. If Joe cracked up, he didn't know what the hell he'd do. When he returned with the cups they sat together without speaking. Jack knew the old poison was working on Eiler, so he stayed there beside him until it passed, out of a sense of duty, which was at that time rather strained. Margaret joined them too, but she knew Jack was unpleasant to talk to until he was completely awake, and she and Joe never had much to say to each other. Jack and Eiler drank the first cups and then two more, all three sitting silently in the still heat and the smell of oil until Cole emerged on deck.

"Look at the happy crew," he quipped. "What year is it, gang? Wrong. That was last year . . . Not talking, uh?" Cole shrugged. He was always playful when he woke up. "Where's the incredible sleeping hulk?"

They did laugh at that. Even Eiler grinned and felt better. Robert referred of course to Billy Delight, who often slept twelve hours. Jack said, "He left word for you to wake him."

Cole grunted. "Sure. Where's the shotgun?"

He went down to get more coffee, and when he came up cursing as he spilled it over his fingers, Margaret was reminding Jack of something she had wanted to do. Jack was not answering much, and Eiler could tell he didn't want to hear it.

"The old man isn't coming today is he, Bob?" Joe inquired as Cole handed him a cup.

"Kurt? No. It's Sunday. But he said he'd have her running sure Monday night."

Kurt was an old Dutchman who owned and ran a shipyard in Otrabanda. They had gone to his yard looking for a part when the engine went bad, and he had taken an interest in them. He had said they had to take one of the big cylinders completely apart and seemed to know they couldn't do it right without him. So he had offered to help, and they started picking him up every evening at five-thirty in the Whaler, and he worked until midnight for nothing but gratitude and Heineken. He had addressed the bunch of them one night as he left, saying in his harsh accents, "I don't know what you fellows are up to and I don't think I want to know. But when I was about your ages, I was trying to get a boat around to California, and an old man in Panama helped me. He didn't ask what I was doing. If he had not helped me, I would probably still be in Panama. So you might say I'm returning the favor." Kurt left quickly that night, without even finishing his last beer.

"Well, hell," Eiler said, "let's go in an' see Ralph. We can get showers an' swim an' do a little drinkin'."

"Fine with me. What do you say, Jack?"

"Yeah. Sure. I don't know what sounds better, the shower or the drinking."

"Maybe we can play some volleyball," Cole said.

"Jack . . ." Margaret spoke in a soft, calculating tone. "I don't feel like drinking today." Jack looked straight ahead and didn't answer.

Joe told her, "Good. You can stay with the boat." She ignored Eiler and spoke with the clear intention of limiting the conversation to the two of them. "But Jack, we were going to drive up to the windward tip of the island today. And take some pictures. Remember?"

"Yes, I remember," Jack replied stiffly. "Does that mean I have to do it?" She took a deep breath and turned away from him. As far as Jack was concerned, on top of everything else, there was far too much "we" in their conversation, and that was what he had feared in the beginning. Margaret could feel his resistance as well as anyone, yet in addition to the fact that she loved him, he had *Leda*.

134

Those two facts put her in a rather desperate position, which should have been sad to witness. But none of them was capable of much empathy then—least of all Joe Eiler.

"I don't mean to interfere with a Sunday outing," he said.

She calmly retorted, "Go to hell, Joe, will you?"

"Sure. Just stay with the boat while I'm gone."

"I don't want to stay here by myself all day and night. Billy can keep watch."

Cole objected to that: "I am personally escorting the incredible stinking hulk to the showers, sweetie." Joe added, "I stayed here last time."

Margaret turned plaintively to Jack. "I don't want to stay by myself, Jack." Her tone went far beyond the mere question of watching the boat.

"Keep the shotgun handy," Jack answered coldly. "You use it as well as any of us. You can take a turn watching. It won't hurt you."

They called ahead to the Holiday Inn to let Ralph know they were coming. That allowed him to advise the appropriate bellmen and maids that his dirty friends were invading again. They usually made some effort to tidy up but always looked like something no one wanted anywhere near their Holiday Inn. Ralph tipped everyone well for their trouble though—otherwise they would have called the police—and the crew generally tried to keep a low profile until they'd had a shower and shave. None of them was much concerned for the other guests, but Ralph had already been thrown out of the Hilton. As it was, Caval's call would have to be forwarded, and having to move again might stretch things too far.

At the Hilton, which was much nicer, they had all gotten pretty loaded one night, and Joe was idly lifting a chair with one arm. It was an insignificant test of strength, but they were bored. Ralph wagered that he could throw the chair farther left-handed than Eiler could. Joe was left-handed. The balcony on the sixth floor looked out over the pool and patio beside the outside bar and provided an excellent site for the contest. Ralph made an admirable throw with one of the room's chairs, but it crashed loudly onto one of the poolside tables attracting a wary crowd. Up in the room they howled with laughter. Joe drew back mightily to throw the other chair and shattered the glass doors. It affected his aim but not his effort. The chair sailed into the bar, terrifying the customers, narrowly missing the barman, and destroying about two hundred dollars worth of liquor. Jack, Margaret, Billy, and Joe managed to sneak out just before the police arrived, in force, and Ralph had to give some lame story about an acquaintance having gone berserk. He had to pay the damages right then to stay out of jail, and that was the last they saw of the Hilton.

Due mostly to Ralph's efforts, they got along better at the Holiday Inn. But the management had asked Ralph not to let his friends play volleyball anymore. Whenever they had played, it had been after numerous beers, which led to a lot of loud foul language. And while they played, Margaret's considerable bosoms seemed to spend a lot more time outside her bikini than in it. And a bunch of big, drunk jocks and a loose broad who played as if their lives depended on it and shouted motherfucker or cocksucker every few minutes was just not the sort of poolside ambience the Holiday Inn had intended. Ralph, in his way, had promised they would be good though, and inflated his tips accordingly.

Ralph was waiting in the lobby and greeted them with his customary exuberance. He loved being a host and hated not being with them on the boat. He had a rare sense of comradeship, and since Katie had left two weeks earlier he was lonely too.

"Hey guys, how ya doin'? Come on in here." He said their names and grabbed a hand or shoulder as each of them came through the door. "There's extra towels an' all up in the room, an' I had 'em bring up some beers too. An' there's doobies rolled up. So we can all go up there if ya want, or else we can sit outside an' have some drinks an' something to eat, an' you guys can go up one at a time for your showers." He spread his arms as they stepped out to the pool area. "Anything you guys wanna do."

Eiler said, "Let's have a drink. Billy can go up an' take a shower. If he stays out here he's liable to fall in the pool an' they'd have to close the hotel."

"If you ever did any work you might get dirty too," Billy groused.

Jack said, "Joe worked all afternoon once. In nineteen sixty-eight."

Ralph roared laughing. "I heard about that," he said. They gave their clean clothes and bathing suits to Billy as he left, then found an umbrella table in the sun and ordered drinks. The wings of the hotel formed a U that opened toward an uninviting beach and enclosed a pool and outdoor bar. The poolside was crowded with sunbathers, and the Sunday smorgasbord was arranged near the bar. The tables around them were full, and a steel band beside the bar whanged out jerky Caribbean rhythms on decorated sections of oil drums. Tiny yellow birds with delicate black markings fluttered among the diners and drinkers and often landed unafraid on the tables.

They discussed the engine awhile, telling Ralph how the work was progressing. He naturally predicted it would run better than ever once repaired. "An' we'll be hearing from Tommy soon," he said. "I know we will. I'm sure there's just been problems down there, ya know? Delays. There always are with those kind of people." Jack and Robert muttered vague obscenities, but with more reference to Caval than Colombians. "Yeah, I know," Ralph said, "I know. If he walked in here right now, I sure might take 'im by the ankles and dip his ol' head in that pool for a few minutes. But you gotta admit no matter what you're thinking that he'd look pretty good walkin' up here right now."

Ralph glanced expectantly around the table, but no one seemed to agree. Jack sat up, stiffened, and frowned a little, as he always did when he had something important to say.

"Well, if in fact he doesn't walk up right about now, it's not going to make much difference. Margaret and I have been figuring times and courses, and unless we actually pick up in the next week or ten days, we'll have to postpone the whole thing until around November."

"Oh, Jesus," Eiler groaned. It was the first he'd heard of this. Cole was nodding his head, rather eagerly.

"No, Jack. Don't say that," Ralph pleaded. "Why?"

"Hurricanes," Jack stated. "It'll be getting into the hurricane season."

"Hell, let's just take our chances," Ralph said. "We're due for good luck."

"They'd be damn lousy chances. Believe me, I hate to have to call it off, but if we don't get going damn soon we'll have very stormy weather. And in the most difficult waters. It just wouldn't be worth it."

There was a painful silence as they sampled the possibility that all the unpleasant waiting was perhaps for nothing but more waiting. Joe grit his teeth and anxiously watched their reactions. Eiler could see that Jack feared it might fall apart, that he was beginning to doubt his ability to hold it together. Joe figured the whole thing would probably be a wash. What a sack of crap, he thought. He sneered malignantly at the others and turned away. They sat for a few moments as if they'd eaten something that had turned their stomachs. Finally Ralph clapped his hands loudly twice, and a waiter rushed to him. "For Christ's sake, bring another round." As the waiter left, he made a crippled effort to regain some sense of enthusiasm. "He'll come. Goddamnit. He'll come soon. I know it."

Jack only mumbled that he hoped so. Just then Joe noticed Billy coming out of Ralph's room on the second floor above them. Delight had a stash of Quaaludes, and from the ponderous way he moved Joe figured he'd taken a couple—Billy's normal dose, but enough to paralyze a normal person. Joe watched him lumber past the stairway and wondered aloud, "What the hell is he doing?" They all turned to see. A wide yellow awning, which shaded the back tables of the patio, extended to just below the railing on the second floor. In his soft bliss, Billy apparently thought he'd take a short cut by simply stepping onto the awning then hopping down among the patio tables. Billy stepped over the railing, and to a sober onlooker, it was like watching an elephant step into a bark canoe. Jack whined, "Oh my god."

The awning parted beneath Delight with a quick scream of ripping canvas, and Billy landed with a sickening thud flat on his back between two tables. A woman shrieked, a little girl began to cry loudly, and all the tiny birds flew away in a sudden yellow blur. Otherwise there was stunned silence, as if a cadaver had fallen from the sky, except for the steel band and Sidell saying, "Don't come to the table. Please don't come to the table."

Delight lay still a moment, semiconscious, then slowly managed a crawling position. Bright crimson blood trickled out of his thick hair. Then he stood up suddenly and like an addled rhino shook his head and shoulders sending little drops of blood flying at the people around him. Guests looked on in horror as he lumbered to the table numbly grinning.

iii

Insinger was stunned by her words, paralyzed by the even tone of her voice, the ease with which she hurt him.

"I've got to," Helen said. She observed it as a matter of fact, as if relating the time. "It's better if I just leave now and stay away from it all. I've been bad for the whole deal. If I stay, I'll probably just cause more trouble. And Jack doesn't want me around it. I don't even want him to know I've been here." She looked away from Mark and shook her head. "And it's bad for me, too."

And what about me, Mark thought. But he couldn't say it. She was being selfish and theatrical, but it made no difference. He loved her, and the prospect of her leaving choked him to the point of tears. He looked back at her silently, in pathetic awe of the power she had to affect his life. If he spoke, he would beg her not to go. He could not do that.

She had waited until he came out of the bathroom, having finished his shower and shave after running, until they sat as usual sipping coffee before the fireplace, the long main room full of early sunlight. Then she had told him that Caval had called, that the deal was postponed, and that she was leaving.

Caval had finally arrived in Curaçao, but the date he had set for a pickup had still been two weeks away. Jack told him flatly that it was too late: it would be hurricane season, and the crew was already in poor shape. Hurricanes meant very little to Caval, but he had no choice. When he found Helen on the phone that morning though, he was happy to give her the blame. "Whatta ya workin' on Mark now?" He had said it with a certain amusement. "I guess you got Cole and Billy so fucked up they want to kill each other and don't even want to do the thing any more."

"I guess I've just been feeding off Jack's deal," she told Mark. "I need to find something of my own to do. I mean, this is over for now, and there's nothing more to do."

"Nothing more to do," he mumbled as if in shock. It had been only four or five nights ago that they had lain together before the bedroom fire and talked of getting married and having children. At the time Helen had meant it; the words had seemed so natural that night. Now things had changed, but not for Mark. "Just like that?"

"I think it's better to just stop now. The deal's over, and—"

"Come to Aspen with me," he blurted. "Everything doesn't have to be over. I live there. I have a law practice. I have an apartment there. There's a lot to do." He hated the sound of his voice, but he was desperate.

"No." She almost whispered, her voice low and soft and subdued by the knowledge that she was injuring him, yet certain that it was inevitable. "It's been fun getting ready for the deal and everything, but I don't want to go to Aspen with you. That would be just another ol' lady trip, and I don't want to do that with you. It would—"

"Fun," he cut her off, uttered the word like a cry of pain. Was it just the excitement of the deal? Wasn't it me at all? "What about this crap we said—" His voice broke, and he stopped himself and looked away from her, taking a deep breath. He could not bear to reduce himself further. You wanted it fast and loose, an inner voice observed cynically. Does that mean you and the chick set up house and live happily ever after? Are you serious? Marriage and kids? You sorry bastard.

The irony turned in the pit of his stomach. He had outdone himself. He had cast himself for her as a strong, cooly independent man whose love was predicated on her desire for him. To confide now the truth of his love and need would only reveal his fraudulence. And Helen did not want that truth, for she was one of those people who bear a tragic sense of life and of themselves. She had never accepted the discrepancy between the way things are in books and movies and the way they really are. She lived in dreams of what might be. And because things never are as they might be, her sad view of life was always justified. Nothing could be beautiful unless it was doomed. That morning Caval had given her the out, the unhappy ending she always looked for.

Mark began to construct reasonable arguments as to why she should stay with him, go with him to Aspen, for her own benefit. It was bullshit, and they each knew it in their own ways. Finally they sat in silence, Helen with her head lowered and eyes averted as if he had told her to get out.

Mark's miserable gaze found the dark green bottle that had held the Bordeaux they had drunk before the fire that night when he had felt with such a mixture of excitement and relief that she would always be with him.

"Gawd," he growled. He grabbed the neck of the bottle and flung it backhand into the fire. It smashed as loudly as everything else. She hurried away in tears, leaving him with the broken glass and settling ashes.

iv

In Curaçao the disappointment was at least balanced by the fact that something had finally happened. There was movement again. The pressure of waiting was over. And more than anything, they looked forward to leaving Otrabanda. Ralph moved onto the boat the same day Caval arrived, and they made plans for berthing *Leda* until they would regroup in November. Cole had been visibly relieved when the decision was made to wait until the fall, but he remained distant all through that afternoon and evening as they drank beer and fought off any feelings of failure by promising each other that it had all been a dress rehearsal, that things would work

140

smoothly next time. Later that night, however, Cole finally told them he was through. "I've had enough," he said, making no attempt at explanation. "You've got time now to find another man, so I'll be checking out. I wish you best luck, but I won't be going." No one said anything. They all knew that for Robert the deal meant only his painful love of Helen, and his humiliation. He was a sad sight the next morning—after uneasy, disjointed goodbyes—heading down the wharf with his grip to look for a ride to the airport.

A few hours later Jack and Margaret caught a flight for Aruba. They had heard of the Nautical Club and other possible moorings there, and were going to see if they could dock *Leda* for a few months. As they left, they had the look of renewed love that comes to bored mates when they travel, anticipating the excitement of new places that the relationship can no longer generate. To both of them, Aruba was going to be a vacation after Otrabanda. With its white sand beaches and hotel strip, Aruba was much more a tourist haven than Curaçao, and they looked forward to a hotel room, some sunbathing and swimming and restaurant meals. Packing and going to the airport, they seemed to agree on every detail. And on the brief plane ride Jack thought perhaps it was only his anger at not hearing from Caval that had made him think he'd had enough of her.

At the airport in Oranjestaad they rented a car and made straight for the Nautical Club. To reach it they had to drive through the grounds of the old Water Works, the abandoned desalinization plant that had become a junkyard with mountains of rusting metal that looked like something from Otrabanda. Then the driveway suddenly reached the small boatyard, beside which the covered veranda and outdoor dance floor of the club looked out toward South America across bright blue waters.

A narrow spit of land extended along the southern edge of the island and made a protected channel in front of the club. There were about a dozen cruisers and sport fishing boats moored along the main dock, but another longer dock reached out into the deeper water and looked like a perfect berth for *Leda.* In addition there were toilet and shower facilities, a short-order kitchen, and a bar. There was nothing very plush about any of it, but after Otrabanda it looked like the finest yacht club. Nevertheless, only members of recognized clubs or guests of club members were welcome, so Jack had to find the master of the club to make arrangements. For Jack Sidell, however, that was no problem. He

141

was eminently acceptable to any sort of boating crowd, and so was Margaret. They could have paddled up in a bathtub and been given a berth.

When Jack inquired at the bar he was told the master of the club happened to be on his way out and should arrive any minute. They sat in armchairs at the front of the veranda and sipped a couple of beers until the man arrived. The warmth, the brightness of the sea and sky, and the occasional breezes all promised a change of luck.

Helmut Voors alighted from his Mercedes with an agility un-common among men his age. He was sixty, rather tall, still slim, and the wavy gray hair combed back from his forehead gave him an elegantly dashing look. He had been Harbor Master of Oranjestaad for several years, and he had numerous business interests on Aruba and Curaçao in everything from cigarettes to real estate. He was chairman of the board of one of the duty-free jewelry chains that operated in the Antilles, and everyone on Aruba knew Helmut Voors. In turn Voors knew everything of significance that tran-spired on the island.

Jack and Margaret introduced themselves and stated their business, saying they were starting a charter in San Diego. They explained that there were troubles among the crew, however, and financial problems that demanded they return to the States for a few months. Voors was immediately taken by this young couple and their business adventure, and he asked numerous questions about their boat, their plans for San Diego, what they needed in the way of accommodations. Finally Voors told them they were not only welcome to dock *Leda* at the club, but that they would be his personal guests. Then, when he had acquainted them with the facilities and taken care of his own business there, he insisted they accompany him to lunch.

They drove with Voors to the Paris Cafe where he introduced them to his other luncheon guests, a kindly old gentleman who was president of one of the larger Antillean banks, and a fierce-looking, bushy-browed executive of Shell Oil, who grinned devilishly at Margaret and nearly broke Jack's hand when they shook. Later, as they sat around a table, the two men shot Jack a fast line of questions as to why he did not run his charters out of Aruba, which they thought preferable in terms of weather, income, and taxes. Jack was still trying to make the adjustment from Otrabanda to the white tablecloths and jacketed waiters, and he winced at the lame-ness of his answers, but ultimately said that from what he had

142

seen so far it was certainly worth considering. Margaret was sandwiched between Voors and the oil executive, who both treated her like a visiting princess. She kept grinning and rolling her eyes at Jack across the table as she sipped her cocktail.

"Charters," the oil man finally snapped at Jack. "The hell with bleeding charter business." He used the rough, simple tone that successful old men always reserve for young men on the make. "If I were your age and had a boat the size of yours, I wouldn't be looking for any bleeding charters." He killed his scotch. "I would get myself to Colombia and fill that bark with marijuana and sail her up to the States and make some bleeding good money."

The other two men chuckled and half-seriously agreed. Margaret snapped her fingers and said, "Why didn't we think of that, Jack?" At that the three men laughed in earnest, and Jack felt as if his own smile were a full confession.

"Well, sir," he touched his mouth with the napkin, "that idea certainly has merit too, but I don't think it's quite that easy."

"Easy, hell," the oil executive snarled.

"In the event you do elect to enter that sort of business," the banker smiled playfully at Jack, "then perhaps you'll want to come see me at the bank sometime. We're very discreet here in the Antilles, you know."

"I have heard it said," Jack replied. The sides of his face were hot. He and Eiler already had over $120,000 in the man's bank.

"It's never easy to make good money, son," the other man stated.

Sidell glanced quickly at Margaret, but instead caught the eyes of Helmut Voors who smiled very curiously at him and winked.

"I'm learning that, sir," Jack nodded. "I'm learning that."

V

The girl was taking a douche behind the paper screen when Eiler heard his name called outside the door. He did not recognize the voice, so he took a pull from the bottle and speculated. Billy had come with him, but it wasn't his voice. Sounded a little like Jack, but Jack was in Aruba. It seemed very unimportant, but then it came again, and it was definitely Jack.

"Well goddamn, Jack," Joe rolled off of the sagging mattress and lurched across the tiny room. The girl grabbed a sad cotton robe off a nail in the plywood wall. Eiler threw open the door and saw Sidell and Thorton. "You cocksuckers," he yelled at them. "What're ya doin' 'ere?"

"Hi, Joe." Jack was stone sober. "You're looking well."

"Eat shit." He swayed naked in the doorway, dirty and unshaven, and thrust out the bottle of scotch. "Look like you need a drink, Jack."

"No thanks," Jack smiled and shook his head.

"Joe baby, you rascal, you're tighter'n a tick," said Ralph. "C'mon and get dressed an' we'll get ya sobered up. We're goin' to Aruba tonight."

"An' I'll kiss a fat lady's ass," Joe replied. "You fuckers get on in here." He headed unsteadily back to the bed where the girl sat with a very wary expression. "We ain't goin' no fuckin' Aruba tonight. Besides that, Ralph, you pigsucker, yer 'posed to be guardin' the boat from Spanish niggers." Eiler fell backwards on the bed laughing and almost spilled the bottle. "They'll be all over the goddamn place, now." He turned to the girl. "No offense, honey. Don't worry 'bout these guys, they're—oh shit, you don't *entiende no Inglés*, do ya doll?"

"Jesus," Jack said to Ralph, "he's wasted. We'll never get him out of here."

They had come in and closed the door and were standing at the foot of the bed.

"*Son amigos,* baby," Eiler railed at the young whore. "*Son amigos mios. No hay problema.* Wanna fuck 'em? Uh? *Quieres?*"

Jack and Margaret had flown in from Aruba a few hours earlier, after a day on the beach and supper with Helmut Voors. They had found Ralph on the boat, and the three of them had decided to sail for Oranjestaad that night, since it would put them there by morning. Leaving Margaret to put things in order on the boat, Ralph and Jack had taken a cab to the whorehouse that Joe and Billy had begun to frequent in the last few weeks. It was a large, battered, stucco house surrounded by a wall topped with broken glass and set amid slums east of town. At one time it must have been a beautiful place. There was still a sense of decayed colonial ease in the curving double stairway that rose to the front door and in the broken shutters on the windows of all three floors. Inside, the lower rooms had been made into a seedy bar and lounge with broken furniture, colored lights, and Latin rock music. The girls were mostly black, from Maracaibo or Barranquilla, and they were cheap and usually fun. But the setting was so depressing, the crew had always taken care to be drunk before visiting. The large rooms upstairs were divided into a hive of tiny plywood cubicles, and behind the house was a double row of small shanties, the less expensive boudoirs. Jack and Ralph had found Billy still languishing in the bar, and he had told them Joe was out back.

Jack said, "Come on Joe, we got to get going."

"Hey Jack," Joe turned from the girl and extended the bottle to him, "will ya jus goddamn relax. Uh? 'Ave a drink. *Tranquilo,* man. *Tranquilo.*"

"I'm plenty *tranquilo,*" he waved at the bottle. He was mildly amused, but found the place disgusting. He had certainly never used himself there.

"We gotta git goin' now, Joe," Ralph grinned. "Hate to tear ya away from this little honey, but we're takin' the boat to Aruba. Now com' on an' git dressed, uh?"

Eiler sat back against the wall, took a thoughtful swig from the bottle and realized they were serious. In his state, however, it seemed like an impossible task, and he had no intention of going.

"You guys're crazy. I ain't goin' no fuckin' Aruba. Why don't we jus'—"

"Damnit, Joe," Jack picked up his pants from the floor and threw them at him on the bed, "get dressed and let's go. We're going tonight."

"My dyin' ass!" Joe threw the pants back on the floor. "Big rush though, huh? Bi-ig business." He took another swig and turned to the girl as though she might understand, or care. "Big fuckin' deal, honey. Lemme tell ya these guys are real bad-ass buccaneers. 'Cept they don't buck nuthin'. And they don't even come very near." Joe howled at his joke. He tried another swig but was laughing too hard and it spilled down his front. "What they do is they got this big-ass, moth-eaten boat, an' they park it in sewers an' play like somethin's gonna happen."

Jack was not laughing. "Come on, Ralph, I'll get his clothes."

Delight squeezed through the narrow doorway, and the garret was full of bodies. The girl slipped fearfully off the bed and into a corner against a fruit crate that held her few belongings. Thorton was coming close.

"Now, Joe baby, if ya wanna be awnry, I'll jus' snatch yer ol' ass up and carry ya—"

"You'll kiss a fat lady's ass!" Joe jumped up so that he was standing on the bed with his head against the low ceiling. The girl began a high pitched chatter of *Popiamento,* and Delight advanced with a mugger's grin on his huge face. Jack gathered up the clothes. "Just grab his ass," he ordered.

"Joe, you know I'll . . ." Ralph reached out to grab Joe's arm, but he jumped off the bed into the corner, knocking down the paper screen. A simple water pipe with one spigot came into the corner through a hole in the plywood, and the douche hose was still on. The girl unleashed a frantic stream of language as Ralph started across the bed. Jack yelled for him to look out, but Joe twisted the spigot full on and the stream of water hit Thorton right in the face. Joe soaked his back as he ducked away, then turned it on Jack. In the shouting and laughter and the girl's screaming, Eiler failed to account for Delight. With characteristic excess, Billy leaped on him across the bed. They crashed into the corner, and there was a crack of breaking wood as the thin plywood wall gave way and they tumbled into the next cubicle. A naked man and woman were screaming like banshees; water was spraying everywhere; and Eiler could not get out from under Delight.

Joe recalled little else other than a chaos of noise and motion, people everywhere, a knot of angry men outside, Jack yelling that he had Joe's clothes. Someone dragged Joe out; Jack was laughing; Delight slugged somebody; Eiler was running naked around to the front of the house; Thorton pushed him into the cab; Delight sat on him; then they were hurtling through narrow streets; Jack was hysterical; Joe still held the bottle of scotch.

They did in fact sail to Aruba that night, but Joe Eiler had no part in it.

vi

It was raining, and there was a chill in the night that gave a certainty to the end of the summer. Beneath an umbrella near the baggage carts at the edge of the wood structure that serves as the Bar Harbor airport, Mark Insinger felt as if he were shrinking in the wet darkness. Motionless, insulated within his dejection, he watched the passengers coming off the flight from Boston, which he would board in a few minutes for the return trip. With only a dull surprise, he saw Jack and Margaret hurrying down the steps, laughing at the weather, then running to the building, happy to be back in New England, to be back on the Maine coast they each knew so well, to be going to Far Prospect. He felt no urge to hail them as they went past. He could not bear to probe his wounds with their happiness. He had talked to Jack on the phone two days before, but he had not expected them to arrive so soon. Jack had given no sense of failure or anguish; he was simply waiting for the weather

146

and would pass the time at Far Prospect and then with friends in Connecticut.

Mark felt alone and outcast, and seeing Jack and Margaret made it worse. He had lost everything, it seemed. Helen, the house, the boat, possibly the whole deal would fall through now. The flight to Boston, passing the night in some hotel, going on to Denver and Aspen the next day all seemed frightening in its loneliness. No one knew or cared where he went, and no one awaited his arrival.

The great smuggling adventure was not so thrilling, and he knew there was more humiliation ahead. The futility of his expenditures over the last several months would be clearest when he could not pay his bills. He would see Melton and his partner Seligson and others. He would have to admit that his big secret operation had not quite started paying off yet. He could see and feel the derision in their smiles. It sickened him every time he thought of it. Mark had always borne a fear of seeming laughable, had always feared that others might see him as comical or falsely daring. He had nearly decided that afternoon not to go back. He had no choice though. He was in the operation only at Caval's pleasure, so he must remain in Caval's service. Mark would have to do anything Tom required. He was sure Tom would make the most of it. He was almost grateful that Helen would not have to see it.

The wind picked up and seemed to swirl, and the rain fell harder and at a slant so that the umbrella did little good. Mark was getting wet and cold, and he went hesitantly to the door of the small terminal. He was about to enter, but saw Jack and Margaret again, waiting for their bags. He stayed outside and got soaked.

Part Two

chapter 9

"STILL raining," Mark mumbled. "Bet it's been raining since I left." His voice sounded odd, as if a strange person were in the car with him. He had not said much more than "Fill it up" for the past two days, and he had just turned off the radio for the first time since St. Louis. He was making a second pass at Kenmore Square and trying to concentrate on making the right turn. In the desperate pace of early morning traffic, the music did not help. He had eaten nothing but Black Mollies and Coca-Cola, and in the rainy gray morning Boston was a sordid place. Everyone seemed to know what he was doing; all the drivers seemed mad at him for not knowing which goddamn lane to stay in if you wanted to get off Storrow Drive at Kenmore; signs seemed unworthy of trust.

He thought he shouldn't have smoked the reefer. It was just dawn when he had lit it, and he could not really remember arriving in Boston, just that suddenly he was in it, dark, wet, hustling, demanding, all around him. For having driven so little in the city, he had come with remarkable directness to Kenmore, only to find himself in the left lane and then funneled downtown, swept all the way to Charles Street before he could conceive another approach. The flight of pedestrians, the workday haste of the traffic, and the sense of universal dislike of it was obscene. Life, particularly his own, seemed reduced to a scurrying unfit for humans.

Having made the correct turn, he spotted the motel not far up Commonwealth Avenue. Then suddenly the destination shocked him, repelled him. He turned abruptly into the filling station beside the place. He told the guy to fill it, and his stomach quivered. He tried to concentrate: I drive in and park at the back. Nearest spot to the right hand corner. Leave the keys in the ashtray. Do something with the window. Some dumb-shit thing. Lower the left rear window. The right? What the hell. Let them figure it out. What if there's cops? Jesus, what if there's cops in there. If they're plainclothes I'm screwed. Christ! Come on. If there's cops . . . I'll just pull in and park and go up to one of the rooms. I'll just knock at one of the rooms, and when nobody answers, I'll just leave. If someone answers . . . Christ, if someone answers, I'll just ask if they want to buy five hundred pounds of dope. Very cheap.

Mark lowered his head and rubbed his face distractedly. The fact was that, if there were cops, they would be waiting for him, and the Colorado plates would end it right there. He was not cut out for this sort of thing. He took a deep breath which did nothing to help his nerves, and he wished earnestly that he had never heard of Tom Caval.

He paid the attendant with a ten dollar bill and told him to keep the change. He thought it might make him feel like something more than a two-bit dope runner wasted on speed and grass, but it didn't work.

ii

Caval played with the pile of cocaine, stirring it with a silver pen knife. He was perched rigidly on the armchair, silently staring at the powder with an expression of demonic intensity. In the half hour since Jack had arrived at the suite, Caval had kept toying with the stuff, drawing and pushing it into shapes, frequently loading the knife and sucking it into a nostril. Jack could see it surging through him. It wired his eyes open, and his lower jaw was set like stone. With his legs pulled up beneath him on the chair, Caval looked like a well-groomed bird of prey. Jack had taken a little when he first arrived. He liked the stuff too, and he and Tom were both making an effort to be amiable, but Caval's excess was repulsive at nine-thirty in the morning.

As he spoke to him, Jack wondered if Caval was even listening. It annoyed him, but not much more than Caval always annoyed him. The girl was something quite different, though, and Jack did

152

not care for her presence at all. She was one of Tom's girlfriends from Aspen, and he had decided to bring her along. She was brown-haired and cute, but just as cocked on the cocaine as Tom. Jack had said they ought to discuss business privately, but Tom insisted the girl was okay. She watched Jack continually. Women often did, but this time it made him nervous.

"We can't go back to the same place. Not this time of year. The weather's too rough there in the winter. Nearly always is." Jack waited for an answer, but Caval kept toying with the powder as if he hadn't heard a word. "It wouldn't be worth the risk," he stated more emphatically. "We need a place further south now. We ought to be looking for something between Florida and, say, Norfolk."

Sidell waited again and was about to repeat himself when Caval snorted a little more dope from the end of the knife and spoke loudly. "Okay. This is what we do. We just go get it. We go get a place. Fly to Norfolk, get a car, drive the coast. Check it all out." Caval snapped the words with mechanical intensity. His mouth scarcely moved, and yet he managed a tone that suggested he had just come up with the idea. "Want you to check out every possible place on that coast. Every town. I want the best possible place. No fuck-ups this time."

Jack seethed at the implications, but he gritted his teeth and said nothing. He was resolved to avoid conflicts with Caval this time and to concentrate solely on getting the job done. It happened to be exactly what Caval wanted. He knew Jack was so committed to the project at this point that he would put up with almost anything.

There was knocking at the door, and Caval jerked. His face became so distorted that Jack had to look away from him. The girl admitted Insinger, fresh from his delivery. He looked tired, thin, and nervous, his body shocked from speed and lack of sleep. He came uncertainly, self-consciously across the room to say hello to Jack. His brow twitched crazily as they shook hands, and Mark smiled as if to say, "Look what I've come down to."

"Well?" Caval demanded. "You get it done?"

"Sure." Mark went to the couch and slumped down beside the girl, glancing at her as if she were a mirage. "Hi honey," he said, remembering her from somewhere. He put his head back and closed his eyes. "Real nice technique, that is."

"So what?"

"I just didn't care for it, that's all."

Caval seemed poised to spring on him. "Yeah? When you start buying the goddamn stuff, then you can decide how to sell it, awright?"

"Sorry, boss," Mark answered sarcastically. "Guess I forgot myself."

Insinger rose unsteadily from the couch and walked to the window, looking out at the old Boston courthouse below. Well-dressed young men hurried along the sidewalks. Mark assumed they were lawyers. "Nice life," he muttered. Caval's fierce eyes stalked him across the room. Mark noticed his canvas and leather hanging bag thrown on the floor, and he immediately picked it up and went to the closet. "Why didn't you hang up my clothes, for Christ's sake?" He unzipped the bag, hung up two suits, and began trying to smooth out the wrinkles. "You tell me I need to look like a straight lawyer, then you throw my clothes on the floor like garbage."

The girl had just taken a long line of cocaine, and Caval had cut out two more for himself. He sucked one into his left nostril with a funneled bill as Mark spoke. He kept his left eye closed when he looked up.

"I'm not your goddamn maid," he snarled. "I got better things to do than take care of your clothes."

"Well then don't be so hot about me looking like a banker."

"You look like whatever the hell I tell you. If I want you to look like a fuckin' Indian, you do it, right?"

Caval was nearly screaming, his features stiff with the cocaine, and Jack could see his pleasure in bullying Insinger. Mark tried to ignore him.

"Matter of fact," Caval went on in a thoughtful tone, "I want you to get a haircut tomorrow. Your hair's too long. I want you to get it cut short tomorrow."

"I don't need a goddamn haircut," Mark turned from the suit he was brushing. His curly brown hair had indeed grown long, but no longer than was currently stylish.

"No, goddamnit," Caval shouted. "I'm tellin' you to get a fuckin' haircut. An' you do it, goddamnit. Tomorrow. Right?"

Insinger stared at him in exasperation for a moment, but then nodded and turned back to the suits. Caval poised carefully and sucked up another line. He sat back with a tight, narrow grin.

iii

They flew into Norfolk and from there drove through a string of small tidewater towns along the North Carolina coast. Despite Caval's sudden desire to examine every town on the way, Jack bought charts of the intercoastal waterway before they left Norfolk, and he and Insinger picked out the most likely spots.

They drove first to the Pamlico Sound area, winding through green pine forests and brown fields, through little backwater towns like Swanquarter, Belhaven, Pantego, and Chocowinity. They attracted so much attention, however—three young dudes and a pretty girl in a big rental car—that they didn't even stop. They went on down to New Bern and spent a day there, but had no luck. They spent two days in the Cape Lookout region, making inquiries in Beaufort, Harker's Island and Moorehead City but still had no luck.

Wherever they stopped, Insinger visited real estate offices. Naturally he never once donned a suit, since virtually no one in the area wore them, especially when looking for vacation property. He told agents that he represented a new corporation introducing charter boat services and other recreational businesses on both coasts. They wanted to rent houses, he would say, for the use of management personnel during the vacation months of December and January. Everyone thought it was pretty strange. People in the area had no great trust for outsiders, particularly those arriving in the winter for purposes difficult to fathom. In addition, people had very strong accents, and Mark had as much trouble understanding them as they did him.

Jack visited the local marinas, when there were any, and learned what he could from locals about the waterway, channels, tides, whatever he could discuss. With his knowledge of boating though, Jack got along better than Insinger. He was a strange Yankee asking questions, but he knew a lot, and that was respected. There is a dependable comradeship almost anywhere among those who know the sea.

They took motel rooms when they stopped, and Caval invariably said he would make some calls from the room, but that never actually occurred. The girl and the cocaine filled his time. He knew damn well he didn't have to do anything.

They had been at it a week when they reached Wilmington on the Cape Fear River, and the prospects did not look good. A real estate agent took Mark to a place called Fort Rhodes Island, however, and it was at least a possibility. It was a narrow sand island about four miles long, open to the Atlantic along its eastern side, and separated from the mainland by the Inland Waterway and a maze of marsh and tidal streams. The land had been developed into an exclusive seaside community, with lots selling for twenty to thirty thousand dollars, and houses worth an average of fifty or sixty thousand.

Mark was shown two houses which were sufficiently large and isolated, but the problems he discussed with Jack as they drove back to their motel were regarding access to the houses from both the water and the highway. The island had a pontoon drawbridge that connected it with the mainland across the waterway, and the bridge was manned day and night by an employee of the island who admitted only owners and their guests, which did not readily facilitate the transfer of ten tons of dope.

Jack had been nosing around in Wrightsville Beach four or five miles south of the island while Mark visited the houses, and he found other problems. Neither of the inlets that bounded Fort Rhodes to the north and south were passable by anything much larger than a skiff. That meant that any boat going to Fort Rhodes had to enter the Masonboro Inlet south of Wrightsville Beach and move up the waterway, which could be a very tricky maneuver at night with a full load. He heard that even veteran tugboat skippers frequently ran aground in the waterway. So by the time they reached the motel, Jack and Mark had decided that Fort Rhodes was a fair prospect but nothing more. Caval did not agree.

"It's perfect," he said. "Perfect. What the hell d'ya want a private harbor? This is fine," he fingered a map of the place in the island's brochure. "I'm not gonna wait around here half a fuckin' year, while you search for a private harbor."

"Are you kidding?" Jack gave him a tired, sarcastic smile. "You mean you don't want to check out every town on the coast anymore?"

"Funny, Jack. Look. This place is just fine. If you guys think you can get a better place, go ahead and keep looking. But I gotta get back to Aspen. I got business to take care of."

"Yeah," said Jack, "and you're almost out of cocaine."

"I *am* outta cocaine," Tom shouted. " 'Cause I was sharin' it with you, goddamnit."

Caval left the next day, and Jack and Mark spent another week searching as far south as Charleston, but without any better luck. They did find two estates that seemed perfect, but one was being used as a movie site and the other was in the midst of prime duck country and would be inundated with hunters during the time they expected to be transferring loads. Finally, they stopped in at Hilton Head Island to think it all over and concluded that Fort Rhodes was their best bet.

iv

"These kinds of channels can be pretty tricky. The bottom is shifting all the time, so your depths change." Jack sipped his beer, looking out across the shallow green water of the channel and the brown marsh grass that separated it from the waterway. On the other side, there were tall pines barely affected by the breeze. The sky was ribboned with faint high clouds, the autumn air cool and quick.

"It's mainly the tides I'll have to learn." Insinger leaned against the railing beside Jack. "But that guy at the marina said there's always about five feet of water in this channel. I won't be drawing four even when I'm loaded, so I can get in here anytime. He said weird things can happen though."

"If it can, it probably will. If there's an unusually low tide, I can always hang off the coast and wait for it to come up. But that wouldn't be too cool. You'll have to figure in advance, so you can tell me by radio before I get here."

Mark only nodded. One of the kids had come within hearing distance again. They were being pleasant and polite to the parents, but they were both too tired from traveling to worry about the kid. They stared at him until he left. His parents were inside, visiting with friends on this Sunday afternoon.

Two long spits extended toward each other at the south end of Fort Rhodes Island, creating a small lagoon with a narrow entrance that opened on to the main channel connecting with the Inland Waterway. There was a house at the end of each spit, and both of them were for rent over the holidays. There were no other houses nearby at that part of the island, and a boat coming in at the back of either house would be easily visible only from the other house. They had decided to rent both places, using one house to live in and the other for storage of the cargo. They stood now on the back deck of one house. It was a simple, boxlike structure with four bedrooms off a large living-dining-kitchen area, making it more suitable for storage than the other place, which was two-story. Jack and Mark had visited briefly with the owners as they showed them through the rooms, but then the guests had arrived. They excused themselves to look at the shoreline and had just returned to the house.

"I'm not worried about the water," Mark said when the little boy had wandered away. "I can learn all that okay. I think our main problem will be attracting attention. We're just not going to blend in with the people here."

"I know it. Have you seen any of the guys Caval's going to have here?"

"Two of them. I guess they'll be alright, if we tell them how to dress. But I don't know who else there'll be. We'll have to have houses off the island somewhere though, so we can keep everyone there most of the time. We'll do business there too, so there shouldn't be a lot of guys hanging around. We can keep the traffic down. I'll get the houses as soon as possible."

"Right. Those houses are damn important. You've got to make Tom understand that. These folks like to know what each other are doing. They've got a lot of money invested in these places. It's their little dream vacation community, and they don't want any bullshit going down. You'll have to make it look right. You might get everybody out on the boat a couple of times and go cruising or fishing. Make it look like a little corporate retreat. Besides, if you get the boat good and loaded, it'll be good practice. But if you let those guys come out here and just lay around the house and smoke dope all . . ."

Mark winked and Jack stopped talking. The wife slid open the glass doors and stepped out to the deck. She was a pretty woman, a mother in her early thirties with a syrupy Carolina accent and bright eyes.

"How y'all doin'? Can I get ya another beer?"

"Thank you," Mark smiled back, "I don't think so. We were just talking about a barbeque we might have out here around New Year's."

"Oh . . ." Her eyes squinted a little. "It's gonna be a bit chilly."

Jack sensed her growing curiosity. He knew she wondered what sort of people did not go home for the holidays.

"Not nearly as cold as it would be where we come from," he said lightly.

"Ah bet." She smiled again.

"In our business, you don't get a chance to take time off during the warm weather."

"Guess so. Well, y'all go ahead an' look aroun' as much as ya like, an' Bill an' I are inside if ya need us, okay?"

"Okay," Mark said. "We'll be leaving in just a few minutes. We appreciate your hospitality."

"Oh sure," she said. She squinted again as she stepped inside.

"Shall we take it?" Mark asked when she had closed the door.

"Yeah. I guess so." Jack kept looking at the doorway as if the woman were still there. "But you guys are going to have to be careful."

"Don't worry, Let's get outta here. I'll give the guy a check, and we'll have to stop out at the office and tell them we're renting both places."

Mark finished his beer and nervously bent the can. He was already worrying about getting another boat, moving it to this area, and learning the waters. Jack was still preoccupied with the woman. He muttered to himself, "I'd bet a thousand dollars she thinks we're smuggling dope."

V

Insinger caught a flight to Denver soon after they came in from Wilmington, and Jack waited alone in the bar of the Atlanta airport. His flight to Miami did not depart for another hour. The next day he would fly on to Aruba and once more prepare for the voyage. Billy Delight was already there, living on *Leda.* Jack had called Thorton half an hour earlier, and Ralph would be there before the end of the week. He had called Margaret, too, up in Maine, and she was leaving for Aruba in two days with Mackenzie, the new crewman. Jack smiled at the thought of Margaret and slowly shook his head.

Soon after Cole had cashed in, Margaret suggested Jack take on Jesse Mackenzie to replace him. Jesse was her old friend and lover who had rebuilt *Leda* with her in Denmark and sailed to the Caribbean—and the only person who knew the boat better than she. But Jack was reticent to approach anyone he did not know well, and Margaret had not seen Mackenzie in over a year. After they had been at Far Prospect a few days, though, Margaret picked up some mail at an old friend's place in Northeast Harbor and found two letters from Jesse. He was living in Ellsworth, only a short distance away, so when Margaret mentioned it again, Jack thought it was worth a try. On the afternoon of the day before they planned to leave, they drove out to his cabin in the rental car. Jack and Jesse hit it off. They stayed up well into the morning, drinking and trading stories, and Jesse was game for the trip. Margaret

159

went to sleep on the couch, and the men made their agreement. The next morning Jack had things to do. They were going on down to Connecticut that day, and there was packing to do at Far Prospect before they started. A week earlier, Jack had thought he wouldn't take Margaret with him, but with the new developments and changes of scene, he was happy with her again. He was virtually on his way to the door when she said she was staying with Jesse. It was one of those moments when no one has an easy word. Jesse looked at him over his coffee with a friendly, knowing smile—not the sort of smile one might expect—and Margaret gazed at him with perfect tranquility. Jack had said something like, "Oh." In another second, the reality established itself as agreeably as if they had planned it, and Jack gave her a hug and kiss. To remark as little as possible seemed best. He shook hands again with Jesse and said goodbye anew. They were all grinning. He hugged Margaret again, told her where he'd leave the key at Far Prospect so she could get her things, and said he'd see them in Aruba. "You're pretty good at this," he told her at the car. As she smiled, her pale blue eyes grew bright as a fine blue sky, and she looked at him with no less affection than ever. Jack felt a good deal more than ever for her.

He had recalled the scene frequently enough that he spent little thought on it that night in Atlanta. There were many other things on his mind. He had called Eiler, too, but as usual got no answer either place and had no idea where Joe was. Jack was sure he would turn up. He always did. Beyond reassembling his crew, there would be a long list of tasks in Aruba: provisions, fuel, complete engine checkout, electronic checks, most likely a good many leaks to patch. Each item occurred to him in detail as he sipped a cognac, and all seemed easy enough to accomplish, the risks mere factors in the equation now. He felt like a general of irregular forces working behind indefinite lines, summoning his operatives by phone calls at night, collecting them from disparate places to a small island at the edge of a hemisphere.

Jack checked the time and yawned. He had another call to make, and he was tired. He was growing weary of endless moving, of having no retreat from the offensive aesthetics of airports, cafes, motels. It was a rather pleasant fatigue though, merely the difficulty of the challenge, and he did not resent it. He accepted it as he had the pain and effort of sport. He accepted the maddening difficulty of working with Caval, the increased danger of the winter voyage, and the risks of Fort Rhodes Island. They had been unexpected, but now he saw them as part of the game, part of the challenge—the strong, feared opponents and the lengthening odds. Vision, he reminded himself, and balls.

Sidell enjoyed thinking of the enterprise as a contest. It justified not having gone to conventional work, not having a regular income; it justified the pleasures and excused the indignities. It was Jack Sidell and his crew against all the elements, the powers. If he persevered and executed well, he could win three hundred grand. To think of it all accomplished was like breaking out of the crowd, taking the long pass, going in for the score, coming from behind to take the lead with one swift strike.

Jack glanced at his watch and put money on the check. It was ten o'clock, so Levering was supposedly available. Hal Levering was the investor Jack had lined up months ago. Through Jack, Levering was buying $100,000 worth of cargo, or at Caval's new price about 3,300 pounds. For arranging this purchase and delivering the dope, Jack was to receive $125,000 as twenty percent of the wholesale value of the load. It would be the major part of Jack's profit.

Hal Levering was the son of a current cabinet member, and a government and business heavyweight of long standing. Jack had met Hal in college, where Hal had been an occasional dealer of marijuana. He did it almost as a hobby though, and because it was a fashionable enterprise, and certainly not because he needed the money. After finishing school, however, Hal had begun to parlay his social connections into a thriving business, selling dope to young Washington bureaucrats and the sons and daughters of office holders. As soon as Jack had advised him that the boat was ready and Far Prospect rented, Hal had quickly produced the hundred thousand. Since then Jack had given him only occasional reports, most recently to advise of the new plans. From a girlfriend in Cambridge, however, whose telephone and address Jack sometimes used, he learned that Levering had been trying to get in touch for the past two weeks. Jack had returned the call several times already, but Hal had been either absent or for some reason unable to speak. Some instinct had told him not to call again. The last time though, this evening, Levering had promised to be available at ten. Jack went downstairs from the bar, picked one of the many booths, and placed his call to Harold Levering, Jr.

"Hello, Hal."

"Hi, Jack. Been trying to get in touch."

"So I've heard. How are you?"

"Really can't complain. You know Washington though. Always running. Been wanting to get away for awhile."

"Yeah." Jack chuckled under his breath. He had never known anyone who flew away more often to stranger places for longer vacations than Levering did. "What's on your mind, Hal?"

"Well, listen, Jack, I'm taking my money out of the deal."

"What?" Jack's face flushed hot. His confidence departed so swiftly he felt weak all over. He nearly dropped the phone.

"Yeah, Jack. Sorry. But I have to do it. Need it for another project. I'm working on a film now. Putting it together with some really good people. They've been with UNESCO last couple of years. It's going to be a film on the ecology movement. Ecology around the world sort of. All the things that are being done in different countries relating to ecology."

"Are you shitting me?"

Levering's voice stiffened. "Not a bit, Jack. We think it's going to be an important film. This is going to be sort of wrap-up to date on the whole movement. Concentrating on the major problems worldwide. And the most notable successes. We're going to go around the world with the film crew to put it together. There's really some amazing things being done now, Jack. A lot of things are starting to —"

"Hey cut this crap, will ya," Jack shouted. "I couldn't care less about the goddamn ecology movement. And you can't just pull your money out at the last minute."

"Well, I think I can, Jack. And I'm going to. And it's not really the last minute either. You're just going down there to get started again, aren't you?"

"That doesn't make any difference. That money is already committed. Plans have been made around that money. It's too late to just say you have another project."

"Jack, I want you to have the money transferred back to me."

Jack wanted to tell him that the money was already in Colombia, make up some story to explain that it was impossible to get the money, but he couldn't. "It's too late to pull out, Hal."

"Well, it better not be. You're not exactly in the position to be telling me what to do, are you, Jack?"

"You punk."

"Just write this down, Jack. Six-oh-three-four-two-two-eight-six-two-seven. That's the account. You got that?"

Jack gripped the receiver as if it were Harold Levering's throat. He held it away from his ear and did not answer.

"Did you get that, Jack? I mean it. Six-oh-three-four . . ."

162

Jack took the pen from his shirt pocket and painfully wrote the number on his cigarette pack.

Levering repeated the numbers once more and reminded Jack of the bank. "Main offices in New York," he said. "And I'll be expecting it soon, Jack."

Jack still said nothing, just held the receiver and stared at it, Levering's voice a distant metallic squeak.

"Sorry to have to do this, Jack, but I can't help it. It's hard to be friends over a hundred thousand bucks."

"It must be," said Jack. He hung up.

chapter 10

i

THE phone was ringing, and Insinger awoke easily and alertly for having drunk so much and having so recently gone to bed. It was as if he were back at Far Prospect, eager again.

Marshall Heard, Caval's assistant, did not even say hello. "Mark, there are some new things you need to do."

Mark asked him to call back in five minutes. Heard repeated, "Five minutes," and hung up.

He turned to see if she had awakened, but she slept soundly, still in the position in which she had rested against him before he slipped away to get the phone. Mark left the bed and went to the bathroom, stood under the shower a moment and then rinsed his mouth. He took his blue flannel robe from the closet, and as he tied the belt, he touched the champagne bucket with his toe and found it still cold, the empty bottle upended. He stood watching the beauty of her face, the softness of her parted lips as she slept. "You're an angel, honey," he murmured. "Just an angel."

Mark had left word of his whereabouts at Caval's house the day before, so he was not surprised to hear from Heard. Walking into the sitting room, he felt little curiosity. Instead, he admired the room, the draperies, the prints of Dutch impressionists and German landscapes, the long mahogany table reflecting the morning sun before the couch, and the silk armchairs. He sat at the letter desk awaiting the call, ran his fingers across the green inlaid leather, and thought that if he were with Caval they'd probably be staying at the Parker House, which Caval thought was better. When Mark had the money, the Ritz-Carlton was the only hotel in Boston.

Four days earlier, Caval had left Colorado for Aruba and then Colombia. Two days later, Mark left Aspen on his way to Miami, to find a new shuttle boat. Caval had decided they would buy a boat and avoid the curiosity of outside parties. But in the Denver airport Mark had changed his mind and flown to Boston. He decided he could just as easily use the boat broker he had done business with before in Boston, and go on to Miami as soon as there were likely prospects. It was expensive and impractical, but he thought there would be plenty of time, and those were not his only considerations.

When Heard called again, plans altered further. He said that $80,000 from the corporate accounts had to be transferred as soon as possible to the account in Curaçao. There had been only $48,000 in the accounts when Mark left Colorado, but Heard said he had just deposited $40,000 more. It all had something to do with withdrawals Sidell had made in Curaçao. Heard didn't know any details, except that Caval wanted Mark to fly to Curaçao to see that the transfer was properly made and to personally make the first deposit to the grower's account, which would be half the purchase price. Their previous plan had been that Mark would conduct the transaction from Miami through San Diego by wire. Caval, accompanied by Umberto and presumably others, was to make the final payment himself in Curaçao, after Sidell had picked up the load. Insinger had never expected to go to Curaçao, and certainly hadn't allowed enough time.

"What the hell does he want me to *be* there for?"

"He sounded pretty uneasy. Said with the delay and all, those guys thought he might be pulling something. He's alone down there you know. They may be pressing him. He wants the bank bit to go without any hitch."

"Well, hell, can you go?"

"I got plenty to do here. I can't operate those accounts anyway. You know that."

"Yeah. Jesus. We're going to be awful pressed for time."

Heard was ominously silent for a moment. "In which case," he spoke slowly and carefully, "I don't know what you're doing in Boston, when you're supposed to be in Miami buying a boat. Don't fuck this up, Mark. Tommy's number in Santa Marta is twenty-nine-oh-six."

164

Insinger got him to repeat the number, and then Heard said a quick goodbye. Mark covered his eyes to concentrate. There just wasn't enough time, but he knew somehow it had to be possible. Yesterday the broker had told him of two boats available in the Miami area. One was a Pacemaker similar to the one he had rented in Maine, and the other was a custom boat, forty-four feet long, with two GM 871 diesels. From the pictures and plans he'd seen, it appeared to have plenty of space. He could go to Miami that day and hope like hell one of the boats was suitable. There would still be enough in the accounts to put down some money. He could get the purchase started, get the boat on slip, and then go on to Curaçao. Marshall had said there would be more money coming in soon that would cover the boat. It would come from the deal Caval had run while they were waiting for the hurricane season to pass. And Marshall said they could borrow quickly in a pinch, but at very high rates. So the money would be there somehow, and he could close the deal on his way back from the Antilles. Still it would leave little time to get the boat up to Fort Rhodes, find distribution houses and learn the waters. He could feel the pressure starting. It scared him, but now every move would begin to count. And he liked that.

When he looked up, Helen was leaning in the bedroom doorway wearing only his shirt. She smiled at him and pulled the fingers of one hand through her chestnut hair. She looked warm.

"Sounds like you're hitting the road."

"The airways as it were." He felt a powerful confusion of emotions. He was like a man who has suffered withdrawal from heroin but seeks again the matchless wonder of its effect, still mindful of its torture. As soon as he had been alone in the Denver airport he had rationalized coming to Boston to see her. Now he did not know if he could bear to stay with her, knowing sooner or later it would end, yet he doubted he was capable of not asking her to come. Then it came involuntarily, as if he had not thought about it at all.

"Why don't you come with me?"

She tilted her head, looked doubtfully at him. "Where? I heard you say Curaçao?" She moved from the doorway across the room to the couch. The sunlight made her hair gleam red as she lay down, tucked the shirttails between her legs, propped her head on one hand.

"Well, I have to go to Miami first. Today. To look at a couple of boats. Then to Curaçao. I'll come back through Miami to pick up a boat and come up the waterway to North Carolina. And then I get ready for business again. I have to get it all done in about ten days at the most."

"Mark, we'd get attached again. I don't know what would happen. I don't want to hurt you."

"I've developed a little immunity."

She loved the sadness of his smile, as if he always had nothing to lose. She had thought of it yesterday when he called. He had come to mind often since they parted in Maine. He was a dreamer like herself, and she missed dreaming with him. She had been working, helping a friend who had a shop specializing in clever, expensive kitchen items, and she had thought for awhile she might open a similar place, perhaps on the Cape somewhere. Go it alone some. It became terribly boring though, and she remembered Mark saying that independence was mostly a state of mind and, in any case, not all it was cracked up to be. She missed the excitement of being around the deal, and she wondered what he was doing. But she missed him too, missed making love to him.

"It'd be a lot of fun." She grinned a little. "Do you have to do anything dangerous?"

"Just a little bank job. Shouldn't be any trouble."

She laughed and rolled onto her back, looking at the ceiling. "Do you think we'd travel well together?"

"I think it'd be tolerable. Just say yes or no, will you?"

She rolled over to face him again. "Yes."

"Okay honey." His smile was wistful. He was rather sure she was going more for the adventure than for his company, but it did not matter a great deal. He would take her any way he could get her. "Well let's get on it," he said. "I've got calls to make and a wire to send. You go out and get us some plane tickets. I'll write down the connections while you get dressed."

She stopped to lean in the bedroom doorway again.

"What are we using for money, lover. I haven't got enough to get to Hartford."

"Take my wallet with you. There's enough to cover the tickets. We'll get along."

"Uhm," she arched her eyebrows. "You sound like Tommy Caval. How do you know I'll come back?"

"Goddamn, honey, I'll be surprised if you do."

ii

Joe Eiler was cold sober when the taxi dropped him at the Nautical Club. It was his first clear look at the place. It inspired a

166

qualified confidence. He found an understated comfort to the wicker armchairs on the veranda, an unpretentious spirit to the small cruisers and sport fishing boats lined up snugly along the simple dock. There was no action visible then in the heat of afternoon, but there was an assurance of it, just as the leaning, layered posture of the Divi Divi trees out on the sandbar gave evidence of steady wind, though it blew only slightly that day. The water inside the sandbar was smooth, pale, passive blue, but the open sea beyond was darker, harder. A long separate dock reached out to the deepest part of the channel, and at the end of it *Leda* dominated the scene. The air was hot and almost still, but expectant.

Billy and Ralph and Eiler had a fond and loud reunion when Joe went aboard. They squeezed each other's hands and laughed and yelled about the last time they'd been together and what they'd done since then, but Joe could feel a seriousness, a nervousness, as if they knew with certainty that the trip would come off this time and it frightened them a little. To Joe's amazement, Billy Delight, who had been washing down the deck when he arrived, went back to work, and Ralph hurried off to make a phone call.

Jack was in Oranjestaad running some errand. Ralph and Billy said the new crewman was in the water, checking the hull. Eiler watched him for a few minutes, bubbling into sight occasionally in the scuba gear. Shortly he surfaced, threw his fins on board, and pulled himself up the rope ladder onto the deck.

"Joe Eiler, I suppose," Mackenzie observed as he took off the mask. When he introduced himself as Jesse, Joe didn't realize who he was.

Mackenzie was of average height and wiry. He had long, dark hair and steady, curious, almost suspicious eyes in a narrow, boyish face. He was quiet and usually soft-spoken, yet formed his opinions with a Yankee strength of mind and stated them in the same manner. He was an excellent marine carpenter. As a sailor, he had less experience than Jack Sidell, but equal ability. Joe found him rather arrogant.

"What'd you find down there?"

"I can't see too much that's a problem now, but she's been sitting a long time. That's not good for the hull, especially on the top side where she's been in the sun. When she sails again, it's likely she'll be opening leaks. She stiffens like a body does without exercise."

"So what's the deal?"

"Drydock. Recaulk."

"Oh Jesus."

"Would you rather sink? It's a possibility."

"You talked to Jack about this?"

"I'm going to. I just now looked at it." He eyed Joe with an impatient sort of contempt, as if he thought Joe was just as half-ass a sailor as he thought Billy and Ralph were. He lifted the tank off his back and settled it decisively on the deck. "You have to do things right on a boat. It's important. And things like the condition of your hull can get damned important."

"I'll try to remember that. I reckon you're the first mate, alright."

"I reckon so," he smirked. "I just like to see things done right. I think it'll be worth it on this trip."

"Well, we could use a little more of that." Joe wanted to change the subject. "Is Margaret still with us?"

"Sure." Jesse smiled, and Joe thought he knew why. "She's up taking a shower."

"Well, that's nice," Eiler cracked. "Nice for the captain to have his piece o' ass handy."

Jesse's smile straightened out. "She sleeps in my cabin."

"Oh." Joe realized who he was. "Well, what's good for the captain is good for the mate, I always say. You'll have to excuse me. Sometimes it's hard to keep up with the couplings on this boat."

Jesse's face brightened with a smile that showed his dimples and a sense of humor akin to Eiler's, and a gap where someone had punched out his lower left incisor.

"So I hear. So I hear." He looked Joe over again as if he'd missed something the first time. "You want to go get a beer?"

They sat on the club porch and told each other a little about themselves. Jesse was not much more inclined than Eiler to talk about himself. He said he worked as a carpenter much of the time, traveled whenever he could, in Europe or Mexico or the western states, and was primarily a wayfarer. He had not much need for money, little interest in any prospect of riches, and none at all in conventional success. Later, through Jack, Eiler learned that Jesse had been quite an eccentric child. His wealthy parents had found it an embarrassing bother and installed him in a sanitarium. After two years there, he sent the family accountant a detailed study demonstrating that it would be much less costly in every respect to merely send him to a medium-priced boarding school. They complied. Jesse had remained pretty much outside the pale of normal society ever since.

As they talked over a few Amstels at the club that afternoon,

168

Joe discovered that the arrogance he had first noted in Mackenzie was that which derives from an independent mind and a not-too-easy life. He also found that Jesse was in the habit of saying what he thought—and regardless of circumstances, as the missing tooth suggested. At one point, he told Joe, "If Jack had you and Billy and Thorton on, you couldn't hit Curaçao from here." Joe let it go; he might have been right. Jesse had a philosophical bent too, though, and he enjoyed a good cynical laugh. He and Joe quickly developed a friendship and a mutual respect.

The others joined them on the veranda as soon as the sun was near enough the horizon to feel like the day was done. The sky softened in color, and the heat let up a few degrees. The pink of sunset glowed on the ragged fringes of wayward clouds. The gang collected around the table like a family reunited. Margaret even gave Joe a kiss. When Jack showed up and saw them assembled there swilling beer, Joe saw an emotion in his smile he had never seen before, and which seemed to surprise even Jack. They were all a little giddy. At some point in the past few months they had each doubted that the deal could be resurrected. But beyond that was the warming realization that the friendship transcended the business at hand. Naturally, Ralph wanted to say it: "I knew we'd get 'er back together again 'cause you all are just good people an' I love ya. An' I would even if we don't or no matter what happens from here on. But by God this time we gonna . . ." He saw Billy Delight playing an imaginary violin, and everyone laughed. Ralph punched him in the shoulder hard enough to cripple a normal man. Billy just kept laughing. "Now, goddamnit, I mean it," Ralph insisted. Eiler said, "I'll drink to it." And they all did. They got greasy hamburgers from the short order shack, sat eating them around a table, loudly recalling excesses in St. Thomas and Curaçao. Jesse was thoughtful enough to wait until the subject was nearly exhausted before telling Jack he thought *Leda* needed drydock.

"Ahh, drydock hell," Ralph groaned. "Let's not start foolin' around again. Let's get down an' go this time. Tommy'll be ready in just a few days or so. If we start crappin' around, somethin' else'll screw up an' then somethin' else, an'—"

"I just don't care to be crapping around on a sinking boat in the middle of the Caribbean."

"She'll make it. Hell, she just come off drydock a few months ago."

"Well, if you think it'll be okay," Jesse answered sarcastically. Thorton glared at him.

"But those months were mostly idle," Margaret spoke. "And

she's just been sitting in the sun these last four months here and in Curaçao. She really could develop some bad leaks. There are already some pretty big ones."

Billy and Eiler stayed out of the discussion and rolled their eyes at each other. Jack looked distant. He knew as well as Jesse what shape the hull was in, but had wanted Jesse's opinion. And yet now he thought of another delay, the time, the money, Caval screaming his head off. He'd just as soon go on. He barely had enough investment to worry about anymore, it seemed. And it wasn't his boat if it did sink.

"The trouble is," he said aloud, "that we won't be able to tell how bad things are until we get going. We won't get going until the stuff is ready to pick up."

"That's why I think we ought to do it here," said Jesse.

"We'd have to go to Curaçao probably, and it would take forever. Caval would scream bloody fucking murder."

"That's the truth," said Ralph. "Let's just go."

They all looked at Jack. He looked like he would rather be somewhere else.

"Alright," he said finally, "there's a big yard in Barranquilla. I can call down and see if they can handle us. Then if it looks bad when we get down there, we can tell them to hold the load for a couple of weeks, and we'll go to drydock."

Sidell and Mackenzie patched the existing leaks over the next few days, and none of them really expected to see Barranquilla. With the exception of Jesse, they shared an unflinching certainty that this time they were going, regardless. Having already done it once, they prepared quickly for the voyage. Then for more than a week there was nothing much to do, but it was a vastly different wait than the one in Curaçao. Life at the Nautical Club was supremely pleasant. They lounged in the sun on deck, swam in the channel, water-skied a few times. They always had music playing; drank beer; there was always a reefer going nearby. It was a great life. The regular members of the club, however, began to grow suspicious. They were mostly retired people, middle-class Americans, savvy enough to be living in Aruba instead of dying slowly in the States from taxes and inflation, and they did not waste much credence on the charter-boat story. For one thing, *Leda* simply looked like a pirate ship, and as Jesse observed one morning as they lay about the deck, the crew did not look capable of anything legitimate. They all sensed a sort of resentment from the club members that came from having worked steadily and long in most

170

cases to own a boat, to be in Aruba. Their welcome there passed long before they did.

Not surprisingly, Helmut Voors received a number of complaints for having allowed this element the run of the club. One occasion was when Billy Delight took two Quaaludes, sat on the porch drinking beer with the afternoon sun in his face, eventually passed out, and no one could move him. But Voors liked Jack, loved Margaret, and presumably did not totally owe his success to having always kept a clean nose. He would tell Jack not to let "the boys" blatantly antagonize anyone, yet even Helmut looked impatient the last few times Joe saw him.

They spent their nights at a place called The Old Mill, and their welcome there was endless. It was owned by Phillip Lindstom, a middle-aged, blonde gentleman who was fascinated by Sidell and his gang. His place was an actual Dutch windmill, four stories high, which had been disassembled and brought to the island by ship years earlier. He had a restaurant and bar on the bottom floor, a discotheque upstairs, and since it was out near the big hotels, he usually had a good crowd. It was a charming place, full of antique furniture, but Phillip was a terrible manager and constantly losing money. Still, he rarely let them pay for a meal after they got to know him, and they never paid for drinks. He was in the process of selling the place and said it didn't matter.

Nearly every night, they took supper privately up on the small third floor of the mill, just beneath the massive wooden gears which creaked loudly as the huge blades outside turned slowly in the breeze. There was a separate entrance to that level via a rickety wooden stairway, and up there they could dress as they pleased, be loud, drink too much, smoke marijuana without offending regular guests, and eat whatever was plentiful that night. In return Billy sometimes collected the cover charge at the discotheque and served as bouncer, and Ralph did what he could to organize the bars a little better.

It was a great life, but they pushed it. One day Thorton and Delight picked up a couple of young black girls and brought them out to the boat. Jack and Jesse and Margaret were gone somewhere, so Joe and Billy and Ralph had a grand time running around the boat naked with the black girls. Unfortunately, it happened to be a busy day at the club, and patrons found the scene less amusing. That night Voors was compelled to come out and ask Jack pointedly when they might be leaving. Soon, Jack promised: He was only waiting for a call which should come any day.

Nevertheless there remained a rather desperate abandon. Despite the outward assurance that they would simply pick up the dope, sail it to Carolina and make a lot of money, none of them knew what would happen. There were enough stories about boats going into Colombian waters to pick up dope and never being seen again. But Jack, apart from his normal worrying about the hull, the radios, the diesel reserves, was in low spirits a lot of the time, seemed distracted, uninterested. When Eiler finally asked him about it, Jack told him Levering had backed out.

"Another two hundred kay out the window," Joe commiserated. "Christ! At least you never actually had it before you lost it."

"Thanks Joe. That helps. It really does."

They were in the forecastle where Joe slept. Joe lay on the bunk, and Jack sat on one of the storage benches. He told Joe when and why Levering had pulled out, and Joe said he had always thought the guy was flakey. Jack said he appreciated that comment, too.

"So what're you going to do?"

"It looks like I'm going to haul Caval's cargo for him. Risk my ass for a hundred thousand lousy bucks."

"Yeah, well, you deserve what you get if you don't do any better than that. Tell the son of a bitch you want part of the cargo. You don't have to tell him you're takin' the boat, just tell him you're leavin' if he doesn't."

"That's not the deal I made, Joe. If we start issuing ultimatums, this deal will really go to hell. There won't be any trust. It'll just be everybody screwing everybody else."

"That's the way it goes sometimes. When you have the power, you screw people a little bit, to keep from gettin' screwed yourself. Hell, Tommy's changed the deal before. And I promise you he will again. You got to fight fire with fire. It's not enough to be a good guy. Honest men usually get screwed real good for their efforts. You got to keep a little edge on things, or a guy like Caval will run all over you. Just tell him what happened. Say you need a piece of the cargo or it's not worth the trip. You don't even have to threaten. He'll see it. Jesus, nobody knows better than Tommy."

"Yeah, Joe, but goddamnit." Jack rubbed his forehead and then nervously chewed the middle finger of his left hand. "I don't want the dope. I want the money. That was the deal with Levering. I would deliver and get the money. So I get a ton of weed from him. I don't want to move a ton. I don't think I could move a ton."

"Brother, I could. Tell 'im—"

"Yeah great. Let's do that again."

"Okay, smartass, go ahead and do it your way."

"I will. This is a big operation, and there are a lot of people involved. The only way it can run smoothly is if the people do what they're expected to do. I'm not going to be the one to start running power plays. God knows where that would end."

Joe gave a slight indulgent smile, but his tired gray eyes collected worried wrinkles. He had developed a combative sense of right and wrong in which right had to oppose wrong. But Jack's notion of honesty was aesthetic. To Jack the deal was a structure built on trust, and it was not in his nature to alter or damage it. Joe figured nobody would appreciate that as much as Tom Caval. Such matters are never quite clear at the times they mean most though, and Joe let it pass. He shrugged and said "You're the boss, Jack."

iii

From the tall leaded windows of the Holland Club, Helen gazed at the yellow-white arches of light on the old bridge. They lit the night with a carnival brightness, reflected garishly on the dark stillness of the canal, illuminated the evening promenade of families, young women in pairs, noisy gangs of boys, lolling young men, old loners, prostitutes, lovers. The warmth of night, an easy confusion of life, the labyrinth of streets, old narrow buildings forced together along the busy fetid channel, gave Curaçao a soft Venetian decadence. She leaned forward at the view, turned her drink between the middle fingers of each hand. Her dark eyes quickened with the sight and feel of it. She savored the low sound of Dutch from other tables, the hurried *Popiamento* of waiters to each other. Mark scarcely noticed; he'd seen it before.

Helen had loved the swift travel of the past few days, the dispatch with which matters were attended to. They had spent two days in Miami, in the old section among the Cubans and the docks, and the old hotels where the blunt reality of hard-earned existence was refreshing after her few months on Newbury Street. They had tested three cruisers, running them out to sea a few miles, pacing off the spaces. From hour to hour there had been an excitement, a sense of separateness and intrigue, of illegal mission.

When Mark had put money down on one of the boats, within an hour they were at the airport awaiting a flight to Curaçao. That night they checked into the Intercontinental on the rocks overlooking the harbor entrance and divided the night between the casino, brief walks, and long moments on the terrace looking out toward South America and the long glow of the moon on the sea.

Mark blinked nervously at her now. "What'd you say, honey?" He jerked his hand at the waiter for another drink.

She tilted her head and searched his unsteady eyes a moment before whispering, "I didn't say anything."

He tried half-heartedly to smile and felt his face twitching. He hoped another drink would calm him. He had risen late that morning and without strength. Three nights of drinking and making love had left him weak, and his nerves were harmed. Life had threatened to exact a price. He had gone to the bank in midafternoon, while Helen waited at the hotel pool. The transfer from California, which he had begun in Miami, had gone through alright, so he had prepared the first transfer to the grower's account in the amount of $175,000. Before making it though, he called Caval in Colombia to make sure everything was okay. He had been surprised and a little resentful that there was no sign of tension in Tom's voice. He even said he'd just come in from water-skiing. Mark wondered why the hell he'd come all that way. He said, "Jesus, man, I thought you were in some kind of trouble. I could've done all this from Miami." Tom replied, "Yeah well my ass is on the line. I don't want any mistakes." On the line, Mark thought. On the end of a goddamn ski rope. Tom wanted to know if the cruiser had been purchased and was ready to go, and Mark lied. The time remaining felt tortuously small. Suddenly all the spendthrift negligence of the past week backed up on him. Flying to Boston to chase Helen instead of doing his work, putting up at the Ritz, spending money like he'd already run the deal, bringing her with him all promised to trap him if the slightest thing went wrong in the boat deal. He cursed himself when he hung up the phone: I hope she thinks you're a cool guy, 'cause if you screw up this deal you'll most likely be dead if Heard has anything to say about it. Ruefully Mark had made the large deposit and kept thinking how easily it could have been done from Miami. If anything went wrong, Mark wanted to feel that it was Caval's fault too, but he could not ignore that the real matter ran much deeper. It had gnawed at him ever since he left the bank. He felt like Caval was just a wild, lucky rich kid who he was risking his ass to emulate. And Helen suddenly seemed like a fickle, naive little girl he'd been chasing around like a horny teenager, trying to make her believe he was something he wasn't. His dreams were turning to shit. All that evening he could not shake the feeling that he'd been running after something that remained always out of reach. And whenever he drew close to it, it was less than he'd expected. And the effort cheapened him. He saw himself seduced by Caval, by Helen, and especially by some imagined glory of fast, rich life that now threatened to make him a fool and a failure, or much worse.

"Wouldn't it be wonderful to just keep on traveling?" Helen wondered, hoping to stir a little conversation. "To go down to South America for a while. Up into the mountains." Her eyes wandered upward in dreams. "Or the coast. To go around the coast. I could do it all right now. I'll bet the coast down there is fantastic." She found his eyes eagerly. "Oh, if we had a boat."

"This'll have to do for now." Mark looked around uncomfortably to see if his drink were coming.

Helen grimaced, shrugged her bare shoulders and looked out the windows again. For the moment she did not care if he were rude. She certainly had her own bleak moments from time to time. She knew he was worried, but he hadn't said anything to explain it. He didn't need her now, but that was alright too. She could fix that easily enough later. Mark's drink was delivered, and his brooding continued. Helen was content to endure it, but then a fearful, almost desperate look crossed Mark's narrow features for an instant and caught her attention. Despite the often nervous moments in his face, which one hardly noticed after awhile, he always bore a studied nonchalance of action and speech, but occasionally, like this evening, a demeanor appeared that showed him endlessly pursuing, or perhaps in flight from, something even he seemed incapable of expressing. She knew he wouldn't say what was wrong if she asked. It was one of the things about him she loved. Beneath his ease he was always trying so hard. And thought no one noticed. But so was she. And she could not come close to saying what it was. She watched him closely for several minutes, knowing he was barely aware of her presence. He had tanned quickly from the few days of sun, and his thick, curly hair was already turning. He wore his shirt half unbuttoned beneath a soft white linen coat he had purchased at the hotel on arrival. He reminded her of that first attraction in St. Thomas. The eccentric mannerisms of his brow and lips made her smile. She wondered if other women found them distasteful. Maybe you had to know how that captive energy translated in bed, she figured. She did love him. She thought she could stay with him indefinitely, if they just kept moving, if things kept up. To stop would end it, sooner or later. Stopping anywhere would inevitably become homemaking, the presumption of permanence and all its false acts, the end of adventure. Within a month she would be unable to come.

Mark took most of his drink in silence. They ordered dinners. When the waiter had departed, Mark sat up stiffly and seemed to speak only from distraction. "Tommy says everything's ready. He's calling Jack tonight. I guess they're going to meet over at the Hilton tomorrow afternoon. It's pretty close. They ought to be picking it up within a week."

Helen listened eagerly. Mark had told her nothing of the phone call that afternoon. "I want to see Jack," she said earnestly.

Mark felt stupid for having told her. "Under the circumstances, I doubt if he wants to see you."

"He's my brother, Mark. It's a dangerous trip. I want to see him."

"That's a lousy idea. You know how he feels." Mark caught the sincerity in her face, though, and changed his tone. "Look, we've got to get out of here ourselves tomorrow. We've got to hustle now. There's a lot to do. We've got to get to Miami, get that boat, and get it up to North Carolina." He hadn't meant to say "we," but it sounded right.

"Okay," she answered softly. "I'd like that. But I'd still like to see Jack."

"I know," Mark nodded. He looked at her straight for the first time that night: the softness of her shoulders, the smoothness of her face, the fragile fineness of her hair and the depth of her eyes. She seemed too beautiful to be so unafraid. It was impossible not to love her. He was ashamed of having blamed her in any way for his troubles.

"Well, if we're going to be working so damn hard," she smiled, "then maybe we should have ourselves a little champagne tonight, eh, *señor*?"

Finally his breath came with ease as he smiled back. If he had fouled things up, it suddenly seemed that he couldn't do anything about it right then.

"Whatever you please, baby."

iv

Jack caught the ALM hop to Willemstad near noon, and spent the brief flight preparing himself to tell Caval they might have to go to drydock in Barranquilla. He planned not to make too much of

176

the matter though. There was still no certainty that it was really necessary, but he had to present the possibility at least. Beyond that was the matter of telling Caval he wanted to be paid for delivering the cargo, which he found humiliating. He had little choice however. He certainly did not intend to go through everything that lay ahead for only $100,000 worth of dope. Nevertheless he hated the idea of working for Tom Caval, but for the wrong reasons.

As it was, Jack was tired and already angry at Caval. He had been awakened at three in the morning by a combination of car headlights and his alias being shouted through a bullhorn. Caval had called Voors's house, and Helmut, quite displeased, had driven to the club in his pajamas, shined the car lights out at *Leda* and called to Jack out the window on his bullhorn. Everyone had gotten pretty ripped at the Old Mill that night, so Jack made his way off the boat unsteadily and in some discomfort. "The international operator called for you at my house," Helmut snapped at him. "From Colombia."

Jack apologized lamely, but it seemed like the last straw with Voors. Nevertheless Helmut gave Jack keys to the bar and said the operator should be calling on that phone any minute, then he backed the car in a sudden arc and sped away. Jack stood around the bar and drank a beer. The call was typical of Caval. In fact, though, Tom had placed the call much earlier, but, as usual in Colombia, it took hours and hours to go through. In any case, Tom would not have cared if someone had been required to rise from their death bed. When the phone finally rang and Jack complained about disturbing Voors, Caval said, "So he had to get up. Big fuckin' deal." Virtually in the same breath Tom said everything was ready to go, and suddenly Jack felt quite sober and a little frightened. He had figured that this might be the reason for the call, but once he actually heard it, nothing else seemed very important. They agreed to meet at the Hilton on Curaçao the next day and hung up. Going back to the boat Jack found himself trembling slightly. It was a combination of fear and excitement he had never felt before, and he didn't sleep again that night. When the others arose one by one and got the news from Jack, there was, along with the hangovers, a seriousness none of them had foreseen. It wasn't going to be any walk-off deal, and they knew it then better than ever. At the very least it would be a voyage of three weeks duration, with no possibility of stopping or turning back. What enthusiasm they expressed was well tempered.

At the Hilton, Jack was told that Mr. Caval awaited him by the pool. Jack found him on a sun chaise. The pool area and the small beach nearby were crowded with American tourists, so they only nodded at each other, smiled as if recognizing that only the prospect of a great deal of money could overcome their mutual dislike. They moved to a table in the empty restaurant area near the bar and began to talk as if they had never really terminated their last conversation.

"You're all ready to go, uh?" Tom's face and voice were as intense as ever, yet he lounged comfortably and seemed relaxed. A resort was his true element.

"Sure I'm ready, but we may have a problem."

Caval said nothing, but his eyes and chest expanded as if he were preparing to scream.

"It's the bottom of the boat," Jack stated simply. His voice was stern. It was Caval's fault if anyone's. Who the hell had he been waiting on all that time in Otrabanda? "It's just been sitting around too damn long. We may have to go to a drydock in Barranquilla once we get down there, and that could hold things up for about two weeks."

"No goddamn way!"

"Keep your voice down, will ya?"

Caval stared at him a moment, fuming, but spoke slightly lower. "Well, that better not happen, because there's no way I can keep the stuff sitting around. Not after this last number we pulled on 'em, waiting for the fuckin' hurricanes. And there's no money. *Entiende?* No fuckin' *plata.* So it better not happen."

Jack nodded at him, unaffected by the outrage. He was growing accustomed to it. If they had to go to drydock, Jack was certain that Caval would come up with the money. He would have bet what he had left that Tom had picked up that portion of the cargo Jack had planned to buy with Levering's money. And time, Jack assumed, was no more important along the Colombian coast than anywhere else in the Caribbean.

"Well, it just may happen," Jack answered him, "and if we don't do anything about it, you could lose your whole load."

He explained what happens to a wood hull when it sits idle for long periods and what can happen when it encounters heavy use again, but Caval looked away impatiently. "I don't care about hearin' all that shit," Tom cut him off. "I'll tell *you* what's gonna happen. If that old tub you bought can't make it, I'm flying that load out. I've had enough of this boat shit, man. I'll just fly it out."

"Bullshit!" Jack leaned close to Caval's face. Tom sat back with a hateful smile.

178

"Bullshit? No, Jack. Bullshit was when I let you buy that fucking fossil of a boat. This ain't bullshit. I haven't been sittin' on my hands down there. I met a guy has a nice Loadstar he keeps on a strip near a place called Rio Hacha. American guy who's made a lot of trips. I can just get Marshall down here to fly up with him an' he'll take that stuff anywhere I want. What it'd cost me'd be worth it."

Sidell's face fell painfully. He couldn't help it. For a moment he'd been sure Tom was lying, but now the plane seemed quite possible. "Look, goddamnit," he spoke desperately, "I've put a hell of a lot of work in this deal, and I don't stand to make a fraction of what you do. I'll get a hundred grand if I'm lucky. And for a hell of a lot of risk."

"That's not my fault," Caval shrugged.

"Well, if we start taking on water on the way down there, I can't get too excited about making the trip without getting to drydock. But like I said, we may not have those problems."

"I hope not." Tom suddenly became a nicer guy. "Look. I know how much time you an' the other guys have got in this thing. I don't want to do the plane, but if the boat screws up . . ." Tom made a casual Colombian gesture with his right hand.

"Hell," Jack turned away. "I should tell you to go ahead and fly the stuff. Even if nothing goes wrong, it's just not worth the work and risk for the amount of money I'm making. I'm hauling your goddamn fortune and not making much for the effort."

"I know it," Tom said quickly. There was a disarming compassion in his voice as he went on. "Look, we didn't have much time to talk when you told me about this guy bailin' out on you. But listen, you get that goddamn boat down there without any bullshit and make this trip an' I'll pay you for it. Okay? I mean, you're right. Why should you do all this for so little?"

"Yeah. That's what I mean." Jack spoke carefully and did not expect Caval's response. "I wanted to talk to you about that."

"Sure. How much ya want?"

Jack looked distrustfully into Caval's dark, shiny eyes. "Two hundred thousand."

Caval was completely expressionless for a moment, then pursed his lips and nodded judiciously. "Okay. You get down there an' pick up without any more drydock and deliver like we planned, an' I'll pay you two hundred grand."

Surprise and suspicion turned Jack's thoughts. He didn't doubt Tom's sincerity, because it wasn't that much to pay out of what he'd be making. But if Jack really had to go to drydock, which seemed likely, he wondered how hard it would be to stall Tom.

179

Could he really run a plane deal that fast? For the moment it seemed best to let it lie.

"I want cash," Jack stipulated. "I don't want cargo."

Caval answered impatiently. "Right. Cash. Dollars."

"And when will I get it?"

"Soon. When the job's done, but not right there in North Carolina. I got my own problems, y'know. My cash is all tied up, but I'll pay you out of profits. It'll be like a month or so after you deliver. That a deal?"

Trust, Jack kept thinking. If I deal straight with him, he'll do the same with me. "Alright," he nodded, "that's a deal."

Tom extended his hand across the table, and as they shook, he smiled very pleasantly. The rest of their conversation was much happier. Tom described the sight of their cargo in a great pile, extolled its quality, the ease with which it would sell at any price. He had a length of rope knotted to show the size of bales, and he gave it to Jack, so he could plan the spacing in *Leda*'s hold. Finally Caval drew a crude map of the Colombian coast near Santa Marta, showed the massive bare rock called Punta Aruja, and made a big X on the second cove east.

chapter 11

i

THE hills behind the bay rose a thousand feet, with steep sides covered in dry, green jungle. The land beyond went higher, grew more lush, more forbidding. Still further rose successively greener, darker, higher mountains ascending in a haze toward the unseen snowy peaks of the Sierra less than forty miles inland. The land descended abruptly on the bay. The water was a deep cool blue, throbbing in the sun like a sensual jewel. The jungle crouched hungrily at the shore, thick, sculptured green and brown. Tall, bright cacti stood everywhere, bunches of long arms reaching for the sun. A soft, hot, carnal smell rested on the air.

It was a large cove, about a mile wide and perhaps two miles long. The innermost shore was pale beach. At one end of it, a half dozen dugout canoes painted red or yellow were pulled up along the shore. Large nets dried on the sand, and simple overhead shelters of fishermen made of long branches were clustered together at the edge of the bush. About one hundred yards away, in the most protected corner of the cove, twisted layered trupillo trees grew out of the sand. Behind them stood an open, palm-roofed cantina with a few empty tables and chairs. Nearby were four small adobe cabanas with neglected pipe roofs. On the other side of the cantina, further from the water and almost hidden in the shadows of giant leaning coconut palms, was a large, two-story house with a long porch, difficult to see. Three jeeps of various sorts were parked here and there in the shade, and a taxi, but there seemed to be no activity.

For the past two hours people had occasionally been visible near the cantina or the fishing camp, generally standing in pairs to gaze out at the strange boat that lay anchored in the middle of the bay, from which Sidell watched them.

The rough beauty of the place equaled anything Jack had ever seen, and yet he distrusted it. It seemed too improbably tranquil, too safe. There was a sense of paradise so near and yet forbidden, which he found unsettling—a feeling immeasurably heightened by the fact that behind him, half a mile away outside the cove, white-capping seas charged endlessly past, taunting him, sadistically awaiting him.

It had been hell coming in from Aruba. The wind had blown hard, and the seas ran steadily at ten and twelve feet, following from the east-northeast, heaving and punishing the old boat, until Billy and Ralph and Eiler were paralyzed with seasickness and almost useless. Leaks had opened in the topsides, and there would surely be more.

Sidell turned from the bow and let the binoculars hang from his neck. He wore a white tee shirt, cut-off pants, and moccasins. He was tired, weathered, but still alert and suspicious. His eyes found Joe sitting sullenly against the forward wall of the trunk cabin. Joe's eyes asked for some news, but Jack shrugged. Nothing to report. They were very quiet, as if they expected to hear something, and in the phenomenal stillness every movement seemed loud. Thorton's bare feet were audible on the deck as he came forward. He wore his flowered, baggy bathing trunks and moved with something less than human posture. He turned a haggard

181

gaze to Sidell, then Eiler, then lay down again across the new deck. *Leda* looked disheveled: mending bodies here and there, odd items of furniture brought up haphazardly from below, remnants of an attempted meal. Jesse soberly prepared to do some patching on the starboard topside. His tools banged sharply on the deck. Nerves responded to every sound. Uneasy glances searched each motion.

Too much weighed on their minds to talk. It had been a much rougher trip than they'd expected. The tough southern Caribbean had kicked their ass all the way from Aruba, and they faced a two-week journey when two days had been brutal. And they were leaking already. But no one wanted to go to Barranquilla. Every time they'd asked about the place in Aruba people had cringed. And above all, they knew anything could happen tonight. There was a pervasive foreknowledge of trouble. And yet around them lay the most beautiful serenity they would probably ever see in their lives. It was a providential refuge but an untrustworthy pleasure, like fine cuisine on the palate of a condemned man.

Jesse went over the side on a makeshift scaffold and began to patch, pounding caulking into open seams, sealing it with lead, then tacking on canvas covers. He and Jack had traced the leaks as they were discovered, and Jack would work on the port side when Jesse finished. The leaking had not been too bad coming in, but there was a very long way left to go.

This morning at sea, Jack and Jesse had conferred about going to drydock. They agreed—for different reasons—that they were not at all eager to go to Barranquilla, and they decided that if they could find some refuge where they could put on temporary patches they would just bandage her up and go for it.

With the strong winds and following seas, *Leda* had made much better time than expected. Jack had swung the course well north allowing for it, yet they had still arrived almost a half day early. They found Punta Aruja, a massive, uninhabited mountain of stone rising from the sea just outside the bay where they now lay anchored, and from which they were to rendezvous in the next cove east. Finding the smooth, protected waters of the bay where they could recuperate and work on the boat, Jack had made his decision to go. He knew his chances were not good, and he knew better than to take any chances on a long trip in an old boat, but in the final analysis Caval was more of a factor than the leaking.

"If I go to drydock," Jack had figured aloud to Eiler that morning as Joe lay suffering in the after cabin, "he'll probably start angling for that airplane. If he hasn't already. The bastard. And

182

with two weeks to do it and four million dollars of dope stacked up and ready to go he'd probably do it. So I guess there's no going to Barranquilla. We'll just have to gut it out."

Joe spent the day mending himself, sitting against the engine house roasting in the sun. He had never been seasick, but it had taken him with a vengeance in the first good swells out of Oranjestaad. It was like some torture from which he could not simply give up and pass out, and the two days had seemed cruelly long. He had moved around, gone on deck, tried to be of use in the galley, but it was no good. Jesse kept slapping his shoulder saying it was the following sea and that everybody got sick at least once, but that did less good. When they finally made that little bay, Joe felt like he'd rounded the cape of Africa in the hold of a slaver. The thought that they had just begun was intolerable. This morning, as he retched up the very last thick fluids in his stomach, it came to him with great clarity of insight that he would really rather be a librarian — and the notion passed slowly.

Jack and Jesse were seasoned sailors, but even they had been tight mouthed and pale with nausea at times. Ralph had been sick too, but it hadn't slowed him down much. Billy Delight took it worse. He had lain in the port cabin and not moved, would not even come on deck to help change the sails. Joe thought that along with the sickness had come Billy's realization that the party was over, that they had ahead of them a great deal of work, risk, and discomfort, and he had never yet reckoned with that. As they lay around the deck, Billy looked like he'd been kidnapped. The sound of the patching registered on his face as if he heard a gallows being built.

In the hot beauty of the cove though, they healed. Jack and Jesse patched the topside, and then Jesse put on the scuba gear and made a few patches underneath. The noise of their labors gradually took on a therapeutic quality. Billy and Eiler finally stirred and helped Ralph dismantle the big table and hoisted the last of the furniture out of the salon, making way for the cargo, collecting it on deck, and lashing it down ahead of the main mast. Jack and Jesse had completed their work by the time that was finished. It was the last hot hour of the afternoon, and they gathered around the new deck, still quiet and nervous, but healthier.

The silence of the place was fantastic. After the steady din of the wind, the humming and whining of the rigging and sails, the wood of the boat working, and the furious waves, it was as if the world caught its breath in that place. Nothing dreadful had occurred to belie the setting. The sickness and fatigue had passed. So for the first time they were able actually to recognize that the thing was at hand. They spoke in awed tones, almost whispers.

"I guess we're about ready. How you feeling, Billy?"

"I'm okay." Billy answered so quickly it sounded like only one word.

"You'll feel a lot better when you see that dope, uh?" Thorton grinned. Billy nodded halfheartedly.

"I'd feel a lot better seeing that other cove again before it gets too dark," Jack said. They all agreed. It was about time to start doing something. But they waited.

"Looks like it'd be a nice place to hang out." Eiler stood up and gazed toward the shore. The few small cabanas and the twisted trees on the beach had a dreamy appearance in the late sun. "Specially if somebody wanted to know where you were." Ralph chuckled a little. Joe winked at Sidell. "Be tough to deliver a subpoena."

"I don't think that's what they deliver down here," Jesse observed.

"I'll bet," said Jack.

"Looks like a pretty friendly place to me," Ralph shrugged.

"Maybe we'll find out." Eiler raised his voice and nodded at the shore. Three men on the beach were pushing a canoe into the water. It was a heavy thing made from a single log, but once in the water the men leaned into the paddles and knifed across the cove toward *Leda.* On deck they watched carefully; Sidell used the binoculars.

"Wonder what they want?" Billy asked uneasily.

"Just coming for a look," said Jack.

Jesse said, "Let's not tell 'em anything."

"Who's talkin'?" Ralph asked.

Joe said, "I will."

When the canoe drew close, they gave a tentative greeting. The three Colombians were dark and wiry and looked happy about something as they waved hello. The one in the middle was the oldest and wore a shirt. He immediately yelled out: "Marijuana. Marijuana. You want marijuana?"

Eyes rolled; there were grunts of disbelief. "Pretty discreet," said Jesse.

Eiler turned his palms up and called back, "No. *Gracias*, no." The man in the canoe grinned at him knowingly, nevertheless. The older one in the middle asked a question in Spanish. When Joe answered, shaking his head, the man began a long, gesticulating speech, pointing and describing something huge. Joe turned to the others when the man stopped. "Seems to be a mountain of dope over in the next cove. I guess they think it's ours. He says everybody's waiting for us over there."

They all smiled a little, but Jack said, "I still wouldn't say anything." Joe turned back to the canoe and made a rather theatrical shrug which caused the Colombians to laugh. The older one kept trying to tell Eiler they were supposed to be in the next cove, but Joe just shook his head. The others on *Leda* remained quiet. Joe finally tossed his pack of Camels down to them, and they got the picture. After a slow turn around the boat they headed back to shore, grinning and waving.

They weren't even out of earshot when Ralph turned to Eiler. "Did they really say a mountain?"

"Something like that," Joe nodded.

"A fuckin' mountain!" Ralph dropped his head back and gave a whoop. They all laughed. Jesse clapped his hands, and Delight went into a little dance. "A fuck-in' mountain!" Joe looked at Sidell and found him laughing, but with worried eyes. Joe still found nothing worth celebrating.

But the mood was broken, and they felt brash and wide open and ready for it all. The relief was giddy. They started kidding each other, laughing, joking that it would take three days to load by canoe, that they'd smoke it all before they got back, that they'd make Caval load it. Jesse got the yellow Colombian courtesy flag out of the cabin, and they ran it up and all saluted. Jack took a few pictures, then Ralph went below to boil some eggs and get cheese and beers for dinner. Even when they got around to putting their billfolds and passports into plastic bags in case of the worst—a shooting bust or a hijack that might force them overboard—the remarks were still careless.

"You think it was bad coming in here," said Billy. "Wait 'til we have to beat through the jungle for a week."

"What the hell," said Joe. "Least we might find a hotel."

The sun had dropped behind the ridge when Ralph came up with boiled eggs, cheese, saltines, and beer. The massive, pale rock of Punta Aruja seemed to glow, and big soft rain clouds slid over the hillsides behind the beach with bright pink edges. Sudden brute gusts of wind, renegades from the northeast trade strengthening outside the bay, ricocheted off the point and blasted at *Leda* from various directions, dancing furiously across the water. They ate in a group, talking about their course that night and the first watches, when a speedboat came into view approaching from the east, bursting over the swell in explosions of spray. Jack quickly checked through the binoculars and announced it was Caval and some Colombian. They went back to eating, kidding about Caval calling off the deal again and enjoyed what they expected to be the last few minutes of stationary calm they would have for a while. The craft roared recklessly alongside, and the wake jarred *Leda* enough to topple Eiler's beer on the deck. He yelled, "Thanks motherfucker."

It was a sleek, white boat with a huge hundred-horsepower outboard. The young, thin-faced Colombian held it close while Ralph pulled Caval aboard. He was soaking wet and looked ridiculous in a bright blue ski parka. He ignored what greetings were offered.

"Glad you guys're havin' a nice time," he cracked. He flung water off his hands and wiped his face. "Gimme a towel, will ya?"

They would have been happy to celebrate the rendezvous if he had said almost anything else. As it was they just laughed.

"Where's the steward?" Jesse asked. Delight called out: "Towel, please." Caval had been at sea all of fifteen minutes, and it amused them to learn he had found it unpleasant.

"Hey. C'mon. I'm soakin'. Somebody get me a goddamn towel."

They only laughed more. Caval's face reddened as if it would burst.

"Listen, I just busted my ass comin' around here in that little fuckin' boat to tell you stupid bastards you're in the wrong goddamn cove."

"My god," said Jack, "you mean it's gotten rough out there?"

"That's odd," Eiler gazed northward, "it was pleasant enough when we came in."

"Is this Colombia?" Jesse asked. He had never seen Caval before and kept watching him with an incredulous expression.

Caval unzipped his jacket and tried to wipe the water out of his hair, realizing no one had any intention of getting him anything and that they knew quite well where they were. The crew went back disgustedly to its sparse meal, and Caval turned to Jack. He gave Jack a walkie-talkie for communication once they reached the next cove, then asked if everything was ready.

"This boat should be in drydock." Jack stared at him hatefully, and the deck was very quiet. "We were already leaking coming in here, and we had to put on patches today. These guys are making a dangerous trip. I'd just like you to remember that. Anybody with good sense would be going on to Barranquilla."

"Yeah, I'll remember that," Tom said wearily. He seemed to resent Jack suggesting that someone other than himself might be important to the operation. "I been takin' chances every day though, so I won't lose much sleep over it."

"I'll bet," said Jack.

"And I believe you picked out the boat. Skipper."

Jack boiled. Thorton stood up quickly, just to be safe. Caval turned to the rest with his shrillest voice.

"Okay, let's can the picnic, whatta ya say. You guys gotta get goin'. We gotta lot of work to do. You gotta get things ready. We're gonna have to make this fast."

"Yeah. Sure thing." Billy Delight spoke with his mouth full. "So you can get back to your hotel, uh?"

"I been workin' like hell gettin' this thing organized over there." He was screaming now. "I want you bastards ready. This loading has got to be fast and smooth. Now let's get goin'."

"Shut up, Tommy," Ralph growled. Caval was shocked. Thorton had never spoken to him like that. "We all been doin' a little work on our end o' things too. We'll be there, and ever'thing'll go just fine. So why don't you jus' si' down and have yourself a beer and calm down. We said nightfall, an' that's when we'll be there."

Tom's dark icy features strained with an almost satanic anger, but then suddenly relaxed. "I don't need a beer," he said in a lowered voice. He leaned against the starboard rail, slowly wiped the water off his hands and face as meticulously as a cat and smiled contemptuously as they finished off the cheese and crackers. A few minutes later, with barely a word, he let himself down to the speedboat, and they raced away.

ii

It was dark and the half moon was well up and glowing between two clouds when Joe Eiler came up on deck from the salon, which was once again a cargo hold. They had nailed up two-by-fours as vertical cargo stays and lined each section with plastic tarp. They would add horizontal stays as the dope was loaded, to keep it from shifting at sea. Billy and Jesse were finishing up. The report of their hammers made sinister percussion with the hard double thud of the diesel. *Leda* pitched restlessly on the swell. The strong wind protested in the darkness against her rigging and furled canvas as Jack took her out in a broad arc to approach the cove head on. A mile away South America lay in black masses of silhouette, yet somehow gave every sense of its vastness.

Jack steered with one hand and tried to raise Caval on the walkie-talkie, but was still too far out. Ralph was pushing shells into the magazine of the twelve-gauge. He had all the weapons out on the top of the aft cabin, giving them a final check. Sliding the shotgun aside, he picked up the magnum, looked at the chambers, handed it to Jack. Jack felt it distractedly, stuck it in his belt a moment, but didn't like the feel of it. He put it on the top step of the companionway just in front of him, beside a thick plastic bag of extra bullets.

Jack had never paid much attention to the weapons. They were only an emergency backup system. If he had thought they would actually be needed, he would not have been there. He was much more concerned with the loading and the prospect of navigating a strange small cove in the darkness with a large, not very maneuverable boat. He wore no shirt beneath the hooded yellow jacket of his foul weather gear, and the sweat ran down his chest and glistened on his face.

Thorton became absorbed in the Thompson. He handled it with a rough affection as he pulled back the bolt and checked the receiver. Ralph was attracted to violence. He did not seek it, but he had a good knowledge of it, so the possibility was not displeasing. In addition, he felt that security was one of his jobs in the deal, and he loved doing his job. He seemed made for a Thompson. They resembled each other: small, heavy, capable of danger and destruction. He had removed the wooden stock, saying it increased the weapon's tendency to rise as it fired. As he held it a moment in firing position, he put it close to his side and gripped only the oily, scarred wood of the pistol grip and the forward horizontal grip, beyond which the black barrel extended only about two inches. Together the two looked very mean, and by nature Ralph would have shot it out with a battleship.

Eiler was not nearly as confident as either of them. He was much less sure that they would not encounter trouble, and if they did he fully expected to be shot. Below deck, when Ralph had said he was going up to ready the weapons, Joe's already wounded stomach had flinched. Suddenly the possibility of gunfire in the dark with unknown forces seemed coldly real and fated.

Sidell made another quarter turn to starboard for the final approach. On that course, *Leda* rolled harder on the waves, as if she didn't want to go. The noise of the diesel was almost drowned in the angry hiss and wash of seas attacking the port side. Ralph had to raise his voice at Eiler. "Anything happens, Joe, you get on up forward," he yelled. "I'll stay back here. Use that windlass for cover. I'll be back here." Joe swallowed and said okay.

He took the AR-15 off the cabin. He liked the weapon. It was light and accurate, and the tumbling little .223 slugs made it cruelly formidable. Joe drained the rest of a beer and threw over the empty. It spread a faint warmth through him and a certain bravado. It felt alright, but he wished fervently for a little scotch. He clicked one clip into the receiver, wedged another in his pocket, and another in the waist of his shorts beneath his shirt. He moved forward unsteadily on the rolling deck to stash the rifle among the headsails in the bow, and promised himself on the way that if there were any trouble he would raise hell. He knew it was only alcohol courage, but it felt better than no courage.

iii

The seas quit and the wind hushed as they came to the narrow entrance of the cove, passed through to the dark, dead-calm waters inside. They were all on deck, silent with anticipation, but able to see nothing of the other party, hearing only the crackle of Caval's voice from the walkie-talkie, then Jack replying loudly, "Show us a light. Show us a light."

A small, yellow flash appeared several times about half a mile off the starboard bow. Just as it stopped a cloud slipped off the moon, and pale light shone on the flat water and the steep, dark hillsides. The cove was much smaller than the other, less than a quarter mile wide at the entrance, perhaps half a mile wide at the center and a mile deep. Jack steered toward the point from which the light had signaled until he made out the white speedboat in the moonlight and a much larger, dark object beside it.

Jack slowed the engine, turned to port, and began a slow counterclockwise circle. Caval's voice broke out of the walkie-talkie again, high and metallic, saying it would be a few minutes yet. Then it came again, shocking the silence, warning Jack of rocks on the shallow far side.

Jack knew that with the steep shore it would most likely be

quite deep even at the edges, but he held his course tight in the center. He kept craning his neck, squinting ahead around the cabin from one spot to another, looking for any sign of rocks. Jesse and Eiler leaned over either side at the bow ready to give warning. The air was heavy and damp with a smell of warm rain. The minutes were empty and maddening. Billy and Ralph, peering into the darkness, quickly grew angry.

"Goddamnit," Ralph hissed, "get 'em on the box again, Jack. See what's the holdup."

"Thought we were in such a damn hurry," Billy groused.

They were coming in toward the shore again five minutes later, when an easy rain began to whisper on the calm water. Then the yellow light ashore flashed again. Caval's voice cracked the stillness, "Get ready. Here you go."

The irregular rumble of a small ill-tuned engine worked its way through the dark and rain. Jack turned away from the shore and slowed almost to an idle. The others gathered along the port side, searching, oblivious to the sprinkle, silent as if awaiting a miracle. The noise grew loud enough to count the strokes of the engine before a giant canoe finally grumbled into view through the curtain of mist and rain. Perhaps forty feet long, its bow was thrust forward in a long curve, like the prow of some ancient war canoe. It was sitting low in the water, with four shirtless Colombians perched atop a cargo of bulging burlap bags. Thorton cursed in amazement. The others stood petrified by the sight.

"I don't believe it," Jack yelled. "Look at that thing. I don't believe it." An old, gaunt man in a thin sweater and a weathered canvas hat sat at the long tiller. He raised his hand to Jack and smiled. Jack grinned and waved back like a kid. All the hassle seemed suddenly worthwhile.

Everyone in both boats started yelling. "*Bueno . . . Hola . . . Buenos noches . . .* Hey, *amigos . . .* Look at all that shit, will ya." Eiler called for them to throw a line. They bumped against the side. One of them threw a bow line. Jesse went forward to fasten it, so the canoe would be pulled parallel to *Leda* while the old man kept close with the tiller. For a moment they stood ogling the cargo, heaped high above the sides of the canoe. In turn the Colombians stared back at *Leda* with wondering eyes. Then before Jesse had even made the line fast, chaos erupted.

The Colombians decided to get along. Working as pairs they each took the end of a bag and started heaving them over as fast as they could.

190

In the face of hurtling fifty-pound bags, the crew protested: "Hey, what the hell? . . . *Momentito,* uh?" It was no use. The loaders were fishermen collected nearby for the night's work, and it was amusement and adventure to them as much as labor. In addition they had about two hundred bags to heave in each load, and they were not being paid by the hour. One after another the bags flew aboard, straight into the crew, over their heads, crashing into the masts, sliding across the wet decks. Eiler railed at them. "Hold it, damnit . . . Hey. *Bastante! Despacio!"* They just laughed and kept heaving.

Ralph and Jesse scrambled below to start stacking. The big skylight hatch was already off, and Billy and Eiler frantically threw bags into the hold while ducking incoming bags and yelling uselessly at the Colombians to slow down.

Nothing bothered Sidell like disorganization, and he fumed at the wheel watching the disaster on deck. He tried to get the Colombians to slow down, but there was too much noise and activity for him to be heard. Delight and Eiler floundered in the barrage. Bags landed everywhere, banging into furniture stacked on deck, flying into the rigging. After only a few minutes they lay all over the deck, soaking up the rain. A few came open as they landed, and occasional gusts strewed the deck with marijuana. "Typical," Jack grumbled.

The rate of delivery slowed for a moment when Caval roared out in a speedboat. As it pulled up, the wake sent the big canoe tossing against *Leda*'s side and nearly put one of the Colombians over. Joe and Billy gained a little on them, but they took it up again hot and heavy. Caval pulled himself aboard, tried with no more luck than the others to regulate things, but then amazingly pitched in and started to work. He had not chucked more than two sacks, when an incoming bag struck him flat across the back, knocked him sprawling over the new deck and nearly into the water. To their amazement, he got up laughing like the others and kept at it. It was just slapstick from then on: the Colombians laughing, shouting in Spanish; Ralph and Jesse calling up unintelligible instructions; the three on deck, wet and bedraggled, staggering, tripping, ducking through the melee, and heaving sacks as best they could.

Sidell finally resigned himself and enjoyed the humor. Somehow they'd managed to get there, he figured. One way or another they'd get the stuff loaded and get out.

When nearly all of the first load was somewhere aboard, two of the Colombians decided to go aboard for a look around. That was too much for Jack, and he yelled at Delight to keep them off. Billy's size did not invite argument, but he moved them affectionately, put his big arms around their shoulders as he turned them back toward their boat, talked to them in English, asked them where they lived, if they'd ever been in the States. They looked back at him mystified.

When the load was finished, the canoe chugged away. Caval followed shortly, to coordinate the second half. Delight chucked the remaining bags, and Joe went below to help stack. The hold was a strange sight. The new lumber of the cargo stays divided it like the preliminary stage of a new house. Between them the bags were stacked three and four feet high on each side, like dikes or hurried battlements. Ralph and Jesse worked like demons relaying and stacking. Wet from rain and sweat, they had become thoroughly powdered with marijuana dust. They lurched and wavered with glazed eyes as they hoisted bags and grew rummy from the *Cannabis* working through their pores.

Several minutes later, Thorton came out of the hatch and tottered on the deck taking deep breaths to clear his head. The rain had stopped; all the bags were below; and Billy had gone down to nail up horizontal stays. Jack kept circling, awaiting the second load.

"Ralph. How does the stuff look?" he called. "Bring me some of it."

"Dynamite, man. Just dynamite," he gasped. "Too much down there breathin' it. Really gets ya."

Ralph called down below, and Billy fetched up a random fistful from an open bag. Jack was impressed. It was the first thing that had really measured up to the plans, and Caval's promises. It was prime, pungent, half-dry dope, bunched on long narrow stems with clusters of seeds and flowers in the tops. The leaves were all a pale green and linen color, greener on the lower leaves, lighter at the tops. On appearance alone, it was fast cash in the States, the sort of weight one dreamed of moving. "It's all like this?" Jack asked. "This is too good to be true."

"All of it I've seen. An' I'll tell ya, man, it's dangerous dope. We hadn't put a match to it yet an' I'm smashed. Just from bein' around it. I can feel it workin' all through my skin. Brother, we gonna make a fortune. This shit's beautiful."

"We ought to." As he steered, Jack peered into his hand again every few seconds, marveled at the nuances of texture and color as if it were precious stones. Finally it seemed that everything would pay off.

Billy turned on his cassette player, and a Carlos Santana tape slashed the thick night air with wild congas and electric guitars. Several reefers went around through the hold and on deck, and against his better judgement, Jack had some. The night seemed dreamlike, the boat alive with noise and careless motion. The old diesel, the hovering jungle, the dark still waters, and crazy music.

Colombians need very little excuse for a party, and the next load came out with two extra men, the whole gang howling and singing. The fiasco resumed as soon as they bumped *Leda*'s hull. Bombarding the boat was sport to the Colombians, and Delight had had time to smoke plenty of the cargo. He lumbered among the chaos like an addled giant and fell on Eiler twice. Caval managed not to return until it was over, so with one less man the dope was piled high all over the deck by the time the Colombians finished at their end. This time Sidell allowed them aboard to give a hand, but after chucking a few bags they started nosing around the deck. Sidell didn't like it, but there was nothing he could do. Billy and Eiler were too busy to stop them, but Eiler kept an eye on the bow where he'd hidden the carbine. By the time most of the sacks had been dumped below, the Colombians were all over the place, in the galley, the engine room, the forecastle, looking through the extra rigging, the food supplies, Billy's cassettes. They were friendly and good natured, but chiefly looking for a few packs of cigarettes, a stray bottle of whiskey, a slicker, or an extra gun. Jack finally yelled at Joe to give them the furniture and get them the hell off. Joe coaxed them on deck, but they were not greatly interested in Margaret's lesser stools and chairs, or even in the nicer ones. In whatever hutments they resided, extra seating was apparently not a problem, but they pitched the stuff down to the canoe anyway. Then to Sidell's delight, Eiler even got them to take Caval's white couch by throwing in a few packs of Camels.

It took nearly an hour after the Colombians left to get the cargo completely stowed and covered with plastic and canvas tarps. Caval returned in the meantime, and he and Jack went over the course, the estimated time of arrival, and procedures for radio communication. Below, when the work was finished, there was nowhere to sit but the narrow center path they had left above the bilge. The two cabins were packed full; on either side the burlap sacks were piled nearly to the deck overhead. Thorton, Eiler, Delight, and Mackenzie sat cramped against the stacks, half-naked, wet, dirty, tired, and stoned, but happy as oil covered wildcatters after a gusher. In the dim light, the hold was like a cave. *Leda*'s slightest movements were ponderous with the load. There was a mesmerizing presence

193

of great riches, the intoxication of a fortune in forbidden treasure.

Jack's shout shattered the reverie. "Jesse, get up here!" There was an alarm in his voice that promised catastrophe. They glanced darkly at each other as they scrambled up.

"Get the glasses," Jack barked as soon as Jesse appeared. "There's a light out there," he pointed. "Outside, maybe two miles. See if you can make it out. What's it doing?"

"Hey, you don't have to worry," Caval insisted. He was standing near Jack at the wheel looking very eager to depart. Jesse ignored him and hurried forward with the glasses. "It can't be *Aduana*, man, an' they're the only thing that'd be out there." Caval sounded too sure to be trusted. "An' they're paid. I know for goddamn sure those bastards are paid. I was with Umberto today when he was talkin' with one of 'em."

"Yeah, well, it could be anybody." Jack kept squinting into the darkness at the far, faint light as he spoke, kept steering the same tight circular course. "Unless you paid off everybody on this fucking coast, I'd like to know damn well what that is."

Caval did not answer but began to gnaw on a thumbnail and moved forward with the others. They followed Jesse along the starboard side as Jack turned, all straining at the distant light, saying nothing, afraid to even guess aloud what it might be. Jesse shuffled slowly aft again as the boat turned, the other four at his elbows, until they were all at the stern again.

"I can't tell anything," he lowered the glasses. "Must be raining still out there. Can't even tell the color. Doesn't seem to be moving though. You just now see it?"

"Yeah, just now," Jack answered gravely.

Thorton breathed deeply beside Eiler as if preparing for anything. Delight cursed under breath, like it was all somehow unfair. Any courage Joe had managed earlier was gone absolutely.

"Hey," Caval called anxiously over to the speedboat grumbling along *Leda*'s side. "What is that?" He spoke Spanish. "What's happening out there."

The driver half stood as he looked back over his shoulder toward the distant light. He turned and shrugged, expressionless. "Possibly a big boat," he suggested without conviction. "Possibly a freighter from Santa Marta." He moved his arm to describe it heading away from the coast.

"Just a freighter," Caval translated.

"*Posiblemente*," Jack repeated the man's word.

"Well, what're we gonna do?" Thorton asked. He wanted orders. Jack took a deep breath. He bit his middle finger a moment as he steered away from shore again toward the center of the cove, then reduced the pitch of the propeller almost to neutral and backed off the throttle to an idle.

"Anybody looking for us out there can probably run us down. We aren't going to outmaneuver anybody in this boat. Let's just sit right here until we see what that thing's doing. If it's going to be trouble let's have it in here. If it's bad we can at least get ashore and have a chance. Out there it'd be all or nothing, and that's stupid."

"What if we just make a run for it?" Thorton ventured.

"Shit yes. Just take off," said Caval. "You got the fuckin' guns."

"This boat doesn't exactly run, Ralph." Jack raised his voice. He ignored Caval. Caval would not be having to face anything three or four miles off shore. "If something comes on us, only two things can happen, damnit. We either scare them off with the guns or we take it in the ass. If we can scare them off, we can do it here as good as anywhere. If we take it in the ass out there, we're dead. Here we got a chance. So let's just wait on it."

"He's right," said Jesse.

Caval said nothing, but Ralph nodded. "Okay. Gimme them binoculars."

Few things affect the passage of time like fear. The minutes labored. They waited in tense, tight-throated silence. Sidell kept to the center of the cove. Locked behind clouds, the moon glowed through only faintly, and the darkness was complete and threatening. Rain fell again for a few moments, stopped, began again. Caval paced the deck, while Ralph and Jesse shared the glasses and made short-lived speculations. Each time they finally believed the light was fainter, it seemed immediately to grow bright. At last, agonizingly, Jack and Thorton and Jesse, taking turns with the glasses, agreed that it was heading away.

"Guess the guy was right," said Jesse. "Probably a freighter heading out slow, at an angle, so it looked like it wasn't moving."

"Yeah." Jack swallowed. "Okay. Let's get the sails up and get the hell out of here."

Caval sauntered back and stood beside the aft cabin. He said nothing but regarded Sidell with the most arrogant smirk. To Joe's knowledge, Jack had never punched anyone, but Joe was certain right then that he was going to slug Caval. Joe thought it was a little late for that though, and he moved between them.

"Guess we'll be seeing you in North Carolina," he said to Tom.

"Yeah, I hope so," he smiled. "Be careful, Jack." He shook his head almost sorrowfully as he headed for the side. He called a curt farewell to Thorton and Delight, let himself down to the speedboat, and departed with a roar.

Jack motored out to the mouth of the cove, and the first breezes snapped hungrily at the sails as they entered the swell. "Here we go, big mama," he spoke aloud to her. "This is it." They cleared the eastern point, and the hard trade hit them. It had come around more to the east, and Jack set a course of 030° north. It was good enough to cut the diesel. It blew as hard as when they had come in, perhaps even harder, but the open sea looked good. They were high and ready, nonstop for Carolina. They sheeted the sails in, set the staysails, and *Leda* heeled to port and really started to move. Jack was bursting. He could feel the weight of the load, the boat low in the water, hard and steady, her old mass crushing ahead like a dreadnought. The hard night seas advanced in silvery black out of a planetary vastness of luminous white caps. With ancient practice, *Leda* rose and reached and settled, and rose and reached and settled, and put the sea behind her with a purpose.

Jesse emerged from the engine room hatch. "She's truckin'," Jack beamed at him.

"Damn right!" Jesse yelled above the sound of the wind and breaking water. "This is her business." He patted the side of the aft cabin, as if it were the hip of an old mare. "You're back at work, old girl. Back at work."

Billy Delight went below and rolled some enormous reefers, a task he always performed with uncharacteristic dexterity, and Thorton broke out the beer. Twice Jesse took the glasses and checked the light that had frightened them in the cove, but it was far away the first time and then gone. They collected around the cabin and drank and smoked and boasted that now nothing could stop them. The seas came more on her bow, and *Leda*'s ride was resolute. Ten tons of weed kept her from rolling much, and the pitch of her weight as she plowed ahead equaled perfectly the way they felt. They were rare. A blood of ages, a scent of wild boundless freedom lent an abandon as timeless and endless as the sea and the night. They breathed it, spoke it, laughed it—and, for a while, they *were* it.

Joe Eiler saw it in their faces, felt it among them on the rough rise and fall of the dark sea. He knew this was it. It was that elusive moment of liberty when one bears his life in his hands and gambles it. He knew suddenly that this was what they had really come for. This moment. The dope was ballast; this was the mission. There would be the money in it, of course, but he knew that would pass from them long before the priceless thrill of this night. And it was so brief.

For a mere split second, there was a dull ripping hum overhead. More than one of them was talking loudly, though, and Jack barely noticed it. Then it came again—identically. Ralph and Eiler heard it and glanced at each other in confusion. Something about the sound. It came again, fainter, off to the side.

"You hear that?" Jack stiffened.

"What?" Jesse asked.

The foot of the mizzensail just above their heads popped as if struck by something borne on the wind. Suddenly the wind made a low whistle through a tear in the heavy cloth. Mackenzie's mouth opened in disbelief.

"What the hell?" someone asked. Jack thought he heard a distant crack. Then there was another hard hum, a flat sound of impact against the hull somewhere near them. "Jesus, is somebody—" Thorton's question was cut off when the corner of the cabin beside him was splintered by a bullet.

"Goddamn," Jack shouted. "Look."

They followed his arm to a large dark object about two hundred fifty yards off the starboard quarter and coming hard. It was without lights but illuminated barely by the shrouded glow of the moon as it broke the waves before it. For an instant they simply froze.

"We're fucked," said Jesse.

"What in hell is it?" Billy cried. With a soft splatter, just after he spoke, his forehead ruptured like a piece of fruit. He lurched, driven backward. Then his huge body thudded full length on the deck and slid against the rail.

There was a moment of purest shock, then of unintelligible shouts, and a horror more palpable than anything that had passed before. Jesse and Eiler lunged around the cabin, gaped at the broken head, the bloody face, the big leg twitching. "Good God," Mackenzie shuddered.

Jack and Ralph crouched by the wheel, staring at the approaching ship. "Is he bad?" Jack yelled.

"He's dead as shit." Joe's voice quavered with panic.

"Get down ya idiots!" Thorton darted into the cabin after the weapons. "Eiler get the carbine and stay up front," he shouted from inside.

They stayed pressed against the side of the cabin though,

staring into the dark at the hulk bearing down on them. "Is it *Aduana*?" said Jesse. "No. Big trawler," Jack answered. He could just make out the broad, snout nose of it, coming in and out of view among the wave troughs, and the tall bridge with long gaffs for nets drawn up vertically as it plowed ahead. There was another hard hum above them. "Goddamn, they're coming too," he yelled. "They know what we got." A bullet struck wood somewhere nearby, then another whined off the mizzenmast. Jack stayed on his knees and used the wheelhouse for cover. "Get the engine started," he called to Jesse.

Thorton emerged with the Thompson and the long extra clip and slipped around behind the cabin. In one motion Jesse went over the top of the cabin and disappeared into the engine room. Joe Eiler glanced at Delight's body, took a deep breath, scrambled across the deck for the main hatch, and went head first down the companionway. By the time he'd gathered the carbine and clips from the forecastle and struggled up through the forward hatch, Jesse had the diesel chugging, and he felt Jack give her full throttle. The extra speed seemed pitifully insufficient. Eiler lay down against the long deck locker just ahead of the mainmast. Ralph knelt to use the cabin for cover; Jesse stayed on the other side near the body, peering over the cabin. The other boat must have seen them scatter because the firing stopped. The diesel slightly cut the rate at which the trawler gained, but it was still overtaking. Men became visible on its decks as the dark form closed to a hundred yards.

"She's pretty damn big," Jesse called to Ralph. "I can see a lot of guys on deck. Maybe eight or ten."

"Don't shoot yet," Thorton yelled back at Eiler. "Wait 'til they get close an' we'll let 'em have it. Maybe we can scare 'em off." Each few seconds the roll of the seas hid all but the trawler's rigging, then lifted the whole thing into view, hid it again, lifted again. It advanced by stages, in and out of sight.

Sidell stayed on his knees at the wheel, worked the old boat for every bit of speed she could manage, which was little. His forearms trembled; he chewed the inside of his mouth. "They could ram us," it came to him suddenly. His thoughts began to run out his mouth, almost yelling. "That's what those bastards will do. They'll ram us. Good Christ, they could break us in two." The pistol in his right hand felt hopelessly inadequate. "No. Maybe they won't do that." Jack tried desperately to keep his head. "If they ram us hard, they sink us, and then they lose the dope. God, they must know we have the dope. What the hell else would they want? Yeah. They just want to run us down. Maybe bump us good. Oh sweet Jesus, for another machine gun." Ralph and Jesse made no replies.

The night and the wind and the heaving sea now seemed rampant and vicious, a perfect setting for a grisly death.

The trawler surged ahead, closing faster. "They're really comin' now," Jesse's voice broke. "They're full on now!"

The trawler was only sixty yards off when a powerful flood light poured out from its bridge. The light fell on the water nearby then unsteadily found the deck and washed everything in an undulating shine. Thorton braced against the starboard side of the cabin, set himself on both knees, and suddenly his body shook and the air was pulverized by the hammering steel blast of the Thompson. For long seconds there was nothing but the brute noise of that gun destroying the night. Simultaneously, Joe Eiler fired the full clip of twenty rounds, four and five shots at a time when the trawler rose on a wave. Ralph fired two long blasts, and before he stopped, the flood light was out. Eiler was still firing when the Thompson quit. Then when he stopped, Jack fired a few more pistol shots. When they quit, the air rang with shock. With all his might Ralph roared at the dark form astern: "Think it over you cocksuckers!"

"They've scattered off the deck," Jesse screamed hoarsely. "We got one I think. Maybe two. I think we got the bridge too. Busted the windshield. They're slowing up. I think they're slowing now."

The trawler did indeed seem to stop, held a mere fifty yards astern, then receded, slowly but steadily, to a hundred then a hundred and fifty yards. On *Leda* they waited silently, afraid to even hope the trawler might give up. Then it changed course, turning away eastward so its full silhouette was visible, about a hundred feet long, with a large bridge and tower and cranes on the rear deck. It fell away to two hundred fifty or three hundred yards, then took up a course nearly parallel to *Leda*'s and began to accelerate again.

"What're they doin' now?" Ralph demanded. He had stretched out on the deck so that the starboard gunwhale gave him a little cover from any rifle volleys.

"They're pulling up with us out there. Maybe they're trying to head us."

"Well let's get this fucker movin'," Jack yelled.

Jesse came forward in a low run, as Jack fell off their course to make the best wind of it. Eiler pushed the carbine and clips beneath the Whaler, and he and Jesse let out the mainsail some, then

199

reset the staysails and adjusted the mizzen. *Leda* noticeably picked up speed, and she heaved and dove across the seas at odd angles, ungainly and desperate. Things crashed below in the galley and forecastle, and Eiler had to flatten out on the deck to keep from sliding. He put the carbine beneath himself as heavy spray began to fall regularly across the forward deck.

Joe never knew how long the trawler remained abreast of them, a sinister form against the wild black of the seas and the glittering starry black of the sky, but it seemed eternal. He kept his face against the planks and did not watch or listen to the others, but kept begging of something he could not have named to please let them go away.

They had come out of the clouds in the preceding half hour, and the moon had passed well out ahead of them in the sky and grown dimmer. Jack finally stood upright looking through the glasses and called out that they were falling off, turning back. The others watched from their places several more minutes and did not move or speak until it was certain.

Wearily Jack held the wheel, then brought them back into the wind until the sails luffed and they slowed, rising and falling fitfully. He gazed at Delight, but then covered his face with one hand and slowly shook his head. He felt as if he had run miles, been pursued for hours in a nightmare.

Jesse stood staring at Billy's corpse. Thorton still squinted into the distance where the trawler had retreated, the Thompson gripped at his side. Eiler looked at Billy a moment but then turned away. He was gruesome, with dried blood thick and dark on his face and chest and on the deck around his head, one hand grotesquely across his middle, the palm upturned as if to pose a question. Eiler sat on the new deck, put the carbine down and lay on his side wishing for sleep.

"They could come back." Ralph spoke grimly as he turned to the others. "They could run up on us again in an hour or so if they wanted."

Jesse and Eiler nodded. There was not relief so much as a mere cessation of terror.

"Ohh, God, Billy," Jack looked upward and spoke slowly and mournfully to no one in particular. "You poor big clumsy bastard." He blew a long, tired breath that was almost a prelude to tears. "He never really knew what he was getting into. He thought it was a goddamn holiday. A dream. He never thought it was real."

Thorton set the Thompson on the deck beside Eiler and moved purposefully to the body. He removed the wristwatch and felt the pockets of the cut-off jeans, pulled out the plastic bag with a passport and billfold. Ralph squatted at the head, his mouth drawn tight, raised the big body by himself from the armpits, and loaded it over the rail and into the black sea.

chapter 12

i

SIDELL awakened just before dawn. He had finally stretched out about three hours earlier for an uneasy rest. In the darkness, he saw Thorton prone on the opposite bunk with the Thompson beside him on the cabin sole, and closed his eyes again. He wished desperately to escape in more sleep but could not.

Many times over the previous months he'd had doubts and reservations about the enterprise, but they had only been worries regarding performance or profit. He had never doubted that the operation was possible, nor that he possessed the ability to execute it. Now, though, he felt a total pessimism, an aching assurance that the trip was doomed.

"You've got to get up," he forced himself to sit. "Got to go check below."

Just before waking, he had dreamed there was three feet of water sloshing in the engine room and forward into the hold. He knew it was only a bad dream, but he still had to go down and check for leakage, and he did not want to do it.

Jesse hung on the wheel as if he would collapse without it. A stocking cap covered the top of his long hair; his narrow features were gaunt with fatigue and the remainder of fear; yet his eyes were still sharp. He and Jack only looked at each other a moment and did not speak when Jack came out of the cabin. God, he's been up for at least forty-eight hours, Jack remembered. I've got to let him get some sleep.

Jack went down the main hatch, and the single light in the engine room cast a dim glow on the piles of cargo. Joe Eiler was asleep atop the stack just ahead of the galley. The galley itself was a depressing sight and mirrored Sidell's own inward disarray. Empty beer bottles rattled in the sink; a forgotten orange half and a wasted hunk of cheese littered the counter among sugar spilled from a fallen sack.

When he moved into the engine room and checked the bilge, Jack set his feet apart and drew a long breath. He lacked the requisite energy for either surprise or alarm. Water was well up on the flywheel, having risen quickly since he had killed the engine before lying down. He merely registered the apparent facts, too weary to calculate their portents, except for the obvious. Staring at the water that slapped around the base of the diesel, he observed aloud with a tone of passive realization, "We'll never make it."

He started an auxiliary pump to clear the bilge so he could start the engine, which would work against the leakage with its two continuously running pumps. Then he went out to the hold and sat on the edge of the counter in the galley. He gazed at the plastic shrouded masses of cargo around him and was reminded of a story he could only barely remember, about a man laden with gold fatally attempting to ford a swift river.

The racket of the pump awakened Eiler. He squinted around the hold until he focused on Sidell hunched sullenly beneath him. Becoming more awake, Joe desired a moment of humor the way Sidell had wanted to retreat into sleep.

"It ain't enough I have to be shot at by beaner pirates and scared half to death, I have to be harassed in the middle of the night by a fuckin' motorcycle. Or whatever that racket is."

Jack glanced at him with an annoyed look. Joe tried again.

"That's the trouble with traveling in steerage, nobody respects you." He waited for Jack to respond but gave up. "Funny guy, uh?"

"Yeah."

"What's the matter?"

"We're leaking like hell."

"Oh, great." Eiler rolled onto his back and envisioned himself puttering around the middle of the ocean in the Whaler while the treasure bubbled to the bottom. At the moment it seemed laughably consonant with prior events in his life. "This is gettin' to be a pain in the ass, Jack. I've tried to be a good sport, but if my clothes get ruined, I'm going to sue the shit out of you."

Jack shouted, "For Christ's sake, Joe!"

"Alright, alright."

ii

Eiler was at the wheel in the early afternoon. The seas had

calmed considerably, and a nice breeze made velvet on the soft swells. The sun beamed out of the endless sky, upon the desolate seriousness of the boat. Eiler however felt tolerably well. He had absorbed some catastrophes in his life, and he could take another if he had to. The pumps were staying ahead of the leakage. He was sure that, at the very least, he could live through it. And to him, that made circumstances acceptable. In addition, he had not been at the helm since the trip into Curaçao, and he enjoyed it. Before, he had thought *Leda* a cantankerous old heap to steer, but with a good load she drove with purpose, responded to the rudder. They were still fairly close-hauled on a northeast course of fifty degrees, heading toward the Dominican Republic to allow for the westward set of the current. Jesse had just turned off the engine, but they still moved well, taking the sea comfortably on the starboard bow. There was a wonderful quiet that was kind to the nerves.

Jesse Mackenzie pulled himself up through the engine room hatch and came around the cabin. The tight set of his jaw seemed to Eiler to promise more bad news. Jesse said nothing to him, only nodded, then reflexively checked the compass to see that Joe was on course, for which Joe grimaced and gave him a stiff middle finger as Jesse entered the cabin. Thorton still lay on one bunk trying fitfully to sleep, and Jack sat at the chart table, dull with depression. He turned in the chair as Mackenzie entered.

"Why'd you cut the engine?"

"The leaks have gotten worse while it's running. The vibration must be loosening the seams. I've got the one gas pump going down there now, but I don't know if it'll clear it by itself. I think we ought to keep the engine off, except when it's absolutely necessary, and just use a couple of the auxiliary pumps to stay ahead of the bilge."

"We can't do that." Jack was exasperated and sounded childish in his insistence. "Without the engine we'd have to go way the hell off course to allow for the current. Besides that, we can only make about four knots at best without it. It would take us forever. We'd run out of supplies. We've got four auxiliary pumps altogether and the deck pump. We can use all of them."

Sidell sounded as if he knew nothing would work and merely wanted to get it over with as quickly as possible. Thorton sat up on his bunk and sleepily massaged his forehead with one hand.

"Sure, we could do that." Jesse measured Sidell coldly before he went on. "But the leaks are getting worse while the engine's running, Jack. If sooner or later it gets ahead of the auxiliaries, it's all over but the praying. And we don't know how much gas the pumps use; we don't know how our gas will hold out. It'll be a hell of a lot safer to just forget the engine. So what if it takes us longer? We're in trouble, man."

"Thank you. I noticed that," Jack snapped. He looked away and chewed at his middle finger. From weariness and distraction, an idea he would have never actually gone through with briefly occurred to him as an easy solution. "Maybe we ought to go back. We could find one of those little coves, dump the load and hide it. Then go to drydock, and come back for the dope."

"No way," Ralph was suddenly awake and stared at Jack in disbelief.

"Are you crazy?" said Jesse. "Go back there? Unload and load again by ourselves, and then risk more shit? And Barranquilla too? Jesus! Once was the limit for me, I promise you. I'm never doing that again."

"Hell yes. No turning back," Ralph insisted. Then a plaintive tone softened his voice, as if he saw that his leader was shaken. "C'mon, Jack. We got to keep going. That's all there is. Muscle it through. We can do it. We're past the worst part."

"Okay, okay." Jack nodded wistfully. He doubted they were even close to the worst of it, whatever that might be. "I guess we can't stop." He thought for a moment and sounded better when he spoke. "Alright, let's still keep the engine going as much as we can. Six hours on and six hours off. And we'll set up the pumps. We can keep close track of the gas consumption and the leakage and just see how it goes."

"Okay. That sounds good." Jesse seemed to relax a little, but grew stern again as he spoke. "But it brings up another matter. It's damn well time we got this crew organized. Like I went down about an hour ago and the main pump on the engine was clogged and water was already high enough so the flywheel was throwing it all over the place. We need to set up regular shifts. Shifts for taking the wheel and for monitoring the pumps. Someone has to be watching those pumps all the time, making sure they don't get clogged and keeping a log on lubrication and gas consumption. We're short-handed now, and we better get organized. We haven't had a god-damn decent meal since Aruba. Somebody needs to be cook. Somebody needs to be in charge of the engine, somebody in charge of the deck. We better get serious."

At the wheel Eiler listened to Ralph and Jack agreeing with Mackenzie. There was a grim resolve in their voices which was heartening. Then Joe laughed, as it occurred to him that he would inevitably be appointed cook.

iii

By noon of the next day, the wind had picked up, and the swell was steepening and getting rough. The chugging diesel and the bawl of an auxiliary pump dominated the air below deck. Eiler spread his feet apart in the gallery to steady himself as he sliced a long bread loaf. He set eight slices in a row, spread mayonnaise on every other one and then mustard on the others. He sealed the bread sack and went to the storeroom at the head of the engine room to get his cheese and canned ham. Joe had no reservations about being the cook. He even liked it. It was necessary. It ordered the time, and until taking over the galley, he had done almost nothing to contribute to the operation. And the siege mentality of the boat gave an importance even to the making of sandwiches. That morning he had contrived a breakfast of french toast, and the others had been happy for a moment in their gratefulness, except that it reminded them of Billy Delight who used to groan regularly for french toast during the misery in Otrabanda. But circumstances allowed little time to think of Delight. They were still stunned by the suddenness, the arbitrary uselessness of his death, but their own continuing danger remained more present in their minds. Still Billy's death weighed on every thought and action, emphasizing the separateness from civilization and the stark reality of no law.

Assigning shifts and duties the previous day had made it easier to deal with their problems. It mobilized the static energy of fear into an organized front, which produced a determination that was almost optimistic. During the day, from six until six, Mackenzie was the engineer, in charge of maintaining the diesel and pumps. Sidell took care of navigation and kept the wheel. Thorton was deck hand, looking after the rigging and adjusting sails when necessary, and Eiler was the cook, responsible for three meals a day. They agreed that Thorton and Eiler would relieve the other two whenever their own jobs gave spare time. The night schedule was a rigid system of three-hour shifts of either taking the wheel or monitoring the pumps, with each man working six hours between sundown and dawn and sleeping whenever he could.

So far the arrangement was working, and the leakage seemed under control. The oldest of the gasoline pumps had given up quickly and was retired for spare parts, leaving only three auxiliaries, but Mackenzie felt they would suffice.

Jesse lay atop the cargo, calculating gas consumption in a

spiral notebook. He looked down at Eiler when the sandwiches were nearly finished.

"What're we getting?"

"Ham an' cheese an' a canned peach. That okay?"

"I guess it'll have to be."

"How we doing on gas?"

"Don't look too good. I can't tell for sure yet, but I don't think it'll last a week at this rate."

Eiler finished opening the peaches before speaking. He wondered if it were really possible that they would not make it. "You get the feeling we weren't supposed to do this?"

Jesse managed to smile. "No. I just keep wondering how the hell I got in it."

"Just as good a question, I guess. What're we gonna do about gas? Use the deck pump?"

"Sure. But I think we're going to have to get some more gas somewhere too."

"At the Shell station?"

Mackenzie chuckled at the sarcasm. "Jamaica somewhere. Maybe. Cuba and Haiti are out. They'd just take the boat—and probably hang us."

Eiler spooned peaches into two aluminum cups. "Shit," was all he replied.

Jesse chuckled again. He believed *Leda* was charmed. He never doubted they would pull through, but he did not know how. He rolled off the cargo and headed for the companionway. He said, "This is a lot of fun, isn't it?"

iv

In the late afternoon, Ralph took the wheel, while Jack took a reading on the sun with the sextant and checked their progress and speed by the taffrail log. The breeze had gradually strengthened through the day until it blew steadily at about twenty knots, and they had taken down the mizzen and jibs and ran only the reefed main and staysail. The seas were six and eight feet, and the sun was still strong. Infrequently overhead were hazy cumuus that combined in the distance to obscure the horizon. *Leda* surged.

"She don't know there's anything wrong," Thorton grinned.

"Yeah. She feels good, doesn't she." Jack was noting the taffrail log. "In fact, I think she's doing better than I thought she would."

Several minutes later when Jesse entered the cabin, Sidell turned eagerly from the chart table.

"We're not set nearly as much by the current as I thought. We're doing alright. We won't have to use the engine as much."

"I'm afraid it won't do any good." Jesse crouched by the bunk.

"Why?"

"The leaking's worse. With the engine off, I've got two pumps going just to keep up with it. At this rate, our gas will only hold out about five more days."

"Son of a bitch." Sidell stabbed his pencil into the table. "You sure?"

"Pretty damn sure. And, man, that's if the leaks don't get worse. And if this weather gets worse . . ." He threw out a hand and shook his head.

"Gas," Jack muttered intently. "We got to get gas." His thoughts strained for possibilities. His depression had passed. He knew somehow they could make it. Aside from the leaks, the boat was going well. They were making good time, and his crew was organized and beginning to work with something like efficiency. He was determined not to fail, no matter what they encountered. Not here, he had insisted to himself the night before; this is the part I know best, the part I wanted. I will not fail here.

"In the Bahamas," he thought aloud. "I know places in the Bahamas we can get gas."

"Jack, I don't think we stand much chance at all of making the Bahamas. If we try we'll probably come up short in the Windward Passage, if we even make it that far, and that'll be the ball game. Let's try Jamaica."

Sidell considered it a moment but shook his head. "I don't know Jamaica, and we haven't got a decent chart. We'd have to nose around. And they're getting weird around there too these days."

"I don't think we have any choice." Mackenzie's voice was hard and insistent.

Jack chewed first on his middle finger than on his thumb and shifted nervously in the chair as he thought.

"We could try to patch her," he said, but as if he did not really mean it.

"In this sea?" Jesse was incredulous. "It's going to get worse."

"Yes," Jack answered as the captain. It was the outside shot, and it would be hard to pull off, but it could be the solution. If they could do it, it would cut the leaking and save gas until they reached the Bahamas. "Yeah," he nodded, "we'll patch this bitch."

V

Sidell wanted to dive beneath the boat himself and get started as soon as possible the next morning. But Thorton would have none of that. It would be a dangerous dive in rough waters, he insisted, and if anything happened to Jack they were through. Ralph had done some diving himself and said he would go first. Jack argued, but Thorton finally made it clear that he was simply not going to permit it. "You be a hero some other time," he said. "Now how do I mark these leaks when I find 'em?"

The pumps howled keeping up with the leaks as they made plans just off the engine room and finished the breakfast of scrambled eggs, Tang, and coffee. They decided Thorton would dive first and tack streamers of red bandana beside the leaks he found, then Jesse, who had the most experience at it, would go down to make the patches.

Thorton donned the scuba, and Jesse and Eiler took down the sails, while Jack pointed them into the stiff morning breeze. They were in the middle of the Caribbean, and the sea was craggy and hard blue, stretching away like an endless rockyard. The pitiless sun emphasized every crude wooden aspect of the boat, every grimace of Sidell's worry, each rough movement of Thorton's as he adjusted the regulator and fixed the hammer and tacks to his belt.

With the bow into them, the swell was diminished as it came past, but Thorton looked tiny as he went over the side and disappeared in the waves. The others waited mostly in silence on deck, but winced at each other with quick glances whenever *Leda*, pitching restlessly without sails or engine, came particularly hard off a swell and crashed into the trough. They had no doubt the massive hull tossing in rough water could knock a man out at the least and quite easily break a skull.

Fifteen minutes passed before Thorton surfaced. Blood flowed with the water down his high, balding forehead as they pulled him over the side. He sat heavily on the deck after shedding his gear. His eyes, as he looked at Mackenzie, showed that the dive had been enough to scare him, and few things did that.

"I found two. And one of 'em's damn big. Like this." He made a rectangle with both hands about three quarters of an inch wide and three inches long. "Right underneath the engine. Must be the main one. But I don't know how the Christ you gonna get a patch on it."

"Think we ought to wait?" Jack asked.

"No. I think the weather's picking up. Let's get it done." Jesse looked like he had prepared himself with some difficulty and did not care to have to do it again.

"What about the blood?" Jack pointed at Ralph's head. It was not a bad cut but it bled freely. "There's plenty of sharks around here. Did you just do that? Were you bleeding down there?"

"Jesus, I whacked my head twenty times. I couldn't say."

"What the hell," said Jesse. "It's not that much. Fire one of the guns. That'll keep them away. Let's get going."

Sidell went to the cabin for the magnum and fired three shots from each side. Mackenzie donned the scuba and collected the patching material. Thorton brought out the carbine just in case.

"You hear a shot," he told Jesse, "you get on back, hear?"

"Don't worry."

He was down nearly thirty minutes, and the wait was excruciating. After twenty minutes Thorton wanted to dive over and make sure Mackenzie was still there, but Jack kept him from it, saying he was more likely to give Jesse a heart attack.

When they finally pulled him back aboard, Jesse was exhausted. The wind and seas had indeed picked up, and he looked like he'd been beaten.

"I got a lot of hemp on it," he said, trying to catch his breath. "Lousy, crude job, though. But I slowed it down."

"Think it'll hold?" Jack asked, as if he were afraid of the answer.

Jesse gave his most sardonic smile. "Nothing could surprise me more."

chapter 13

i

"I HOPE it's like this," Mark spoke above the brooding growl of the twin diesels. Helen got to her knees on the couch, where she had been reading a magazine and sipping a 7-Up. She looked out the windows beside her and then forward through the windshield.

"I guess so," she answered. "There's not a soul out here."

"Yeah, but it'll be close to Christmas. There'll be a lot more people around then."

She dropped the magazine and moved up behind him at the wheel, put her arms around his stomach and hooked her chin over his shoulder.

"But didn't the kid say there still wasn't that much activity around here then?"

"There may be, if the weather's like this. I hope it isn't rough though. I wouldn't mind it just like this."

"I hope it is too, sugar. It's not easy holding two boats together. I'd hate to do it in rough water." She rubbed her lips and nose softly up and down his neck. "We almost there?"

"Just about. A few minutes more."

It was crisp but not cold for early December. The yellow winter sun was veiled with high, delicate clouds, and the dull blue Atlantic was choppy but tame. Insinger was on his first trial run since returning to Fort Rhodes Island. He had flown back to Miami from the Antilles soon after Caval's meeting with Sidell in Curaçao. From Miami, once the boat had been purchased, he had hired one of the broker's agents to familiarize him with the craft while piloting them to North Carolina. They had run at sea as far as Charleston where a mild northeaster had forced them to the Inland Waterway, and they stayed in the channel up to Fort Rhodes.

The previous day had been their first on the island, and while Helen bought groceries and supplies, Mark had found a local guide. A nineteen-year-old marine diesel mechanic, who worked in a shop at Wrightsville Beach, had given him a rundown on the boat's engines, then shown him the inlets and channels around Fort Rhodes.

Mark switched on the Loran set to his left. He read the unsteady electronic lines on its small screen and figured his position on the chart. He was almost sixteen miles offshore and near enough to the mark he had aimed for on the chart to be able to see it if it were a boat.

"There we are," he pointed. "Not bad, uh?"

"Pretty good, Admiral. Want a drink?"

"Sure." He pulled back the throttle levers to an idle so that the broad bow dropped as if landing, and then he figured a course for returning.

Helen broke ice at the wet bar in the rear of the cabin. It was a luxurious salon with a liquor cabinet, a small refrigerator beneath the bar, sumptuous carpeting, a stereo tape system, a settee, two fixed swivel chairs, and good light provided by large windows.

Mark decided to return by heading for a buoy well north of Fort Rhodes, then move southward, staying close to the shore for a good look at the island and the nearby coast, until he reached Masonboro Inlet.

The inlet worried Mark as he left the wheel, letting the boat toss freely, and went out to the afterdeck. The shoreline was faint in the distance, but he could see the taller hotels and condominiums at Wrightsville Beach. Masonboro Inlet was just to the south of them, the busy main passage in that area for boats coming and going from the open sea. There was a Coast Guard station just inside the channel, however, and Mark would have to pass it when he brought in the cargo, unless he could reach the waterway by another inlet. He feared that the cruiser, riding low in the water under five-ton loads, would attract attention coming in at night. Mason Inlet, at the south end of Fort Rhodes quite near the houses, was a possible alternative, but a dangerous one. There was always surf across the inlet, and it was usually too shallow to allow anything larger than a speedboat to pass, and even then the surf made it precarious. When Mark had asked about it the previous day as they passed by it, the kid had smiled at his ignorance. He said he had often fished in the inlet and that at high tide when the wind came either from the east or northeast there was enough water on the north side for anything to pass. "But 'at surf's purdy rough then too, an' wuth a nice boat lack this un, anybody'd jus go on down Masonboro." The kid talked like he had a mouth full of grits. "You could do it, but 'ere wouldn' be no point riskin' it." Mark had smiled back at him.

Helen put on a tape before coming out, and strains of electric guitar reverberated and lingered over the water. It did not distract Insinger as he resolved to make a study of Mason Inlet and thought again of the Coast Guard.

"What are you thinking?" Helen asked. She sat in the fighting chair and propped her feet on the transom. She wore faded corduroy pants and sailing moccasins with heavy socks. She looked a little bundled, with a thick New England sweater over a turtleneck. Her hair was straight but teased full by the wind, and her face was rosy in the winter air. Mark thought perhaps she looked her best when she had been outdoors, but there was no way she ever looked that he didn't like.

"Coast Guard," Mark replied distantly as he studied her. "I wonder if they can see us."

"You mean with a telescope or something? I'm sure they could if they wanted to. Why don't you plan to meet further north."

"I think I will. But I just wonder what kind of equipment they have for observation. I'm sure they'll notice *Leda* when it gets here."

"I know." Helen sounded peeved suddenly and a little frightened. "I still can't believe you guys got a place right beside the Coast Guard. Even if they don't see you, you have to go right by them. Going in at night will probably attract attention around here. And if they take a look at you, you're going to be loaded down like a camel."

"I may not go in there."

"Oh Mark, you're crazy if you try to go in that other inlet. You don't know how dangerous that is. Through that surf. If you ran aground in there, it'd be all over. For you and Jack too, probably. You'd be lucky if you didn't drown."

"If I go in there, I'll know damn well what I'm doing." Mark was touchy whenever she implied that he had little knowledge of boating. He had begun to realize that she measured all men against her brother.

"Promise me you won't try to do that," she said plaintively.

"No," he said resentfully. He turned away from her and sipped the vodka and tonic as he stared toward the shore. "I'm not going in there if it's more dangerous than passing the Coast Guard," he told himself, "but if it's possible, I'll do it if I have to."

"We'd better get back," he said a few moments later. "Caval ought to be calling. I should have had you stay at the house in case he called while I was out."

When he started up the ladder to the bridge, Helen said, "Why don't you stay down here?"

"I want to be on the bridge going in. That's where I'll be when we're loaded."

"It's no different," she said impatiently.

"Unless you're going to be driving this thing, I think I'll do it my way."

The pressure of recent events and the rapidity with which his responsibilities were concentrating had begun to change Insinger. He had always acted with a certain hesitation, a concern for how his actions might be viewed by others. Through much of the deal he had been so enamoured of what he was doing—and what it looked like to others—that it was as if he stood to the side of himself judging, criticizing, admiring whatever he did. In recent months, though, he had learned well that despite its high points, the operation was no glory ride. Unless he prepared and executed, unless he dealt carefully with Caval, in short, unless he worked damn hard, he could very easily get killed, go to prison, or perhaps worse—finish with nothing but the memory of how close he had been. So he was in gear now. He had a lot to do, and he did not care how it looked or sounded to anyone else.

Similarly he was no longer so captivated by Helen. He loved her still and felt capable of loving her forever, but he still expected to be hurt again, so he had defenses. He had been burned badly enough the first time to have been cauterized a little. And yet she had come back to him. She was human to him now, no longer a dream. They had traveled together too, which had revealed a great deal, sometimes too much, and they knew each other well. He could speak his mind to her, was not afraid to grow angry at her. And Helen preferred the change. She had had doting men enough. And she appreciated Mark's awareness that inevitably they would part again, because it acknowledged her freedom, left a door open. He had been accurate back in Boston that morning. She was largely along for the ride.

Insinger headed back on a course almost due north. He had taken off the canopy above the bridge, because the boat looked better without it, and it felt good to be in the open with his jacket zipped tight and the wind sharp in his face.

If I had more time, he thought, I'd know this job perfectly. I'd know the tides, the weather. I'd know this boat like I know my body. I'd damn well know the Coast Guard. I'd know when and why and where they go out. I'd know if they notice boats coming in at night. I should have had more time. Tom's always in such a goddamn hurry. Millions of bucks at stake, and he has to rush it. And I thought he was so cool. Thought he knew everything. He's good, okay, or we wouldn't be this far along, but Sidell's got better sense. Tommy'd say it doesn't take good sense—it just takes guts. But I wouldn't mind a little good sense in the bargain. Rush, rush, rush. The old man used to say that, if a deal has to happen fast, you probably ought to steer clear of it. Yeah. Must be nice to be able to say that. But he's right. Look at this damn boat deal. Had to happen so goddamn fast. Now my ass is hanging bare in the breeze. There could be a real tough lesson in that one.

Back in Miami, when Mark and Helen had returned from

Curaçao, the money for the boat had come in at the last minute. Everything had to be hurried. And in the process the papers had come back with his name on them in addition to that of the corporation. There had been no time to change it. If anything went wrong, Mark's would be the only real name connected with the operation. That error had lent the most bracing seriousness to the work.

It was a good boat, though, and Mark liked it even more than the Pacemaker he'd had in Maine. It was a forty-four-foot custom boat built five years earlier by a yard in New Jersey. Its owner in Florida had been one of many who were flooding the power-boat market at that time, in panic over expected rises in fuel costs. It was well worth $60,000, and Mark had gotten it for $42,500. Ahead of the salon, a companionway led down to a full galley, head, and shower on the starboard side. Opposite the galley was a dinette and a good-sized port cabin. With a large forecastle as well, it was a well-appointed boat and had plenty of room for the load. Mark especially liked the power of the two GM 871 diesels. And he liked its name: *Errant.*

He reached the buoy on his course and headed southwest a half mile off the coast. When he had passed along Fort Rhodes, Mark slowed, drew even with Mason Inlet. The wind was northerly that afternoon and only slight, but the surf across the inlet was threatening nevertheless. It gave Mark a thrill to envision himself powering recklessly through the breakers, knowing that he had the room to make it, knowing in the darkness just when to make the turn into the channel that would bring them right up behind the house.

Helen had come up to the bridge when he slowed down. His hands were tight on the wheel, as he saw himself crashing out of the surf, and giving full throttle on the port engine, as he wheeled into the channel. When she saw why he had stopped, Helen gazed cooly at him from the corners of her eyes and imagined his thoughts.

"It'd be a hell of a ride," he grinned at her.

They moved on down to the Masonboro Inlet and then up the waterway toward the drawbridge, which was the entrance to the island from the mainland. One hundred yards before the bridge, however, there was a small triangular piece of marshland always visible. The local kid had showed Mark that, by turning just before or after it, one entered the deep channel that curved behind the island, passed in back of the houses Mark had rented, and then reached the Mason Inlet.

214

Mark moved slowly down the channel, making sure no one was outside any of the houses. Reaching the house they would use for storage, he veered away and turned toward the house, approaching slowly. The sandy shore behind the house sloped into the channel at roughly a thirty-degree angle. Mark had determined the previous day that he could probably beach the cruiser for the unloading. He moved the boat cautiously toward shore, until the bow scraped snugly into the sand.

"Plenty of room," he said happily as he put the engines in neutral and felt the boat fast against the shore. He could have jumped easily from the deck to dry land. "As long as my props are in the water enough, I'll be able to pull off in reverse. I could go up further than this."

Helen nodded. "But you won't have any props if you try to come through that little inlet."

Mark laughed and pulled her close to him and kissed the side of her face. He felt he had things well in hand.

He reversed his engines, pulled easily off the shore, and moved on down the channel. At its end, as he turned in toward the waterway, he again confronted Mason Inlet, seeing its surf curl slowly into white foam. As he turned away from it, he kept well to starboard where the inlet channel had been deepest the day before. He could see the waterway not far ahead and nothing seemed very difficult. He pushed the throttles forward a little more, and looked back over his shoulder at the inlet one more time. Although it was shallow enough along the south side, he could tell from the smaller surf that it was much deeper near the island. I could make it in there, he told himself. And it's not even high tide yet. Hell, I could run this baby out there right now.

"Mark!" Helen screamed from the afterdeck. "Get over. It's shallow here. It's shifted."

He wasted a split second looking up to determine which way to go when there was only one way to go. They were already scraping bottom when he turned hard to port. In the space of two seconds, the grinding grew louder and louder. He pulled back the throttles, but too late. The engines died just as the boat scraped to a halt.

Mark said nothing but closed his eyes and pounded the control panel. "Reverse," he finally shouted instead of cursing. "Should've reversed it, you stupid bastard."

"I'm sorry," said Helen. "I should've been watching, I should've told you sooner."

"No. Hell. It was my fault. What're you going to do, ride on the bow for me all the time?"

"I would."

Mark managed to smile at her. He was not ashamed before her, because she knew him much too well, and he was not angry over the mistake, because inevitably he would make errors. But he was sure he had damaged a prop, and that would cost him precious days of practice.

Gradually, over the next hour, helped by the rising tide, Insinger manipulated the cruiser back and forth with the port engine until they were finally free. He started the starboard engine as they headed carefully on to the waterway, but it screeched horribly when he put it in gear. They returned to the marina in a desultory silence, and the next morning Mark motored down to the Bradley Creek Marina near Wrightsville. By paying a virtual bribe and insisting that he had a special party of guests arriving, he managed to get the shaft straightened by the next day.

When Helen picked him up at the marina in their rental car, she told him that Caval had called and would call again. Typically the call did not come until almost one in the morning, and then the voice at the other end sounded like an old woman. "Tom?" Mark asked incredulously.

"Yeah," the voice wheezed. "How's it going?"

"Where in hell are you?" Mark demanded, ignoring the unusual sound of Caval's voice.

"I'm in Santa Marta. I've been in the hospital." Tom spoke as if with his last effort.

"Jesus, man, you were supposed to be here before me. We've got to get those houses. We've got all kinds of arrangements to be making. What're you doing in the hospital?"

"I've been really sick, Mark. It's some kind of brain fever. They don't know what it is."

Oh, for Christ's sake, Mark thought. "What d'ya mean brain fever? Who's they."

"The doctors. It's really been bad, Mark. They thought I was gonna die."

From what he knew of Tom Caval, Insinger simply could not believe the story. Tom was a man who traveled and lived with twenty different bottles of pills and had two or three medical conditions always ready to afflict him when he needed an excuse, or did not care to perform some necessary labor, and wanted a means of getting someone else to do it for him. It seemed much more likely to Insinger that life at Playa Blanca accounted for the delay.

"Well, I hope you're feeling better because you've got to hurry up and get here. We have to get those houses, and we have to set up the radio on the boat. There's not much time."

"I won't be able to get the houses," Tom said pitifully. "I don't have the money anymore. Somebody broke into the house and ripped me off. We won't be able to do those houses. I've got heavy hospital bills here too. We just can't get those extra houses."

"We have to have those houses," Mark said tensely.

"Can't do it. Just can't do it."

I don't believe it, Mark thought, one thing after another. I just don't believe it.

"When are you coming in? You've got to get back here. Just get on a plane. You can be taken care of here if you have to."

"I've tried, but they wouldn't let me travel. I'm gonna try it again Friday though. Could you pick me up in Charleston?"

"Charleston?"

"I can't hassle with making four stops on Piedmont to get to Wilmington. I'm really sick, man,"

"Alright. Okay. When, in Charleston?"

Caval gave him the information, and shortly they hung up. Insinger sat stunned at the kitchen table. All that dope's going to be on this island with god knows what goons traipsing out here to load it up. It'll be a fucking circus. And I'm the figurehead. That son of a bitch has got my head out in front of this thing. He got me right out front. I'm on the boat. I rented the houses. Jesus Christ. And I don't have a deal. I don't have anything yet.

chapter 14

i

A BRUTE gust of wind slammed into *Leda* and made her heel hard to port for almost a full minute. About forty knots, Jack reckoned with a low whistle. Thorton, trying to sleep in the after cabin, cussed at it as he had at all the big ones for the past two days. It was stiff weather and still picking up, but it was strong enough to really move the boat, so they were making good time. Since patching the previous morning, Jack figured the average wind had increased gradually from about fifteen to twenty knots. Gusts had been frequent and were starting to get mean. Sidell knew people who would have called it—with trepidation—half a gale, but to him it was good hardass sailing. The leaking had not been cut to a safe level, but the patches were holding even in the tough seas. Since the patching, the bilge had been under control with only one of the gas pumps when the engine was off, so matters at least seemed to be vastly improved. With each hour, Jack grew a little more amazed, tentatively confident, yet still slightly afraid that something had to bust. The gustiness of the wind kept the seas high, rough, hard-blue, and white-capping at ten feet and more. Old *Leda* worked hard in it, and still the leaking did not increase. At moments Sidell felt almost invincible in the strength of her mass against the collision of a sudden gust or the threatening smash of a big wave. Yet in the shadows of his thought, there was the abiding precognition that over each glassy, foaming hump of water he moved closer to some inescapable trouble.

Joe Eiler came on deck near noon, emerging unsteadily as he carried a bowl of canned chili over rice, with crackers and a cup of powdered milk for Sidell's lunch. He staggered coming around to the stern as *Leda* dove off a big swell, and he had to fall against the cabin to keep from losing the dishes. Jack laughed at him.

"I'll throw this shit on ya," Joe yelled back over the rushing water. "Here, le' me drive."

Joe took the helm, while Jack stayed at one side of the wheelhouse and gobbled the hot meal, grunting a few times with a full mouth that it was delicious. "Good meal," he stated when he finished, wiping chili out of a week's growth of beard with the back of his hand. Jack was very dark from his days at the wheel, but his hair had lightened and the beard made his face larger and more determined.

"We're hanging in here pretty good," he yelled at Eiler. Joe turned at the understatement. Jack grinned and spoke stronger. "Pretty damn good."

The sun emerged suddenly and hot from behind one of the strange, ragged clouds proceeding overhead in nervous haste. Standing in its heat, Sidell passed one of those moments when a man can feel the nature of his life, the temper of his spirit in the physical elements around him, and is inspired by a oneness with the world.

The decks reflected the attitude of their enterprise. They were reefed twice against the strong wind, and the main and mizzen were each sheeted off to the strongest holds available. Preventing lines were tied from each gaff and boom, to keep the motion of the boat from jerking the sails too violently against the masts and rigging. Everything else visible was made fast enough, with Thorton's love of ropes and knots, to withstand an explosion. Ahead of him, the maze of rigging towered straining, heavy red sails bent to the wind, shrouds, halyards, preventing ropes pulled taut in every direction, the scarred yellow and brown wood of the great masts, the aged strength of the booms each fringed with a perfect line of short ropes from the reef ties curving with the wind. Beneath it, the oak deck swept forward, busy with the cabin, the hatches, skylights, lockers, equipment lashed down, forward to the Whaler, made fast against the starboard gunwhale, to the big iron windlass, the headsails tied down on the bowsprit. It might have seemed huge if it were not always lifting and rolling and falling in an infinity of restless, steel-blue water, which continually rose around them to block the horizon, foaming as if it awaited some meal, thrusting them up again for a view of its vastness, and pulling them down again. And if the wind were not always flexing its mysterious muscles to demonstrate the possibilities of its dominance. And if the sky were not so endless, and if the sun had not seen centuries of strong men and fine ships go down, then there might have been real confidence. As it was, there was too much assurance of smallness and frailty. Jack knew it well, but knew also that theirs was an ancient effort, and men had done far greater things against far larger odds. They were tiny and patched and bandaged and virtually tied together, but it could be done. They might just do it.

A furious gust pushed them off balance and tore whining through the rigging. It bullied them off course, and before Eiler could right them a huge odd wave leaped over the starboard side, sent its spray all over Jack and Eiler and washed across the deck.

"Got to stay right on her," Jack yelled, shaken from his thoughts. "She means business."

Eiler nodded and worked at keeping their course in the strong waves that seemed to pursue the gust. It was like driving a big truck over a tough road and required a continuous exertion. "Some of these babies are about twenty feet, aren't they?"

"Closer to half that," Jack yelled back with a smile. "Seas are generally about half what they seem. Same with the wind usually. But not many people like to admit it. She's honkin' pretty good today, though."

"You don't mind if I lie about it when we get home, do ya?"

"It's a great tradition."

ii

Eiler discarded the five of hearts, and Jesse thought it over. He had the five of diamonds but with two trios and a pair already. Something told him to take it though. Fives had usually been good to him. It was early in the game, too, and he had a feeling he was going to gin. Eiler observed the move and made his own, taking a draw. Jesse was perched on a milk crate, leaning back against the galley counter, and they placed their cards on an upended one-gallon fruit tin. Eiler was more comfortable in one of Margaret's cane chairs, but his right elbow was braced against the cargo supports for balance against the boat's motion. A lantern in the galley challenged the unsteady darkness of the hold with a dreamy yellow light. A single bulb in the engine room gave little help. Two auxiliary pumps growled wearily and loudly, but their noise was easier to get used to than the acrid smell of their exhaust. Massive timbers and the great dark bulk of cargo around them heaved in constant rhythm with the rushing wind and sea. It was four-thirty in the morning, and they paid dull but practiced attention to the game.

Near sundown, just when Sidell and Mackenzie had speculated that it could not blow much longer, the weather had again increased. The wind was averaging well over twenty knots by midnight, and seas arrived with a momentum that seemed to have accumulated over the past three days. In the forecastle, Eiler had been awakened by the hard pitching of the boat, felt nauseous as he lay there, and had to move about. He had found Mackenzie on the pump watch, and they resumed their running game of rummy. Mackenzie had been on the losing end of it since their first games back in Aruba and, at a nickel a point, owed a fair amount of money, but he was always ready for a chance to change his luck. He was growing a little suspicious over the fact that it never altered.

Jesse glanced at a draw and threw it away. The irregular, sometimes violent pitch and roll of the boat barely phased him, but Eiler felt like he was in the belly of a whale and invariably groaned some long obscenity whenever the motion was sudden or hard. Joe took Mackenzie's discard and threw a seven. Jesse promptly added it to his other three sevens, and had to decide whether to keep his pair of fives or the pair of threes. Stick with the fives, he figured. He was certain he could gin, and the game was quite young, the discard pile not yet large enough to slide much. He would kill Eiler this time; his luck had to change. He threw the three. Joe picked it up, thought a moment, and showed Mackenzie the five of spades.

"I guess you'd hurt me with that one," he ruminated, then put the card face down. "I'll just go for nine."

"No," Jesse whined incredulously. Seeing he could not play off, he flung his cards at the can. "Goddamn son of a bitch," he stormed. "One fucking point." He stood angrily and headed for the engine room.

"That all?" Joe asked disinterestedly. He was bored and bilious and tired. "Where you going?"

"One of the goddamn pumps is clogged. Can't ya hear, ya lucky, fucking . . ."

A long description of Eiler merged into the racket of the pumps. Mackenzie killed one of them and deftly removed its intake filter, cleaned it, replaced it, and started the thing again. A constant necessity in monitoring the pumps was to clean debris from the intakes, and everyone knew the muffled sound of a clogged pump and could fix it blindfolded.

In his anger Mackenzie had not bothered to check the bilge before fixing the pump. But once he took a look the money he owed Joe became insignificant. In the early evening, the rough seas had begun to take their toll, and new leaks forward and around the stern tube had forced him to start a second auxiliary pump when the engine was off. Now as he looked, the water was coming high in the bilge, clearly outstripping the discharge. "Here we go again," he muttered painfully. "Come 'ere you poor, tired bastard," he addressed the third auxiliary, as he pulled it into place along the port side of the engine. It had sounded bad earlier in the day, so he had used the others instead, betting there would be time to fix it later. He pulled the rope to start it, and it joined the noise of the other two with an uneven hollow sound. The compression was going, he figured, maybe the carburetor. He was too tired to hassle with it, and at the moment it seemed useless.

Jesse skulked into the half light of the galley, poured himself another cup of coffee, and puttered with the sugar.

"You better get over here an' get crackin'," Joe kidded him without much spirit. He glanced at the score sheet. "You're down about five hundred. Uh, four hundred eighty-six—"

"Piss on you and your lucky goddamn five hundred bucks."

Jesse wandered wearily around to his seat again, nevertheless.

"We leakin' again?" Joe inquired. The dark hold was particularly oppressive just then, filled with his question, Jesse's anger, the endless roll and pitch, the abominable din of the two-cycle pump engines, and the stench of their exhaust.

"Yup." Mackenzie looked straight at him, his mouth very tight and thin.

"What's wrong with this pump?" Joe jerked his thumb toward the noise. "Sounds fucked."

"It is. Deal."

iii

The wind slackened during the first hours of daylight, but by eleven it resumed with a vengeance. The seas had not rested a moment. They were twelve and fourteen feet, and with narrower troughs dividing them, they charged at *Leda*. The yellow-white sun blazed, and gray clouds careened overhead like garbage blown across a great emptiness. The discomfort of the waves and the schedule of watches was telling on the crew. To everyone the thing of primary importance was sleep. Joe was trying desperately to keep eyes closed for a few minutes before having to concoct a lunch. Ralph had finished his watch at six o'clock and lain down immediately in the aft cabin. Mackenzie, tired and disgusted and further in debt, decided to work on the bad pump later. He had started the engine at eight-thirty, then took the other bunk in the cabin.

Sidell, alone at the wheel, was getting punchy. He had been there since six, except when Jesse relieved him briefly for breakfast and a look at the leakage and pumps. From the endlessness of churning sea and the slow struggle of the boat's motion, his mind sought shelter. Even in the strong weather, whole hours had passed during which he seemed not to have paid a moment of attention to what was going on around him. Instead he had thought of Charlotte or Aspen or other things far away. He spoke aloud a few times and laughed at himself. By noon the weather was requiring more concentration though, and Jack tried to pick his way through the steepening swell, laying off the wind a bit over the bigger ones to hit the next a little easier. With the main and mizzen both completely reefed and only the forestaysail up, they were still making close to seven knots. Each wave parted with a solid bump

222

and a fan of splash above the bow that showered the deck. *Leda* lurched over them and dropped suddenly, met the next wave with another jolt and another explosion of spray. Then rose and dropped and struck the next one, rose and dropped and struck the next one. Hour after hour.

It was just after noon when they came over a particularly steep sea and the constant hum of wind and roar of waves and whistle and clatter of rigging was ripped by a tremendous metallic screeching. The whole aft end of the boat shuddered with the sound and shook Jack utterly awake. So sudden was *Leda*'s descent from the wave that her prop had come out of the water, revving wildly in the air. Sidell stiffened with alarm and instinctively fell off the wind a little, to take the swell more angularly. The troughs were deep and brief though. He no sooner crashed through one and rose like an elevator on the next wave, than the prop came out again and the shaft shook the boat and screeched like a banshee. Jack started to yell but the noise had already raised Ralph and Jesse, and they scrambled out with shocked faces.

"Get up there on the sheets," Jack ordered. "Get Joe up here. We got to change course. Free the damn sheets."

Mackenzie and Thorton, scared out of half-sleeps, rushed awkwardly to the work. Bringing the prop out a few more times would damage the diesel at the very least, and more likely shake out every ounce of caulking in the stern hull.

The first time it happened, Sidell thought it was only a freak wave. After the second time, coming so soon upon the first, he could not take any chances, yet still thought it was merely a few odd seas. For a half hour, though, the seas came close together and steep as cliff walls, and every fifth or sixth one, and sometimes twice in a row, the air was rent by the squall of the exposed shaft and propeller. Each time Sidell stiffened as if he'd been stabbed, shouted wild curses, and changed the course slightly more. He could not believe what was occurring. It was simply not supposed to happen.

Struggling on the deck to change sails as Sidell ordered, Mackenzie, Eiler, and Thorton staggered wearily with the boat's violent motion. Jack moved off the wind until the waves threatened to throw the boat on her side, came up again gradually looking for a safe slant, and finally even came completely about to a port tack. Yet every few minutes, the capricious seas threw *Leda*'s stern into the air, and she screamed and shook like an old woman goosed. The waves that loomed above them each time the bow fell seemed not like water at all but like the hard scaled back of some undulating monster.

"Turn the goddamn thing off," Sidell shouted at last. Thorton went below with Jesse to kill the engine and start the auxiliary pumps.

"Jesus, look at it comin' in," said Ralph. They both peered into the bilge where water rose steadily around the engine. "I bet we loosened up ever' one of them engine mounts."

"Yeah." Jesse sounded too tired to care. "We're in for it now."

They hurriedly started the gas pumps, but the lame one barely ran. They agreed quickly it was the carburetor and heaved the thing onto the workbench to fix it. The engine room throbbed with the howl of the pumps, filled with acrid carbon monoxide. As the boat rose and fell, they kept colliding clumsily as they tried to fathom what was wrong.

"I just can't figure the thing out," Mackenzie said after several minutes. He turned away toward the other pumps to see what he might learn looking at them. The bilge was completely full and water was up on the floorboards. It was as if the pumps were doing nothing. "Well, shit," Jesse spoke slowly and despondently. "I guess this is it. You better get Joe and get on the deck pump. Tell Jack we're sinking."

As he came to the wheel, Thorton's features behind the beard grown thick and brown since Aruba begged Jack for orders, planning, direction, as he told him what had happened. Eiler too looked for some assessment, some hope. Was it really possible they were sinking? Was this the finish? But Jack merely stared past them toward some indefinite point far ahead and saw at the moment no alternative, no possibility of reprieve. He shook his head almost sadly and simply said, "Pump like hell."

It was much like hell. For hours, through the heat and gusting wind of the afternoon and the relentless pitch and roll of the deck, they took turns at the pump. When the wind picked up still more and it became nearly as hard to keep footing as to keep working the pump, Mackenzie came up, and he and Eiler lowered the mainsail altogether. *Leda* hardly slowed at all, but steadied somewhat and the pumping went on while Jesse returned to the engine room.

The deck pump was a heavy, manual beast set flush with the boards just ahead of the mizzenmast and operated by a long steel lever usually kept fastened against the rear of the new deck. To force water up from the bilge required a full downward thrust from the shoulders to the knees again and again and again, an effort

224

that discharged the water freely onto the deck to flow away out the scuppers. It was brute labor, exhausting as chopping wood, yet with never a real sign of progress. Going fast or slow at it made little difference, but while the most furious efforts were of course the most wilting, they did manage to reduce the rate of discharge. Yet only a few moments later, a new thrust on the lever sent a broad stream across the deck. To go slowly was easier on the body, but then the depressing volume of sea transferred through the boat never lessened.

Below, Mackenzie worked diligently on the third gas pump, although it would only reduce slightly the immediate labor and certainly not solve the problem. He repaired the carburetor, only to find that it still lacked power and that the piston rings were shot, so he had to completely dismantle the thing. The fumes and the boat's motion and the complication were as taxing as the slavery above him. Time and again, the movement and his fatigue required an entire maddening minute just to line up a screwdriver or fit a wrench to a nut.

By late afternoon, after four grueling hours, it seemed that the sea would win. Sidell and Thorton and Eiler were stuporous, sagging over the lever as they worked. There was no strength for talking, and they relieved each other only when the one working became so wretched with fatigue that he was accomplishing nothing but to further tire himself. The physical strain accumulated in a dizziness, a strange sharpness of vision, black flecks rising before the eyes, and the screaming of muscles. Every sense and tendon protested the hopelessness of the situation.

Eiler finally voiced it, as he took over the lever for another turn. "We can't just keep doing this."

"What the hell else we gonna do?" Thorton yelled at him from the wheel. Sidell lay face down across the skylights of the new deck having just finished fifteen minutes at the pump, his lungs heaving. "We're gonna pump all the way to North Carolina if we have to. Now git goin', Joe."

Joe pumped. He pumped with an amazement that his body could continue, as if it knew separately that there was no alternative but to be as resolute as the seas that demanded the work.

Just before six o'clock, Jesse finally had the third pump running. It did not greatly diminish the labor on deck, but enough to allow an occasional break and added Jesse's back to the task, which seemed like divine intervention.

Sidell finished another turn at the pump and, for the first time in many hours, had a few moments to wonder where he was. Taking the sextant, he wedged himself against the cabin for stability and took a fix on the departing sun. Several minutes later at the chart table, he found that Haiti was only eighty miles to the north-northwest. In his exhaustion he found it difficult to believe he was still making good time and was well on course for Navassa Island, off the southeast tip of Haiti, and the approach to the Windward Passage.

His thoughts brightened for a moment. He thought he had noticed the wind slackening. They might get a break. They would raise Haiti easily by morning. They could take the chance of looking for a cove. Patch again. They'd done it in rough seas; they could do it well if they could find calm water. But Haitian authorities were known to occasionally board and sometimes seize odd vessels coming close to their shores. And that would be curtains. Probably the most dismal of prisons. But there was no choice but to risk it. They could do it fast, rest a bit, then get moving again, around the point and into the passage.

"Windward Passage," he muttered. His brief optimism dissolved in misery at the prospect. How the hell are we ever going to make it through there?

The Windward is the main passage between the Caribbean and the North Atlantic, crossing from the Bahamas toward Jamaica between Haiti and Cuba. Its principal boundaries, Punta Maisí and Cap á Foux, concentrate prevailing winds and currents and send them rushing to the southwest through a tight stretch only fifty miles wide, producing characteristically treacherous seas, hence its name, coined with no affection.

Leda would probably have to spend two full days beating into the teeth of steadily strengthening wind and current, merely to reach the main eastern stretch of the passage, where conditions were always roughest. Heavier than normal weather would make it virtually impossible, while the political natures of Cuba and Haiti would make seeking refuge nearly as dangerous. Sidell recalled frequent stories of massive container cargoes being bucked from the decks of large freighters during storms in the passage. And I'm going through there with a bunch of goddamn Band-Aids on the hull? he thought. It did not seem possible that he had actually placed himself, step by step, in these circumstances. For months the Windward Passage had been an enigma in his thoughts and plans, yet now it loomed diabolically, representing the consequences of all his errors coming due. Acquiescing to Caval's haste, to his disregard for precautions, his refusal to put the boat in drydock again, taking chances with his investment, not insuring that his reward would justify the danger, all promised to compress against him as surely as the wind and sea.

Desperately he desired some possibility of an alternative route. He stared at the chart until it swam in the fatigue of his eyes. Finally the crank and wash of the deck pump, the noise of auxiliaries from the engine room, then Thorton calling from the wheel about their position brought him back to immediate reality. There was simply no turning back, nothing but pressing on, somehow. "First things first," he whispered firmly to himself getting up. "I better just see if I can keep from sinking tonight."

The wind began to subside by about eight o'clock and, over the next three hours, nearly vanished. The seas kept up, running ten and twelve feet, but without the wind they gradually lengthened and seemed comfortable compared to the swell of the afternoon. The last of the hateful wind swept away the clouds, so that the night awoke with stars, and the world seemed pleased with itself.

Thorton spoke of the break in weather with an almost religious awe. "Like a miracle, ain't it? Just when we had to have it." But Joe Eiler found it unworthy of trust and a rather frightening indication of the capriciousness of the sea.

The pumping continued all through the night. Conditions were much better, but bodies were wracked from the day's ordeal. Nevertheless, smoother waters diminished the leaking, and Mackenzie divided a watch. Each man steered an hour, monitored the pumps an hour, spent an hour at the deck pump, working five or ten minutes out of each twenty, and finally slept an hour. Exhaustion was monumental, but the watch was effective. In the early morning hours, in the silence left by the weather, they played some of Delight's tapes. Billy seemed to have died years ago.

iv

At dawn Eiler was on the deck pump. His back, shoulders, arms, and thighs had come to the point at which they were not in pain only when he was pumping. As he stopped, having again reduced the discharge to a dribble for what seemed like the thousandth time, he could stand upright only with agonizing care. He found Sidell looking at him from the wheel over the top of the cabin. Jack smiled at the sight of him, standing in underwear, sweating, arms suspended from his sides by taut tendons, his russet hair faded and thickened by sun and salt, standing almost on end, hard gray eyes glazed like old porcelain. He stared back like a zombie until Sidell pointed ahead and called: "Hispañola."

Out of a thin mist over the gray water, Haiti rose dark and mysterius five miles off against the charcoal sky. If Joe had seen the gates of heaven he would not have been more relieved or surprised. "We made it," he gasped.

"This far, anyway," Jack corrected.

The first real light showed dense green jungle climbing steeply out of the water, without any sign of life other than a few twists of smoke from morning campfires far apart. The merest breeze carried *Leda* close to the shore, and Jesse and Ralph lowered her sails about a mile off Baie Anglais. They dropped anchor in about twenty fathoms of nearly flat water. The prospect of making good repairs and the fact that no one cared to spend much time hanging around Haitian shores brought out the patching supplies and scuba equipment with amazing energy.

Jesse was ready to get started when Eiler came forward from the cabin with the .41 magnum in his hand. Jack was uneasy seeing Joe Eiler half-naked clutching the big revolver.

Jack said, "Hang on, Joe. I don't think we ought to fire any shots around here."

"Okay," Joe shrugged. He turned the pistol up and glanced down the barrel, then nodded at Mackenzie. "Think the sharks'd like us to rub a little mayonnaise on him?"

"Jesus Christ!" Jesse snapped. He already had on the tank and fins and was adjusting the mask.

"We want to attract as little attention as possible," Jack said firmly. No one had cared for Joe's remark. "We'll keep watch with the carbine. If we see anything we'll fire. And you get your ass back up."

Jesse closed his eyes and said, "Splendid." He gave Eiler a contemptuous look as he went over the side.

Mackenzie disappeared dreamily into the quiet water, and he and Thorton spent the next three hours trading time beneath the hull. They found serious leaks around each engine mount and another hole almost as big as a fist. In addition they patched a few smaller leaks along the starboard topside, while Eiler and Sidell took turns between the pumps and keeping watch with the carbine. By eleven o'clock, with the heat rising, they lay around the deck, and the bilge was emptying with only one gas pump.

228

The green mountains lay peaceful and beautiful against the clear sky, and the indigo water was flat and soft and only occasionally traveled by an errant breeze. They lay quietly beneath the warm sun, weary to the bones, but now pleasantly so. A freighter that had appeared earlier passed close enough on its way into the passage that crewmen were visible waving from an upper deck in the stern. The ship was small, white, clean, civilized. From *Leda* they gaped back at it without a gesture. It was the first sign of other humanity they had seen since the attack off Colombia. It felt as if for the past five days they had been traveling some bleak and dangerous highway in the middle of night. And, given the normal shipping routes and the time of year, that was roughly what they had done. A tanker appeared not long after the other ship, heading southwest out of the passage, slow, distant, and alien.

A vacuous calm followed their travail, and it seemed to extend from their very marrow through the strong worn oak of the deck to the calm water stretching toward an infinite horizon in the west. In the stillness, Hispañola loomed like a silent planet. Unseen in the distance lay Cuba, the converging seas, and—with equal certainty—more travail.

The somnolent tranquility continued until Mackenzie bestirred himself near noon to check below and returned to say incredulously that the bilge was almost dry. They began to talk again and to move around a little as if returned from the dead. Sidell slept like a rock on the deck, but Jesse went below to turn on some music and roll up a joint. Eiler made coffee, toast, and scrambled eggs, and Thorton found a hand fishing line with a large lure that Mackenzie had used years before and began casting off the stern, singing along with the music. Just before Eiler delivered the breakfast, Ralph felt a heavy tug on his line and started yelling like a kid as he hauled it in hand over hand until he produced, flopping on the deck, a silvery blue six-pound Mahi Mahi that glistened in the sunlight. The catch and the prospect of a big fresh meal that evening added considerably to the reviving spirits. They spent another hour on the deck after the breakfast, smoked more dope, and drank another pot of coffee while they listened to music and a few times even laughed. At about one o'clock, Sidell came happily out of the cabin to say he had picked up a weather report from the Bahamas.

"There's a good high-pressure zone. I figure it will be easy weather for at least the next twenty-four hours. So let's get moving."

An hour later they had rounded the tip of Haiti to find the waters approaching Windward Passage in one of their rare benevolent moods. Long easy swells stretched endlessly before them beneath a clear sky, and the water seemed thick and soft after the mean seas of the last few days. They set full sail against a soft easterly breeze and motored on course for Punta Maisí. Sleeping two at a time, they passed by far the most pleasant day of their voyage, waving at passing freighters, taking pictures, lying on deck with nothing to do and—for the moment, at least—nothing to fear. When the evening began to cool, Eiler stuffed the big fish with canned tomatoes, lemons, and a little bit of everything else he could find in the galley, wrapped it in foil, and baked what was acclaimed without dissent a masterpiece. The last warm bottles of Amstel beer, stashed away since Aruba, came out for dessert, and once again they were riding high.

chapter 15

i

THEY neared the end of the road, just before the turn that headed back to the house, and Insinger could feel the overcast sky merging with the gray Atlantic beyond the beach. He pulled his folded arms defensively against his chest. The drive from the marina was not long enough to warm up the heater, and he could not overcome the chill he had gotten on the boat. The island seemed utterly without warmth. The open spaces with tall, light brown grass and pale sand were as cold to him as the starkly weathered wood of houses along the beach and the curious stares of residents arrived for the holidays. "What's he out on a boat alone for on a day like this?" he imagined them asking one another. "There's a bunch of other weird looking people staying at that house too."

It had not been a very good day. He had navigated the channels well and was beginning to know them with confidence, but going out to sea he had miscalculated the current of the Gulf Stream, which was strong that day and close to shore, and he had missed his mark by miles. The Loran had been unsteady and difficult to read, so he'd had virtually no idea where he was. They had an automatic directional finder, which he could have used if he had actually been out to meet *Leda*, but they had not installed it yet, and Mark rather doubted that Caval really knew how to use it. Heading back to shore he had finally found a buoy and located himself far north of the island, almost to Cape Lookout, then nearly froze coming back on the bridge.

Only Helen seemed warm, and he watched her as she drove, always fast, always with an intent, slightly harried expression. She drove the way she made love, it occurred to him, and that made him feel better, even though he knew she was not happy with him at present. He wished it were just the two of them again. The simplicity of living alone with her had made the house a refuge in the evenings against the pressure and the paranoia. They'd had it to themselves only a handful of days, but it seemed much longer. When Caval arrived, then others, that was all gone, and now there were problems all the time.

She disliked returning to the house as much as he did. She had just said her piece about it as they drove from the marina, and Mark felt acutely the inadequacy of his response and the impossibility of doing what she had suggested, although it was exactly right. Exactly right and yet impossible, he thought—the special attribute of female advice.

They were both trying to say something to change the subject. They did not want to argue. That would spoil the refuge altogether.

"Want to walk on the beach a little while?" she asked just before the turn. To her thicker Yankee blood, the weather was merely brisk.

"No, honey. I'm freezing. Let's get back."

"Okay." She turned the car with resignation. "I was out there all afternoon anyway."

The other two rental cars were parked in the open circular drive. The house was unpainted and weathered—the motif of the island—and like the others it bore the angular geometry of contemporary design, although much more modestly than homes along the beach. It was a two-story structure, built well above the sand to provide a view of the ocean, allow storage of recreational equipment beneath the rear of the house, and perhaps escape freak tides. The living area on the lower floor had full glass doors and a large deck facing the sound, and there were three bedrooms upstairs.

Caval was to be contended with as soon as they had climbed the front steps and opened the door. He sat at a large captain's table in a corner of the room, talking on the phone. Marshall Heard sat beside him and played a game of backgammon with a man named Harry Amian. Through the glass doors near the table Mark could see the other man, whose name he could never remember, Henderson or Hendrickson—they called him Don—sitting on the deck with his girlfriend Marilyn. The air was pungent and blue with marijuana.

"Well, the newlyweds are back," Caval quipped over the receiver. Amian laughed eagerly, but Heard merely looked up a moment and nodded at them as they entered the room. Caval seemed to appreciate the flashes of disdain he produced on their faces. He grinned and said, "Whatsa matter? You wreck the boat again?"

Amian laughed harder than before, and Mark started to reply, but Caval spoke to the phone again. "No," he said, "just one of my guys here. Now listen, believe me, you're gonna wanna come out here for this stuff. Yeah. Sure. But . . ."

Mark sat at the table and spoke briefly with Heard about the practice run he'd made. Heard and Amian were supposed to have gone with him to get the feel of the boat and the sea in preparation for the real off-loading, but they had decided it was too cold. Mark told Marshall of the trouble he had that afternoon and repeated that they needed to practice, that they all had to be familiar with the waters and with navigation, but Marshall did not seem very interested. "Current out there, uh?" he asked.

Amian leered and said, "Well, at least you didn't run aground again." Mark wanted to punch him in the mouth. His anger at Caval and his resentment of the others boiled in him. Amian wanted to kid a little more: "Maybe we could fix up a thing on the boat so that you—"

"Shut your fuckin' mouth," Insinger cut him off.

Amian mocked his anger with a low whistle, and they stared for a moment. But when Heard said, "Take it easy Mark," Amian smiled to himself and took his turn at backgammon. Insinger sat fuming, his brow twitching with a rage as he heard Caval on the phone.

". . . No, it's not gonna be cheap. I told ya man, this is the primo-primo stuff. No. I don't wanna talk figures now. The shit ain't even here, but when you get out we'll . . ."

Insinger felt a thorough hatred for him as he watched him talk, smug, conniving, leaning back in the chair, rubbing one of his bare feet with his free hand. Mark wondered how the son of a bitch could go barefoot in that weather. Goddamn reptile, he thought.

Since Caval had arrived, Mark's distrust and dislike had grown with that sudden speed which seems reserved for those who have been recently admired. Mark felt taken in, lied to, exploited. He had been angry that Tom stayed in Colombia instead of coming to Fort Rhodes for preparations, but he had finally accepted the idea that Caval had been seriously ill. He had driven all the way to Charleston, having fixed up the rented van to accommodate an invalid, and then Caval had come roaring off the plane as manic and domineering as ever—and suddenly healthy. Nevertheless, although Tom had the radio set with him, he had not stopped anywhere in the islands or in Florida, as they had planned to do, to make contact with *Leda*. He still refused to spend the money to rent houses off the island for distributing the load, saying he didn't have it. He had Heard and Harry Amian and the other guy meet him at the island, so he could have a proper circle of retainers about him. And they had done nothing but lie around the house smoking dope. Their comportment angered Mark as much as not getting the distribution houses, since that too had been a crucial ground rule for using Fort Rhodes. They had agreed on the necessity of mixing in with the normal family residents of the island, especially regarding dress and activities, yet Caval and his crew were as alien as Indians.

Harry Amian was an old friend of Caval's, a dealer from the East Coast, who happened to be on parole for a federal narcotics rap and was illegally outside New York. Harry was in his thirties and had a dark Armenian complexion and black hair, which often made him seem like a parody of Caval. His face was rounder than Tom's, though, and the eyes less formidable, and he was far from Caval's equal. He had a strong New York accent, having spent most of his life in Manhattan and Queens, and he seemed to dress for the part of a dealer with long hair, hip clothes, and flashy turquoise jewelry.

The other guy, named Don Hendrickson, was from Miami. He was in his late twenties, blonde and tanned, and he was as flashily attired as his friend Harry Amian, down to the turquoise. Marilyn, his blonde girlfriend, looked and acted like a hundred-dollar whore.

Marshall Heard always dressed conservatively in slacks and sportshirts, even in Aspen, but his quietness, stern narrow features, and suspicious eyes produced a threatening air that attracted attention anywhere. Caval, always in knit shirts and tennis shoes, looked more like a regular resident than any of them, but the only time he had been away from the house he went to the marina clubhouse with the others and made loud jokes about the island and its bourgeois family lifestyle. "Where are the kids?" he had cried out at one point. "Oh, my gawd," the blonde had gasped, "we left them at the airport." They had laughed hysterically, and the bar had grown quiet around them.

Mark had complained to all of them the next day, but Tom ridiculed him, said he was getting paranoid, freaking out. Tom enjoyed toying with Mark, demonstrating to the others that Mark, the attorney, was a minion. He dictated lists of supplies and errands, kidded him about his worries while the others laughed along.

On top of everything else, Mark thought, as he watched Caval on the phone, the bastard is setting up deals on the goddamn house phone. Mark was becoming truly frightened of Caval's irrationality. It was as if Tom was seeing how much he could get away with. It was like speeding through red lights for fun.

Mark caught a glimpse of Helen lighting a cigarette across the room. She looked at him with hard eyes, but he avoided her. She added to the pressure he felt to challenge Caval, to threaten him, to take over and make things run as they had agreed. But she didn't understand. He would have loved to do it, even dreamed of it, pictured himself telling Tom and Marshall that he was giving the orders from then on, even brandishing a gun, telling them he damn well meant business. But it was so impossible. He thought of it only to compensate for the fact that he could not do what he should.

An hour or so earlier, as he came in from his practice run, Helen had met him on the dock, caught his stern lines and helped him tie up. The cruiser was still their refuge, and they had listened to music and had a few drinks in the salon before going back to the house. He had asked her as they left what the others had been doing, and she replied irritably, "Same as always." They complained about it together, and again Mark catalogued the broken agreements. "I know all that," Helen told him. Lately they had talked of little else. "I can't see why you don't call him on it. Just make him do it. Tell him to get his ass in gear. Like those houses. Make him get them. He can get money somewhere."

Again Mark realized he was in no position to demand anything of Caval. But he could not admit to Helen that he had no power in the deal, so he had retreated. He had said perhaps it was not really so bad, maybe he was just getting nervous. But he did not sound

234

convincing, and she had looked at him suspiciously as they drove away from the marina. "You and Jack could both go to prison," she said. She was upset, but less because of Mark than from a sense that things were turning sour again, that there were always forces that fouled the promise of her dreams. "Just stand up to him," she had begged.

"It's not so easy," Mark had answered miserably.

When Caval finally hung up, Mark felt like lunging for his throat. "If I had rammed the goddamn Coast Guard station, it would probably attract less attention than a bunch of people hanging out smoking dope all day. And it'd certainly be less of a hazard than running down deals on the house phone."

"Why don't ya relax, Mark." Caval spoke in his coolest, friendliest tone. He could be thoroughly disarming, even charming when he wanted to be. Since arriving three days earlier, Tom had behaved with a complete assurance that they had not a problem in the world. "Don't worry about it, okay? Nobody cares what we're doing. When people are on vacation they do whatever they want. If we don't want to do anything, who cares? But if it'll make you feel better, Marshall an' I'll go out an' catch crabs on the beach tomorrow."

Heard snorted, and Caval and Amian laughed together and then made jokes about playing badminton or holding a barbecue for the island residents or going in town to catch crabs. Tom was in a jovial mood, but as always his humor had a victim—Insinger.

Mark made no comment, but suddenly he was neutralized, trapped between two forces. Without seeing them he could feel Helen's eyes, knew her thoughts, and she seemed like the part of him that wanted to be careful, exacting, to control the possibility of error. Yet Tom Caval still had a power over him. The hell with 'em, he seemed to say. You wanna sit around worryin' about whether everybody on the island thinks you're a nice person? We don't need more houses. We run the stuff right outta here.

Mark still wanted to be capable of that daring, that abandon, that bold assurance of success, and as Tom joked about the shmucks on the island, he turned to Mark with a special grin as if to remind him.

Caval leaned back in his chair and stretched his bare toes before him, luxuriating in his audacity. Eager for another subject, his fast eyes found Helen across the room.

"What's for dinner tonight, sweetheart?"

She smoked her cigarette and looked back at him with an

expression beyond contempt, merely uninterested and wishing to be elsewhere. The first two nights Caval and the others had been there, she had cooked meals. But no one said a word of thanks except Marshall, and no one offered to help. Tom made her feel like she was being paid to do it, and that demolished her prior notion of taking care of the group.

"I'm not your cook," she told him quietly.

"Oh, I forgot," he said, "you're on vacation."

"Why don't you surprise everyone sometime and say something nice?" She seemed honestly to wonder.

"I thought it was nice enough that I provide this honeymoon cottage."

"Hey, ease up on her, will ya, Tommy," Marshall looked up.

"Yeah," said Mark. His tone was quiet, almost friendly. "Cut this honeymoon shit."

"I'd like to," Caval snapped.

The conflict of emotions, Caval's smiling depredation, Mark's helplessness, and Helen's disappointment filled the room with a discomfort that only Caval could contain. There was silence, except for Heard and Amian nervously organizing another game, as if to avoid witnessing a sacrifice. Caval watched Insinger with a curious, expectant pleasure as Mark in turn watched Helen. She seemed to wander in a corner of the room looking for an exit, and Mark felt as though he saw her drifting away in a solitude left by his impotence. He knew she would put up with almost anything, any risk, any unpleasantness, would not even care when Jack learned she was present, if only he would make a stand. Alone, there was only one thing she could do. He knew that, even if he could not challenge Caval on the logistical matters, he should tell him clearly that Helen was his woman and not to be abused. If he would not defend himself, he must still somehow defend the woman he said he loved. She required that of a man, at least, and she had been woman enough to him to expect it.

Yet Caval smiled across the table to remind him, and Mark felt with a slow cold nausea that he was in too deep. He saw her distractedly pick up a cigarette box from the counter that extended along one side of the kitchen area, then look at it as if that ordinary object was suddenly as alien to her as the people in that room. She tossed it down and turned to leave the room, and he saw in her movements a finality, a surrender, a letting go of the rope. Passing to the stairs she looked at him through eyes burdened with a vast disappointment, and he looked back across an impossible void and knew the emptiness of never seeing her again.

236

As she ascended the stairs, Caval suddenly began to talk about the boat, about who would comprise the loading crew and how they would proceed upon hearing from *Leda*. He seemed satisfied that Insinger was rid of any encumbrance, and now he was willing to work with him. Mark managed to make replies, but distantly and with his thoughts still on Helen.

Why did you bring her here? She wanted you. You could have had each other later. You didn't have to bring her here, into this lie, with her believing you were a leader of the thing. You lied to her by not telling her. And now you had to let her watch you eat shit. You deserve that.

For a moment he thought he should tell her the truth about his position, tell her that he was in up to his neck, had almost no money, was more vulnerable than anyone, and was therefore under Caval's power. But that would not change anything, and he could not bear further degradation in her eyes. It was better if she left, he concluded. The place would probably become a snakepit before they got out, and Jack would want to kill him when he found her there. And he would deserve that too.

Mark gradually absorbed himself in Caval's sudden desire to make plans and even prolonged the discussion to avoid facing Helen. It was late when he went up, and the room was dark, and she lay on the bed in ruins. The disturbed covers seemed to blend with her wrinkled clothes and disheveled hair as though she had lain there in despair for years. Mark sat beside her, leaning against the headboard, but did not touch her. He waited for her to speak the inevitable. Sitting in the darkness he marveled resentfully at the turmoil that had erupted that evening, at how inexorably his dream had been crushed, at how cruelly events had conspired to expose him. How swiftly it collapses, he thought, and the words came to him again with a familiarity. How swiftly it collapses.

Finally, without prelude, she murmured, "I'm leaving tomorrow."

Mark took a deep breath and said, "I guess you should. It's going to get pretty gamey here. We can get back together again when all this bullshit is over." He waited for her to answer but there was nothing. "Let's go back down to the islands when this is finished."

"Sure," she said. There was not a whimper in her voice but the effort to restrain one. She seemed further depleted, molested by the fact that he did not argue, made no plea, not even a suggestion that she stay with him.

You'll never forgive yourself for this, he thought. But he saw no other way. He knew she had nowhere to go, except some dismal return to a sister or parents. He had let her down completely. By going back to her, loving her, persuading her to accompany him, he had joined their lives, and there was a promise in it that now he could not live up to. Yet regardless of the damage, it seemed better to end it quickly, at least for a time, than to prolong the pain. Like most men, he did not realize that in matters of the heart the bravery of quick death is a cowardice in disguise.

A silence endured. He thought she was asleep, but at last she stirred and reached to the night stand for her cigarettes.

"I love you," he said. He knew it was a worthless thing to say as soon as he heard himself, and the truth of it was of no avail. She kept the cigarette but did not light it and turned closer to the pillow.

"Yeah. Everyone's in love." Her voice was slightly hoarse. "But nobody wants to bet on it. The first time it gets difficult, they bail out and want to try it again later on. But it's never as good and you never get to go back."

Her words sounded too true to answer. He wanted to prove her wrong somehow but knew it was impossible that night. He found nothing at all to say, and a few minutes later fell asleep in his clothes.

ii

Driving back from the airport the next afternoon, Insinger knew a desperate relief. The injury, the veiled pleading in her eyes, which he had borne like the prospect of death all that day and through their long wait for the delayed flight, was finally over. The fall was ended and he had struck bottom at last. Sending her away seemed to have completed the destruction of his images and dreams of flamboyant romantic conquest in the dope business. His money was gone, his dignity, much of his self-respect, and now Helen too. He might have her again sometime, or perhaps not, but he had to take the chance. He could no longer fight the mental skirmishes of how things could be or should be. By sending Helen away he seemed to have put all illusions aside, and life was refracted to a cold simplicity.

But the sad sweet remembrance of being with her lingered on, composed itself beautifully in his mind, tortured the body with the aching of his heart. Yet her absence emphasized a passage—from what he wanted life to be to what it really was. Life with Helen had

238

been the artistry of Mark's dreams, but reality was waiting. He felt emotionally stripped down for action, looked to the future with a vengeance. Driving out of Wilmington toward the island, Insinger believed he had nothing to lose, and was a little surprised to find with it a feeling of power.

"Where is everybody?" Mark shut the front door behind himself.

Caval looked him over critically and said, "Down at that clubhouse thing. Gettin' some dinner."

Caval lounged in a chair, dressed in light brown pants and a thin suede shirt. He wore white running shoes and propped his feet on the table. A pro football playoff game from the West Coast was on the TV beside the stairway, but the volume was quite low.

"Good." Mark moved confidently to the table, aware that Tom watched him with his usual expression of amused curiosity. "I want to talk to you."

"Sure." Tom's eyes narrowed slightly. "I think it's about time we got our deal straight. That what you wanna talk about?"

Insinger nodded. Caval's steady smile seemed to know everything about him. Tom always knew when someone was ready to talk business, was always prepared, waiting like a spider. Mark was no longer intimidated though. He knew what he wanted and in his present mind was prepared to demand it, to take nothing less. Failure seemed too close to be frightening, and he knew what cards he held—knowledge of the boat and the local waters. He was ready to play as hard as he had to, and his brow began to twitch slightly at the prospect. On the way back from the airport he had realized that there was always one other card Caval would have to consider if Mark threatened to walk out—the fact that he was after all an officer of the court.

"Yeah, I'd say it was about time we firmed up the arrangement. We've put if off quite awhile now." The more tension Insinger felt, the more quietly and carefully he spoke.

"If we'd made a hard deal in the beginning, you wouldn've known how much you wanted, would ya?" Caval asked pleasantly. "You wouldn've known how much work you'd be doin'. Isn't that right? Don't you want more now than you would've then?"

"Maybe so. It's getting hard to remember what I wanted when we started this thing."

"Well, do ya know what ya want now?" Caval leaned forward a little.

"Yeah. I think so. I know how much money I want."

Mark had planned to state his terms abruptly, but now he

spoke slowly and studied the jewel-like intensity of Caval's eyes. Tommy had something up his sleeve.

"Okay. Good. Let's hear what ya think of this." Tom's entire body seemed to flex with his love of dictating a deal. "I'm movin' a big piece of this to Amian. He's gettin' the biggest piece. I'm frontin' him six thousand pounds."

"That's a lot," Mark affected only a mild interest, but he was appalled. He thought Amian was an incompetent fool. Nevertheless, Harry was pretty big in the business. There were a lot of fools and incompetents in the business. Mark had begun to realize that Caval liked them, because he could awe and control them.

"Goddamn right it is. It's a helluva lot. I'm frontin' the whole thing to 'im for two hundred a pound. That's a million an' two. A million bucks." Insinger nodded warily and lit a cigarette as Caval went on.

"You gotta stay on top of it to collect that kinda money. Really stay on top of it. I know," he patted his chest. "But I'm gonna have a lot of collecting to do. I'm frontin' most of this shit. An' there's gonna be a lotta cash movin' around. A lot of it. An' I don't wanna be jugglin' dough like a fuckin' banker if anything happens. I wanna keep some of this money away from me until I'm ready to handle it."

"Good idea," Insinger allowed.

Caval stared silently at him for a second, then fell back in his chair, suddenly relaxed. He inclined his head slightly, regarded Mark's impassive face, knew that he was being cagey, and laughed quickly through his nose.

"So I want you to collect it for me. I want ya to stay right with him all the way. Keep track of who he moves it to and when an' how much he takes in. See? An' be there to collect my money when he gets his. I know the people he'll be movin' most of it to. He's got the contacts to take care of that much, but he ain't organized, ya know? You don't have to see his stuff or be around the deals, just keep up with him, right? Make sure the money comes in, and make sure I get mine."

"And?"

"And . . ." Caval sat back again and his eyes came loose in their sockets a moment as he appeared to settle on one of several figures he had been considering. "You keep half of it. Six hundred grand."

"That's interesting." Mark looked away. "That's interesting." His stomach closed like a fist.

"Yeah." Caval laughed again. "Yeah."

Caval kept talking, adding the details of the job, and Insinger weighed the proposal suspiciously. He's pulling the string again,

Mark thought, drawing me in further. The job would be a lot of work, and God only knew what kind of work, but still it was more money than he had planned to demand. Any demand for cash could bring only a promise at best, and Mark was rather sure that none of Caval's promises were much better than his promises regarding Fort Rhodes. The money would come much quicker too—and not through Caval. He could not imagine Harry Amian handling a million dollars, though. But Mark had dreamed of it himself enough times in the past year to be confident at least of holding on to it. And he could always hold over Amian and his friends Caval's old collection buggaboo about his family's syndicate contacts. But of course Caval had that over Mark too. A curious proposition, Mark thought, and a fast cash flow of a million bucks.

"Harry know about this?" he asked when Caval finished.

"Sure. I talked it over with him."

"And what about rip-offs?" Insinger stood slowly and went to the kitchen for a beer.

"If Harry gets ripped, it's off my half," Tom called after him. "If you get it, it's off yours. Fair enough?"

Amazing, Mark thought. As he took out a beer he noticed part of the casserole Helen had made a few nights earlier. It seemed she had been there long ago, before he became serious. His thoughts collected quickly as he returned to the table. He and Tom had always discussed his cut in terms of a cash payment. Now Tom was talking about more work, deeper involvement when he clearly knew Mark was sick of it all, or at least thought he knew. He's expecting a beef, Mark thought; he can't expect me to want this deal.

Insinger looked forward to the expression on Caval's face. He sat down and took a swig of the beer, then smiled as if they had just agreed that the weather was pleasant.

"Sure. That's fair enough. We got a deal," Mark stated. And, to his uneasy surprise, Caval beamed back at him and said, "Great."

chapter 16

i

"COM'ON you bitch," Thorton growled. "Drive, will ya." *Leda* gained speed again coming off one of the long steepening swells and veered to port. Thorton's massive arms stiffened as he cranked the wheel to get her back on course. The compass came unevenly around to 320°, halted a moment as they bore through the wide trough, but then without perceptible movement by the boat, the dial turned deliberately on toward due north. Ralph cursed again and hauled the wheel back to port, straining to adjust the rudder against the pressure of following sea.

Behind thick brown whiskers, the tight set of Ralph's mouth showed the effort of keeping on course with the seas pushing erratically from behind and the wind shifting out of the southwest as unpredictably as a snake. Since eight o'clock, when Sidell had gone below to eat before taking the first nightwatch, Thorton had struggled with the wheel, correcting, oversteering, recorrecting. He stayed to one side of the wheel, and his eyes darted between the seas rushing and crashing around the stern as he crossed them, and the maddeningly unsteady dial of the compass. It was as though they had passed a great hump in the ocean and now sped downhill over the seas with little control. Through the afternoon the winds had swung around from the northeast, picking up in the process to a tough thirty-five knots. The cloud cover had grown close overhead and ominously dark in the west. Finally, with the wind behind them, Jack had Ralph and Eiler bring down the headsails and goosewing the main and mizzen, extending them to either side so *Leda* ran before the weather like a huge ungainly waterfowl. The spread of scarlet sails blocked the forward view and convinced Thorton that *Leda* fled beneath the threatening sky with a mind of her own.

Sidell came up through the main hatch and flinched at the lowering sky and the throbbing, dark-purple squall line that blocked the sunset. By God, we're moving though, he thought. This is better than six knots, I'll bet. He was pretty sure the bad weather would keep to the west, but he knew better than to trust it in that region.

"This is strange." Thorton glared at him as Jack went back to the wheel. "Wind's movin' all over behind us. Feels like we're outta control." He hauled angrily at the wheel again and gritted his teeth, wanting to be as close as he could to the course of 320° when he gave the helm back to Sidell. "Damn hard to hold course," he said gravely as Sidell took over.

Jack nodded, and Thorton stepped aside to gaze along the horizon with a mixture of wonder and fear. Seeing Jack wrestle with the wheel as he had, Ralph said, "It's strange, ain't it? The way that wind's shiftin' and she won't steer."

"There's a big low-pressure system moving northwest toward Florida." Jack did not care to acknowledge strangeness; there was nothing he could do about strangeness. "We're catching the tail end of it behind us, it looks like. Always hard to steer when the wind is behind you, and even harder if the seas are on your tail too. Remember on the way to Colombia?"

Thorton agreed halfheartedly, but thought instead of unearthly forces. It was the twelfth day of their voyage, and they were northwest of the Bahamas, almost three hundred miles off the Florida coast, hard in the middle of the Bermuda Triangle, that region of the Atlantic roughly bounded by Bermuda, Florida, and Puerto Rico, and known for deadly occurrences without explanations. Ralph had never heard of it before Jack and Mackenzie spoke of it at length a few nights earlier, and now that the weather gave an eerie feel to the evening he had a morbid curiosity that Sidell did not share. Sidell had been through the Triangle a few times, had encountered sudden rough weather, had heard all the tales of vanishing ships and planes, spinning compasses, confused instruments, chilling Mayday calls, but it was not in his nature to waste much time considering the inexplicable. Nevertheless Ralph was right. It was strange.

In the waning light, clouds overhead rolled in a slow boil; the horizon appeared higher and closer than it should be. Everywhere was a changing brightness, a yellowish glow of varying intensity that seemed to match the indecisive shifting of the wind and gave unsettling luminescence to the green sea. *Leda* rolled and bucked, halted and surged as if frightened, pursued by an angry ocean. But even the waves making tumultuous, confused canyons around them seemed to rise up in fear of something.

"The Devil's Triangle," Thorton invoked above the rush of wind. Attributing it to the devil partially satisfied his wonder. "It sure is weird. Whatta ya think it is?"

Jack shook his head. "The really weird stuff, nobody knows. Weather causes some strange effects. Right now, it's a big low."

Sidell pulled at the wheel and ignored another of Ralph's questions. He was relieved to see Mackenzie emerge from the cabin. Jesse had lost weight on the trip and looked like a man emerging from some dark prison to view the sky for the first time in many years. His arms were still muscular, but his bare chest was bony and his middle was thin. Without the watchcap, his long black hair fell on his shoulders, and his beard was scraggly around his mouth.

"Hell of a sky," he said, warily looking around.

"What'd you get?"

"Low's still moving north-northwest to Florida. There's storm warnings out on the coast and in the islands. Maybe we ought to head east and steer clear of it. We don't need any o' that."

"We need to make some time." Raising his voice above the wind hardened Sidell's words. "Let's just keep running off its ass-end like this. We're doing okay."

"We're truckin', that's for sure. But I'd hate to test those patches in a storm."

"You think I want to? The way it's going, the storm won't hit us. We'll get some rough weather though."

"If it's possible, I'm sure we will."

Joe Eiler came on deck and like the others was struck by the appearance of the weather and an uneasy eminence in the atmosphere.

"Gonna be a real nice night," he said, as he came around the cabin. "I'd like to put in for shore leave."

"You may get it," Thorton laughed, but Sidell glanced irritably at Joe.

"What're we eating tonight?" Jesse asked.

"Soup," Eiler answered. He smirked as Mackenzie frowned distastefully, being bored enough to enjoy seeing someone annoyed.

"It's not bad," Jack said. "Got carrots and onions in it."

The level of their voices made every word sound angry. Sudden movements of the deck kept them off balance, as they held the cabin top, falling off half a step to one side or another. The strangely luminescent seas rose and fell around them with a disquieting hum.

"You put those goddamn old carrots in it? I wouldn't have fed those to a dog. What about those cans of meat stew?"

"I'm savin' 'em," Joe yelled back. "When it starts gettin' cold, you'll damn well thank me."

"An' I guess split pea soup is for hot weather."

"You wanna cook, Jesse? Why don't you cook?"

Mackenzie nodded sardonically. "You'll navigate, I suppose."

"Maybe I ought to. Looks like we're in the wrong spot right now."

Sidell pressed his full weight against the wheel as they surged and rolled into another trough. The sea rose high above them. Jack jerked his head to snarl at the others, "Let's cut the bullshit and get this boat squared away." The seas abruptly fell away as they mounted another wave and viewed the sinister horizon. "This wind's going to be building."

Two nights before, Mackenzie had idly listed "Serious Shortages" on a page of his log, including "diesel (about 600 gals.); cigarettes (1 pack); milk (1 glass); paper towels (done); batteries; patience."

ii

Through the six days since they had cleared the Windward Passage, the crew had grown restless and short-tempered. After the exhausting trials of the Caribbean crossing, the passage had seemed to mark a halfway point from which the remainder of the trip promised to be easier. Instead there had been boring days of little wind and trials that were slight by comparison with those already endured, yet were tedious and bothersome.

The first two days after clearing Windward Passage had been almost celebratory. The patches had held well, and they were rested. Beneath big blue skies and idle clouds, the sea was kind with fair winds, and they made good time toward the southern Bahamas to gain the Atlantic through Crooked Island Passage. Shifts were kept loosely, and they lay in the sun on deck or sat in the after cabin smoking dope and listening to tapes. They ate constantly, as if there were only a few days left in the voyage. At night they smoked more grass and marveled at the skies, repeated to each other—always with humor—how they had felt when the boat was sinking or at the most dismal point of their exhaustion over the deck pump or upon the sight of Haiti. Like most difficulties, their troubles were not so bad in the past tense, and they even spoke of making the trip again. But at those moments the memory of Billy Delight cast its shadow, and the conversation would grind down, and they would find things to do. Still they laughed and joked a lot and took almost nothing seriously, as if Carolina was only a few days off, success and riches just beyond them.

Sidell was slightly worried that they received no word by radio from Caval, but he was too happy to be out of danger and back in good Bahama sailing to be bothered much. He or Mackenzie kept the single-sideband set open for an hour each day between noon and one, Greenwich time, but there was nothing. It annoyed Jack, but did not surprise him.

The morning of December 16 began a tortuous day. Sidell and Mackenzie decided they had to get more gasoline. The engine's pumps were sufficient to control the leaking when it was running, but without it they still had to run a gas pump ten or fifteen minutes out of each hour. There was plenty of gas for the one auxiliary, but there was still the likelihood of new leaks or patches giving way in rough weather. Studying the coast pilot manual, they had located a small fishing village on Landrail Point of Crooked Island, where fuel could be purchased with little worry of attracting serious attention if they were quick.

As they made for the island that morning, though, the sea and sky were ravaged with squalls. They had to motor all the way through sudden cloudbursts and ferocious assaults of wind and did not reach the island until early afternoon. Holding four to five hundred yards off the village, *Leda* tossed violently on mean craggy swells, and lowering the Whaler with any control was nearly impossible. One moment the water seemed ten feet below the Whaler, and the next moment it shot up to knock the skiff crosswise or smash it against *Leda*'s side. Once in the water, another squall blew up while Thorton tried to start the outboard, and several times he and the Whaler were nearly crushed beneath the larger boat as the sea and wind drove them together. In the beating rain as they tried to keep the Whaler clear, start the motor, and keep *Leda* in position, there was a promise of catastrophe in the air, in the futility of their efforts, the opposition of nature. They shouted instructions and advice at each other with mounting intensity and cursed like dire enemies.

Finally Sidell had joined Thorton in the Whaler, and they let themselves out astern of *Leda* on a line and worked feverishly at starting the wet motor while the Whaler bucked crazily on the waves at the end of its tether. Fearing the curiosity of some Bahamian authority or other they had planned to make a quick trip of it to Landrail Point, but it was already late afternoon. There was no choice but to run *Leda*'s engine to hold her position, but the steep seas whipped by a full day of squalls were starting to throw her prop out of the water, and the crankshaft screamed as if to announce the whole bottom coming loose. When the outboard finally started and Jack headed ashore with Ralph and eight five-gallon jerry cans, his nerves were shot.

There was neither a bay nor a cove really, but shallow protected

246

water, and when they reached a short wooden dock extending from the beach and tied the Whaler beside two small crude fishing scows, the world was abruptly tame and pleasant. A crowd of black shiny-faced children had gathered to watch the strange ship pitching wildly off the shore, and the handful of local fishermen greeted them with bemused friendly smiles at the struggles they had witnessed for the past two hours. An old man was happy to sell them fuel and even asked them to his house for dinner. They regretted sincerely. With the only denomination of currency on the boat, a hundred dollar bill, Thorton went off with the old man in a rickety old pickup of unidentifiable origin, and Sidell lay down wearily on the sand. He watched the children playing with sticks at the water's edge; the men picked debris from a broad net before gathering it in the stern of one boat in preparation for the next day; another man about Jack's age squatted on the dock and cleaned his catch. As he watched them, Jack found a vast wisdom in the simplicity of their lives, and it forced him to wonder if, in all his struggling, he were not a fool. It was not a comfortable question. Against what seemed like an ageless dignity, he compared the exhausting, high-stakes hustle in which he sneaked across the seas at any cost. The measure weakened him further. He looked out at *Leda* fighting with the mean sea and wished earnestly not to go back. It was one of those unprotected moments, when a person is tortured by a longing for some irretrievable past and feels imprisoned by forces he himself has set in motion.

There was the smell of rain in the air, a coolness to the frequent gusts, and a promise of more rain. It was an afternoon rich with the desire of going home, of lying alone with a woman all night, making love and promises, guarded from the passage of storms. Jack thought inescapably of Claire and their years together in the mountains outside Boulder—back when the game was football. The memory came with that homeward scent on the breeze, and his sadness coincided with the aching of his muscles. The wish of having her beside him right there, his nose in her hair, the smell of her, of having the house up on Sugarloaf to return to, of any house to go home to, to be with Claire again, anywhere, thickened his throat with the knowledge that it could not happen.

There was no time for revisions or conclusions though, nothing to do but go ahead. The rickety truck returned too soon. They loaded and were about to depart when Jack took another longing look at the shore and the children. The man his own age stopped working a moment to lift his chin in anonymous farewell. Beside them on the dock the old man smiled with paternal compassion. Perhaps he saw something in Jack's eyes, or it may have been that Ralph gave him a hundred dollars for forty gallons of gas, but he said, "You got marijuana, eh?"

Ralph stiffened, but Jack shrugged and said, "Nope. No marijuana."

The old man smiled so his bare gums showed, and his face crinkled as if it had been worn thin from years and years of smiling in the sun. "No-o-o-o-o marijuana," he laughed.

The next two days were overcast and long. The only wind came in series of gusts and never from a serviceable direction. They motored forty hours straight, uncomfortably crosswise with the seas, and averaged not even two knots creeping over the Tropic of Cancer past Rum Cay and finally past San Salvador and into the Atlantic. December 19th, however, was a real sailing day. In the morning a good breeze came up from the northeast and blew well all day. The seas were in their favor for the first time as they aimed northwest, hoping to catch help from the Gulf Stream. They ran up every square inch of canvas and made a steady five knots. *Leda* was in her glory, loaded with cargo, ploughing the Atlantic beneath a splendor of swollen red sails brilliant against the crisp sky.

They were still making good time near one in the morning. Thorton was at the wheel. The world was looking much better to Sidell, and he slept soundly in the cabin. Below deck Joe Eiler was on engine room watch, and a Paul Butterfield tape filled the darkened hold with solid driving rhythms while Mackenzie slipped further into debt.

Jesse threw a card on the upended milk crate and said, "I wish we'd had a few more days like this one."

"Yeah," said Joe, tapping his foot and nodding to the music as he picked up Mackenzie's discard. "Rummy."

"S-s-s-s-son of a bitch," Jesse hissed and threw down his cards. "Thirteen, you . . ." He decided not to say it and tipped back on the jerry can that was his chair. He stretched and yawned and spoke dreamily. "Few more days like this one and we'd 'ave been home for Christmas. Maybe. Such a great time of year, y'know. I always like to be home for Christmas, don't you?"

Joe kept looking down, figuring the score, multiplying the points by a nickel.

"I guess I'd like to want to be someplace for Christmas." He did not care to pursue the question. The mere idea of Christmas held more painful memories than he could tolerate.

248

Jesse looked curiously at him. Joe never said much about himself, but Jesse suspected he was playing some mysterious role. Yet Eiler had a rootless quality and never spoke of family or a home.

"Where is home, Joe?"

"I don' know. San Francisco."

"Didn't you tell me you'd lived in Boulder?"

"I didn't tell ya. I lived there though. Yeah." He still looked downward, tallying the damage. "I was married. I lived up there for four or five years."

"You were married, uh? What happened?"

Joe looked up and studied Jesse's face a moment.

"You owe me six hundred an' eighty-three dollars."

Jesse shook his head and smiled with a sort of resignation.

"Awright, Joe. I'm gonna catch some sack. *Mañana*, uh?"

On the deck Jesse stopped to take a deep breath of the sharp night and a look at the stars. Eiler always had a way of making him feel lonely, as if he had been drawn into some vacuum, in which Joe lived a life that seemed to have no end and yet no permanence, nothing solid, nothing to hold onto. It made him miss his home and friends all the more.

Rounding the cabin as he headed for bed, he was shocked to see no one at the wheel. It sent a jolt like electricity through him. Then he saw that the wheel was tied off to the davits that held the dinghy over the stern. Turning to look for Thorton he heard a sharp whistle from the bow, and then another.

"What the hell?" he muttered and started forward at a low run, imagining some catastrophe, calling, "Ralph? Ralph?" He could see nothing in the darkness until he was past the mainmast almost to the bow, and then he saw Thorton, perched out on the nodding bowsprit like a monkey, with one hand gripping a forestay. He grinned at Mackenzie with a strange look in his eyes. Jesse stared in wonder for a moment.

"What in the world are you doing?"

"Listenin' to 'er," Ralph called back above the whoosh of sea parting beneath them.

"Jesus," Jesse exhaled. He had done the same thing many times when he and Margaret had brought the boat from Europe. But never from the bowsprit, with the wheel lashed off in good winds. Only Ralph would do that, he thought.

Thorton inclined his head again with an expression of perfect contemplation. He had studied the music of the old boat until he knew each of the sounds separately and which part of the deck or rigging made them, like the instruments combined in a symphony. Timbers and planking groaned or creaked with the slow undulation of the deck; rigging scratched against masts or cut the wind with a range of whistles. The wind itself hissed low and high, groaned against the sails, which hummed back and sometimes popped along the luff. And all around was the uneven low wash of broken sea.

"I used to do this," Mackenzie called to him and seemed to break a spell. Uncharacteristically, he chose not to mention that they were probably way off course. "Not like this, though. We get an odd wave, and there'll be some swimming to do."

Ralph patted the sprit with great seriousness and said, "She wouldn' do that to me. Not this gal." Nimbly he returned to the deck and stopped beside Jesse, setting himself purposefully before him. "I want to tell ya somethin', Jess," he seized Mackenzie's eyes with a fervor. "We got a fine boat here, pal, an' I love 'er. I didn't think much of 'er at first. An' to tell you the real truth, I didn' think much o' you either at first. I thought ya had a pretty high opinion of yerself. But I know that's just yer way, an' you prob'ly didn' think much of me at first. But I feel like we've gotten to know each other good, an' we've sure worked together, an' I want ya to know I feel like we're brothers now. I really do, Jess. An' there's just not much I wouldn' do for ya. I really mean that. And, uh . . . I just wanted to tell ya. So . . ." Ralph seemed embarrassed himself for a moment and did not know how to finish, but thrust forth his hand. "So put 'er there, pal."

Mackenzie was overwhelmed, as people usually were when Thorton suddenly bared his heart. He was moved by Ralph's expression and felt much the same way, but he would never have said it.

"Thanks, Ralph." He gripped the hand and nodded into those fierce eyes. "I feel the same way. I really do. But whatta ya say we go steer this girl, uh?"

"Sure," Thorton practically shouted, "come on, Jesse." He suddenly roared with laughter and pounded Mackenzie's back, as if to let off some residue of passion he had been unable to express.

Once in the cabin, Mackenzie decided to make an entry in the log before sleeping. Jack sat up as he entered and glanced at the compass to check the course, then returned immediately to sleep. Jesse normally entered only the mileage on the taffrail log, their position, course, sails, and the wind force and direction. Occasionally, without literary pretension, he commented on the crew's

250

behavior or noted his own thoughts. This night he felt a certain melancholy romanticism after talking to Eiler and Thorton. He rambled for half a page about the first good day of sailing they'd had since leaving Aruba:

It was great. It felt like it ought to feel. It finally overcame the feeling of death. But that will never be forgotten. The boat is good now. But different. I feel closer to these guys than I do with people I've known years. Because we've been through a lot already. There will probably be a lot more. And maybe because this is the first adventure I've known where there hasn't been a woman along. Especially on this boat, but anytime. My soul requires a woman's presence, and I miss that. Margaret has left a shadow here and there. And, of course, there's *Leda* herself. Look at us now, lady—four salty guys and ten tons of dope.

iii

At eight-thirty that night, there was still a faint lilac glow in the air and a tactile assurance of trouble somewhere. Seas had steepened to twelve feet and better but were still far apart and rarely breaking. It was a punishing ride. Big swells pushed and pulled as erratically as the wind blew. Every few seconds *Leda* plunged ahead into a trough, then struck the back of the next waves with a burst of water over the bow and seemed to stop. Then a pursuing wave would strike from behind, with a shower of water over the stern, and send them rushing ahead into another trough.

Mackenzie worked the radio inside the cabin, trying to get another report, but reception was poor. The wind at Sidell's back was a hard thirty-five knots, but it feinted, gusting and halting, and changed directions to blow at one of his shoulders and then the other. According to the last report, Jack figured they were all right. With the low continuing northwesterly, he figured he should be able to keep the present course. On the known facts he expected it to get rougher but not unmanageable. Nevertheless he had the feeling they were piling recklessly ahead into something—but he did not know what.

For the past two hours, as is not uncommon in the Bermuda Triangle, a secondary low, more intense than the main system, had developed in the southern Bahamas well south and west of *Leda*'s position. It formed faster than the satellites and the Coast Guard and the weather bureaus could detect it and issue warnings. It had traveled rapidly to northeastward, wheeling on the larger primary system, until their counterclockwise winds merged north of the Bahamas in a broad, dual storm front, like vast armies in the atmosphere combining for a swift campaign.

At nine o'clock Jesse was sure he could get some sort of report. Joe Eiler hung expectantly in the cabin doorway, but heard only the wind and shrill static as Mackenzie worked the radio. Joe's stomach suffered, empty and nervous, as he swayed with the boat's motion. He hated having to wait for danger, and he sensed Sidell's uncertainty. Jack saw the fear in the severe features of Eiler's face, accentuated by the growth of beard that had accumulated thickly along the sharp edge of his jaw.

"We're going to get it, but I don't think it'll be bad." Jack's voice was loud above the other noise and encouraging, yet still uncertain. Eiler nodded, but had a hard time swallowing.

"Shouldn't we get some of this laundry down?"

"I don't think it'll be that bad," Jack shook his head. "We can get it down if we have to."

Joe nodded again and looked back to the west. For the past half hour he had been watching dull flashes of lightning in the distance, but it seemed quickly to have grown more intense. As he turned to ask Sidell if the storm seemed closer, the wind behind them suddenly died to almost nothing. Their faces went blank. They stared at each other in absolute confusion. Then off the port side came a sharply rising hum of furious approach. It struck like a cannon blast of wind and water. The boat was nearly driven on its side from the impact. Sidell clung desperately to the wheel, just to keep from being blown over the side. Eiler was thrown backwards into the cabin and collided with Mackenzie, knocking both of them onto the starboard bunk. In an instant, the boat was consumed in screeching wind and a horizontal, beating rain.

Just as Sidell regained his balance, the force of the squall jibed the mizzen, snapped a preventing rope, and sent the boom flying across the top of the cabin. The gaff preventer still held the top of the sail, and the canvas twisted diagonally with such strain Jack thought it might be ripped off the mast. When Eiler and Mackenzie scrambled out of the cabin, the boom of the contorted sail thrashed overhead like the limb of a huge wounded animal.

"Free the gaff," Jack shouted at them. He knew it would be hell getting the sails down. He had felt gusts of sixty miles per hour before, and this wind was at least that. For the moment, until the sails were freed, there was nothing to do but try to hold course. They floundered ahead, heeled over by the wind.

252

Bent against the storm Mackenzie and Eiler released the gaff and sheet of the mizzen, fighting for their footing on the steeply inclined deck. The sail flew away from them until it was parallel to the wind but still whipping crazily. Thorton came on deck, and the three of them struggled to pull the sail down. The boom kicked violently from side to side as the boat's motion threw it against the wind every few seconds. In the darkness and turmoil, they wrestled the canvas as if it were a wild beast. It seemed like an hour before they had it tied down.

Mackenzie fetched the portable floodlamp for Sidell when they finished the mizzen. Eiler and Thorton moved forward toward the main, catching handholds wherever they could to keep from being blown off the deck. They stayed low, waiting for Sidell to come about. As the boat plunged into a trough Jack managed to bring the bow into the wind, and the huge mainsail swung back over the deck with terrifying force. With the bow to the storm, the boat lay at odd angles to the tumultuous seas, though. And, as it rose and fell, it rolled with the waves, and the boom swung dangerously back and forth.

They tried fitfully to lower the sail, struggling simply to keep their feet on the heaving wet deck. But the wind was so strong that even with the halyards slack, the sail would not come down. While Mackenzie and Eiler held the lines. Thorton pulled helplessly at the canvas, and the shifting boom threatened to knock him overboard any second. At the wheel Sidell strained to judge oncoming waves and to keep them into the wind with only one hand and held the lamp aloft with the other.

The wind began gusting unsteadily, and the waves grew steeper and confused, cresting onto the boat and washing across the deck. The rain hammered their faces as they floundered around the thrashing sail. As conditions worsened, there were long minutes when they could do nothing but hold on in the face of vicious gusts. Eyes closed and hands clutching halyards or anything near enough, they cowered against the blasts until slight lulls allowed another try at the sail. They jerked and slackened the lines and pulled frantically at the canvas, but the wooden hoops that held the sail to the mast seemed riveted by the wind. Each time they covered up, they believed it could not rain harder, that the wind could not possibly blow with more strength, and yet it did. And when they could squint upward again through the darkness and the onslaught of weather, the huge sail was still up and lurching from side to side like a monster in agony. The growing seas began to wash across the deck regularly, and the deck itself moved beneath them so suddenly and violently that fear of going overboard matched the futility of trying to control the sail.

One particularly strong gust passed as suddenly as it began, but then was followed by another. The boat dove into the trough of a sea at the same moment, and Mackenzie was thrown against a corner of the new deck, tearing his knee so that blood flowed instantly down his leg. Eiler moved toward him to give a hand, slackening the throat halyard as he did. Before either could brace themselves to stop it, the rope sped through their hands and the gaff came crashing down like a guillotine. It dropped forty feet in an instant, covering the deck with flapping canvas. Mackenzie tried painfully to regain his footing on the lame knee, while Eiler tried to gather the slack sail. Thinking only that once the sail was tied he could get off the deck, Eiler wrestled it desperately, trying to pull it all through to one side so they could gather it up, until he heard Mackenzie shouting at him, "Get Ralph."

Eiler looked across the whipping sail but saw nothing, then looked astern and saw only the light moving frantically as Sidell tried to signal them. For an instant the wind subdued the sail enough for Joe to see Thorton's head and one arm precariously above the rail. Using the sail as a hand line, Eiler pulled himself around the front of the mast and down the other side of the deck, until he came even with Thorton. As the boat rolled to port Joe dropped on his butt and braced his feet against the rail, grabbed Thorton's leg, which was hooked over the rail, and gripped his right arm at the elbow. He did not have the strength to pull him. He just hung on.

From the wheel Sidell had seen the wave breaking on deck that knocked Mackenzie down, freed the gaff, felled Thorton, and nearly washed him over. For an endless half minute he had shouted uselessly into the wind, swinging the light, while Ralph clung to the lifeline with one hand and managed to kick one leg back up over the rail. He had thought Ralph lost. A rescue would be impossible, and the sense of doom in the chaos on deck and the fury of the storm was absolute. The waves steepened and broke more menacingly, and the wind howled louder, as if the gale could smell blood. As if only saving Thorton could avoid total disaster, Jack kept shouting hysterically even after Eiler reached him, "Pull him in, Goddamnit. Pull him in." By the jerking beam of the floodlamp, Jack watched Mackenzie crawl over the new deck and plant himself against the rail beside Eiler and take Ralph by the belt. Even with the two of them pulling, they were too exhausted to get him up and simply clung to each other, while the heaving deck tried to throw them off. The huge untended canvas of the mainsail flailed them like a dark attacking spirit.

A breaking sea, fourteen or fifteen feet above the deck, rose off the port side. When Eiler saw it, the phosphorescent foam seemed twenty stories high, and he screamed for them to hang on as if it were his last utterance. Jack had brought the bow slightly into it. They seemed to strike granite, rode up it only an instant before the crest broke over the bow like thunder and buried the three men with violent water. Sidell waited in horror through the seconds it took the water to subside. Then, as he steered back into the storm, the wild mainsail blocked them from view before he saw at last that all three were somehow back on deck.

As Eiler and Mackenzie hung on, the motion of the wave had lifted Thorton above the rail, and the effort with which they held him was enough to pull him back aboard. Then the force of water had deposited the three of them like flotsam in a tangle with the crazed sail. For a few seconds they lay beside each other amid the chaos, in surprise and exhaustion, and the howl and blast of the storm and the agonized thrashing of the boat suddenly seemed as if it had always been there. Then without a single word they went after the sail again. For the next fifteen minutes, barely slowing down for even the worst gusts, they fought the sail and finally gathered it and tied it up with a vengeance.

Sidell had two options, each as threatening as the weather. There was no way of guessing how long the storm would last. Clearly it was no squall but a full-on gale, and he began to figure what had happened. If a secondary low had developed, as he suspected, then the storm front had broadened, and they might be in it as long as twenty-four hours. Run off with it, he thought at first. Keep the wind and seas on the starboard quarter and just ride it out. But *Leda* was not built for running with a storm, and the idea retreated. With her broad, blunt stern and outhung rudder, she would be hammered by waves and very difficult to steer. She could easily broach, be driven broadside to the storm, could even be blown over if that happened. And then, if the cargo shifted, they would certainly be finished.

The violence of the storm was rising. The dull, hungry glow of breaking water leaped and fell furiously in the darkness around him, and there seemed to be no sky, no place outside the murderous intent of the elements. *Leda* crashed and floundered as if in death throes. The world seemed to have converged on him completely, and Jack was truly frightened for his life. He feared pitting himself against the storm, and instead thought: just heave to. He could set the bow into the storm and take it all head on, even though that was possibly as ill-fated as running. The seas were twenty feet, steepening and drawing closer together and promising to get worse. The ride would be a brutal pounding, and he doubted that the seams and especially the patches could take it. And yet if he heaved to, he could tie off the wheel, go into the cabin and hang on, pit the boat against the storm, and settle for whatever came.

Mackenzie struggled back to the wheel when Thorton and Eiler had nearly finished securing the sail. He bent over to catch his breath in the small lee of the cabin, and as he looked up at Sidell, his features were rigid with fright and exertion.

"Shall we heave her to?" A blast of wind drowned his words and he had to yell again, his face only a yard from Sidell's. "Heave her to?"

Jack could not answer. He glanced at the ugly gash in Mackenzie's knee, from which blood still flowed steadily into the water that ran in rivulets down his leg.

"You alright?"

Jesse looked back at him with harried impatience, as if his knee were surely the very least of their problems. He nodded, but the gesture demanded an answer to the real question. Still afraid but suddenly resolved, Jack made up his mind. He could no more tie off the wheel and retreat to the cabin than Jesse would have gone below because his leg was injured. For an instant the choice seemed like everything else. It was no choice at all. He had made his choice long ago. He could not simply stop and take his medicine, or even his chances. He had to keep going, keep executing, play it out.

"We'll run with it," he said.

"That'll be hell. If we broach to a big one, it's all over."

"No choice," Jack shouted into the pelting rain. "It's hell already."

Jesse did not believe him at first. Then he shook his head slowly and almost grinned. The decision seemed to inspire him. He turned away, bent to the wind and limping, and hurried forward to set the forestaysail.

It was ten o'clock by the time Sidell brought the boat around and began to run before the gale. He kept roughly a north-northeasterly course. The wind howled at his right shoulder, blowing at least fifty knots steadily and gusting much higher. The seas raged behind him, smashed against the stern, and several times nearly ripped the dinghy off its davits. But the wind was so strong the staysail drove them ahead faster than the waves and kept them from breaking over the stern. But *Leda* rode like a matchbox on the water, and the storm tossed her with awesome ease. Steering was a deadly contest of strength and endurance. Every roaring wave forced the big rudder to one side or the other and sent *Leda* veering crosswise to the storm, where the wind threatened to blow her down and the seas to consume her like a small meal. Against unlimited tons of water crashing against the rudder, Jack had to use every ounce of strength to try to hold the wheel steady, then to correct the result of each battering sea before they broached. He was blinded by the enraged elements, and from one second to the next it was a desperate, brute struggle.

By twelve o'clock, Sidell was exhausted, but Mackenzie had had time to bandage his leg, check the pumps, put on dry clothes and foul-weather gear. Jesse took the helm for awhile. But, since he weighed less than one hundred fifty pounds and did not have the full strength of one leg to steady himself, the wheel and the seas had gotten the best of him after forty-five minutes. Hanging onto his bunk, bound miserably in the yellow, rubberized foul-weather gear, Jack felt as if he had lain down only a few minutes when Mackenzie kicked the cabin door and he had to go back out.

Below deck it was a purgatory of violent motion, nausea, and carbon monoxide. Soon after the storm began, the bilges had started to fill. So they started another of the gas pumps. The hold and the engine room were putrid with exhaust, and the tortured movement of the boat quickly made Thorton and Eiler sick. It was dark except for the faint engine-room light, and everything was wet from condensation and leaking. Articles from the galley were strewn across the floorboards.

Thorton staggered into the engine room, falling one way then another. "I'll do it for awhile," he said to Eiler, seeming to groan more than speak.

Joe pulled himself up from the milk crate he was sitting on and said, "Clean the filters," as he headed weakly out to the cargo area.

Thorton gripped Joe's shoulder as he moved past, and he said, "We gotta hang in there, Joe. Gotta hang in."

Ralph's face was ugly from seasickness, and Eiler couldn't look at him. "Yeah," he answered. "Sure."

Eiler lurched forward to the cargo stacks and hung on a vertical support for several minutes, trying to think of some way to lie down. The impact of waves and the jolting motion was like one car wreck after another. Finally he headed toward the forecastle, but lay down for only a moment before the extreme pitching of the bow made him feel worse than ever. Nevertheless it was several more minutes before he had the strength to get up. He felt his way back through the darkness among the cargo and slumped to the floorboards with his back against one of the stacks. From the corner of his eye he saw Thorton lean over and puke into the bilge between the pumps, then mutter, "Oh God," and lean against one of the diesel tanks with closed eyes. Eiler began to wish the storm would destroy them. "Come on, blow harder," he muttered perversely. "Bust this goddamn thing. Smash it up. Scatter this fuckin' heap across the sea." Strangely, though, the more Eiler wished for destruction, the better he felt. He began to concentrate on the violence and chaos roaring around him, and it seemed to absorb him, and he became a part of it. And, as if he had struck a bargain with the devil, he found it tolerable.

Sidell kept the wheel for almost two more hours and felt as if he had never stopped. The wind had come around gradually to the south, as the pressure system moved northward and away from them. And now it attacked from south-southwest. The wind had risen to a steady sixty knots and blew too hard for the seas to break. Without diminishing in size, the waves flattened on top and showed the wild patterns of the wind. They came as black and rock hard as the surface of a dark planet. The task at the wheel was no different, though. The rain pounded him. The wind screeched. He strained furiously over the wheel. And evil seas advanced endlessly out of the night.

Thoughts passed through Jack's mind like the storm waves. In the worst of it, he thought of Claire again. He wished he could go back to her. He imagined ways of atoning for having put her aside in Aspen, cast adrift among hustlers when he began this deal. As if she were an object he could put on a shelf and use again later. In the parade of images and unkind memories, Jack found himself a taker. He wanted earnestly to recall some time when he had truly given of himself, given more than he had taken. But he couldn't, and he had to wonder instead if he deserved to live. He thought of his parents, too, of how he had told them to stay out of his life when they only wanted to know where he was, what he'd been doing for the past year. He tried to think of ways to make up for that, too. But the madness around him seemed to forbid it. It seemed too late. He thought of Helen and wished he had spent more time with her. And then he thought of Claire again, as if searching for arguments to justify survival. In the turmoil he found no forgiveness.

Jesse relieved him for about an hour, and after a fitful, bilious rest, Jack took the wheel once more near four in the morning.

Bearing north-northeast, as the wind continued to come around gradually to the west, his mind stopped almost completely. The deep consuming fatigue of his body overwhelmed it, and he continued by instinct, hunched over the wheel and staring ahead as if mesmerized. After another hour, he began to think the storm had peaked. The rain had lessened; the wind seemed not quite so strong. He tried to ignore it at first, thinking it was only a delusion. But after another hour had almost passed, the rain had nearly stopped, and the seas, though still averaging twenty feet, did not charge so viciously. Finally he kicked the cabin door and called Mackenzie. Jesse agreed that the storm had begun to subside, and he started the engine, so Jack could bring them around to the wind, and they tied off the wheel.

Sidell crouched along the cabin side for a few more minutes, still flinching at the hard wind. He watched the staysail pull the bow into the waves. Then the rudder steered back to the wind. Then the staysail pulled back to the waves, again and again.

"If it gets worse, I'll come out and drive some more," he promised himself wearily, "but that's enough for now."

For the next nine hours, they were hove to, hanging on wherever they could, suffering through the jarring motion, hearing the gale outside, raging as if over the agonizingly slow loss of its power. After a few hours they had to start up the third gas pump, but the leaking stayed under control. They took more or less hourly turns in the grating noise and acrid stench of the engine room. And occasionally they looked on deck to see if it was still secure. For hour after hour though, there was nothing but the swift, wrenching ascent as a wave lifted the boat, followed by the stomach-lifting plummet into the trough, the bone-jarring impact and the rasping howl of the pumps. The whine of the wind sometimes rose to such a fury it seemed that some engine of the earth would burst.

By the dead gray of midafternoon the seas were more uncomfortable than ever, though perhaps less dangerous. The wind had lessened to about thirty-five, but blew from the west, disturbing the progress of the seas, so they grew steeper and closer. Sidell had Thorton and Mackenzie help him raise the mizzensail and reef it to provide more stability. Then he adjusted their position toward the waves and tied off the wheel again. They continued more or less hove to, being set further northeast and off their course.

Once the mizzen was up, Mackenzie went below to relieve Eiler at the pumps.

"What's it like out?" Joe asked him. He did not really seem interested.

"Still rough as hell, but it's passing. Go look. You're gonna die from these fumes."

Slowly Eiler navigated the gangway, slid back the hatch and climbed on deck. He saw Sidell standing forward with one arm around the bare mainmast to brace himself. The deck still heaved and rolled, washed by waves breaking over either side of the bow, and the wind was mean. Eiler took deep breaths and watched Sidell staring thoughtfully across the rough water, clad in the worn pants and jacket of his weather suit. Eiler moved up beside him and set his feet apart for balance. They lifted their heads at each other in a sort of recognition. Jack's hair was still wet and flattened against his head, and the fullness of his beard gave a sadness to his eyes. When he turned to Jack, Joe's hair blew wildly above his head, bleached from sun and stiff with dirt and salt. His eyes were the gray of the sky at the end of the storm.

"What're you lookin' at?"

Jack studied him uncertainly and thought he found Joe slightly changed.

"Little blue sky out there," Jack pointed. A tiny patch of blue peeked out timidly from behind the still angry movement of the dark sky.

"Well, I'll be damned." Joe smiled for an instant, then shrugged hopelessly. "Where the hell are we?" He looked around at the stiff charcoal Atlantic, rolling in glassy waves and cracking, smashing everywhere. "Pretty shitty looking water."

Sidell nodded with a thin smile. "Yeah. Sargasso Sea. We got blown pretty far out. Cold out here, too."

"Is it?" Joe wondered. Numb from the long ordeal, he wore only a pair of soiled shorts and his slicker, open in front.

"Yes, it's cold out here."

chapter 17

i

INSINGER nibbled tensely at his bottom lip as he maneuvered the cruiser into its slip at the marina. Trim little fishing cruisers and a sprinkling of sailboats formed neat ranks on either side. Mark shifted into forward, edged the throttles forward with his other hand, then shifted to reverse and slowly backed in.

"Okay, floor it," Amian called out from the afterdeck. He and Don broke up laughing. In their ignorance of the boat, everything was a joke. But Mark laughed with them now, admiring at the same time the ease with which he docked.

Things had been getting better in the last three or four days. He missed Helen terribly, but he still believed he could repair the damage, so he tried not to think of her too much. And without her, he found it easier to cope with the factors he could not control, easier to be one of the guys and not to worry. For the past three days Marshall and Amian and Don had gone out on the *Errant* with him as crew, and they'd had a good time and worked well together. Mark had regained a sense of confidence.

He backed almost to the dock, then steadied the boat by shifting again to forward for a moment as Heard jumped onto the dock. Mark killed the engines and watched Heard get the stern lines. He admired Heard's capability. Marshall was the oldest and he had learned to be serious and careful about whatever he did. He was also tough and smart, with experience inside and outside the law, and Insinger liked having him on the boat. In a tight spot, he was sure Heard would be the only one of the group worth a damn.

As he fastened the lines, Heard not only seemed to know what he was doing but also looked like he knew what he was doing. When the time had come to begin working on the boat, Heard made a point of looking around the Fort Rhodes marina and the one at Bradley Creek. Then he had gone into Wilmington and bought a pair of khaki pants, which he washed twice at a laundromat, a nylon windbreaker and a pair of white-soled boating shoes. The first day he went out with Mark, he had studied the way other people docked their boats, which lines they fastened first and what knots they used.

"Good work, sailor," Mark smiled at him as he finished.

Heard winked back at him. "Thanks, skipper." He was a quick study and looked like he'd been around boats for years.

Often Mark felt he and Marshall were the only ones who took the project seriously, but he was beginning to feel that they could handle it by themselves if they had to.

"Hey, Mark, is this right?" Don yelled. He was on the dock, with one of the bow lines around his waist.

"No, your neck," Amian laughed. "Your neck."

"Yeah, and make it tight," said Mark. "It may be rough tonight."

261

Heard and Insinger secured the bow, and the four of them kept kidding each other. They'd had a good time that afternoon, drinking beer and listening to tapes as they cruised out fifteen miles, and to Don and Harry it was all a party. Their presence was required on the boat only to help stow the cargo once it arrived, and they were doing that only because Caval, in his way, had promised them each an unspecific better deal on the dope. Still, Mark usually felt self-conscious about them around the marina because they each looked so alien, yet they had to gain some familiarity with the feel of the boat at sea. They both wore longer hair than anyone around Fort Rhodes, and this afternoon Harry Amian wore hiking boots and a tailored leather jacket, while Don wore a yellow ski parka. More than their clothing though, there was something in their jewelry, in their hip good looks, and the way they laughed at everything that seemed to promise normal people that they had never done, and would never do, any honest labor. To Mark they looked like a couple of blackjack dealers from Tahoe who didn't know where they were.

The four went back into the cabin for another beer before heading back to the house, and just then Insinger didn't give a damn what people were thinking. It was Christmas Eve, and there were very few people around the marina. The afternoon was bright and sharp and expectant, as if the day belonged particularly to children, and it was hard to imagine anyone caring what other people did.

Hinton Roberts stood on the dock a few slips away though, and suspiciously watched the *Errant*. He had been talking to two island residents when Insinger came in, and the conversation changed quickly.

"I wonder what those birds are up to," Roberts muttered as he watched them tie up. He was in his late thirties, and his blonde hair stood up a little in the breeze. The other two men were older, in their fifties, and all three wore mildly plaid slacks and rubber sole shoes and held drinks in plastic cups.

"They're the ones in the Pearson place, uh? This is the first time I've actually seen 'em," said one of the older men, who wore glasses.

"The Pearson place *and* the Garwood place," Roberts emphasized. " 'Cept that nobody's *in* the Garwood place."

"Looks like they're just havin' a good time to me," said the third man. He was the oldest and wore a billed golf cap.

"Your wife says you think they might be smugglin'," said the other.

"They could be," Roberts nodded judiciously. "They could be. Say they're a leisure corporation," his accent drew out the words sarcastically, "but there's sure somethin' peculiar about 'em."

"Com'on Hinton," the man with the cap shook his head, smiling.

"Well, they're not doin' any fishin' with that big ol' boat, I know that."

"What do you care what they're doin', if they're not botherin' anyone?"

"If they're breakin' the law, they're botherin' people," the man with glasses insisted. " Why don't we see what they got to say, Hinton?"

"Sure. Let's do that."

Roberts was an architect by profession, and he had taken the job as manager of Fort Rhodes Island a year earlier when a recession slowed his business. The economy, however, had also kept business at Fort Rhodes on a low level, and Roberts was not a happy man. He had resented Insinger, whom he knew as Mark Templin, from their first meeting. To Roberts, Mark was a young outsider who had little to say about his business, but had enough money to rent not only one expensive house but two. His curiosity had increased considerably when Mark arrived on the biggest yacht in the marina with a beautiful young woman who had soon departed. He was also certain Insinger was a Jew, and he had kept a critical eye on Insinger's activities, eager for some grounds to show he was not legitimate. Roberts had quickly warned a few residents that these new tenants might be up to no good — as if early discovery might provide some pardon for having rented to them. And that, along with the unusual situation at the Pearson house, had spawned a number of rumors, which accounted for the curious stares Mark frequently noted around the island.

" 'Lo there, Mister Templin," Roberts called as he approached the *Errant*. He was followed closely by the man with glasses and rather hesitantly by the third man.

"Hello," Mark nodded carefully. "How are you gentlemen this evening." He could not remember Roberts' name. The four of them were just preparing to leave the boat, and thought Roberts was making only a casual greeting, so everyone nodded hello and Mark made no introductions.

"How was the fishing?" Roberts asked pointedly. There was a sardonic challenge in his tone, and everyone felt it. Heard's eyes snapped at him reflexively with a menacing intensity that made the man with glasses look quickly at his feet then away at other boats.

263

Heard hated people poking their noses into other people's business, especially his.

"We were just taking a little cruise," Mark smiled. "It was a pretty nice day for it."

"Oh, I see," said Roberts.

Don and Harry glanced uneasily at each other, then said they'd better be getting back to the house, nodded goodbye, and walked away.

"Aren't you fishin' when I see you out here?" Roberts asked as Don and Harry left, pointing toward the channel that ran behind the houses. Roberts had never seen Mark fishing.

"Sometimes. Yes."

"What're you gettin' back there?"

"Not much," Insinger shrugged. "I'm not really much of a fisherman."

Heard sat on the transom and folded his arms and watched the faces of the other men as carefully as they watched Insinger's.

"Well, y'all sure got a nice boat for it though. What're you usin' to fish back there?"

Mark did not know what he meant at first, and there was an uncomfortable pause for several seconds. "Lures," he answered finally.

"Lures?" Roberts repeated. He turned his head to the other men. "Ever use lures? Out there behind the Garwood place in the channel?" The man with glasses grumbled and shook his head, and the other drew a deep, embarrassed breath. Roberts turned back to Insinger. "Y'all not usin' the Garwood place?"

"Not yet. We're expecting more people in a day or two." Mark's nervousness was beginning to harden his words. Heard still smiled thinly at the other men, but they avoided his eyes.

"I see. This must be a fairly large corporation y'all have."

"No. Rather small." Mark was suddenly aware that his voice was growing irritable, and he turned away for a moment to lock the cabin, hoping it might end the conversation.

"What is it the corporation does, Mr. Templin?"

Mark stepped up on the transom and then to the dock. With a great effort he managed to speak pleasantly.

"Well, we mainly charter two large sailboats out of San Diego, for trips down to Mexico and Central America. Lately we've been working on a project to expand. Perhaps to the Caribbean or along the East Coast somewhere. That's why we decided to spend the holidays here."

Roberts was about to say something else, but Heard stood

deliberately and joined Mark on the dock. His mere motion seemed to demand a halt to the interrogation. No one was under the impression that anyone thought it was idle conversation.

"Well," the man in the golf cap said loudly, as if to cut through the thick atmosphere, "we ought to be gettin' on up to the clubhouse, shouldn't we Hinton?"

"Yes. We have to be getting back to dinner ourselves," said Mark.

"Surely," Roberts smiled. To Insinger his face bore the root indignance of a man who had always played by the rules and been beaten. "Y'all coming by the Christmas party tonight?" Roberts added challengingly.

"Perhaps later. We're having a big dinner tonight."

"We'll see y'all later then." Roberts moved past them on the dock.

"Merry Christmas to y'all now," said the man in the cap as he went by. His tone seemed to apologize for what he considered rude behavior.

"Merry Christmas to you," Marshall Heard smiled. He had not used the expression in years.

"Oh yes. I almost forgot," Roberts turned back with a sarcastic smile in which he took great pleasure. "Have a Merry Christmas."

ii

Eiler checked the baked beans and thought them just hot enough. "Not bad," he remarked after a taste, "not bad at all." He reduced the burner on the small galley stove to its smallest flame, but then the thin circle of fire sputtered a second. At the same time the fire beneath his pot of water faltered.

"Not now. Good God, honey, not now," he begged, fearing the end of the propane was finally at hand. Both burners resumed strength almost immediately, but Joe flipped open the little oven door, and whistled in relief when he felt that the heat was steady and saw the burner still on. For a few moments, squatting before the stove, he looked with great pride upon his pie.

"A masterpiece," he announced to himself as he stood up again. "Too good for these heathens." A few moments later, the water was boiling, and he added nearly the entire remainder of the spaghetti noodles. "Got the entree, the pasta, the pie. Damn. Oughta be on a ship o' the line."

"Eiler you losin' yer shit in there?" Thorton called. He was in the engine room, repairing the clutch on the troublesome third pump. "Yer rattlin' around like an ol' woman."

"I oughta be. Your mother couldn' make a meal like this."

"Gawd, I hope not. What is it?"

"Pure delights, my friend." The word stuck a little, and Joe quickly added, "Go tell 'em the escargot's ready."

When Ralph came into the hold to go up on deck, Eiler was stacking sacks of marijuana. He had taken back the plastic tarps on one section of the cargo, and he laid out three bales in a close row over the bilge and stacked it three deep to make a table. Thorton watched him industriously arranging the burlap bags and shook his head.

"I don't believe what I'm seein'," he chuckled.

"Well, hell, it's Christmas, man," Eiler grunted as he lifted on the last bale.

"That don't matter. I still don't believe it."

After the travail of the storm and the bad days that followed it, spirits were finally rising that day, but hesitantly, and with an accumulated distrust of optimism or any sense of well-being. For two days after the storm the sea had been nearly dead calm, and they were beset with the wet, Atlantic cold of late December. They had not been out of foul weather gear since the storm began, and nothing would dry out completely. The occasional sun seemed as tired as they were and less resolute. Stores were low. There were no more eggs, no more powdered milk, no canned stews left, and no more cigarettes.

Yesterday, the twenty-fourth, light breezes had come up in the morning and freshened through the afternoon, so they finally began to make decent headway. But in the evening when they decided to get help from the engine, it had died after a few minutes. Off and on all night Mackenzie and Sidell worked on it. It was after dawn when they discovered the problem in the injection pump of the forward cylinder, and well into the morning before they got it running again.

Just after the old diesel came back to life, Sidell had gotten a Loran fix showing them less than thirty miles south of the Frying Pan shoals and therefore only about sixty miles from Fort Rhodes. The proximity seemed to have sneaked up on them. And almost in the same moment they realized it was Christmas.

Surprising even himself, Eiler had become rather excited and promised a special meal that afternoon. When he started on it though, Joe found, as he had in preparing each recent meal, that there was very little to work with. Besides beans and spaghetti he had only a large can of peaches. But finally he located the last of the pancake mix. Adding a little water, he fashioned a crust in a frying pan and baked it. He added the peaches, chopped up and soaked with the last of the maple syrup. Then, thoroughly carried away, he formed strips of crust, crisscrossed them over the peaches and felt at least the equal of any chef.

"He's ready." As he approached Sidell on deck, Thorton was still grinning at the sight of Eiler scurrying around the galley.

"I hope it's good," said Jack. "I'm so goddamn hungry."

"Well, it ain't turkey, but you'd think it was if you saw 'im putterin' around down there."

Jack was temporarily tying down the furled mainsail, and as he finished, he and Ralph speculated about being within unloading distance of Fort Rhodes by noon the next day. Several minutes earlier, Jesse had pointed them into the wind and tied off the wheel. Then they had taken in the jibs and lowered the main and mizzen so they could heave to with the staysail for a while, and all eat together. At first Jack had thought it was a little silly to pull up when they were making good time again, but he had been touched by Joe's enthusiasm—it was not unlike seeing Ebenezer Scrooge inspired to generosity. Besides it would be only a brief pause, and it would be the first break together since Haiti. And there was no telling what was ahead. Even the elements seemed to encourage a rest. The swell was long gaited and friendly. The easterly breeze felt dependable. The thin gray overcast had broken in an area to the west, and sharp angular sunrays knifed through to the dark, blue sea.

"Hey, Jack," Thorton stated solemnly after they had gazed out at the light a moment. "I been thinkin' that, since we're so close to bein' there, maybe we oughta say somethin' about Billy."

Jack's embarrassment before the intense honesty of Thorton's feelings made his face flush.

"You know what I mean? I know it'd be kinda weird, but we could do it if we wanted." Ralph's eyes were passionate. "Ol' Bill wa'nt too smart, an' in fact he was a pain in the ass sometimes, I know that. But he was good people. An' he was one of us, Jack."

"I know that, Ralph. I do."

They faced each other, standing effortlessly against the easy motion of the deck, but Billy's death came hard between them. The vast difference between what it meant to each of them was insurmountable.

"But what is there to say?"

"Well . . ." Ralph's eyes narrowed. "I guess I just know what I'd say. Maybe that's enough."

"Ralph, I know what—"

"No, it's awright. I just wondered what you thought." Ralph turned away quickly, as if to avoid further discomfort, saying, "Come on, let's eat."

Jack stayed a second and knew in a way he had insulted Ralph. But he could not have lied to him and patronized him, and certainly not in front of Eiler and Mackenzie.

When Jack followed Thorton below, his mood changed quickly. Mackenzie had preceded them and was already riding Eiler about the dinner. "What the hell? Where's the tablecloth? Think I'm going to eat off these bags?"

"Shut up an' go wash yer hands," Joe retorted.

Mackenzie was still filthy with grease from the engine work as he leered at Eiler's table. There was little room between the stacks of cargo, but Joe had put out the milk crate and two jerry cans for chairs and already placed the loaded plates on the dope bags.

"Hey, how 'bout this. Spaghetti noodles. Special meal, uh?"

"Sets a pretty table, don't she?" Thorton laughed.

"Yeah. I get it, it's make-believe."

Sidell put a cassette in the tape deck, and the jokes and laughter grew louder with the music.

"Couldn't we hear the pumps instead?" Jesse asked. "It'd go along with the indigestion."

"Slave all day over a hot stove," Joe dropped his head into one hand, "an' not a complimentary word."

"Aww, come on Auntie Joe," said Jack, "the dressing's great. Would you pass the gravy please?"

The same line of humor continued as they ate but could not grow old. Joe laughed along with them and enjoyed the kidding as much as anyone—and everyone enjoyed it more than the food. To Joe these men had become more of a family than anything he'd known in the last few years.

"More mash potatoes, Ralph? . . . Thanks, could I have the green beans too? . . . Stuffing anyone? . . . Are these cranberries? . . . This turkey is absolutely delicious . . . I'd like another roll . . . Fuck you, man, ya wanna eat 'em all? . . . More wine please . . . I think you've had enough, Jack . . . Aunt Joe, this is wonderful . . ."

Sidell kept looking around at the faces as they laughed and ate: Thorton's high forehead that always reminded Jack of the top of a fire hydrant and the scar beneath his eye looking meaner as his beard grew thicker and long; Jesse's uneven scraggle of beard on his hungry features, the knit cap always over his long black hair and his careful calculating eyes; Eiler's hair a bleached out tangle, his smile crooked and sad, something desperate in his eyes.

Suddenly Jack recognized that it really felt like Christmas. And it felt better to him than any he could remember, better than arriving somewhere by obligation to eat food somebody else bought and somebody else cooked, and with people whom he had little in common with except history. But there in the shadowy hold, with the cargo stacked close and high around him, the big timbers overhead, the heavy gentle motion of the old boat, the loud voices, and the sense of survival and a promise of accomplishment, he could feel his life. And in it, he discovered an authentic sense of celebration.

When the plates were finished, Joe went quickly to the stove and a moment later proudly placed his pie in the middle of their plates.

"*La pièce de résistance*," he announced.

"I can feel the resistance," said Mackenzie.

Thorton made a low whistle. "I don' know, Joe."

Jack inclined his head doubtfully. "Fun's fun, Joe, but—"

Eiler was genuinely wounded. "That's a beautiful goddamn pie."

In fact it was not. The crust was puffed up, and the strips across the center had nearly sunk. The peach chunks had turned a rather menacing orange, and the syrup resembled thin engine oil.

"Oh well, hell, a pie. I thought it was macaroni," Jack shrugged.

"Eat shit," said Joe.

"That's just it," Mackenzie laughed, "we'd rather not."

Joe looked up and shook his head. "I don't believe it."

"Neither do I," said Jesse. Thorton covered his face and shook with laughter. "Is that those fuckin' carrots?" Mackenzie went on. "Is that what that is?"

"Carrots an' diesel fuel," Jack erupted in laughter.

"Seriously, Joe, it was a good idea, but we're low on fuel as it is. Let's save this."

"You assholes."

Ralph wiped his eyes and suggested in utter seriousness, "Maybe if we smoked a reefer first . . ."

Mackenzie howled, and even Eiler broke up and laughed. It

was nearly a full minute before they recovered, then Sidell suddenly remembered something. "Wait a second," he said, hurrying up to the hatchway.

Mackenzie went into a brief dissertation on the pie's resemblance to decomposed human flesh, while Sidell hurried back to the cabin. He reappeared a few moments later and ceremoniously produced from beneath his slicker the beloved shape of a bottle of Mount Gay rum, about one-third full.

"My God," Mackenzie gasped, "the Holy Grail!"

"Where'd you get that?" Thorton demanded.

"You been hoardin' that, you son of a bitch," Joe accused him.

"No. I swear. I found it down here in one of the galley lockers right after we left Aruba, and I just stuck it down in my bag an' forgot about it."

There were loud statements of disbelief, but it seemed superfluous. They clamored around each other to find a glass or a coffee cup that wasn't too dirty, and then measured out all of the pale amber prize.

Eiler took a full gulp, savored it a moment and felt its searing progress down his throat. "A miracle of the Nativity," he breathed.

They carried on loudly for several minutes before Thorton made a loud guttural sound and looked around at them with wondrous eyes. "You won't believe this," he said with a full mouth, "but this pie ain't bad."

iii

"This is Gambler. Come in, Rainbow." Sidell cleared his throat and then spoke louder and more distinctly. "This is Gambler. Come in, Rainbow."

It was a few minutes after noon on the day after Christmas, and Jack had just begun to transmit. Thorton moved about nervously behind him in the cabin, leaning in the doorway, perching for a moment on the bunk. There was no response, and Sidell repeated the transmission almost angrily.

"Com'on you guys, goddamnit," Ralph growled. They were so close to Fort Rhodes Island that the only excuse for not being in touch was either incompetence or real trouble. Jack was raising the mike for another transmission when the voice cut loudly through the scratch and hiss of static.

"Hello Gambler. Hello Gambler . . ." It was Insinger, and his voice was steady, but with a high pitch of excitement. "This is the Rainbow, this is the Rainbow. What is your position?"

Thorton clapped his hands, and Jack could hear Mackenzie's shrill whistle at the wheel as he gave Insinger the figures. "North thirty-four-zero-three," he enunciated. "West seventy-seven-twenty."

Jack had taken a reading on the Loran before transmitting, and the set was still on. But as he glanced at the small screen as he repeated their position, the lines were fuzzing and breaking into a trellis of erratic signals. "Goddamnit," he muttered as Insinger replied. Mark excitedly remarked how close they were, but Jack's reply was dulled by the prospect of a broken Loran.

"Rendezvous fourteen-hundred." Insinger repeated Jack's suggestion. "Rendezvous fourteen-hundred. Can you hold position?"

"We will try. We are being set north-northeast by the current. Being set north-northeast by current. Having difficulty with Loran. Difficulty with Loran. Do you have Automatic Directional Finder?"

"Roger. Have ADF. If you transmit at fourteen-hundred, we will meet you north-northeast of your present position."

"Okay. We will try to stay close, but I cannot promise. May be fog later. May be some fog."

"Transmit at fourteen-hundred, and we'll find you." Insinger seemed not to hear about the fog or else not to be much concerned. "Anything else?"

"Transmit to you at fourteen-hundred."

"Look for you then. Roger out."

"Right," said Jack. "Gambler out."

Thorton and Mackenzie were talking excitedly at the wheel, but Jack looked at the small, greenish screen of the Loran, the unsteady mess of its lines, and shook his head. There'll be fog too, he thought. I hope they know what the hell they're doing.

chapter 18

INSINGER came out of the cabin, locked it, then stood on *Errant*'s afterdeck and looked around the dock. He had just turned off the radio set after talking to Jack. When he had come to the boat half an hour earlier, two men were just going out in a skiff, but there was no one around now. It was not the sort of day when anyone would be going out, especially in the larger boats.

He zipped up his nylon airman's jacket and stiffened himself against the cold breeze, drawing his hands into fists inside the pockets. Instead of enthusiasm at the arrival of *Leda*, he felt a grim anxiety, and every muscle of his body was taut. It would not be easy. He had never been out in fog. Already the air seemed hazy, as if the fringes of amorphous gray sky close overhead extended to the ground. He registered the wind from the northeast, and that would make the swell rough. He was sure the ADF would work, but he wished like hell he had practiced with it. The worst part about the weather, though, was the attention he would attract by going out. It would compliment every rumor and suspicion he read in faces around the island. Roberts would certainly be poking around, and he would notice they were out. Sooner or later, Mark was sure there would be heat. It seemed as inevitable as the bad weather, but there could be no turning back. "Pull it off," he told himself. He jumped to the dock and started for the car, and kept repeating, just loud enough to hear himself, mesmerizing himself to overcome the worry and fear, "Pull it off . . . Pull it off . . . Pull it off . . ."

When Mark opened the front door at the house, Caval stood there in his thick brown robe, staring with an anticipation that seemed to know what Mark would say. The intense certainty in his features shocked Mark for a moment.

"They're here."

"Awright." Caval struck his hands together with a ringing clap. "You ready to go?"

"Yeah. Anybody out of bed yet?" They had all been up late, and only Caval, who never drank, had been stirring when Mark left.

"They're startin'." He turned quickly to the dining table where Heard was nursing a cup of coffee. "Let's get goin'. Marshall, get 'em movin' up there."

Heard nodded slowly and took another sip. "What's it like outside?" he asked.

"Good breeze." Mark went to the kitchen to make himself a cup. "It's going to be pretty rough. Jack says there'll be fog, and it looks like he's right."

Marshall raised his eyebrows and nodded as if only good luck would surprise him.

"Com'on Marshall, get up there an' get 'em goin'." There was something whirring and metallic about Caval's excitement. "You got gas an' everything?"

"Yeah, I'm all set." Mark poured hot water onto the instant coffee and stirred in a spoonful of sugar. The nervous twitch in his forehead began as he moved to the table. "We're going to look pretty strange going out today."

"So what. You can go out any time you want. Just because that manager's a nosy son-of-a-bitch don't mean everybody around here is watchin' us. If you go about yer business you attract a lot less attention than tryin' to sneak around."

Mark nodded quickly. He did not agree, but there was nothing he could do about it. "That ADF is going to be crucial," he said instead. "You're sure it's working okay? If it's not we'll be—"

"Works fine." Tom grinned as he pounced on Mark's reservations. "What the hell? I told ya how to use the thing. It's easy. Set the compass card on top to your course, tune in the station, y'know, tune in their radio, and that arm thing on top points in their direction. It's—"

"Points to the compass bearing of their direction?"

Caval hesitated a moment and looked agitated. "Yeah. Right. The compass bearing. It points to what direction ya go to find 'em. Jesus, a fuckin' monkey could do it."

"Look . . ." Mark stared for a second at his left hand on the cup and found he was trembling slightly. "Since you know how to work the thing, why don't you come with us?"

"No way, man. This is your job," Caval snapped. "I don't know how to work it any better than you do. Goddamnit, it's simple. An' I got plenty of things to do here."

"Okay, okay. Don't worry about it. I'll get it done."

"Damn right," Caval grinned again. "You all ready on the beach over there?"

"Yeah. It'll be dark though. You stand on that little jetty I made when we come in and I'll beach just beside it."

"I'll be there. This has got to be fast. I mean fast," he snapped his fingers. "We gotta get that stuff offa there an' inside, awright?"

Insinger agreed, but infinite uncertainties preceded that prospect.

For the next half hour Caval was up and down the stairs like a demon, shouting, threatening, giving orders. He had been quiet and rather passive for the last few days, but now he came alive with the pressure of the moment. When he wasn't exercising his high pitched voice, shrieking at someone to hurry, he paced the living room with a distant smile and occasionally, elated at his power and the nearness of his fortune, unburdened himself of that unnerving nasal laugh. It radiated electric charges that filled the house. Insinger received them at the table with shudders and tried fitfully to concentrate on what lay ahead. Mentally he navigated the inlet at Masonboro and then the waterway approaching the island. The tide would be ebbing by the time he returned. But with the wind from the northeast, he would have plenty of water. The difficulties would be at sea in the fog.

Don and Harry barely got down half cups of coffee before Caval hustled them all out the door. Once inside the car, the seriousness of Heard and Insinger imposed a nervous, reflective quiet.

"Sure as hell is cold," Don observed as they left. But Heard quickly replied, "It'll get a lot colder." Those were the only remarks as they drove toward the marina. They turned past the clubhouse to reach the dock and saw Hinton Roberts standing outside, watching the car approach. Insinger cursed him under his breath, but Heard was quick to smile and wave as they moved by him. "Don't you dare come down to the dock," he growled through his teeth.

They cast off nervously, but with difficult attempts to seem carefree since they assumed that Roberts, though he was no longer visible, was viewing them from inside the clubhouse. When they had grumbled out the narrow channel which led to the waterway, Insinger signaled the bridgekeeper, who raised the double drawbridge for them to pass.

"Where y'all goin' on a day like this?" the old black man called as they went through. He and Mark had become familiar, and his voice was friendly and merely curious.

"Just down to Bradley Creek," Heard called back from the after deck. "See ya later."

There were small craft advisories on the weather station and sure predictions of rain and fog along the coast by early evening. The wind offshore was blowing twenty knots, and Insinger could feel it against the boat before they even reached the mouth of Masonboro Inlet. Whitecapped waves were everywhere ahead of them, crests blown in foamy S's. And even with the cabin closed up, it was cold.

Heard set up the ADF and then raised *Leda* on the radio. Through loud grating static Sidell reported that they were probably three or four miles northeast of their former position. Their Loran was almost useless, he said, and they were motoring occasionally against the current, but fuel was low so they were mostly drifting.

Leda's side-band radio produced a weak signal, and Insinger had a hard time tuning it in on the directional finder. He got it, but when he did, the rotor arm indicated unsteadily in a direction of one hundred seventy degrees—almost due south. Mark asked if Jack's last reading on the Loran could have been faulty, but Sidell was sure it had been accurate. They had to be almost due east of Masonboro. They yelled at each other in short sentences through the wild static. Mark finally replied that they would head east until they were close enough to get a stronger signal and would make radio contact again in about an hour. He signed off, and he and Heard stared apprehensively at each other. He pushed the throttle levers forward to just more than three-quarters power, and the big cruiser sat back in the water and drove ahead defiantly.

"Okay, let's just get out there," Mark mustered himself. "We'll find 'em."

Heard kept his eyes ahead of them but raised a fist and nodded.

For the first two miles the chop was uncomfortable but not bad. They moved through it at ten knots, and the thumping of waves against the hull grew slowly louder. The salon was deadly quiet compared to the way it had been on their previous outings. Don put on a tape, but—except for a few nervous questions about storing the cargo that had already been asked and answered several times—they spoke very little. It was a hard scene, and Insinger rather liked it when he looked around from the wheel. The cabin was closed tight. Heard sat in the swivel easy chair with arms folded stoically. Harry Amian smoked steadily on the couch, and beside him Don lay with his head back, trying to sleep. The music combined with the contralto growl of the diesels and the uneven beating of the boat against the sea. The United States receded out the rear windows, and the restless steel-blue Atlantic thrashed ahead toward the dark horizon, where a man could do anything he was able to accomplish. There was a concentration of energy in the cabin, a confined equilibrium of fear and resolve as they rushed toward the twelve-mile limit. And for the moment, it inspired Insinger, thrilled him. He had waited a year to do it.

They reached the big swell suddenly. There was no gradation, it seemed, between the steady, oncoming roughness of the coast and the fast rolling lift and descent of the farther waters. "Ohhhh shi-it," Don groaned when the first hard motion displaced his stomach. He was instantly ill, and Amian had to let him lie full length on the couch. The waves were only about six to eight feet, but the northeast wind made them close and steep and breaking. Mark slowed the engines to about eight knots, but it made little difference. The seas hit them on the starboard bow, and the boat seemed to lurch continuously in every possible direction. Amian was quickly ill too and lay down on the cabin sole beside the couch, and Heard's normally reddish features occasionally turned pale and empty. Talking subsided completely.

Soon the fog embraced them as if they had departed the world, and visibility was abruptly reduced to about two hundred yards. Without any horizon the motion of the boat was crueler than ever. They endured it chiefly by moaning long obscenities at the worst waves, and the cabin grew dismal with a biological pessimism impossible to overcome. Insinger became slightly nauseous but not sick. Yet he could not imagine several more hours of blind discomfort and plenty of hard labor. He kept at it only by dreaming of cash in huge sums and of himself and Helen in love again beneath the sun of some warm island—all of which seemed so distant that by comparison the rigors ahead would be brief.

The further east they struggled, the more the fog thickened, and the harder the waves grew, jarring the boat with increasing force. Gusts of wind ripped angrily, and it was like being wrapped in a gray blanket and shaken by an invisible pitiless machine. Insinger had never been in rough seas, and he fought the wheel to remain on course, tormented constantly by recollection of a conversation with an old man at Bradley Creek who had told him of boating deaths that occurred each year to people who "just didn' b'lieve the weather." Insinger began to believe with a sense of terror, as if in a vengeful god.

When an hour had passed, Don and Harry were very seasick, regularly complaining and asking like children how much longer it would be. "How goddamn far are they, for Christ's sake?. . . This is crazy, man." Heard, himself clinging to the chair and suffering, kept telling them to hang on. Mark made no attempt to use the radio but bore ahead through the fog, far more willing to trust

276

Sidell's sense of their position than the ADF. It was after three o'clock when he figured he was close. He slowed to get a Loran fix, and they tossed harder than ever. Amian barely made it down the companionway to the head before vomiting loudly. The Loran reading was unclear, but Mark was sure it was close to Sidell's reckoning. He raised Jack on the radio, and Heard grudgingly prepared to go up on the bridge as a lookout.

Jack agreed they must be close, but the ADF was again confusing. When it registered *Leda*'s weak signal, it gave a course of north-northwest. Jack doubted it was right, but the reading was more definite than before and Mark reasoned that he must have passed them and miscalculated the set of the current. They agreed to make contact again in half an hour, and Insinger set off on the new course with Heard on the bridge.

They jounced to northwestward for half an hour and saw nothing. "The hell with it," Don moaned from the couch. "We can do it tomorrow." Amian started agreeing, and in their misery they became nearly hysterical.

"Tell 'em we've gotta go back," Harry insisted.

"Yeah, fuck it. This is crazy," Don was nearly screaming. "Tell 'em we just—"

"Shut up, goddamnit," Mark snarled back. He was frightened himself and harried to distraction. He radioed *Leda* again.

Sidell demanded his position as soon as they made contact, and when Mark took a reading and reported it, Jack answered loudly and carefully with a rising anger that cut clearly through the static: "You could not possibly be near us."

"Maybe we should wait for better weather. My crew is sick."

"No way. No way. We will play a tape and keep transmitting constantly to give you better signal. Got that?"

"Yes," Mark answered, "but there is difficulty with ADF."

"Figure out the machine," Jack's voice again crackled loud and angry, "and get your ass over here." Then suddenly his voice disappeared and was replaced by sudden electric music distorted by interference but strong and insistent. It heightened the almost frantic chaos in *Errant*'s cabin.

"Jesus Christ man," Harry started up again, "why don't we just—"

"I said shut up," Insinger yelled. "Now keep quiet and let me figure this damn thing out."

He took a deep breath and tried to clear his mind enough to comprehend how the directional finder worked. The boat was still moving slowly northwest, with the seas bullying the stern. And as he tuned in the more constant signal of the music he got a pretty steady reading of almost due south again. He was desperately confused. It did not seem possible, even in the fog, that he had passed them again. Keeping the directional unit on, he brought the boat around to the south. The rotor slid around the compass card to point westward. "This piece of shit," he railed. But then he began to realize what was happening. It could not be a magnetic reading if it changed as his boat moved. He feverishly studied the unit once more and finally saw that one of the knobs was to indicate either magnetic or relative. It was set to relative. Prayerfully he switched it to magnetic and caught his breath. He whispered, "Come on baby." The rotor adjusted slowly to show one hundred ten degrees east-southeast. It made sense. Then as he headed the boat on the southeast course and the arm stayed put he suddenly understood. With the compass card set for a magnetic reading, he had been picking up a direction relative to his own course. "You stupid bastard," he derided himself. "Now let's get going." The sea and fog seemed not so invincible just then. "Harry," he ordered, "get up there and tell Marshall I got it figured out and we'll be there soon."

For another half hour they pounded eastward, and the salon was intense with the music from *Leda* mangled in static over the radio and the hollow hammer of the hull against the waves. Insinger managed to get Harry and Don up and moving around, insisting they would feel better. He kept his eyes shifting from the empty fog ahead to the arm of the directional finder and the dial of the compass. The broken music over the radio was unintelligible, but in the margin of his thoughts Mark kept remembering sounds of lyrics or pieces of different tunes as it went on. Finally he recognized one song and simultaneously recalled the others. It was Elton John's album "Madman Across the Water." Mark started laughing. Don and Harry, bilious and not at all sure that they weren't in grave danger, thought he was crazy.

Insinger saw her just as Marshall shouted from the bridge. Two hundred yards ahead, veiled in the fog, *Leda* sat with her bow to the waves. Turning off the commotion of the radio, Mark got Harry to hold the wheel while he went to the bridge to steer them up to her. It was after four o'clock, and the overcast and fog produced a silvery dusk as they moved in. *Leda*'s broad black hull was low and steady in the swell, and her bare masts and rigging loomed like a dark phantom displaced from a time long past.

"Pretty nice sight, uh?" Mark's voice was ecstatic as they closed the last hundred yards. Marshall, who had never seen the boat, stared open-mouthed, as if it were an apparition, and said nothing.

Leda's crew had the grizzled aspect of survivors, waving in a group from the stern with grinning, hungry, bearded faces and glinting eyes. They laughed and shouted wild greetings when Mark moved alongside. Even Harry and Don snapped out of their torpor and yelled back and forth with them. Mark kept the cruiser at a distance of about fifteen or twenty yards. *Leda* had appeared to be steady as a rock as he approached her, but close-by she was a huge mass rising and falling with frightening force.

Eiler and Mackenzie started yelling for cigarettes. Mark moved close enough to *Leda* so Don and Marshall could throw their packs to them, but Mark was ashamed of having brought nothing to reward the long journey. They had even drunk up all the beer and liquor on *Errant*. The resentment in Thorton's face was fierce. "We out here riskin' our asses, an' you guys don't even bring us a fuckin' beer!" he snarled.

"Hey man, it was all we could do just to get here," Don called.

Thorton threw a hand at them disgustedly, and he and Eiler cast a hail of epithets. "You pussies! This is calm!" Ralph yelled. Nevertheless the energy of the rendezvous produced a celebratory mood, and they yelled and laughed at each other for several more minutes. Briefly even the sea felt more comfortable as it seesawed the two boats. Then a light rain began to fall, and things abruptly grew serious. Mark thought he noticed someone missing. He asked obliquely if everyone was okay. They turned quiet aboard *Leda*.

"We lost Delight," Sidell called. "He's dead."

"What happened?" Heard yelled back. The sea awoke with a big wave, and the rain picked up as they struggled for footing aboard *Errant*.

"Trouble in Colombia. Tell you later. Let's get this moving," Jack shouted. They started hustling on *Leda*. "Don't you have any tires?" Jack demanded.

Insinger cringed. He had never thought of tires again since they'd discussed it months ago. Before Mark had a chance to reply, Sidell yelled angrily, "You're going to smash shit out of that boat! Jesus Christ. You better be careful. Let's go. We'll both move ahead slow."

On the *Errant* they were all dumbstruck by the news of Delight and by the threatening sea. The task ahead seemed impossible, but

279

the crew on *Leda* acted like it was nothing. Mark and Heard were still gaping at each other, uncertain what to do next, when Sidell yelled at them again to hurry up, he didn't have much fuel.

Mark moved cautiously closer. The flying bridge where he steered was above the deck of the old ketch, but they traded heights regularly in the waves, and it was difficult for Mark to tell how close he was. With the wind blowing counter to the current, the waves were confused and unpredictable. He had no sooner moved within five yards of *Leda* than the two boats were thrown together by the sea with a grinding crash. Flustered and frightened by *Leda*'s threatening size and weight, Mark moved away in a panic and could not hear Sidell's advice. He approached again, held a good position for a few moments, then the boats smashed together once more. In the hassle of it, Jack's instructions were merely shouts. He tried it again with the same result and began to fear he might do serious damage. Exasperated, he shouted at Sidell that they should wait for better weather.

"Hell no!" Eiler and Thorton yelled back at once.

"This fog is good cover," Sidell called. "Just control your goddamn boat. This sea's not bad."

"This is nothin'," Thorton screamed.

Finally with Sidell's advice Insinger managed to hold a decent position by using his engines separately. Mackenzie took *Leda*'s helm while Sidell and Thorton started to feed the sacks on deck to Eiler, who heaved them onto the afterdeck of the cruiser as fast as he could. The process was slow and exhausting. Thorton hefted one sack at a time to Sidell, and Jack lifted them through the hatch. When Eiler threw them down to the cruiser, Amian in turn threw them into the salon where Don passed them to Heard as they filled the forward sections first. There was no kidding around once they started, and barely any talking. Footing was uneasy, especially on *Errant*, and hefting the fifty-pound sacks one after another was tough work. It grew dark quickly as they labored, and the wind and rain increased. The aroused elements became far more threatening to Insinger and his crew than the prospect of a bust. The Coast Guard would not drown them.

The two boats lurched violently, scraping and colliding several times as they worked and once splintered the corner of the cruiser's stern. It took them an hour and a half to transfer two hundred bales, and when they finished it was dark and foreboding. The wind gusted and the rain flattened to a tormenting angle. Everyone was cold and wet.

Insinger was more exhausted than anyone else when it was

done. The mental and physical exertion of handling the boat had left him wasted, and he had not eaten all day. He moved the cruiser slowly away from *Leda* and tried to restore himself with deep breaths. He couldn't tell whether he was shivering or trembling. He feared he had damaged the hull colliding with *Leda*, and with the five-ton load, they already sat low in the water and clumsy as an elephant. Fort Rhodes Island seemed terribly distant. He could not believe it when Sidell shouted that he should come back for the second load that night. Just getting back to the island seemed impossible. Below him on the afterdeck, they were still stashing the last few sacks. The forward section was overloaded and the salon was packed. Hunched against the rain, Insinger gathered his wits to figure a course. He needed a Loran fix. That thought produced a convulsion of desperate fear, as he realized the Loran set was buried behind a couple of tons of dope. He had only a vague idea of his position and visibility was nearly zero. The darkness and weather seemed suddenly to increase by a hungry leap.

He maneuvered close to *Leda* again and yelled to Jack that he would reach him by radio at ten o'clock, ignoring the idea of returning for another load. Jack yelled back at him, but Mark paid no attention and brought the boat around to the west. At the same time he heard Marshall and the others closing the cabin door, wedging themselves against the cargo in the salon, and he felt absolutely alone.

He tried to keep to a course of west-southwest, angling slightly across the waves as he started back. He hoped to power ahead until he neared the coast and then figure out where he was, but he quickly found that the boat would not steer. The first waves pushed his bow around and then filled the afterdeck with water. And when he turned the wheel, nothing happened. For a few seconds of sheer panic he believed they were swamped. Cursing at the top of his voice, he pushed the starboard throttle lever forward, and the boat lurched around. But when he increased the other throttle, his speed did not increase. Instead the bow drove deeper into the water, as if it were a submarine beginning to dive. He pulled back the levers, and the elements converging on him were hopeless and overwhelming. The wind and rain tore at him from one side and the sea combated from the other. Unable to see further than about thirty yards, the night seemed endless. He eased the throttles forward again, though, and this time the cruiser floundered ponderously ahead. The sea was growing in the gusting wind, and a wave crested over the low bow, pushing them off course and blinding Mark with spray. But as he increased the starboard engine, the

281

boat recovered, and he saw that the only way to get through was by steering with the engines, and simply struggling back one wave at a time.

The best speed he could maintain was only four knots. He was soaked, and aching cold from the rain. He shuddered uncontrollably. Each time he looked back at the afterdeck, there appeared to be a foot of swirling foaming water in it. A few times he shouted crazily at the others, yelled Heard's name, but it was useless. He was alone in it. "Chickenshits," he muttered hatefully. "Marshall Heard, big deal!" He gripped the throttle levers, bent against the driving rain, and drove ahead, in constant fear that the overloaded boat would swamp or capsize as the storm gathered strength.

In the worst of it, after about an hour, Mark became consumed with a hatred of Tom Caval. And it produced a fortitude at least equalling the force of the elements. Everything about his immediate situation was perfectly indicative of his dealings with Caval. "This is the whole thing," he kept telling himself. "This is the whole goddamn thing. Sent out with false directions about the ADF, caught out in a storm transferring Caval's treasure, in danger while Caval is warm and dry. I'm going to beat that bastard," he swore to himself, and the same vengeful resolve propelled him through the darkness.

Two and a half nightmare hours passed. Then, gradually, Mark made out the faint roar of surf perhaps a half mile ahead. Instead of an ominous sound, though, it was the promise of salvation, and he edged the throttles forward a little. He was rather sure he lay somewhere south of Fort Rhodes, but when he had come as near land as he dared, there were no lights visible, no dim flash from the Masonboro buoy, no glow from Wrightsville. He slowed and turned northeastward into the wind to follow the coast and look for a bearing. Heard came out of the cabin, as if emerging from a tomb, and climbed to the bridge.

"I knew you'd make it," he gripped Mark's shoulder and raised his voice in the wind. Wet and shivering and sick, he looked pathetic. "I couldn't do anything. I'm sorry. Do you know where we are?"

"We gotta find some light. Stay up here and help me."

They made their way along the coast, with the growl of surf not far off the port side, for only fifteen minutes before they saw the flash of a light buoy, faint and small through the weather, but glowing unevenly and dim every few seconds.

"That's gotta be Masonboro," Mark shouted. He was elated for a moment, then realized that if it were Masonboro he should also be able to see the glow of Wrightsville. He felt totally lost again, but he knew the buoys along the coast and headed recklessly straight at it. In a few more minutes he was near, and he brought the cruiser dangerously close off the port side. Hanging over the side from the afterdeck and gripping the pinrail, Heard strained to read its letters as it went past. "N.T." he shouted. "It's N.T."

New Topsail inlet, Mark thought. He was far north of Masonboro and twenty miles from home.

" That's New Topsail," Heard yelled as he scrambled back to the bridge. "That's an inlet. We can go in here."

Mark knew exactly what it was, but he had never been in there. He would have to navigate six miles of a strange section of the waterway, then go through the Fort Rhodes bridge loaded down like a mule, and bypass the marina. It was tempting, but the hazards were immense. Without answering Heard, he turned out to sea again to start back down the coast, trying to steel himself for another two-hour ordeal.

"Whatta you doin'?" Heard grabbed his arm. "Let's go in here. We can go in here an' get down to the island."

"Get your goddamn hands off me," Mark wrenched himself free. Heard did not seem so large as usual. They stared at each other for a moment, with the rain pelting their faces, and the wind beating wet hair flat against their heads.

"I'm running this thing, and I'm not going through waters I don't know in this weather. I'm not taking the chance of running aground, and I'm not going under the bridge. We're going to Masonboro. If you can't take it, get yer ass back down below."

Marshall glared threateningly at him, but Mark turned away and set the throttles up as high as the boat could manage.

Two hours later, in an area that was partially protected from the wind, the rain was heavy and vertical as they approached the narrow channel that cut off the waterway toward the houses. Mark slowed the engines, and it felt warmer. The waterway was disturbed by the weather, but seemed flat calm compared to the sea, and the fog was not as thick. Mark could see the lights of the Fort Rhodes drawbridge ahead. Heard was out on the bow to spot the triangle of marsh grass that marked the channel, and Don and Harry had come out of the salon and were commiserating on the afterdeck about what a rough journey it had been.

Marshall saw the tiny grass island drawing near and raised one arm. Mark slowed the starboard engine so that the boat veered gradually to the right and into the channel. He had cut the lights several minutes earlier and moved toward the houses by memory. He motored down the narrow inner sound past the lights of several houses at the lowest, quietest speed possible and soon saw a flashlight blinking at him from the spit of land on which the storage house sat. A few minutes later the bow ground up onto the sandbank, and before he even killed the engines Mark could hear Tom Caval.

"What the hell took ya? Jesus Christ, I was scared to death. What the hell happened? Man, we gotta get this shit unloaded."

Mark made no effort to answer and simply jumped over the side into the ankle deep water and trudged slowly onto the shore. There was a steep sandbank several feet from the water, and Mark sat down heavily against it. His knees trembled from fatigue as he listened to Harry and Don clamoring about how it was, telling Caval all about it. When they reported that Delight had been killed, Caval quickly checked it with Heard, then stood perfectly still. To Mark he seemed to glow in the dark. One of Tom's men had been killed in service, and Tom absorbed the importance. It made his business more serious, his power greater.

Marshall ran a line from the bow up to the rented van that Caval had parked behind the house. Caval started ordering everyone to get busy. Mark sat against the sand and stared at him.

"Com'on, goddamnit," Caval hissed at him. "We got a lot o' work to do."

Mark laughed rancorously at him. He wanted to get up and slug him or throw him in the water. But that would never be good enough. He smiled back into Caval's intense, angry features and silently promised, "I'm going to screw you to death."

"I said com'on, damnit. Now—"

"Let 'im rest, Tommy," Heard spoke quietly as he walked back to the boat. "This shit wouldn' even be here if it wasn't for him."

Caval's eyes squinted fiercely for a moment, as if he feared not knowing what Insinger thought, and Mark kept smiling back.

It was ten o'clock by the time they began to transfer the dope to the house. Insinger had no intention of going out again, and he made no effort at radio contact. Jack could take care of himself, he figured. He would talk to him tomorrow. As soon as the boat was empty, he and Marshall motored back to the marina, pausing to tell the old bridgekeeper they had gotten in a good poker game down at Bradley Creek and their two friends were still there. When the cruiser was tied up and clean, Mark dropped Heard off to help finish storing the dope and then drove back to the other house and went to bed.

284

chapter 19

"BY God, I remember this bag. The ol' chief," said Harry. He pulled the burlap sack out of the corner from among several others and dragged it toward the table, where Caval sat with his papers. The sack bore the faded markings of its original use, in the center of which was a large red and black stencil of an Indian's head, like the profile of Calarcá on old Colombian ten-centavo pieces.

"I was layin' against this one las' night," Amian continued. "I thought the chief was gonna be the eternal pillow."

"I guess you did," Heard said. He was dragging a wet bag over to the stove. The large square room that was the kitchen, living, and dining area of the house was crowded with burlap sacks arranged in groups, and the oven and burners of the stove were on to help dry the wet ones. "Hell, I heard you talkin' to 'im."

"Damn right I was," Harry laughed. He was almost always laughing. "I thought we were headed for the deep six."

Caval looked up from his figures while they laughed. He was surrounded by sacks. "Looks like you puked on it," he quipped with a baseless adolescent perversity and then laughed at his own comment.

"I would have, man. Believe me. But I didn't have anything left by then."

"You guys had it tough alright," Insinger observed sarcastically. He sat casually on the kitchen counter, sipping a bottle of beer. "Laid out down there on a dry bed."

"Not exactly," Heard objected.

"You should've been up on that bridge."

"Thanks, I had plenty."

"You couldn've drug me up there," said Amian. "I don't know how you did it, man."

"Just wasn't a whole lot of choice."

"Yeah," said Heard, "and I was more than happy to let you be the hero."

"I appreciate that," Mark smiled.

Heard moved routinely to the front windows for a look outside, and Insinger took a pleasant swig from his bottle, enjoying the respect his efforts had earned. As he lowered the bottle he found

Caval leering at him across the room. "The man of the hour," Tom nodded slightly. Mark shrugged, and they stared for a moment, smiling curiously, distrustfully.

Since early in the morning Caval had had Marshall and Harry and Don shifting, examining, and separating bags of weed, while he made figures on a legal pad. The previous night he had them pile all the load into two of the four bedrooms, which lay off hallways on either side of the main room. Through the morning, they had placed wet bags near the stove and the heating vents in the kitchen and transferred the dope from torn sacks into green plastic garbage bags. Each of the burlap sacks was opened at one end to check the quality, and Caval had the best stuff collected in a separate group and kept count of them.

The heating had been on full since the night before, and the room was hot and stale and murky with smoke. The place reeked of fresh marijuana. Heard and Amian had taken off their shirts and were sweaty from hefting bags all morning. Insinger stayed to the side, relishing his role as momentary hero. He had smoked a joint of the stuff when he arrived, and the scene around him was dreamlike. The cargo he had landed stood everywhere in the room, the sacks open at the top and packed with fine Colombian weed. In the middle of it Caval sat like a lord receiving and judging sacks of grain from tenants.

"Jesus! Would you look at this stuff," Harry said when he had pulled open the stapled burlap of the bag with the Indian head on it. He pulled out a double handful of thick tops on narrow stems, clustered and stuck together with resin, pale brown and yellow and green.

"Yeah, that's one of the best ones awright." Caval reached out and pulled away part of the bunch and examined it with fascinated eyes.

"This stuff'll go," Heard said as he dragged another sack toward the table.

"Well I'm claimin' this bag for my load." Harry kept staring wonderously into the sack. "An' I may just keep it all for myself."

"You ain't claimin' shit." Caval tossed the clusters back to the bag. "I'm decidin' who gets what. An' I'm not decidin' 'til it's all here, an' 'til I know how much everybody's gonna take. So just put it over there with the other ones." Amian glared at him resentfully, and Caval seemed to like that. "An' I want ya to start puttin' those good bags in this front room up here," Caval went on, pointing toward the hallway on his left. "That's where we'll keep all the best stuff outta this first load. Then start bringin' 'em in outta that other room."

"What the hell? If I don't get to claim some of the good stuff, what in hell am I doin' all this work for, huh?"

" 'Cause you're gettin' the best chance. We awready said that." Caval's face reddened as his voice rose. "Yer gettin' better consideration. If you don't like it, don't do it. But if somebody else wants to work or somebody else wants to pay more, they're the ones that'll get the best stuff. See? So you help me an' I help you."

"Sure, but—"

"No." Caval thrust out his chin. "That's the way it is."

Insinger watched the exasperation in the tight redness of Amian's face as he jerked the bag across the floor and stood it upright against more than twenty others crowded along the front side of the room. It was similar to the look Don had worn as he left to perform a long list of errands for Caval just as Mark had arrived. Temporarily immune from Caval's power Mark could see how it worked and, in a moment of cognition, saw himself reflected in Amian. Caval attracted people into his circle, let them walk among the treasure, handle it, and led them to believe part of it could be theirs if only they did his bidding. Then he ultimately charged them as if they had done nothing. Mark had no doubt that Harry would get the same deal out of Caval as everyone else. Tom had a rare ability to sell someone something and make them believe he had done them a favor. Insinger found it bitterly amusing for a few moments, but he wondered too how Caval would ultimately deal with him.

Amian dragged in two more bags from the other room and scowled at Insinger as he went by. Heard was getting other bags.

"You cripple or sumthin'?" Harry asked.

"Not at all," Mark told him.

Caval looked up from his figures. "Yeah. What the hell, Mark, give 'em a hand."

"No. I got things to do." He took a sip from the beer. "I have to go down and check the boat and get on the radio."

Mark smiled at Caval as he refused him. For the time being, he held the cards. No one else was going to bring in the load, so Caval could save his orders for the others. Mark knew it would only last another day, but it was too sweet to pass up. Caval looked him over, and slowly he too smiled. As usual he knew Mark's position exactly, and he appreciated it because it would be over so soon. Caval said nothing but turned back to his pad.

A few minutes later Insinger left. It was fogged in so thickly, he could barely make out the road. That morning he had awakened to find the weather still bad and small craft warnings still in effect. Heard and the others had absolutely refused to go out in it again, and Mark had not been too eager himself. He had made no effort to contact Sidell though, and he had no intention of doing so now. Jack would only give him hell about not coming, and Mark did not care to hear it. Jack could take care of himself. Mark drove down to the clubhouse and had a drink.

ii

Leda lay blanketed by the fog in a small circle of restless gray sea. She was hove to against the northeast wind, drifting nervously in the chop, with forestaysail standing up bright as blood in the overcast light. There was a constant drizzle in the air, which only occasionally stiffened into rain, and the cold was inescapable.

Thorton climbed up through the engine room hatch, having just killed the auxiliary pumps. He looked around briefly at the conspiracy of weather, felt the affront of mist in his face, and damned everything about it as he moved around the cabin.

Eiler sat facing astern with his back against the cabin. Jesse perched on the companionway just out of the drizzle, and Sidell lay quietly on his bunk. The yellow foul weather gear they each wore was soiled with dirt and grease; their faces were grim and bearded; and they were all stiff against the cold. Imprisoned by the weather and the silence on the radio, they waited like men in jail.

"Goddamn that Insinger," Thorton railed. He struck the wheel-housing with the flat of his hand so the chains rattled inside. "Why don't he radio? What the hell's wrong with him?"

Eiler and Mackenzie grunted in agreement. The same questions had been asked fifty times since the previous night.

"Anything could come up on us in this fuckin' weather. Hell, anything coulda happened to them too. They could be busted fer all we know." He glared at Eiler as he spoke, and Joe nodded indulgently.

"I know that, Ralph, but there ain't much we can do about it. So let's just take it easy, uh? We'll hear from 'em."

"But shit, they coulda wrecked in that weather las' night. An' if they did, here we sit." He gripped the port rail as if he meant to tear it off and beat away the fog. Then he turned suddenly. "Joe, why don't you an' me take the Whaler an' head in to shore. We could take

288

the fishin' rod an' just be like we was out fishin'. Jack's got the goddamn telephone number at the house. We could call up an' see what the hell. Nobody's gonna be aroun' shore on a day like this. Whatta ya say?"

"No way you're doing that yet," Sidell called from the cabin.

"Just relax," said Mackenzie. "You know damn well what's the matter. They were sick as dogs yesterday. They thought it was a goddamn typhoon. They're just not coming back out in it, that's all. And they don't have the nerve to get on the radio and say so."

They were all silent for a few moments, and Thorton moved into the cabin to sit on Jesse's bunk. Fog seemed to mute the hum of wind, but the waves slapped hard at *Leda*'s sides. In the cabin there was only low whispering static on the radio, and the dramatic tick of the chronometer.

"They'll be in touch as soon as the weather breaks," Jack said finally. "With some damn excuse." There was another minute without talking, and the sense of nervous apprehension built, as if unattended matters were accumulating dangerously. "I wonder what they're going to do when we report Billy lost?" Jack looked ahead morosely. Since Delight had been on the crew list out of Aruba, there would be no avoiding the matter when they cleared Customs. "I guess we'll have to make out some forms or something for the Coast Guard." Jack's voice grew more dismal with each word. "They may want to look into it."

They had discussed the problem numerous times already, but it was a thing that would not rest and haunted them with the prospect of an uncontrollable chain of inquiries.

"I think our story's good," said Jesse. "We lost him in the storm. He was gone before we could do anything, and it would've been impossible to save him anyway. We lost our antenna too and didn't have any transmitting power to report it. And if we had, it wouldn't have changed anything anyway. What the hell could we do? People are lost at sea all the time."

"I know. But there's going to be a lot of questions, and they're going to get damn curious about what we were doing."

"Just stick to the story," Eiler leaned in front of the cabin door to speak. "That's all we can do."

Jack nodded silently. "We've got to tell his family though. And do it right too. So they won't get nosy and want an investigation." Jack flinched a little at his own cynicism, but he knew the situation would require a good deal more of it. "And who the hell's going to have time for it."

"Well, goddamnit, I'll go if I have to," Thorton blurted. Then his sudden resolve trailed off, as he realized that when he left Fort Rhodes it would be with a great deal of dope and no time for consoling anyone's mother. "I mean . . . couldn' we just . . . oh shit!" He rolled wearily onto his back. "It's so . . . fucking . . . I don' know . . . sloppy."

The agreement was their silence and the heartless tick of the chronometer.

Jack finally said, "I'll go. I can fly out as soon as we clear. I guess that'd be best. I could get back the same night or the next morning."

The others mumbled in agreement, but a thorough feeling of disgust abided and mixed uneasily in their stomachs with the anxiety and the discomfort of the elements.

"I better get back to work on the Loran," Jesse said halfheartedly a few minutes later, "before we drift to Nova Scotia."

"Why don't you let me try it a while," Jack stirred himself to a sitting position on the bunk. "I watched my father fix one once."

Mackenzie shrugged and shifted around on the companionway to look out into the slow-moving gray miasma of fog.

"Wanna play some gin rummy?" Eiler asked him.

"Go to hell," said Jesse.

iii

A man stepped suddenly out of the darkness and fog from beside the road and beckoned stiffly with both arms. Startled, the driver hit his brake, and the big Ford ground to a halt on the gravel. "Damn fool," he muttered. The man in the fog came quickly to the driver's window as he lowered it.

"You Jeff Culleney?" the man asked furtively.

"That's right," said the driver.

"I'm Roberts. Uh . . ." He thought of asking to see a badge but saw the radio unit beneath the dash. "Why don't ya pull your car up over here, an' we'll take mine. So we don't alert 'em."

Culleney breathed heavily. "Okay." He drove to the left, into a small parking lot in front of the island's management office. It was after nine o'clock, and he wanted only to go home and eat dinner. For the past week he had been required to hold down the Customs office in Wilmington with only two secretaries to help. The temporary agent-in-charge had been transferred back to Norfolk, but the former SAC had not yet returned to work after a brief stint with the

Drug Enforcement Administration. Meanwhile the other agent in the office had been attending a strategy conference in Florida, so Culleney had been saddled with everyone else's work. Having just returned that morning from a case in Charlotte, he had spent the entire day attending to paperwork. He had not returned Roberts' call because it seemed insubstantial, but Hinton Roberts had spent the afternoon harrying the local D.A. and the U.S. Attorney until they in turn pressed Culleney to go check it out. All Roberts had to offer, though, was personal suspicion and a charge of strange behavior against a group of tenants on the island. So Culleney viewed the visit as his final tribulation of the day.

"Now I'm askin' you," Roberts began as soon as Culleney got into his station wagon, "what in the world would four guys be doin' goin' out for a cru-uise," he drew out the word emphatically, "on a day like yesterday when there's fog comin' and small craft advisories? Now I know they weren't fishin', because they've as much as tol' me they don't know nuthin' about fishin'."

"Did you ask them?"

"What they were doin'? Well o' course not. They tol' our bridgekeeper—when they came back nearly at midnight—that they'd been playin' poker down at Bradley Creek, and two of 'em wasn't on the boat. Well I happen to know 'bout every poker player between here an' Myrtle Beach, an' I have never heard o' any games goin' on at Bradley Creek marina, for heaven sake."

Culleney did not even waste the effort to say that those circumstances were not exactly grounds for calling in U.S. Customs. With an effort he listened as Roberts drove across the bridge and onto the island.

"To begin with, they're just not the sort o' people that come here. They say they're from Cali-fornia. Out here representing some cor-po-ration or something. But now, here's four young guys don't know anything about this area, and yet they're here over Christ-mas. Well, they don't do a fiddlin' thing but go out in that boat, which happens to be just about the biggest cruiser we've had here, and they've got *two* houses. An' they don't use one of 'em, except that they started to las' night, which was the night they went out in that fool weatha'. Well I've also seen 'em cruisin' around behind the houses in the channel, and *not* fishin' either."

"So you figure they're smugglin' marijuana, uh?"

"I know as certainly as I'm drivin' this car that they're up to somethin', and that's what makes sense."

When Roberts parked at the marina, they got out and Roberts

identified the *Errant*, raising his eyebrows at Culleney as he pronounced the name. He noted that Mr. Templin and his associates were the only people who locked their boat, and he pointed out the damaged transom and long black scrapes along the port hull.

"I figure they whacked that cruiser into another boat while they were transferrin' the stuff in that weatha'."

"Could've gotten drunk playing poker and run up on something in the waterway too, couldn't they?" Culleney had rarely seen a case actually constructed out of clues, and he thought Roberts had a wonderful imagination. Roberts wanted him to examine the boat closely, but the agent passed it off.

"Why, think of the prints there must be."

"Uh-huh," Culleney smiled faintly. "That might be rushing things a little. Where are these houses they have?"

Rather disappointed, Roberts drove toward the houses. On the way, he kept trying to describe the basis of his suspicions, and Culleney listened with the last of his patience.

". . . Another thing that don't make sense," he said after rambling a little, "is that here ya have four decent lookin' young guys. They don't appear to be fruits. They're here over the holidays, and there's only one gal with 'em. One gal. Was another one with this Templin when he first came, and she was a beautiful little thing, supposed to be his wife I guess, but didn' look old enough if you ask me. And then she up an' left."

The presence of only one woman in the company of young men who apparently had a lot of money caught Culleney's attention, and he nodded and wrinkled his forehead as Roberts went on. Rich guys didn't have trouble finding chicks; he knew that. Still it was only a curious point and nothing to go on. He had learned that there is something strange about everyone's life. But more than that, he was tired and, for the moment at least, had no real desire to uncover a big case. Anyway, if he were running a deal, Fort Rhodes Island would be the last place he would pick.

At the first house, where Roberts knew that Templin and his friends had been staying, they made a slow pass around the circular end of the road. All the lights were on, and three cars were in front. Roberts moved quickly to the other house, the Garwood place, which he described to Culleney as "their warehouse."

The lights were on in that house too, and a rented Ford sedan was parked in the drive. Cutting his headlights, Roberts stopped just before the driveway.

"Now there's a van been parked here all day. Where do ya figure that van is?"

292

"I can't imagine," said Culleney. "The place doesn't look too mysterious to me. How would they get the stuff from the cruiser to the house?"

"That channel I spoke of runs right behind here. Coulda used a little skiff or just beached that yacht. Look! Look there at the winda' left o' the door. Someone's peekin' out."

"I'm not surprised. What would you do if somebody pulled up in front of your house and killed the lights?"

"Well, I'll bet your odds that that place is full of marijuana." Roberts spoke the word with deep aversion. "Why don't you jus' go up to the door an' ask 'em a few questions?"

"Mister Roberts, I just can't do that. If there was more evidence . . ."

In five years with Customs, Culleney had acquired the habit of trusting his instinct, and nothing Roberts had told him or anything he had seen had alarmed those senses. There was that bit about no women, but that was so little.

Heard let the curtain fall back in place. Open bags covered almost every inch of the kitchen floor except for a narrow space in front of the refrigerator to the stove. He had knocked over two bags rushing to the window at the sound of a car.

"Roberts," he said aloud. "You son of a bitch . . ." Heard suddenly felt an emptiness in his stomach and a thin metallic flavor to his saliva which he had known before. "Awright Roberts," he spoke softly. He slammed home the bolt, sending a cartridge into the chamber of the .308. "You wanna be a hero just come on up."

Heard parted the curtain again slightly and kept watching. A nerve began to twitch in his right bicep and the right side of his neck. Thirty seconds passed before the darkened car backed around and departed.

"Too bad, Roberts," Heard spoke louder as the car moved away, and he suddenly sweated profusely. "You missed the big chance."

iv

The fog had thickened around *Leda* by eight o'clock, so that from the stern, where Sidell and Eiler leaned shivering in the darkness against the rail, it was not possible to see the bowsprit. Thorton, standing silently against the mainmast, looked out into the deep, gray oblivion and was a blurred ghostly figure.

"I'm starting to get worried too. I was just mad before," said Jack, "but Ralph could be right. Anything could've happened.

Maybe you guys should have run into shore this afternoon. I can't believe they wouldn't get in touch for this long. It's really starting to bother me."

A few moments passed before Joe answered.

"I'll tell ya what bothers me, Jack," he spoke thoughtfully but with a dim smile. "It's bein' so damn close to a bottle o' scotch. Ya know it?"

"Jesus." Sidell looked away.

"Really. Knowing that it's right out there somewhere, not far away. In a store or somebody's house or something. And knowing that nobody could possibly appreciate it right now as much as I would."

"Always nice to have you to talk to about something serious."

"Yeah, well I'd like to have me a bottle o' scotch and be layin' in some lady's arms. And not have anything serious to think about."

"Sure. I guess that would be nice."

"I'm tired of all this bullshit. I'm tired of business being such a hassle all the time."

Jack grunted in response as he shuddered at a cold gust. He was not yet tired though. He was weary from the trip, but not like Joe, who to Sidell sometimes seemed totally worn out. Jack still had energy. He still had plans, and looked forward to completing them.

"It would be nice, but we've got this to finish first." He could not bring himself to address Joe's melancholy, as if it would encourage a weakness neither of them could afford.

"Oh yeah." Joe nodded rather dejectedly.

"Hey. You guys hear that? You hear somethin'?" It was Thorton yelling back at them, and there was an edge on his low voice, as if he hated them.

Sidell and Eiler glanced at each other and listened a moment but heard only the slap and splash of waves and the old boat creaking and the mournful strains of wind against the rigging.

"Still hear it?" Jack called.

"No. Sounded like breakers though."

"Couldn't be."

"It could be *any* goddamn thing," Ralph shouted back. He had grown steadily angrier since the previous night. After all they had been through, he knew things were not being done properly on the island. And after they had risked their lives on *Leda*, Caval and Insinger would not come out in the fog and would not even radio to tell them what was happening. The groaning anticlimax of waiting blindly in the fog for twenty-four hours had affected the others differently. They had lain about doing almost nothing, drifting in every respect, and that ran profoundly counter to Thorton's spirit. He had grown angry, and angry at the others for not taking some action. They had stayed clear of him all day. He was a dangerous man when he was mad. Now he stood with his back against the mast and arms folded, and he listened intently.

Half an hour later, Sidell was talking about getting into a drydock in Wilmington after the second load was off. It would take a few days, then they could pick up their shares of cargo and be gone. Jesse and Margaret would take care of the boat after that, moving either to Norfolk or down to Charleston. As Jack spoke, Eiler watched the dark fog overhead. It had begun to swirl slowly, and the night seemed mysterious and the future unknown. He was startled by Thorton storming back toward the cabin.

"Goddamnit, you can hear it now," he roared at them. His hair stood up in a long wisp above his high, broad forehead, and his face was mean behind the beard.

"What the hell are you—"

"—That's surf, damnit. Listen!"

Eiler and Sidell both recoiled at Thorton's rage, but listened intently. There was a deep whispering somewhere ahead. Thorton bristled before them with his jaw set and eyes blazing. Sidell moved past him and hurried forward with Thorton and Eiler behind. At the bow they could hear the faint hum and roar of waves breaking in the distance.

"Jesus, it is," Jack mumbled. His brow furrowed nervously, as he tried to think while Thorton fumed menacingly at his side.

"That's northeast, isn't it?" said Eiler.

"No shit," Thorton growled. "Now where the fuck are we?"

"Just a minute, damnit." Sidell gnawed at the nail of a middle finger. "That's the shoals. Got to be the Cape Lookout shoals. How in hell could we have—"

"I don't know how we done anything," Thorton exploded, "but fix that goddamn Loran and find out where the hell we are!"

Jack stared back at him. He did not care to be yelled at.

"Take it easy," said Joe.

"Easy my ass. I didn' come through all this shit to run this fuckin' boat aground. Now let's git this goddamn thing together an'—"

"Quit yelling," Sidell yelled back at him. " Go start the engine." He turned away quickly and headed for the wheel.

On a south-southwest heading they sailed all night, saving the last of the diesel fuel for reaching harbor once the cargo was off. Around midnight the wind began to expire, and the seas lengthened and relaxed. The fog began to dissipate during the last hours before dawn and departed quickly at sunrise. There was a flawless brilliance to the sky in the first good light, and the sea lay placid and blue green, as if the planet were making amends.

Clutching cups of coffee in the sharp early air, they moved close along the shore and by about eight o'clock identified Fort Rhodes Island.

"I guess we better head back out, uh?" said Mackenzie.

"Hell no," said Jack. "I want those bastards to get their asses out here. We can sit right off there," he pointed toward the Mason Inlet, remembering where the houses stood on the island. "They'll be able to see us if they just look out the goddamn window."

"We'll attract all kinds of attention, though," Jesse argued.

"Less than we would sitting twelve miles out, looking guilty as hell. I'd fire off a cannon if I had one."

V

Insinger lay half awake for several minutes before fully realizing that there was sunlight in the room. It fell across his bed in a distorted rectangle that extended across the floor. He sat up and thrust himself toward the window. In amazement at the sparkling flat sea and bright sky, he saw nothing else at first. Then his breath stuttered in shock when he saw *Leda* lying patiently under bare masts a quarter mile off the inlet. "Incredible," he gasped.

The next time Insinger saw her, he was on the bridge of the cruiser cleaving the glassy water at almost full throttle as he came up on her about fifteen miles off shore. He had burst out of bed yelling after he'd seen her from his window, then sped to the marina before any of them were ready. He and Jack had been curt on the radio. It was no place or time to complain. Jack said he would simply move away from Mason Inlet on a course of 120°, adding heavily that he would see him whenever Mark felt comfortably ready.

Everything was different when Insinger moved alongside though. Heard and Harry and Don were well; the boats were easy to control; and the long wait of the previous day was almost forgotten. There was a hail of obscene accusations along with the first greetings, especially from Thorton, but they faded quickly before the certainty of getting the job done at last. In addition, Insinger had purchased a case of beer and things like pretzels, potato chips, cookies, and cigarettes, which were received aboard *Leda* with reverent thanks.

The job itself was so swift and pleasant compared with almost every other aspect of the journey that it seemed over too soon. When it was finished, Thorton climbed on deck again, opened a beer, and took Joe Eiler in his arms like a lover. "We figured you guys had been up to that," Amian yelled at them from the cruiser. Ralph dropped his head back and laughed from the depth of his soul. Then he and Joe waltzed around the deck amid a boundless hilarity and several flying beer cans.

Part Three

chapter 20

THE sun was distant; a thin haze gave uncertain direction to the day. It was cold again. Insinger cringed against the morning wind. He balanced a moment on the damaged afterdeck of the *Errant* and poked at the splintered corner of the transom with his right foot. The boat was injured, beat up after two brutal tasks.

The planks beneath him were bowed and broken away from the gunwhales, after catching ten tons of dope thrown down from *Leda*. Inside, a dozen things were bent or broken. The sides of the hull were scarred and battered. The *Errant* did not look so classy anymore.

Emotionally, Insinger was similarly worn. His face had two days' growth of beard. His darkened, narrow features were smooth with a layer of nervous oil and carried a look of confusion and disappointment. The *Errant* had been his promise and refuge, but that seemed to have vanished now, expired too quickly. He had looked forward to his role in transferring the cargo, as if it would be the thrill of his life. And now, on the morning after the second load, it seemed to have passed as clumsily and quickly as a first attempt at sex. He felt let down and cheated. Now he was back under Caval's power, and all that remained were Caval's orders and the task of overseeing Amian. His liberty was still far in the distance. Yet the prospect of riches was not enough to keep him going now. The desire for sudden cash wealth had certainly been the main factor all along, but Insinger was beginning to realize that what he had wanted more was the exultation of triumph, of having conquered convention, the strictures of normal life and the law. That had turned out to be a fleeting conflict though—and a small victory. He felt that Caval had known it would be, that Caval had hung it before his nose as bait, and he had followed it like a dog.

Now, more than the money, he looked forward to beating Caval and being with Helen again. He could endure anything to gain satisfaction from Tom Caval, but Helen's absence was an emptiness in which he suffered like a man awaiting death. He agonized over having sent her away, always remembered that repudiated longing in her eyes before the plane, and saw in it the failure of his love for her. Constantly he thought of her alone, without anyone who loved her enough to oppose her belief that life was unalterably tragic. He ached for her body, and he worried deeply, not over her safety or her fidelity, but for her happiness. And he knew it was the first time he had ever been truly in love. So there was a torturous sense of danger in her absence, as if that previous precarious balance of perfection he had known so briefly with her would fall subject to the natural disorder of life. He had tried three times to call her since she left, but could not find her. For a moment, though, he thought it might actually be best not to talk to her. There was still a great deal ahead of him, he believed, before he would be free to have her again.

Mark sat heavily on the port rail and blew out his breath in a long, mournful whistle that the wind snatched away. Life seemed insidiously difficult. He could not bear the thought of returning to the house. New people had begun to arrive the night before, and the place was a madhouse. Caval was wild with power, and the house was taut with fear of him and distrust. There was nothing there for Mark except Caval's further domination, and just then he felt he might never escape it.

A few minutes later, in a sort of half thinking desperation, an idea came to him. He glanced around at the damaged deck. He could take the boat for repairs. It had to be fixed. Hell, he could go to Norfolk. No, Charleston. He could have Helen meet him there for a few days before he had to start following Amian. It would be perfect. He believed that urgently. It could be just as it had been before.

When Mark had hurried to the phone booth outside the clubhouse, there was no answer at the apartment of Helen's sister. Then as he dialed her parents' number he felt a rising sense of emergency, as if he had waited too long. After several empty rings, she answered, her voice tired and resigned, and he was struck by it with a sense of guilt, abandonment.

302

"Hi, it's Mark." He prayed for some brightness in her reply.

"Hello," she said again, softly. There was an irony in her voice and a barrier around it.

"How are you, honey?"

"I'm okay, I guess."

"Uh . . . your brother's here. He's alright. They got here a few days ago. They had some trouble, but he's alright."

"Good. I was worried." It seemed that she did not want to say more but added as if only in politeness, "How is everything?"

"We had a pretty rough time at first, but it turned out."

"I'm glad." The absence of feeling and her brevity held him away like a sword.

"Gawd, I miss you, baby. I really want to see you." He waited for some reciprocation, but hurried on when there was none. "I've got to get *Errant* down to, uh, Charleston. I tore it up a little. I thought you could meet me down there. We wouldn't have a lot of time. I've still got a lot of things to do, but it would be better than this. You could fly down in a day or two."

"Mark, I don't want to do that." There was a deep ennui in her words.

"Why not?" Mark spoke helplessly, like a blind man groping in darkness. "Charleston is nice. Remember? We'd be alone."

The silence before she answered stretched a void between them.

"I can't just keep running around . . . trying to have a romance . . . whenever nothing gets in the way . . . I just can't do—"

"We don't have to. We don't have to," he cut her off fearing what she might say next. "I don't want it to be like that. You know I don't. I've told you that. It has to be for a little while longer, but not always. Meet me in Charleston, baby." His voice nearly broke. "I've got to see you."

"Mark, let's just let it go."

"Whatta ya mean? Let it go? I love you Helen. What . . . you . . ." She felt so distant he could barely go on. "Baby, you're so far away. Come see me. We can get it together again."

"Oh Mark . . . trying to get it together again. I don't want that. I know it sounds stupid, but I don't know what I want."

"Helen, please come down. We want the same thing. I know we do."

There was a silence like the last cigarette.

"I'm going up to Marblehead tomorrow, Mark. I'm going up to see Robert."

It was as if she had held the gun cocked throughout the halting painful conversation, and now had fired. She waited for him to answer, but he was like a dumb animal finally put out of misery. The struggling stopped, the thrashing about for some word or expression to try to restrike some chord of love ceased. And the void proceeded infinitely. In his own silence, he knew it was just like Far Prospect, just like the airport several days ago. Insist, entreat, beg her, something told him, but he could not do it. As before, he could not suffer further pain. He feared more humiliation; some total loss of dignity threatened him. He knew he must risk that for her love. But when he spoke, it was not possible.

"Is that what you want?" He asked it in the reflex of defense, and it came out as surrender, as acknowledgement of defeat, and sounded like the first spade of earth on a coffin. And she sighed "Yes" as hopelessly mournful as a mother at the grave.

They stumbled through a sequence of tired old phrases, each missing the mark of their emotions as carefully as a eulogy.

"I'll always love you," he said finally, and she said, "No you won't," and the thing was gone.

ii

All who passed through the Garwood house once the entire shipment was stashed became intoxicated by a mixture of greed, fear and mistrust, as if they all breathed the same gas, which was Caval's passion for control.

By that time of course, the marijuana business was already old and had changed considerably. Not much remained anywhere of that sense of hippie brotherhood that had guided most of the market for several years. All kinds of people were in it. Nevertheless, throughout the business there was a feeling of togetherness outside the law, the necessity of trust, and not a lot of selfish grinding over every point of percent. And there was still a looseness to the commerce befitting the exigencies of the enterprise, which were chiefly to get the deal down with everyone happy as quickly as possible, before the cops came.

But to Tom Caval that was all bullshit. Like everyone, he was in the trade because there was more excitement, more money and no taxes, but the reason Tom *loved* it was because there were ultimately no rules. To him the business was an animal test of wits—a level at which few people care to operate, but where Caval excelled.

By necessity, large shipments were mainly fronted. So trust

was implicit. As always when there is no formal means of redress, the rule of self-protection was to deal with people you knew, but accounts receivable were inherently risky. How breach of contract would be dealt with was rarely mentioned in the construction of a deal. It remained the unmentionable, so honesty was made sacrosanct, and more than in conventional affairs, a man's word was his honor. Honor may be the most unstable of human qualities, though, and it is in no greater evidence on one side of the law than the other. Rip-offs had always been a regular occurrence, but there had never been many violent people in the marijuana trade. And mayhem, as a form of reprisal, was a rarity. There was always plenty of grumbling about violence but a nearly universal reluctance to apply it. A greater force for keeping bargains was, first, the fear of acquiring the reputation of being a cheat and, then, the need of finding new unknown people to deal with. So it was in those days anyway.

Tom Caval, however, had ripped people off prominently. He had that reputation, and he never flinched at it. He always had his own version, his own justification—facts were nothing before his powers of rationalization—and he did not give a damn what anyone thought. Moreover, he was never squeamish about new associates, and he was never scared. In addition he loved to talk about violence. He seldom advanced dope to anyone without alluding somehow to his well-nurtured role of having underworld connections, connections that could easily be turned to the painful demise of one who crossed him. One time in Boulder, Joe Eiler heard Tom tell a guy, "Two weeks. That's our deal. An' I want that dough then. Where I come from, people's knees bend the wrong way when they fuck off. And that's for reminders." Most people knew that his family had such acquaintances, but some, like Sidell and Eiler and a few others, doubted that Caval could put them to any use. Still there was always just enough material for Caval to weave his threat, and no one ever really knew if it were true. A year earlier a young man had driven over a cliff on his way to Independence Pass outside Aspen, and since he had owed Caval money, Tom discreetly allowed the rumor that he had been responsible. Before that, there had been another guy who had not paid Caval a large debt, and after he disappeared, Caval was quick to say that he would never be around again. He never was. Another similar rumor arose in connection with a young man in Tucson whose car exploded one day, although he was not in it. Whenever the story came up, Caval merely smiled, which was all people needed. A few tales like those go a long way, and Caval made the best of them. He was rarely content to leave the matter unstated. He would bluntly demand to be paid within a certain time and did not care what problems the other party might encounter. He wanted his money he would say, "or else you know what happens."

He was content to deal through fear and discomfort. It fed his ego and his self-image to order and browbeat, and he would have rather not been in the business at all than give it up. If some people didn't like it, that was fine. Tom Caval never had trouble attracting new partners. Those captivating looks and his style and confidence dependably drew people who were just daring enough to want to join him or try to be like him, but generally not quick or ruthless enough to keep up with him. Their fascination usually lasted until the time for real bargaining was at hand.

Caval's business practices had generally been complimented, and partly necessitated, by the fact that he rarely had good merchandise to sell. Conventional wisdom in the field held that the only way to do well consistently was to deal in quality with moderate but assured profits and eliminate the problem of getting stuck with a lot of weight. Tom Caval had a simpler understanding: buy cheap and sell dear. To that end, he did not care how long it took to move a load, and if it required screwing the source, cutting the weight, or lying about the quality, well, that was simply business. He figured, when you're outside the law, you watch your ass. He always watched his ass. Anyone who did not and bitched about it later was not worth bothering over.

So with ten tons of the finest quality on hand at Fort Rhodes, Tom Caval was in a fervor of cunning and avarice. A house full of contraband generates a high feel of intrigue and considerable possibility of danger. And in this case, the dope was very special and the seller was equally rare. Colombian weed was still unusual, and every dealer who came to the island was hot to get some. So all of Caval's unendearing talents reached an apex, and the Garwood house was a treacherous place.

After talking to Helen, it had taken Insinger another hour before he could bring himself to return to the house. When he reached the door, he was numb and silent. Heard opened the door before Mark reached it and admitted him with no greeting other than a slight jerk of the chin and a curious squint. The .308 stood beside him against the wall. It was stifling inside from the heaters and the stove, still burning at maximum. The air was thick with smoke and ridden with the smells of dope and sweat, the sense of tension and paranoia. Voices were high with competitive anger,

306

and dope was stacked everywhere, some bags piled in high banks against the walls and others standing open revealing the pale-brown treasure packed inside. Except for narrow passages giving access to the stove, refrigerator, and hallways, the floor was completely taken up with the bags. There was another clearing around the table, where Caval sat using two chairs in order to prop up his bare feet, and an old pump shotgun lay beside him on the floor.

Les Batalli had arrived from Kansas City the night before and stood in front of Caval as if he were being interrogated. He was a small muscular man and a good dresser, but he looked harried from the effort of bargaining with Caval, and his square face was wet with perspiration and darkened by a heavy shadow of beard. Two men who had accompanied Batalli stood nearby, shifting uncomfortably against the sacks and looking very nervous. Don and Harry were present as always, Amian sitting at the table, and Don on the floor with his back against the sacks. They were waiting to see what they would ultimately get from Caval, languishing like dogs around the back door at dinnertime. Behind Caval at the hallway entrance, Ralph Thorton sat in the doorway nodding in and out of sleep. He had come to the island early that morning after a hard-drinking celebration with Sidell, Eiler, and Mackenzie.

No one spoke to Insinger as he came in and looked around disinterestedly. Batalli stopped talking a moment to glance at him, then resumed his argument. The atmosphere was charged with a sense of futile waiting, as if it were the first round of negotiations between bitterly opposed parties, wherein everyone knew that an agreement would be reached sometime but not yet. Batalli knew Caval was like that. And Caval knew that Batalli would bargain for two or three days, grow tired, then paranoiac, and finally take what was offered.

"Well now what the hell does that mean?" Batalli raised his voice after Caval had merely shrugged in answer to his last expostulation. "I can move a ton of this stuff. You know damn well I can. I can do it in a week. Two weeks at the very most. With the money. *With* the money."

Without answering, Caval turned to see who had come in, and Batalli shook his head in exasperation.

"Where the hell you been?" Caval demanded.

"Checking the boat," Mark replied distantly.

"Great. What for?"

"She's pretty busted up. I think I ought to run her down to Charleston to a boatyard."

"My dyin' ass." Caval took the opportunity for a display of

toughness. "You crazy? We got work to do, man. The party's over. You're workin' for me now." He paused a moment to let that sink in. The cargo was in, and he was back in control. He wanted Mark to understand that as clearly as Mark had known his own position two days ago. "I want you around here all the time now. I want you keepin' a record of everything that goes outta here. Y'know? Weights and prices. You're gonna be my secretary, man. Got that? You're the secretary now." He grinned viciously at Insinger as he finished, and his eyes were bright and blinking, as if they worked on some electronic circuitry.

Mark nodded slowly at him. At the moment, nothing in the room made much difference to him, except that the tension and turmoil seemed unbearable. He felt as if the purpose of everything had been suddenly erased, as if he kept from breaking down completely only from one minute to the next. Barely focusing on the mass of objects around him, he scarcely noticed Caval still chastising him.

". . . Charleston. I don't believe it. Sure ya don't wanna go back to Aspen an' get a little skiing in while I wrap this up?"

"Think we could get back to work, Tommy?" Batalli asked irritably. "I got a few arrangements to make ya know."

"Awright, I'm listenin'." Caval turned his grin to Batalli and smugly folded his arms.

"Listenin'. Come on, Tommy. I already told ya." Batalli could barely keep from shouting. He was one of several people who hated dealing with Caval, but could seldom resist it—and certainly could not in this case. "Let me take two thousand of it."

"Well, I don' know if I should."

"Damnit. You said a month ago I could take a ton."

"Maybe," Caval snarled. "I said maybe. A lotta people want a piece of this. Why the hell should I give you that much? What're you doin' for me, huh?"

"I'm movin' your dope for a hundred an' fifty bucks a pound that's what. Whatta ya want? That's a lotta dough. Three hundred grand, man. And I can get it back to ya quick."

"Alright. I'll think it over." Caval turned away and looked at his note pad, leaving Batalli staring in a speechless rage. "Go on back to the Ramada an' I'll call ya tonight. Maybe in the morning."

"Whatta ya think I'm doin' out here, takin' a fuckin' vacation?" Batalli shouted. "You tell me to come out here an' pick up a ton of this shit, an' you want me to hang around like a fool. What kinda bullshit is this?"

"It's my dope, that's what." Caval's face was a red mask as he screamed back at Batalli. "*My* dope. You got that? I don't have to give you anything." His voice reached a pitch that paralyzed the room. "Nothing!"

Batalli furrowed his brow and recoiled at the outburst. He did not say another word but looked sidelong at Caval, as if he had just seen sheer madness for the first time. The room was possessed by a pervasive fright as Caval stared at Batalli, his breath hissing through his nose, as if they all were shocked by the tantrum and suddenly fearful of their own safety in the company of such a man surrounded with guns and dope. Insinger was shaken from his torpor and looked around in the acute silence. The eyes of Batalli's friends were wide with disbelief. Amian and Don shifted their glances uneasily from Caval to each other. Thorton had come completely awake during the noise and sat stiffly against the door jamb, slowly shaking his head with a bewildered, disdainful look.

Insinger watched each of the expressions for a moment and took a perverse pleasure in seeing them suffer under Caval's wild capriciousness. Then he looked over his shoulders toward the front door. Heard was just turning back to the room after a quick glance out the small curtained windows of the door, gnawing at a hangnail. His eyes caught Insinger's, and they smiled at each other.

The next seventy-two hours ran together in chaos, so that whenever Insinger had cause to go outside or by chance looked out a window, he was surprised by either darkness or light and generally could not estimate the hour. He became a counsel, an assistant, in a more subservient role than any he had known in his distant tenure in Chicago. And he was resigned to it. At the same time, it allowed him an immunity from Caval and diversion from the melancholy of his own affairs. He became Caval's shadow, was rarely away from him, slept only when Tom did and kept scrupulous account of each contact, advance, transaction; of prices and qualities and amounts; of names and phone numbers; and of every change and rechange that occurred with the spasms of Caval's whim. He was quiet and dutiful to his client and spoke only when his opinion was asked. And in the meantime, he buffered himself from the tension around him and salved his heart with long dreams of Helen in the sweet drama of reunion played over and over in his mind, word by word in half a dozen settings, each of which came out so much better than the prospects of reality.

Caval took advantage of Mark's passivity whenever it allowed him to impress someone by referring to Mark as his attorney or bookkeeper or secretary and by issuing curt orders. At which Mark would simply raise his eyebrows, purse his lips slightly, and then smile and perform his function. Around him at every hour people came and went, were insulted, lied to, screamed at, threatened, and always played off against each other, until Caval had them buffaloed to his satisfaction. All of it Mark recorded with a mercenary objectivity, sometimes observing that Caval abused people for no apparent purpose other than his own amusement.

Batalli finally agreed almost gratefully to pay two hundred dollars each for two thousand pounds, just so he could get out of town. Caval kept another man waiting at a Wilmington hotel for three days. When Caval finally decided he could not force the guy to pay his price, he woke him up on the telephone at three-thirty one morning and told him that if he didn't pick up the load in an hour's time there would be no deal at all. Fearing some impending disaster, the guy drove his Winnebago motor home onto the island before dawn, loaded it in a near panic, and departed—with Caval laughing at him in the doorway.

The chief result of Caval's behavior was steady movement across the island's single bridge of rental cars, vans, campers, and alien nervous faces at unusual hours, which became prominent even among the heightened traffic of the holidays. The atmosphere of the houses and the temper of each transaction became more and more strained, both in fear of a bust and of Caval's caprice. Paranoia grew each day, with each tortured agreement, with each of Caval's screaming rages, with each assertion of his power to do anything he wanted, until Don, in darkest humor, began to call him the mad prince.

Everyone, if they wanted a piece of the action, was forced to treat Caval with great caution and deference. Harry Amian became a model of servility, getting meals for Caval and running his errands, in order to protect his position. Ralph Thorton, who slept in the Garwood house each night with the Thompson at his side, had known Caval too long and faithfully to be bullied by him. He too grew almost obsequious in his presence, eager to agree with him and ready to serve, but Ralph did it with the felicity of a big brother who feared that the young prodigy might run amok and hurt himself more than others and out of his characteristic respect for the figure he identified as boss—and certainly to protect his own considerable stake in it all.

Don, however, was a little too cynical and had a little too much self-respect and not enough desire for wealth to meet the circumstances. In addition to the services he had already performed by the time the entire cargo had reached the island, he continued to be of use to Caval, shuttling van loads to contact points on the mainland, while still trying to make his own deal. Gradually the strain began to crack his patience, as Caval kept putting him off to pursue less certain, more lucrative possibilities. He started responding angrily to Caval's orders or not responding at all. Then in the early hours of one morning, when Don wanted only to sleep but Caval wanted him to move a load off the island, Don yelled at him: "Goddamnit, I want to get my own fucking load and get out of here. I'm sick of your shit!" And Caval smiled at him and said, "Are you?" Don went ahead and delivered the load, but by the afternoon of New Year's Eve, Insinger could see from his record of remaining inventory and the list of potential takers that nobody needed Don. That evening just as Caval was returning from a shower, the phone rang in the crowded Garwood house. Don picked it up and answered, "Cutthroat Hotel." No one had a chance to laugh. He had barely delivered another word when Caval ripped the receiver from his hand, told the party he would call back, and turned ferociously on Don.

"You stupid cocksucker," he shouted, "whatta ya mean answerin' the phone like that? You don' know who it's gonna be, you dumb shit. You're smart-assin' around, an' that coulda been the cops, an' maybe that'd be all they needed to come over an' pay a visit. Huh, what about that, funny boy?"

Don and everyone else in the place, except Insinger, was dumbfounded that Caval of all people would suddenly acquire such a fierce interest in security.

"Oh and you've been so careful—" Don attempted, but Caval cut him off.

"You think I'm a cutthroat, you motherfucker, after the deal I was gonna give you? Huh?" Caval was perhaps fifty pounds lighter than Don but advanced on him as if Don were a child. "And you're sick of my shit, too? Huh? Then just get your fuckin' ass outta here. Go on, cocksucker. You hear me?" he screeched. "Get goin'!"

The room was dead silent. As Don backed before the onslaught, his ruddy, bright-cheeked features looked ready to burst into tears. He tried to argue in his defense, but Caval overwhelmed him again each time, until finally he slammed the door behind him, and Don never returned.

At the table, Insinger looked across at Marshall Heard, who

was busy eating a cheeseburger that Don had just delivered. They shrugged wistfully at each other, and Mark drew a line through Don's name on the list.

The next morning Mark thought it was all over. Sidell called the house early. He wanted to meet Caval at a cafe in Wilmington. After the call, Mark observed Caval steadily growing angrier and more preoccupied. For the past three days any mention of Sidell or utterance of admiration for the feat of having sailed the shipment from Colombia had set Tom off. "Well, it's my dope," he would insist, "and I'm the one who's runnin' this number so you better dig *that* now." Even Thorton learned to suppress his desire to tell of the struggles and adventure they had encountered. That morning it was as if the mere thought of Sidell was an affront to Caval's power and control, and Mark watched him develop a dangerous mood.

A man came to the Garwood house near nine o'clock to make final arrangements for a load, but Caval kept him waiting while he took a long, brooding shower at the other house. By the time Caval showed up, another man had arrived for the same purpose. The earlier arrival was a young man in his mid twenties from Miami. He was a gentle, happy kid with a round face and heavy glasses who was something of a rich hippie involved in the business rather as a hobby. He had met Caval in Aspen and had dealt with him a few times without great aversion, but the guns and tension at Fort Rhodes terrified him. The other guy was a streetwise character from Providence, Rhode Island, who had come up in the business from nickel bags and was frightened by almost nothing. He had never met Caval, but was working with people from Connecticut who did know him and therefore had not cared to go all the way to Carolina to encounter him. The man was in his thirties, had a bristling black mustache and narrow eyes like a snake. Both of the men wanted five hundred pounds.

When Caval stalked in, he threw his parka on the floor and cursed the heat and thick air of the house. He sat as if preparing to convene another session of his court-market and pulled off his shirt. A vein was standing out slightly in his forehead, and the muscles of his chest and arms were taut.

"I've changed my mind on this stuff," he began angrily without apparent provocation. He had not said a word of greeting. The younger man seemed willing to excuse himself and leave immediately, but not the other.

"On what?" he countered contemptuously.

312

Caval looked him over with a hateful gaze, and the air deadened.

"Both you guys want five hundred at a hundred an' fifty bucks. Well, fuck that. I been damn near givin' this stuff away, an' I'm sick of it. This is the best stuff in the country," he gestured around him. "It's the best in the goddamn world. So you guys tell me what the weight's worth to ya. Yer both right here, so what the hell. Whoever wants to pay the most can have the whole thousand. There ya go."

"You kiddin' me?" snapped the guy from Providence. "Is this a joke or a fuckin' game show. I been waitin' on yer ass, man, an' my deal with you was fer five hundred at one fifty."

"Well that deal's over with now, an' this is the way it is. You want it er not?"

"Hey, listen," said the kid, who wanted only to be gone, "I don't want to cause any—"

"You fuckin' punk," the other guy cut him off, nodding at Caval as he spoke. "I heard you been runnin' shit like this. What the fuck you think you are? Where I come from somebody'd just take you off for this stuff."

Caval erupted from his chair.

"Nobody's taken me offa anything," he shouted at the absolute limit of his voice. "Got that, motherfucker?" He bent down suddenly and grabbed the shotgun from the floor. Coming up, he leveled it straight at the man's face. Everyone seemed to draw in their breath until there was no oxygen left in the room. "Wanna see who gets taken off?" Caval screamed. "Huh? Wanna see where I come from, tough guy?"

Insinger heard nothing of the nervous shuffling of feet and did not see the unbelieving horror in the face of the guy from Providence as he looked in the barrel of the twelve gauge, or hear Thorton softly pleading, "No, Tommy, com'on now . . ." Instead, Mark turned his head away and peered thoughtfully at the ceiling, as his brow began to twitch, and his thoughts proceeded swiftly. "If he shoots him, I can get to the marina and take the boat. I can gas it up full and head out to open sea and then down the coast. I could get to the Bahamas. Get the boat fixed up and sell it. Make it to Brazil, maybe Paraguay, until it blows by." Then, suddenly, he began to imagine a shotgun blast blowing everything open and exploding his life free again, and he wanted earnestly to hear it. "Go on," he thought, "kill the son of a bitch. Blow his head off."

He heard a much duller sound though, and when he turned, the kid from Miami had fainted onto the floor. The man from

Providence kept looking at Caval and at the shotgun straight on, without ever blinking or making a sound until Caval, his chest heaving, lowered the gun. Then the guy just turned and walked out.

chapter 21

i

NEW Year's Day was quick and sunny when Eiler and Sidell entered the Anchor Cafe, which lay within sight of the river. It was near one o'clock, and the place was almost full. Four hours earlier, when they had eaten breakfast, there were only a few other customers, but now the patrons had risen from the previous night's debaucheries to attempt the day. The crowd was familiar, and there was a camaraderie, as if they had endured a blitz. Voices were louder than usual and faces more expressive. They were laughing too hard or gesturing too much, as the last of alcohol numbed final excesses before real hangovers set in later in the afternoon. They were the hard-drinking working folk of the area, and the Anchor was where they ate breakfast, lunch, sometimes dinner, and often recuperated. They were an odd collection of janitors, dockworkers, carpenters, retired men, and truck drivers. Wives with weary smiles accompanied many of them and enhanced the simplicity of the holiday mood.

Joe nodded to a couple of people as they moved inside. He looked out of place, with his beard and his hair bleached by the sun and grown long, and they knew he was off the strange boat. But he had eaten nearly all his meals there, so he was not completely alien. Joe even succumbed to the conceit of believing that if they knew what he was really doing—and he was not so sure some of them did not suspect it—they would not care.

Jack drew some curious looks. He had shaved his beard a few days earlier and wore a clean shirt, and he generally stood out in a crowd. He moved with a resolution no one else in the place possessed as he prepared to execute the last stage of the enterprise. And although he looked openly into the faces of people they passed, there was no mistaking that he had business far out of the ordinary of their lives. In an instant Eiler realized that this was not the place to meet Tom Caval.

When they had found a table and ordered coffee, Joe said, "Ya know, this is a hell of a place to be seein' Caval. I don't know what we were thinkin' about."

"I know it." Jack's face clouded and he looked at the other people instead of at Joe. "It seemed simple this morning though. There was no one here. Why didn't you tell me this was the god-damn clubhouse?"

"I didn't think it would be today. I reckon it's too late to call him. You wanna wait outside for him an' go somewhere else?"

Jack took a deep breath and pressed his mouth so that his lips disappeared for a moment. "No. If he's not cool we can just leave. But we might as well wait now. This is not very smart though."

Eiler's gaze fell to the table as he wondered if there were other mistakes. He tried to remember if anything had been overlooked, but nothing came to mind. It was just Jack worrying, he figured, and he remembered also that this part of the deal was foreign to Jack. "It's okay," he said. "No harm done. We better get sharp, though. You're right about that."

Joe grew thoughtful as the coffee arrived, and a dull unease came on him. What Jack had said reminded him of the afternoon four days earlier when they had finished the second load. They had hurriedly cleaned the hold and then begun to drink up the beer. They reconstructed the large table and tried to make things resemble something normal. They had put music on and laughed a lot as they spoke of reaching shore that night, and the feel of earth beneath their feet, and the desire for steaks, shrimp, salads, potatoes, whisky, and above all the prospect of pussy.

They had been pretty ripe, Joe recalled, but before they got underway for Wilmington they had found themselves all together on deck. It was an odd situation. They were sinking bags of trash and sweepings, and when they stopped, it seemed as if there was nothing to say. For several minutes, the four of them stood or sat there along the new deck, not awkwardly but merely not inclined to say as much as they thought they might. And yet that seemed the time to proclaim the feat accomplished. The moment invited it. But they seemed to mistrust it. "Well, goddamn, we did it awright," Thorton bellowed, but a little self-consciously for once, and they didn't go far in agreeing. A few moments later, Mackenzie said gravely, "We'll never make a sail like that again," and they only muttered in accord. Joe remembered an inquisitive look on Jack's face at that moment, as if in a way he were recognizing that there would be no more cheering, no more neatly measured contests, no final guns saluting victors. To all of them the trip had promised that nothing ended, that they were never really out of danger. Each time they had believed they were delivered, it seemed that something worse had happened. Now that the entire ordeal had apparently been overcome, there was a feeling that perhaps the greatest danger lay ahead. It conflicted not so much with their happiness, though, as with their sense of accomplishment. They seemed to know it was not over. In addition, what they had done was for money, and one of them had died in the quest, and none of them had any of it yet. So it had been an odd sensation, to be finished and not yet finished, happy and still serious. It left the flesh content but the soul in need.

Joe had thought about those feelings for a few days afterward, but without understanding them. He had even thought it was some murky precognition of a bust. But just now, at the Anchor, it began to make sense. He looked up brightly at Jack for a moment, but it was too large and miasmic to attempt describing. Sidell sipped his coffee warily and considered other matters.

Jack was tired, and thoughts hurtled through his mind too swiftly for reason. He could not imagine negotiating easily with Caval, but there were a dozen matters to discuss. The boat: money for fuel, drydock, general repairs, docking. How and when could he pick up his load. What about the salary? The prospect of each one was a struggle, and Jack lacked the strength for it then. But he could never admit it, even to himself. Earlier that day, he had wondered whether Caval would be troublesome. Joe had said, "Now it's just a question of *how* he'll try to screw you. I figure he'll be pretty out front about it at this point." Jack had not cared much for that. It only made the prospect more difficult to reckon, added more variables. He grew a little irritable as he ordered another coffee. He felt as if he had not had time to think anything out, that it all proceeded recklessly.

When they had finished the unloading, the calm afternoon had offered the finest possibilities for planning. They had all been fairly quiet, and Jack had rarely seen the sea so flat, seen its color so perfectly Atlantic or the winter sky so inspiring. He had believed at that moment that he could plan a war or compose a symphony. The world seemed like a great plaything, huge and rough and difficult—like *Leda*—but completely within his ability. And yet

316

the Gulf Stream had been carrying him inexorably to the north, and there was nothing he could do about that. Regardless of the apparent maleability of the day and his desire to rest there, he was low on fuel. And that was a simple and cruelly immutable fact. If he drifted much further, there was an excellent chance that he would not have fuel enough to reach Cape Fear, and that would invite another disaster. So finally he had bestirred himself from that solicitous quiet and the possibilities of that rare calm and hurried to port, and everything had run together since then.

The old engine had missed and coughed and died on the very last drop of diesel just as they glided into a small fuel dock near the point of Cape Fear. Under the circumstances Jack had had to more or less ram the dock. Eiler and Thorton, delivered from the teeth of another catastrophe and pretty tight on several beers, laughed hysterically, and the terrified old operator of the dock had threatened to call the Coast Guard.

It became dark as they motored up the river to Wilmington. Jack steered, and they all hung around the stern and laughed at each other's comments as the lights of the city grew brighter. At the drawbridge guarding the harbor, they had to wait almost a half hour, and once it admitted them, there was again the matter of Billy Delight. They tied up quietly at the Customs dock, and waited for an inspector. If they had dropped the load in the Bahamas there would still have been the grim nervousness and the fear of something forgotten. When no inspector appeared, Sidell finally went ashore and called the bureau, and an official showed up forty-five minutes later. They were tired and sullen by then, with the worry and the beer wearing off. When they reported Delight's fate, the Customs man made profuse apologies, as if he had killed him by taking so long to arrive. He checked the ship quickly, looking around innocently in the dark, and muttering constantly about what a strange old thing she was. Eventually they learned the name of a man who would watch the boat that night, so when the inspector had cleared them and was out of sight, they came alive again, loud and eager. The new Hilton Inn was within sight not far away, and in short order they had rooms on the top floor. They bought a bottle of whisky on the way and ordered up oysters and shrimp cocktails and took turns at great length in the showers. Finally looking not much different than when they had arrived, they ate dinner in the hotel restaurant. Thorton devoured two steaks, and they were all drunk and noisy. Their table was a collection of big shoulders and arms and hair and bearded leering faces and a din of raw language. They handled one waitress until she was nearly in tears, but she was replaced by another, somewhat older, who rather liked it. The management of the place and the clientele seemed uniformly shocked and yet fascinated by such open misbehavior, as if they were witnessing the reenactment of some rude history.

After the meal Mackenzie and Thorton went off in a taxi in search of a few whores, which were not in great supply in that area, and Eiler and Sidell adjourned to the bar, to await the second waitress. Eiler had managed to interest her in a little party following her shift, and she had promised a friend for Sidell. By eleven o'clock, though, Joe had gone up to the room with her, and the friend had not appeared. Jack decided not to waste more time and joined Eiler and the waitress in bed. Shortly thereafter, by sneaking in through the kitchen, Thorton and Mackenzie reappeared with two black girls who meant business, and no possible expression of desire went neglected.

There had been no real interest in continued existence the next morning. Life seemed too painful and too difficult. Nevertheless, Thorton had headed for Fort Rhodes, and Jack had gone to the Coast Guard offices to file a routine report and answer questions regarding Delight's death. Eiler and Mackenzie limped back to the boat and slept. The next day Jack had departed for St. Petersburg, Florida, to see Delight's family, and Jesse had begun to make plans for getting *Leda* to drydock and assembling another crew for that purpose. Joe Eiler passed two days very carefully, with coffee in the morning, beer in the afternoon and scotch at night, cauterizing his senses against the approaching task of hustling a big load. And he found frequent occasion to wonder if there were not something else he might do with his life. He did not feel fit for anything else just then, but it was still a possibility, though he recognized, as a person does with morphine, that there might soon be no turning back.

Sidell went to St. Petersburg, arrived in the afternoon, and found the address of Delight's parents, but no one was home. He took a motel room nearby and kept calling the house without success. He returned to the address after dark and inquired at neighbors' houses and about half an hour later found Billy's mother in a shabby estaminet several blocks away. She had no apparent plans to leave the place, so he gave her the news, and the woman cried out her son's name with what seemed to Jack like happiness. Bunny Delight, as she had introduced herself, was a big woman, nearly as big as Jack, and she looked like Billy grown old and wearing a wig, except for her veiny and angular nose. Jack learned later that her husband had departed years before, and she had since led the tavern life. "My boy is dead," she bellowed drunkenly into each face along the bar, then embraced Sidell and wept on him. A moment later, the bartender had given her a new drink, and she put half of it away at once with such satisfaction that Jack identified the quality of sorrow he had noted in her outburst. It was appreciation for having a solidly negotiable purpose for drinking, and Jack had delivered her at least a year of guiltless drunks. Her companions at the bar, all of whom were drinking to the end in the most unattractive fashion, took up the cause, and they carried on about death and the family and drank like hell. Jack told them the whole bullshit story in great false detail and then had a few himself. He felt as if he were attending a party of corpses toasting with embalming fluid.

"Ohh Billy," the mother whined with dim amusement when the place fell silent a moment. It was the sort of tone with which people recall a high school teacher. "You ever get the son of a bitch to do anything right?" she slurred at Jack without looking at him. "Hell, I never did."

"Sure. Quite a few things," Jack answered.

She said nothing, as if the curiosity had passed quickly.

When Bunny was sufficiently wiped out, Jack took her home, and she begged him in desperate slurs to return the next day and help her. It was noon before Jack could force himself to go back to the house, and he found her already loaded again. He helped her contact a local church regarding a service, and then she wanted him to write down all the names of people she wanted to notify. She carefully listed two persons, then lapsed into a stuporous silence. Jack suggested she think it over and offered to carry out the trash. There was at least a month of garbage collected in the rear kitchen, and when he had removed it all he found her passed out face down on the table. He sat down again and wondered if he had any further obligation. The room was empty as a vacuum except for the labored breathing from the broad back and tousled head beside him. Suddenly the quilted blue robe rose with a long breath and then gave way to a muffled belch, whereupon a semicircle of watery vomit advanced across the table. Jack stood and walked out of the house, went to the airport, caught a flight to Charleston that night, and went on to Wilmington by bus.

The waitress at the Anchor looked down at him, and her worn

features took him back to St. Petersburg. "No thanks," he snapped about the coffee. It all seemed out of control, and he looked at Eiler as if for help. Eiler looked back and smirked, as if to say there is no help.

"Here he is," said Joe.

Caval climbed hurriedly out of the rented Cougar and came in. He had just finished threatening the guy from Providence with the shotgun. He caught every eye in the place, shaking his head derisively as he marched up to the table.

"Nice place," he said loudly. "This your idea, Joe?"

"I knew you'd like it."

"They got decent coffee?" Tom sat.

Even Eiler had thought there might be a few passing pleasantries before the venom, but Caval seemed barely able to tolerate Sidell's presence.

"Where you been?" he demanded, when Eiler had signaled for one more coffee.

"I had a few things to attend to," Jack replied incredulously. He could not believe Caval would say nothing about the voyage, the transfer, Delight.

"Hey, tell me about it, will ya? I been holed up on that fuckin' island in a little house piled to the ceiling with shit an' it's eighty goddamn degrees. An' hasslin' every thimble full of that stuff 'til—"

"Keep your voice down," Joe told him. People were watching them from all over the place.

Caval glared back at him, but waited until the waitress brought his cup before continuing.

"So anyway, you ain't the only guy that's done some stuff, okay?"

"This isn't a contest." Jack's tone pleaded with Caval to be rational.

"Oh it isn't?" Tom's voice fired up. "You oughta see that fuckin' house an' then tell me it's no contest."

"Whatever the hell it is . . . I just want to get together and figure some things out. We have to take care of the boat. We have some money to talk over, and I want to know where you want to deliver our load or if you want us to come get it."

Caval gritted his teeth and nearly exploded.

"That goddamn boat is your responsibility. I'm sick of that thing. I don' wanna hear another fuckin' thing about it."

"Would you be quiet?" Jack demanded.

"Everybody in here can hear you," said Joe.

"Fuck 'em. What the hell you guys think I'm doin' out there, layin' on my ass? That goddamn boat. Jesus. An' you think we've got all your stuff piled up an' waiting, you're crazy. You were supposed to be out there and pick out your own stuff. Everything can't wait 'til you assholes decide to come over an' do some business."

"Let's get outta here," Joe whispered. He was trembling. He had thought Caval could not irritate him much anymore, but now he wanted to kill him.

"Well, our stuff better be there, and it better be good."

"Oh sure, we just set the best stuff over on one side an' said, 'Hey, this is for Jack an' Joe. Okay?' Get serious."

"Everyone in this place can hear this—"

"Well that'd be about the very least we deserve," Jack growled at Caval. "Somebody had to take care of the boat and another little matter you might have heard about, so—"

"I'm sick of hearin' what people think they deserve. All I been hearin' is what some asshole thinks he deserves from me." Caval's voice rose steadily, and Eiler was already standing, laying money on the table. "You better understand nobody deserves anything. That stuff is mine! You got that?"

Everyone in the cafe had turned to watch their table as Caval finished, red faced and glaring. Jack too had stood up by then, and Caval rose and followed them outside.

Joe stepped in front of Caval as he came outside, and Jack stayed to one side, too angry to speak.

"What the hell you makin' a scene like that?"

"Get outta my way," Caval demanded.

Joe stared at the fine features a moment and weighed the idea of slugging him before he let him pass. Sidell found his tongue as they followed Caval to his car. "What are we going to do about this stuff?"

"I got things to do." Tom slammed the door and started the engine. "I'm gonna be at the Holiday Inn tonight. We can talk there if you guys don't think it'll offend anyone."

"What the hell does that mean? What time? Where?"

"The room's under Davis. Nine o'clock."

Tom suddenly floored the accelerator and roared away. Sidell stood blankly in the street as if he had narrowly missed being hit by a train.

ii

All afternoon and evening Jack tried to calm down, to accept the situation and regroup himself. He recognized that there was simply no functioning appreciation for what he had done. After all they had endured, he might be left with the lousy dope. No quality, he kept thinking. That was of one piece with all the rest of it, he concluded. It seemed ultimately an accurate appraisal of his own performance. He had done the job, but not without great strife, and now all of it seemed rotten. The deals he had made and the people he had made them with all seemed foolishly poor choices. Several times he was able to swallow it and look ahead, but each time he was struck with a sickening certainty that Caval would not pay him.

Joe Eiler did Jack the favor of keeping away all afternoon, so his mere presence would not remind Jack that he had warned him all along. Joe stayed on *Leda* or wandered the docks, while Jack had taken a room at the old Cape Fear Hotel so he could make phone calls. That night, when they had taken a cab to the Holiday Inn, Joe waited in the parking lot while Jack checked the desk for the Davis room. They walked around to the rear wing of the place and entered. Before they had even reached the room they could hear laughter and loud voices, and the hallway reeked of marijuana. Jack turned to Eiler and exhaled sadly.

"Who is it?" a voice yelled after Sidell knocked.

"Jack."

"Who the hell's Jack?" the voice inquired of others within. There were replies, then the door opened. They entered, but Eiler remained close to the door, leaning against the wall, knowing they would not stay long. Sidell looked around the smoky room and saw three men, roughly his own age and completely unknown to him, empty beer bottles on the floor, and a large handful of marijuana in crumpled newspaper on the table. The radio was playing loudly on a local AM station. A prospect came suddenly to him that he had not considered, even in the depths of his depression that afternoon—that they would be busted. He saw it with such clarity that it froze him a moment, and he thought, if you had any sense at all you'd get out of this town tonight.

"How ya doin', Jack? You don't look any better than ya did this morning." Caval sat in a chair leaned back against a desk with his feet on one of the double beds and smoked a reefer. "These are friends."

"I don't know 'bout that," said one of them. He was a tall guy with coarse blonde hair and mean, careless expression, who by his bearing seemed in charge of the other two.

"Yeah, well, maybe friends," Caval went on with Jack scowling at him. "They're like everybody else. They think they deserve some kind of special treatment. I'm beginnin' to wonder what the hell I deserve," he laughed.

"You—" Jack started to answer that for him but did not. "I thought we were going to talk."

"So talk. You gotta have privacy we can go to another room. They got another room. I'm pretty sure they all sleep together, but they got another room for front."

The other three laughed hard, and it was evident they had been drinking beer and smoking for some time.

"Sure." Jack cut in angrily enough to douse the laughter. "This is just great. You're running a party in here with dope and the hallway stinks of it. That's real cool. I'm just dying to hang around for awhile and talk it all over. I hope you know you're going to bust this whole thing the way you're going."

"Oh wow," one of the friends moaned.

"Better clean up the act, Tommy," the blonde guy quipped.

Jack roared at him: "Shut yer fucking mouth, buddy. I got a little more stake in this than you do."

The guy tried to keep his composure, but eyed Sidell nervously. The other two looked plainly worried, and Caval smiled. Eiler stood up straight. It was about time Jack lost his temper, he figured.

"You're always such a pain in the ass, Jack." Caval grinned as he said it, and Jack started to yell again but did not.

"I'll see you at the house tomorrow," he snapped and turned away.

"Awright. Jesus," breathed Caval as Joe opened the door and followed Jack out. "Bring your lawyers," Caval yelled as the door shut, and there was laughter behind them as they went down the hall.

iii

"Let's get down to it, Ralph," Jack spoke seriously as they reached the Fort Rhodes bridge. "What's going on out here? How much is left?"

Jack had called the island that morning and gotten Thorton to pick him and Joe up and take them to the house. They had been bullshitting all the way out, recalling their voyage with a good deal more humor than they had known at the time. Ralph had particularly seemed to want to avoid the real matter, but Jack finally gave him no choice.

"I don' know . . ." He shifted uncomfortably behind the wheel, stopped to wave at the bridge tender, who nodded back dourly. "He's bein' crazy, Jack. He's runnin' all kinds of deals, usin' the phones, got a lotta people in there I never seen before, and actin' wild too. Too much goin' on, ya know? I'm gettin' worried. He's even keepin' me hangin'," he spoke with a sorrowful indignation. "I figure there's maybe five tons left. Only Insinger knows for sure though, an' he's like Tommy's bookie or sumthin. Hell, he won't tell me straight how much he'll let me take. Won't give me a straight answer on a price. An' I don' care. I jus' wanna git outta there. It's crazy. He wants me to hang on 'til the end. It's crazy. It's like we didn' do nothin'." He shook his head in resignation. "You're not gonna like it, Jack."

Heard opened the door when they reached the Garwood house.

"Hello, captain," he smiled at Jack. They shook hands warmly and spoke quietly a moment as Thorton went inside. They had become friends skiing together at Aspen. They were about the same size, and they skied the same, which was wide open and straight down the hill.

"I hear you did quite a job," Marshall nodded.

"Somebody sure doesn't think so."

Marshall inclined his head and shrugged sympathetically but said nothing. Jack moved on into the room, saying curt hellos to Caval and Insinger.

Joe had gone immediately to the refrigerator to see if there was a beer. He found one, opened it, and moved back toward Heard. Joe hated Marshall Heard. He had seen him serve as enforcer for too many of Caval's rip-offs.

"Hello, Marshall," he smiled imitating the rapport between Sidell and Heard, "you low-life bastard." Joe took a leisurely sip of the beer as he watched Heard's face tighten. "Ever find out which one of those southside whores is your mother?"

"Yeah," Heard replied through his teeth, "step outside a minute, an' I'll tell you."

Joe chuckled and took another sip.

"Not today, big boy." He nodded at the .308 standing by the door. "Armed an' dangerous, uh?"

Heard said nothing. His face had grown crimson and quivered slightly. His cloudy eyes bore down on Eiler.

"Guess I better watch my back," Joe said, and he turned away.

The main room was less crowded than it had been. There were still a dozen or so bags collected in the kitchen drying before the stove, but the rest of the area was fairly clear. Another group of bags stood in the corner near the table, and it was still uncomfortably warm. Harry Amian and the blonde guy from the Holiday Inn shifted nervously in their places. Insinger had risen from the table and gone forward to shake Jack's hand. "Nice to see you on solid ground again, *amigo*."

Caval looked on scornfully, but he alone—aside from Joe Eiler perhaps—was relaxed. Insinger, Amian, Thorton, even Heard were all self-conscious, waiting like men who desired only an excuse to be elsewhere. There was a feeling of unfairness in the place. They all knew what Sidell's role had been. They knew how difficult the job had been, but knew also that Jack was getting no consideration for the trouble. There was an inevitability of dishonorable conflict in the air, and a pervasive sense of guilt.

" 'Bout time you got here," Caval thrust.

Insinger moved to one side of Sidell and sat on the kitchen counter. Jack set himself firmly before Caval. He had never had any intention of being there.

"Let's not go over the same old stuff," he said.

"Course not," Tom smiled. "Hell, we're successful partners. I'd offer you somethin' to eat, but there ain't anything. It'd be a lot homier if your little sister was still around. She was takin' good care of us there for awhile."

"What?" Jack demanded.

"I don' know why she split. Ask Romeo here," Caval gestured at Insinger.

"You brought my sister here," he turned on Insinger.

Mark's brow flinched nervously, but he looked steadily at Jack. "I sent her home before anything started." He would almost have blurted out that he loved her and would not have let anything happen, but that was impossible.

"Well you guys have really been cool," Jack growled at him in disgust. "I hope you impressed her."

Insinger looked back helplessly at Jack, and Caval smiled at the exchange. Eiler, standing with arms folded in the doorway to one hall, wistfully shook his head at the scene around him. Caval slipped this poison to Insinger and Sidell and prevented any possibility of collusion, but more importantly he simply played with his power. The others he had already isolated by means of their own ambition. He loved, craved, the ability to control.

"So what's goin' on?" Joe broke in loudly. "Don't we have a little business to take care of?"

"Joe Eiler, the great businessman," Caval smiled contemptuously. "Yeah, I guess we do. You guys own seven hundred pounds of this stuff. It's in this back room here," he pointed to the hallway on his right. "Take your pick of it. Mark the bags if you like. There's a hundred pounds in each of 'em. You're a little late, though. I awready tol' you that."

"Late, my ass," Jack retorted. He disappeared angrily toward the back room. Joe did not follow him. He knew what the reaction would be, just as Caval did, and they gazed curiously at each other in waiting.

In the rear bedroom Jack found large, green plastic bags. He went from one to another, peering, turning the contents, reaching deep inside to pull up handfuls. It was all the dregs. It was the stuff that had gotten wet, the bottom leaves, the big sticks, the stuff from ripped sacks that had been swept up with dirt or sand. It was still good dope by popular standards and not at all hard to move, but the worst of the lot.

"This is shit!" Jack stalked back into the room and slapped a large handful of it on the table in front of Caval. "You expect me to take this? This is the garbage, man. The garbage!"

"That's tough luck." Caval yelled back at him. "You shoulda' been here. You could've claimed your stuff. You didn' have to be screwin' around. You just didn' wanna come over that's all. You thought everybody'd look out for ya, but that ain't the way it goes."

"I'm not taking this shit," Jack pointed at the pile on the table. "I risked my life to get this stuff here, and I'm not going to take the crap that's left after a bunch of punks I never saw before get to pick it over."

"Yer fuckin' life. You had some bad weather. Big fuckin' deal. I was riskin' my life every day I was down there. I had my ass on the line every day . . ."

They argued viciously back and forth for several more minutes. Eiler had noticed that there were still a lot of bags in the rooms off the other hallway where he stood, and he moved quietly into the front room. It was still packed with about two tons of cargo in the original burlap but open at the tops. Grabbing samples from bags nearest the door he found the prime stuff, pale clustered tops packed solid like herbal gold. It was the dope Caval had separated

326

during the first two days, the dope he was saving for his own load, for Amian's big load, and to give to Thorton if he stayed on obediently to the end. Joe examined a few bags and knew exactly what was happening. He hoisted the nearest one, stalked back to the main room, and set it before Caval.

"What's this, your personal smoking stash?"

"That's spoken for," Caval screamed at him. "You keep yer goddamn hands off that stuff."

"Who *spoke* for it?" Jack inquired with bitter anger.

"None of yer fuckin' business. That's my dope, an' I've already sold it." Caval looked feverish, his red face snarling in one direction then another.

"So what?" said Joe. "They haven't got it yet. They can take the other stuff."

"Fuck you!" Caval shrieked like a madman.

"Who's stuff is it?" Jack looked first at Thorton then at Insinger. "Who gets the good stuff? Some punks who didn't do anything? Is that the way you guys want to do this?"

The others said nothing, and Caval breathed like a deranged animal as he watched their faces.

"Come on, Ralph." Jack could not believe his eyes. "What's it going to be?"

"It ain't my dope, Jack," Thorton said slowly.

"Jesus Christ, I don't believe it." Jack turned away and stared hotly at the ceiling.

The silence was suddenly prodigious. And in it Thorton and Insinger wore expressions of nausea and self-contempt. Yet each of them was trying only to insure his own profit, just as Sidell and Eiler were, in the only ways they could. It was every man for himself. But they inevitably felt a party to the screwing of Sidell—Joe Eiler never being one to inspire much compassion—and that was a most unpleasant role to stomach, although impossible to escape. Self-sacrifice appeals to no man.

Eiler watched a cagey smile form slowly on Tom Caval's face. His eyes rolled with possibilities as the corners of his artistic mouth seemed to sample the pleasure of some option.

"Listen Jack, I'll tell you what," he suddenly spoke in an almost friendly tone.

"Yeah, you tell me what you'll do for me, okay?"

"No, com'on. I'm tired of this hasslin'. Let's quit fightin' like this." Tom was instantly friendly and compassionate, and Sidell furrowed his brow distrustfully, as if regarding an apparition. "Tell ya what," Caval went on. "Instead of that other business we talked about in Curaçao, you go ahead an' take a ton of this stuff. A ton. Take it out of the best stuff here. You pick it. Now your seven hundred still comes outta the stuff left over in there. That's just the way it is. But I'll let you have a ton of this other for a hundred bucks. That's two hundred grand. You can make a bundle."

Both Sidell and Eiler and everyone else present gaped at Caval in utter bewilderment.

"Our deal was cash," Jack stated indignantly.

"Sure it was," Caval's voice hardened slightly. "But we didn't say when. I said I didn't know when I'd pay ya, an' you said okay. There's no time on the deal."

Caval seemed to be warning him to take the new offer or get nothing, and Sidell shouted at him.

"Don't tell me that. You said out of profits. You liar."

"But we didn't say when." Caval was screaming again, supremely offended that Sidell spurned his magnanimity. "I don' know what's gonna happen. Take yer pick. I may never be able to pay ya."

Eiler thought, for Christ's sake, take it, Jack, take it. His immediate inclination was to take the ton as payment richly deserved and never pay a cent for it—which was why Caval would never have made the same offer to him, or anyone else besides Jack Sidell. But Jack had been manipulated and maneuvered by Caval too much, and he could not tolerate another altered agreement.

"You punk," Jack railed at him, towering over Caval's chair in a rage. "I'm sick of your lying. You expect me to take that crap and then sell the good stuff for you. I want the money you owe me, and I want the good dope that belongs to me."

"You want this?" Caval screeched back at him. He jumped out of his chair and grabbed a fistful of grass from the sack Eiler put down. "You eat it!" He flung the stuff in Sidell's face.

chapter 22

i

BROLEY stood over a cardboard box of six or eight framed photographs and gazed at the wall behind his desk. Hanging photos and certificates always annoyed him. It was vanity, but it was better than bare wall. He thought for a moment that a painting or a print, perhaps a couple of them, would be better, something to give it a little class. He needed a little class after the DEA.

The office was a nice one, at the top of the tallest building in Wilmington, with panelled walls and long bookshelves in the wall opposite the deck, and a broad view of the river and well beyond. The view caught his eye, and he stood for a few minutes absorbed in it. He was fond of the scene, and he had missed it in his absence. A long barge approached the dark, old drawbridge, and a skiff came up on the other side. The brown salt marshes in the distance were peaceful, and there was not much movement in the harbor. The old battleship *North Carolina* sat hulking and gray in the middle of it all, and he always wondered why they did not get rid of the damn thing. The main streets near the river were busy, and the battleship in the background was ridiculous, as if it were defending this model of American enterprise, when in fact it was a shell. He had been a naval officer in the war, but this was bullshit, and Broley did not have much tolerance for bullshit. Before he turned away from the windows he noted an old ketch, black hulled and patched like old blue jeans, moored among the commercial docks. He had a veteran customs agent's curiosity about it, but was not quite back in harness enough yet to feel suspicion.

It was the first working day of the new year, and Broley was returning to his former job as Special Agent-in-Charge of the U.S. Customs detachment in Wilmington. He had just finished a brief stint with the newly formed Drug Enforcement Administration and was happy to be back. DEA had been created as part of a national crackdown on narcotics, and the Justice Department had put into it any government agent with experience in that field. So Broley had been transferred, but after three months he threatened to resign if they did not put him back in Customs. He despised DEA. It had collected every lowdown narc in the country, and Broley could not stand to be in the same room with some of them. Agents with rank equal to his own, and with whom he was expected to work, had played both sides of the street so long they were worse than most of the criminals they sought, often less principled, and always more dangerous. As far as Broley was concerned, most of them were scum. And he had not spent twenty years in law enforcement to come to that.

On the other hand he was proud of Customs. It had a tradition, dignity. Customs agents did not sneak around in the gutter and mingle with the people they pursued. It was an honorable profession, and that was important to Carl Broley. He thought of himself as a gentleman, and he was.

Broley's father had been a policeman in New York back when that was a well-respected position, and a sense of that pride had been crucial in Carl's career. He had distinguished himself in New York in his early years with Customs and then on the Mexican border. For several years subsequent to his Mexican tour, he had been in charge of Customs for the port of New York. During his first stint in New York he had been the model for a movie about a customs agent, due as much to his appearance as his record. Broley looked like a government agent. Moreover he looked like what everyone wants a government agent to look like. He was six-foot-three, with dark hair and a deep voice, and he had a big Irish face with a stern jaw and brown eyes. He was forty-three, and his hair was graying and he was growing in the middle. But he could still kick somebody's ass if he had to. That necessity did not often materialize anymore. There was plenty to keep him busy in the Wilmington office, but it was not New York or the border. That was fine with Broley. He had two young boys to raise, and he had done his time in the combat zones.

"Well, hello there. Welcome back."

The voice was soft, and the enthusiasm in it was unusual. Broley turned with a big grin and a sparkle in his eyes.

"You're late," he grumbled, then winked at her.

"I am not," said Nancy, as if scolding a child. She had just come to the office and still carried her coat and purse as they moved to each other and embraced. She was the secretary and manager of the office, and she and Carl had been good friends for several years. The DEA office was only on the other side of town but they had not met in almost two months. So they asked each other how they had been and hugged with an affection that went just beyond that of a brother and sister.

"Missed pattin' your ass, honey." He reached behind her and did that.

"Cut that out." She pulled away from him. "You want some coffee?"

"Hell, that's the only reason I came back." The remains of a New York accent made Broley's *t*'s sound faintly like *d*'s. "The stuff over there's terrible."

"And I thought it was my ass."

Broley started to say something as she went out of the room but only chuckled, as much from happiness at seeing her again as at what they were saying. He was very fond of her, and he admired her as she went out. She was good-looking but not striking in any conventional sense. She was slender and not very tall, and she didn't have big bosoms or much else about her body that drew attention. But to Carl she was beautiful. She had light-brown hair that turned lighter in the slightest sunlight so that wisps and strands combed back from her high, smooth forehead were yellow-white against the rest of it. She had furthered this process with bleach for years, but then had quit, with a characteristic resolution to make the best of it with what she had. Her face was unusual, with bright green eyes, a sharp nose, and prominent bones, which made her cheeks seem a little sunken, her face a bit long. There was a steady, cynical intelligence in her gaze that most men found rather threatening. All of this Carl Broley found quite appealing, once he got to know her, and he liked not only working with her but being with her. He had missed her at DEA.

When she returned with a mug of coffee, they spoke a few moments about the bare walls, and she said she'd help him find some prints.

"Well, anything happening around here?" he asked finally.

"Not much. That Fort Rhodes Island thing. You see Culleney's report on that?" Nancy spoke slowly with a very slight southern accent. Carl had not heard of it, since he had just left DEA before Christmas when Roberts began making his calls. So Nancy filled him in about the two houses, the group of young men unaccompanied by women, and the cruiser movement.

Broley squinted and considered the information but did not find it very suspicious.

"And Jeff didn't think much of it, huh?" he mumbled. "But I guess you do." She merely arched her eyebrows in response, and his tone became lighter. "So why didn' you look into it?"

"I have work to do," she said.

Broley was more serious than joking. For the past year he had been urging her to apply for status as a special agent. He thought it might rescue her from the hazy depression in which she existed, and he knew she would be good at it. Three years earlier, when Broley had taken over the office, Nancy's three-year-old son had just died of a circulatory disease. Within a few months she had decided it was time to settle accounts with her husband. He had married her because she was fairly attractive, and she was never properly sure why she had married him. To produce a child more than anything, and he had seemed as likely a father as any. It seemed that, as soon as he had found out she was smarter than he, he began to do his act elsewhere. She had put up with it, but once the child was dead, she saw no reason to continue. She had made a few inquiries of Broley regarding techniques of investigation, and within a month, caught her husband *in flagrante* and sued successfully for divorce. Since then, Carl had used her whenever he needed help and wherever a woman could do the job better, and she had proved cagey and quick. Nevertheless, when Carl frequently suggested she become a full-time agent, she always shrugged it off.

"You just wanna be a secretary, right?" he said now.

She laughed, a brief self-deprecating chuckle. "I may help you out a little if you need it." Her sharp eyes flashed at him as she turned to go.

"Well, hold it now." More than he cared about anything on Fort Rhodes Island, Broley wanted to see if he could make her smile. He loved her smile, and it rarely appeared. "You never even answered my question. Think there's anything to this or not? At least gimme a little intuition, huh?"

She did smile at him, sharply and full of brief happiness, turning to him with her hands on her hips, then rolling her eyes thoughtfully upward.

"Carl, I think if they were legitimate they'd be down at Hilton Head, maybe Myrtle Beach. No one knows Fort Rhodes. You'd have to be looking for it. It seems pretty fishy to me. I think there's probably a lot to it."

Broley nodded agreeably as she went out, and an hour later he called Roberts out at the island. He listened to a flood of minutiae about comings and goings at the Garwood place, then had to decline a half dozen strategies for "taking" the house. He instructed Roberts to have his bridge tenders carefully note the license number of every vehicle visiting the houses and to call if anything particularly suspicious occurred. Broley said he'd be in touch.

ii

Leda was docked on the river above the main part of town in a run-down boatyard that was the only one having either the room or the inclination to let her park. No one else had been willing to admit a hulking old bark of rather sinister appearance, patched all around with an air of desperation, pumps howling below the decks, piloted by scruffy looking young dogs who could be depended upon to vanish as soon as she sank. The boatyard owner who finally had let them tie up did so on terms so temporary that he had never really agreed to let them do more than pause. And he continually had wanted them out yesterday.

So tired, battered old *Leda* lay low in dark, oily water off a rotten dock, surrounded by some old fishing trawlers, a few little sport cruisers, and right beside a monstrous, black, homemade salvage boat. The beast was probably fifty feet long, stood up out of the water almost fifteen feet, was crisscrossed all over with raw welding seams, and looked like the cockpit of an old steam locomotive stuck somehow on the end of a big coal bin. How it managed to float utterly confounded Sidell. Black as tar and loaded with a mountain of indescribable rusted things, it loomed beside *Leda* like a huge, filthy, iron vulture.

It was cold down on the water, and in the after cabin Joe Eiler sat at the chart table bundled in two sweaters beneath his foul weather jacket. Beside him, Sidell lay brooding on the bunk like a Biblical warrior prince attempting to understand the trials placed before him by a once-benevolent god.

"If you'd just killed that little son of a bitch, there wouldn' be much problem," Joe observed.

"Oh sure," Jack sighed. "You have a great sense of reality."

"You prefer this reality?" Joe spoke in a monotone of regret and did not look at Sidell. "We all could've divied up that good stuff. Hell, even Heard would've gone for it, I'll bet. Y'know, after the fact. Could've just buried Caval."

"Right, Joe," Jack said impatiently, but his eyes grew distant for a moment, and he could not resist thinking how simple, for the immediate present, that would have made things.

"That punch you cranked up would've just about done the job," Joe muttered on, as if to himself, "if you'd've just hit 'im. You missed 'im about a yard."

"I had that goddamn dope in my eyes."

"Yeah." Joe nodded sadly. He knew Jack was not a fighter. He had never had to be, and it was simply not his style. But you have to have an instinct for the throat, Joe thought.

At the house the day before, Thorton had started moving as soon as he saw what Caval was going to do, and he could be credited certainly with saving Caval's life. When he had thrown that dope in Jack's face, everyone else in the place had frozen at the madness of it, at the invitation of mayhem. Thorton had seen plenty of mayhem, though, and he arrived at Sidell just as Jack—before the weed had even fallen from his face—cleaved the air with a whistling right that would have shattered the skull of an ox, had it only struck. But Caval had retreated slightly, had actually made a very nice move, kept his eyes open, fell back just enough to let that large fist rocket past, and simultaneously unleashed a squalling blast of obscenities. He had never seemed to feel endangered. And of course, once Thorton got hold of him, Sidell was not doing anything, and a second later Heard was there too.

Eiler had not moved a muscle, largely out of certainty that Heard would take the slightest excuse to sunder the back of his own head with that rifle butt. Once they had Jack under control, though, Joe happened to meet Insinger's eyes across the room, and there was a mutuality of disappointment so deep it surprised them both.

Thorton and Heard had hustled Jack outside, the way teammates drag a star player away from a fight. Ralph drove them off the island, and that afternoon and into the night Jack really tied one on, drinking straight bourbon until he decided it would do no real good and then collapsed. He had not risen until after noon, and it was about three o'clock now. He felt a torturously thorough sense of shame. He was ashamed of his wretched hangover, of the condition of his boat, of his failure to put Tom Caval at least in a hospital, and deeply ashamed of the shambles of his enterprise.

"Let's just go over there an' get our stuff an' take that ton too an' get the hell outta here," Joe suggested.

"Sure. I'll say I changed my mind. I've decided to take it."

"Hell yes," Joe argued. "Ralph said he'd help us load it up. On the way back yesterday, he said he'd help us put it in that van an' drive wherever we wanted to transfer it. Let's jus' go get it."

"I'm not going to rip the stuff off."

"You're not, goddamnit. He made the deal." Joe was growing very sick of Jack's insistence on integrity in the face of Caval's behavior.

"Well, you know damn well he won't do it now."

"Let's jus' go get it. Not even Heard would—"

"That little punk would do something really crazy," Jack cut him off loudly. "You know he would. He'd grab that shotgun or something and then . . . God . . ." He shook his head at the specter of violent chaos.

"Look," Joe leaned plaintively forward, "you know he's not going to pay you. You can't possibly believe he will. So what're we gonna do? Take that lousy seven hundred pounds?"

334

"I don't know." Jack sounded hopeless. "Man, right now, I'd almost pack it out of here and forget the whole thing. I mean it. I would. I've had it, Joe."

"Yeah, well . . ." Joe had a certain compassion for Jack and the endless tribulations he had encountered, but he was not listening to any more of that talk. He was about to point out very clearly that part of the dope was his and that Jack owed him money as a crewman, but just then he heard footsteps on deck hurrying back toward the cabin.

"What's that?" Jack stiffened on the bunk.

Eiler shrugged impatiently. Jesse Mackenzie appeared in the cabin door.

"They throw ya out?" Joe asked.

Jesse had an old girlfriend from Boston whose parents often spent holidays with southern relatives who had a house on Fort Rhodes Island. Jesse had even visited there twice with her several years before. Eager to get away from the boat and Wilmington, Jesse had called that house, found the girl there, and had gone out to spend the afternoon and have dinner. Now he hung in the cabin door short of breath and stared darkly for a moment before saying, "You won't believe this."

"What?!" Jack demanded, and Joe said, "Oh I think we will."

Mackenzie took a deep breath and talked fast. "I'm sitting there with the family, right? One of the young kids is looking out the window. There are these other little kids who are friends of theirs on the island. 'Is that it?' says this kid. 'Is that the pot house?' The pot house!" Jesse almost shouted. "I about shit in my britches. I mean . . . the Pot House! Jesus Louise! The other kids are all looking, saying, 'Yeah, that's it over there, see?' Her parents—her mother!—says to me, 'Yes, we seem to have real dope smugglers on the island.' I mean . . . like it's a goddamn curiosity."

Sidell lay stricken. He looked like he expected in the next few minutes to go blind.

"Fuck that," said Joe. "Whatta they know?"

"Jesus, they're telling me about the cruiser coming and going. Beaching behind the house. Telling me one house is being used for storage, and they're living in the other one. I say, 'Let's see,' and they've got these binoculars and I look over there," Jesse's voice mounted to a crescendo, "and I see Ralph standing in the goddamn window!"

"Oh my god," Jack moaned.

"They say some guy who's manager of the island is trying to catch them. Say he's already had an FBI guy or something out there once. They say they're going to bust them all at once. Hell, I waited as long as I could, then I made up some story about not leaving a bilge pump on here and the boat'll sink. So I got Phyllis to bring me in. She'll be down here in a minute. She's just parking the car. Goddamnit, I hear her coming. I'll talk to you later. I'll be back tonight. I'll get back early. I'll see if I can learn anything more."

They sat stunned for a minute or so, and Eiler cursed slowly and carefully under his breath.

"Well . . ." he finally drawled. "I guess we better get somethin' on."

Jack shook his head one last time and got up quickly from the bunk.

"Yeah, we better get moving. Let's get the dope and get the hell out of here."

"Awright," Joe nodded.

"I'm going to get us a truck. You get ahold of Ralph and see what's going on over there. Tell him what Jesse said and that we're getting out of here. You figure out with him what's the best way to get that stuff. I'll meet you back here."

"The ton too? We gonna get that too?"

"Hell yes. We'll need it. For attorneys' fees."

iii

"You're bullshittin'!" Caval accused.

"No," said Eiler. He reclined comfortably in one of the chairs at the main house, and Caval paced before him on the living room carpet. When Joe had called the island from a pay phone near the boat, Thorton had told him he ought to come out. There were a couple of loads leaving that night, and Ralph said he'd better come out and sit on that ton if they wanted it. Jack had gone to the Hilton with several calls to make before getting a van, so Joe went back to the boat and left a message telling him to call the island. Then Joe had taken a cab to the Yucca Motel, a little place on the highway at the Fort Rhodes turnoff that sported one cactus in favor of its name, and Ralph had picked him up there.

"Okay, so they think they know something." Caval stopped moving and stared defiantly at Eiler. "Big deal. If an agent came out here, why didn' he bust us? They can't, that's why. 'Cause they don't know enough."

"Sure. Maybe. I'm just tellin' ya, Tom. Y'oughta watch out."

"I always watch out." Caval grinned suddenly as if he enjoyed the increase of pressure. Eiler knew he would use the heat to his benefit. Joe had tried to think of some way to warn Thorton without letting Caval know, but Ralph would have told Tom himself. If the FBI moved artillery into position around the house, Caval would spend the last five minutes before they started firing screwing somebody out of another five dollars a pound. And then he would get away. He had a marvelous confidence in his luck.

Mark Insinger, sitting at the table beside Eiler, had a good deal less confidence, but he was in much too far to call his bet. He said nothing, but his face was in constant nervous motion, his brow twitching, lips pursing, his eyes occasionally blinking in flurries as he considered the news.

"Damn, Tommy. Maybe we oughta get the hell outa here," Thorton suddenly blurted. He had been anxious for days at the way things were going, and this was almost the limit. "You can't ever tell when them bastards'll get a warrant."

"Sure," Caval snapped at him. "And go where? So that asshole got a cop to come out here. So those people can look at us. They can't see the other house. They're just talkin'. I ain't freakin' out."

"Yeah, but what if—"

"You can leave any time, Ralph." Caval turned irritably to Eiler. "So whatta ya want? Besides just wantin' to make sure I was alright."

"I wanna get that dope."

"So get it. It's yours. Get it outta here."

"And that ton you were talkin' about," Joe said gently.

"Ohhh. Oh sure." Caval's face seemed to burn with pleasure. "How nice." His features instantly grew livid. "The crazy bastard tries to kill me yesterday, an' now he wants to deal!"

Eiler said nothing and looked back at Caval as if with no interest in the matter at all.

"Awright. Okay." Tom suddenly relaxed. "I'll still give it to him. It'll be worth it. I can't think of anything nicer than having Sidell paying me off."

"You're a wonderful guy, Tom. I knew you'd want to do the fair thing."

Caval snickered through his nose so annoyingly that Joe thought Thorton would scream at him to stop. Insinger's face suddenly grew wet with perspiration. It was a snicker that promised Eiler he had seen nothing yet.

"Okay, listen," Joe spoke up loud enough to halt Caval's laughter, "Jack's gettin' a van this afternoon. Let me or Ralph load the stuff in your van here an' I'll meet Jack with it somewhere later tonight."

Thorton spoke edgily to Insinger regarding some other load moving that night, mentioning names Eiler had not heard before. "Yeah, later though," he said to Joe. "Pretty late."

"Wait a minute," Caval broke in. "What the hell? If Jack's got a van he can bring his ass out here an' get the shit. We got other stuff to do with that van tonight."

"No. We could do it awright," said Ralph. "We just meet 'em somewhere an'—"

"No way. I want Sidell to come here." Caval leered like an animal circling for the kill. "I wanna tell 'im it's not a hundred a pound anymore. It's a hundred and *fifty* now. I wanna tell 'im that punch he threw at me yesterday cost 'im one hundred thousand bucks."

Sidell did not call until an hour later, and then his voice was so fraught with exasperation over trouble renting a van that Joe did not hint about the change in price. As it was, he had to tell him to come out to the island to get the load, but Jack thought, at that point, that it was a small matter. He said he had to discuss a few things with Mackenzie, then he would get their bags, be out to the island as soon as possible, and they would drive out that night. Their plan was to drive the stuff to the house of a friend an hour north of Boston just over the New Hampshire border, and not until he had hung up the phone did Joe fully realize how long a journey that would be. Another precarious passage infinite with possibilities of disaster. He wondered for a moment if the deal would ever end, and then he lay down on the floor and managed to sleep until Thorton called from the Garwood house to say Jack was there.

Tom Caval took great pleasure in confronting Sidell as soon as he arrived with the fact that he was gouging him an extra fifty dollars per pound. But Jack was so numbed by accumulation of cruel fortune that he merely glared at Caval and shrugged. "Is that supposed to surprise me?" he snarled. Events hurtled forward with such abandon that one hundred thousand dollars seemed like scraps of paper in the wind.

They loaded very fast. It was dark by then. Everyone but Caval gave a hand, as if it assuaged their guilt at witnessing the fact that Sidell and Eiler, for all their trouble, got no better a deal than anyone else. The big garbage bags of dreg went in first, and then forty bags of the primo, packed tight and salted with four bags of charcoal to absorb the smell. Jack had got a pile of padded moving blankets from the rental agent, and they covered the stuff completely. Eiler rigged one so that it separated the cargo from the seats. It was cold and foggy by the time they finished, and there was fearful haste in every moment. They all thought they were being watched. The farewell was bitter and brief. Without a word, Sidell jumped in and drove away. Thorton and Insinger watched them depart with haggard, longing faces, like stragglers on a sinking ship, for whom there was no room in the last lifeboat.

As they made for the bridge, Jack explained nervously that two friends of Mackenzie from Maine were going to help Jesse and Margaret move the boat to Norfolk, and they would drive down in the van and return it to the agency.

"Alright," Joe mumbled. He could not have cared less, yet it reminded him of something. "Why'd you have trouble getting the van?"

"I don't have a goddamn credit card. They wouldn't rent it without a card for the deposit. Nobody in the damn county would rent a truck without a credit card. They wouldn't take a cash deposit. No way. None of them would."

The strain in Jack's voice made Eiler sit up and look intently at his face.

"So what'd ya do?"

"I went back to the boat and got the papers. I gave them the papers to the boat to hold."

"Ohhh Jesus."

"Well, what the hell would you have done?"

"I don' know. Don't yell at me." Joe folded his arms thoughtfully and turned to look into the passing darkness outside the truck. He could not figure it out with any certainty, but he was sure they would regret the leaving of those papers.

The bridge was down as they reached it, and Jack barely slowed as they rattled over it. As they passed, the old black man waved at them with a stage smile, then squinted after them, made out the license plate, nodded to himself, and corrected the prior entry on his log.

chapter 23

i

THEY were shadow figures in the dark stillness of early morning. The hard cold held everything in motionless silence except their breathless haste. Dark against the dark background, they carried objects with animal stealth to the silhouette of a car, and frozen breath marked the air with their fright.

The last four days had been insane with fear and conniving. Everyone who came through the house knew or sensed a bust was coming, so they were willing to pay almost anything Caval demanded, just to get the stuff and escape. And Caval became more capricious and avaricious than ever as he assigned the last of the cargo. He used the fear to enforce higher prices and to browbeat Thorton, Amian, and Insinger.

Neither Mark nor Caval had slept more than six hours in the last three days, as they schemed around the clock to dispose of the last tons. In that time, they and the others had snorted almost constantly through cut plastic straws, rolled bills, or off the tip of knives, inhaling a half ounce of cocaine that Caval had had his driver bring out from Aspen. Instead of sleep or food they fueled themselves with the coke, until their nerves were blistered. By the last two days their minds raced irrationally. They moved in jerks and sudden starts, afraid of every noise, suspicious of every statement or comment. By the last day, their faces had become livid, locked grimaces like characters in each other's nightmares.

Caval turned the key, and the engine seemed to scream in pain, like a helpless animal whipped toward some impossible task. The starter sawed hysterically at the air, but the engine would not catch. Caval kept trying, as if mesmerized by the sound. Bent over the wheel with his teeth bared, he stopped a moment but then tried again and again for long periods that rasped whatever remained of nerves, until Insinger finally screamed, "For God's sake—"

"Goddamn this fucking thing!" Caval shouted. "It's outta gas."

There was panic suddenly with the fear. Neither of them could imagine that another hour—much less another day—would pass without an attack of federal agents. They were to catch an eight o'clock flight to Atlanta, and there was already very little time.

Crazily Caval tried to start the car again, rupturing the dark with the futile sound. "Come on," he hissed finally. "We'll take Thorton's car. Write him a note," he ordered, scrambling out. It was as if they had just robbed a bank. "Tell 'im we'll turn it in at the airport."

Mark did not even feel capable of getting his bag out of the back seat. "What's Ralph going to do?"

"I don't know. He's supposed to clean things up anyway. I made him a good deal. He can do this."

Ralph had left the island an hour earlier in the van to deliver Caval's personal load to the driver, who would transport it to Aspen. Half of Ralph's own load had departed for Cleveland with an old associate of his a few hours earlier, and Ralph planned to drive the rest of it to Chicago in the van. Harry Amian had finally been allowed to take his weight the day before, and he had left with friends in a large truck for Miami, where Insinger would meet him. As part of his deal with Caval, Thorton was left with the huge task of sweeping out the houses, replacing furniture, and destroying any remaining evidence. The last arrangements had been made in unthinking haste, and to Insinger it seemed to assume the inevitability of disaster. It was disorderly retreat.

They struggled to the other car, dragging luggage, and threw it haphazardly in the back seat. Mark had not shut his door when Caval sped out of the driveway in reverse, went off the pavement into deep sand, tried to go forward, but only spun the tires. Cursing at the top of his voice, he floored the accelerator and the wheels howled desperately.

ii

Carl Broley went over the scraps of paper another time, looking for the one bit of information that could tie it all together or indicate some significant next stage. There were plenty of figures, sets of initials, amounts of money, and even one sheet of stationary from the Irotama Hotel in Rodadero, Colombia. It was still scraps, he thought. There was nothing really hot yet, but he was a patient man.

Broley sat at the round table in the very chair where Tom Caval, several hours earlier, had arranged his last consignments.

"How are you coming in there?" he called to an assistant from the office who was sweeping the two bedrooms off the hallway to Carl's left.

"Pretty good," came the voice. "Got nearly an ounce behind one of the doors. Hell, the stuff's everywhere. I'll have a half a pound easy, I imagine. There's even some of it on the darn walls. Must've been stacked about waist deep all over here."

Instead of answering, Broley nodded to himself. From the papers they had found wadded in a small bathroom waste basket, he figured the load was eight to ten tons, and that could certainly have filled most of the place to waist height. It was a huge load and from what Broley had been told about the cruiser *Errant*, he figured it had been a "mother ship" operation. Broley had been predicting for the past year that, since the main federal attention was being directed at airplanes and boats coming to port, smugglers would begin to transport larger loads by boat and shuttle them ashore from outside the twelve-mile limit in small pleasure craft. As yet, however, there was not much way of catching such deals, so Broley felt no great anger that this load had come and gone beneath their noses. He had some evidence, and he had no doubt there would be more, so he still had a good chance of getting them, even though he felt sure the mother ship was long gone. They were lucky, he figured, and stuffed the papers in a pocket of his coat. But he didn't think they were very smart.

He called to his assistant that he would see him later at the office and went out to check the other house. An hour earlier, Broley had received a call from Hinton Roberts. The island manager had passed Caval and Insinger as they headed for the airport and had seen their bags in the back. He had gone by the houses a little later and seen Thorton going to the van carrying a bag. As soon as Thorton had left, Roberts went to the Garwood place twice, but left because the car was still parked there. Finally he called both houses several times, got no answer, and went to have a look at the Garwood house. He approached carefully and saw through a window that furniture was crowded into one of the bedrooms. Going around the house, he found the other bedrooms empty. He had gotten a high school kid who took care of a few boats at the marina to jimmy a window and enter. When the boy, as instructed by Roberts, looked around and found marijuana in a few places on the floor, Roberts had made his triumphant call to Customs.

Broley found a few items of interest in the other house, more scraps of papers with figures and initials, and one or two phone numbers. He went to Bradley Creek Marina next and located and boarded the *Errant*. The bowed deck, the damaged transom, scarred hull, disturbed interior, and small amounts of marijuana in the forward spaces left no doubt in Broley's mind how the operation had transpired. He took descriptions of a Mark Templin and associates from operators of the marina, learned that Templin planned to come back in the near future, and asked that his office be notified if and when that happened. Broley rather doubted Mark Templin—whoever that might be—would ever again set foot in North Carolina. They already had millions worth of dope, what the hell did they want with a beat-up cruiser? But stranger things had occurred. Next Broley made calls to the Coast Guard to determine the registered owners of the *Errant*, and they promised to give the information to his office as soon as possible.

iii

Matt stirred a thickening stew on the stove in *Leda*'s galley. He was a large, broad-shouldered man, and black and gray hair fell down his back. He was an old hippie, almost forty-five, who had worked every sort of job there is, and in far more places than most people ever manage to see. He had met Margaret Emery in Bequia years earlier and had lived on the boat a few months, and they had been good friends since. He had a beefy red face, clever eyes, and a salt and pepper beard that matched his hair. He was one of those rare characters who are seldom met and never forgotten. When Margaret had heard he was in Boston, she insisted he come help move *Leda*. Being rich in free time, he was not difficult to persuade, and he loved the old boat.

Matt had been at various times a stockbroker, merchant seaman, housepainter, lettuce picker, and a hundred things in between. He had been successful once, with a family in Westchester, but he had not held a bank account in ten years. He became a traveler, a vagabond in search of a bottle of whisky, a few friends, and a good time—a raconteur with endless material, a bawdy sense of humor, and a boundless ability to take life as it came. All of which made him a sort of elder statesman in Margaret's circle.

She had flown down with Matt the day before, paid his fare, and she sat at the table as he worked over his stew, kidding with him, listening to tapes, content with the feeling that *Leda* was hers—theirs—again. She had hoped Jack would still be there when she arrived, that he could somehow be part of the life she shared with Matt and Jesse, Chris, who was a musician, and Eric, a carpenter and fellow traveler. They were not so extravagant or fast, not aflame with wild aspiration. They were laid back, liked uncommon simplicity, and disdained the trappings of wealth and success. They did not drive rented cars or stay in hotels or risk their lives to become rich. They were explorers of life, and they savored it and were not often in a hurry. Margaret sat at her reassembled table and, in her happiness, never let herself think that Tom Caval owned the boat.

Margaret had been growing ill over the last two days and suffered a sore throat and a congestion in her lungs that threatened any moment to begin a rending cough. In the past year, she had been getting sick more often. Chris sat beside her and occasionally blew his harmonica along with a Doc Watson tape. He was drinking beer like everyone else and in good spirits. His black hair was thick and curly, wild on his head and around his small dark face. He was a carpenter too, from time to time, and a good musician.

Chris and Eric, a larger, younger man with slow searching eyes who worked with Jesse in Maine, had driven Sidell's van from New Hampshire and retrieved the boat's papers. The trip was a holiday to them. It was dead winter, so there was no real work at home, but they had some money. So they celebrated *Leda*'s successful return from commerce and enjoyed a vicarious triumph in Jesse's adventure. Most of all, like Margaret, they loved being together again, having a party again on *Leda*.

They sang along with parts of the songs they knew, laughed about old times, and joked about what they might do when the boat was fixed. Jesse and Eric moved busily back and forth from the engine room to the forecastle and up and down through the hatch as they prepared to leave. There was a fine sense of togetherness, and it was a setting that embodied their collective view of life — outside the normal bounds of society on a vessel that had successfully flouted the rules.

Jesse came into the salon, snapped his fingers to the music a few times and said the stew smelled good. He went to the table and bent over Margaret from behind, put his arms around her and his face next to hers. "Eh, babe, how you feeling?"

She hugged his arms. "I'm okay." Her voice was hoarse and weak. "Are we ready to go?"

"You sure you shouldn't see a doctor? Get some pills or something?" Chris asked.

"No," she replied. "I'll be alright. I want to get out of here."

Her hoarseness sounded worse though. Jesse moved around to face her. "I think maybe we should wait 'til morning and see if you feel better. If you are, we'll leave first thing. If not, I want you to see a doctor."

"Oh Jesse," she argued weakly. "Remember how sick I got that time in the Atlantic? And I got over that fine."

"It's cold out there now, babe. I don't want you to get worse. You could get pneumonia out there tonight. If you're better, we'll leave first thing tomorrow."

"I want to leave tonight," she said. "I'll stay in the aft cabin and keep warm. We won't be out long. And I want to get out of here. I'm scared to stay here."

"I don't know," Jesse scratched his head. "I really think you ought to see a doctor."

Margaret shook her head. Matt turned in the galley and said, "This stew'll fix her up. If she stays warm, it'll be okay. Let's get the hell out of here."

"Yeah. You're right," Jesse decided suddenly. "We gotta get outta here fast. We can pull in someplace tomorrow if you're not better." Margaret nodded with closed eyes. "Come on," he told Eric, "let's get the engine started and get going."

iv

Broley had not even been part of Customs at the time the deal had happened, so he suffered no personal professional pangs over not having made a good bust. Nevertheless, when he returned to his office in the late afternoon, he was bitter. He told Nancy rather curtly she had been right about the thing, but that did not bother him either. She felt worse about that than he did. What grated with Carl Broley was that the mother ship had gotten away. And although he could surely produce the names of some of those involved, he would probably have to give the case over to the DEA.

"Those bastards," he grumbled to Nancy. "They'll play a bunch of silly tricks and spend a fortune chasing them around." He shook his head with a cynical smile. "Then they'll probably steal the money from them."

"Pretty big case, Carl." Nancy had a way of raising one eyebrow. "Sure you're not jealous?"

"No. Hell. I don't care." Carl turned and looked out his window at the river. "I just don't like the way DEA works."

"Somebody has to catch these people." Nancy thought Carl must be tired. She usually knew how he thought. She knew there were many narcs he didn't care for and that he did not personally care for undercover work. Yet he had always said it was necessary.

"Yeah, but when you throw the book away," Carl turned back to her, "you're no different than they are. Hell, I almost hope they get away."

Nancy flinched at his words. She had always thought he was too strong to talk like that. That was why he had become important to her. She trusted him, could depend on him.

"I don't like hearing you talk like that." She started back to the outer office. "I didn't ever think I'd hear that crap from you."

Broley replied rather sadly, "You just haven't seen any DEA crap."

With an effort Broley began to finish the day's work. He went over the traffic log he had picked up from the island's bridge tender and separated the rental cars by license numbers, then called about the ones from local agencies. They had nothing very unusual to report but made arrangements to advise Customs when and where each car had been rented and returned and send them copies of the rental agreements. A few of the licenses were rentals from other states, and Carl left those for the next day and called a truck rental company not far away in Wilmington.

"Yessir, they brought that one back in here this very afternoon."

"Is that right?" Carl sat up carefully at his desk, as if catching a scent.

"Yessir, it is. Kinda odd deal too, y'know. They had gone an' left us the papers to a big ol' sailin' boat, instead of usin' a credit card or sumthin', y'know? Is there anything we—"

"And they just returned the vehicle today?"

"This afternoon."

"What kind of boat?" Carl inquired very calmly, and he rose out of his chair as the man answered.

"I remember when we went over the papers. It was an old Baltic ketch, it said. A big one too. Eighty feet or so, I b'lieve it was. An' it was right down here at the docks. I wish we'd've made a copy of them papers for ya, sir."

"Oh, I think it'll be alright." Broley smiled. He was looking out his window at the boat.

V

Margaret laughed at one of Matt's remarks, and her cough finally broke with a bad bronchial sound and a ripping feel in her throat, then a dizziness and aching in her arms. She bent over the table and the blood left her face. Matt turned from the stew, and Chris said she ought to lie down. Just then, there was noise above and a strong challenging voice called, "Hallo *Leda*. This is United States Customs."

Alarm unspoken but strong as thunder shocked the air, and all eyes met in a flurry of glances. Several footsteps sounded on the deck above, and Jesse hurried out of the engine room.

"Where's the master?" It was Carl Broley's deep voice over the main hatch. Clearly not a friendly visit.

"Right here." Jesse started up the companionway, anxious to keep them on deck if he could.

"That's okay," Broley stopped him. "I'll come down." He spoke quickly over his shoulder to the men with him before going below, ominously large as he appeared in the salon, looking into the grim surprise in each face, perfectly attuned to the crisp antagonism. With the five of them in his view he asked, "Is anyone else on this boat?"

"No." Jesse answered tersely. "What can I do for you?"

"Yes. My goodness," Chris spoke with a quick attempt at levity, which under the circumstances was transparent to Broley, "to what do we owe this honor?"

They had all drunk enough beer to laugh a little at the remark, as Broley looked around. Matt remained at the stove but turned and said, "We aren't familiar with the customs around here." They laughed hard at that. As quickly as they had been frightened, they became certain again that they were immune from trouble. Hell, the deal had already gone down. The cops were comically late. There was still some dope aboard—a good size sack of the cargo in a galley locker near Matt—but that would merely require outsmarting them again.

"I'm glad you're all still having a good time," Broley said pleasantly. He stepped very close to Jesse Mackenzie and stood over him in a way that achieved silence among the others. "Had a good time off Fort Rhodes Island too, didn't you? Huh? When the *Errant* met you guys out there. That must've been a good time. Just back from Colombia and everything?"

Jesse was cool. "You're going way too fast, mister."

Broley saw in Mackenzie a pugnacious dislike of authority—which he did not necessarily mind—but he wondered if the arrogance would last very long once he'd slapped him silly. Broley took his eyes away and gazed around them a moment.

"I guess this is where you carried the dope, uh? About this high," Broley gestured at shoulder height, "all around?"

There was a loud chorus of moans, less in denial than to express how banal they thought Broley's tactics. Jesse stared straight into his eyes, as if acknowledging: Okay, I know you know and you know I know, but you won't get me to say anything, asshole.

"I don't like this at all," he said aloud.

"Neither do I," Margaret added weakly.

"You have some business," Jesse went on, "or you just down here to dream?"

Now? Broley considered. Should he throw the kid against the bulkhead so hard his teeth came loose and clamp the cuffs on so hard he begged? Not yet. So far the kid was just being cool.

"Yeah, I got some business."

Broley called up through the hatch, and a moment later two Customs inspectors attired in long white mechanic's coats with "U.S. Customs" lettered across the back came down through the hatch. They entered to cynical snickers, and Matt said, "Hey, you guys're from Midas Muffler aren't ya? Could ya take a look at the diesel?" The others broke up, but the agents ignored them. Broley directed them to begin as usual in the forepeak. As he did, Matt deftly went into the locker beside his right knee, brought out the clear plastic bag filled with about four ounces of grass, and quickly stirred the contents and the bag into the stew. When Broley turned around, he found them laughing like school children behind the teacher's back, and they regarded him with contempt.

"Just one good time after another, uh?" he nodded at them. "Okay, let's all sit down here at the table and stay put."

"May I have another beer, colonel?" Matt inquired stiffly, and the others laughed again.

"Sure. Get one for everybody if ya want. Hell, get drunk. I love a party."

Matt brought an armload of bottles to the table. They were almost enjoying themselves when Broley began to question Mackenzie.

Broley asked what they had been doing in Aruba and why the

other crew had departed, and Jesse fed him the story of the corporation and the charter business. Chris interrupted: "Tell him about the heroin, Jess. Show 'im that great junk we got." Then Matt said, "You got a joint on ya, colonel? No? Wouldja care for one?" Margaret and Eric laughed at it all, but Jesse kept his eyes steadily on Broley.

Soon the inspectors had checked the forecastle and staterooms and swept the forward part of the salon, and one of them came to Broley with white paper full of sweepings.

"There's a little bit of it just about everywhere, Carl." They each poked a finger in the debris.

"What?" Jesse demanded. He rose angrily from the table to look at the stuff. "I don't know where the hell you're getting that."

Both Broley and the inspector ignored Mackenzie and the others' contentions that it was a setup.

"They've cleaned up pretty well," said the inspector, "but it appears to have been stacked all over the place."

"And you folks just don't know a thing about it, uh?" Broley asked them.

They all stared back at him, and then Margaret started to answer him, but Jesse stopped her.

"Don't bother, honey," he said to her, "just let them play it out." He turned to Broley. "I'd like to know what we're charged with, if you guys still observe those formalities."

"Now I've gone and made you all mad, haven't I," Broley kidded them back, and they did not care for it.

"I asked if we're charged with anything," Jesse raised his voice.

"I'm not sure yet." Now Broley was enjoying himself. "But I know goddamn well you brought several tons of marijuana up here from Colombia, ran it ashore in the *Errant*, and moved it out of two houses on Fort Rhodes Island, so I don't have to be in much of a hurry. And I don't think you should be either."

"You oughta write a novel," said Chris.

"You're dreamin', man," Jesse snapped contemptuously. "You're asleep and dreamin'."

Broley thought, all right pal. He took the quick breath he always took before administering a fast loosening up to a smartass, but he heard his name spoken behind him. He turned to find Jeff Culleney, the agent who had first gone out to Fort Rhodes. Culleney wondered how things were going, and Broley winked at him but said it seemed to be in the bag. Then he pointed out that they had a woman in the bargain, so Culleney ought to call Nancy to come out and perform the search.

"Alright," Broley turned to the group as Culleney departed, "let's everybody go up on deck while they sweep up the rest of it down here."

There were groans over that, and Matt, with a slur creeping into his voice, said, "Hey, man, it's cold out there."

Broley had had enough. His voice promised that someone was going to get hammered.

"Look, sweetheart," he turned on Matt, "I got enough to put you in the slammer right now, and I can be very unpleasant about that process. So I don' want any more of your shit. Now move your ass."

Sullenly, they trooped up to the deck, but Margaret was wracked again by coughing. She recovered, short of breath, holding her elbows and bent at the waist, and asked Broley if she could stay below. He looked her over and said alright.

It was well after dark when Nancy arrived. Culleney had reached her at home, so she wore blue jeans and boots beneath a light brown trench coat wrapped up against the chill. A dark rust scarf was around her neck and pulled her hair smoothly over her head. She jumped onto *Leda* and seemed very short beside Broley, but she looked like she meant business. There were a few comments about her from the four squatting, nervous and cold, around the new deck. "Could ya have her search me, colonel?" Matt called out. But there was not a lot of humor left in the others, and Nancy ignored it.

"Whatcha got?" she asked Carl.

"There's dope," he turned his head so his speech could not be seen. "It's okay, but there's nothing sexy yet, y'know?"

She nodded, knowing that in a case like this you had to find something that tied it all together and made plain saleable truth of it, something to inspire the U.S. Attorney and promise him a victory, headlines, notice—and certainly not a lot of work that might come to nothing.

One of the inspectors approached, having finished a search of the aft cabin. "Can't find much back there," he said to Carl. "There's a lot of books and scraps of paper, though. We ought to take those in and check them closer."

"Sure," Broley answered. "Okay Nancy, why don't you get the girl from down below. You can search her in the cabin over there. Sorry to call you out like this, but we have to search her."

"It's okay," she said, "I was watching TV."

After Nancy had followed her to the cabin, Margaret tried to make the sickness as apparent as possible, but without the result she had hoped for. Nancy had never had much sympathy for sickness and thought Margaret was trying to look helpless. Beside that, she disliked Margaret on sight—a rich chick who had never worked a day in her life, cruising around having a good time. She didn't mind that so much—she had no great love of work—but she resented the fact that Margaret and her friends turned to crime as part of their recreation. Nancy knew all the popular arguments in favor of striking down the laws against marijuana, but she rarely thought in a popular vein. She might have agreed that what somebody did in the privacy of their home was their own business. But when you brought the stuff into the country by the ton, you didn't pay taxes, and you had no idea where it would end up. That was a crime on the books, and to Nancy it was a moral crime.

"You sail a lot?" she inquired as she looked around the aft cabin.

"As much as possible," Margaret answered softly. "This was my boat for several years. I bought it in Denmark and rebuilt it, restored it. It was my whole life. But I had to sell it. I sold it to this corporation, and they've hired me to help move it to drydock now. I've been working a lot, though, so I don't get to sail much anymore."

Nancy suddenly remembered seeing an article about Margaret a few years ago in a fashion magazine, about her living a very chic life on her boat down in the islands.

"Working? Doing what?"

"A lot of things really." Margaret's voice hardened with a resentment of the bitch cop enforcing her bullshit. In it Nancy saw the arrogance of the jet-set hippie.

"Like what?"

"Well . . . I've been writing."

"Is that work?" Nancy almost laughed.

"You should try it," Margaret turned away.

"I'd love to." Nancy closed the door. "Take your clothes off."

Nancy went through the stack of charts, photographs, books, magazines that the inspectors had piled together on the chart table. Margaret laid her parka on one of the bunks and pulled her blouse over her head then held it before her breasts, shivering a little. Nancy set down a chart and picked up a thick spiral notebook and was about to look through it.

"Are you an agent?" Margaret asked.

Nancy regarded her curiously. It seemed a quick question and insincere. She merely nodded and looked at the notebook again.

"Is it interesting work? I'd love to have a job working on the waterfront. Inspecting boats coming in."

Nancy smiled. She thumbed through the notebook a moment more then asked, "Whose is this?"

"I don't know. I haven't been aboard in months."

What a terrible liar, Nancy thought. Margaret convulsed in a spasm of painful coughs and held her breasts and turned away in pain and humility. Nancy did not rush her.

"Do I have to undress completely?" Margaret asked when she recovered.

"That's right, lady. This is for real."

Nancy looked coldly upon Margaret as she removed the rest of her clothing and then stood naked, staring at Nancy as she looked over her clothes. Nancy took her time, and when she looked up again, Margaret watched her hatefully.

"Turn around," said Nancy.

Grudgingly Margaret turned. "I hope you enjoy this."

"Sure. Bend over."

A few moments later, as Margaret dressed, Nancy looked again at the spiral notebook and found that it was a log and that the dates were quite recent. She smiled a little realizing that it was very useful and turned slowly through the pages. A look of wonder struck her features as she read one of the entries.

"Here's your sex, Carl," Nancy quipped as she approached him on the deck. "Read this little observation."

Broley took the notebook and read with some difficulty the disturbed script with which Jesse had made the melancholy note that ended " . . . Look at us now, lady—four salty guys and ten tons of dope."

Broley closed his eyes and let a long whistle.

"Look at the beginning and at the last entries too. He talks about the coast of Colombia, then about letting off the first part of the load, the whole bit."

He leafed through most of the pages very quickly and looked up.

"Thanks, honey."

She smiled for an instant and shrugged her shoulders.

352

chapter 24

JACK came inside from the sunny, cold morning and poured another cup of coffee. It was good to be back in New England, and it felt like years since he had been content. It was good to be in the big kitchen of the drafty old house that had rooms and sections of different ages, like well-spaced brothers. There was a fire in the wood stove on its brick platform at the end of the kitchen. As he stood with his back to it and sipped the coffee, he looked out the window at the snow and the crisp birch and pine forest across the rocky dirt road. In the thrill of the morning, and the blood familiarity of New Hampshire and warm old havens from cold, he felt at last that the struggle was over.

The dope was in the attic. It was divided into ten-pound bags, and there was only the seven hundred fifty good pounds left. The previous day he had delivered in Cambridge the whole of the five hundred pounds that had been left as his share of the cargo. He had made the deal with people who were associates of old friends, and they had snapped up the stuff at three hundred a pound and given seventy thousand in front. So now Jack had seventy grand in cash, eighty more coming soon, and the primo stuff he had left could bring four fifty a pound. At last he was certain to make out. Not the million, but plenty.

His friends had just left for the daily drive to Boston, and Jack had walked out to see them off as if it were his house. They were a married couple, and Jack had known them for years. Their house was perfect for moving weight in the Boston area. They were no strangers to the business and were both in graduate school, so they could use the money Jack offered for their risks.

Joe had left the previous day. They had settled up, and Joe took two hundred fifty of the thousand pounds they bought from Caval, along with his own two hundred pounds and put it all in a steamer trunk he picked up at a second-hand store in one of the little villages along the Merrimack River. Swearing he would never again drive further than the nearest liquor store, Joe chartered a twin-engine Cessna for the trip to Denver.

Joe had shrugged when neither of them could think what to say on parting. "How about Utah?" Eiler mused.

"A little powder skiing?" Jack grinned.

"And a little discussion of foreign banking."

"Sounds good. Try for once to keep in touch."

They had chosen, as they rarely did, to shake hands.

Finishing his coffee Jack took great pleasure not only in the fact that he was happy, that he liked where he was, but that there was nothing he had to do. He decided to take a hike through the new snow up to a high hill he remembered from his last visit, from which you could see the White Mountains in the north and the Green Mountains to the west. Then he would come back and build a blazing birch fire and make a few sketches. He had not begun a design in almost a year.

The telephone rang like an alarm, as if Jack's satisfaction had exceeded some limit. He knew it was bad news of some sort. He had developed a nose for it, but he had no idea it would be Margaret's voice, ill and frightened, saying in one breath that Customs had seized *Leda* and Jesse was in jail.

He leaned back his head as if in agony, but then laughed. It all seemed absurd. There was a confused silence at the other end before Margaret spoke again with all her might, as if to prevent Jack from delirium.

"They know everything, Jack. Everything! They know about *Errant*, about Fort Rhodes . . . and everything, Jack."

"Jesus," he shouted. His composure was utterly shattered. He felt as if he might cry next. "Who else was busted? Did they bust anybody at the houses?" he demanded. "How the hell could they know about *Leda*?" He had nearly forgotten about leaving the papers.

"I don't know, Jack. They booked us all." She sounded out of breath and weak. "They only kept Jesse, though, because he was on board when you cleared."

"Goddamnit, I don't know how they could know everything."

Margaret coughed horribly before she could answer.

"Me neither," she wheezed, then gasped for breath a moment before saying, "Jack, they found the log, Jesse's log."

"No."

"Yes. They found it, Jack. Oh, Jack, I'm so sick. It just happened last night. I haven't been to sleep, and they say—"

"We're fucked," Jack pronounced. He was incapable of pity for Margaret's bronchitis. He knew they should have pitched the log, but Jesse had thought he might write something about it all one day. That had seemed so aesthetic. When are you going to learn? Jack reproached himself with a bitterness that bordered on self-hatred. Aesthetics are for novelists. This is business.

"I'm scared for Jesse," she said.

"Don't worry. I'll get him out."

As Margaret stumbled through the information about the jail and charges and bail, the worst of it struck Jack. He had given Jesse the number of this telephone, which was now surely in the hands of the cops.

"How did you get this number?" he snapped.

"Jesse wrote it down for me yesterday morning."

"Jesus Christ, he's still got it on him."

"What? Jack, what are you going to do about Jesse?"

"I don't know yet. Let your mother know where you are. I've got to get out of here right now, or I won't be able to do anything."

"But Jack, I'm scared for Jesse. I think they might—"

"Don't worry," Jack cut her off loudly. "I'll help him. I've got to go. Bye."

As he hung up he heard her crying "Jack—" But for all he knew the heat could have been coming up the road right then. He tried to think for a moment, but he had no time, and there was very little to consider. He had to get out of there immediately, warn his friends, get another truck, get the stuff out of there somehow, find another place, tell Joe, tell the others, hide. He took his coat, and a few minutes later he was walking down the road toward town, cursing the harsh weather.

ii

It was three weeks later when Carl Broley considered throwing his coffee, mug and all, into the outer office. "What're we payin' that bitch for," he grumbled. "Can't make decent coffee. Hell, that's all I need her for. I can do the rest of it myself." He grimaced at another sip of the stuff. The goddamn DEA, he thought. Why had he ever encouraged Nancy to become an agent?

One thing after another had seemed to go wrong ever since he had returned to Customs. The first good case he got into was turned over to DEA. "Get a good case," he had growled at the time, "and they give it to a bunch of armed hippies with badges." Then Nancy had been transferred and didn't even seem to care. Right after they had busted *Leda*, she had applied for the higher status. Given the newness of DEA, and the policies designed to hire women, she had been told that by joining the narcotics agency she could almost start working right away. Carl had tried to stop her, but she seemed to resent his objections. It had made him feel like her father and reminded him that he was about twenty years older than she, and he hadn't liked that either. "After awhile," he had warned her rather heatedly, "you won't know the difference between right and wrong." She had replied, "I'm beginning to wonder if you know the difference." That was their final exchange on the matter. He had taken her out to dinner after her last day in the office, but he hadn't heard from her since. Then they sent this incompetent broad to replace her. He ought to retire, he had begun to think. He damn well ought to retire.

The previous day, a nineteen-year-old kid from Miami had returned a car that had been rented in his name a month earlier to help some of Harry Amian's associates move weed into Florida. The rental agency had called Broley, and Broley arrested him, but he was appalled that DEA had not even left instructions with the agency. He thought of calling DEA, to see what they planned to do with the guy, but he couldn't even stand to talk to them. So he called the U.S. Attorney instead.

"I mean, what the hell?" he raised his voice at the telephone a few minutes later. "These bums have got two cars out that still need to be returned, and DEA don't even leave a number with the agency."

"Carl, you're just pissed off 'cause they got that little secretary that worked for you."

"Oh go to hell, huh? I just wanna know what's goin' on. I busted this crew in the first place, and I didn't like havin' the case jerked on me. And now they can't even do it right. What the hell are they gonna do with this guy? Have they busted anybody else yet? I mean they've had three weeks now. Hell, I gave 'em the phone numbers of two of 'em. They coulda called 'em up."

"They're going to let this kid go," the attorney replied and then spoke loudly to overcome Broley's groaning curses. "They're just going to keep an eye on him, Carl. They know where these others guys are, most of them anyway. They're going to wait 'til they know the whole operation and then bust."

"That's crazy. Why the hell don't they start bustin' people. That's the way you find out who's runnin' things. Not by screwin' around an' followin' people. Hell, they'll move all that shit by the time those bums get around to doin' something."

"I don't make their rules, Carl," the attorney said wearily.

"Who the hell does?"

"Jesus, I don't know."

iii

Joe Eiler went quickly up the steps of the subway exit. He carried no bag, although he had just flown in from Denver. He wore gray wool slacks, black cowboy boots and a dark blue ski parka, and he had shaved since North Carolina and cut his hair so that he looked like a nice young man from one of the local colleges, unless you saw the severity of his eyes. He smiled crookedly when he saw Jack standing impatiently along the windows of a men's store huddled in gloves and a scarf in a short leather jacket. The last snow remained in brief discolored drifts against the building.

"You look like a fugitive," said Joe.

"I am, for Christ's sake." Jack looked around quickly. They stood in a stream of pedestrians flowing hurriedly on either side, and a cold wind sneaked among the buildings and occasionally attacked. "I think they picked me up this morning when I came out of my sister's place."

"No shit." Joe stiffened. He was afraid to look around.

"Yeah. Three people in a blue Ford. I saw them park as I was on the doorstep, and then they pulled away behind me just as I left. They could be watching now for all I know."

Joe simply shrugged and shook his head. He was very tired and could not understand what was going on. The previous day he had managed to locate Jack at a friend's house in Connecticut. It was their first contact since they had parted, and Jack went to a pay phone and called him back, and Joe told him that he was being followed. They had gotten on him in San Francisco, but Joe had thought it was just a local deal. He got away to Denver, but others turned up on his trail there. He had heard nothing of the bust in Wilmington, so Jack told him he better come out for a visit. Joe had taken the earliest flight that morning, and Jack had come up from Connecticut the day before.

"You're not still holdin' that stuff, are you?" Joe asked.

"No. It went fast." Jack perked up for a moment. "Hell, I'd leave the country for awhile, but I've got too much to collect." Jack's distaste for the common work of dope-dealing was suddenly more striking than the worry in his face: "I hate collecting money," he growled. "I don't care how well you know somebody, it's a pain in the ass."

"I've heard," said Joe. "Let's get something to eat."

They walked through the Boston Public Gardens toward Charles Street to cut over to the Hampshire House. Jack told Eiler about the seizure of *Leda* and *Errant*, the arrest of Mackenzie, discovery of Mackenzie's log, and the howling headlines the story earned, quoting Jesse's log:

FOUR SALTY GUYS AND TEN TONS OF DOPE

Joe had known nothing of any of it, especially Jesse's log, and he was dumbfounded. He moved along silently as Jack talked, beneath bare branches of huge trees that seemed hysterical against the winter sky. Ugly old people shivered on benches. A giant mechanical swan used for taking people on rides around the lily pond was retired for winter and lay on its side on the shore, an expired fantasy.

Eiler felt the world closing in on him. Everything he saw and felt and heard assaulted him, and there was no refuge. The pressure weighed on his mind like an irresistible force and increased with each word of bad news Sidell spoke. There had been moments in Curaçao and Wilmington when Joe had sensed that the venture would ultimately part the narrow thread that seemed to suspend his life over a fearful chasm. Now it seemed certain.

"I don't understand," he said as they walked. "They must know all of us. They're probably watchin' us right now. Why the hell don't they bust us?"

"Because they didn't get the dope, I guess. I can't figure it out either. I think they're just trying to find out where we've got the stuff or where it went. Or else just trying to get a case together to indict for importation, maybe conspiracy." Joe nodded so that Jack would keep talking. Jack thought well under pressure, and Joe was afraid to try.

"We've got to get a good lawyer. We've got to keep everyone together and get a good laywer. If they start busting and get somebody isolated, no telling what will happen. We were lucky they got Mackenzie and not somebody else."

"Lucky as hell," said Joe. Anger made him feel a little more stable. "Remind me to do business with a fuckin' writer again."

"He didn't talk."

"He didn't have to. You know what a lawyer will cost us with all that shit the cops know?"

"The moon. But we've got to get one. And it's Caval's job to pay for it."

"Oh come on. What else has Tommy made good on?"

"He'll have to do this. It's his ass too. But we've damn well got to pay him for that dope."

"Goddamnit," Joe raised his voice. He was on the verge of screaming. "Fifty thousand bucks to that little bastard. I'd rather get my own lawyer. I can't stand to pay him."

"I have to pay him three times that much."

"That's different. You're honest. I don't want—"

"Damnit Joe, you said you'd pay him." Jack stopped on the pathway and glared at Eiler. "We have to keep this thing together. If we get our own lawyer, one guy could crack and screw us all. We need one good lawyer for everybody. And if we pay Caval, he'll take care of it." Jack paused a moment. "Because we could screw him if he doesn't."

"Sure." Eiler nodded sarcastically and walked on. "You'd turn state's witness against him, uh?"

"At this point I really don't know."

"Bullshit."

They went into the lower level of the Hampshire House below the street. It was midafternoon early in the week so there were few people there, and the place was always dark. They ordered hamburgers and a couple of beers then decided to play a game of darts.

"I think I'll go down to New York tomorrow or the next day and get this straight with Caval," Jack said as he took a few practice throws. "He was scared to death the first time I talked to him a couple of weeks ago, but he sounded back to normal the other day when he called."

"What's he doin' in New York?" Joe asked, but three people entering the bar just then caught his eye and he barely heard Jack's reply.

"He's down there for a ski convention or something. Probably shooting off his mouth."

The three newcomers—two men and a woman—sat at the bar close by. Joe could feel their presence as he threw, and he heard nothing of Jack's conversation. The three had looked Joe over carefully as they came in and were speaking under their breath.

When Joe finished, he found them still watching him. He cautioned himself against delusions, but he kept an eye on them, and his jaws grew tight.

The man nearest Eiler was medium height and heavy, with sandy coarse hair and round puggish features. He wore a vinyl imitation-of-leather jacket and seemed angry about everything, except when he was looking toward Joe, and then he smiled a little. The other man was older, about forty, with dark hair conventionally cut, and he wore a dark raincoat. The woman between them appeared to be in her late twenties, but with a worldly look about her and plenty of cosmetics.

Joe said nothing to Jack and tried to ignore them, until the sandy haired man reached for an ashtray across the bar. Then Joe saw the pistol outlined through his coat beneath his left arm. Eiler's arms quivered, and his thoughts raced madly. He could have bolted out the door that instant, but if he had a gun himself he might have killed three people very quickly. There was nothing in the world he hated more than undercover police.

"Check that," Jack nodded toward his first round score—four twenties. The game raised his spirits a little, but his smile dropped when he saw Joe's face. "What?" he demanded.

"Look what walked in."

When Jack turned, he found all three of them looking straight at him. He looked back at them for a moment and went cold all over, thinking they might pull something right there, but it passed. He turned coolly back toward Joe who was getting the darts and said, "I'm sure they were in that car this morning."

"Sure they were," Joe spoke through his teeth, then threw the first dart as hard as he could. "And here they come."

"How're you fellas?" The man with the blonde hair and vinyl jacket approached Sidell, smiling like an old acquaintance. Jack looked him over and said nothing.

Joe threw another dart very hard and answered without looking at the man, "Gee, hi."

The second man followed his partner, nodding at Sidell as he came up, but the woman stayed in her seat.

"How 'bout lettin' us play?" said the first one.

"Why not wait 'til we finish?" Sidell looked away from him.

"Naw, hell, let's just play doubles." There was a loud rude familiarity in the man's voice, and he stepped forward as if to simply enter the game. Sidell, however, did not move an inch, and the man nearly walked into him. Eiler threw another dart as if the board were a hundred yards away.

"Hey. Easy there," said the bartender. He seemed to feel something strange in the offing. Eiler ignored him. The agents chuckled.

"There's another board in the back room," said Jack.

"Hey, com'on, just a friendly game, uh?"

"No thanks." Sidell turned away from him but stayed in the same place to prevent him from getting closer.

Joe collected the darts quickly. As he gave them to Jack, he looked at the men with undisguised hatred. He was on the verge of telling them he knew damn well they were a pair of scumbag narcs. But despite his acute dislike of them, Eiler was seldom jittery about police. He knew what his rights were, but he also knew that when you are implicated in a large smuggling operation and are hopping around the country—the world—with no apparent means of support and no address your rights are not worth much. He had no choice but to endure them.

"Hey, what're you guys," the first man persisted, "a couple of assholes, you won't play a little game of darts?"

"Hey, you guys, this is Marilyn," said the first man, as she sat on a stool beside him.

Jack paid no attention, and the woman caught Joe's eye with a curious smile and said, "Hi. What's your name?"

Eiler stared back at her. "Fine, how're you?"

"Not very friendly are ya?" the first man snarled.

"No," Eiler snapped. Jack glanced at him over his shoulder with a warning in his eyes: don't push them.

"I don't like guys who aren't nice to ladies," the blonde man said.

"Oh, come on now," she said to him. "He just doesn't know us." She smiled again at Joe, and the second man examined Sidell very closely. Joe exchanged a glance with Sidell, and Jack seemed as indecisive for the moment as Joe was. Joe wanted simply to leave, but he felt the necessity of seeing what they had in mind, although it was getting harder.

"Where are you from?" the woman had a friendly tone, but Joe ignored her.

"The lady asked you a question." The tone of the blonde agent's voice made Joe want to smash his beer bottle in the guy's face.

"I thought she was talkin' to you," he said.

"I asked where you're from," she tried again very sweetly. "Are you from Denver? You look like you're from Denver. I know some guys from there."

Joe ignored her again. It was getting a little ridiculous.

"The lady's talkin' to you, buddy."

"Talkin' to my buddy?" Joe wondered without looking at either of them.

The first man's pug face was livid, and the woman dropped her smile. The second man seemed mildly amused though. He approached Jack as he gave the darts to Joe, and he fished something out of the pocket of his raincoat while the other two whispered.

"Your name's Jack, isn't it? I think I've seen you in here before." He came very close, but Jack did not answer. "You guys speak English or not? Isn't your name Jack?"

The air was becoming very tense. Eiler threw the darts like he was hunting boar. There were three men at the other end of the bar and two tables were occupied nearby, but every eye and ear was on the loud exchanges near the dart board.

"Look, I asked—"

"Whatta you care what my name is?" Jack turned toward him, which pleased the man. He raised the object from his raincoat. Jack saw it was an Instamatic camera, and he turned away abruptly and rested his arm against a pole running from the corner of the bar to the ceiling to block his face from the side.

"Mind if I take your picture?"

"Yeah, you guys're a piece o' work. We never seen any millionaires before," the other one taunted.

"I mind," Jack said loudly.

Sleazy bastard, Joe thought. He stood still and breathed deeply before he threw again. He had boundless contempt for them, too stupid to steal a decent shot or use a good undercover camera. Beside that, he figured they were more concerned that he and Jack made a lot of money—more than they would ever make—than how they got it.

"I just want the practice, you know." The man spoke with the camera at his eye. "I just got this camera."

"I asked him to take one for me," the woman offered.

Jack turned his head slightly to see what was going on, and the guy pushed the shutter button. The flash cube didn't fire though, and the agent angrily examined the camera. "Stinkin' narc," Joe grumbled as he threw the last dart.

"Huh? Talkin' to us?" the first man asked. "You say sumthin?"

Joe went forward to retrieve the darts, and the man moved a

little to one side and snapped another shot but again without a flash. He muttered something to himself.

"Why don't ya take one of yourself," Joe asked angrily.

As Joe took the darts, the man clicked the camera again, but there was still no flash. Sidell and Eiler looked at each other, and Jack jerked his head for Eiler to follow. They pushed past the agent as he tried to put in another flashcube and went quickly toward the far dark corner table.

"Hey, you guys leavin'?" the first man asked.

"Yeah," said Joe, "it's all yours Sherlock."

They sat looking at each other for a few moments before speaking.

"It's goddamn scary to have guys that clumsy and obnoxious following you," Jack whispered through his teeth. Joe just nodded. His heart was beating so fast it was hard to breathe. "What're we going to do if they come over here with that fucking camera."

"Leave."

"Think they'd try anything outside?" Jack watched the three agents talking in low voices at the bar.

"I doubt it. What would they do?"

The hamburgers came a few moments later, and Joe gave the waiter ten dollars for the check and told him to keep the change so he and Jack could leave with as little notice as possible. It didn't work though. The woman noticed, and the three spoke together briefly, then she went to the phone.

"We better get this over with," said Joe. He spoke with his mouth full, but he wasn't hungry anymore.

"I'm going to New York in the morning. We got to get a lawyer. This is crazy. I wonder if they're on Caval."

"Wouldn't be very hard to do. I guess I'll call you in Connecticut, okay?"

Jack nodded and tried to speak without moving his mouth. "How you getting out of here?"

"By cab, I guess. Why don't you go on foot. I don't think they'll do anything, but be careful."

They each took a last bite and another sip of beer, then Jack said, "Now?" Joe shrugged sadly, and they stood and walked toward the door.

"See ya, fellas," the blonde agent smiled.

They hurried up the steps to the street, and as Jack turned to the right, Joe looked nervously for a cab.

"Hey," Jack came back a step. "Where you going?"

"I don't know. You better get outta here."

Joe beckoned a cab only seconds after Sidell disappeared around the corner, and he told him to go to the Statler Hilton. It came to him quickly. He had never been followed and all he knew about it was from late movies. When he looked out the rear window and actually saw a metallic brown Ford leaving the curb a half block behind them, he cursed them, but to his amazement, he found it rather amusing too. He sat sideways and kept an eye on them until they reached the Hilton, then he gave the driver a five and jumped out quickly and went inside. His idea was to rush through the lobby to the other entrance and catch another cab, but as he looked back he saw the brown Ford hurry past the glass doors and realized that it must be one of the older ploys. He stood there a moment, taut and empty, and no longer in any slightest sense amused. By some physical instinct he reversed his field and hurried back to the doors he'd entered, went out to the first cab in line, looked around the street, but did not see the other car, and jumped inside.

"Go to the airport!" He startled himself with the loudness of voice and terrified the driver. "And haul ass!" He barely touched the seat before pitching himself lengthwise on the floor. The astonished driver said nothing, so Joe yelled, "Come on damnit. My wife's lawyers are tailin' me. I'll give ya twenty bucks."

"A-right, a-right, Jesus, let's go," said the driver, and the car lurched away, "Jump in 'ere like bank robbahs, an' I'm s'pose to . . ."

The man babbled, and Eiler lay on the floor breathing like a trapped animal. The man sounded as if he spoke from within a separate set of dimensions. Joe could not think of anywhere to go. The thread parted, and Joe felt himself plummet into the emptiness.

chapter 25

i

BY ten o'clock Sidell was in a nervous stupor. He sat on the motel bed with his legs outstretched, one hand tightly at his side, while his teeth explored what remained of fingernails on the other. His eyes were unblinking, his stomach empty and numb. The room was dark except for a dull glow from the bathroom light, and he inhabited the place with every stray sound from outside, which he identified like a sentry. He had been there, in roughly the same position, since around four in the afternoon.

When Eiler had beckoned a taxi, Jack had gone around the first corner to his right and hurried down the back street without knowing whether he was actually being followed or not. He considered returning to his sister's apartment like an innocent man, but if they stayed on him how would he collect his money, how would he reach Caval to discuss a lawyer? Worst of all they might actually arrest him, sock him with a huge bail, and then everything would go to hell. Beside that, his money was at his sister's. He had kept it with him locked in his suitcase and changed it into larger bills whenever he had the chance, but finally it was too much worry. The night before, while his sister was out, he had taken up the runner on the narrow stairway that went up to her bedroom. He dismantled a lower stair and stashed the money in a shoe box inside. He had worked carefully at it for two hours, using the old nails and trying not to mark the paint, but if someone good really searched the place, they might still find it. So he had to lead them away from there if he could.

He had kept from running the last block before he cut to his left toward the Storrow Drive freeway and reached a pedestrian overpass that led to the narrow stretch of park that extended along the Charles River. He had no coherent notion of where he was going, except to flee.

As soon as he reached the ground below the overpass he began to jog upriver. A gray detritus of snow marked the dead grass, and the river lay dark and cold. Every few steps he looked back to see if there were a figure on the overpass, and even though he saw none he ran faster, fast enough to attract attention from the few strollers braving the cold afternoon. Finally he forced himself to slow down, then stopped altogether. On sheer impulse he turned and ran back in the direction he came, though not as fast. At the footbridge he crossed back over the freeway and cut over to Charles Street then across Beacon Hill and finally, still acting merely from one impulse to the next, he had gone to the Holiday Inn and taken a room.

All evening he sat on the bed, stiffening at the sound of voices or footsteps in the hallway. He imagined them staking out his sister's place, waiting at the airport, patrolling the area. He imprisoned himself with the inability to decide where to go or what to do next.

His mind was almost blank by ten o'clock, but he still followed a pair of footsteps down the hall. Then he heard other feet behind the first ones. Still, he had grown so used to them continuing toward the exit that he jerked convulsively when they stopped at his door. There was a solid purposeful knocking. What the hell are they going to do? His thoughts clawed at the walls, yet he sat perfectly still. The knocking came again, shocking as gunfire.

"Jack? . . . Jack?" Sidell thought he recognized the voice from the bar. He knew he couldn't get out a window. What the hell would they do? "Jack? . . . Jack, you in there?"

Two low voices conversed briefly outside the door. Then, sarcastically, one called, "G'night, Jack."

Jack's heart pounded so wildly he could barely catch his breath. His face burned with the indignity. They were playing with him. They knew him, knew what he'd done, but were not even going to arrest him. They were going to play with him, drag it out. His failure seemed absolute. Hunted down now and hiding in a motel room, he could see the remaining downward spiral arriving finally in some dismal cell. Utter disgrace had warned him with feints and starts for a year. But now it seemed to occur like a bomb exploding. Every aspect of it tormented him for some indistinguishable period of time, perhaps two hours—time was without significance. He waited for them to come back. They would break the door down, maybe use a pass key. Jerk him off the bed and beat the shit out of him. Take him to his sister's. Throw her around until he showed them where the money was. Then put him away. Put her in jail too. Demolished, he rolled onto his side and somehow slept.

He awoke the next morning and managed a desperate resolution. He had no better opinion of his position and still did not doubt that sooner or later he would lose completely. But being followed was almost purely a physical matter, he decided, and he did not believe he could be followed by anyone for long. He took a shower and left by the front door. It was cold and steel gray outside, and Jack walked the distance to the Charles Street MTA station in plain view and unhurried. He mounted the stairs to the downtown side of the tracks where the wind tormented the early crowd of workers.

Sidell walked slowly among the crowd studying faces from one end to the other. Finally near the stairs, Jack saw her, turning away as if she were speaking with two other women, and he nearly laughed. He called, "Hello Marilyn," but she did not acknowledge. The whole thing became ridiculous to him as he turned away. They seemed crude and witless to him, and he wasn't frightened anymore.

Sidell moved to the other end of the platform and stood among the crowd until he saw Marilyn approach just as the train was arriving. People surged forward with the crash and roar of the cars as they halted, and Jack watched her nonchalantly wait to see which car he would take. When the entire crowd had nearly boarded, Jack was close to the door of one car and Marilyn was just behind him. The bell rang and he stepped forward to enter, then at the last moment hurried to the next car and jumped inside. He was a second too early, though, and she made it into the car just as the doors closed. Jack smiled at her and nodded, as if admiringly. She looked back only for an instant, with a cool businesslike gaze, then looked elsewhere. As the train roared on, Jack was close enough to touch her.

The next stop was Park station, only a few minutes away, where all passengers connect with other lines, and Jack tensed as they pulled in. He thought: Alright sweetie, this is where we part company.

The doors slid open, and Jack moved forward with the crowd, keeping very near her. He timed the shift of his weight, planted his left foot, and kneed her in the thigh as hard as he could. She let out an animal groan and fell to the floor among legs and shoes. In the same motion Jack forced his way through the exit and could just hear the snarling protests of witnesses as he raced down the platform. He pushed through the crowd like a thief, reached the stairs to the lower level, descended, and darted to his right into a small space between the stairway and a pillar. Only about twenty seconds passed before she came into view at the foot of the stairs. She limped like a cripple, and her face was shocked with pain, her mouth hanging open, but Jack was amazed. He had felt the muscle and bone against his knee when he hit her, and he had not thought she'd be getting up. She looked around for a few seconds, then struggled on toward the phone booths. Sidell slipped around the other end of the stairs to catch another train for Government Center and then a connection for the airport. He knew they would still be around, though, if not this morning then another day.

On the long line to the airport, Jack got off and on the trains twice to see if anyone new was with him. He was satisfied he was alone when he finally arrived. Buses take MTA passengers from the trains to the terminals, however, and as Jack approached the waiting bus, he noticed a man reading a newspaper. He was about forty, balding on top and wore a black overcoat, and he was apparently waiting to board the bus, except that no one waits for the airport bus. There is almost always a bus standing ready, and with rare exceptions, people proceed straight from the trains to the bus. So Jack stopped and looked at the man, and his stomach began to flutter. Impossible, he thought. The fright crawled over him like clammy animals. For a moment he thought of getting back on the MTA, but that seemed hopeless. When all the other passengers had boarded, the man glanced at Jack and then there was no doubt. At the last minute Jack walked to the bus, and the man followed.

The agent sat on one of the two front seats which face the side of the bus, and Jack sat nearby facing the front, looking directly at him. By the first stop, which is the shuttle terminal for flights to New York, Jack had stopped thinking of New York. He was trying to keep himself from believing that they would never get off him. By the next stop though, he had decided to see how quick the guy was. When everyone leaving seemed to have gotten off Jack stood up and went quickly toward the door. He was down the small steps and ready to get off when the man rose and followed, whereupon Jack stopped and turned to face him.

He could tell by a slight jerk of the body that the agent was surprised, but his face betrayed nothing. Jack stared into his eyes and found them cold and calculating as a cat's. Because Jack was blocking the exit, the man had no choice but to stop. Jack smirked at him, but still the man's expression did not change. He was trained, and he did not play games with the opposition.

"You guys gettin' off heah, or not?" the driver demanded.

"Is this TWA?" the man asked, still staring at Jack.

The driver said no, and Jack, mesmerized by the agent's eyes, moved back up the steps. When the doors shut and the bus proceeded, he wanted to kick himself. He'd had the son of a bitch right there, he thought. He could've run him around in a circle, and he blew it. Something in the bloodless depth of the agent's eyes had unnerved him. It suggested an army of men appearing without end to wear him down like the forces of a nightmare.

By the time they reached the TWA stop, Jack was ready to run for it across the parking lot, but he drew a deep breath and went inside with the man close behind him. With his thoughts whirling he stood in the ticket line. The man remained nearby, within hearing distance, as if waiting to meet someone. Jack kept groping for some tactic but nothing beside a bold dash came to mind. Finally he was at the counter and paid cash for a one-way ticket for Hawaii. As soon as the ticket was handed to him, he turned and walked briskly toward the staircase to the upper level. Turning slightly he saw he had some distance on the agent and suddenly sprinted for the stairs, took them four at a time to the top and raced around the corner and into the broad concourse, certain that something would offer itself. As soon as he turned the corner he saw a janitor with a mop and a wheeled bucket opening the door of a custodial closet. The man was only about fifteen yards ahead, so Jack slowed to the speed of a normal person late for a flight, took a last look over his shoulder as he reached the door and darted inside pulling the door shut behind him.

The place was a good deal smaller than Jack had thought, though, and he found himself straddling the bucket and wedged belly to belly with the janitor, who turned out to be about six feet tall and well over two hundred pounds.

"What the hell you doin'?" the man growled down into Jack's face. He was pressed back against shelves, startled and angry.

"Sorry," Jack gasped into the glowering black features. "I just need to get out of the hall for a second. I'll only—"

"I don't care what you doin'."

"Look, I just need a couple of seconds."

"I said I don't—"

"Come on, man, they're some guys chasing me."

"Jesus Christ!" The man's eyes closed for an instant. He grabbed Jack by the coat.

"Alright." Jack placed his hand lightly against the man's hands and thought: Just a few more seconds. "I'm going. I'm going."

Jack turned carefully in the small space and opened the door while the janitor grumbled about losing his job and being arrested and how he ought to hold Jack for the police. To his right, down the concourse, Jack saw the agent moving quickly, checking the crowd from side to side. Sidell shot out of the closet, and a minute later he was in a taxi heading in to the train station.

ii

Even the day after he had been there, Mark Insinger could remember little of the Park Lane Hotel. He recalled it was down the street from the Plaza, across from Central Park, opulent in a way that made his favorite, the Ritz-Carlton, seem slightly provincial, but he had been too weary and harried to register much else.

He was admitted to Caval's suite by a young woman he had never seen, who spoke English with difficulty in an accent he assumed was French and whose tight jiggle of bosom reminded him painfully how long it had been. There were eight or ten people in the room, all of whom seemed connected in some way with the ski convention that brought Caval to New York. Tom was not present, but his guests enjoyed themselves in plenty. Cocaine was in evidence, as were marijuana and tequila, and Mark had the impression everyone was talking at once. He could not have guessed within two hours either way of the correct time, but sunlight streamed angularly from the windows, accentuating a sense of decadent chic about the gathering. A few of them asked him questions—essentially who he was and where he was from—and the vagueness of his answers amused them. He listened like an eavesdropper to their talk of skiing. They discussed the Alps as opposed to Colorado, and people and equipment and the competitive circuit. Mark felt like a servant intruding on the party. He disdained them as trivial and frivolous, at the same time that he envied them. He kept waiting for Caval to return from somewhere and was tired enough but too nervous to sleep.

When Sidell appeared, Mark greeted him the way one would discover an old friend in hell. Small talk was not possible. The merest greeting introduced heavier personal matters, and Jack had no more use for the party than Mark did, so very quickly they went to a bedroom.

Mark heard of Jack's adventures of the last two days with the usual admiration he felt for the way Sidell's life ran. Jack lay on the bed when he finished telling about it, in the same wrinkled clothes in which he had met Joe Eiler. He was two days without a shave. He looked mysterious somehow, rather than dirty as most people would have.

Mark couldn't manage much sympathy for Jack's problem though. If anything, he envied him. The only reason Mark had not been tailed was because he had not had the luxury of being able to slow down long enough for them to locate him. Beside that, Jack had already sold nearly his whole load—and to people he at least knew something about. Jack did not have to ride herd on Harry Amian twenty-four hours a day, collect money like a Brinks guard, and chase people all over the country. And Jack did not have Caval breathing over every penny he made. Mark would have been happy to trade him. They could chase him anywhere they wanted.

They talked for another hour, speculating in low, tired voices about how the bust had occurred, how the DEA was proceeding, what a grand jury might do. The dark bedroom fit their mood, with the curtain drawn and only a small light on by the bed. It provided a decent place to rest, comfortable and secure. They agreed, like two newsmen considering a political likelihood, that sooner or later the grand jury would indict.

The door opened suddenly, and light and heightened voices fell into the somber room, and Caval entered. He was resplendent in a closely fitted suit of pale blue leather, and he appeared relaxed and calm. He kept the door open for a moment so he could see Mark and Jack, and as though he knew the look of splendor the backlighting gave him. He smiled at the squinted terse greetings before he shut the door, and it was not the detestable smirk he usually rendered but a normal human expression of pleasure. He even said hello, which seemed equally rare, and asked how they were. Mark thought perhaps it was not really Caval.

"You don't look too good, Jack." Caval remained standing. He seemed to be modeling the suit.

"I've been chased around Boston for two days. Hard to keep my wardrobe straight." Jack's voice was aggressive and short. He had just finished telling Mark he thought the heat was completely Caval's fault, for not living up to their plans regarding Fort Rhodes.

Caval further amazed Insinger by inquiring how Jack had been followed, and then actually listening to the reply.

"Yeah, it's a bitch alright," Tom shook his head. He seemed a little confused, unable to decide if there were really a chance of being defeated by the law. He had taken care to keep his name off everything, so he had felt no heat himself as yet. To no one in particular, he wondered, "Why the hell don't they bust?"

"Because they're going to get us all at once. What the hell do you think? They're just putting a case together. That's why I came down here. We need to get a lawyer. We need a lawyer on this right away. Representing everybody. A good one too, or they're going to blow us out of the water. Hell, with all the . . ."

Jack let it trail off, and Mark knew he'd been about to berate Caval for the bust, but figured it would do no good then.

Tom said he had the lawyer in Denver who took care of whatever troubles he encountered, and that brought Sidell off the bed.

"That guy's nothing." Jack paced back and forth. "Goddamnit, they've got a big case on us. They've got two boats, two houses and a log that tells—"

"Tells everything. I like that." Caval's old rattlesnake meanness flashed for a moment. "That fuckin' friend o' yours an' his diary."

"The bust had already gone down. And you know damn well how it started. It started at the houses."

Caval shrugged his shoulders and looked bored. He stood close to the large window, and Sidell coursed past him in one direction and then another, large and tense and threatening like a shark. But though Caval was as unimpressed as usual with Sidell, the scrap and the offensiveness seemed to have left him, as if the deal had at least partially vented some demonic passion in him and left him softer.

"You had guys out there I've never seen before," Jack spoke without looking at Tom. "We've got to keep this thing together. Hell, they seem to know all of us. They're following Eiler, too. If some of those other guys get busted when the cops finally start doing something and somebody turns state's witness, we've had it. Now you know where these guys are, and you said from the beginning you'd take care of attorneys."

"I know that, Jack." Caval's voice rose slightly, and a more familiar grin came on his face. "They're followin' Joe too, uh?" That seemed to please him. He slipped off his coat, tossed it on the chair like a nineteenth-century gentleman preparing to duel, and jumped on the bed with sudden boyish enthusiasm. He sat against the headboard as Sidell had earlier, and the delicate shirt clung to his build. "Awright," he began loudly. "Lawyers cost money. They cost a lot. And if they hear the dope didn' get popped, you won't believe what they'll cost."

Insinger watched his smile and saw the old Tommy reemerging.

"Well, I ain't seen a penny o' my money from you yet, Sidell . . . fer somebody who wants the best lawyers in the country."

"I've got a lot of it. Don't worry. I didn't know where the hell you were. And it's not too easy to move when it's red hot."

"Well I *am* worryin'. An' I want my fuckin' money before I start lettin' some lawyer start bleeding me. Awright? When I start gettin' my money, I'll start lookin' for a lawyer."

Insinger sat in an armchair in one corner of the room and made only a handful of comments throughout the discussion that followed of lawyers, tactics, money, deliveries, and messages. He could not bring himself to consider the prospect of dealing with the matter in court. He had no idea what he might do when and if he were indicted, but for the moment he had no time to consider any legal strategies beyond traveling by night. He had too much to do.

372

For the past month Mark's life had been a marathon of confusion, constant travel and worry, and very little sleep. By the time he learned about the bust, which was only a few days after leaving Fort Rhodes, he had already learned that Amian was, by his standards, incompetent. Harry kept no records, which was generally a good idea in the business but a disaster in a deal that size. He had a lousy memory and was soft as putty on a bargain. Harry let people tell him they didn't know what had happened to large amounts, where they could be found, or when they would deliver money. His connections were good—he'd been around long enough to know people who could sell dope—but his techniques were terrible. Mark had quickly understood why Caval had wanted him to oversee the deal. And it turned out to be the same old story. Caval was getting a lot more out of him than Mark had planned.

In the last days at Fort Rhodes Island, the original arrangement of six thousand pounds had been whittled down to forty-five hundred. The front which Mark was to collect became $900,000, so Mark's take—half the front—had dwindled before he even started. At that point though there had been no time to argue.

Two loads of Amian's stuff had left the island before either Harry or Mark departed. Two guys had taken fifteen hundred to Miami, and another guy took eight hundred to Atlanta, with pretty vague plans in both cases. Harry took the remaining twenty-two hundred pounds to Nashville, and Mark met him there as soon as he got away from Fort Rhodes. By that time though, Harry had already fronted most of it at $350 and $375 a pound, but he could only account for eighteen hundred and fifty pounds. Things were already a mess by then, so Mark had just written that off.

In spite of the sloppy distribution and high prices, the stuff had moved fast. Dealers had snapped it up from Amian at roughly twenty dollars an ounce. It was far better than anything on the market, and after the dry summer, people were eagerly paying forty dollars an ounce or twenty or twenty-five for half-ounce lids. The stuff was producing money, but it was a scramble to collect. Nevertheless, out of any money they got, Harry dutifully gave Caval's share to Mark without argument. Harry was no chiseler, and that had been one of Caval's main considerations in fronting him so much.

After stashing a little over a hundred and fifteen thousand dollars in a Nashville safe-deposit box, Mark and Amian had gone on to Atlanta and then Miami. Matters had been in no better shape in either of those places. A week later, they had been back in

Nashville, and Mark put more money in another deposit box before heading back to Atlanta. Overall, things had gone pretty smoothly in Atlanta, and Mark put away seventy thousand dollars more or less. In Miami though, things were wild. By sending the load ahead, Amian had lost control of it, and his associates there kept no better track of things than Harry did. For days they ran down weight from one person to another, but a lot of it seemed to have gotten lost in the shuffle. In the beginning, back in Nashville, Mark had started to realize that things in the dope trade simply never work out like they do on paper. He had started figuring rough minimums that became his goals in the operation. The figures varied from day to day, as Mark used up half a dozen small spiral notebooks, but after a while he determined that if he got three hundred and sixty thousand dollars out of the Nashville fronts, three hundred thousand out of Miami and a hundred sixty thousand from Atlanta he'd be damned successful under the circumstances.

It had all seemed so manageable back at Fort Rhodes Island. Amian had wanted to work out of the southeast because he knew it well and had the parole problem up in New York. But the people he had fronted to had no such reluctance, and they took off in every direction: L.A., Dallas, St. Louis, New York.

In the last two weeks before he'd come to the Park Lane to make his first delivery to Caval, Mark had been in eight cities running down money with Amian. Carrying the loot in his suitcases or coat pockets, he'd brought it back to his safe-deposit boxes. Before leaving for New York, he had over two hundred thousand dollars in Nashville, a hundred and sixteen thousand and change in Atlanta. By then he was having a hard time figuring how much he had in Miami. Each time he'd gone to the box there, he hadn't had time to count it, but he thought there must be a hundred and eighty or a hundred and seventy-five thousand. So he had collected half a million bucks, but that was a long way from the million he and Caval had first discussed or the subsequent nine hundred grand. There was still a lot out there he could get—maybe another three hundred thousand, maybe more—but Mark was exhausted and starting to get scared.

When he'd finally gotten a hold of Caval and Tom had wanted him to come to New York with as much of the money as he could carry, Mark had been quite ready for a break. He had just returned from running down one of Amian's loose deals in Puerto Rico, and that account plus a few others that remained to be settled promised to be unpleasant business at best. Mark had gone through

Nashville and taken out one hundred thousand to give Tom. It was stuck in a pair of boots back in his hotel room.

The thought of his money made Insinger feel a little better. That alone had retained its appeal through the struggles and disappointment. The cash. Cash in bundles. Cash in packets with rubber bands. Cash loose in big envelopes. Old, soft, streetsmelly, small-bill cash. Fifty thousand. A hundred grand. The images flickered pleasantly through Mark's mind. Cash packed tight in a pair of boots, stashed all over his suitcase, bulging in the pockets of a suit coat. Cash wedged tight in a safe-deposit box and the feel of the key in his pocket. The cash still thrilled him. But it was no easy matter to come by. And he was so tired. And there was so far left to go.

The thought of his money lessened Mark's fatigue though. The twitching in his brow relaxed. He was not so tired of running around. To a certain extent he had gotten in shape for it and for a few minutes he missed it, like a fighter who gets nervous if he doesn't work out. As he sat half listening to prospects of impending disaster, he felt like getting on it again and getting as much as he could of what was left—and he didn't feel like handing any over.

The room had grown darker while Mark sat listening to Caval and Sidell. He envied them and watched them with a sort of resentment. Hell, Jack had already moved most of his stuff. Caval probably had moved his, probably already had collected the first increments of his millions. No wonder he was relaxed and almost pleasant for once. Hell, neither of them had had their name all over the damn deal, he thought. Followed. Shit. Mark was so hot he glowed in the dark.

But as he watched them across the shadowed room, he could not help admiring them. Some of the old idolatry which had first drawn him to both Jack and Tom returned. They always seemed to be better off, to be in better positions, to come out better in the end. In the strain of his present situation, he was susceptible again to the notion that, if he could only be like them, he could have the things he wanted. If he were as bold as Sidell; if he possessed the daring to take things on the way Jack did. And if he had the gall and the balls that Tommy had, the audacity to screw someone as brazenly as he did, as he undoubtedly would screw Jack again in some fashion over the lawyers. Mark chuckled aloud to himself. If Tom Caval paid lawyers for everybody, he'd eat their briefcases.

Caval turned at the chuckle. In the near darkness he was a delicate eminence on the bed.

"Speakin' o' hot, for Christ's sake. You gotta get outta here.

You were all over that thing. All I need is you hangin' around my hotel."

Mark flinched a little at being addressed—even by Caval—as if he were a dog that might soil the rugs. The twitch began in his upper lip.

"So where's that money?"

Mark felt something like a winter draught sweep across the room. His body temperature seemed to drop ten degrees.

"I don't have it. I didn't get a chance to stop. I just got in from Puerto Rico and decided to come on up and see what this bust was doing. See if you could still handle the cash."

Caval's eyes narrowed at him. The mention of Puerto Rico did not divert him. "I told ya. I told ya the other day." His voice rose. "I told ya to bring it. What the fuck?"

"It's no problem. I have to go back down there. I'll bring it all to you in Aspen next week if you like."

"Yeah, I like," Tom spoke crisply, still staring at Mark.

"Well then, I'll take off. I'll be in touch." He rose and moved toward the door and could feel Caval's eyes on him all the way. "Take care, Jack." Mark noticed almost nothing of the scene in the other room as he went out.

iii

"Wanna die young, motherfucker?" Insinger spoke from the foot of the bed. He wore only his pants and boots, and his chest muscles, built up with weight devices, were flexed and moved quickly with his breathing. But he was still not a very imposing sight. "Huh? You wanna die young, motherfucker?" His voice came harder than before. "If you think I'm alone, you're outta yer skull. There's people waitin' fer me, an' they know exactly where I am. An' they can sure as hell find you again." He stared for a moment and nodded slightly. "So cut the funny shit. I came for the money."

Mark exhaled loudly, with about as much relief as if the situation he imagined had actually occurred and was now over. That would do it, he figured. Then he corrected himself—*might* do it. Mark turned from the mirror to the plush comfort of his hotel room. Unnecessarily it reminded him how different the real thing would be.

He had already given the warning once, although certainly not

376

in the same words, so Jerzy knew. He wouldn't be setting up this meeting, Mark assured himself, if he were not worried about Caval's ability at vengeance.

"You guys know how Tom Caval operates." Mark had said that two days earlier when he accosted Jerzy on the sidewalk, his speech very slow as it always was when he was afraid, or very serious, or particularly both, as he had been then. "He has a lot of friends. You're not just dealing with Amian."

"I guess I know damn well who I'm dealing with, okay?" Jerzy had barked back at him. The predatory hook of his nose had seemed a yard above Mark's face. "An' it's Harry Amian. If Amian's got some deal with Caval, that's his problem. I got nothing doing with Caval. And besides Caval don't cut any shit around here."

Mark had answered that remark with a smile, but he tended to agree. Nevertheless, Jerzy wouldn't be meeting him tonight if he did not think Tommy could have a load of buckshot delivered.

But that was not the issue. It was merely a factor, however large, in the strategy. The issue was a great deal of cash. And, as Mark had had lengthy opportunity to consider in the past two days, a large sum of cash was like a very unstable chemical solution that can easily explode. It is not dangerous if handled properly, but if the conditions of its transfer are violated, it can be very destructive.

Back in Miami, Jerzy Koss had gotten Amian to front him three hundred and fifty pounds of their load, and he owed over a hundred twenty-seven thousand dollars for it. Mark would never have allowed it himself, but while he had been in Nashville and Atlanta arranging some places to hold money, Jerzy had managed to bully Amian into it. Mark had been enraged when he returned to Miami and learned of it and learned also that Amian had made no real arrangements for payment. Worse than that, though, was the fact that Amian had let Jerzy scare him into the deal. Mark had been at Amian's the first night Jerzy showed up looking for some weight. Typical of Amian's style, everyone in town seemed to know he had big Colombian. Jerzy was a big, strong, mean-looking New York Jew with tight kinky hair on an enormous head. Amian— again in character—had apparently sucked up to him once by promising that they would get together on Harry's next big deal. So Jerzy had showed up wanting some action, and he was a very driving, intimidating young man. So Amian not only knuckled under once Insinger was out of town, he let Jerzy get off with some of the best blonde they had left.

Harry had kept saying not to worry, that Jerzy would pay, but they soon discovered that Jerzy, who had been living and dealing out of Miami for two years, had moved out of his apartment and gone back to New York with the dope, retreating to his native turf. Amian would have let it go. The deal was broken, and if Jerzy meant to rip them off, he damn well meant to back it up too, and that was out of Harry's league. But Mark hated being muscled. He had grown up with the small person's hatred of a big guy who throws his weight around, and under certain circumstances he was not afraid to call it. Like small men who are determined to be or at least to seem tough, Mark knew that the value of bravado generally increases in direct proportion to the size and threat of the opposition. If a smaller man is not afraid, the larger man must wonder why. And the prospect of violent insanity is frightening to anyone. It often backfires. But even in extreme cases, the most formidable foes may be amused by senseless courage and will at least elect not to maim seriously.

So Mark had wanted to face him. He had already developed a very personal attitude toward Amian's load, and he was not going to let some musclehead steal from him. He wanted to confront him unexpectedly, let him know that someone wasn't afraid of him and especially that he could be found.

Mark forced Amian to help him track down Jerzy by calling mutual friends in Miami and New York until they finally learned that he was in Puerto Rico, where he and a few partners kept a house along the coast near Ponce. Mark went down to the island immediately, chartered a small plane, and found the house without much trouble. But Jerzy had gone. Through some wondrous lying about federal agents hot on the trail, Mark managed to get Jerzy's address in New York.

But once he actually knew where Jerzy was, Mark had started to lose his nerve. He had not really expected to find him in Puerto Rico, and the pilot he had there had served as an armed bodyguard too, but to take him on in New York was a different matter. And Amian was certainly right about one thing—Jerzy meant business.

Mark had been ready to write it all off the afternoon he went to Caval's suite at the Park Lane. But he decided that night that, if he were going to start writing things off, he'd do it well. He had to admit that he had really done none of what he had been seeking in this enterprise. He had been a lackey, and he'd had it with that. He had a notion, an image of how he wanted to end the deal, but he doubted he could ever pull it off unless he could collect from Jerzy

Koss. That seemed as if it would atone for all that he had previously endured and at last provide a chance to prove himself to himself.

The next morning he went to that address in the East Seventies on a tree-lined block of solid old buildings guarded by wrought iron on the sidewalks, with brass on the doors and sparkling glass in leaded windows. Doing well with my money, Mark had observed. Mark waited an hour before Jerzy came, and then he stopped him on the sidewalk. From the way Jerzy's face came alive with fear when Mark called his name, it was obvious that he would not have been surprised to be shot at. He was larger than Mark remembered and looked as if he didn't understand the language when Mark said, "How are you?" Mark felt stupid as hell, but he said, "You owe us a hundred and twenty-seven thousand seven hundred fifty dollars."

"Who's *us*?" Koss snarled at him.

"Me. And Amian and Tom Caval."

Koss had made his pronouncements about not fearing Caval, but Mark finally said, "Well, we came to get the money." He had let the "we" sink in and had marveled at how unafraid he sounded. But now in his room at the Sherry-Netherlands, where he had passed the last three days, he was actually nauseous with fear. He lay on his back and stared at the ceiling but could not relax. His eyes blinked regularly. Jerzy would be ready now, and Mark had made a grievous error. When he had got in touch again with Jerzy by phone, Jerzy said he had the money together and Mark started to tell him where to deliver it, but Jerzy said he wasn't delivering anywhere. He'd heard about the bust, he said, and he was hot himself and wasn't going out with money and wasn't trusting anyone else with it. Mark had been so eager not to betray fear he said okay, so Jerzy said to call him back that night.

Mark had made the call only fifteen minutes earlier, and a voice he had never heard before gave the time of nine-thirty and an address. He didn't know New York very well, but the address sounded gruesome. He was starting to feel as if he might throw up before nine o'clock.

But as tactically horrendous as it was, he had to do it. Men sometimes find that the worth of their lives depends on the performance of some feat that can establish—perhaps only in their own eyes—that they are greater than they have been. Thus Mark Insinger had to place himself in danger. That would justify him.

Yet, he kept imagining Jerzy's voice talking to Caval: "Hell. I don't know what happened. How do I know, uh? He was crazy, the crazy bastard. Came an' got it alone, y'know. I gave it to 'im, sure. But alone? With all that dough? Aroun' there? Hell, they eat people aroun' there!"

And even then Mark was getting carried away with his own ruse, because no one would be checking on him. No one even knew where he was. Jerzy could simply kill him or have him killed and keep the money. And a hundred and twenty-seven thousand made that very easy.

Half an hour later he picked out a sturdy-looking driver among the taxis out front. But when he gave the address the guy said, "Are you shittin' me?"

"You heard me." Mark repeated the numbers. He thought, I don't need this.

"Why in God's name—"

"I have some business there. You want to go or not. I'll make it worth it."

"Jeeeee-sus," the guy moaned, but motioned Mark inside. They pulled away, and the car even seemed reluctant.

Mark gave him twenty bucks over the fare right away and promised him fifty more if he would keep cruising around the block while Mark was inside. The guy carried on as if it would disinter his mother, but he finally agreed.

It was a neighborhood one would wish only on worst enemies. Accentuated by moonless dark and deserted streets, it seemed that no one dared go out and even street creatures hid from each other. It was the no-man's land of the South Bronx. The last few blocks they drove were lined with big, hard, uncaring buildings redolent of obscure misery and useless death, like some East European war zone.

The driver swore he would not stay very long for fifty bucks. Mark spotted a young man in front of the building as they stopped, so when he got out he looked around and made a gesture as if signaling to someone down the grim street. He nodded knowingly to the lookout as he entered the building and shivered at its filth and emptiness and damage and the tomblike echo of his footsteps on the stairs as he went to the third floor.

When he reached the door it was not as bad as he had thought it would be. His face was twitching at the lips and brow, and his stomach was hell, but it wasn't so bad. The door opened to Jerzy's challenging features, and Mark spoke very slowly.

"Hello, gentlemen."

Jerzy stood back a step and regarded Insinger contemptuously as he entered. There were two others present, a clever-looking young guy with a round face and a hungry smile, and an older man, sullen with heavy jowls, crepe-soled shoes, and a cheap overcoat that resembled a rug pad. A ratty couch and a card table with two chairs were the only furniture in the main room.

"You alone?" Jerzy demanded in a tone of disbelief.

"Well . . . sort of alone. Why?" Mark's effort at unconcern was as if his life depended on it.

"This is a lot of money." Jerzy glanced at the others.

"Yeah. You're right." Mark looked around the room a moment. The young guy stood anxiously, and the older one stared from the couch. "But I don't see it."

Jerzy snorted angrily, and the old guy got up as though on a signal and went to the window for a look past the edge of the shade. Jerzy stepped to a small closet near the door and opened it, bent over, and reached in. The moon-faced kid began to talk to Mark about Miami. And just then the fear overwhelmed him without warning. It had collected behind his pretense until it finally burst forth and engulfed him. He could feel the sweat run suddenly all over him, did not understand how his legs remained beneath him, and his stomach collapsed. The sounds and movements around him occurred in a visual setting so bright and intense they seemed unreal, and then he saw Jerzy turn from the closet with a large black revolver. There was a thing on the end of it that looked like the choke on his grandfather's shotgun that Mark remembered from when he was a kid. And he heard distant singing and laughter from something he recognized perfectly, and then the high, shredding, nightmare squall of the shots.

Mark opened his eyes and saw Jerzy standing there saying, "Well here," and holding an old brown suitcase. He heard the moon-faced kid saying, "Ya know? Ya know?" And he was certain he had lost his mind.

He was dizzy. Saliva poured into his mouth as he sat at the card table. The suitcase was heavy, and when he opened it the sight was stunning. It was the largest amount he had collected at once, and it was almost too heady, like an overdose of some narcotic far beyond his tolerance. There were all sorts of bills, all in packets with rubber bands laid flat and stacked, and it nearly filled the bag completely.

"Bundles 're a grand," said Jerzy, and that brought Mark around. He put a tremulous hand to the contents and began to handle the packets at random. Finally he took one and counted it very carefully and therapeutically and was amazed to find that it did hold a thousand dollars. He thought he might actually get away with it. He tried a deep breath, but couldn't manage it. A single knock at the door was heard just then, and the old guy admitted the young man from downstairs. He looked about twenty and like he'd never been in sunlight, and he gave each of the others a confused and troubled look. Glances were exchanged around the room, and then they all looked at Mark. He was not sure he could speak and in fact was unable to on first attempt, but he cleared his throat and asked, "How many packs are here?"

Jerzy stared at him. "Dere's a hundret an' thirteen. An' another one's only about six hundret an' fifty."

Mark looked into the bag and stroked his chin very carefully, and his lips pursed endlessly. He figured he had really no choice of action.

"That makes you light about fourteen thousand."

Mark looked up, and Jerzy stared viciously at him. Mark looked back at his eyes and was not afraid of blinking. In fact, he did so profusely. There were glances all over the room and an air of transcendent expectation. The fear came back on Mark again like a swift disease, rotting his very bones.

"You think I sell dis shit in a fuckin' supa' market?" Jerzy barked indignantly.

There was a rupture in the tenor of things, another flurry of longer glances. Jerzy stared more angrily, but avoided the others. In the air was a surprise of dismay.

In a stroke of clarity Mark saw the moment turn. Jerzy had told them he was going to say this was all he was paying. Now he was backing off. Maybe he hadn't planned on paying at all, if he could get away with it, but they couldn't figure it out, didn't know what was happening. And now the son of a bitch was worrying about the rest of it. Shit, Mark thought, you can keep it, you punk. He sucked a deep breath through his nose, and it was sweet.

"When you going to have the rest?"

"I don' know. Some big hurry?"

"It's been a month." Mark arranged the stacks a little better, snapped the case shut. "I doubt this is all you've made."

"What the hell is this? Whatta ya wanna see my fuckin' books?" Jerzy's face reddened. He was not so angry anymore as humiliated.

Mark closed the bag. "I just want the money." It was the first time he had dared to use the singular.

"Don't press me, buddy."

Okay, Mark told himself. Okay, okay, okay, okay, okay. "I wouldn't think of it," he said aloud, as he stood, pulled the bag off the table, and adjusted himself to its weight. Ominous looks still darted around the room, but Mark could see the finish and headed for the door past Jerzy. "Thank you, gentlemen." He spoke like a lawyer leaving the mildest of conferences. "I'll be in touch."

The six grimey flights of stair were each an orgasm of terror and release. Each step felt like he had picked his way torturously through a minefield then had finally given up and run wildly. Each escaping footfall gave a silent scream of surprised delight. He was going to make it. He could barely believe it. The bag was so joyously heavy. He was in such exquisite danger. He was so close. No faithful child ever awaited Christmas as eagerly as Mark stood at the filthy cracked window beside the door in the dingy foyer, and no hapless man ever awaited a firing squad with more intense desire. The nearness of rich triumph and the possibility that the cab would not come produced a final crescendo of anxiety that raced his heart until he emitted a high metallic hysterical whine. And then the thing appeared. He was unaware of passing between the building and the automobile, only of the speeding gushing relief and the wildness of his own voice, as if he had never heard it happy. Shouting: "Go, man. Jesus. Go to the hotel. Go on, man. Let's get it." Howling: "Whowwwwwwwwwwww-hoooooo. Floor it, man. Gawd, I love it. Whooww. Haul ass."

V

It was a rough flight, and Mark put the oxygen mask to his face and held on. He was on his way into Aspen and the twin de Havilland banged into air pockets and was belted by gusts. Mountains loomed threateningly on either side, shrouded eerily in untouched snow, and reached for the tiny machine with windy arms.

The half dozen other passengers complained fearfully, but Mark did not mind it. The last dozen days had been so pleasant it felt good to be unsettled, to be threatened a little. And it was certainly only the beginning of that. After the business with Jerzy Koss, he had moved into the Plaza for two days, bought some nice clothes, and some nice women, and lived with two suitcases full of cash. It had been rich. Then he went on to Atlanta and met a little doll of a woman there, only about four feet eleven with big blue eyes, and she had gone with him to Miami then to Nassau for some banking and further recreation, then back through Miami. He had

383

left her at the Brown Palace in Denver less than two hours ago, telling her he'd be back that night.

Mark was frightened at what lay ahead, and the rough flight added to the queasiness of his stomach, but it wasn't bad. Once you've been terribly afraid of something and still done it, he realized, you may be afraid of it again but never as badly.

Caval had been trying to get in touch with Mark for the past two weeks. Everywhere Mark had gone, there had been messages. Tommy was going to be apoplectic. Tommy might even have a stroke, Mark thought. Behind the oxygen mask he dared to grin. It might turn out to be a very enjoyable journey. But there was the threat of course. There was always the question of whether or not Tommy was for real. But then none of it would be the same if it were not for the evidence that he was. Insinger raised his eyebrows and recognized that his life had become very serious sport.

Mark Insinger was a wealthy man now. After the collection from Jerzy Koss, he had collected a little over sixty-eight thousand more in Miami. At last count, before he'd left for Nassau, he had six hundred ninety-nine thousand dollars in cash. Plus a few hundred change. He looked forward to Caribbean banking and leisurely travel. He wanted to see Banff and the Canadian capitals, perhaps Hawaii, and then the South Seas. Pleasant prospects, but first there was today's work. "The ceremony," he said aloud. And yet he looked forward to that too. Now that he had the things he wanted, he felt compelled to risk them, as if he could sense their value only if they were in danger of loss. He could not determine what lay ahead, though. When he had finally returned one of Caval's messages a few days ago, he had spoken to Marshall. The next day Mark spoke to Caval and said he would be arriving, but the conversation had been weaved around long silences.

The sharp thrilling recklessness of the landing at Aspen, the improved shack of a terminal, then driving into town knowing that it was late in the season and only the hard core would still be around made him homesick for his old town, and he wished he could stay. Very quickly the taxi passed through and wound its way slowly up Red Mountain. Mark prepared himself, studied his hands for any tremble, and felt fit and well-tuned.

Teresa answered the door. Mark was struck by the fact that she no longer looked like a rich sweetheart but like the wife of a millionaire. She was a little older looking and more elegant. And she spoke: "Hello Mark. Come in."

Beyond her Mark saw two men, one of whom he vaguely recognized, standing together in the large main room. Caval appeared quickly, stylish in wide wool pants and a white turtleneck but barefoot. He examined Mark skeptically. He always knows, Mark remembered. He always knows.

"Let's go in here." Caval turned impatiently toward the far room, the paneled den with fire and stereo, thick rugs, and a leather couch, where Mark had been summoned a year earlier to hear that they were going to Colombia. Caval sat angrily on the couch, almost jumped on it like a spoiled child. Mark stood near the fire, warming.

"Let's make this quick, uh. I don't wanna hear your philosophy."

"I don't have any, Tom. I'm just keeping it, that's all." Mark's breath came short, but he spoke thoughtfully, as if they had no serious argument. "Hell, I earned it. You know that. And right now I've got the worst risks too."

"Shit!" Caval screamed at him. The loudness stiffened Mark a little, but it did not startle him. He'd heard Caval scream too often before. "Bull-fuckin'-shit!" Tom stared fiercely, then his voice was low. "How much you got?"

We're like kids fighting over marbles, Mark thought.

"About seven hundred grand."

"Shit!" He screamed with astounding volume. His nostrils flared and his face grew dark red. "You fuckin' Jew." Tom savored the venom in each word. "You're a shit-eatin' thievin' Jew, you cocksucker. I should've known better than ever do business with a fuckin' Jew."

Mark felt suddenly very Jewish. His father was a Jew, but his mother was an indeterminate Christian who hated Jews. Mark had attended some Jewish services as a child and a few cultural functions, but he had never felt Jewish or thought of himself as Jewish until he entered college and was rushed by a fraternity. He was popular with them until the last moment, when a few of the fraternity's elders inquired whether he could take an oath to the cross. The question had been fraught with their concern that he might be a Jew, and he had felt like a Jew then and told them to shove their cross. And now he felt very Jewish. If what he had finally brought himself to do was Jewish—or Polish or Australian—he was that and he loved it. And if Caval hated it, all the better. So he replied with what he hoped was a deeply Hasidic smile.

Caval was not finished though. "You ain't gettin' away with

this." He was full of a searing indignation that Insinger was not in fear of his power.

"No, I don't know that."

"Well you can't, you Jew motherfucker."

"I'll remember that." Mark started to leave. He did not care to hear this stuff. He would be spending plenty of time thinking about it without hearing it all from Tommy.

"Don't ever turn your fuckin' back." Caval sprang off the couch and followed him down the hall. Mark heard the dogs barking somewhere near and had a chilling flash of Caval turning his shepherds loose on him as he left. He moved more hurriedly toward the door, and Caval threatened loudly at his heels. "Don't ever turn your back, 'cause I'm gonna make it worthwhile for somebody, believe me motherfucker." Mark reached the door and opened it. "Remember," Caval screamed at him as he walked away. "Your ass is cheap!"

Mark swallowed with difficulty as he reached the road. Caval's assurances had been a little more unnerving than he had expected. Tommy had the money to make it happen, and it was not hard to have someone killed.

He did not even think about transportation but just kept walking, his feet making soft, steady sounds in the spring snow as he went down the hill toward town, unconscious of the distance he covered. It was cold and fresh out, and the afternoon sun was warm. His heart pounded on the thin air.

chapter 26

i

IT was springtime in Boston, and the smell of it was in the air, even downtown. There was the look of it on people's faces and a feel of it in the way they moved along the streets. Sidell paused several minutes outside the law offices and sampled it. People with everyday jobs seemed happy, fortunate. The waywardness of days and boredom of nights was getting to him. For the first time in his life he envied someone's forty-hour week. The past month had been spent on the floors and extra beds of a succession of friends and in another dozen unremembered hotels. His friends' lives all seemed occupied and moving somewhere, with school or jobs or starting professions, and his was sneaking—and he was not sure where. His occupation was the chasing down of last accounts, calls from phone booths to other phone booths to see if anyone else had been busted, and a great deal of worrying. Nothing that could be discussed in polite company. On the rare occasions when he saw the families of his friends or his own, he knew he was regarded as a ne'er-do-well. He had his stories, of course, but they were vague. His ready cash and travels had become an embarrassment. So much wasted, they clearly thought. He was beginning to believe it.

So the new season had no promise for Jack Sidell. What little of the future he could see was not inviting, and the lawyer he'd just seen had assured him of that.

Since Jack saw him in New York, Caval had shifted ownership of his businesses in Colorado and been incommunicado. Even when Jack made arrangements with Heard for his payments, Marshall would not tell him where Caval was, and Jack knew Caval had made no attempt to hire counsel. Meanwhile Jesse and Margaret had been summoned before a federal grand jury in Wilmington. Although they had given information about themselves and *Leda*, they had mostly taken the fifth. But the prosecutors and local press were salivating. Margaret and Jesse had only a local lawyer to assist them, and the man knew nothing of the others involved in the deal. Jack knew that when the net dropped they would all be easy meat.

In the overthoughtful discomfort of waiting, he had begun to think Caval might have enough money now to ignore an indictment, to get out of the country until things cooled down, or even permanently if necessary. So Jack had made a trip to Boston to see an old friend who was in law school. The friend had been busted for a little pot back in his undergraduate years, and as a result he knew a man who had become the foremost dope lawyer in the country, Ted Zarl.

Jack made an appointment, but saw one of Zarl's assistants, an unreconstructed cop who mainly marveled at what a fine case the government had. At one point he said, "Jee-sus, North Carolina? You could do twenty years." Jack had said he was already pretty sure of that prospect, but would Zarl take the case and for how much? Jack smarted at the mention of a hundred thousand as a possible minimum for himself alone, and the guy said, "For a case like this, that's nuthin'. Hell, what'd ya do with all 'at boo?"

Jack had a phone call to make that he'd been putting off for several days. He began to walk down the hill toward Government

Center. He looked at the buildings with the interest of an architect, but now they oppressed him. The Government Center had always been a place he enjoyed and admired, especially the long, curving colonnade toward which he walked. Now it merely reminded him how far he lay from his original goals. He boiled with resentment and frustration as he walked, Caval was doing nothing, and Jack expected to end up spending all his money on lawyers. He was not surprised any more though. And he was even aware that his inner rage at all of it had altered somehow. It was not really anger he felt anymore, but a seething, uncharacteristic vengeance, as if the continuum of conniving and disappointment had changed his chemistry.

When he had reached a phone booth and called Heard and Heard in turn had called him back five minutes later, Jack spoke with a distant astonishment at his own words. The idea must have existed in his mind, but not consciously, until he actually said, "I can't pay the last part. One of my guys got ripped off for cash and the rest of his stuff. There's nothing I can do about it. I lose on it too."

Heard was curiously quiet but said he would pass it along to Caval when he heard from him.

"Well, tell him to let you give me his number goddamnit, so I can talk to him. If we don't get a lawyer on this we're going to be shit out of luck. And that means everybody too, Marshall. So tell him we better get going on it."

"I will," said Marshall and hung up.

"I never thought you'd do that," Jack mumbled to himself, as he turned from the phone. He felt a plummeting depression. For an instant, he sensed the point at which a person's character collapses, the point beyond which his convictions and beliefs are ruined. Jack sensed it the way an animal knows a danger it has never seen, and he feared it in a way he had never feared anything physical.

ii

Joe Eiler sat reading the sports pages in the small second room of his studio in San Francisco. He flinched when the phone rang. He had acquaintances around the city, but rarely got calls.

Joe had kept the apartment for nearly two years, but he was

never able to spend as much time there as he'd have liked. It had a brief entryway and then a large main room in which Joe had an old burl bedstead, a few overstuffed chairs, a beat-up stereo, a big new TV, and a horde of paperbacks and second-hand books jammed into two old bookcases. In addition to a kitchen, there was the second room with a bay window overlooking the street. Joe kept his bar in it and a short couch and coffee table all littered with whatever newspapers, magazines, or books he'd been reading for the past week or so. The walls were white with old-style heavy woodwork darkly stained, and Joe had paintings on the walls that he'd bought at the Art Institute or the artists' cooperative. It was a cozy place with good light and cheap enough to keep no matter what Joe was up to. It lay on Washington Street over the hill toward Chinatown and North Beach, and Joe loved the narrow view of the bay and the Oakland bridge, the clamour and crash and little ringing bell of the cable car as it went down the hill beneath him, and the anonymity of life among predominantly Chinese neighbors.

He let the phone ring twice more before picking it up.

"Yeah?" He said it pleasantly, but as if someone had been yelling at him.

"How are you?" It was Sidell.

"I'm great as a matter of fact. I know I've felt this good before. I just can't remember when it was." Joe's voice was full of an enthusiasm it very rarely held.

"A little early to be drunk isn't it. Even for you?"

"Hell, it's springtime, man. And I'm in love. Can you believe that?"

"Do I have to?" Joe laughed, and Jack went on impatiently. He asked Joe to call him back at the number he'd given him a few weeks earlier. Joe agreed, hung up, grabbed his leather pouch of change and went out and down the hill to a little Chinese grocery on the corner. He stood in the corner among the cookies and crackers and potato chips, which were always stale, and used the pay phone. On the line again, Jack said, "Glad to hear you're happy, but we have a little problem."

"We got a thousand fuckin' problems," Joe quipped. "We always do. Why don't ya come out. You oughta—"

"Hang on, will you? I still haven't talked to our friend, and he hasn't done anything."

Joe blew a loud sigh into the receiver. He knew Jack meant he had not heard from Caval, and there were as yet no lawyers.

"Goddamnit. So did you go see Zarl?"

"I saw some asshole that works with him. Guy scared the shit out of me. I felt like I was talking to the U.S. Attorney."

"An' he wants a bundle."

"He wants an arm and a testicle."

"Did ya tell 'im your testicles belong to Tommy?" Joe gave a burst of cynical laughter.

"Very funny. Except they don't anymore."

"Oh lord," Joe recovered. "They don't uh? How's that?"

"I didn't settle with him. Told him I had some trouble out here and couldn't. I'm not going to."

Eiler replied in high tone of amazement. "Well you son-of-a-bitch."

"Well hell—"

"Hey man, don't tell me. I said it from the beginning. From before the beginning. Well if that doesn't . . . you bastard, after making me promise about that. And I just settled up. Just finished that up with him the other day." Under the circumstances Joe was mildly angry, but more amused. "I'll be damned. What happened to that incurable integrity?"

"Kiss my ass. I didn't like doing it." Jack didn't sound good, and Joe eased up on him.

"I understand. I'm glad somebody got 'im. He deserved it. Was it very much."

"No. I just did it because of this lawyer business," Jack insisted. "Which reminds me, can you be in Chicago tomorrow night?"

"To see Zarl?"

"Yeah. You, me, and Mark. I'm trying to get Caval and Ralph, but I don't know."

Joe said he'd be there, and then Jack asked tiredly, "Who the hell are you in love with?"

"This little lady I ran into down here. I met her over in that place where Claire's working. She works there, too. They're friends. I had a drink with her after work one night, then again the other night, then she had to leave town for a few days, but she's back. I'm waitin' to go see her tonight as a matter o' fact. She's cool. She really is. I'm kind of, uh, excited. I really like her, ya know? I haven't felt that way for . . . for a long time."

"Well, that's good. I'm glad for you. How's Claire?"

"She's okay. She'd like to see ya, y'know. She's worried about ya. Why don't ya come out an' see 'er? We'd have a good time."

"Yeah, I don't know. I think I've screwed her life up enough already."

"Maybe so, but she's kind of strung out on it. What the hell, come on out."

"I might. After Chicago, maybe. I'll see you there. I've got to go."

"Where?" Joe inquired doubtfully.

"Goodbye."

Joe laughed as he hung up. He wandered outside and leaned against a mailbox on the corner, smiled down the street at the last purple of sunset retreating from the north bay. The trouble did not bother him much. At least, he didn't fear it. It was almost too late for them to do any serious damage by busting him. He'd moved the load and handled it pretty well. He had plenty of money. There was only one thing Joe had really been afraid of for the past few years and hadn't even realized it—that he would never be in love again. He still wasn't, but it felt possible, and he was game. He walked down into Chinatown in the gathering darkness and then back up the hill. It was a still, quiet evening, warm for San Francisco, and the air bore a sweet combination of the city and the sea. Joe walked in a deep sentimental warmth where life seemed magic, his heart resurrected.

Back on the couch, Joe looked out at the bridge lights in the distance and the steep street with its shiny rails plunging through the fog. He envisioned her face for a moment: off-blonde hair, clever eyes, her lips always parted slightly in a canny, almost tough expression. It was the first woman's face he had thought of with affection in years, and he was impatient to see her. He glanced at his watch though and saw it would be about three more hours yet before she was off. He went back to the sports pages. He thought the Giants might have a decent team that season. It was hard to believe, but to Joe it seemed possible.

iii

Near midnight Martha approached his seat at the bar. She had her hands thrust into the pockets of a loose skirt which moved as she walked so that he could see her legs. Her expression was harried from working, but also rather arrogant, and she did not smile when she saw Joe but merely arched her eyebrows and mouthed Hi.

The place was a French restaurant on Union Street called The

Vineyard. There was a bar area in front darkened by the heavy wood motif of a wine cellar and stained glass fixtures that gave a softened light. Joe had frequented the place for some time, and when Claire, the woman Jack had lived with in Boulder and Aspen, had moved to town a few months earlier, he had introduced her to the owner and gotten her a job there. Claire was a buxom, voluptuous woman of great humor and rare spirits, and she and Joe were old buddies. When Martha started to work there two weeks ago, she and Claire became friends, and Claire introduced her to Joe.

There had been a mutual interest, a curiosity between Joe and Martha when they met. Joe liked the way she looked, but more than that the way she acted, a coolness, a distance about her, a sense of self-respect, and a face that had seen something of the world. Joe himself was not unattractive to women, but he seldom gave them a chance to like him and cared for very few. From the beginning they seemed to have something in common.

Joe had asked her to have a drink with him after work that first night they met, and they stayed around and talked as the place closed up. She was from Atlanta and had lived in a few other places Joe knew, like San Antonio. She had been a secretary with a law firm, and she hated waitressing. Claire had told him that Martha had left a boyfriend she'd been living with in L.A. and seemed a little wounded. Joe drew her out on the subject that night. She said she'd moved to L.A. with the guy from Atlanta, that he'd been a TV cameraman who wanted to get into films but ended up dealing cocaine. "I didn't mind that much," she said. "It was other things. I don't think he ever told me the truth about himself." Joe replied, "Maybe he didn't know what the truth was."

In his customary manner Joe had said very little about himself, but chiefly because he preferred listening to her, her mild accent, watching her eyes. He could see she was interested in him, but she seemed slightly resentful of his interest in her. He wanted to take her home, but she preferred a taxi, so he walked her outside. He attempted cavalierly to kiss her cheek, but she leaned away, seemed insulted by the advance. Joe didn't mind.

He had gone to Denver for a few days to wrap up the sale of his load and pay Heard the remainder of what he owed Caval. He had found himself thinking of her and was compelled to find her upon his return. He had met her at work again, late, when they were closing, and asked her to go out to dinner or something, but she said she didn't feel like it. She told him she didn't want to go out with anybody yet. They didn't talk much that night but had a few

392

drinks, and Joe took her home to an apartment she had sublet through the summer. They paused at the door, and she seemed to wait for him to leave. Joe shook his head at her.

"I like you, honey," he told her. "I'm sorry you got the blues, or whatever's bothering you. But hell, I'm sort of damaged goods myself. Why don't we get together sometime and have some fun. What d'ya say?"

She had looked at him for the first time with affection in her eyes, but confusion also. Joe put his finger against her stomach while they kept each other's eyes, and the feel of it thrilled him. She moved her hand down to remove it, but left it there a moment. Joe started to kiss her. She stiffened, and her eyes seemed to darken, and she did move his hand. "Joe, come on. Don't." She said she'd see him again, but she had to go to L.A. for a few days.

Now, as she came toward him in the bar, making love to her occurred to him more than anything else. It was the way she moved, with an understanding that her body was not outstanding in any particular regard but with an assurance that it was appealing, her litheness, her control of it. He did not mind waiting. Her hair was pulled back on top with two barrettes. She inclined her head and looked at him from the corners of her eyes as she took the stool beside him, as if he were a difficulty, but a vaguely pleasant one. Martha was always self-possessed, preoccupied, perhaps distrustful. Her face sloped smoothly from high cheeks and gave a rather sad expression unless she smiled.

"Hi honey." Joe's face felt hot. He could have laughed at himself.

"Hi, Joe. Could I have a cigarette?" She kept her head tilted and watched his face as he lit it for her. She always spoke in a low voice and seemed to say less than she was thinking. Her slight accent smoothed off the corners of words. "How've you been?" she asked and blew the smoke out.

"Good. How'd it go in L.A.?"

"Alright." She paused and looked at the cigarette. "I never used to smoke."

"Why'd ya start?"

She just shrugged and shook her head, looking tired and dissatisfied.

"So what'd you do down there?"

"Just stuff."

"Pretty mysterious."

"Not at all. I had to store my things. Clothes and furniture. Sort of finish up that relationship. It wasn't very pleasant. Kind of like divorce." She made a vague gesture with her cigarette and studied Joe a moment. "You ever been married?"

"Yeah."

"Yeahhh," she mimicked him. " What happened?"

"I'm not married any more."

Martha turned impatiently to the bar. "Look who's mysterious. The other night you wouldn't even say what kind of work you do."

"You writin' a book?" Joe was more interested in her eyes and mouth than the conversation.

"Never heard that line before." She turned away again and put out the cigarette.

"I didn't think you'd be very interested. I don't work here in the city. I work with an outfit in Dallas that researches property rights for pipeline companies. You know. Utilities or oil companies. We find out who owns the property they need to cross and arrange right-of-ways. I get a lot of time off, so I keep a place here. I prefer it to Dallas."

It was Joe's most dependable story. Whenever the question of his occupation came up—although he'd gotten pretty good at keeping it from coming up—he'd trot out that line, or say he had a few small oil leases back in Texas. He could deliver a quick anecdote about the bayou country around Galveston or some parish in Louisiana and steer the conversation to something else. He gave Martha the story with misgivings, though. The ladies at the Vineyard were pretty savvy, and Joe figured knowledge of his business got around. It's a small world, and people who knew people were always passing through town and knew someone else who perhaps knew Joe. Very few things are secret for any length of time.

Martha asked a few questions, and Joe told her about it. He had actually done that sort of work with his father and, more recently for short periods, with an old friend in Fort Worth.

"It must pay pretty well," she commented.

"Well enough that I don't have to do it all the time."

"So I hear. Don't you have a boat? I thought Claire said you and her friend Jack bought a boat or something."

Joe made a face as if it were nothing. "Aaah, we moved a boat for this corporation down south. We've been thinking about going in business with them. Maybe do a charter business in the Caribbean." Joe warmed to the subject, and he saw she was curious. "Nice kind of business, ya know. Work half the year maybe, down in

394

the islands. Sort of break away from normal crap. Beat the everyday grind."

"Sounds like you already have."

"Not really. Don't you ever want to do that?" He wished she'd say yes, say, "Hell yes, let's go to South America." Because with her he would have left in a minute.

"I guess so." Her eyes were distant as she looked at him, and then there was the confusion he had seen before. "Oh, I don't know. I'm really pretty straight. I've always worked." Her voice hardened with a certain indignance. "Some people have to work every day, you know."

"I didn't make you."

"Nobody makes you."

"Oh yeah. You make yourself."

"I don't need any philosophy, Joe."

"Yeah, well I guess it's easy to get caught up, but I don't think you have to. Not all the time, anyway. It can't ever give you anything you really want. You just get caught up in somebody else's game. The things you really want you have to go out an' get yourself."

"Sure. If you have the money to go out and get."

Joe smiled at her. He thought she had a pretty good head. "That's the easy part," he said, knowing it wasn't true.

"Bullshit."

"Bullshit yourself, honey." He chuckled at her. "You want a drink?" She nodded. "B and B?" She said yes, and he called it to the bartender and a scotch for himself, then he picked her hand up from her lap. "You're a pretty tough broad," he kidded her and squeezed her hand a little. She looked at him distrustfully and would not really take his hand. "Come on, honey," he squeezed a little more, "I know you got more grip than that." She squeezed back and smiled the slightest bit, and her green eyes looked fierce. Joe could tell she didn't want to get involved. He recognized the condition; he had felt that way about all women for a long time. He knew the attraction was mutual though, and he wasn't going to let her slip him. Her hand felt soft and hard at once. He felt capable of transferring something to her but didn't know what it was exactly, just a feeling.

"Wait 'til I get a couple of drinks down," she said.

"Oh yeah?"

"Then I really get tough."

"I can't wait."

She took her hand back as the drinks arrived, and when Joe had paid she said, "So how come you're moving somebody else's boat if you're so damn independent?"

Joe laughed at himself in earnest. "That's a good question. But I wanted to do it. For awhile anyway."

"Maybe I want to do what I do."

"You said you didn't like it."

"I don't always do this," she answered impatiently.

"I'm beginning to think you do. Why don't we go out on the town some night. Like tonight maybe. I know some very dangerous places."

She loosened up a little but gave him a sideways glance. "That's what I'm afraid of."

"Are you really?"

She shrugged, shook her head, and took some of the B&B.

"Let's get outta here then." He finished his own drink. "We'll get another one somewhere else."

"No, I really don't want to." She sounded vulnerable. "I'll have another one with you here, but then I want to go home. I've been working all night. I'm tired."

"Hell, I'm tired too," Joe grinned. "I've been waiting to see you all night. I'm exhausted."

She did not answer but looked astonished at the way he came on. Joe enjoyed the look in her eyes though and especially the way it made her mouth open a little. He wanted very badly to kiss her.

They had two more drinks there and talked about San Francisco, and Joe was bothered that she had seen so little of it and seemed not terribly interested. Joe, the old cynic, began to feel that Martha was the callous one. When they left, he took her out to his car, an old blue Bonneville convertible that he kept at a friend's place in Marin county and retrieved whenever he was in town long enough to use it. It was almost impossible to park it where he lived, and someone was always smashing into it, and he had hundreds of dollars in parking tickets, but he loved it. He insisted on driving around to Diamond Heights. When they came over the hill, the city lay below like a jeweled citadel on a field of smaller sparkling gems, an ermine cloud of fog around it like some celestial kingdom.

"Ohh God," she breathed when the vista appeared. She said nothing more when Joe pulled over, but gazed in a sort of sad wonder. He watched her distant dreamlike smile. Then suddenly it disappeared, and she covered her face with both hands.

"What's the matter?"

"I'm freezing to death," she answered, still covering her face.

"I'll put the top up. I'll turn the heater on. I'll put my arms around you."

"Just take me back would you, Joe?"

Joe pulled the car away irritably but in a moment figured she had some reason to be upset. Driving back, he kept glancing at her profile as she stared ahead. Before he reached her building near the marina she came around some and apologized, said she had a lot on her mind. She asked some things about the city, and they started talking again. As Joe walked with her up the stairs to her apartment, she asked him where he and Jack had moved the boat.

"Just up from the islands to the East Coast."

"You don't like to talk about business do you?"

"Not much," he said. "I like talking about starting a charter business down in the islands though, with a nice big sailboat, out of Martinique or Guadalupe. Be nice wouldn't it?"

She agreed but again with a troubled sense of longing. They were at the door, when Joe said, "What's this dying swan routine?"

"There's just some things bothering me."

"It's not very becoming."

"Maybe we're just not good company, Joe."

"Wrong. Maybe you oughta invite me in before I beat the shit out of you."

She laughed but with her hand over her mouth like a little girl who'd been told not to laugh, and then they went inside. There was a hallway with a bedroom off to the right, and the living room lay at the end of the hall and the kitchen beyond. It was a comfortable place decorated by a woman, and Martha turned the radio on. They sat on the couch, but there seemed to be nothing to say. Instead, they looked at each other with the curiosity of two people who have discovered a growing attraction. There was only one thing to do, and Joe moved closer to her to do it. But she stopped him again, simply raising her hand in an almost pleading expression. Joe smiled and stood up.

"You've hardened your heart somehow, for some reason. Or you're doing it now. I know something about that. And I'm going to make you stop it. I am."

"Are you, Joe?" She looked nearly happy, but still very skeptical.

"Yeah, I am." He turned to leave but stopped. "I'll see you in a couple of days. Think about me, will ya? I need it."

"Poor Joe Eiler."

"I'll think about you," he offered. "That a deal?"

She really smiled at him for the first time, and it blossomed across her face.

"My God, what a smile."

"Be careful, Joe." She put away the smile with an effort.

"Why do you say that?"

"I don't know," she shook her head. "Whatever you do."

He winked at her and went out. Alone on the street Joe found every sense tuned to the prospect of delirious excitement. He could have run down the street, leaped in the air, swum the bay. "Damn," he threw back his head and laughed, "in love again. At last."

iv

Theodore Zarl, like many good criminal lawyers, had a presence about him, only part of which was due to appearance. He was somewhere in his fifties, and his thick, well-kept mustache was gray, yet his hair, worn long for a man his age, was still very black. He had a large nose and blunt masculine features, with a trellis of wrinkles at the corner of each eye, and he seemed thickly set and large. He was not in fact very big, but even when people stood beside him he was still imposing physically.

Zarl had great energy and quick wits and sharp perceptive eyes. In addition, he had a rare personality that seemed at once crude and refined and was capable of either gutter toughness or a drawing-room polish. He had come from a poor Boston family in the North End, had worked his way through college as a cop, then went to law school at night, and, in effect, had bet on the dope business when the chances were cheap. In the early sixties, when marijuana and LSD were at the most unsavory aspect of social estimation, Ted Zarl took the cases of young users and dealers and publicly maintained that the use of drugs was not limited to degenerates. But due to the nature of the offenses and the overzealous loathing with which police pursued them, Zarl's cases were usually so flawed with unconstitutional arrests and searches that he seldom had to address a jury on social or philosophical matters. Whenever he did encounter twelve honest persons, he generally convinced them there was no harm done in blowing a little weed, and, moreover, that he would never be associated with real criminals. Mainly however, he employed his energy, perception, and ambition to explore every possibility of escape from the law by reason of technical impropriety. After only a few years, it became very difficult to bring a Zarl defendant to trial, an unpleasantly difficult operation if it did occur, and therefore an expensive proposition all around. Especially for the defendants. As a further result, Zarl became able to represent the most blatantly guilty subjects. And by virtue of his reputation and its inherent promise of great aggravation, prosecutors would agree to the most astonishing bargains, allowing defendants to plead guilty to reduced charges and serve comparatively fleeting sentences. So Zarl made a great deal of money, and a reputation as one of the finest lawyers for any sort of criminal case—but above all as the best dope lawyer in the country.

But Zarl's money did not come quickly or without hard work. And along with his wealth he acquired refined tastes and some nice social connections. Nevertheless, he retained the meaner instincts of the North End, and this combination accounted for a certain charm and a reliable attraction for the ladies.

Joe Eiler knew some of this, since Zarl was well known in Eiler's circles, and he sensed much of the rest. Joe had found Sidell waiting for him at O'Hare when he got off the plane, and they went on to Zarl's Palmer House suite together. Zarl happened to be in Chicago on another case, so he preferred to meet them at night, and they found him in his shirttails and stocking feet after a long day. He was casual as they met, yet reserved and almost formal in the manner in which he mentioned their "problem." He felt them out, Eiler noticed, and became familiar only as they desired. He said of the case that his investigator had just returned from North Carolina with reports indicating that the government certainly did have evidence, but there were still flaws that might well change the story. For the moment though, he preferred to go into detail only after Caval and Insinger arrived.

Joe Eiler had never cared for lawyers. He characterized the more expensive kind—like Zarl—as "Bleedem and Pleadem," yet he liked Zarl. Zarl seemed to respect them, and from a few comments he made, Joe could see that at least one reason he had made a living from narcotics cases was that he admired the subjects. Smuggling seemed to be something Zarl had always wanted to do himself.

There was a bar in the room, and Zarl had good whisky and Danish beer to pass the time. He and Sidell discovered a mutual passion when they learned the Boston Bruins were playing the Chicago Black Hawks on TV. They screamed and cursed at the set, while Eiler, who thought hockey was ridiculous, slept on the couch. He awoke at the sound of Insinger's voice. Mark entered with his eyes probing every corner of the place, unusually nervous, even for him. Zarl introduced himself and made about the same preliminary presentments as he had to Jack and Eiler and then went back to the TV. Mark, clearly apprehensive, asked Eiler if they had heard anything from Caval, and Joe replied, "You look like you owe Tommy some money."

Mark poured himself a triple bourbon and told Joe, with whom he had never been very close, that he had finally taken from Caval what was rightfully his share of the venture. Mark feared Caval had said he would meet them in Chicago only to set a trap for him. He said Tom had sworn to get him. Joe simply listened; he did not know if Caval would or could get Mark.

"Man, if he doesn't show up tonight," Mark hissed nervously, "I don't know what to do. What would you do? I think he's crazy. I really do, Joe. I've spent more time with that little bastard than you have. He could buy me a coffin, Joe. He's got plenty of money to do it. He could buy me easy."

Insinger's nervousness and the general subject irritated Eiler. He was tired of hearing about rip-offs. He had already learned that Thorton would not be there because he had been burned by some people in Buffalo, of all places, and was chasing them down. And all Joe could think of was that he was paid up in full.

"I guess when you do that to somebody," he told Mark, "you ought to have the guts to look at the consequences."

Insinger turned from him distrustfully, as if Joe might pick up the contract. He watched the hockey with discomfort, as if it presaged the violence in his future. When the next person to arrive was not Tom Caval but Caval's lawyer from Aspen, Insinger did not look good at all. He glanced at Joe and took a deep unsettled breath. Mark knew the guy, a hip snakelike character named Neal Eskeridge who had been involved in more shady operations than any other lawyer Mark had ever heard of. Eskeridge impatiently greeted everyone but Mark, to whom he gave a quick contemptuous look. Eskeridge was visibly displeased by the hockey game, but Zarl and Sidell were too far gone in it to pay attention to him.

It was a strange scene to Joe Eiler: Eskeridge stewing angrily among enemies of his client; Jack and Ted Zarl cheering in front of a television; himself wondering if Martha were thinking of him and trying to recollect that smile and wishing that somehow they could be far away together; and Insinger beside him worried for his life because of a twenty-three-year-old kid.

When the game was ended, there were new drinks. Then, with

the strong Boston accent he used in tough business, Zarl addressed himself to the case. From what Jack had told his associate and what his investigator uncovered, he thought the government had good evidence. But there appeared to be a good defense possible on the basis of illegal searches made of the Fort Rhodes houses and the *Errant*. However, he would not know anything with certainty unless they actually retained him, and he and his partners could begin to research it. To do that, he wanted two hundred thousand dollars in front. He paused to let the figure sink in, for the smoke to clear. He paced thoughtfully to the bar, then back to his chair. He seemed to feel no need to explain himself. They were in trouble and needed the best counsel available, which was expensive.

They asked a hundred impossible questions about "the charges," drank more, and the room grew dim with cigarette smoke and dismal thoughts. Zarl doubted they could ever win a trial in Carolina, but the chances of getting the case thrown out or winning it on appeal were much better. Meanwhile, everyone involved had to stay in touch with each other and out of the way of subpoenas. It would be a long and expensive proposition. Eiler closed his eyes and stopped listening after five or ten minutes. He sat up when Sidell demanded of Eskeridge whether Caval intended to pay the retainer. Eskeridge said he knew nothing about it, but that Tom would be in touch, and then he quickly left. There was nothing for the other three to do but agree to be responsible for their own share of the fees, but they sat a long time in near silence before saying it. They all liked Zarl and felt a good deal more secure in his alliance, but it was a lousy night and a very expensive one.

"Where are you guys going from here?" Mark inquired edgily when it all seemed over.

"Get a room," Joe shrugged.

"No, I mean are you going back to California?" Mark's face was troubled and urgent.

"Oh. Yeah, I guess. How 'bout you, Jack? You goin'?"

"San Francisco?" Sidell muttered. It was as if he could not recall where he was or why he had once thought of going there. "Yeah. Sure. For awhile," he nodded.

Eiler could see that Zarl was rather intrigued by the conversation, although he kept a discreet distance.

"Well, listen, let's go tonight. I'll pay. I need to go to L.A., but I don't want to travel alone. Not around here."

"Sure. What the hell." Eiler finished his drink on the couch.

"As expensive as this guy is," he nodded toward Zarl, "I could use a free ride." Zarl smiled back at him.

"Goddamn, I'm tired." Jack did not know what to make of Insinger's fear, but in any case he did not care for running. "Why not just go in the morning?"

"No, come on. Let's go tonight." Mark's voice became severe. "I'll pay. Really. And I've got some good toot in my bag."

"You do?" Jack's eyebrows shot up.

Eiler laughed and turned to Zarl. "Call the cops, damnit." Sidell looked at Joe irritably. Zarl said, "I didn't hear anything."

Eiler and Sidell had another drink while Mark made arrangements by phone. Half an hour later, they slipped out a service entrance into a cab. It had begun to rain. They crossed town to Midway Airport and caught a chartered Cessna twin to St. Louis in time to catch the late plane to L.A. Every fifteen minutes along the way, they dipped a pocket knife into Mark's film can of cocaine and discussed the case until it seemed to have been in progress for years. In Los Angeles, they stayed at one of the airport hotels. They finally turned in after breakfast in broad daylight. Jack had never really believed any of the stories about Caval being dangerous, and the whole journey was extreme to him and ludicrous. Jack was tired of rootless drifting and skullduggery. But to Joe and Mark, it no longer seemed out of the ordinary.

V

"Let's go on a trip," he called to her from the kitchen.

"Where?" She answered indulgently, as if it were impossible.

"I don' know. Central America. Costa Rica maybe, or the Caribbean somewhere."

"To get away from all your hard work?"

"You don' know whether I work hard or not."

"I can imagine."

"Yeah, so can some other people."

Eiler poured pineapple juice from a can into the blender with the rum and ice, held the cracked top with a towel and switched it on. The uneven grind of the thing reminded him vaguely of *Leda*'s pumps. He wondered where the old girl was and if the feds had let her sink. He wanted to tell Martha about it, for a moment even thought of actually doing it. He had already told her some things that afternoon that he would not normally have told anyone, especially a woman. She seemed to know other things. She certainly wasn't stupid. He wanted to tell her everything, but it still clashed with old instincts. And in the kitchen then, he thought there'd already been enough heavy talk for one day.

They had been on the beach off Fort Point all afternoon, and it was evening now. The sun was setting. The angular light on one side of the apartment seemed to change from one moment to the next, and they had already shared two daiquiris from a tall glass. He had called from Los Angeles and asked her to go find the extra key hidden in the old Bonneville and then to drive it out to the airport to pick him up. Sidell had stayed in L.A. another day with Insinger, but Joe had wanted to see her. They drove around the city and then wound through the Presidio and out to the deserted little beach near the Coast Guard dock that looked across the bay toward Marin and the Golden Gate and Alcatraz. They had talked of weightless unimportant things and laughed a lot. Joe loved it when she laughed. Before he met her, he had started to wonder if he had ever really made a woman happy. Other than a hooker. But when Martha looked into his eyes, it was still as if he were a brother or the husband of a close friend, something forbidden. Yet it added to the excitement he felt with her.

Joe had talked for awhile about traveling, about exotic business ventures outside the country. Something about her kept him thinking like that. He knew it would take some disturbance of her life to allow him in it, and sooner or later he had to learn where she stood. He had already inquired once if she cared for some good Colombian marijuana, but she'd said she did not use drugs much anymore. And for that matter, neither did he. It came up again when Joe was rambling about buying a sport fishing boat and running a charter out of Aruba. He had thought there was good opportunity for it when he was there.

"Would you really leave the country?" she'd asked.

"Who the hell needs it? I'd like to get down there where things are smaller and wide open. You can be your own man an' not always be running into some damn law or other. Get away from all this crap."

"It's not just crap, Joe." She was offended, defensive, as if he'd pilloried her religion, condemned her security. "Is that all society is to you?"

"It's to organize people who want to be organized, I guess," he told her. "It wasn't my idea."

She had found that an exasperating notion.

"Oh Joe, if you get a fishing boat down in Aruba, or wherever, you're really talking about smuggling, aren't you?"

Joe's face had hardened and he looked at her carefully.

"Maybe," he said. He hadn't really been thinking of that, but thought perhaps the subject ought to be aired.

She rolled onto her back in the sand. Her skirt slid down the knee of one bent leg. The majestic expanse of the bridge was behind her, and her breasts and stomach moved with annoyed breath.

"You're an outlaw, Joe."

"Outlaw." He laughed. "Thought you had to wear at least two guns to be an outlaw. Where do you get this outlaw bit?"

"You are." She would not look at him.

"Who you been talking to?" Joe's voice rose suddenly. "Where'd you get this stuff?"

"Everybody in that restaurant knows. And the way you live. It's so damn obvious, Joe. You're a dope dealer."

She turned her head to him. Her features trembled as if she might cry, but with anger too. Where could she get that? Joe wondered. Claire may have let something slip, and maybe some others said things or heard things, but nobody *knew*. So what, he figured. She was bummed on the business because boyfriend had been a jerk. Well, Joe was rather bummed on it himself. It was not important. He would have said, "Okay I quit the business," and meant it. In a way, he had awaited another chance to do that.

"I am not." He spoke steadily and stared at her with a fierce intensity. "I'm a rhinoceros." Her face was stunned; he didn't bat an eye. "It's true. I didn't want you to know. I knew it'd only upset you. I've been a rhinoceros for years."

Her head disappeared in her arms and she rolled onto her stomach. "For Christ's sake, Joe." Her body began to shake with laughter.

"Funny as hell. You think it's easy? You know what it's like being a rhino?"

"Oh, stop it, Joe." He had not been able to tell if she were laughing or crying.

It was one of those afternoons that just get heavier. They were due for it. The attraction had to be tested. They had to show some cards. They had walked down the beach to Aquatic Park, but the crowd repelled them. They went back along the edge of the bay, and she said, "What happened to your wife, Joe?"

Joe hadn't answered that question for a long time. But she had caught him, and it slipped through his myriad defenses. He told her the whole thing. They stopped on the narrow strip of sand with the grand vista of the bay on one hand and the army warehouses of the Presidio on the other. He couldn't walk and tell it at the same time. The wind blew her hair and she squinted at him as though he were far away. His voice had cracked a little at the end. He wished he'd told her something else. She had turned away and gazed out at the bay a long time.

Joe poured the drink and went back to the other room. She stood beside his bed looking at a painting. Her shoes were off, and she wore a long manila colored corduroy skirt with brown buttons down one side and a blue denim blouse. He had noticed her appearance change slightly since he first met her. She was more casual, more San Francisco. He damn well wanted her.

"This is better than the last," she said after a good sip. "I'll be bombed if I have another of these."

"Oh no," he grinned. "So we'll leave in the morning, uh?" He playfully took hold of the waist of her skirt, and the feel of her stomach excited him.

"Joe . . ."

"I'm gonna change my goddamn name if you keep saying it like that." He pulled her a little closer. "Stay here tonight, and you can decide in the morning."

Her eyes fell to the floor. She moved away from him. He sat on the bed with his back against the headboard.

"Come on, sit down. Where you wanna go?"

She gave him the drink. He took a long sip and put it on the side table.

"I can't go anywhere with you, Joe. I think I'm going to leave here pretty soon. I'm going back East."

"Bullshit. What're you going East for? Will ya si'down?"

She sat tentatively on the edge by his legs, still facing the wall.

"I just need to go back there."

"You haven't got anything to do back there."

"I don't know." Her voice became lower. "Maybe I just need to get some things straightened out."

"Welcome to the club." Joe's voice was agitated. "Look at me, goddamnit. Straighten what out?"

"I don't know. Just you, maybe. You do this too fast." She turned further away. "I can't figure anything out."

Just then his resolve not to force her to do more than she

wished became nothing before his desire for her and a sudden fear of losing her—and perhaps some long harbored vengeance against the sadness and the finitude of love. She resisted him with a pathetic high noise in her throat, her body rigid and arms clutched before her. It was strange to him, frightening, as if he struggled with a child that had lost its mind. But he pulled her, forced her to him, kissed her face as softly as he could, and she closed her eyes, then looked at him with such panic that it made him tremble, and the energy between and around them felt dangerous.

He brought her backwards down to the bed, kissed her harder, until with something close to violence she opened her mouth and her hands clasped the back of his neck. They kissed with a hunger, tasted each other a long time. By the small of her back he moved her closer, more onto the bed, and there was a fevered abandon in the way she pressed against him, kissed as if not to stop and think what it was.

For a man like Eiler, there is a point at which he knows and from which he will not turn. She did not seem to notice when he unfastened the buttons of her skirt. He barely noticed himself. Then he touched the warm soft inside of her thigh, and their passion seemed impossible, torturous. He found the nylon of her underwear full and hot between her legs.

Then suddenly she lurched from his arms, broke free with an urgency and desperation that shocked him.

"Joe, I just can't do this." She sat up, pulling distractedly at the back of her hair, hard of breath, her skirt parted around the naked crook of one leg. "Don't ask me why. Alright? Please."

"What the hell is it?" He forced her to look at him.

She began to speak, he began to say it again, but the force of their attraction prevented anything but itself. They came together again. The sweetness of her mouth was all there was. They lay back again on the bed, and there seemed no end to desire. He put his hand between her legs again, to that damp heat. Again she wrestled her face from his in near panic. "Joe don't. Please don't. I mean it. I don't want to." But he pulled her underwear aside and felt her so wanting that nothing else was possible. He undid his pants. He was so hard he was in pain. He could not stop. "Joe. Stop it." She almost screamed at him then, struggled in earnest, but he kept her with one arm, kept her legs down with his. He just pulled her panties to one side. She stopped. Her mouth half open gasped, her green eyes in his face wild with anger, love, fear until he put it there. Then she swallowed, closed her eyes, gripped him with a fury, pushed with him until it was all there. Then she gasped in exquisite relief, "Joe, I don't care . . . I don't care . . . I don't care . . ."

chapter 27

i

"I HATE this place," said Eiler. He laughed though.

"You just wish you could dress like those guys." Jack nodded at two gaudy young blades with air-blown hair cut in shaggy layers and cascading on their shoulders. They stood in the entrance with the pouty expressions of magazine models, perusing the loud and colorful Friday night crowd.

"He can have those gauze pants, but I like his neopreme shoes with the six-inch heels."

They laughed as they had at almost everyone who had come through the door near their table. Jack waved at them and called, "Over here guys," but they ignored him. Joe had not seen Jack so loose since St. Thomas.

"Stop it, Jack." Claire was laughing herself. "I knew if I wanted to come in and see what this place is like, I could depend on you two to behave like this."

"At least you could introduce us to some of these people," Joe complained. "We could give 'em our phone numbers."

"Oh, you wouldn't want to know hers at all, I suppose." Claire gestured toward a black haired woman with a scarf around her neck a few tables away.

"Yeah, I might need her later." Joe glanced at Martha, and she grinned meanly at him, that grin with which she seemed to dislike him as much as she liked him. "Maybe not," Joe added.

"Well, at least tell her you'll make it some other night, Joe," Claire pleaded.

"Oh, okay, I'll fuck 'er," Jack stood up. "Which one is it?"

They erupted in laughter. They had had a few drinks at another bar, and then Claire had wanted to come to Henry Africa's because she'd heard of it often. It was a fern bar, one of the first, and there were mirrors and colorful glass and plants hung everywhere. Moreover it was a meat locker, crammed with the unattached of either sex, attired in their hippest finery, constantly aware of being watched, relentlessly exchanging lines, phone numbers. It had the reputation of being a spot where fast San Francisco singles met prior to embarking on enviable sex adventures. It looked like the action existed in inverse proportion to the talk of it though, and they found the clientele comical.

"And where did you want to go, Joe?" Claire challenged. "To that saloon you took me to down on Grant Street?"

"Why not?"

"Ohh gawd." Claire laughed again. She was in boundless good spirits, being with Jack again. She had not seen him since almost the beginning of the deal. Jack had gotten his car out of storage in San Diego and driven up the previous night, and they were still celebrating the reunion.

Jack was rather fascinated with Martha, as if he'd always known only one kind of woman would suit Eiler, but doubted he would ever meet another. He was nice to her, curious about her, solicitous of her thoughts. She did not speak much to him, but as women always were with Sidell, she was charmed.

It had been three days since they made love at Joe's apartment, and her mood had been more uneven than ever. She was at times negligently happy, eager to talk, drink, play, go to bed. Yet at other times she was nervous and apprehensive. She had asked Joe twice if he were afraid of going to jail because of what he did. He had told her he had no intention of ever seeing the inside of one again. Other times she had been silently depressed.

She had spent that first night with Joe, then the next day and night also. The day after that, though, she had left to work lunch at the restaurant, and he did not hear from her again all that night. For some reason he thought he had seen the last of her. He drank a great deal, and was sullen and sleepless when she finally called the next morning and said she had merely needed some time to herself.

"I must love you," he had said.

"I love you, Joe, but I don't know what I'm doing."

Tonight, though, she was easy. A few drinks always brought her around, and she enjoyed the company. As they sat there, she hooked her arm inside Joe's on the table and kept her face close to him. They kept making fun of the place, getting louder about it. The four of them could have been happy anywhere that night.

Joe thought he recognized a face that flashed in the mirror behind the bar for a moment. He was only curious at first. He

408

searched among the crush of noisy people. Jack was telling the story of the chair-throwing contest at the Curaçao Hilton, and when Claire and Martha stopped laughing, he began to relate the debacle a month later at the brothel. Joe chuckled momentarily at the vague memory, but then he saw the face again and squinted and was sure he knew it. Then it was again eclipsed by other bodies. Joe's stomach felt empty; the mood of the evening froze. Sidell was describing Delight and Joe going through the wall and breaking the water pipe at the whorehouse. The girls were hysterical, but Joe was only half aware of it or of the bodies and torrent of voices around him. The Rolling Stones were howling over the sound system. Joe glimpsed the guy again, hustling some chick at the bar. Joe did not really hear Jack asking, "Do you remember Delight punching that guy that tried to stop us?" Jack made an excited flat gesture with his hands. "Just laid him out." The way Joe looked back at him sobered Jack's face quickly.

"Look at that guy down there along the bar." Joe was quiet and serious. "The guy with blonde hair, wearing a leather coat. Who does that remind you of?"

Their table was suddenly quiet amid all the noise, and Jack searched carefully.

"Right there. That guy," Joe said. "That look like anybody you know?"

Sidell's brow furrowed in disbelief or confusion. Joe could not tell which. When he looked back at Joe, though, his lips were pressed into a thin angry line—he seemed to object to Joe having brought it to his attention. But without a word, he stood up and made his way through the crowd as if heading for the restroom. Joe sat perfectly still and watched the guy in the bar mirror. Martha and Claire said nothing. They were shocked by the abrupt interest. In the reflections, Joe saw Jack come near the man and stop a moment. The man seemed to look twice at him, then Jack was not visible. When Joe could see the man again, he was looking carefully among the crowd. Then Jack was making his way back, looking intently at Joe.

"Mind telling us what's going on? Which guy are you talking about?" asked Claire. She kept her voice down though and recognized that it was serious. Martha had an expression that expected pain, but Joe looked past her at Jack as he sat.

"Is that him?" Joe asked. He was already positive it was.

Jack seemed unsure. He didn't really recognize him yet. "What is it about him?"

"He dyed his hair."

There was a moment of pregnant silence at the table. Jack nodded slowly into Joe's eyes with grim wonder in his face, as though the discovery posed a horrible question.

"Look," Claire snapped, then lowered her voice, "is that the guy right there?"

All four of them turned. The man had stepped away from the bar into the thicker crowd. Among tossing heads and laughter he stood out, expressionless, looking straight at their table. His eyes met Joe's for an instant, and there was no doubt. Then smoothly his eyes went past Joe, then to the next table, then the next, as if he were looking for someone. Then he stepped out of sight again behind others, but a moment later Joe saw him pushing through to the side exit.

"He's leavin'," Joe stated. He stood and went to the front door. There was a shadow at the corner of the building, and as Joe stood in it, he saw Cavin O'Neal peering in the rear side windows toward their table. Then he looked quickly down the sidewalk toward Joe, but apparently did not see him. He walked away hurriedly, looking back twice before he reached a dark Jaguar coupe parked near the side door. He pulled out, jerked it through a tight turnabout, and whined up to the corner, turned left and sped away to the north.

Eiler was smiling dreamily as he returned to the table. Jack regarded him uncertainly. Claire and Martha were silently expectant of some explanation.

"A chocolate-brown X-KE," Joe enunciated.

Sidell sneered, but the antipathy in his eyes did not change.

"What's the matter?" Claire looked at Jack, then Joe. "Who is that guy?"

"It's nothin'," Joe addressed Martha's worried features in a tone he hoped would calm her. "Just an ol' friend we thought had disappeared. Just nice to know he's still with us. Hey, sweetheart," he called to the bar maid passing by, "need another round here." Joe took a long breath and felt his heart pounding.

ii

Joe and Martha made love fitfully that night, too passionately at first, as if there were not enough time, then slower and slower until at different times each seemed to wander. A delicate sense of each other seemed violated by distraction, and ultimately it came

410

to nothing much. They gave it up, and Joe lay on his back, listening to fog horns on the bay through the open windows, a mournful deep bleat every twenty seconds, followed every other time by a sadder two-part blast. There were sounds of traffic and random Chinese voices in the street. Occasionally the night was startled with loud reports, and in that neighborhood one never knew if they were gunshots or firecrackers. Martha lay on her side facing him, and his hand rubbed the smoothness of her back.

"I feel so far away when I don't know what you're thinking," she murmured.

"Hell, I rarely know what you're thinkin'." Wondering about O'Neal made his voice sharper than he meant it. He turned to her to apologize and saw the small, round breast he loved, elongated by the way she lay.

"I know. I know it," she said in painful frustration before he could prevent it. She turned over and pressed her face into the mattress. "We're like strangers, Joe. I feel so lost. I feel like there's no place to go."

"It'll be okay, honey." He did not know how or when, but he felt it would be. "Let's just stick together. It'll be alright if we just stick together."

She would not let him pull her closer when he tried, and her back moved slightly as she began to cry. Then he made her come closer and held her to him, her face soft against his chest and warm with tears. "Come on, honey. Don't worry. There's nothin' to cry about."

iii

Joe found Sidell sitting in the bay window when he returned to his apartment. He walked past him through the room and tossed a newspaper on the couch.

"Where have you been?" Jack frowned suspiciously. "What're you doing with that car?"

Joe did not answer. He eyed Jack clinically and went on to the kitchen. He took a bottle of beer from the refrigerator and downed about half of it at once. Jack waited for an answer. He had not been able to get Joe for two days. They had not discussed O'Neal at all the night they had seen him, had only given each other frequent probing looks. The next day Jack had gotten no answer at Joe's apartment all afternoon. He couldn't raise him that night either, and Martha was working and had no idea where he was. She spent the night at her own place. Today he had called several times and finally had come over and got inside with the extra keys Joe had given him. He had been looking out the window as Joe drove past looking for a parking space in a rental car.

"I found him," Joe smiled. He sat triumphantly on the couch.

Jack was incredulous. "You talked to him?"

"No." Joe shook his head and seemed preoccupied, then spoke slowly. "I don't know why I never thought of it before. Before, ya know? When I was lookin' for him. Windy. His girlfriend, remember. In Aspen? Windy. But I thought of her the other night when I saw him talkin' to that number at the bar, and I got a flash he was still screwin' that poor broad around. So then yesterday I thought that's who he's living with, so he can keep it all in her name but handle her, y'know? But I couldn't remember her name. Lenticum," Joe nodded. "Windy Lenticum. And where would they live?" Joe smiled. "Marin, where else? So I looked 'er up. Went up to the county recorder's office and looked her up in the name index of property owners. There she was. Big as hell. Mill Valley." Jack looked mesmerized. "I looked it up on the plot maps an' got an address an' everything. I just went over there. Saw his car an' everything. Little love nest."

Eiler's grin was so venomous that it disturbed Jack, and he looked away.

" And so what's that car for?" Jack still looked away.

"Shit, man, we're gonna go see 'im," Joe's voice rose.

"Well what—"

"I don' know what the hell he'll do. He stole a lotta dough, man."

Jack was very uncomfortable, unable to sit. He stood abruptly, and squared off to face Joe, his feet apart.

"What the hell can we really do about it though?"

Joe studied him a moment. He had not considered the situation from that point of view. He simply knew that he had caught the man at last and that he had the power to deal with him almost any way he wanted.

"One way or another, I'm gonna make the son of a bitch produce whatever he's got left. What the hell d'you think? Or I'll take property or somethin', loot his place, make him sign over that car, whatever it takes, I don't care. I can get Sleig on him if he tries to run, but he won't do that now. I can threaten to put the IRS on him."

There was always the ultimate too, Joe thought, but he did not

412

mention it, because that seemed to be what bothered Jack. It bothered Joe enough that he had not really looked that prospect in the face, but the possibility had been coldly prevalent in his thoughts.

"If you're just talking about beating the shit out of him, or scaring him, is there really any—"

"I'm takin' my pistol for sure, Jack. What the hell? I'm not gonna take any shit from him."

"That's what I'm afraid of," Jack answered angrily, then turned to face into the other room.

"What the hell? What if he's got a gun or something?"

"Goddamnit," Jack whirled and shouted, "I knew when I saw that son of a bitch that something like this was going to happen."

"Now listen," Joe yelled back at him, "that son of a bitch . . ." Joe stopped and sat back on the couch, finished his beer, and tried to cool off. "Alright, let's slow down, fer Christ's sake. Come on." Jack only stared at him though. "He ripped us off plenty. Now what're we going to do about it?"

"I'd just as soon let it go, Joe. I don't need any more trouble. I've had enough."

"You'd just let him go?"

"I don't know," Jack replied wearily, full of frustration. The thing was out of control again. "When you get right down to it . . ." He stopped, started to speak again, but could not, as though he lacked words capable of expressing his thoughts.

"When you get down to it, there's this," Joe stated. "He stole about twenty-five thousand dollars of dope from us. It could've been nearly two hundred grand once it was turned. Gawd, I've forgotten what that could've brought us in the Colombian." Joe was suddenly mastered by a paroxysm of anger that seemed to spring him off the couch. "When I think of what that fuckin' sneak thief pulled off on us, man, I could break his goddamn neck with my hands!"

"Right. Right." Jack was yelling again. "But what good is that going to do."

Joe turned away from him and went to the kitchen for another beer. He took a long drink of it and calmed himself. As he returned to the couch, his thoughts and feelings focused for a moment, and he spoke quickly before emotion disturbed them again.

"What's the use of keeping a bargain, Jack? What the hell's the use of going through with a deal? Why don't we give our money to the poor? What law is there governing us? Huh? I mean, beyond

413

our word, what do we have to regulate a deal? What do we have to enforce a deal? There's no structure. There's no cops. There's nobody to go to. What the hell do you do? It's honor, man. That's what we're talkin' about. Honor." The word, his tone and volume, seemed to invoke great powers. "But what do we do about dishonor? What's the enforcer? There has to be something out there to keep it together. And there is. It's there. You always know it's there. You and I and everybody else knows it. You can feel it. It's instinctual. Violence, man. It's violence."

Sidell gaped at him in wonder. Yet the disbelief in his eyes was not at what Joe said, but at the fact that things had come to this.

"How the hell else do ya do it?" Joe went on with a resigned, thoughtful voice. "You either let it go or do something about it. You go along with it, and you might as well have done the same thing yourself. But if you do something about it, you have to at least threaten violence of some kind. There isn't anything else. And you gotta be ready to back it up. If you don't, I can't see that any of it makes any sense at all."

There was a ponderous quiet for a few moments, and Joe knew Sidell was thinking he had not paid Caval, had in effect stolen from him, and that Joe had talked several times about ripping Tom off. It did not bother Eiler, though. There had been infinite provocation. Those had been justified. He knew neither he nor Jack had ever done anything remotely like what O'Neal did.

Joe had come to a sort of working understanding of good and evil. After his wife's death, it had become a necessity for continued existence. He knew that good and evil existed in the world independently of man's social rules, regardless of whose God was said to have defined them. They existed like polar entities, exerting forces on every action. A man could only master them by himself, and only when he realized that the two forces do not exist separately, that one assumes the other. A man must be capable of both. But most importantly, Joe felt that good could not be achieved or defended without meeting evil with evil. Honor was the integrity with which a man dealt with the polarity. But the understanding was difficult and insidious, and Joe could rarely state it clearly, even to himself. Nevertheless, he felt it, but he could not have attempted to say it to Jack—certainly not that afternoon.

Joe sat back on the couch with a sad, wistful smile. "Are we honorable men, Jack? That's a good question, isn't it? I think we are." The question gained momentum. "I think we try to be. I think we must be. We must try to be. And so, what do we do about dishonor?"

414

Jack closed his eyes a moment and clenched both fists. He was no philosopher, but he was not afraid to think, and he had a hard confidence in his ability to do that.

"Joe, what you're saying makes sense. But I don't see it that way. Okay. We are separate from the law in this thing. We are outside of it because marijuana is outside of it, and there's big business in marijuana. But it's a pretty damn widely acceptable thing, and we're just sort of skirting regulations that still apply to it. That does not make me feel like I'm in some no-man's land where I have to create a whole new moral code. Especially about killing people, goddamnit. I'm not a criminal, Joe. Except for this deal, I'm not an outlaw."

Joe nodded. That was indeed the difference. He had forgotten that line existed between them. Jack still had some alternative, could still turn back. Joe felt too far gone.

"I'm not talking about assassinating the bastard," Joe said plaintively. "I mean to get from him what he took from me, if I can. And that's gonna take a threat, but let's be realistic. He won't push it. You know he won't. He's a punk."

"I don't know." Jack shook his head. "I guess he won't. It's just the whole idea."

"Well, hell, that's just the way it is. I'm not letting this go." Joe's voice grew tougher. They looked passionately in each other's eyes. "After all this crap, I'm not letting it slide. I'm going out there tonight. You comin'?"

iv

They spoke very little crossing the Golden Gate, then driving up the freeway. At the top of Waldo Grade high above the bay, as they descended to Marin, white plumes of fog rushed through the darkness across the freeway and vanished. They had finally cooled off enough to discuss the thing and agreed to tell O'Neal they already had Sleig on him if he tried to run again, that they wanted all the cash he had remaining and the car and house.

"If the violence is such a damn obvious deal," Jack had finally said, "then let him assume it too, alright? Don't make him panic, so he does something crazy."

Joe had readily agreed. He did not think O'Neal would try anything because there was not anything to try. Nevertheless, he had taken the pistol, for his own safety if necessary, and in case he needed it to make the point. It was a little five-shot nickel-plated .32

that Joe had owned for years and carried a few times in unpleasant situations. But he had never used it on anything other than bottles and beer cans. It was a safe revolver to carry in a pocket, a Smith & Wesson with a safety grip and a firing pin instead of a hammer, so it could not be fired without intention.

The road narrowed and darkened beneath tall redwoods as they neared the house. Joe was aware of the gun in the pocket of his parka. As he had several times in the past half hour, he thought O'Neal might not be home. Each time his stomach turned with a sinking incongruity of feeling. He said, "It's right up here a little." Jack, at the wheel, said nothing. A moment later Joe directed him off the main road that climbed the ridges up to Mount Tamalpais and into one of the dark lanes that twisted among the lower slopes. There was an abandoned stillness to the area. It was a suburban neighborhood of tiny $100,000 homes with no one on the street at night. Houses, further darkened by large trees, were built only on the downhill side of the street to Joe's right. They all had carport decks, and most entrances were reached by descending steps.

Joe tersely identified the house and told Jack to drive ahead, until he could turn around, then park in the shadows a few houses down the road wherever he could. Joe said he would flash the front light if it was okay for Jack to come to the house. Jack merely nodded, but as Joe closed the door, he wanted to say something. The effort, either to say it or not to, tightened his jaw muscles, but he shook his head and drove on.

O'Neal's Jaguar sat in the carport close to the road. Beside it to the left was a hedge of shiny privet parted by a lamp post illuminating a wooden stairway. A dozen broad steps bounded by ivy and raspberry vines led down to the cottage.

Joe approached with the same resentment he had known that afternoon when he saw it, with its red-stained shingles and white trim. He was taut with anger, but he felt no fear. He stood before the door a moment and listened. A car passed by and sounded phenomenally loud. He could hear wind in the trees, a dog barking somewhere, a rustle in the bushes. A television was on inside and gave forth urgent voices. Joe knocked five times, and the whole county seemed to bristle and listen.

"Who is it?" The voice came from beside the door, hard and startled.

"It's Joe." He paused a second. "Open up, Cavin."

There was a gripping silence that seemed to precede some sudden action, so Joe called again.

416

"Come on, Cavin. If I was gonna hurt ya, I wouldn' come to your damn house. I'm alone. Come on. Open up."

There was silence again, and Joe sensed a grave error. Then the lock turned. The door opened slightly, then all the way. There was no screen, so suddenly they stood face to face.

Joe had forgotten how big O'Neal was. It startled him a little. With his hands in his jacket pockets, right hand on the gun, Joe stepped past him carefully into the room. O'Neal said nothing and merely glared at Joe. There was a convulsion of anger, resentment, shame, and fear in O'Neal's face.

O'Neal was slightly less than six feet tall, and he was a good-looking young man built better than average. He had always had dark brown hair and long, handsome, almost pretty features. Joe always thought pretty guys believed they could get away with things. But now O'Neal's hair was dyed incongruously pale blonde and clashed with his dark eyes and complexion. He had been a rather good slalom racer for awhile, but he was mainly one of those guys who was always waiting to parlay his attractiveness for a part in someone else's success. Joe had known that and therefore never liked him much, but he was clean-looking for transportation jobs, and Joe never thought he had the guts to rip him off, or more likely, to put himself in a position where he could not return to Aspen and show himself off to horny wives from Dallas and Tulsa.

"So how you been Cavin? Huh? What the hell? You don't even say hello."

O'Neal stared at him, stood still near the door, with his shirttail out and only socks on his feet. A puppy, apparently a shepherd-husky mix about two months old yipped and barked and cavorted between them.

"You're not gonna talk? Nice place you got. Glad to see you're comfortable."

Behind O'Neal was a small dining room with an antique oak table. The kitchen lay off it, bright yellow and white. They stood in the living room. Off the left of it seemed to be a short hallway with a bath between two bedrooms. There was a woman's touch, with old wood chairs newly stained, a couch and coffee table with flowers in a vase. There was stereo equipment on shelves, about a dozen books, wall to wall carpeting, the TV still on but turned down now, a mounted poster from Aspen, a gaudy seascape behind the couch, pictures of Cavin and Windy on the slopes. It was a contemporary little home, with candles and a mobile and other current tastes.

"Where's Windy?"

"She's working." His words emitted weakly.

"Where?" Joe demanded.

"The Trident."

Joe nodded with a smile and sat on the coffee table. The bum, he thought, all that money and he makes her work at night so he can screw around.

"You're a little late delivering the load, Cavin." Joe toyed with him perversely, saw the shock in his eyes, and would have enjoyed it if he fell on the floor groveling. "Where you been?" O'Neal just stared back at him, and his face grew so livid with fear that it frightened Joe in turn. He decided he had better come to the point. He stood up. His arms began to tremble.

"Okay Cavin, this is what's happening." Joe's voice quaked. "I've got people on you. I'm paying them plenty, and they're good. You can't lose them. So I want the dough you owe me. However much you got left. And I can find out. I want the car too." The puppy gamboled across the rug and began to jump against Joe's leg. "And this house is for sale."

"I got ripped off too, Joe. I did. That's the truth. I swear to God. I don't have any cash." He extended his palms. "A lot of it got ripped off. We just rent this house. You can have the car."

O'Neal's voice was pathetic, but it only made Joe hate him more.

"You lyin' motherfucker," he snarled. He gripped the gun inside his pocket. "You own this place. You got it in Windy's name. You're a lyin' thief. The car. Don't make me laugh. I'm takin' everything you've got."

"No," O'Neal screamed. The puppy ran in a small circle, then cowered at the foot of the couch. "You are not. You're not gettin' anything." His tone was suddenly so wild that Joe braced himself. "I'll go to the cops. I will. I swear it." He leered at Joe, as if he had just thought of that ploy. "I'll go to the fuckin' cops."

"You won't do shit," Joe said confidently, but he had never thought of that possibility. "You're gonna get the rest of—"

"You think I won't?" O'Neal suddenly came forward, his face desperate, the fear making it maniacal now, as if it had crept through his life like syphilis for the past year, until it finally drove him mad. "You'll go to jail, Joe. You're the one who's in trouble, Joe."

O'Neal came forward so abruptly that Joe had to lurch backward to keep a distance, and he drew out the pistol and poised it waist high. O'Neal stopped dead, cringed, half turned away and made a sickening groan.

418

"I think you're just going to do exactly what I tell you." Joe's voice trembled audibly, but his hand was steady. O'Neal made another groaning sound, still turned away, and Joe was horrified, as if by the sight of a person gone completely insane. He could not think what to do. It struck him then that he had forgotten to signal Jack. Should he do it now, he wondered. Should he leave? What the hell should he say? O'Neal hunched his shoulders, made a longer moaning sound and began to cry.

"Shut up," Joe shouted at him. "Turn around goddamnit. Now listen, you're gonna—"

"Please don't," O'Neal shrieked. "I couldn't help it. Just leave me alone. Please. Don't do it." He was blubbering and looked grotesque with his bleached hair, his reddened face, and his mouth loose and wet with tears.

"Shut up," Joe shouted again. He was sickened by the sight.

"Please, Joe. You don't need it. You don't want any of this stuff." He was hysterical now. "I've got a nice life. Please, Joe. Just leave me alone. Please. You don't want any of this stuff."

"You sorry bastard," Joe moved toward the door. His hatred of O'Neal returned completely, and he decided to signal Jack. They could scare him enough that he would produce every penny he could get his hands on. There was a light switch by the door, and Joe went to it.

"Just leave me alone. Please. Can't you just—"

"Is this the porch light?"

O'Neal froze for a second, uncomprehending. Joe glanced out the window as he flicked the switch and saw the outside light go off and on. O'Neal's eyes grew to a wild intensity. He gave a high, almost inhuman cry and burst across the room toward the bedrooms. There was only an enormous ringing in Joe's ears when he fired. O'Neal turned and fell in the hall doorway, clutching at his lower back. The terrified puppy ran back and forth across the room yelping. O'Neal twisted on the floor and let out an agonized squall. Joe stood paralyzed, the pistol still extended, and closed his eyes until the noise lessened. He opened them to see O'Neal contorted on the floor, his face turned pitifully. As Joe crossed the room, the puppy had stopped in the dining area, but still yelped hysterically. The bullet had knocked the breath out of O'Neal, and he gasped and heaved to regain it. Finally he blurted desperately: "Caval took it . . . Caval got it . . . Oh, Joe, help me . . . I gave it to Caval . . . He ripped me off . . . Joe, please help me . . . I didn't get much . . ."

He lost his breath again and fought for it at Joe's feet. The blood was all over his hands and back and the rug. Joe was still stunned by the act. It precluded any thought, any reaction to what he'd just heard.

O'Neal partially relaxed and begged with a sort of whimper between each word. "Please, Joe . . . don't kill me. . . . Don't let me die. . . . I'm sorry. . . . Windy's pregnant. . . . She is. . . . Please . . ."

Joe knew instantly as O'Neal spoke again that there was only one thing he could do worse than killing him. It did not bother Joe to look at the pleading, wall-eyed face. He could not have said why. The puppy was still whining, but it stopped when Joe fired again. The bullet struck just beside the nose, and for an instant only disfigured the face. Then blood seemed to gush from every orifice.

V

"Goddamn you," Jack growled. "Goddamn you. I knew you'd do that. I knew when you walked away from the car you'd do that. Goddamn you."

All the way back, coming out of Mill Valley and on the freeway and bridge, Jack had hung his head or covered his face with his hands, muttering, "I don't believe it. I don't believe it." Joe was so shocked himself, it was all he could do to drive. Only once he recalled what O'Neal had said about Caval, but he couldn't bring himself to add that to what already horrified Jack. Now they were back in the city, driving up Lombard, with Joe at the wheel and bright garish motel and restaurant signs on either side. Joe glanced at him and saw the same stricken, bottomless disbelief he had seen when he walked out of the house. Jack had been on the wood steps, frozen by the screaming and shots, and Joe had walked past him toward the car as if nothing had happened.

"What the hell good did that do, Joe? What goddamn good? Huh? Why? Tell me."

Joe stopped for a traffic light and turned to face him.

"The son of a bitch ran for the other room. I told ya that," he shouted. "He could've been going for a gun or anything. I just shot him. What else could I do? Tough shit. He ripped me off. I'm gettin' sick of that shit. All I see is a bunch o' punks rippin' each other off, and nobody's got balls to do anything about it. Well, nobody's rippin' me off again. That's for sure."

Jack looked at him with utter disgust. It seemed as if he had never really seen Joe Eiler before, as if Joe had been an imposter of some kind all those years. Worst of all, Jack saw himself reflected in Joe and found the image base and ugly.

420

The light changed and with a jerk Joe accelerated away.

"Gawd, Joe, I can't believe it. All your talk about honor. Honor." Jack was on the verge of tears. He spoke with the bitterness of thorough betrayal. "Honor. Shit on you. Shit on you, Joe. You're the dishonor. It doesn't matter anything what some punk steals. You made something dirty out of everything we did. Goddamn," he finally shouted. "Pull over. Pull over, damnit. I'm gettin' out."

Joe cut across the right lane and stopped hard against the curb. There was nothing he could say, but as Jack threw open the door, Joe blurted, "Where you gonna be?"

"I'm not telling you," he snarled. He quivered with rage. "I hope I never see your fucking face again."

Jack slammed the door and hurried up a side street.

chapter 28

i

THE road wound among huge redwoods near the coast. Jack kept the Citroen howling in the third gear, pressing it to the red line whenever he had room. Again now he rocketed through a curve, thrilled at the fine variation in engine tone and the knife thrust of speed he could produce with the slightest touch of his foot. Sunlight slivered by the trees danced crazily on the hood. Then suddenly there was a big American sedan moving deliberately through the turns, and it seemed stationary as Jack shot up on it, downshifted, socked the brakes hard to keep from hitting it. He was about to scoot around it, then decided there were too many curves right there, so he relaxed. He saw a bumper sticker on the Chevrolet, hurriedly applied like most of the others he had seen. The right half of it hung down unstuck and popped in the wake so the thing read only, "Discover . . ." All through Oregon and into California there had been those stickers urging discovery of a cave or a lake or some damn wonder where people sold hot dogs and key chains. The banalities of the summer roadside reminded him that he had discovered he was less than he had thought, that he was not really capable of rising above normal life, that he was just another tourist. He had accepted it, though, and was resolved to work from there, with a little more wisdom than he'd started.

Since that night with Joe at Cavin O'Neal's, three weeks had passed, solitary and slow. He had taken a cab to Claire's apartment that night, gotten his clothes, left a quick note, and then headed north. He had driven all that night, and when his thoughts had finally come together in the early morning, he had decided to leave everything behind, not to see anyone he knew, to go on to Seattle, get a job, make new friends, leave everything else.

He discovered that he did not like Seattle at all. He went on to Vancouver, British Columbia. It was an intriguing city, surrounded by fantastic country, but always overcast and usually drizzling. The first week there had been full of excursions, great dreams, and fervent resolve. The next several days had come closer to reality. The fear over O'Neal mounted, the creeping dread of an indictment, a sense of idleness, and the need of friends. The last week he had spent there was full of worrying, calling Zarl's office, trying to reach Insinger or Thorton, wondering what had become of Joe. Ultimately, he discovered he could not strike out on his own, could not leave everything behind. He hated being alone. He needed his friends, whatever they were. He elected in the end to go back to San Francisco and work things out. If there was trouble over O'Neal, or if the indictment came out in North Carolina, he would deal with it. But he could not tolerate being alone, and he was desperately tired of a pointless life.

As they will after tense decisions, things fell into place. He made phone calls to old professors back in Boulder and was fairly honest with them. They were impressed and eager to help him in San Francisco, offering a few introductions for employment, counseling him to take part-time courses at the university in Berkeley until, perhaps with their influence, he might gain admittance to a master's program. It seemed miraculous. He had spoken to Zarl the next day, and the attorney sounded proud and confident. In their first two meetings, he had given the prosecutors hell. He thought he had convinced them he could beat their case on illegal search of the houses and the *Errant*, which, if proven, would taint the rest of their evidence. Then some of the evidence from the storage house had apparently been lost, and the chief prosecutor in any event was a pussy. Zarl virtually promised Jack the case would be dropped.

That had been only two days ago, and Jack spent a pleasant

last day in Victoria, then had departed near dawn that morning and hauled ass for San Francisco.

The traffic was backing up a little by the time Jack neared Eureka, so he stopped for some dinner. There was nothing pressing, so he went out to the docks, walked around awhile, then found a restaurant. He had a fresh salmon steak and a few beers. On the way out, he decided he would call his mother. He had not spoken to her in more than two months and had felt guilty about it for weeks. He thought he'd tell her his new plans, let her know he was going to be good after all. He placed the call from a booth outside the restaurant and dialed it straight through.

"Hi Mother." The cheer in his voice surprised even him.

"Ohhh Jack," she cried. "Goddamn! What have you done."

"Huh?" She never cursed. "Mother, what's—"

"What have you done?" she sobbed. "It was all in the paper. I'm just so—"

"What. What the hell are you talking about? What's in the paper?"

"*The Globe*, Jack. On the front page. You've been indicted for smuggling and conspiracy and . . ."

"Mother, stop crying. It's okay," he lied. "I promise you it's okay. What else did it say?"

"Oh, I don't remember all of it. Don't you know, for God's sake?"

She asked him continuous questions, told him federal agents had come to the house, that friends and relatives had been calling. She was distraught, completely humiliated, and more than anything frightened for her only and prodigal son. Finally, she managed a composure. "What in the world did you do, Jack? And where are you now?"

"I'll tell you everything, Mother. I'll be there tomorrow."

"Jack, please—"

"I'll be there tomorrow, Mother. Now don't worry."

He hung up and stood for several minutes staring at the rotten, beaten, but still strong planks of the long dock. "San Francisco, sure," he smirked. "You're going to prison."

ii

For two days Joe and Martha had their best time together. Joe felt no fear, and he had no guilt, but he knew without question that he was through with the business. He felt free, and they were in

423

love. In the mornings they had cappuccino at the Cafe Italia in North Beach, where she was the only woman and everyone spoke Italian. They took idle walks through Chinatown. They took the ferry to Marin one day, and seals came alongside between Alcatraz and Richardson Bay. At other times they were perfectly content to sit and do nothing. They never spoke of their pasts, except in fleeting anecdotes, strange little stories that an only-child recalls. They preferred to stick to the present, as if they felt themselves changing each other and feared the past could only damage the sweet adventure. In terms of the future, they kept to travel, talked dreamily of going somewhere out of the country, as though they might leave the next day. Joe's desires had become simple. He was sure he could do anything if she were with him. She took it up, too. She said she'd go anywhere with him. The prospects of South America or the Pacific or Africa or Beirut, as they wandered through Joe's atlas, fascinated her.

Joe was so far beyond nervousness, he felt like a visitor from another planet, at least another epoch. But when she went to work those nights, he was desperate in her absence, full of terror, almost held his breath until she returned. She came back both nights, after the six-hour separation, like her old self, distrustful, afraid. Yet in a short time they could calm each other and resume. It felt miraculous. Those two days were timeless. Their love peaked from moment to moment. The third day it came apart so completely that Joe felt cast out from the human race.

Martha departed around ten-thirty that morning to work lunch. She called him before noon. "Joe," she began in a distant voice, "I've gotten some bad news. I have to leave town. My father died just yesterday. I have to go to Atlanta. My mother really needs me. I have to leave right away."

"Jesus, I'm sorry. I'll come get you and take you to the airport. Where are you?"

"I'm at my apartment. But I just called a cab. I'm just gonna go out by myself. The plane leaves real soon."

"Well, hell, I can get ya there faster than a damn cab. I'll go with ya. I can be ready to go in—"

"No. You can't go, Joe. I have to go by myself."

"Well, I'll fly out in a day or two an' meet ya."

"I think it's better if I call you from there. I'm not sure what it'll be like."

"Alright. But where are you going to be? Gimme their name."

"Just let me call you, Joe."

He waited a long moment before replying. In her breathing at the other end he felt her former fear and confusion. He said, "You're running away."

"I have to go. I'm not. I'll call you. I promise—"

"You're running away, goddamnit."

"I have to, Joe. I can't help it."

"Why!"

"I can't tell you. Please. I promise I'll call you."

Joe stiffened with betrayal, hardened reflexively at the pain. He said, "Sure."

"Please Joe. I'm telling you the truth. I have to go. I have to go by myself. I'll call. I promise. I do love you."

There was another long silence, in which she waited for him to say he loved her too, but he breathed emptily into the phone. Finally she said, "I have to go. Bye." He hung up.

He sat numbly through the afternoon, but gradually his desperation grew so complete that he felt the approach of some action so wild he could not even imagine it. He had no choice but to await it. Near five o'clock his doorbell buzzed. When he let them up and opened the door, it was two detectives from Homicide. They were middle aged, fairly well dressed, and had veinous, hard-drinking noses and tough, scrutinizing eyes. Eiler was almost happy to see them. They had saved him from isolation with himself. They in turn so clearly smelled murder on him they looked shocked as they came inside. There was a mutuality of perception that made the exchange bitterly pleasurable, and Joe lied belligerently. There had been no accurate description of O'Neal in the paper, so Joe said he'd known someone by that name in Aspen once but had no idea he was in the area. When they advised him that Windy had described him as an enemy whom O'Neal had seen a few nights before and feared, Joe merely glared at them and curled his lip in disinterest.

"So he's dead, uh?" Joe asked. They had not specifically mentioned that he was.

"Didn't you know that?" the older, meaner-looking one asked.

"Rather obvious," Joe sneered. "Did I give myself away?"

The man stood up and measured Joe with a veteran, skeptical gaze. "Oh no, you're too smart," he smiled sarcastically. "What do you do for a living, Mister Eiler?"

"I mind my own business."

The man regarded Joe with something like sadness and shook his head. "Do you have a cute one for what you were doing Tuesday night?"

"I'm sure I can find a lawyer who does."

The man turned slowly to his partner, and they raised their eyebrows at each other. "Yeah. Very good," he told Joe and motioned casually toward the door.

Eiler retained an attorney he knew of and maintained to the police that he'd been alone at home reading on the night in question. Joe could tell they had little to go on. He had figured Windy wouldn't talk much, and apparently she hadn't. At least she hadn't for awhile, or the cops would have been on Joe much sooner. He also knew that the cops thought this kind of case, where a wife won't talk and the victim was obviously on the run from something, was a kettle of fish and certainly no front-page story. Joe was pretty sure of his position. He had wiped the light switch and door knob in Mill Valley before leaving. After Jack left him in the city, Joe had returned the rental car at the airport and picked up his own. For over a year Joe had kept a set of false identification—California driver's license, Social Security and passport—made from the birth certificates of a deceased person. He had also set up accounts at the Bank of America in that alias and kept enough money in them to have a BankAmericard for emergencies. He had rented the car with it. Near dawn that morning, he had thrown the .32 and his box of shells into the bay off Fort Point, mailed the credit card and false license to his post office box in San Francisco, then woke up Martha, and took her to breakfast at the Garden Court. Joe always kept his apartment pretty free of notes or lists, but he had cleaned it better before ditching the gun and had flushed the few ounces of grass he had. They searched the place while Joe was interviewed, but it didn't worry him.

Joe acknowledged that he'd been in Henry Africa's one night, but said he'd been accompanied only by a Martha Vickers and had not seen O'Neal, whom he described as having brown hair. Joe wasn't sure how he'd cover for Jack and Claire. If Martha called, he would tell her not to say anything. If she never called, Joe felt he wouldn't be worrying about anything. When he told them Miss Vickers had had to leave town and he didn't know where she was or how to reach her, the detectives stared at him across the scarred table in the small, pale-green room that stunk of tobacco smoke and indigestion, then stared at each other. Joe told them where she worked though. As for his own employment, Joe gave the name of the pipeline company in Fort Worth owned by his old friend, for whom he had actually worked about six weeks the previous fall when Caval's deal had bogged down after Curaçao. They had been close since high school, and the friend had said he could cover Joe over several months if anyone asked. Joe said prior to that job he'd

426

made good money working on offshore rigs in the Gulf and made a little more through some drilling investments. He pushed it all the way and invited them to check his tax returns, which of course did not exist. They told Joe to stay in town until the matter was cleared.

Back at his apartment Joe entered a state of siege. He went nowhere, except infrequently to eat, and did almost nothing. He read some and watched TV and sat still in the darkened rooms for hours on end. Three days after he had first been questioned, his attorney called to say the local authorities were temporarily sitting on the case because of a federal interest stemming from a grand jury in North Carolina, but that Joe was still under investigation.

The proximity of disaster demanded some move, but Joe was paralyzed. He could have acted, put into use any of a number of strategies he'd worked up over the years, but he was numbed, emotionally shocked. Without knowing where Martha stood he was powerless to do anything. At times he was sure she was gone, and he didn't care about anything. Yet moment to moment, he wondered if she would call. When she finally did, it was worse than if she hadn't. She sounded stiff, defensive, said her mother was very upset and there was a lot she had to do there. They were nice to each other and it felt terrible. Finally Joe said the police were asking questions about somebody who got killed, and they might get in touch with her.

". . . if you ever come back. It was that guy we saw at Henry Africa's that night. He disappeared from Aspen awhile back. Nobody knew why. Nobody really cared. But that's why I thought it was strange to see him. I guess somebody was after him. Apparently he told his ol' lady he saw me, so the cops wanted to see if I knew anything." Martha was dead silent. "I really didn't even want to say I knew the jerk. I figured he'd ripped somebody off. I said I didn't know he'd been in the bar." She was still silent. "I just didn't wanna get messed up with it. I don't think the guy even knew Jack. I said I was just there with you. I figured I'd keep Jack and Claire out of it."

"Oh for Christ's sake, Joe . . ." She seemed to break down.

"Look. It's no problem. I'll tell them the truth if they really press it. Guys like that get killed, honey. It's just a lousy coincidence."

"Don't talk like that," she begged. "You're going to get in trouble over this."

"No. It's nothing. Come on. If they wanna talk to you just don't say anything. I've got a lawyer here. He'll tell you what to do. I don't think it's anything, but I had to tell you."

"Then why did you lie to them? You know they'll find out."

"I just didn't want to get mixed up in some punk's mess. I'll tell them the truth if it comes to that."

She fell silent again, and Joe waited for her to give a phone number or say she wanted him to come there or would come back soon. When she didn't, he said, "Aren't you going to say when you're coming? Don't you think I need to know that?"

Her voice was flat. "I need to know it, too, Joe. And I don't . . . I can't really talk now. I'll call you again soon."

"Wonderful. I'll wait. There's nothing pressing."

"You really are in trouble, aren't you? Please tell me what's happening."

"No. You're the only trouble I've got right now, honey. I'll tell ya anything you want, if I ever see ya again. Bye-bye."

For the next several days Joe was tormented by his isolation and the sordid threat of his fate. He had heard the optimism from Zarl's office, but that and the O'Neal business were a house of cards he knew would fall. He never felt remorse for Cavin O'Neal, though. One certainty alone maintained him, which was that Cavin got what he deserved. Joe was sickened sometimes by the recollection of it, the pathetic quarry O'Neal became, the disgusting level of energy Joe had been required to assume. But he did not retreat from what he'd told Jack that evening. Everyone knew the rules, whether or not they acknowledged it. No one minded talking about it. To suggest violence, allude to it, know something of it, was thought to be cool, was accepted to be necessary in most levels of the business. But people are squeamish about enforcing moral judgements on either side of the law. Joe knew that. To take a stand or press a point too far makes others uncomfortable, is uncool. Joe had been around plenty enough to learn that those who dare to be righteous must be ready to suffer for it. Thus he assimilated being abandoned by Sidell. He was ready to endure the loss of Martha if he had to. He could not give up, adjust, make allowances or apologies. His life advanced too swiftly, with too many precarious factors, and to relinquish control seemed to invite chaos, like turning loose the wheel of a speeding car.

So he waited alone for some climax. He could not have accounted for the passage of days. He read, walked around the city, sat emptily at home, or drove aimlessly up and down the coast, and drank each night until he could sleep. He missed Sidell and mourned the loss of his friendship, but convinced himself it was inevitable. Missing Martha was infinitely worse. There were organic chemical properties about his affection, and without her he

428

suffered a disease that weakened him a little more each day, reduced his will, further darkened his future. Being in love with her had resurrected him. His life had meant something. Sometimes he wanted to go to Atlanta and find her, yet wondered if he should draw her further into the grim prospect of his life.

It was about a week after she had called that Joe was awakened one morning by the telephone. It was Zarl's office, advising him he had been indicted, should come to Boston with the others to surrender. Joe barely listened. He could feel forces closing in, himself closing in, all careening toward some junction that would be his demise. As he made coffee, he tried to persuade himself to forget Martha, and he found something in the finality of his solitude and the sense of impending disaster that was at last satisfying. He thought he should just take it on the lam. He had enough money. He had made about forty-five thousand selling his portion of the cargo. The good stuff they had bought from Caval, Joe sold easily for three hundred a pound. He had paid Caval thirty-seven thousand five hundred for it, and when all was done netted about thirty-five himself. So Joe had made some eighty thousand dollars in the deal—more money than he'd ever had at one time. Yet it felt small. He had most of it, sixty-eight thousand, in a deposit box at the Bank of America, held under his alias, where he also kept his false identificaion, credit card, and passport. The ten thousand or so remaining was divided between the Bank of America checking and saving accounts and another deposit box for expense money, which he rented at the Bank of Marin in Sausalito.

Tactics, strategy, logistics, options, cities, countries, hemispheres proceeded too swiftly in his thoughts that morning. He could come to no conclusion. He kept feeling that the chips were not quite down yet. He had been sitting on the couch for more than two hours when the doorbell rang. In no hurry he buzzed the door downstairs and awaited the knock at his door. He knew it was police. He asked who it was, and the sound of her voice was hard to believe. When he opened up, she stood there beside a large suitcase, in a raincoat and pants. He looked at her in wonder a few moments. The wheat colored hair was a little straggly, her cheeks a bit sunken, her green eyes tired but bright, as though she had finished a long journey. She tilted her head and winked at him with that paradoxical smile and said, "I got the stuff."

The feel and scent of her in his arms eclipsed everything else. They played with each other's faces like children and were almost embarrassed at themselves. They talked about small stuff. She had just flown in and took a cab to surprise him. She wanted to know what he'd been doing, if he'd been going down for cappuccino in the mornings, or to other places they'd known. He kidded her that he'd been hanging out with Chinese hookers, but she smiled and shook her head. Perhaps to avoid the inevitable unpleasant matter, she even wanted to know how the weather had been. And to the best of his memory he told her. Joe suddenly felt invincible. Her presence created a determination to survive anything. After awhile, one of her sidelong glances suggested the bed.

Afterward the other things closed in on him again. He lay wasted, physically spent, and preoccupied with hopelessness. Her eyes were closed. She stretched her back and took pleasure in the muscles of her neck and shoulders.

"You're frightened, aren't you?" she asked. There was a calm in her voice he'd never heard.

He turned his head to her and hoarsely muttered, "Yeah, I guess so." He caressed her bosom with his nose and held her.

"You're so tight," she breathed. "You're just rigid." She kissed his head. "Relax Joe." He kept his arms around her middle, though, as if he awaited an earthquake. "You're in trouble over lying to the police about that guy aren't you?" He didn't reply. "I knew you would be. You'd better just square it with them, Joe, and—"

"Oh, honey, stop it." He let go of her and rolled onto his back and stared at the ceiling. "It's endless."

"Nothing's endless."

"I'll try to remember that."

She recoiled a little at his tone. He wondered if he could tell her and, in an instant, realized he had to tell her, had to see if she would try to make it through with him. Everything hinged on that. Love seemed the only possibility of salvation, unless he'd already ruined it.

"I've been indicted by a federal grand jury in North Carolina."

"No." She sat up so abruptly and with such disbelief that it rather startled Eiler.

"Yeah. The whole shmere. Conspiracy, smuggling, possession, an' I don't know what all else."

"You've already been indicted? A grand jury has actually made an indictment?" There was clinical skepticism in her voice, but she looked hurt, and her face dropped sadly.

"That's what I said, honey."

She slumped down against the headboard, drew the sheet up

430

over her breasts, and gazed defeatedly across the room. "I knew you were in trouble. I mean, I could tell. But I thought it was going to be all right. I had a feeling it would be. I just knew it would be."

"I'm afraid it'll be everything but that." Joe stirred himself suddenly and got off the bed. He stood for a few moments naked, like he was lost somewhere, and wondered if he should go ahead and tell her all of it.

"I moved a boatload of dope with some guys." He turned to face her, but she closed her eyes as he went on. "That's what I do, honey. That's what that deal was with—"

"Joe, don't tell me about it. I don't want to hear about it."

"Yeah, well maybe you better hear," he raised his voice to a challenge, "cause you're part of the problem. Because I love you." She opened her eyes when he said that and watched him as he went on. "And the goddamn feds have got me pegged in this deal, an' if I stay around here I'm going to prison."

They kept looking at each other, and he expected her to say something but she didn't. You better have a drink, he thought. As he left the room, he mumbled, "So, for starters, that's what's the matter." He threw ice cubes haphazardly into a glass and poured at least a double scotch. When he returned to the room she lay forlornly beneath the sheet. Joe sat at the foot of the bed to face her and took a good belt of his drink. They merely sat though, occasionally searched each other's eyes, but did not talk. They remained that way long enough for Joe to finish his drink and begin another, and the sun departed, and the room grew dark.

"Let's just leave, Joe," she said finally. The room felt like they'd been there for days, weathering a disaster. "Why don't we? What the hell? I don't want to go back to Atlanta. I don't, really. I'm not going back. I want to be with you, Joe. Let's do. Let's just leave. We could go to Europe or something. You're the one that's always—"

"Goddamn honey, that's not easy." You better tell her all of it, he thought.

"We could do it, couldn't we?" she implored. "You could get a fake passport or something if you had to. Couldn't you do that? They don't even chase marijuana cases that hard anymore."

A toughness in the set of her mouth and the desire in her eyes captivated him anew, as she was always able to do.

He knocked back the remainder of his drink. "I would go anywhere with you," he stated. His mouth languished open, and she waited for him to go on, but he could not. He exhaled heavily instead, got up again, and headed for the kitchen.

"Don't start drinking like that, Joe."

"Yeah? Why not?"

He threw two more ice cubes into the glass and doused them with scotch. He returned to the bed with a cruel expression that made her watch him apprehensively.

"Hell, this is one of the nicer things I do."

"No it's not," she said softly.

"Oh yeah it is." He nodded at her and spoke loudly. He had to make her react. "You know this guy the cops are asking about? This guy that got killed?" Joe kept nodding as he spoke, nearly yelling. "The guy we saw at Henry Africa's? Remember the guy?" Martha bit her lower lip and turned away. "Look at me damnit!"

"Don't yell at me."

"You oughta know this."

"I don't want to know anything more."

"Well, you better. Because I'm the one who killed him, honey."

Martha gasped, seemed to choke on the knowledge, as if he'd shot her too. The horror that filled her eyes made Joe tremble. He had to talk again to stop shaking.

"A couple o' weeks ago I went into that guy's house and I killed him."

She screamed, "Stop it, Joe," and turned into the pillow.

"You think I'm kiddin'?" He took a swallow of scotch and nodded again as he spoke. "It's true, honey. He stole dope from me, an' I killed him."

Martha covered her ears like a child and yelled angrily, "I don't want to hear it! Please don't—"

"I want you to hear it," he yelled back at her. His voice was shrill and uneven. If she was going to react the same as Jack had, then he wanted to know now. He stood and walked around to the side of the bed where she lay cringing. The sound of his own voice shocked Joe, but he could not stop it. "He stole a hundred thousand bucks worth of grass from me, so I shot 'im. Killed him. Ya hear me?"

"Don't tell me, please," she begged into the pillow. "Don't tell me."

Joe pulled her arm so that she had to look at him, and her face was red and wet with tears.

"It was real nice. You should've heard him beg me not to kill 'im because his ol' lady was pregnant." Martha's face contorted pathetically to resist what he yelled at her. "You should've heard that. That was great."

He let go of her arm, and she fell away from him into the pillow.

432

He finished the drink in a gulp, then lay across the foot of the bed. Just leave her alone, he told himself. Why do you always have to fuck everything up?

Some immeasurable space of empty time elapsed before he heard her roll over to look at him, but he did not lift his face.

"Please don't say any more about it, Joe. You can tell me later if you want. I don't care. I may have done things you think are worse. I have. But don't tell me anything more now. I just don't want somebody to make me testify against you, that's all." She swallowed and closed her eyes. "I don't care what you've done or why. It's just that business. You know that, don't you? It's all that stuff. That's what happens with all that stuff."

Joe gazed across the rumpled sheets. Her face was ravaged. He said, "I'm sorry I upset you." He felt depleted. He could feel the scotch on his empty stomach. He thought, man, your nerves are shot. You shouldn't drink. "The guy didn't leave me any choice, honey. I didn't go there to kill him. I just got in a position where I couldn't do anything else. I don't think the D.A. will be too philosophical about it though." Some of the horror still remained in her eyes, and he wondered if it would ever leave.

"To me, it's like someone else did that, Joe. If you told me the truth about quitting that stuff, then what you did doesn't make any difference. I don't even care about that guy. I'm just sorry you did that to yourself. You'll never get over it."

Joe moved closer to her and touched her face, smeared a tear around her cheek. Oh God how he wanted to see her smile again.

"Let's just get out of here," she said. "If they don't know about that yet, let's just leave the country. I could go tonight. Isn't there one of those islands you talk about where they wouldn't find us until all this is over?"

"Maybe so," he murmured. "Maybe we could do that. It isn't so easy hiding from a murder though. No place is friendly then."

"But if you don't wait until they indict you or something, there must be somewhere. Brazil or Africa or someplace."

He smiled carelessly at her. He thought: listen to her. Hell, if you can't do it with her, you couldn't do it at all. He pondered a moment.

"Yeah. Maybe we'll do that. But I have to go to Boston first. I have to go back and surrender on the dope thing and make bail, or they'll grab me out here. I got a lawyer back there who'll handle it. They're watching me here for sure now. I'd never make it onto an international flight."

She was already shaking her head before he stopped talking.

"Don't go back there, Joe. Let's just go. I'm afraid for you to go back there."

"No. Come on now. Be serious. I'd never make it out of here. I'll just be back there a day or two. There won't be any problem. And I can talk to some people about where we can go."

She was still shaking her head, her face distraught again.

"You don't have to go. We could get away from them. They're not that good."

"Come on, honey. You don't know what you're talking about. Just stay here 'til I get back. No. Wait a minute. Those guys'll probably be back here. Can you still stay in your place?"

She lay her head down again and nodded. She looked at him with such saddened longing that, after a moment, he moved closer to her and took the sheet off. Her body was tired and limp across the bed, like a soft painting. He moved against her, felt how warm she was, and he ached with hardness. She was feverishly warm, as if the emotion of their revelation inflamed her. Her face was soft and hot and damp. Everywhere else she was loose and hot. Between her legs she was on fire, and her breath seared his ear, and it burned when he put it in.

iii

Ted Zarl's secretary entered his spacious, slightly darkened office carrying two bright-green bottles of beer and chilled ceramic mugs. She placed them before Mark Insinger and Joe Eiler, who sat on the chair and couch awaiting their attorney, and she and Mark traded a few playful comments. They had just returned from surrendering to federal marshals and being booked, and Zarl's assistant who accompanied them had said Zarl wished to see them briefly. Eiler acted as if it were a waste of time, but Mark was happy enough. Zarl took care to achieve a casual comfort in his offices, which were appealingly decorated and functionally arranged with bright artwork and modern furniture, in which his clients were treated with a personal deference. The two main secretaries were also hostesses, ready to provide a speedy cocktail, a good beer, have a sandwich delivered, or a full meal catered. There was a sauna too, and a workout room. Five minutes of business could be attended with hours of extracurricular pleasure, so that retaining Zarl's legal services, in addition to other attributes, was like joining a small men's club. Mark savored the treatment, particularly his status as a big client and being served in the manner in which he had once had to serve old men whose problem was having too much money.

"Nice," Mark nodded at the Heineken as he poured it. "I like the way Ted runs his office."

"You ought to," Joe said. He drank from the bottle and thought a lot of Zarl's trappings were more than he had cared to afford. "That's the most expensive beer you'll ever drink."

Mark laughed. The comment was more like Eiler, and Mark had been wondering what was wrong with him. Through the procedures at the federal building, Joe had been sullen. Everyone else had surrendered the previous day or night, so Mark and Joe had met unexpectedly at the office a few hours ago. They had talked very little, though, and when Mark asked about Jack—why he and Joe had not come to Boston together, where Jack was, why didn't they call him at his sister's, all go out, etc.—Joe kept scowling and virtually ignored him.

"You know, I wondered if you'd show up or not," said Mark. He sipped his beer and fit himself into a corner of the couch to face Joe. "When I talked to Ted on the phone yesterday and he said you hadn't been with the other guys, I thought that bastard probably won't show."

Eiler looked bored and picked at a cuticle while he studied the room. "Caval hasn't been in touch either, has he?"

"Oh, hell, that's different. That son-of-a-bitch is just waiting to see if we'll pay the fees before he gets here. Or maybe waiting to see if we'll take enough raps so that the thing will blow over." Mark snickered a little, and his lips and brow flinched. Then, suddenly wistful, he said, "I almost didn't come myself, though."

"Oh yeah?" Joe's eyes shifted quickly.

"Yeah." Mark pursed his lips a few times, as though requiring a moment to reassure himself Eiler was safe. "I don't care to go to prison. Nor to have the IRS on my ass for eternity. And I don't think they're going to waste much time on us in Wilmington, North Carolina. And appeals, in case you haven't heard, are long and expensive."

"Yeah," Joe sneered, "I can't wait to get down in Dixie with our Boston lawyer. So what're you doing here?"

Mark adjusted his position. "Running is not easy, man. I gave it a lot of thought, in detail. It requires a succession of additional crimes. Covers. You got to keep moving 'til you find a place, and then pay people off who are always going to be able to lean on you in the future. And you can't get back to the States without hassles and risks. Jesus, I think it'd be a lot of trouble."

"I know." Joe's tone was short. He did not enjoy being reminded of these things. Now that he'd had time to think about it, it didn't seem so easy. And taking Martha with him kept reminding him of something. He was not quite sure if it reminded him of his wife or of Sidell. Perhaps it was both.

"You got to want to do it," Mark concluded.

"Gotta *need* to do it."

Mark chuckled curiously at the way Joe snapped. Something had changed about Eiler, he thought. There was a toughness, an animal caution and alertness about him that had not been so evident before.

"I think a lot of it would be having a woman you could move with," Mark observed thoughtfully. "That'd make things a lot easier on the lam, y'know. A good, smart, capable chick." Joe merely nodded, and Mark took a long swig of beer and rambled on, relaxed and glad of having someone to whom he could talk unguardedly. "That lady I told you about earlier, she's a good woman. She's Dutch, y'know. She has a funny accent. Pretty sweet looker, too." His forehead twitched. "And she can use it. But she's a good one for moving around. We've been traveling a lot. Hell, I met her down there in L.A., right after we got back from Chicago, and we drove all across the West, up through Canada, up to the mountains. But she's good, y'know. She takes care of stuff. She gets the laundry done. Always reminding me of things. Lists phone calls I need to make and tells me when it's time. She's really something. Ought to meet her."

Mark paused a few moments and found Eiler watching him the way a smart dog might watch you if you were telling it something, as if it knew everything innately and only wondered why you troubled to say it. Mark smiled and continued. "But she's got some immigration beef that makes her hot. I guess they'd deport her if they caught her. And she's been running with dealers of one kind or another for a long time, too. And she's just a kid. Twenty years old. And she thinks I'm straight. Thinks I'm a lawyer, y'know. So she's telling me how great it is to finally find somebody the cops aren't after. She doesn't know anything about this shit. But she really loves me. I think she really does. Hell, we even talked about getting married and kids and all that. I always get into that rap. These days, anyway. I don't know why. I guess it feels good, y'know.

But I still couldn't tell her about this shit. I could've, I guess. But hell, you know, just because you meet a chick and you're gettin' it on real good, you can't go telling her your life story, right?" Mark finished off his beer and was impatient for Joe to say something. "How's that lady of yours you were hot about?"

"She's real good," Joe smiled. "Just fine. She's one of those women that move with you. Move right along with you."

"Doesn't need a history, uh?" Joe shook his head, and Mark said, "Why don't you get her to fly out? Really. Get her to fly out, and we'll go up north. We've got a cabin in the mountains, up in the Laurentians. We've been there a week. Hell, we're moved in. We could all hang out and have a good time. Talk over long-term possibilities." He started to laugh a little and his eyes blinked. "Look over some travel brochures."

They had a good laugh at that, and Joe said, "Okay, I'll get ahold of her and get her to come. She'd like that. We were talking about going someplace."

Mark smiled at him and liked feeling they were on the same frequency. He had never been close to Eiler and had never thought anyone else was except Jack. Now he saw something in Eiler he liked, and he was curious about it and wondered if it had always been there. As with Caval and Sidell, Mark saw a little of himself in Joe Eiler and a lot more of what, for the present at least, he would like to be—a species of lone wolf, unallied, predatory, hunted.

"You got any blow?" Joe asked him.

"I happen to have a toot 'r two over there." He gestured, grinning, at the briefcase he'd left at the office while they surrendered. "Where do you suggest we do it?"

"For the money we're payin', I suggest this table'd be just fine."

Mark laughed and blinked. "Why not?"

Zarl appeared about ten minutes later and apologized for their wait. The three of them made small talk about the federal procedures, and then the attorney stated abruptly, "I can't believe they indicted." He folded his arms and seemed large, pacing before them. "We're ready nevertheless. Don't worry about that. But I didn't think they'd do it. Jeez, I even called Jack last week and told him they wouldn't, told him it was in the bag. They have the thing all screwed up. I mean, I really think they're kind of dumb." Zarl turned dramatically and made a sharp gesture with a clenched fist saying, "And I told them I'd stick that Customs search right up their ass." He let the statement sink in a moment, not because he was snowing them but because it had become his style to speak so.

437

"And I will. We're still going to, believe me. Hell, even our sources at DEA said they were going to have to let the case go by. Then I guess some smart-ass bitch from Washington got sent down there to help on the case or something and got hot pants. Her and this Customs guy Broley, who thinks he's the king's knight or something and can jack up somebody's boat anytime he wants."

Zarl talked on, warning that in all probability they could not win in Wilmington. It would have to be on appeal. Then he went over the plans for their arraignment. Mark asked questions and enjoyed bantering with the great lawyer.

Eiler enjoyed listening to Zarl speak but not particularly to what he was saying, all of which in his own case seemed beside the point. Abruptly he excused himself to go get a meal. Insinger said he wanted to stay and would catch Joe later at his hotel.

But Zarl said, "Wait a minute, Joe. One more thing before you go." He went back to his desk and took something from their enormous file and returned to the couch. "This could be pretty serious. I have it that DEA put some chick on this case undercover. They'll do shit like that, so all you guys should take care, especially now this indictment's out. Anyway, we hear they got her next to somebody. We don't know to what extent she's inside with anybody or even if she really is. But our investigator knows a few folks over there, and he managed to get this photo. It's supposed to be the chick, so take a look and see if you've seen her. Or she might try to pick you up sometime in a bar. Hell, they'll do anything."

Mark glanced at Joe, who was standing to leave, and saw a faint, slightly mesmerized smile. Then Zarl thrust the picture before Mark, an institutional identification photo. Mark checked it a moment and said, "Not bad, but, uh, I guess I'm clean."

Joe took the photo without interest and said nothing. His eyebrows rose very slowly as he gazed at it. Mark watched his dull smile change to an expression that he had never seen before on anyone. Joe seemed to regard something horrible, yet with no surprise. He leaned slowly against the door and studied the picture for a long time. Finally he tossed it on the couch. "It's my mother," he said, and walked out.

iv

If Eiler could have seen himself, it would probably have snapped him right then. He never considered the front entrance, took only one cursory look up and down Steiner Street, then in one movement pulled himself up and went over the iron gate of the narrow alley that garbagemen used, went resolutely through the scattered residue of trash with the buildings high on either side, back to the big battered cans and old wooden rear stairway. He stepped over dog feces on the first landing, smudged by feet on the next stairs, heard voices steady and civilized at the second floor, then music at the third. By then, some faintly surviving rational thought made him hope she would not be there.

All night on the plane back he had thought wildly of catching her, of what he would say and do. Dialogues and scenes had played in swift tormenting imagery. And then in the dark loneliness of the half-empty overnight flight, he had lapsed occasionally into over-whelming, soul-crushing depression. By four-thirty that morning in the San Francisco airport, sitting for three hours over coffee, he wished a hundred times that it were possible that he'd never see her again. Then finally he had to go, and he knew she would be there.

He was taut as drawn wire from sleeplessness and caffeine, burnt out within from fierce emotion, and in anger and humilia-tion and betrayal, no longer quite human. He stopped perfectly still at the fourth landing to identify a noise, a strange, sharp, rushing sound that just then seemed to him as alien as the very air. It was the shower, he comprehended a moment later, and stepped to the bathroom window beside the door, heard it clearly, saw through the clouded glass the curtain and steam and the blurred shape. The most deep and thorough imperative of self-preservation and a vengeance of the heart and soul combusted in every inch of his body. He felt the handle of the back door, an unattended wooden thing weakened by rainy seasons, and his first kick splintered the lock from the jamb. The safety chain held, but the second blow ripped it out.

With the sound of the door hammering open against the wall the shower ceased. There was silence so definite the air seemed petrified. He could feel her terror resonate in every molecule of the place.

She did not utter a sound when he jerked the curtain so hard the rod came out of the wall and clattered down around her. She stood there in the tub, soaked, naked, stiff, clutching a towel, her hair wet against her head. She saw the knowledge that transfig-ured his face, and the terror in her eyes became the horror Joe had seen before. Then her scream split the air, rang off the walls. "Joe!"

she screamed, screamed only his name as she might have cried out to him for help in a nightmare. But she saw the impossibility in his crazed eyes and wilted, dropped back her head and screamed again with every longing and fear of the human heart, "Joe, I love you, I love you."

His hand cut off the sound as it struck beneath her chin and gripped her throat. He dragged her stumbling and falling out of the tub and over the fallen curtain and rod, and by that hold flung her at the door like a ball. She hit and scattered through and struck the stove, then hung there, dripping, jerking with muffled chokes. He kicked her with a full swing of his leg and the boot struck her side. Her weight seemed like nothing. The only sound was the dull slap of the blow and her breath leaving. Before she could reach the floor he caught her by the hair and beneath the arm and threw her across the kitchen against a table and sent utensils and silverware cascading onto the floor, where she fell limp as a corpse. A second later she was gasping, convulsive, wounded. She tried to scream again, but once more cried only, "Joe."

He kicked her again, as hard as the first time and hit her shoulder and drove her beneath the table. Before she could regain the breath of another noise he shouted, "You fuckin' filthy bitch. You filthy goddamn narc whore."

He stood heaving and for an instant speechless above her, lying wracked on the wet floor.

"Where's your badge, you cunt? Where's your badge and gun? Huh? Why don't y'arrest me, ya fucking bitch narc?"

Before he had finished shouting he was on the way to her bedroom. Beside the unmade bed he found her purse, emptied its contents on the wrinkled sheets, stirred them viciously but found nothing. He tore out each drawer from the dresser and upended them over the bed and ripped through the clothes but still found nothing. Then he took the suitcase from against the wall and turned it up on the bed too. Out fell a heavy zippered cosmetic bag, which he nearly ripped open. The plastic wallet with her badge and cards was stuck in the stiff newish leather of the holster with the short-barreled .38.

He was back in the kitchen with the stuff in an instant. Martha had managed to emerge partially from beneath the table but lay injured, pulled up into herself, sobbing as though it were difficult to breathe.

"You fucking bitch." He threw the holster and wallet at her face. She could only gasp, struggling in pain to be audible. "I swear I love you, Joe. I was going to . . ."

440

The last of it trailed off in low, unintelligible sounds.

"Were you going to love me with this?" he yelled. "Huh? With this?"

He bent and thrust the barrel hard against her cheek, which was wet and pale as fright against the dark steel. Her eyes were desperately closed, and her body, marked from the beating, throbbed silently, He bent there with his finger closed on the trigger for some indefinable period of time, until he became aware of an odd grinding bleating sound and realized it was himself. He saw one fall to the floor and realized there were tears all over his face. With a noise, a cry and shout together that were an utterance of complete abandon, he whirled and threw the gun against the couch in the other room and departed, fled, leaving her there on the floor, in what seemed to be the litter, the trash that remained of their lives.

chapter 29

i

TED Zarl was held up in court and did not get back to his hotel until matters were beyond repair. His assistant and partner Freddie Westheimer was a tough, aggressive young guy who could usually handle people, but he looked like a man being swept out to sea through the cloud of smoke and the tempest of voices. Sidell, Insinger, Thorton, and Caval were there, meeting at Zarl's Palmer House suite in Chicago for a strategy session, and to that combustible mixture of humans was added Zarl's well-stocked bar. The attorney might have thought that in midafternoon they would go easy, but time of day had long ceased to be a factor of importance in any of their lives. Upon his arrival, the situation resembled nothing in which he had ever attempted business. Something about the scene, the disturbance of furniture, the noise, indulgence, the young men intoxicated and shouting angrily, howling in laughter a moment later, struck Zarl as primeval, like a war council of heathen princes.

Jack had arrived first, from Boston, and Thorton had come just after him, having driven in from his hideout on a lake in upper

Michigan. They had missed each other at the arraignment in Wilmington three weeks earlier, so this was their reunion, worthy of celebration despite the circumstances, and the whisky came out right away. Then Caval entered, and the polarity of feeling he created in Ralph and Jack began to charge the air. Spawned by Thorton, there were great loud rushes of comradeship that even the antipathy between Caval and Sidell did not diminish. They had been successful after all; they had pulled off a big one. The feds had caught the tail of it by luck, but they had still pulled it off. "An' this damn indictment is just another obstacle," Ralph swore, "and we can just keep bustin' through it just like we did ever' thing else." Caval and Sidell actually laughed together and drank to that. With his next breath, Caval made a crack about Jack leaving the boat's papers, and then they were shouting viciously. "You son-of-a-bitch, you're the one who . . ." Westheimer, perceiving the trend of things, said they'd probably get more accomplished with less yelling and less drinking. Jack and Tom did not even hear him. Thorton took a slug of bourbon straight from the bottle.

Insinger showed up about a half hour before Zarl, and his mere presence there with Caval further charged the air, more so because Mark was surer, not so nervous, not so afraid of Caval. Mark's greeting with Jack and Ralph was raucous and loud. They were aware of their overexuberance and its incongruity with the purpose of this gathering, but the last meeting they recalled had been at sea off Carolina. And since then they had been hiding and hustling and lonely for friends. And it was not in their natures simply to collect themselves and do business.

Caval moved to one side. While the other three made their hellos, he seemed to position himself for dramatic effect upon Insinger. Then in response to some remark by Thorton, he interjected, "That was before he became a rip-off Jew."

Mark only smirked at him, but Sidell turned and said, "You're a great one to talk. If you weren't so goddamn greedy and tight, you'd have gotten those houses off the island like we planned, and we wouldn't be here now."

"Fuck you, Jack. Wasn't any of your fault, right?" Tom's voice calmed suddenly, and he showed his calculating grin. "You always do right, don't you Jack?"

Jack shouted back at him and began to catalogue Caval's errors, but Ralph got between them and said, "Hey, come on now. Let's cut this shit, uh? We can't be fightin' among ourselves now."

"Don't start kissing his ass again, Ralph. I saw enough of that at Fort Rhodes."

442

They exploded on that spark and almost came to blows, advanced on each other with raging accusations, as though flung together by some valency of nerves. It took a few minutes for Westheimer to calm them, and then swelling with emotion, Thorton said, "I'd stomp yer ass for sayin' that if we hadn' been pirates together." They all roared laughing. " 'Member that? 'Member that day, you an' me an' ol' Joe sittin' on deck when we was goin' to Caruso?" Ralph's eyes burned with a passion to recall the kinship of spirit they had felt that now seemed so different. Jack smiled back, remembering, and laughed at the way Thorton always pronounced Curaçao as if it were the great singer's name. Ralph began recalling episodes of the long adventure: the trouble approaching Curaçao, some crazy night in Aruba, and then "the night they got Billy." It seemed he would break down and cry as he stood before Jack's chair describing it cryptically, as if the others should never know all of it. "Hearin' 'em . . . 'Member how we heard 'em. An' then it hit 'im just like that." He snapped his fingers and stared at Jack like a mystic. "An' then seein' 'em out there all dark as hell comin' up on us. Goddamn! I'll never forget that! Never!" He turned suddenly to Insinger and Caval and said fiercely, "We let those bastards have it though, by God. We sure as hell let 'em have it. Didn' we, Jack?"

Jack nodded gravely. He did not care for the recollection, just one in a string of progressively sordid events as he saw it now, and it gave him no thrill in retelling. Sidell was the sort of man who could spend a year in combat and never speak a word of it the rest of his life. But he turned to Caval and snarled, "Yeah, Tom, tell us who did the rough part."

More arguing ensued. Jack knew the importance of preserving what little alliance remained among them, but he could not restrain his resentment of Caval. And he was more worn than ever by the ordeal now, felt as if he had not slept in a year, and he could not tolerate Caval. He began to wonder, though, if they would be able to agree on anything enough to keep themselves out of prison.

When Ted Zarl finally opened the door on the smoky, noisy chaos of his rooms, Jack saw the same doubts reflected in his face. But Zarl was the man, the weapon they had hired to hold off the government, and he got their attention—but not before two good scotches and some loud bullshitting, just to get on the same wavelength. When he came to the business, though, he did not have good news.

The government was getting tough, he told them. The woman they had sent down from Washington was putting together a pretty formidable case, and the only chance of victory lay in appeals, and only a chance. He paced among the disarray of chairs and bags, half-full glasses, and sullen faces as he told them that an appeal would be a long and expensive proposition during which they might be in jail. If the government was forced to spend a lot of effort and money in a trial, they would want longer sentences. And the length of time required for a trial raised the chances of someone being lured or trapped into turning state's evidence.

"When they get on somebody the way they got this chick on Joe Eiler, hell, sometimes they can make them do anything."

They had all learned about Joe at their arraignment in Wilmington, for which Joe had appeared a week late, to avoid them. The story had so thoroughly shocked Jack that it began to inspire strange irrational thoughts of Joe as some evil force. And the love he had seen between Joe and Martha only added to those feelings.

"Now, Joe told me he never told her much, and I'm not saying Joe would go over on us," Zarl retreated a little. "But that's the kind of thing that can happen. Hell, they may have a bundle on him, and those guys can screw you to the wall."

Ralph declared it impossible that Eiler would ever testify, and Insinger agreed, though cautiously. Caval said, "Sure. Why isn't he here, then?" That made Jack turn uncomfortably in his chair. None of them knew what he knew. Joe was not a human being to him anymore but a strange menace, an enigma of grim revelations.

Ted Zarl then came to the point of the meeting. He wanted them to consider changing their pleas to guilty and accepting sentences of six months to a year. They would spend a lot less money, he told them, get it over with and perhaps avoid some really big raps.

If they were not deeply, innately opposed to copping pleas they would not have been there at all, and they erupted at the idea. Ralph thundered against it, and Jack denounced it too, although the prospect of putting an end to it all was appealing. Caval glared furiously at Zarl. He already felt saddled with an expensive lawyer that Sidell had picked out like another costly safety precaution. "I thought you said you could win the fucking thing. What the hell are we paying you for?"

It became a shouting match again. Only Insinger remained relatively calm and kept his questions to Zarl in a civil tone. It went on and on, well past dinner and into the night. They insisted naively on knowing how evidence would be used, what their chances were, how the judge would view certain matters. Futilely,

Zarl tried to make them understand there was not much telling. The place grew more agitated, smokier, louder, more drunken. There were complaints from the desk, but Zarl could only swim with the current and hope the whisky would slow them down before it started a brawl.

Caval, who rarely drank at all and had only one or two if any, was the first to depart. The cost of a trial had come up, and Jack turned to Caval: "That's not my worry. That's your responsibility."

Thorton addressed him like Caval was a child. "Hell yes, Tommy. You know that's right."

Tom ignored Thorton, and, of course, he had no intention of paying Insinger's way. But he looked at Sidell and said, "You're real big on responsibility, Jack. And on sticking to deals. I'd almost forgotten that." He stood as he said it, and a moment later left the room.

Jack's mind reeled at Caval's implication. He felt like an animal in a trap. He had not paid Caval the last twenty-eight thousand he owed him, because he'd been afraid at the time that Tom wouldn't take care of the lawyers. And in fact Caval hadn't. If Jack hadn't made contact with Zarl and organized the group to meet with him and put together a defense, they might all be in jail already. Then at the arraignment Caval had reiterated that he'd pay the legal fees, but Jack could not find a way to explain what he'd done. At the same time, his fears over Eiler and the killing of O'Neal had mounted immeasurably once he learned about Martha. He was afraid he'd have to get another lawyer for that matter, so he finally rationalized never paying Caval. To his surprise, Caval had never mentioned the matter.

They continued for hours more, into the morning. Zarl went to sleep in his chair, then moved to the couch, and Westheimer finally took another room on a different floor. At three in the morning, when the bourbon was gone, they went out to look for dinner.

The next afternoon when they managed to straggle together once more, hangovers and fatigue made the idea of copping at least considerable, like the prospect of rest after sleepless nights. But they had only begun to discuss it when Zarl revealed that, in his first meeting with them, the feds had demanded felonies for all six major defendants and three-year sentences for each. Their reaction the previous night would have blown out the windows, but now they cursed in low voices and swore they would never make that deal. Zarl quickly promised there would be further negotiations, that it would likely come down to four felonies with one-year

445

sentences and misdemeanors or probation with longer periods for the others. That of course began the argument over who deserved the felonies. It had barely begun when there was a knock at the door, and Westheimer admitted Joe Eiler.

No one said more than his name and hello, and the skepticism and apprehension curdled the air. Jack's eyes met Eiler's for an instant, but they repelled each other. Joe simply stood in the doorway gauging the mood, aware of the distrust with which they watched him. He looked different, exhausted and quiet, but keen. His face was thin, and he had grown back the beard along the sharp edge of his jaw and up into his mustache. He wore a gray suit, with a vest but no tie, and his black cowboy boots. Thorton jumped up as soon as he overcame his surprise and gave Eiler a bear hug, but it seemed as tenuous as the other greetings, restrained by the general uneasiness. Joe pulled a chair up to the group with a calmness that made Sidell think he had either been to a Zen camp or gone quietly mad.

As he sat, Joe inquired deferentially, "Anyone object to me sitting in?"

Quickly they said no, but Caval loudly remarked, "I only object to your taste in women." He made the remark with a strained nastiness; it made up for his diminished power over the others. "You brought some great people into this deal, Jack."

Joe regarded Caval with no visible reaction. The room was dead silent. Joe could hear Cavin O'Neal's gasping voice saying, "Caval took it . . . Caval got it." With a deep breath Joe turned away. He felt no obligation to explain himself to the group. Two weeks ago he had finally forced himself to call Zarl, and he'd told the lawyer everything, except about O'Neal, of course. Given the nature of their relationship, Zarl was sure the government would never dare bring Martha into court.

They started in again on the question of blame and who deserved to take the felonies, and there was a long and bitter discussion of their errors: Caval's not getting the houses and attracting attention on the island; Insinger's letting his name turn up on the papers of the *Errant* and harming the boat so that it was in Bradley Creek for repairs when Customs came around; Mackenzie's writing in his diary; Jack's leaving *Leda*'s papers with the rental agency. It was an exercise in acrimony and hindsight, and finally Sidell said, "We're not going to get anywhere this way. We're all to blame. One way or another we're all responsible. So why don't we—"

446

"Bullshit!" Thorton cut him off. It was the sort of statement that Thorton might have made himself, but now it affronted him. "I did my job! An' so did Joe, even if this gal did get onto him. 'Cause that could've happened to anybody, an' I don't think he or I should be takin' felonies. No way. We didn' make no mistakes. We did our jobs. All you guys fucked up one way or another, an' I say you oughta own up to it an' take yer raps."

Jack could not accept it. He had begun to reason with a bias he made little attempt to hide. He thought of the deal as a bad episode in his life, one that was almost over now, but that would never end if it resulted in a felony conviction. He could think of a hundred ways that would harm him with schools, jobs, business—and if he ever did get to it—architecture.

"But the harm is already done, and punishing people won't really change anything," he argued. "I think, if we're going to cop pleas, we ought to arrange it so the guys who can afford it take the felonies."

"What the hell does that mean?" Ralph demanded. He had just finished a stiff drink and was growing surly.

"I can't have a felony on my record," Jack insisted. "It would ruin my career. I'd never be able to do a lot of the things I plan to do. If Mark takes a felony he'd be disbarred." Jack spoke too heatedly, as he had often begun to do under the pressure of the last few months, and with too high a regard for his own opinions. "But what difference does it make to you whether you take a misdemeanor or a felony?"

Ralph stared at him, wounded. Everyone would have agreed to some extent with Jack's reasoning, but they also saw how it affected Thorton, and there was a regretful silence. Sidell stood up nervously and regarded Thorton with conflicting emotions. He loved Ralph. They had been through a lot, and he even felt Ralph might be the only decent man in the bunch. But there was no time left to worry about hurt feelings.

"What are you going to do where having a felony record would make a difference?"

"No," Ralph yelled. His voice was burdened with betrayal. "I'm not coppin' to a felony." He had become a wealthy man through the deal, and it had been the adventure of his life. He had been through more with these men than anyone he'd ever known. Yet Jack seemed to say that he could be sacrificed as a person of lesser importance than his educated friends from wealthy families. "I did my job," he shouted.

Joe Eiler said, "I think you got a good idea, Jack. Let's decide it on the basis of social standing."

Sidell whirled on him with absolute contempt. "Well how the hell could you care?"

Very quickly the place became a snake pit that made the previous meeting seem almost tame. There was little Zarl could do but let them fight it out. The whisky came out again, but this time they drank with anger and grew uglier with each drink. In addition, Eiler started taking occasional snorts of coke in one of the bathrooms and shared some with Thorton, and Insinger was doing the same with Sidell. The combination only heightened their arguments, until the atmosphere became a maelstrom of resentment and self-interest.

Only Caval remained sober, and he seemed to take pleasure in the rancor and division. Finally he employed the last power he held over the others—that of paying the attorney's fees. "Awright," he raised his voice, "maybe I can settle all this by just paying for the guys who take the felonies."

Both Jack and Ralph attacked him, but Caval seemed to enjoy it, and any kind of agreement looked more impossible than ever. Then Jack said, "Hell, let's face it. The issue is money." He said to Caval, "You say they don't have much evidence on you, so you don't want a felony. I can't afford to have it on my record. But what's it worth to you? What's it worth to me? Let's get realistic." He turned to Ralph Thorton. "You'd take a felony for money, wouldn't you?"

Ralph was speechless. In his own terms, he had as much to lose as Sidell: respect. His family would be humiliated; his image among friends would be diminished as a loser. Yet he felt he was being sentenced by his own friends on a class distinction. For a moment, he was conscious with a vengeful pride that his mother had been a maid in this hotel for nineteen years.

"Fuck you, Jack," he finally blurted. "My freedom's worth something too. You're not the only one who counts." He said something more, but it was unintelligible as he headed for the door. Then he stopped and said, "You fuckin' rich kids think you can buy anything." He slammed the door behind him like a cannon shot.

Ralph's departure quieted everyone. The arguments seemed to expire from lack of interest. Jack did not say another word. He believed that his intentions had been right, but that he had no choice but to state them badly. He had felt a few moments earlier that he had to be blunt in self-defense, but now he began to wonder if he were really worth defending.

The meeting faded to a close again without any concrete plans, but with a general agreement, which no one cared to enunciate just then, that those who pleaded to felonies would be paid by the others. Jack stared out a window while the others gradually dispersed, Insinger and Westheimer departing for a late supper, Zarl to make some calls. When Jack finally turned to leave with no specific destination, he almost bumped into Eiler.

"How you been?" Joe asked him.

"I don't know," Jack mumbled. From the rigidity of Joe's features, Jack could tell he had been using a lot of cocaine lately. Under the circumstances though, Jack thought he would probably do the same himself. Looking at Joe's eyes, which seemed duller but harder than he remembered them, his emotions were paradoxical. He still felt estrangement and disgust over what had happened back in California, yet he wanted to say something about Martha. He could not forget that he had seen his old friend in love again and had been touched by it and happy for him. But now that affair had been transformed into something loathsome, just as Joe himself had been transformed in Jack's eyes. In Joe's mere presence Jack felt a menace, as if someone were offering him a drug he was trying to kick. It was Joe who had got him into the business in the first place; Joe had begun the deal with O'Neal; and Joe had ultimately shown him what business outside the law was all about and had pushed him into it up to his neck. And now the only way Jack could protect himself might be by burning Joe. Jack had no idea what the cops had linking him to the murder, but he was not taking any rap for it. He hadn't killed anyone. If he had to, if it came down to that, he'd tell them the truth. He had no choice. And he hated Joe for that.

So they just stared at each other. Joe was about to tell Jack the San Francisco cops had nothing on him, but Tom Caval seemed to materialize at their side, his dark, handsome face hungry and intent.

"I need to talk to you guys," he said. "Come 'ere a minute."

It was one of the vacant moments when suggestion is powerful, and they followed him into the bedroom Westheimer used. When they got there Jack was suddenly uneasy. He was always distrustful of Caval, but there were a number of things they had to talk over sooner or later. Mainly he did not want anything to do with Eiler, or anything to suggest they had been friends and partners. Caval dropped into a chair and grinned cleverly at Sidell.

"I think you made a mistake, Jack." Jack said nothing, but his

449

face tensed, and Caval kept smiling. "You did. You made a mistake on the phone with Marshall awhile back."

Eiler exhaled loudly and sat on the bed.

"What the hell is this?" Jack snapped.

"Oh come on, you remember. You said you got ripped off. You said Jim Bains got ripped off with some of your stuff, so you couldn't pay me. So you shorted me about thirty thousand, right?" Jack's face darkened, but he remained silent. Caval's smile evaporated as he went on, but his enjoyment of the moment was clearly great. "Well, you made a mistake about that because I know Jim Bains. You didn't know that, did ya? Well, I sure do, an' he tol' me he never got ripped off fer anything." Caval began to nod. "Yeah. I'm the one got ripped. You ripped me off. After all this bullshit of yours about keeping bargains, you turned around an' ripped me off. Didn't ya? Well, didn't ya?"

Jack made no reply. He folded his arms and looked at Caval's grinning face with more hatred than he ever thought he could feel for anything. The hatred made his face redden, but it was embarrassment as well, because his humiliation was complete at last. Finally he caught you in his web, Jack thought. You finally sank to his level, and then he beat you. All the other times he only cheated you, but now you let him beat you as an equal.

When Caval saw Jack was not going to give him the satisfaction of a reply, he said, "So don't expect me to pay a cent of your attorney fees." Then he turned to Eiler. "Or yours either."

"I paid you everything I owed you, you bastard, an' you know it." Joe was just on the verge of yelling, "Who bought our dope from Cavin O'Neal?" But other thoughts hurtled through his mind to prevent it. Should he reveal he'd seen O'Neal again? If he did, would it further harm Jack? If he brought up any of it, would an agreement ever be possible? Before he even approached a conclusion, Caval spoke again.

"You guys were partners in this thing all the way, so yer still partners now, so you can kiss my ass."

"I paid you." Joe stiffened and sat up straight on the bed. "You better not do this."

"Yeah? Bullshit. What're you gonna do about it?"

Jack still stood silent with his arms folded, stunned, his thoughts almost empty, as if he were in shock. Then the grim challenge of Caval's last question caused him to look at Eiler, and he recognized the look in Joe's eyes. His mouth fell open for an instant. "Goddamn," he shouted and left the room.

450

ii

Insinger was still flashing, still rolling high. He thought he would never tire of it. He wore a custom-made denim suit and new tan boots as he came off the plane in Miami, and his brown curly hair was bleached from the sun and bushy. He carried only his briefcase, as he headed for the baggage area, but he got a porter to transport his single bag. The porter asked where he was going and said that hotel had limo service, but Mark took a cab.

Mark and his Dutch girlfriend Gretta had gone back to California soon after Mark and Eiler had met in Boston to surrender, and they had moved into a house in La Jolla. Despite the legal troubles, every day was a new adventure, and he was happy. He had money and fast friends, and life was challenging and full of schemes. He had begun to admire himself for an ability to cope with nearly anything, to get things done, to deal with any problem. Moreover, he knew that his friends and people he met respected him and considered him a man who could make things happen. He was a good scammer and proud of it.

Mark had considerable problems now, though, some of which he could barely understand yet. But he was still confident he could handle them. He was smiling and felt good as he left the airport and drove out toward Miami Beach. What made him smile was the assurance that none of the others were as capable of handling Tom Caval as he was now. He had finally begun to think like that.

The group of defendants had met only once more in Chicago, although without Thorton, but there had been numerous telephone conferences during the weeks that had passed since then. The central issue was settled now. The chances of winning the case were hardly worth the risk. Thorton and Caval had kept wanting to fight it, and Mark had even met Sidell in Boston to pore over the evidence and search for any scrap of precedent in their favor. But finally they had decided to cop, and then convinced Caval and Thorton of it. Zarl's crafty dealing with the government had been a great inducement, especially when considered against the prosecution's evidence and the certain wrath of any jury that realized what ten tons of dope were worth.

After several sessions, Zarl had negotiated a deal by which the government would accept three misdemeanors and three felonies, all except one of the felony charges carrying only one-year sentences. In addition he had secured promises that all of the defendants would serve time in minimum-security federal prisons.

Thorton was taking one of the felonies, because characteristically he thought his cohorts felt he should, but he was still hurt and angry. No one had seen Joe Eiler since the Chicago meetings, but he had talked to Zarl recently and said he did not give a damn if he got a felony or the plague.

It was that third felony that was on Mark's mind as he rode with the windows down through the soft thick warmth of evening air. Back in Chicago, Zarl had warned that the government would want to say it had nabbed the ringleader of the deal. In their bargaining since then, the prosecutors had kept insisting someone admit to that role and serve a two-year sentence. Plainly it had to be either Caval or Insinger, and the evidence suggested Mark. His was the only name that appeared in every phase of the operation—the corporation, the houses, the *Errant*—but Mark of course had no intention of taking Caval's rap and never considered it.

Mark knew from his record-keeping at Fort Rhodes Island how much Tom stood to make from the deal, and several extra months in any slammer was worth it for that kind of money. And in the past few months, Mark had heard through mutual acquaintances that Caval was absolutely socked with dough. He had come out with about three million dollars. Mark had never been able to grasp it completely, although he never doubted it was true. Every time he thought of it, though, he would speak the words to himself in amazement—three million dollars! Successful men did not make that in all their paychecks put together. And Mark would think of Tommy Caval somewhere, in jeans and a tennis shirt and running shoes, driving a Bentley, building a new house in the mountains and making exotic banking arrangements through Luxembourg and Switzerland. It fascinated him—still fascinated him—but he was busy with his own success and never thought of the third felony charge.

Then Zarl had called to tell him about the final deal with the prosectuion. He said they would all meet in Wilmington on the date of their preliminary trial and change their pleas. But he also said it was about time Mark and Caval settled the ringleader bit. Mark laughed. There was nothing to settle, he said, but Zarl answered that Tom did not see it that way. And if it did not get settled, the government certainly had the evidence to pin it on Mark. Moreover, if Tom and Mark would not agree, then the government might well bring them all to trial, and everyone would get screwed.

Zarl said he would be in Miami finishing up another case

before going to Wilmington for the final plea bargaining, so why didn't Mark meet him and Caval there before going to Wilmington and they'd figure it out.

"Meet you and Caval?" Mark had carefully repeated.

"Yeah," Zarl said brusquely, "Tommy's coming down there to discuss a few things with me before we go up."

"Tommy," Mark thought, ". . . before we go up." He agreed to meet them. It had been a startling conversation, and as he hung up, he had thought, Caval bought that son of a bitch and they're going to screw me good.

The situation had scared him for awhile. He respected Zarl, but Caval had a lot of money, and you never know. Each time he came to believe he was being paranoiac about Zarl, he would not be able to get him on the phone or Westheimer would not return his call. It grew quite uncomfortable.

Moving up the strip now though, with buildings jammed along the sea and jutting into the sky like unearthly geological thrusts, the straits luminous and metallic beneath a thin haze, the setting sun reflected flaming orange in hotel windows, he felt sure. Be dangerous, he thought. You've got to be dangerous. Tell them you'll stand up in court and say Caval set the whole thing up. Tell them you'll fuck up the whole party. You don't care. You're a dangerous man.

There was a message at the desk asking Mark to join the others in the restaurant. Zarl preferred to eat early, so he could work or make calls later. Mark opened only his bag and spent a fraction of his usual time freshening up in the bathroom. The dining room was a noisy, gaudy place, but he had no trouble picking them out. They were certainly the most flamboyant table among a crowd that aspired to just that. Their voices were loud, and they caught the eye. Zarl and Westheimer were both handling a cocktail waitress as Mark approached, and he joined them in it from behind, causing the young lady to jump and producing a roar of laughter from several tables nearby. It was a fitting beginning to the meal, and they were continuously attracting attention with their laughter and bold voices. In addition, Zarl, although not a particularly handsome man, possessed a vitality in appearance and behavior that made people watch him. Caval however was a show-stopper that night in a pale, lemon-colored linen suit and a white silk shirt open at the chest. He was accompanied by a gorgeous little blonde, who could not have been more than twenty years old, giggled continuously, and said nothing, but produced a complimentary

453

prop for Caval. Mark constantly noticed people watching Tom, as though trying to recall what TV or movie star he was. Mark liked drawing attention, no matter who he was with, and he enjoyed himself immensely.

They ate and drank with boisterous happy conversation, which managed to steer clear of the case except for one brief exchange. In response to some joke, Zarl spoke in that Boston accent that lent interest to everything he said: "Yeah sure, I'll live that long, if I don't have another case like these guys. You guys're too hard on my nerves."

"Hell, it's almost over now," Mark said. "You'll be bored."

"Over my ass," he retorted. "It's not over 'til you guys figure out what you're gonna do. An' if you screw this thing up now, which you could easily do, I'm goina knock your heads together like a couple o' monkeys."

Mark and Tom both laughed, but there was an edge on their eyes as they looked across the table. By that time, Mark was sure there was no skullduggery between Zarl and Caval, but he could see that both attorneys had been drawn in by Caval, charmed by his beauty and wealth and adventures, which might still be a problem if he did not play his cards well.

The lawyers excused themselves after coffee, saying they might meet again in the bar, and while Mark ordered a cognac, Caval's girlfriend found some reason to return to the room. Suddenly they faced each other alone for the first time since their meeting in Aspen, and Tom leered at Mark with rather amiable contempt.

"Look," Caval said abruptly, "Zarl says we're both gonna get screwed, if one of us doesn't take the big rap." Mark merely lifted his eyebrows and shrugged, awaiting more. Tom smiled, less friendly than before. "Don't gi' me that shit. You know what's happenin'. They got you all over this thing. All over it. So why don't you not be an asshole an' take the rap?"

" 'Cause I don't want to."

"'Cause I don' want to,' " Caval mimicked him in a high voice. "You dumb shit, they're gonna jump on you anyway, with the evidence they got. If you cop to it, you can probably get out the same time as everybody else. If you don't, they'll bust yer ass."

"Sounds to me like I get screwed either way," said Mark. From their first words he had thought this exchange was out of character for Caval, so he had decided to be passive until he learned what was up Caval's sleeve. He had learned that from Tom: save your strength.

"That's right. So why don't ya take it?"

" 'Cause I didn' do it. I wasn't the head guy. That's your rap, Tommy. You'll have to take it." Mark sipped his cognac and, above the snifter, saw Caval seething.

"You asshole. Whatta ya want? You rip me off a bundle. I brought ya into the goddamn deal. You get rich. You rip me off, an' now 'cause you gotta go down, you wanna take me with ya. Look, I awready said I'd pay attorney fees for whoever took felonies. I'll pay yours too."

"I can afford to pay my lawyers, Tom." Mark was beginning to enjoy himself again, and he was intrigued to learn what made Tom deal so desperately. Maybe he's afraid of prison, Mark thought.

"Whatta ya want, goddamnit?" Tom's voice rose with his exasperation, and Mark loved making him angry.

"I don't want anything," he replied innocently. "I just can't plead to something I didn't do. After all, I am an officer of the court, you know."

"Funny as hell," Tom railed at him. He stood up and said it again even louder. "Funny as hell!" No one in the place failed to hear him, and he stalked away, proud and mad as a fine cock. Mark sat alone, red-faced but smiling, as he finished his cognac.

iii

As he was riding into Wilmington from the airport the next day, alone in a cab, the town—hot and sleepy and laden with throbbing trees and grass in late summer—was unsettling to Mark. After all the traveling, the rare places, the adventure, and the money, they were all being brought to ground in this little town, deserted in the midday heat. He knew it was just the breaks, but it still posed a fundamental challenge to his perception of life. He tried to shake it, but nothing else he thought of was any better.

Everyone was coming into town that day. They were to meet with the judge that afternoon to discuss their pleas. The sentencing would be tomorrow. All the faces came to mind—Margaret, Jesse, Jack, Ralph, Joe—but this would be their most cheerless gathering, divided with aversions and objections, poisoned with broken promises and spoiled dreams, to be sentenced now, to repudiate that wild notion they had shared of romantic danger and invincibility. As he passed through the town, this last meeting reminded him of a funeral, but there was no body of an old friend over which they could unite once more. They were only burying that notion.

They had all flown up together from Miami, and Mark had sat with Westheimer, away from Caval. Then he had contrived to go into the town by himself, so he could think, plan. But he concluded there was nothing to do but wait. When he had checked in at the Hilton down by the river, Mark called Zarl's room to check the time of their appointment with the judge, and he could hear Caval talking in the background. Again Zarl said, "You guys have got to get this main plea settled . . . I don't think they'll accept anything until you guys make up your minds."

Mark drew the curtains in his room and waited. He looked through a *Playboy* and an *Esquire* he picked up at the airport, but mainly he sat on the bed thinking, wondering what prison would be like, and then after awhile wondering what it would be worth to Caval.

Zarl kept calling from the courthouse, where he was taking Margaret and Jesse before the judge, then Jack and Ralph. He implored Mark to find Caval and settle the matter before the judge killed the whole deal, but Mark told him to tell that to Tom. The hour of their appointment came and passed, but without word from Caval. Westheimer called around four o'clock to say Zarl had managed to stall the judge until the next morning, but that the judge didn't like it. He said Caval had been on the phone all afternoon, "like an options broker." They laughed, and Mark said, "Guess he's getting his shit together."

Half an hour later, someone pounded on the door. It was Thorton, with his hair cut shorter than Mark had ever seen it and his tie loose around his neck so that he looked like someone's bodyguard. "Where's Tommy?" he demanded.

"I don't know, Ralph. How you doing?" Mark punched him playfully on the shoulder, but Ralph bristled.

"I'm gettin' ready to plead to a felony," Ralph growled. Mark could tell he'd had a few belts, and he sounded mean. "What're you gettin', probation?"

Mark returned to the bed and sat. "I haven't heard yet. I may get the main rap, maybe a couple of years."

Thorton moved around the room for a few moments, like he was looking for something to destroy, and it scared Mark a little. "Where the hell is Tommy?" Ralph demanded again, but Mark said he didn't know. "What the hell's goin' on?" There was suddenly a

456

plaintive note in Ralph's voice and a childlike resentment. "I can't find out what his room number is. Those fuckin' lawyers won't tell me where he is. I can't find out at the desk."

Mark knew Caval had told Thorton he would pay him for taking the felony. Mark didn't know how much exactly, but thought it was fifty thousand. To placate him Mark said, "Don't worry, he'll pay you."

Ralph glared at him, and Mark was sure he would throw something through the window. He yelled, "We were friends too, ya know. Is it just fuckin' money now? Ever'body's hidin' around, sittin' aroun' by 'emselves, not talking to each other. What the hell happened to us?"

Mark looked back at him with real compassion, but he had no desire to answer the question. He did not know the answer and did not have time to try. Ralph finally grumbled, "Ahh, fuck it," and turned to the door.

"I'm waitin' for Tom, too. I'll tell him to get in touch. Where you going to be?"

"In the bar, where d'ya think?"

Another hour passed and Caval had not called, nor Zarl nor Westheimer. Mark nearly jumped off the bed when someone knocked at the door, but then he stopped a moment to collect himself and recall the things he had planned to say. But it was Jack. He had just come from the courthouse, where he was prepared to plea to the misdemeanor. He described to Mark how the judge had given him a slip of paper stating his conviction and sentence and signed at the bottom. He said Eiler had not showed up, that Jesse would get only five years probation. The charges were dropped against Margaret, but she and Jesse were in a motel nearby, soured on the entire affair, with no desire to see any of their codefendants. "Who the hell does?" Mark asked.

Jack was nervous at the nearness of an end to what he now regarded only as a long ordeal, and he paced the room, edgier than Mark, chewing his fingertips. He was concerned about Mark's tactics in the war of nerves with Caval and feared the two of them might somehow ruin his chance to get it all over with at last. They argued about it, and even though they had become good friends in the past months, Mark was on the verge of telling him to get out.

"You're not the only one with something to lose," Jack finally insisted. "Would you just call him and get it straight?"

"No way." Mark shook his head. "He's coming to me."

"That's just your ego trip," Jack countered. "You guys are going to foul up everything."

"That's tough," Mark raised his voice. He no longer cared about either Jack or Caval. He was dangerous. "I'm not taking any more shit, especially not from him. If I get screwed, I don't care who goes with me. So go talk to Caval."

"Sure. That'd do a lot of good. He's doing the same thing you are." Jack opened the door to leave. "I hope you both get the rap."

Mark was glad to see him go, angry or not, and he settled back onto the bed. He was consumed in the contest again, and for the moment at least, he would not have cared if it cost every friend he had. His thoughts returned to Caval and pictured him on the phone, imagined his dealing with his banks, arranging his fortune. Mark felt rather puny by comparison. He had put some money in a Cayman account and a little in a Bahamian bank, mostly to impress the lady he'd been traveling with at that time, but he'd stuck most of it in Mexico. As the dusk advanced and the room began to darken, he toyed with an idea, considered its worth. The more he thought about it, the better it seemed. But when he had plotted its implementation it made him more nervous than ever. Finally he got into his dop kit and took some Valium to keep him calm. The next thing he knew the phone was ringing and the room was dark and he was not sure where he was. There was a lengthy silence on the other end when he managed to answer.

"You asleep?" Caval asked. Mark said he was, his mouth thick from barbiturate. "I'm comin' down." Mark kept thinking of throwing some water on his face, but he was still on the bed when Caval knocked.

"You better wake up an' start thinkin'," Tom spoke loudly. "It's gonna be all over tomorrow. Zarl says the government's gonna fuck us an' everybody else if we don't get this straight."

Mark was still disoriented as he sat on the edge of the bed rubbing his eyes and looking around the room. Another hotel room, he thought. He felt like he'd been through the same scene a hundred times, like some kind of athlete on an endless road trip, constantly playing in opponents' towns.

"He didn't tell me that," Mark said at last.

"Use yer head." Caval sat on the desk, put his feet on the chair, and still spoke loudly. "They're gonna sentence everybody tomorrow. If somebody doesn't take this rap, they're gonna call the whole thing off. They'll screw everybody. Or else they won't settle, an' then

458

we'll have to go to trial. An' with the evidence they got," he pointed at Mark, "you'll go down the goddamn river."

Mark blinked as he looked back at him. "I'm sure you're not worried about me. If you're concerned about the others or just yourself, I suggest you take the rap. I wouldn't take it for two hundred grand." They stared at each other through the darkness. "You couldn't pay me to take it."

"Why not? What the hell?" Caval demanded. There was a tone in his voice Mark had never heard before. Fear. "Whatta ya want? You aweady been paid. I coulda had you killed. I let you rip me off. I let you get away with that," he shouted. "You owe me fer that, man. You owe me."

"I don't think so." Mark mumbled because he was watching Tom closely. He's scared to death, Mark thought. "I appreciate your letting me live, but they're going to make this rap two full years. They're going to get somebody, but it's not going to be me. It'll be no parole," Mark's voice rose, "and it won't be in any country-club federal camp either." Mark knew it was not true, but he was positive that what Caval feared was prison. "They're going to put you in there with the rough boys," Mark grinned meanly. "That's what you're scared of."

Caval's face reddened and distorted with rage.

"I was on the street with the rough boys when you were in law school, motherfucker."

"Yeah, but when you get inside with that mug of yours—in Atlanta or someplace—they'll run everything but the guard's hat up your ass." Mark laughed. "They'll be turning you out for gang bangs!"

"You Jew son of a bitch," Caval screamed. "You don' know when to quit do ya?" He sprang off the desk knocking the chair away and headed for the door. "I'm gonna get you now, you cocksucker."

"You aren't getting me. I'll tell the judge, man." Caval froze in the doorway with a crazed look, and Mark's arms trembled as he spoke. "Try that on. I'll tell the judge the whole trip. Think about it."

iv

Eiler came out of the judge's chambers and went down the

main hallway toward the restroom. Before seeing the judge, he had gone in there and tapped out a few lines of coke on his billfold and snorted them up through a rolled bill. He thought he might as well have a couple more now.

He had only spent about twenty minutes with the judge, accompanied by Zarl. The judge was a middle-aged man, with glinting eyes and short black hair and bushy eyebrows that looked like tufts of pubic hair growing out of his forehead. He and Joe looked each other over as if they were from different planets, and Joe nearly laughed at him. Joe was given a piece of paper describing a felony charge for possession of marijuana for sale and a one-year sentence, to which he could plead guilty in exchange for having the rest of the charges against him dropped. The judge said that Joe and the others would change their pleas formally at eleven o'clock, "if these other two associates of yours can remember who ran this little operation." He had looked distrustfully at Zarl as he said it. Then, instead of lecturing Joe as he had the others about the leniency of the court, his good fortune, and the awesome wrath he would invoke next time, the man said that Joe's sentencing might be held up because the government believed there was another matter in California that might be connected to this case. The man referred to the murder as if it were misplaced paperwork. Joe had merely nodded, and then brushed off Zarl on his way out. He knew where he stood and did not need Zarl to tell him it was grim, and he did not care if they sentenced him or not. He had only come at the last minute, just in case. And right now he just wanted a couple more lines. He had been using the stuff every day for almost two months. Since the last time he'd seen Martha. He was aware that it had put a permanent grimace on his face, his hands were usually clutched, his eyes had darkened, and he had lost weight. His nose was ruined, and decongestant sprays had become the most important thing in his life. He was sure he could quit the coke when he wanted, but figured he was hooked on Afrin forever.

Walking through the broad front hall crowded with men in conservative dress holding briefcases, Joe was aware of people looking at him. Comments made as he passed identified him as one of the smugglers, who the local folk thought were going virtually scot-free. With his hair shaggy and the beard collected in a thick brown line around the edge of his jaw, Joe knew he had finally come down to looking like a dope dealer. He didn't like that, but then he didn't like anything else either. Anyway, the coke steeled

460

him against it all. He felt impervious to the things he knew were relentlessly closing in, and he was not afraid. But a couple more lines would make it better. The strange voice startled him as he passed the front doors. His nerves were fried.

"So you're Joe Eiler." It was a deep New York voice. "Little jumpy, aren't you?"

Joe faced a large man standing alone, taller than Joe and looking down at him with acute distaste—obviously some kind of cop.

"What do you care?"

"Beautiful. I knew you'd say that." Amusement marked his contempt for an instant.

"Who are you?"

"Carl Broley. I'm with Customs."

"Oh yeah. Broley. Good job, Broley. If I paid taxes, I'd appreciate the work you did." Joe looked him over and realized they were wearing the same sort of brown woven tie. Joe fingered his own and smirked at the coincidence. "Good taste."

Broley did not care to recognize it. He tested Joe's eyes with a practiced stare. "I bet I could bust you for snort right now." He said it with a challenge, but also as if it were too petty for him to bother.

"I wish you would." Joe loosened his tie and unbuttoned his collar. "I been trying to kick it for weeks." He started to walk away, still toward the restroom.

"What the hell did she see in a cocky punk like you?" Broley seemed to ask the question of someone else, but Joe stopped and squinted at him suspiciously. "I don't understand it," he went on. "The last guy she fell for was a louse, too."

"What're you talking about?"

"Nancy."

Joe nodded. His empty stomach flinched from the conflict of emotion. "Her name was Martha when she was workin' on me." Broley merely shrugged. "Where is she now?"

"Still with DEA. Why? You wanna beat 'er up again?"

Joe could see and feel more than mere professional allegiance in Broley's interest. "I was pretty pissed off," Joe remarked quietly, stunned by the subject. "You would've been too."

"Yeah. Like right now. I'd like to take you outside an' break yer back."

Eiler watched his hands carefully. He seemed to mean business. "What is she to you?"

461

"She's a good friend. We used to work together. An' you're damn lucky they transferred her out to DEA, 'cause if she was still with us," he stuck a large finger in Joe's face, "I'd've found you an'—"

"Awright." Joe moved away from the finger. "Come on. You're scarin' me to death. But she deserved it."

"Sure."

"You ever do undercover work?" Joe snapped. Broley just stared at him. "Yeah. That's what I thought. It's real nice. And I loved her too, man, so I was a little angry."

Broley looked away, as though sorry he had stopped Joe.

"You must have a real bad temper," he said. "I hear they're about to hang a murder rap on you back in California. Some people seem to believe you shot one of your partners or something like that . . . speaking of nice work."

"She tell you that?"

"She didn't say anything about you. Maybe you two deserve each other. But I hope not. She's suspended now, anyway. That oughta make you happy."

"What for?" He was almost ready to defend her.

"Because you beat 'er up an' she was in the hospital to begin with." The anger returned to Broley's face, but he took a deep breath, and it passed. He seemed to have decided that slugging Eiler would not be worth the trouble. "Then she wouldn't file a report or something, I don't know."

Joe looked away down the hall and felt utterly miserable.

"I loved her, you know it?" He looked Broley straight in the eyes. "An' I still do. Ain't that a bitch? I do. I still love her. You know, I find myself thinkin' about her, like she was coming back." Joe saw the disbelief and confusion in Broley's face and wondered, what the hell am I telling him this stuff for? "It's true," he nodded anyway. "An' I was good to her. I was. I just got so mad that time . . . you know."

Broley was disarmed suddenly and stuck his hands uncomfortably in his pockets. His features bore a certain compassion but a repulsion at the same time. He seemed disappointed, disappointed in Nancy, and especially in what Joe was, and perhaps even in himself and what he was. For a moment or so, there was nothing to say.

"So you think they got me in California, huh?"

"I don' know," Broley shrugged, but he searched Joe's eyes again. "I just heard about it."

"Well, I hope justice is done."

"Oh Jesus," Broley turned. They were both cynical enough to smile at the prospect though. "Like now?"

"Hell, they're sendin' me up," said Joe. "Whatta ya want?"

Broley snorted and shook his head. He knew where they were going. Joe liked him though, and respected him. He was about to suggest they get a beer, but that would have been too much.

"Nice meetin' ya, Mister Broley." Joe looked him in the eyes again and extended his hand. "We just met her from different directions, I guess."

"Sure." Broley clearly did not care much for that attitude, but he took Joe's hand a moment. "Good luck in California. You'll need it." Joe nodded, smiled forlornly, and went on to the restroom.

V

"I will," said Mark. There was shaving cream on his face, and he stood naked except for a towel around him and held the receiver away and talked loudly at it. "I am hurrying. I can meet you at the judge's chambers in about fifteen minutes. But I haven't talked to Tom again . . . No . . . No . . . I'm just pleading the misdemeanor . . . That's his problem . . . Maybe you ought to explain that to Tom. I'm just going to go down there. I guess we'll have to see what happens . . . I know. I know . . . All right I'll hurry."

He hung up and sat uncomfortably on the bed. It was not happening. The situation was out of control. He had no idea what to do next. Maybe Caval had called his bluff, he thought. Maybe he was going to get screwed after all, and maybe he was only making it worse. Zarl had just told him that, until he and Tom agreed on the pleas and told Zarl so that he could make the arrangements with the judge, the judge would not allow Mark to plead to a misdemeanor. Nor would the judge allow any of the others—Jack, Ralph, Margaret, Jesse, all waiting angrily at the courthouse—to change their pleas formally. For the moment the pressure was paralyzing, yet neither that nor fear of the penalty possessed him as much as the contest with Caval.

He always spoke to himself in tight situations and now he said, "Keep going, man. Keep going," and made himself get up. He had to take it all the way, but the courthouse was going to be a very unpleasant place.

Before the bathroom mirror, the worry in his eyes reflected. As he raised the razor to his face, his hand trembled. He watched it shaking in his fingers, tried to hold it still, and then nearly dropped it when there was a loud knocking at the door.

He yelled that it was open, and the anticipation brutalized his empty stomach for the mere second he waited. In the mirror he saw Caval enter the room. Quickly he began to shave, as if he had been normally occupied, and took a knick out beneath his ear that started bleeding down his neck. Caval approached silently and put down the lid of the toilet and sat behind Mark without a word. The taut, dark features of Caval's reflected face studied Mark's reflected face as he scraped away the lather, dipped the razor beneath the faucet. There seemed to be a dull ringing sound of the slowness with which each second passed. Their eyes kept meeting, and Mark felt as though Caval could hypnotize him, and he glanced away each time with an effort.

"You're late," Caval said finally. He made no attempt at disinterest. "You're always late."

Mark shrugged and said nothing, but dared a longer look at Caval in the mirror. Tom looked like he had something terribly distasteful in his mouth, and his eyes were enraged. The brown sport coat and a pale champagne tie he wore for court looked as foreign to him as this situation.

"A hundred grand," Tom snapped. He said it as if flinging himself out a high window. "Whatta ya say?"

Part of Mark relaxed, but his breathing shortened as he took the last strokes of his shave slowly and carefully. Don't blow it, he warned himself. He had concluded the night before that he could be out after sixteen months, and if he could get the money it was worth it. It would be hard; it would be torture, but he would be a rich man when he got out, almost a millionaire. For two hundred thousand tax-free, sixteen months of almost anything was good work. The IRS would never get off his ass, but he knew how to handle that. As for the felony, he never intended to practice law again anyway. He took a few final passes at his neck and tossed the razor on the counter.

"*Two* hundred thousand," he countered at Caval's face waiting in the mirror. He bent and splashed water on his own face, then grabbed the towel and turned. "Two hundred thousand," he said again, like ordering a hamburger from an indolent waitress.

Caval waited for Mark to towel off before saying, "All right." He looked relieved as much as defeated.

"Two hundred thousand," Mark repeated.

"Two hundred fuckin' thousand goddamn dollars."

"You sound like a kid, Tom," Mark observed pleasantly. Hell, he is a kid, he thought, just a kid.

"Fuck you, you goddamn rip-off son of a bitch."

"I'm a Jew." Mark shrugged. "What can I say?"

"Would ya just hurry up, damnit? You're gonna screw this thing up yet. That judge is pissed."

Mark continued to lounge against the lavatory though, awaiting what he knew was obvious.

"I can give ya the money cash in a few days, no problem." Tom stood up and moved nervously around the small space.

"I don't want cash."

"What the hell, you don't want cash?" Tom whirled and glared at him.

"Cash is a pain in the ass, Tom, you know that."

"What the fuck you want, traveler's cheques? Don't start tryin' to jerk me around again, man, I can still—"

"I'll tell you what we'll do," Mark stopped him loudly but then explained in a calm voice. "We're going to call your bank and my bank and send telegrams and have that money transferred by wire today. Nice an' neat."

Tom stared at him. "You're crazy."

"No, I'm not," Mark smiled.

"We'll never get back to goddamn court on time," Tom exploded, pointing in some vague direction as if an army approached. "Everybody's waitin' on us, man. They're about to sock us with contempt right now. I'll get it to you cash in two days. You can come with me. This whole goddamn thing's waitin' on us."

"Calm down," Mark said. His own heart was fluttering though. "We can do it pretty quick. I've done it before." He was lying, but he was pretty sure he knew how to swing it. "We can say the car broke down or anything."

Caval started pacing fitfully, handling the doorknob, wiping his face, kicking the toilet base.

"They'll wait for us," Mark stated confidently, trying to convince himself as well. "I don't care if it takes until three o'clock. They're in this as far as we are now. Contempt of court. Big deal."

"Okay goddamnit," Tom shouted at him. "Will ya just hurry up, though?"

Mark turned and smiled at himself in the mirror as he patted after-shave on his face. He could barely catch his breath.

"I am hurrying," he said. "Relax."

chapter 30

EILER drove into Carolina Beach, turned left at a gas station, then right into a neglected vacant lot that fronted on one of the least appealing inlets in the area. The sun was setting behind him, and two other rental cars blocked his view, except for the familiar masts. In the dusk he could see the dirt-banked inlet with its shabby houses and small trailers, its weeds and litter growing together everywhere. Even gulls seemed to eschew the place, except for one, standing on a jagged branch near the mud bank, an outcast who appeared not to care much for the spot himself. After Caneel Bay, Joe thought, this.

He saw someone standing ahead by the bank as he stopped the car and then recognized Margaret as soon as he got out. She wore a heavy sweater and folded her arms against the autumn cold in the wind that blew her hair. Her head was inclined, burdened, as he reached her, and they merely glanced at each other and said nothing, being too taken by the sight before them.

In a shallow slough scraped out of the bank for a slip lay what remained of *Leda*, like a great discarded toy. Customs had seized her when they made the bust. Not long afterward, while still at the Wilmington docks, she had broken loose in a wind one night and gone crashing among other boats like a captured beast free on a final rampage. She had sunk two boats and damaged several. They had put her at auction a few weeks later, and some local shark with a scheme for making her into a restaurant had picked her up for fifteen thousand. He had run out of money or interest quickly but had to get the boat out of Wilmington, so he had motored her to this dismal spot not far from his small hotel, which had a penny arcade for a lobby. At the first low tide she settled on a large rock and broke open her bottom. With her other leaks, that was enough to leave her sitting in the mud, so that now the tide rose and fell within her. She had been stripped and plundered and played upon by local youths and unpainted for so long that she was barely more than a wretched corpse of her former self. The great windlass was rusted; the decks were scarred and sunbleached; the skylights were broken; she listed miserably to port, as if staggering from abuse and age and sad fate; and her rigging was fouled and cut so it dangled

466

and blew in the wind like the few last wisps of hair on the battered head of some old hag. To see her was like finding the body of a dear friend, decaying in a ditch.

Joe stood beside Margaret a few minutes, at the end of a board laid from the bank to the deck, and suffered the view, but when he turned to her at last, the worst of it seemed to be in her eyes. Those fine blue eyes glistened with tears that reflected much more than the passing of a well-loved boat. They showed the death of dreams. Everything she had thought would happen when she fell in love with Jack in St. Thomas and sold him the boat had come out bitterly. She had lost Jack; she had lost the boat; this afternoon Jesse had left her to meet a new girlfriend in New York; she was alone; and the party was over. The strength of her features, the glint of her eyes were much less than they had been. She was heavier and not so proud. Joe, even in the numbness of cocaine, was struck by the realization that these two ladies—Margaret and *Leda*—were the worst casualties, almost equally damaged by events. Delight, in his view, had merely been spared a life of further mishappenings. And Joe could not consider himself. But Margaret and *Leda* were suffering.

After they had finally been in court that afternoon, Ralph had asked Joe to meet him out at the boat and have a drink and bullshit a little. It was the sort of thing Ralph loved, and everyone else was steering clear of Joe, and he had not seen the old girl since the previous January.

"First time you seen her?" he asked Margaret. She merely nodded. "Well, Ralph's on 'er somewhere. Let's go on board an' have a snort with him."

"He already called to me. I don't want to go on."

"Oh, hell, Margaret," he spoke softly with compassion but chided her too. "It's better than standing here crying. Now come on."

"No, Joe." She recoiled when he touched her arm. "You go if you want to."

Joe stood silently a moment, cold and uncomfortable and aware that Margaret would much rather be alone.

"Honey, when you ride high, you fall hard. It's just part of the deal. You have to take yer licks."

"Damnit, I know that. I'd just rather be alone."

"Just come on aboard an' get in the middle of it an' get it over with."

He coaxed her a little more, and finally they went across the plank. They wandered slowly among the disarray toward the stern, and Margaret stopped to look at things or grasp some hanging piece of stray line. By the time they came to the after cabin, she seemed to feel a little better, and Joe was glad he had been so glib. They found Thorton there, sitting with his back against the cabin and a bottle of bourbon beside him, staring off the port quarter. He stood up as they came near, and Margaret fondly embraced him. She loved rough men who were sweet, and Ralph had always treated her like a princess. She even snuggled up to him, because it was getting chilly, and laughed about something, then had a good slug of bourbon.

Joe and Ralph tried to think of something heartening to say about the boat, but it was impossible. There was a painful silence, during which *Leda* seemed to ache beneath them, and Margaret finally said, "I can't believe my boat is here like this."

"It's not yours anymore," said Joe. He took a shot of bourbon and glanced at the label with shock. "You just got to let it go."

"Best you sold 'er like this," said Ralph. The whisky was making him terse. "Made a great trip. Best way to get out." He smiled at her, sad and tight. "It be awright. You get another one."

"Sure. If I ever get the money for her."

"What?" Joe turned.

"Customs made more than I did." She looked out across the darkening inlet, ashamed to reveal her further loss, but needing to. "I got fourteen from Caval in Puerto Rico, and they wanted me to wait until the deal was completed for the rest. I didn't want to foul things up for Jack. Now, Caval says he's got all these lawyer costs to pay so he'll have to pay me later. I'll bet I never see another penny of it."

" 'At li' son o' bitch," Ralph growled drunkenly.

Joe shook his head slowly and asked Ralph, "Did he settle with you?"

"No. Shit no," Ralph muttered. "Payin' my lawyer, but he owe me more'n'at, ya know. An' he's duckin' me now, like he never knowed me." His voice sank lower. "I don't b'lieve it. I don't think he'll pay. I don' think he will." Then Ralph raised his head suddenly, wanting a brighter side of the matter. "Hey, didn' Mark get'im though? Wa'n' that great? I like to die when I see 'at look on 'is face when 'at judge give ol' Mark 'at sen'ence." Ralph laughed meanly.

"He didn't pay for the boat," Joe stated, as though for some official accounting. "He caused the bust in the first place. He screwed you, Ralph. And Jack. Jesus, what he did to Jack, you couldn't even call a screw. But by God, he screwed me."

Joe made the last appraisal with a gravity that caused Ralph to lean forward, squinting at him as if he saw double from the drinking. Margaret smiled curiously at Joe and with a certain fearful fascination, as though watching a poisonous snake in a cage. She and Ralph were both aware of the talk about Joe and Cavin O'Neal, but not even Ralph had asked him about it. The air was prevalent with their wonder. That afternoon his sentencing had been postponed, and federal agents had tried to question him again after the court session.

Joe did not notice either of them looking at him, any more than he had been bothered by the inquiries earlier that afternoon. He stared into some abstract void, in which, with the urgency of cocaine, his mind strove for some conclusion.

It was all one, he realized. It was all for the moment fabulously interlocking. It ran from the death of his wife through all the hassles of dealing and the transgressions of this long enterprise to Tom Caval. It was people who do ill and know they will be unopposed. It was clear. Evil went unopposed because no one had the guts to call it.

"Tommy gon' take a real hard fall one o' these days," Ralph muttered, still studying Joe's passive face. So did Margaret, and she observed distantly, "People like that usually get what they deserve."

Joe said, "Not unless someone sees to it." He was thinking aloud. It was the cocaine and the whisky on top of it, but for the moment it was all perfectly plain to him.

ii

Ralph lay on his back on the couch, and Katie sat across the small room on one of the new chairs. The TV was on, one of those situation comedy series, and Katie laughed a moment at something that happened. Ralph was looking at the set, but his thoughts were distant, and he made no sound. In the last few months he had let Katie buy some new furniture, and their house was nicer now, more comfortable, and yet still rather simple despite all the money Ralph had made. They did not live much differently than if Ralph were still working high construction.

Ralph's thoughts were on prison. His orders had come in the

mail the previous day, and he was to report in two days to the federal penitentiary at Lewisburg, Pennsylvania. He would be there about nine months, he figured, through the winter, could be out by midsummer, back up on the lake, if he was good. He knew he would be good. He had planned it. He would not take any shit, but he would not get in trouble. Nobody would run any games on him. He had quit drinking only a few days after the sentencing and been sober now for eleven days. He never expected to be called this soon, but he was glad of it now.

He was prepared and felt positive about it, and he was not afraid or worried. He did his job. Even before the sentencing, he had arranged the sale of his liquor license and rental of his bar within his family, and the deal had worked out well for everyone and looked good on paper. Everything was clear, and there would be no problems. His parents would be cared for. All his good friends, his old friends, knew what was happening and why, and they were ready if the folks needed any help, because they knew Ralph would do the same for them. Katie had plenty of money, and she was a good woman. She knew how to see that the final papers went through on the bar, and how to check the books regularly and send him the figures. His income from the deal was safely banked.

The felony continued to pain him though. He could not get over the stigma of failure and inability it marked him with. In addition, he could not quite shake a sense of having lost himself, of having run with a rich crowd, of having made it up to fast company and big money, only to feel in the end that he was not part of that, and to feel now that he would never again be part of what he had come from, would be lost somewhere in the middle instead.

It was that and the betrayal of friends that hurt him most, hurt him more than the felony he could always explain, even though he'd hate it. He had not seen or heard from anyone since the sentencing. The greatest adventure of his life had ultimately burst open, and there was nothing, just prison, penalty, mistrust. And the money. Hell, he liked to spend money, loved to, but he didn't *need* it. He'd trade the fortune he had made to be with Jack Sidell and Joe Eiler right then, bullshitting over some Heinekens on the deck of ol' *Leda* in the hot sun down in St. Tom. Goddamn.

A car pulled in the driveway, and its lights played across the wall above Katie, then went out. They sat up quickly to identify it. Not recognizing it, they both stiffened with a long-trained reflex. If the stove had exploded in the kitchen, neither would have turned attention from the window until they knew who was there. As soon as the car lurched to a halt though, Ralph knew it was Caval. He always put a car in "park" before it had quite stopped. He glanced at Katie with only a residue of anger.

He had managed to track down Caval and learned that he had moved into a house not far away, in a higher-class suburb along the lake, playing straight until the case was settled. Ralph had gone by there several times. He had been mad as hell then. He wanted his money, the money Tom owed him for this indignity, and he had wanted Margaret paid. He had never found Tom there though, and it had become too demeaning, so he let it go.

When Ralph let him in, Caval made no remark at all to Katie, so she left the room, and he barely said even hello to Ralph. Caval's hair was messed up, and his face was disturbed. He looked to Ralph like a small, frightened animal, and it offended the respect Ralph had kept for so long. He almost threw him out as soon as he started talking, his voice shrill and panicky.

"Man, I got my fuckin' orders today. Today! They said we'd have time to take care of things. They said we'd have a month or so. Those motherfuckers. I gotta report the end of this week! Man, they sent me up! They're sendin' me up!" The hysteria in Caval's voice disgusted Ralph, and he turned away. "They're puttin' me in Leavenworth. I gotta fuckin' one-year rap on a misdemeanor, an' they're puttin' me in Leavenworth!"

"They know you was runnin' it, Tommy. You can't buy your way through ever'thing."

"Buy shit," Caval screamed. "I didn' buy nuthin'. Insinger pleaded to the felony. He said he ran the thing. He told 'em. What the fuck? An' that cocksucker got off with nuthin'!"

"Don't yell at me, Tommy. I got my own problems." Ralph did not face him, because if he had, he would have slugged him. "My orders come yesterday. An' I got a felony." He turned to challenge him. "You remember that, don't ya? Huh?"

He stared into Caval's electric eyes, but they no longer seemed capable of comprehending anything. He turned away again and lay on the couch and stared at the ceiling.

"Hey look, man," Caval came around beside the couch, but Ralph wouldn't look at him. "I'm gonna pay ya that money tomorrow. Fifty grand. Cash. Just like I said. Cash. An' more too. I need ya to do somethin' for me though, okay? I gotta have ya do somethin'."

The words and the tone of Tom's voice and the realization that Caval had been talking to him like that for years turned Ralph's stomach. He said, "I don't want the money."

"I'm not jus' talkin' fifty grand. I'm talkin' a lot more." Ralph could not bear the intensity of Caval's eyes. "I got a lotta money I can't put away. I didn' expect to be goin' this soon. That fuckin' Jew Insinger screwed me. I had it all set, man, an' that fuckin' Jew screwed everything up."

"I don't wanna hear it, Tommy." Ralph's voice was getting tough.

"No. Now look." Tom exhorted him through the tension with which he poised above him. "I'm talkin' about a lotta dough, man. There's two hundred ten thousand, Ralph. Two hundred an' ten thousand! Now fifty of it's yours, but I need ya to hold the rest of it for me. You gotta do this. It's a hundred an' sixty over what's yours. You jus' keep it for me while we're in, an' then you can have half of it when we get out. Half of it, man. That's eighty grand jus' for keepin' it."

Ralph glared at the ceiling and shook his head without a word.

"Ralph, come on." Caval turned a complete circle before him. "Whatta ya talkin' about? That's great dough. You know people who'll keep it for ya. Your family. That won't be any problem. They don't even have to know what it is. They jus' get a deposit box an' slip in the package, an' you'll make—"

"No, Tommy. I'm not involvin' anybody else in this stuff. You got family. You got lawyers. You know people who can take care of it for ya."

"Ralph, I can't trust anybody except you. I can't trust 'em, man. I gotta—"

"I'm not surprised," Ralph shouted. He stood up suddenly, and Caval was driven back a step by the sheer force of his indignation. "If you got so damn much money, how come you don't pay back Margaret for her boat? How come you don't pay her lawyer fees? An' ya damn well better pay Eiler's fees."

"Eiler?" Caval's eyes rolled wildly. "Eiler ripped me off." His voice rose. "Eiler ripped me off! Everybody's been tryin' to rip me off. Except you, Ralph. An' I'm gonna pay them. I swear, I'm gonna pay Margaret. I jus' don't have time." His voice kept rising. "I don't have any fuckin' time. They're sendin' me to Leavenworth." He was completely undone.

"Si'down, for Christ's sake," Ralph ordered him. "An' jus' slow down."

"I can't. I haven't got any time. You gotta help me with this money. I don't have any—"

"Tommy, you been screwin' an' screwin' an' screwin', 'til you got so damn much money you can't hide it all! I don't care if you flush it down the goddamn toilet. I don't want it. I don't want any of it!"

Caval cringed as Ralph roared at him, but then a fierce resentment burned through.

"Awright, Ralph," he almost whispered, "awright, you turn on me. You go ahead an' turn on me." He went quickly to the door, with the car keys clicking in his hand. "But you're gonna be out, man. You're gonna be completely *out*."

Ralph said, "I already am."

iii

People floated by like asteroids passing in space. Joe made his way up the long concourse toward the huge main terminals at O'Hare mindful only of his plans, barely noticing other humans. He wore a raincoat and carried nothing. He had checked the bag that now comprised the totality of his possessions. He never checked it, could not remember ever having checked it before, but travel had become so endless now that he longed to believe it would be over someday and checking the bag had at least been a change. He kept telling himself though, that this was the last trip, the last heavy one anyway. The bag even had the last of his on-hand money in it— about six thousand—but he didn't worry about that anymore. If it were lost or stolen, that could only accelerate the final stage. The other thing was in there too though—the instrument—and that could be a problem if he lost it.

When Joe left Wilmington, he had not gone back to California. The feds were watching him. The court had set a date one month away for him to reappear for sentencing, presumably after California authorities had decided something on the murder case and made their moves. So Joe had begun to make his own moves, to take action at last. That was how he thought of them—the final acts.

He knew that if he returned to California he would have to face the grand jury and the DA and probably the U.S. Attorney now, would be indicted sooner or later, and arrested. He had almost been ready to go back, just as he had gone to Wilmington at the last minute to make an end of that business. Briefly he reached points where he wanted everything to be finished. Fitfully he had begun to want to be caught, convicted, taken away, and locked up. Sometimes that had seemed to promise an end, a stop to traveling, worrying, loneliness, cocaine, the absurdity, the strangeness of other human beings. At least being convicted of a crime and being sentenced seemed orderly, made conventional sense. He could have surrendered control—or what remained of it—and let the machinery of the system take him over.

Then on *Leda*, that evening with Ralph and Margaret, he had snapped out of it and begun to realize that he had too much invested, believed too deeply in himself as the only entity truly able to determine right and wrong in his own life. That view of life, that sense of the world, extending from himself, had become too powerful, too established in him by action and longevity ever to allow him to surrender himself to the judgement of the state. If he believed the state was worthy of that power, he would never have done the things he had done in past years. Moreover, he had become almost biologically incapable of giving up to them, just as centuries of social and legal inertia prevented them from ever letting him continue to be free.

Joe Eiler had become a knight-errant. He was a sovereign individual in a medieval realm of contemporary legal powers. In the pressure of forces currently impending, he understood it as he never had before. He had become this thing and could not undo it and would not. Despite the weariness and danger, he would not let it go. If it were the right way to live—and he believed it to be—then he could not stop. But there was more to it than that. There were responsibilities. When a man is his own standard, Joe reckoned, a fealty to the self is required, a necessity to serve the standard. There were obligations. And Joe concluded that there was one more item of business to take care of, one more salient of honor required before the strategy of retreat.

Out of Wilmington, Joe had held tickets for San Francisco. But on the first leg of the flight, he pulled a little maneuver at the Atlanta airport to elude any federal agents. He paid a cab driver to speed like a madman toward the city, where he caught a train to Miami. From there he took a flight to Nassau, then a little six-seater over to Eleuthera. The money it all cost meant nothing anymore. He still had enough on him to cover his plans. Weeks earlier, he had taken money out of his Bank of America deposit box to buy another set of identification in L.A. and procure a second false passport. The cash remaining by then, about forty-six thousand, he had paid to Ted Zarl and still owed him almost five thousand more, which he planned to pay when he closed the accounts that supported his false BankAmericard. There would be very little money remaining when he finished, but that seemed like the least of his problems.

He had found a small hotel in Spanish Wells, deserted in the off season. For eight days he lay in the sun, gazed out to sea, drank beer, used cocaine. He forced himself to exercise and eat well. He ran and swam and did push-ups. The hotel maid was seventeen years old, her hair in tiny braids close to her head, her skin so black it glistened, and after the second day, she and Joe fucked each afternoon. If he were not waiting, she would whistle lightly from the glass doors of his room, and the high notes seemed to float out through the hot air until they found him, even when he was far down the beach. He would go in and find her kneeling naked on the bed, her back straight, presenting big, pointed, primitive tits, a grin, her eyes dark, her pubic hair steely coarse and dense as forbidden jungle. They sweated at it. There were a few other women around, Canadian or American, but Joe had no interest. What would he say to them?

In the evenings, he would have some dinner at the Harbor Club, return to his room to snort a few long thin rails of cocaine, then stick a chair in the sand outside and look out across the darkening water and ask himself again, "Do you really want to play for these stakes?" Each time he reached the same conclusion: he could not escape from himself; he could not surrender control of his life. But to control life required making decisions, judging good and evil. Who else would judge for him? The government? Whose philosophy and behavior should be his model? That of Jesus Christ? Christ was killed. Sacrificed. He ascended, but Joe believed every spirit ascended. To the right hand of God, as it were. But Christ had been promoted since his death to the spiritual demise of a civilization! In which the church had the franchise on your soul.

Joe found he had to judge for himself, and that every act counted. He had always believed, based on knowledge he could never identify, that life continued eternally, that it extended and accumulated act by act as immutable, inexhaustible, infinite energy, the totality of which comprised his eternal being. Beyond that, he knew nothing of the ultimate significance, but he was powerfully bound to what he did know, because it was all he had. All else had fallen away in repudiation.

Joe hadn't reached these conclusions through the cerebral momentum of cocaine. They had been building for years, demanded by his business and the events of his life. He'd started the coke almost as a sedative after Martha. At night in Eleuthera, he rarely went back for more. Though undoubtedly it affected him, he had quit getting wired on the stuff. He spent too much time alone to keep doing that. And once in the very pits of his life, in a Los Angeles hotel after he last saw Martha, he had burned the stuff until he finally found himself on the floor, holding onto the floor. Every muscle, nerve, and organ revolted. He had thought he was still, and yet it seemed he was heaving, shaken by invisible murderous forces. Then he had begun to move, slowly at first like a dog beginning to wretch, then faster and faster into convulsion and out of control. His stomach, empty for days, heaved without anything to give up; his blistered throat gagged until he couldn't breathe. Then his throat muscles had cramped and pulled his tongue back. He fought it, clawed at it, but every muscle in his body, his very heart had strained against him to draw his tongue into his throat, as if only that could end the spasm and turn the page on his life.

Joe could never recall how it ended or how long it lasted. He knew only that it seemed like days, but could have been mere seconds. He did know absolutely that he had struggled against his own body—against his entire physical life, it seemed—when it was resolved to death. He had been sore for days, as though he'd been clubbed, and he only used the stuff rarely now and in little bits, except with Ralph during that bad session with Zarl in Chicago. He had beaten the stuff, but there had been a victory in it so transcendent that the cocaine seemed only a tiny factor. He kept using the stuff, but never like before. He did it because he liked it, a couple of toots every once in awhile, normally only twice or three times a day.

It became instructive in his life, a continuing lesson in his philosophy. Because he regarded the stuff as evil. He had learned it on the floor that long night. But he could control it, use it, as long as he understood what it was.

Joe's view of the drug fit his understanding of life: building the eternal soul; the struggle between good and evil. It was a philosophy that attempted to fathom the opposition of law and the individual, the body and the spirit. Now finally in the past months, he had had to make some hard sense of those things. He found that good did not exist alone or there would be no law. And yet there were bad laws; entire legal structures and whole societies could be bad. Great worldwide religions existed that were based on suppression and control of the human spirit for power. And yet these same powers were capable of good. He saw that good and evil existed in duality like magnetic poles, in insidious subjectivity.

476

Understanding this duality became the riddle of his existence. And he knew that only the free individual could hope to grow to that knowledge.

Through those isolated nights in Eleuthera, he had gone further. He found that good alone was stagnant, except in the face of evil. Good was prey to evil unless it opposed evil. But evil was opposed only by evil. Good had to be capable of evil, use it, control it. To do that one had to become evil to fight evil, and prevail. He must strive to make good the ascendant produced by the conflict. But who could judge that result? In answer, Joe again discovered no one but himself. The revelation locked him in far lonely orbit. He left the island knowing that he must believe ultimately in himself. And to believe in himself, he must act on his principles or accept and surrender to others.

He stayed in Miami for several days when he returned. There was information he had to get there—and shopping to do for one particular item. When he left for Chicago, everything was set.

Near the end of the concourse at O'Hare, just as he reached the enormous terminal and began to think of car rental agencies, he saw Ralph Thorton approaching. Ralph did not see him though, and Joe stayed to the right to avoid him, but slowed and watched him, saw his eyes sullenly ahead, his tough old face indicating unmistakably that he was on his way to prison. They were almost abreast of each other, only ten yards apart, when Ralph did see him, and his great smile revived his features. Ralph opened his mouth to speak and started forward toward him, but Joe made no expression of greeting, did not smile or gesture. It stopped Ralph cold and dissolved his smile. His shoulders appeared to settle beneath a weight. They looked at each other a moment longer, then Ralph gave a tight-lipped nod of sad recognition and went on toward his plane.

iv

When Caval entered and shut the large front door behind him, he was visibly nervous. He looked around quickly with a frightened expression, as if he had been chased here, but the large half-empty house seemed to offer no refuge. It was a spacious four-bedroom house in Lakeshore he had rented with characteristic extravagance, shortly after the meetings with Zarl in Chicago a few months earlier, to distract attention from his real addresses while he came to terms with the government. He had rented furniture, but only enough for a few rooms, enough to make it seem as if he lived there, and to make it liveable when he actually did.

It was not the best section of the suburb, but the house was well off the street and at a private distance from the neighbors. A broad foyer extended toward the rear of the house from the front door, where Caval remained a moment scowling like he hated the place. The foyer expanded into a dining room off the kitchen. There was a dining table in front of glass doors leading to the back yard and patio, but the curtains were drawn. To Caval's left was a sunken den with a fireplace, and it was arranged with a couch, end tables, lamps, easy chairs, and a large gaming table with arm chairs. To his right were double louvred doors, shut now, but giving access to a formal size living room which was completely empty. Beyond these doors and before the dining room was the hallway to the bedrooms. The emptiness produced a sterility in which Caval was tormented by loneliness. He had never been able to be alone; he was too paranoiac and hyperactive. But now, isolated by distrust and fearing what lay ahead, he was trapped. He pulled off his parka and went toward the few broad steps leading down toward the den, but stopped at the top of them, as though he could not decide what to do. He kept glancing around with the tormented look of a snared animal. Then suddenly he sensed something wrong, something dangerous, and his eyes jerked excitedly. Eiler stepped out of the dark hallway, and Caval lurched in shock.

Joe stared at him, amused by the way he stiffened in speechless surprise. He felt good. He had not had to wait long, and he had just taken a few snorts off the tip of his pocket knife. He had seen the address among Zarl's papers while they were meeting with the judge in Wilmington and memorized it, with no clear purpose at the time. He had arrived less than an hour ago, at about nine-thirty. He had hoped Caval would be there and simply took the chance that he would be alone—he could have waited longer if he weren't—but finding the place empty he broke in and waited, prepared to leave unnoticed if necessary. Now it had happened perfectly. Everything had come together even better than he had planned. He felt strong, powerful, precisely directed. In the long, rarefied seconds before they spoke, Joe felt that everything in the past year had gradually accelerated toward this moment and now combined in a final settling stroke, like the last thrilling strains of a bolero. He had a sense of pure action, high justice.

"What's the matter, Tom?"

"What the fuck are you doin' here?" he demanded. His voice was tremulous.

"Just came to see ya." Joe stepped out to the middle of the carpeted foyer and stopped. "I would've waited outside but I'm a little hot these days."

"How'd you get in here?"

"Bedroom window. I didn't think you'd mind."

Caval's eyes were wild with suspicion, and Joe stood before him a few yards away, his coat pushed back, and his hands poised lightly in the pockets of his pants. He could feel the weight of the instrument in his coat pocket, touching his hip. It was an old .38 calibre Smith & Wesson he had bought without record in Miami. It would be loud, but that didn't matter anymore. He had a stocking cap in the other coat pocket, and his car was parked a block away in the shadow of some large elms. There were plenty of trees in the area, nearly continuous shadows through which he could sprint to the car when the time came. He had rented the car with the false credit card. Then he'd picked off a pair of license plates in a deserted corner of the airport parking garage. The deal was balls-out.

"Well, look, uh . . . it's good you came," Caval said quickly. He tossed his parka on the floor and spoke hurriedly, his eyes searching Eiler's face. "I wanted to get in touch with ya. I meant to get in touch. But I didn' know where you were. I changed my mind about those attorney's fees. For you and Jack both." There was an embarrassed, defensive tone to his words. "Things turned out a little differently than I thought. I figured I'd go ahead an' pay 'em for ya. It's a good thing you came 'cause I gotta go to the goddamn joint the end of the week."

"Decided to pay us anyway, huh?"

Tom's face fell. He studied Joe a moment. He was thoroughly vulnerable, and to him that was a strange sensation, which he did not care for at all. He spoke tentatively. "Yeah, that's right. I came out a little better than I thought I would. So I figured what the hell, you guys did your job. We can forget the hassles now. In fact I can get ya the money—"

"Did ya tell Jack about this?"

"No. I haven't had a chance. Man, I've really been hustlin'. I didn't know they'd make me go this soon. An' I don' know where Jack is. Ya know? I mean I don't have any number for 'im anymore. You got a number for 'im?"

Joe stared back disgustedly. The urgency of Caval's lies sickened him. He only hoped he did not start begging, but he had rather hoped Caval would try to buy him off, offer him great sums of money.

"Well . . . I'm serious, Joe. You know where he is?" Tom faltered a little. Joe's silence threatened him with more than he first suspected. "I mean, ya got a number for 'im?"

"It doesn't matter."

Caval blinked and turned his head and squinted at Eiler with a look of momentous discovery. Caval's mouth opened a little, and Eiler smiled at him with the pleasure of the hunter once the prey is at hand. You son of a bitch, Joe thought, what do ya think of that?

Then a grim smile turned Caval's face, and his shoulders relaxed. In seconds, every vestige of anxiety or fear departed from him as if some drug had been administered. It gave Joe an odd twinge in his stomach. He's gonna flip, he thought. He's gonna flip big as hell. Do it now. Do it right now.

Eiler watched him, though, and there was no possibility that Caval did not understand. Yet he seemed fascinated by it and strangely calmed. He looked like he had expected this for years, even desired it to justify his own behavior, but had at some point given up on it. Now it stared him in the face real as death, and he gazed back at it in wonder.

Eiler's thoughts proceeded like the cars of a speeding train flashing beneath a light as they howled past into a dark night. Crazy. Son of a bitch is crazy. He likes it. What the hell's he smiling about? Is he smiling? Take the piece out. He's gonna flip. No, leave it a minute. What's he looking at? Don't let him suck you in. Don't explain. He knows.

Caval's eyes wandered for a moment as if he played with images of what was to follow. Then he turned to the steps beside him, but Joe straightened, stopped him with his eyes and the way he flexed as he snatched his right hand from his pocket. Caval froze, but looked at Eiler with phenomenal contempt and condescension. Then Caval turned slowly and went down the steps to the den. Eiler stalked him, eyed the ease of his movement, the fineness of his hair, his neck, the perfection of his clothes, and saw him as a trophy. Now, he thought. Right now.

Cooler than ever Caval sat, lounged on the long couch. His nonchalance captured Joe's attention, intrigued him. He reached the last step and watched Caval peruse the room, question it with the sharpness of his vision, judge it with an expression of his lips. Then with a breath, he disapproved of the setting.

"So, what's the beef?" Caval asked. On either side, there was absolutely no doubt now.

"You cheated me," Joe stated. He had stopped before Caval near the middle of the room with the gaming table behind him and an easy chair to his left. "I paid you off, an' you didn't pay my lawyer. I end up with chicken feed. But that was just your last mistake. You been askin' for this all along. You're a worthless goddamn animal."

Caval snapped back at him, "I think you're a great guy, Joe." The room rang with his sarcasm. "I been meanin' to tell ya that for a long time." He sneered at Eiler, dared him. "You're just wonderful."

A voice in Joe kept telling him not to say anything, just do it and get out of there. But he couldn't. "You draw people to you, an' you use them an' cheat them. I've seen you do it too many times. You get people who are honest an' trust you, because you know you can screw 'em. And because you know they won't do anything about it. You're rotten. You ruined that whole deal. We could all have been rich. And you'd still have made more than anybody. That was the least of it. You ruined people's lives. You should've been killed ten different times for the stuff you did. You fouled the whole thing. You're rotten."

Caval listened with no particular expression, certainly with no look of denial. Then all he said was, "Yeah?" He spread his arms across the back of the couch as though to present a better target. "Tell me this," he demanded. "Did you know Sidell didn't pay me? Did you know he cheated me on that deal? On that deal you *both* took? Were you in on that?"

Eiler stared back without answering. He knew there was no point in explaining. There was only the urgent voice: shoot the bastard now.

"That's what I thought," Tom sneered. "And I'm sure there were a lot of times you would have screwed me if Jack had gone along with it. Huh?"

"You would've deserved that just as much." Joe understood all that and had at the time. There was no conflict. He started to tell Tom, but he felt the cocaine surge. He felt it in himself like a hum of electrical current. His hands stiffened; his face felt wired; the room seemed bright. There was suddenly a great desire to tell Caval in precise detail why, under the circumstances, taking *Leda* would have been just. But the coke pushed other thoughts at him one after another. "And what about O'Neal? That was another mistake you made. You knew he ripped us off. He went to you with the dope, you son of a bitch."

"So what?" Tom snarled. "You give a load to a punk like that, an' you don't even watch him. That's my fault? You're full o' shit. You try an' run a fast deal an' you get burned, so I'm supposed to watch out for you? Bullshit. You just didn' watch your ass, that's all. Don't hang that one on me. That one's your rap. You're just like everyone else. You tripped over your own shit."

The cocaine ebbed. It was one of those moments when its drive relaxes and leaves an empty sinking sensation. Joe's fingers clutched in his pockets. He pulled them out and put them in raincoat pockets and felt the gun. Caval's mouth opened.

The words spun in Joe's mind: "You tripped over your own shit . . . tripped over your own shit." It was true. Even at the time, he'd cursed himself for trying to be like Caval. But that was just one thing. He tried to think of the real matter, but the cocaine wouldn't let him. He kept feeling it in him, and it frightened him. He'd been using it so long, controlling it so well, but now it was all over him, sneaked up on him. It undermined him, kept him from thinking. Everything he'd reasoned so clearly broke from focus, stirred and muddled by the dope.

Caval's open mouth suddenly became a grin. "You killed him didn't you? O'Neal. You off'd 'im." Tom found it amusing. "They were sayin' you did, but I didn' really know. But you did, didn' you?"

"Shut up!" Joe started to take the piece out but felt his finger clutched so tightly on the trigger he thought it might go off. He jerked, and Caval flinched back on the couch. Eiler just stared at him and realized he did not know what he was going to do.

Caval straightened. He seemed to know the moment was at hand.

"You do what you're gonna do, Joe, but don't give me this crap. Don't tell me this shit about me bein' the bad guy. You been in this stuff too long. I've heard all that crap. I been hearin' it all through this thing. All this whinin' an' bitchin' about me. I made this thing happen," he thumbed his chest indignantly. "All those crybabies got in this deal because they wanted to be like me. Well, it doesn't work that way, an' you know it. Everybody doesn't get to be on top. The reason I get to be on top is because I don't let them be on top. Man, they wanted it. They wanted to try it. Anything bad happened to them, it was only because they tripped over their own shit."

Caval breathed heavily, and his dark eyes squinted at Joe. "An' all this about cheatin' an' breakin' rules. Bullshit! Where you been, man? This is outside the rules. Everybody agreed to play a game without rules, an' now they don't like it. Well tough shit! All this about truth an' trust an' honor. Well there ain't no honor among thieves, an' there ain't no truth outside the law except that. Maybe they had their rules, but I never made any deal about that. They can talk that crap all they want, but trust is a longshot bet, an' you only do it when you think you can get away with it. The only real rule is watch yer ass." Caval finished with his face thrust forward, out of breath. "So do what the hell you came to do, but don't play God with me."

All of it whirled in Eiler's mind. Was it true? Had Caval just beaten them all? Was Caval lying, tricking him? The dope drove again, and Joe could not stop his thoughts long enough to decide. Caval stared so expectantly before him that Joe's mind felt out of control. It was the first time he had considered that he might be wrong, and if he were, then he was nothing but a punk killer. The unassailable assurance that he was leveling a cosmic balance turned fraudulently soft. He knew the dope deluded him. An incidental agent, which he knew was evil in excess and which he had once fought to the death, controlled him. He was afraid, not afraid of killing, because he had known too long that it was necessary sometimes, but afraid of indecision, of the possibility that he was wrong. He saw Caval at least sticking to whatever predatory principles he held, but saw himself gone to hell on cocaine until he could not think straight. He had a sudden horror of killing Caval for the wrong reason, had a vision of himself as a demented murderer, images of those last grisly moments in Mill Valley with O'Neal begging him, of Jack's revulsion as though he had seen Joe for the first time. But most of all, Joe saw the possibility of destroying himself, of fouling irreparably his own honor, if anything remained of it. Those things were all he had left now. Finally, he could not risk them.

"Well . . .?" At last Caval's voice trembled.

"I don' know." Joe took his hands out of his coat and stepped to the easy chair on his left and sat down. "You'll have to figure it out, Tom." Joe felt so wired, but so weary, that he wished he could be anywhere else, even in jail. And yet he also wished that he did not have to leave, could just sit until somehow it was all over.

"Yeah, thanks a lot, Joe." Caval looked away at the floor and scowled as if in disappointment. Then he looked at Joe for a long

483

time. Joe gazed at the ceiling. Finally, Tom got a cigarette from his shirt pocket. "Got a match?" Joe fished in the coat pocket beside the stocking cap and threw him a pack. His thoughts were empty, as if he had turned them off the way one turns off lights to go to sleep. Tom paused, though, as he lit the cigarette, and his eyes darted from the matches to Eiler. When Joe looked at him again, he found Tom studying him with his usual devilish grin. Joe turned away. Right then he could not summon the effort to fathom it. He stood to leave and said, out of distraction only, as if he had to say something, "Nice place you got here, Tommy. Glad I stopped by."

Caval laughed, blew smoke out in a cloud. "You kiddin'? This place sucks. You got shit for taste, Eiler. Always did." Joe was on the stairs and stopped to turn back. "I just rent it 'cause I had stuff to do here. I got a beautiful new house up in Steamboat Springs goin' to waste. Just Teresa sittin' up there gettin' ready to spend my money while I'm rottin' in prison." Caval seemed eager to talk, as though he had hoped for someone to talk to. The shrill insistence returned to his voice. "It's a bitch ain't it? You get a bunch of nice stuff, lotta money, an' ya can't use it. Ya go to the joint instead, 'cause some dumb fuck wants to write a diary. Got plenty of dough, an' ya can't use it, or the goddamn IRS pops ya."

"Yeah, it's too bad about you." Joe went on up the steps. He was sarcastic but also amazed. He hadn't phased him. But there was nothing more to say. Joe just had to get out, had to get away, but when Caval spoke again he stopped at the door.

"Nobody wins at this shit, Joe." His dark, handsome face looked older as he frowned. Joe had never seen age in that face. Caval flicked his ashes on the carpet. He seemed truly disappointed, as though he had really hoped that Eiler would finally provide the climax it all kept seeming to lead to but never did. "They just come out with different amounts of money. Unless some crazy fucker like you dusts 'em off."

Joe shook his head. He would have laughed, but his face was too taut with cocaine to allow it. "You do amaze me," he said, then turned again to leave. Caval would not let him.

"Me?" he demanded. "What about you? What're you?" Tom jumped off the couch and stood pointing at him. "You're not even real." Caval laughed his short, sawing, nervous laugh. "What name you using now? Huh? What's your name now?"

Joe looked back at him, hating him no less than ever, but conceded the point with a weary nod. "Yeah. Paul Morrison," he muttered. A dead person, it occurred to Joe, resurrected by him until he was of no further use.

484

Caval grinned. "See ya around, Joe." Joe opened the door and went out, numb to every thought and sensation except the sound of Caval laughing.

V

It was after ten o'clock when Joe awoke in the hotel room the next day. Several hours before, he had finally reached a state resembling sleep. He was not rested though. It had been too fitful, too full of rushing images instead of dreams. He hurried to the bathroom. His nose was so cauterized from the coke that he had breathed through his mouth as he always did now, until his throat was parched and sore. He brushed his teeth and gargled mouthwash, then bathed his face for several minutes in hot water in a futile effort to clear the passages of his nose.

Back on the bed, he sat for nearly an hour wondering where to go next. He could still come to no conclusion regarding Caval and what Caval had said and what he himself had finally chosen. He still could not organize his thoughts, but that at least served to suppress the desire for a few of the narrow white lines with which he had come to begin each day. You couldn't think straight, he told himself. You still can't think straight. You never will if you stay on that shit. And with what you've got ahead of you, you'd better think damn straight.

He got the remainder of the supply from the lining of his bag. Together with what he carried, which he added to the plastic bag, it was about six or seven grams. When he turned it up slowly and carefully, it snowed onto the flat water of the toilet and landed with a sort of muted effervescence. A dull cloud permeated the water for a moment, then it was clear again. "Five hundred bucks," was all he thought. He shrugged. He should have sold the stuff, he thought. No, there wouldn't be time. Probably get busted. That struck him as supremely funny, and he laughed for the first time in months. He felt good, not quite free yet, but almost. You'll make it, he told himself. You'll make it all right. He wanted to throw the goddamn nose spray out the window, but figured he would need it more than ever in the next few days. That made him laugh at himself, and he liked it.

A second later, there was a solid knock at the door. Joe stepped out of the bathroom so that he stood before the door and said, "Yeah?" The voice called his name: "Joe . . . open up." Every thought and question, every breath of air and bodily function felt suspended suddenly as though he stood in an absolute vacuum. Like a hypnotized man responding to orders, he opened the door.

Tom Caval grinned at him. Then Joe saw the other man, much bigger than Tom, angular with dirty hair, dull eyes, veins prominent in his nose, his mouth a thin line, the heavy object in his left hand. Tom said, "My turn, Joe."

chapter 31

i

THE light morning fog was dispersing, and the broad half-circle of the bay at La Jolla reached out to the calm Pacific and continued into distant, infinite haze. From the indefinite horizon, the sky came back in steadily strengthening blue until overhead, contrasted by retreating wisps of fog, it was brilliant. The sun was just cresting the coastal hills, and the bay and the sea and the sky were all one great sparkling jewel. Set around it on the lush hillsides that rose from the bay like a huge amphitheatre were the fine homes with their inlay of bright green gardens, bushes, trees and well-kept lawns, the earth eager to grow things. The smell of it all, of the sea commingled with wet soil and ripe flora, was pure and sweet and stole all your thought if you let it.

Mark lay in the hammock on the side deck of his house high up the hill and gazed at the scene, absorbed the smell and feel of it, listened to the shrill optimism of tiny birds with a rich pleasant melancholy. He had lived there for only two months, but at one time actually thought he might live there forever. But this morning he took his coffee alone, as he had for the past few days, and had no more notions of perpetuity. In fact he was rather sure this was the last morning he would ever spend in the place. The next morning he would be hurrying down one cup and departing for prison. That might also be the last time he saw Gretta. She came into his view from time to time, through the big windows of the living room, moving back and forth through the room, cleaning things, straightening up as she always did in the morning, but not calling to him, reminding him of calls or appointments or suggesting things as she used to, just continuing with an unspoken resentment. Another little domestic interlude was over. Mark was acutely aware of not having done very well at it, not in the end anyway. He looked away from the windows again and turned back to the impassive beauty that urged him to consider the more pleasing past. He summoned again the images and the counterpoint of thrill and drama in his last victory over Tom Caval, then dwelt on the princely, triumphant outlook it allowed him.

They had not returned to court that afternoon in Wilmington until after three o'clock, and it was a mean-spirited group that awaited them. The judge was boiling and, despite Zarl's efforts, began the last proceedings by fining Mark and Tom each five hundred dollars for contempt of court. Jesse Mackenzie laughed aloud. Even the judge was a little embarrassed when he thought about it, as though he had been petty. The others then entered their pleas and received their sentences, and Caval had taken the misdemeanor and, like the others, was directed by the judge to serve a full year. Mark had stood before the bench last and received his six-year sentence for felonious conspiracy, then waited in nervous agony for the judge to stipulate how much of it he must serve. The man leafed among his papers with an ugly expression. He looked up suddenly to say he did not care at all for the outcome of the case, that he had serious doubts they had accurately identified the leadership in the matter. Mark felt faint. He had to bend his knees to remain standing. Then the judge looked Mark sternly in the eyes, said he saw no reason why Mark should do more time than his codefendants, and accordingly reduced the sentence to one year. There were mutterings and sardonic laughter among the crowded defense table, and Mark could not resist a look at Caval. Tom sat still and expressionless, his eyes burning the judge and his face scarlet with anger. A moment later, he had marched out of the courtroom, and Mark had not seen him again. The clincher had come from the government, when Mark learned from Westheimer that Caval was going to Leavenworth. He learned it the same day he had received orders to report to Lompoc, the minimal federal prison camp on the California coast just north of Santa Barbara, a pleasant place to do penance for having made so much money. Mark was almost happy to go and, in fact, viewed it with little more trepidation than most men do paying taxes, which was how he chose to view it. In all, the long deal left him not so much with a feeling of accomplishment as of great adventure and rich conquest. On occasion, and right now, he was sorry it was over.

Mark heard a car pull in the driveway, but he had many friends in the area and thought only that it was early for a visitor, not yet nine-thirty. A few moments later, through the living room windows, Mark watched him come around the walkway to the front door. Then, seeing Mark in the hammock, he came on around the corner. Mark barely recognized him, and had not at first. He was shaven, had gotten a decent haircut and gained some weight. He wore a tennis shirt and light trousers and looked relaxed.

"Well goddamn, Joe, I was beginning to wonder." Mark got up and they shook hands, and Mark joked about how nice Joe looked. They laughed, but with some nervous reservation. Joe Eiler was a wanted man and not necessarily desirable company. He and Mark had begun a close friendship in the last few months though, and Mark was happy for Joe's company on his last day.

"I thought I'd stop in an' say hello," Joe told him, as though to explain the liability of the visit. His hair seemed redder against the blue background of sea and sky. His pale eyes carried the same sad fatigue, but in the rest of his face there was a certain whimsical happiness.

"Hello?" Mark smiled ironically.

"Well . . . ," Joe fluttered one hand and smiled back at him, "you know. I kind of wanted to see Jack, too. I thought he might be around. D'you know?"

"He's in San Francisco." Mark climbed back in the hammock. "There were some other friends of yours around here the other day. Nice guys. A little inquisitive," Mark winked, "but nice guys." Joe nodded thoughtfully and said nothing. "You're aware that you've been indicted for murder? And for interstate flight to avoid prosecution?"

"I uh . . . heard something about it," Joe replied. "I won't be here long. I just wanted—"

"Oh hell, it doesn't matter. Why don't you hang around. You can spend the night. I'm going to the joint tomorrow."

They talked it over, and Mark insisted he stay, so Joe had a seat and said he'd have a cup of coffee. Gretta came out when Mark brought the coffee, and he introduced her. She was a sexy-looking lady, only twenty years old but mature and easygoing and very well traveled. She was a bit taller than Mark, but not busty, and had a nice slim figure. She had blue eyes and speech that seemed concocted of Negro, New York, and Dutch accents. Mark tried to be lighthearted and affectionate as he introduced them, but there was already a distance between them, the scar tissue of emotional wounds. He wished Joe could have been with them when they were in love, but now there was only the dull routine that is left at the end. He knew Joe could see it.

When Gretta went back inside, Joe suggested, "Listen, maybe you guys oughta be alone tonight. An' I should prob'ly get going anyway."

"There ain't much left in that jug," Mark told him. Joe laughed at the expression, and Mark put his hands behind his head and stared into the sky, shook his head a little and smiled and spoke slowly. "I feel like I'm trying to come back to earth, Joe, you know it? We were in a real high orbit. Really fast. I guess you still are. But all that flying around, all the time, the different places. And spending money. I loved it. I did. It made me high. I really felt hot, really felt like I could make things happen." He glanced at Joe a moment and grinned self-consciously. "You make your own reality. I used to tell myself that all the time. You make your own reality. You can make things happen any way you want, if you get your shit together. You really can. I made some crazy things happen." He nodded to himself and recollected Jerzy Koss, the first load at Fort Rhodes, jacking up Tom Caval—not once but twice. Things you had no business doing, he thought. "I made some crazy things happen. I got pretty hot there for awhile. I really had it in gear. Incredible feeling of power." He took a deep breath. "But, hell, you can't live like that all the time. You just can't keep flying all over the place, hustling all the time, spending money like crazy. And you certainly can't do it with the *federales* on your ass."

Joe arched his eyebrows. "I hope so." Mark smiled at him and said, "I'll bet you do." Joe kicked off his shoes and propped his feet up on the low brick wall that ran along the side of the house. He settled back in the chair and gazed out at the Pacific as Mark talked. Mark knew Joe did not care much for this sort of thing, but he wanted to talk to someone who knew what he was talking about. And he wondered what the hell Joe was going to do.

"You can't keep flashing," Mark went on. "You can't keep doing it all the time. It's got to run out, you know? Sooner or later you've got to make it happen in some kind of normal human situation. You have to come back to earth. A few months ago, before it was even sure we were going to take a fall, I started thinking, 'What the hell have I got to show for my life!' Ya know? A lot of money, but not a damn thing else."

"Why don't ya get married?" Joe suggested easily.

"Well, hell . . ." On his back in the hammock, Mark shrugged, and his face twitched for a moment as it rarely did anymore. "I know. I wanted to. I honestly did. Gret an' I were going to get married. We were going to wait 'til I got out and have a good wedding, you know. I was all for it. I was. She's a good lady, a real good lady. I've told you that. And I loved her. I don't know if I still do. I don't know if I still can, but I sure did. You know, I like to be with her, she takes care of me. She's hot in the sack. I told her all this. Told her I wanted to have a kid. I wanted a son. I really did. We talked about getting married, the whole bit. Where we'd live. All that crap. An' then I don't know, man." Mark covered his face with his hands, and Joe moved uncomfortably in his chair. "About a week ago. More than that maybe. After the sentencing, I guess it started. I just started getting on her ass. Treating her like shit. Gawd. I was drinking a hell of a lot. Gave her some read bad shit a couple of nights. Told her I wasn't going to marry her. That she was just with me for the dough. And a lot of other stuff. Mean shit. Just spoiled it. Just ruined the whole thing. Told her I didn't want to see her when I got out." He turned to look at Joe, but Joe did not look back, kept staring out at the ocean. "So what happened?" Joe finally asked.

"I don't know. I can't really figure it out. I guess I just started feeling like I was closing myself in. I just freaked out. I think I got that old feeling that I want to be the cool guy, the fast operator. So I turned on her. I really thought I'd gotten over that. You know, letting some dream push me around, trying to be something I'm not. I really thought I'd gotten that straight, that I could be myself. That I could control my life. Shit. It's like old dreams sneaking up on me."

"Make it up to her," Joe offered.

"Naa," Mark lay on his back again. "I tried. Kind of. You can't fix things like that, though. She's going to keep living here after I go, until she figures something out. And I'm giving her the car I got for her. But you can't go back. Not after stuff like that. Hell, I learned that from Helen. You got to try all the time. You got to keep it alive. You can't drop it awhile or kick it around and make it right later. It just doesn't work that way."

Eiler nodded slowly and turned around to Mark. "Sounds like you're going to be back in the business."

"No thanks. No way. I've had enough of that. I think I have anyway." He winked at Joe. "I think I have. There's plenty of action inside the law." He put his feet on the ground and got up to get

490

another cup of coffee. "You're the one who'll keep traveling fast. I think I'll try it on the earth for awhile."

"Yeah." Joe picked up his own empty cup and looked into it. Mark stood watching. For a long time he had wanted Joe to talk to him, tell him what he thought of life, what he believed, but Joe never talked. What does he know? Mark wondered. Does he know anything? Then Joe looked up, and his tired gray eyes with crow's feet wrinkles grown deeper around the corners promised he would not reveal that answer.

"Yeah, I guess I will be," Joe said. "Not for long though, maybe. I wondered if you could give me a little advice anyway though. About some logistical matters, as Jack would say. About carrying money. Transferring it, ya know?"

"Yeah. Sure." Mark looked deeply into Joe's eyes, trying to see. "I could help you on that." He felt it come over again, sweep over him like fever. Joe didn't have enough cash for that kind of stuff, Mark thought. He must have a lot of dough now. What the hell did he do? It grew in him now, and Mark could feel it—the old blood. He wished he was doing what Joe was doing. Moving fast. He knew suddenly he would never get that out of his system, and just as quickly he knew he never wanted to.

ii

When Sidell opened the door of Claire's apartment the next evening, he winced as if in pain. "Can I come in, or you wanna stand around in public with me?" Joe asked him.

"What's the difference?" Jack let him in quickly, shutting the door behind him as though it were a war zone. "You're full-on crazy," Jack protested again while they were still standing in the entryway off the living room. Claire was already at work. "They've got to be looking for you." The nail of Jack's left middle finger went instinctively between his teeth. "They want you on murder and some federal thing about splitting."

"I know it," Joe told him. "I won't stay long."

"Joe they're probably watching this place. I can't even believe you'd come back to town at this point."

"I'll take that chance. It won't cause you any trouble. I just now drove up from San Diego. I was . . ."

Jack took a good look at him as Joe told him where he had

been, and the tone of Joe's voice made Jack relax. Hell, he's not worried at all, Jack thought. With affection and a little surprise, Jack recalled the understated boldness that had always been Eiler's style. Maybe I should have listened to Joe's ideas, Jack wondered for the first time. I bet I'd have a lot more money right now. If I was alive. More than anything though, the old sense of their friendship returned, and Jack felt like he had been having a long feud with a brother over some principle that had since receded into obscurity. He wanted truly to say, "Screw it Joe, it doesn't matter any more. O'Neal was just something that happened. We disagreed. I don't care if you're hot, we're still friends. We've been through a lot and nothing else comes before that."

But he couldn't do it. Other things did matter. What evidence might they already have linking him to the O'Neal killing? What about aiding and abetting? How would he like another year or so struck on his sentence? Other things always mattered. Life was not aesthetic.

"Come on, Joe. Let's sit down." Jack stepped into the larger room. "But I'm not letting you stay long." Jack had to say it, so it did not bother him, and Joe smiled at him, understanding. "You want a beer?"

When he had opened the bottles and sat down, Jack could tell quickly that Joe had just wanted to be with him again, to bullshit awhile one more time. No telling what's ahead of him now, Jack thought. He did not intend to ask. He told him he had not heard anything from the government yet, but that he knew he would be going to Lompac.

"Ol' Mark was getting pretty philosophical," Joe recalled with a smile a few moments later. "Trying to figure it all out. I didn't feel much like helping him."

"I guess I'll hear some of that if we're going to be in stir together." Jack almost asked Joe where he would be in, but stopped. Joe started talking about the Caribbean to change the subject, and they became engrossed in it as they always did. After awhile, Jack knew he should make Eiler leave, but he couldn't. He got a couple more beers instead. Something about Joe's presence intrigued him, beyond the friendship. They talked on about getting back down to the islands, and then about starting a charter service, which was Jack's favorite subject. But other things ran through Jack's mind, as they spoke.

It was hard to believe he was sitting with Joe again. It felt like a dream, and the evening light from the windows as the room dark-

492

ened made it look like a dream. Gradually Jack realized that Joe's mere presence spoke a great deal about what he had been through in the last eighteen months. For years Jack's images and ideas about the dope business had been embodied in Joe Eiler. They had been friends, had a lot in common, were really much alike. It had made the business seem close, manageable, easy to figure. Jack had always thought it was simply a matter of performance, of execution. He had always been able to see that Joe, despite his competence, never put himself in the right position, never executed properly. Everything had been so clear then. Caval had seemed like the perfect backer, Jack recalled. All I had to do was perform. It had been lurking in the background though. All the heavy stuff, the real stuff. Just like Joe. What a shock Joe had been. One night in Mill Valley after everything else, Joe had finally taken him by the scruff of the neck and said look at *this*, Jack. You don't just get to perform. People don't play that way out here. It gets messy.

"Well, if you ever get that together," Joe finished his beer and his tone demanded all Jack's attention, "I'll be the chef, uh?"

"No. I said a *good* cook, Joe."

"Well, you ungrateful bastard."

"Yeah. No shit." They both laughed. "Thanks for everything, Joe." Jack dropped the sarcasm quickly and looked Eiler in the eyes. "You know where you're going to be?"

Joe shook his head, his lips pressed in a tight line. "I'll have to get in touch with you."

"Okay," Jack said. He saw Joe getting a little upset, but he did not know what he could say.

Joe turned for the door as if he were only going out for a six-pack. "Got to keep moving," he said.

"Good luck," Jack told him at the door. They didn't shake hands. "I'm sorry it came out this way."

"I'm not," Joe said, and he went quickly out the door.

Jack was startled by the suddenness with which Joe was gone, with which everything seemed finally terminated. He wished he had thrown his arms around him. He wondered if he'd ever see him again. A second later he pulled open the door and went out on the landing. Joe was just reaching the sidewalk below him. Jack called his name just loud enough that Joe stopped without fright and looked up. On the high landing, Sidell was perfectly framed by the soft San Francisco evening, always so handsome and pleasantly dressed, and Joe knew Jack would always make out, would always make out even better now. It made Joe feel good, and he was truly not sorry for any of it. Jack smiled down at him a moment and called, "Neither am I, Joe."

iii

It took Joe nearly all night in the hotel room to overcome a sense of cosmic unfairness and bad fate. On and off, he wished he had never stopped to see Jack and Mark, to be tortured by the envious knowledge that their lives would turn out alright, that they inevitably had gotten a better deal. It had been nearly morning, almost time to get a cab for the airport by the time he got it straight. Then he was glad he had seen them. They were not bitter. They had accepted what they had done, what they had won or lost and what they had each become. They were going to play it out. The government had defeated them in the end and might yet defeat them further. But they acknowledged it and succumbed only for the moment, and they were not giving up. Inside or outside the law, he knew they would never relinquish a determination to make life an adventure. He was certain they would never relax their antipathy toward a safe, sure existence. They would always go out and try to win their lives, risk them against the odds, so that in the most important respects—the freedom of the spirit and the energy of life—Joe doubted they would ever really lose.

He could do no less himself, he decided. In the end he felt inspired by them and with them, and he managed to renew himself one more time.

He had raised the stakes almost impossibly, but he had to play it out too. He had not only jousted with the law, he had repudiated it altogether. He had separated himself from every social criterion and set himself up as the only standard to which he must answer or be judged. He could still not turn back on that. The knight-errant must always keep moving, he concluded. And thus he accepted his exile.

At the airport, he checked in at Pan Am with the false passport and felt no fear or nervousness left in himself. He checked the bag through and saw it trundled out of sight by the conveyor belt.

At the security checkpoint on the way to the gate, he surprised himself with the casual manner in which he placed the heavy new leather briefcase on the table. He already knew they no longer opened carry-on luggage, merely x-rayed it, yet there was a great

494

deal in it nevertheless. "Do you even care about that stuff any-more?" he asked himself. He had not the mental strength left to plumb that question. There would be plenty of time.

He checked in at the gate like a normal human but felt like something totally alien as he sat among the large crowd of other passengers. There were laden tourists, noisy dark-skinned families going home in bright clothes, and a handful of the strange solitary characters who are always found on international flights, among whom, he realized, was himself.

He sat with his back to the wide hallway against the odd chance someone he knew—or worse—might recognize him. He thought of nothing except how strange it would be when he landed. Once he was out of the airport and free of the briefcase though, he convinced himself it would be heaven. Heaven of a lonely sort, but sanctuary at last.

He was not far from the check-in counter, so he was vaguely aware, amid the din of voices around him, of a rather unusual exchange with the agent there. Something he could not quite hear. He did not turn around though. In all that other noise, he did hear the footsteps coming toward him. His saliva had a steely taste as he tried to swallow. He felt anesthetized. He saw the shoes first, as they stopped before him, and the ankles and calves in nylon stock-ings. He could not look up. Her voice exploded in his consciousness like the flash of a nuclear blast. "Mister Eiler you're under arrest."

When he looked up, he was so numb with shock she might as well have walked up with a pistol and blown out his brains. He said nothing, just looked at her. Her hair was longer, below the shoul-ders now, and even blonder than he remembered at the edges of her face, pulled back on top by sunglasses resting on top of her head. Her face repelled him. The delicate chin and mouth were set hard, too hard. But the green of her eyes was fantastic and bright. And yet so painfully sad, he thought they could pull out his heart through his chest.

She looked like an agent now, though, wore a dark blue suit with a loose skirt, a cotton blouse. She seemed taller to him too, perhaps a little thinner and without much bosom, and her face was still narrow but so much harder than before. She shifted the purse on her left shoulder and started to reach inside it.

"Don't bother with the badge, honey. I've seen it."

When she answered, he saw her teeth gritted angrily.

"Let's go, Joe."

"Where we going?"

"You know. Come on. Up."

"You still don't sound very mean." He heard his voice quiver a little. He did not care if she answered, made the observation mainly to himself. "I guess that was it. You never sounded very mean."

"I don't have to. Let's go." She stood back from him on one locked hip and folded her arms, right hand over the purse. The noise around them was muted by the emotional cataclysm of their reunion. A few people nearby whispered about them. Joe got up, and they went past the check-in desk and into the broad concourse, which was busy but as yet uncrowded at that hour. He would have run if he were sure she would shoot him.

He turned toward the terminal, but she said, "No, over here," and then followed him across the hallway to an empty gate. He set down the briefcase and leaned against the railing. The others would be there in a moment he figured.

"How much in the case?" she asked in a flat professional tone. He kept looking uselessly at her eyes. No possible response seemed to matter.

"I quit counting at about a hundred an' ninety thousand. Didn't seem to make any difference."

"I guess it doesn't. What'd you have to do to get that?"

"Guy gave it to me in a hotel." He looked away from her down the concourse, and everyone coming looked like an agent. "Guess he didn't want it anymore."

"Caval?"

"None of your business."

The way she smirked at him, standing there again with her arms folded, her weight on one leg, he would still have taken her in his arms. And yet he would have spent the rest of his life in prison to be spared another minute with her like this. She looked quickly to either side. He tried but could not summon any rancor, or even fear. It was all over. "Your friends coming?" he asked.

"None of your business."

"How'd you get me?"

"I knew you'd go to Jack's. I knew you would." Her voice cracked slightly. Something on top of everything else suddenly confounded Eiler, but he was too shocked to think. She grit her teeth again harder and shook her head with bitter disappointment. "Why didn't you give yourself up?" she demanded.

"I couldn't." Her own anguish made him feel as if he was being choked. How in God's name could she do this? He could have screamed that at her. He could have broken down and cried, but

496

warned himself as he had so often before: Don't start now, man. You'll never stop. "I love you," he said suddenly, raising his voice to overcome the emotion, so that he nearly shouted, "I still love you, you no-good bitch."

She kept her mouth set a moment, as though to withstand his assault and, when she opened it to speak, moved her jaw a little to each side. "I told you that once. You didn't believe me."

"I couldn't hear you."

They made the first announcement for his flight, and people at the gate began to line up noisily. He looked at the deep green sadness of her eyes and could have howled like a wounded beast.

"Joe, you could still surrender." She spoke coolly, but her voice cracked again as she hurried on. "If you just went down, you could—"

"No way." He looked away from her, could not bear to keep looking at her. "You turn me loose, I'll just keep goin'. For Christ's sake, do your fuckin' job this time. There's nothing left."

She was silent until he turned back to her. He kept looking down the concourse and couldn't understand. "Where the hell are they?" he demanded, still not looking at her.

"They're here. I asked them to let me talk to you first. You can surrender, Joe. You still can."

Joe squinted hard into her troubled eyes. "Who's here? Who're you with?" His voice mounted excitedly. "DEA? This isn't any of their business anymore."

Her voice cracked slightly. "What difference does it make who does it, Joe? If it's me or somebody else, what's the difference? They'll get you anyway. Sooner or later, someplace, they'll catch you."

Joe began to tremble. He kept glancing from her eyes to the broad halls of the concourse, searching the faces that approached.

"What the hell is this?" he turned back to her. "Am I under arrest or not? Where are they?" He delved her eyes with desperate confusion. "Are you workin'?"

She opened her mouth but couldn't speak. Joe suffered before her like a trapped animal, and she wanted to put her arms out to him, save him. He was on the very edge of bolting, running—he didn't know where.

"Come on, damnit. What is this? Are you workin' or not?"

Her lips trembled. She couldn't talk. She just stared at him.

"You bitch, just—"

"I'm pregnant, Joe."

"Ohh, gawd." He closed his eyes and dropped back against the railing as if she'd shot him. How much more? he thought. How much more? Five minutes ago he had felt like he'd been thrown from an airplane. Now he had struck earth, but was not yet dead. He was battered, destroyed. "Honey," he touched his forehead distractedly, "it's your ballgame now. I can't take any more. Run me in or let me go, but don't put me through this. I don't deserve this."

"And I do?" Her face finally broke. The feelings in her eyes ignited, and she screamed at him. "I do?"

Just then, he saw one last distant glimmer of a chance, and he thought in that instant that she waited for it too, but he was terrified to suggest it.

"Can you get a ticket for this flight? Can you get them to hold the—"

"And go down there to the end of the damn world with you and deal dope?"

"I've had enough of that. You want to stay here an' do this shit?"

She stared at him hopelessly and then muttered, as if only to herself, "I don't think we'd stand a chance."

Her answer baffled him, but he was already too demolished by everything else to try to understand it. He spoke with panicked urgency. "Can you get a ticket?"

With incredible calm, she replied, "I've already got one."

He actually held the railing behind him. Except for her face, everything around him whirled like a gyro. He did not hear the last call for the flight or see the passengers begin filing into the passageway. When he finally stepped forward to her, they embraced very carefully, very gently, as if surely the roof would cave in if they dared more.

A moment later he reached down for the briefcase, and she glanced fearfully at it.

"What the hell are they going to do when we get off the plane with that briefcase?"

"I really haven't the faintest idea."

She took a deep breath and another fevered glance at the case and then finally gave him one of those smiles he loved, a good deal wizened now, but undiminished enough that at last Joe felt it save him. She said, "Well hell, let's try it."